P9-BYG-242

ARCHER
IN
JEOPARDY

ARCHER IN JEOPARDY

by

Ross Macdonald

THE DOOMSTERS
THE ZEBRA-STRIPED HEARSE
THE INSTANT ENEMY

With a Foreword by the Author

Alfred A. Knopf
New York

FOREWORD

Most fiction is shaped by geography and permeated by autobiography, even when it is trying not to be. Both my father and his father were Scots-Canadian newspaper writers and editors. But I was born about five miles from San Jose, California.

At the dim early edge of memory my parents' marriage broke up, and I became a persistent visitor in the homes of other relatives. The ones I loved most were Aunt Beth and Uncle Rob, with whom I spent two happy years on the shores of Georgian Bay in Ontario.

Rob was an electrician, and held the key to several popular arts. He possessed the only radio in town—he had built it himself—and "Yes-sir, She's My Baby" echoed through my pre-adolescent dreams. On Saturday afternoons it was Rob who opened the movie theater, which had stood dark all week, and admitted any boy or girl who possessed a dime.

For an hour or two, in the flickering semi-darkness, Rob showed us an imaginary world that was realer than the actual one. Chaplin taught us to laugh and cry. Pearl White outwitted the gothic villains who continually threatened her and us. Together they demonstrated that laughter and pain can follow very closely on each other, in a world much like our own but sharper and darker and more brilliant.

Sharper and darker than our world? Perhaps not. Almost before Pearl White had enacted the final escape of her current serial, Aunt Beth died. I was given a train ticket to Winnipeg and placed in a private school by another aunt. There I learned how to grieve for Beth, and for myself, without being noticed by my fellow students or our stoic English masters.

The crash of 1929 propelled me out of Winnipeg and sent me farther west. Before I was out of my teens I had lived with relatives and friends in several dozen houses. I am old enough to be grateful to them now, even to the dangerous one who carried a heavy handgun in his Packard. He may have inspired some of my best work. But I won't name him.

The dead require us to remember and write about them, but I think not to expose them too completely. Though their looming images stay in our minds and become virtually a part of us, they keep their own secrets. Their privacy is necessary to their continuing reality, and to ours. We reinvent them and ourselves out of memory and dreams. And we learn as we grow older to be grateful to the dead. They have cast their flickering shadows across ours, and quicken our reality and their own.

As if they were in adjoining rooms I can hear them talking (not necessarily to each other)—dear Adeline and Uncle Rob who was not my uncle, my two Uncle Edwins who were, my grandmothers and their grandchildren living and dead, my dying father. I can hear them talking in Scots dialect and German and Pennsylvania Dutch and plain English, explaining themselves through six feet of earth impacted over half a century. I hope my books echo (but not too plainly) the feelings which moved my kin when they were alive, the things they were ready to die for, money and music, paintings and each other, fear of God, and their fundamental wish to be remembered, if possible loved.

I love them better now than I did then, and through my stories I understand them better. Sometimes I feel that the stories were written by them to me, asking me to communicate their sorrows and explain their dreams.

My dreams. The underlying theme of these three novels, as I read them now, is the migration of a mind from one place and culture to another. Its purpose, like the dominant purpose of my young life, was to repossess my American birthplace by imaginative means and heal the schizophrenic pain which is clearly posed as the problem of *The Doomsters*. In the other two novels reprinted here, the problem tended to become its own solution. It surrounded itself with character and accreted circumstance, and provided itself with the means of becoming fiction. In the end I possess my birthplace and am possessed by its language.

Ross Macdonald
May 9, 1979

THE
DOOMSTERS

I WAS dreaming about a hairless ape who lived in a cage by himself. His trouble was that people were always trying to get in. It kept the ape in a state of nervous tension. I came out of sleep sweating, aware that somebody was at the door. Not the front door, but the side door that opened into the garage. Crossing the cold kitchen linoleum in my bare feet, I saw first dawn at the window over the sink. Whoever it was on the other side of the door was tapping now, quietly and persistently. I turned on the outside light, unlocked the door, and opened it.

A very large young man in dungarees stepped awkwardly backward under the naked garage bulb. There was dirt in his stubble of light hair. His unblinking pale blue eyes looked up at the light in an oddly pathetic way.

"Turn it off, will you?"

"I like to be able to see."

"That's just it." He glanced through the open garage door, out to the quiet gray street. "I don't want to be seen."

"You could always go away again." Then I took another look at him, and regretted my surliness. There was a kind of oily yellowish glaze on his skin which was more than a trick of the light. He could be in a bad way.

He looked again at the hostile street. "May I come in? You're Mr. Archer, aren't you?"

"It's kind of early for visiting. I don't know your name."

"Carl Hallman. I know it's early. I've been up all night."

He swayed, and steadied himself against the doorpost. His hand was black with grime, and there were bleeding scratches on the back of it.

"Been in an accident, Hallman?"

"No." He hesitated, and spoke more slowly: "There was an accident. It didn't happen to me. Not the way you mean."

"Who did it happen to?"

"My father. My father was killed."

"Last night?"

"Six months ago. It's one of the things I want to ask you—speak to you about. Can't you give me a few moments?"

A pre-breakfast client was the last thing I needed that morning. But it was one of those times when you have to decide between your own convenience and the unknown quantity of another man's trouble. Besides, the other man and his way of talking didn't go with his ragbag clothes, his mud-stained work shoes. It made me curious.

"Come in then."

He didn't seem to hear me. His glazed eyes stayed on my face too long.

"Come in, Hallman. It's cold in these pajamas."

"Oh. Sorry." He stepped up into the kitchen, almost as broad as the door. "It's hellish of me to bother you like this."

"No bother if it's urgent."

I shut the door and plugged in the coffee-maker. Carl Hallman remained standing in the middle of the kitchen floor. I pulled out a chair for him. He smelled of country.

"Sit down and tell me about it."

"That's just it. I don't *know* anything. I don't even know if it is urgent."

"Well, what's all the excitement about?"

"I'm sorry. I don't make much sense, do I? I've been running half the night."

"Where from?"

"A certain place. It doesn't matter where." His face closed up in blankness, almost stuporous. He was remembering that certain place.

A thought I'd been suppressing forced its way through. Carl Hallman's clothes were the kind of clothes they give you to wear in prison. He had the awkward humility men acquire there. And there was a strangeness in him, stranger than fear, which might be one of guilt's chameleon forms. I changed my approach:

"Did somebody send you to me?"

"Yes. A friend gave me your name. You *are* a private detective?"

I nodded. "Your friend has a name?"

"I don't know if you'd remember him." Carl Hallman was embarrassed. He popped his dirty knuckles and looked at the floor. "I don't know if my friend would want me to use his name."

"He used mine."

"That's a little different, isn't it? You hold a—sort of a public job."

"So I'm a public servant, eh? Well, we won't play guessing games, Carl."

The water in the coffee-maker boiled. It reminded me how cold I was. I went to my bedroom for a bathrobe and slippers. Looked at the gun in my closet, decided against it. When I came back to the kitchen, Carl Hallman was sitting in the same position.

"What are you going to do?" he asked me dully.

"Have a cup of coffee. How about you?"

"No, thanks. I don't care for anything."

I poured him a cup, anyway, and he drank it greedily.

"Hungry?"

"You're very kind, but I couldn't possibly accept—"

"I'll fry a couple of eggs."

"No! I don't want you to." His voice was suddenly high, out of control. It came queerly out of his broad barrel chest, like the voice of a little boy calling from hiding. "You're angry with me."

I spoke to the little boy: "I don't burn so easy. I asked for a name, you wouldn't give it. You have your reasons. All right. What's the matter, Carl?"

"I don't know. When you brushed me off, just now, all I could think of was Father. He was always getting angry. That last night—"

I waited, but that was all. He made a noise in his throat which might have been a sob, or a growl of pain. Turned away from me and gazed at the coffee-maker on the breakfast bar. The grounds in its upper half were like black sand in a static hourglass that wouldn't let time pass. I fried six eggs in butter, and made some toast. Carl gobbled his. I gobbled mine, and poured the rest of the coffee.

"You're treating me very well," he said over his cup. "Better than I deserve."

"It's a little service we provide for clients. Feeling better?"

"Physically, yes. Mentally—" He caught himself on the downbeat, and held steady. "That's good coffee you make. The coffee on the ward was terrible, loaded with chicory."

"You've been in a hospital?"

"Yes. The State Hospital." He added, with some defiance: "I'm not ashamed of it." But he was watching closely for my reaction.

"What was the trouble?"

"The diagnosis was manic-depressive. I don't think I *am* manic-depressive. I know I was disturbed. But that's all past."

"They released you?"

He hung his head over his coffee cup and looked at me from underneath, on the slant.

"Are you on the run from the hospital?"

"Yes. I am." The words came hard to him. "But it's not the way you imagine. I was virtually cured, ready to be discharged, but my brother wouldn't let them. He wants to keep me locked up." His voice fell into a singsong rhythm: "As far as Jerry is concerned, I could stay there until I rotted."

The melody was familiar: incarcerated people always had to be blaming someone, preferably a close relative. I said:

"Do you know for a fact your brother was keeping you there?"

"I'm certain of it. He had me put away. He and Dr. Grantland made Mildred sign the commitment papers. Once I was there, he cut me off entirely. He wouldn't visit me. He made them censor my mail so I couldn't even write letters." The words had been rushing faster and faster, tumbling out of his mouth. He paused and gulped. His Adam's apple bobbed like a ball valve under the skin of his throat.

"You don't know what it's like being cut off like that, not knowing what goes on. Of course, Mildred came to see me, every chance she got, but she didn't know what it was all about, either. And we couldn't talk freely about family matters. They made her visit me on the ward, and they always kept a nurse there, within hearing. As if I couldn't be trusted with my own wife."

"Why, Carl? Were you violent?"

Suddenly and heavily, as if I'd rabbit-punched him, his head sank low between his shoulders. I looked him over, thinking that he could be formidable in a violent mood. His shoulders were overlaid with laminated muscle, and wide enough to yoke a pair of oxen. He was saying:

"I made a fool of myself the first few days—tore up a couple of mattresses, things like that. They put me in wet packs. But I never hurt anyone. At least I don't remember, if I did." His voice had sunk almost out of hearing. He raised it, and lifted his head. "Anyway, I never stepped out of line after that, not once. I wasn't going to give them any excuse to keep me locked up. But they did. And they had no right to."

"So you came over the wall."

He looked at me in surprise, his pale eyes wide. "How did you know we came over the wall?"

I didn't bother explaining that it was only an expression, which seemed to have hit the literal truth. "More than one of you broke out, eh?"

He didn't answer. His eyes narrowed suspiciously, still watching my face.

"Where are the others, Carl?"

"There's only the one other," he said haltingly. "Who he is doesn't matter. You'll read about it in the papers, anyway."

"Not necessarily. They don't publicize these things unless the escapees are dangerous."

>>>>>>>>
>>>>>>>> *chapter* 2
>>>>>>>>

 I LET that last word hang in the silence, turning this way and that, a question and a threat and a request. Carl Hallman looked at the window over the sink, where morning shone unhampered. Sounds of sporadic traffic came from the street. He turned to look at the door he had come in by. His body was taut, and the cords in his neck stood out. His face was thoughtful.

He got up suddenly, in a brusque movement which sent his chair over backwards, crossed in two strides to the door. I said sharply:

"Pick up the chair."

He paused with his hand on the knob, tension vibrating through him. "Don't give me orders. I don't take orders from you."

"It's a suggestion, boy."

"I'm not a boy."

"To me you are. I'm forty. How old are you?"

"It's none of your—" He paused, in conflict with himself. "I'm twenty-four."

"Act your age, then. Pick up the chair and sit down and we'll talk this over. You don't want to go on running."

"I don't intend to. I never wanted to. It's just—I have to get home and clean up the mess. Then I don't care what happens to me."

"You should. You're young. You have a wife, and a future."

"Mildred deserves someone better than me—than I. My future is in the past."

But he turned from the door, from the bright and fearful morning on the other side of it, and picked up the chair and sat in it. I sat on the kitchen table, looking down at him. His tension had wrung sweat out of his body. It stood in droplets on his face, and darkened the front of his shirt. He said very youngly:

"You think I'm crazy, don't you?"

"What I think doesn't matter, I'm not your head-shrinker. But if you are, you need the hospital. If you're not, this is a hell of a way to prove you're not. You should go back and get yourself checked out."

"Go back? You must be cr—" He caught himself.

I laughed in his face, partly because I thought he was funny and partly because I thought he needed it. "I must be crazy? Go ahead and say it. I'm not proud. I've got a friend in psychiatry who says they should build mental hospitals with hinged corners. Every now and then they should turn them inside out, so the people on the outside are in, and the people on the inside are out. I think he's got something."

"You're making fun of me."

"What if I am? It's a free country."

"Yes, it is a free country. And you can't make me go back there."

"I think you should. This way, you're headed for more trouble."

"I can't go back. They'd never let me out, now."

"They will when you're ready. If you turn yourself in voluntarily, it shouldn't go against you very hard. When did you break out?"

"Last night—early last evening, after supper. We didn't exactly break out. We piled the benches against the wall of the courtyard. I hoisted the other fellow up to the top and he helped me up after him, with a knotted sheet. We got away without being seen, I think. Tom —the other fellow—had a car waiting. They gave me a ride part of the way. I walked the rest."

"Do you have a special doctor you can see, if you go back?"

"Doctor!" It was a dirty word in his vocabulary. "I've seen too many doctors. They're all a bunch of shysters, and Dr. Grantland is the worst of them. He shouldn't even be allowed to practice."

"Okay, we'll take away his license."

He looked up, startled. He was easy to startle. Then anger rose in him. "You don't take me seriously. I came to you for help in a serious matter, and all I get is cheap wisecracks. It makes me mad."

"All right. It's a free country."

"God damn you."

I let that pass. He sat with his head down for several minutes, holding himself still. Finally he said: "My father was Senator Hallman of Purissima. Does the name mean anything to you?"

"I read in the papers that he died last spring."

He nodded jerkily. "They locked me up the next day, and wouldn't even let me go to his funeral. I know I blew my top, but they had no right to do that. They did it because they didn't want me snooping."

"Who are 'they'?"

"Jerry and Zinnie. Zinnie is my sister-in-law. She's always hated me, and Jerry's under her thumb. They want to keep me shut up for the rest of their lives, so that they can have the property to themselves."

"How do you know that?"

"I've had a lot of time to think. I've been putting things together for six months. When I got the word on Dr. Grantland— Well, it's obvious they paid him to have me committed. They may even have paid him to kill Father."

"I thought your father's death was accidental."

"It was, according to Dr. Grantland." Carl's eyes were hot and sly, and I didn't like the look of them. "It's possible it really was an accident. But I happen to know that Dr. Grantland has a bad record. I just found that out last week."

It was hard to tell if he was fantasying. Like any other private detective, I'd had to do with my share of mental cases, but I was no expert. Sometimes even the experts had a hard time distinguishing between justified suspicion and paranoid symptoms. I tried to stay neutral:

"How did you get the word on Dr. Grantland?"

"I promised never to divulge that fact. There's a—there are other people involved."

"Have you talked to anybody else about these suspicions of yours?"

"I talked to Mildred, last time she visited me. Last Sunday. I couldn't say very much, with those hospital eavesdroppers around. I don't *know* very much. It's why I had to *do* something." He was getting tense again.

"Take it easy, Carl. Do you mind if I talk to your wife?"

"What about?"

"Things in general. Your family. You."

"I don't object if she doesn't."

"Where does she live?"

"On the ranch, outside Purissima— No, she doesn't live there now. After I went to the hospital, Mildred couldn't go on sharing the house with Jerry and Zinnie. So she moved back into Purissima, with her mother. They live at 220 Grant—but I'll show you, I'll come along."

"I don't think so."

"But I must. There are so many things to be cleared up. I can't wait any longer."

"You're going to have to wait, if you want my help. I'll make you a proposition, Carl. Let me take you back to the hospital. It's more or less on the way to Purissima. Then I'll talk to your wife, see what she thinks about these suspicions of yours—"

"She doesn't take me seriously, either."

"Well, I do. Up to a point. I'll circulate and find out what I can. If there's any real indication that your brother's trying to cheat you, or that Dr. Grantland pitched any low curves, I'll do something about it. Incidentally, I charge fifty a day and expenses."

"I have no money now. I'll have plenty when I get what's coming to me."

"Is it a deal then? You go back to the hospital, let me do the legwork?"

He gave me a reluctant yes. It was clear that he didn't like the plan, but he was too tired and confused to argue about it.

>>>>>>>>>>
>>>>>>>>>> *chapter* 3
>>>>>>>>>>

THE morning turned hot and bright. The brown September hills on the horizon looked like broken adobe walls you could almost reach out and touch. My car went miles before the hills changed position.

As we drove through the valley, Carl Hallman talked to me about his family. His father had come west before the first war, with enough inherited money to buy a small orange grove outside of Purissima. The old man was a frugal Pennsylvania German, and by the time of his death he'd expanded his holdings to several thousand acres. The main single addition to the original grove had come from his wife, Alicia, who was the descendant of an old land-grant family.

I asked Carl if his mother was still alive.

"No. Mother died, a long time ago."

He didn't want to talk about his mother. Perhaps he had loved her too much, or not enough. He went on talking about his father instead, with a kind of rebellious passion, as though he was still living in his father's shadow. Jeremiah Hallman had been a power in the county, to some extent in the state: founding head of the water association, secretary of the growers' co-operative, head of his party's county central committee, state senator for a decade, and local political boss to the end of his life.

A successful man who had failed to transmit the genes of success to his two sons.

Carl's older brother Jerry was a non-practicing lawyer. For a few months after he graduated from law school, Jerry had had his shingle out in Purissima. He'd lost several cases, made several enemies and no friends, and retired to the family ranch. There he consoled himself with a greenhouseful of cymbidium orchids and dreams of eventual greatness in some unnamed field of activity. Prematurely old in his middle thirties, Jerry was dominated by his wife, Zinnie, a blonde divorcee of uncertain origin who had married him five years ago.

Carl was bitter on the subject of his brother and sister-in-law, and almost equally bitter about himself. He believed that he'd failed his father all the way down the line. When Jerry petered out, the Senator planned to turn over the ranch to Carl, and sent Carl to Davis to study agriculture. Not being interested in agriculture, Carl flunked out. His real interest was philosophy, he said.

Carl managed to talk his father into letting him go to Berkeley. There he met his present wife, a girl he'd known in high school, and shortly after his twenty-first birthday he married her, in spite of the family's objections. It was a dirty trick to play on Mildred. Mildred was another of the people he had failed. She thought that she was getting a whole man, but right at the start of their marriage, within a couple of months, he had his first big breakdown.

Carl spoke in bitter self-contempt. I took my eyes from the road and looked at him. He wouldn't meet my look:

"I didn't mean to tell you about my other—that other breakdown. Anyway, it doesn't prove I'm crazy. Mildred never thought I was, and she knows me better than anybody. It was the strain I was under —working all day and studying half the night. I wanted to be something great, someone even Father would respect—a medical missionary or something like that. I was trying to get together enough credits for admission to medical school, and studying theology at the same time, and— Well, it was too much for me. I cracked up, and had to be taken home. So there we were."

I glanced at him again. We'd passed through the last of the long string of suburbs, and were in the open country. To the right of the highway, the valley lay wide and peaceful under the bright sky, and the hills had stepped backwards into blueness. Carl was paying no attention to the external world. He had a queer air of being confined, almost as though he were trapped in the past, or in himself. He said:

"It was a rough two years, for all of us. Especially for Mildred. She did her best to put a good face on it, but it wasn't what she had planned to do with her life, keeping house for in-laws in a dead country hole. And I was no use to her. For months I was so depressed that I could hardly bear to get up and face the daylight. What there was of it. I know it can't be true, but the way I remember those months, it was cloudy and dark every day. So dark that I could hardly see to shave when I got up at noon.

"The other people in the house were like gray ghosts around me, even Mildred, and I was the grayest ghost of all. Even the house was rotting away. I used to wish for an earthquake, to knock it down and bury us all at once—Father and me and Mildred and Jerry and Zinnie. I thought a good deal about killing myself, but I didn't have the gumption.

"If I'd had any gumption, or any sense, I'd have gone for treatment then. Mildred wanted me to, but I was too ashamed to admit I needed it. Father wouldn't have stood for it, anyway. It would have disgraced the family. He thought psychiatry was a confidence game, that all I really needed was hard work. He kept telling me that I was pampering myself, just as Mother had, and that I'd come to the same bad end if I didn't get out in the open air and make a man of myself."

He snickered dolefully, and paused. I wanted to ask him how his mother had died. I hesitated to. The boy was digging pretty deep as it was, and I didn't want him to break through into something he couldn't handle. Since he'd told me of his earlier breakdown and the suicidal depression that followed it, my main idea was to get him back to the hospital in one mental piece. It was only a few miles more to the turnoff, and I could hardly wait.

"Eventually," Carl was saying, "I did go to work on the ranch. Father had been slowing down, with some sort of heart condition, and I took over some of his supervisory duties. I didn't mind the work itself, out in the groves with the pickers, and I suppose it did me some good at that. But in the long run it only led to more trouble.

"Father and I could never see eye to eye on anything. He was in orange-growing to make money, the more money the better. He never thought in terms of the human cost. I couldn't stand to see the way the orange-pickers were treated. Whole families, men and women and kids, herded into open trucks and hauled around like cattle. Paid by the box, hired by the day, then shunted on their way. A lot of them were wetbacks, without any legal rights. Which suited Father fine. It didn't suit me at all. I told Father what I thought of his lousy labor policy. I told him that this was a civilized country in the middle of the twentieth century and he had no right to push people around like peons, cut them off from employment if they asked for a living wage. I told him he was a spoiled old man, and I wasn't going to sit idly by and let him oppress the Mexican people, and defraud the Japanese!"

"The Japanese?" I said.

Carl's speech had been coming in a faster rhythm, so fast that I could hardly follow it. There was an evangelical light in his eye. His face was flushed and hot.

"Yes. I'm ashamed to say it, but my father cheated some of his own best friends, Japanese people. When I was a kid, before the War, there used to be quite a few of them in our county. They had hundreds of acres of truck gardens between our ranch and town. They're nearly all gone now. They were driven out during the War, and never came back. Father bought up their land at a few cents on the dollar.

"I told him when I got my share of the ranch, I'd give those people their property back. I'd hire detectives to trace them and bring them back and give them what was theirs. I intended to do it, too. That's why I'm not going to let Jerry cheat me out of the property. It doesn't *belong* to us, you see. We've got to give it back. We've got to set things right, between us and the land, between us and other people.

"Father said that was nonsense, that he'd bought the land perfectly honestly. In fact, he thought that my ideas were crazy. They all did, even Mildred. We had a big scene about it that last night. It was terrible, with Jerry and Zinnie trying to turn him against me, and Mildred in the middle, trying to make peace. Poor Mildred, she was always in the middle. And I guess she was right, I *wasn't* making too much sense. If I had been, I'd have realized that Father was a sick man. Whether I was right or wrong—and of course I *was* right—Father couldn't stand that kind of a family ruction."

I turned off the highway to the right, onto a road which curved back through an underpass, across flat fields, past a giant hedge of eucalyptus trees. The trees looked ancient and sorrowful; the fields were empty.

chapter 4

CARL sat tense and quiet in the seat beside me. After a while he said:

"Did you know that words can kill, Mr. Archer? You can kill an old man by arguing with him. I did it to my father. At least," he added on a different note, "I've thought for the last six months that I was responsible. Father died in his bath that night. When Dr. Grantland examined him, he said he'd had a heart attack, brought on by overexcitement. I blamed myself for his death. Jerry and Zinnie blamed me, too. Is it any wonder I blew my top? I thought I was a parricide.

"But now I don't know," he said. "When I found out about Dr. Grantland, it started me thinking back all over again. Why should I go by the word of a man like that? He hasn't even the right to call himself a doctor. It's the strain of not knowing that I can't stand. You see, if Father died of a heart attack, then I'm responsible."

"Not necessarily. Old men die every day."

"Don't try to confuse me," he said peremptorily. "I can see the issue quite clearly. If Father died of a heart attack, I killed him with my words, and I'm a murderer. But if he died of something else, then someone else is the murderer. And Dr. Grantland is covering up for them."

I was pretty certain by now that I was listening to paranoid delusions. I handled them with kid gloves:

"That doesn't sound too likely, Carl. Why don't you give it a rest for now? Think about something else."

"I can't!" he cried. "You've got to help me get at the truth. You promised to help me."

"I will—" I started to say.

Carl grabbed my right elbow. The car veered onto the shoulder, churning gravel. I braked, wrestling the wheel and Carl's clutching

hands. The car came to a stop at a tilt, one side in the shallow ditch.
I shook him off.

"That was a smart thing to do."

He was careless or unaware of what had happened. "You've got to
believe me," he said. "Somebody's got to believe me."

"You don't believe yourself. You've told me two stories already.
How many others are there?"

"You're calling me a liar."

"No. But your thinking needs some shaking out. You're the only
one who can do that. And the hospital is the place to do it in."

The buildings of the great hospital were visible ahead, in the gap
between two hills. We noticed them at the same time. Carl said:

"No. I'm not going back there. You promised to help me, but you
don't intend to. You're just like all the others. So I'll have to do it
myself."

"Do what?"

"Find out the truth. Find out who killed my father, and bring him
to justice."

I said as gently as possible: "You're talking a little wild, kid. Now
you keep your half of the bargain, and I'll keep mine. You go back in
and get well, I'll see what I can find out."

"You're only trying to humor me. You don't intend to do anything."

"Don't I?"

He was silent. By way of proving that I was on his side, I said:

"It will probably help if you'd tell me what you know about this
Grantland. This morning you mentioned a record."

"Yes, and I wasn't lying. I got it from a good source—a man who
knows him."

"Another patient?"

"He's a patient, yes. That doesn't prove anything. He's perfectly
sane, there's nothing the matter with his mind."

"Is that what he says?"

"The doctors say it, too. He's in for narcotic addiction."

"That hardly recommends him as a witness."

"He was telling me the *truth*," Carl said. "He's known Dr. Grantland for years, and all about him. Grantland used to supply him
with narcotics."

"Bad enough, if true. But it's still a long way to murder."

"I see." His tone was disconsolate. "You want me to think I did it. You give me no hope."

"Listen to me," I said.

But he was deep in himself, examining a secret horror. He sobbed once in dry pain. Without any other warning, he turned on me. Dull sorrow filmed his eyes. His hooked hands swung together reaching for my throat. Immobilized behind the steering wheel, I reached for the doorhandle to gain some freedom of action. Carl was too quick for me. His large hands closed on my neck. I struck at his face with my right hand, but he was almost oblivious.

His close-up face was immense and bland, spotted with clear drops of sweat. He shook me. Daylight began to wane.

"Lay off," I said. "Damn fool." But the words were a rusty cawing.

I hit at him again, ineffectually, without leverage. One of his hands left my neck and came up hard against the point of my jaw. I went out.

I came to in the dry ditch, beside the tiremarks where my car had stood. As I got up the checkerboard fields fell into place around me, teetering slightly. I felt remarkably small, like a pin on a map.

>>>>>>>>>
>>>>>>>>> *chapter* 5
>>>>>>>>>

I TOOK off my jacket and slapped the dust out of it and started to walk toward the hospital. It lay, like a city state, in the middle of its own fields. It had no walls. Perhaps their place was taken by the hills which stood around it, jagged and naked, on three sides. Broad avenues divided the concrete buildings which gave no outward indication of their use. The people walking on the sidewalks looked not much different from people anywhere, except that there was no hurry, nowhere to hurry to. The sun-stopped place with its massive, inscrutable buildings had an unreal quality; perhaps it was only hurry that was missing.

A fat man in blue jeans appeared from behind a parked car and approached me confidentially. In a low genteel voice he asked me if I wanted to buy a leather case for my car keys. "It's very good hand-carved leather, sir, hand-crafted in the hospital." He displayed it.

"Sorry, I don't have any use for it. Where do I go to get some information, about a patient?"

"Depends what ward he's on."

"I don't know the ward."

"You'd better ask at Administration." He pointed toward a new-looking off-white building at the intersection of two streets. But he was unwilling to let me go. "Did you come by bus?"

"I walked."

"From Los Angeles?"

"Part of the way."

"No car, eh?"

"My car was stolen."

"That's too bad. I live in Los Angeles, you know. I have a Buick station wagon, pretty good car. My wife keeps it up on blocks in the garage. They say that keeps the tires from deteriorating."

"Good idea."

"Yes," he said. "I want that car to be in good condition."

Broad concrete steps led up to the entrance of the administration building. I put on my jacket over my wet shirt, and went in through the glass doors. The highly groomed brunette at the information desk gave me a bright professional smile. "Can I help you, sir?"

"I'd like to see the superintendent."

Her smile hardened a little. "His schedule is very full today. May I have your name, please?"

"Archer."

"And what do you wish to see him about, Mr. Archer?"

"A confidential matter."

"One of our patients?"

"Yes, as a matter of fact."

"Are you a relative?"

"No."

"Which patient are you interested in, and what exactly is your interest, sir?"

"I'd better save that for the superintendent."

"You might have to wait all morning to see him. He has a series of conferences. I couldn't promise even then that he could find time for you."

It was gently administered, but it was the brush-off. There was no way to get around her quiet watchdog poise, so I gave it a frontal push:

"One of your patients escaped last night. He's violent."

She was unruffled. "You wish to lodge a complaint?"

"Not necessarily. I need some advice."

"Perhaps I can help you to it, if you'll give me the patient's name. Otherwise, I have no way of knowing which doctor is responsible for him."

"Carl Hallman."

Her thin eyebrows twitched upward: she recognized the name. "If you'll sit down, sir, I'll try to get the information for you."

She picked up one of her telephones. I sat down and lit a cigarette. It was still early in the morning, and I was the only one in the waiting-room. Its colored furniture and shiny waxed tile floors were insistently cheerful. I cheered up slightly myself when a covey of bright young nurses came in, and went twittering down a corridor.

The woman behind the desk put down her telephone and crooked a finger at me. "Dr. Brockley will see you. He's in his office now. You'll find it in the building behind this one, in the main corridor."

The second building was enormous. Its central corridor looked long enough to stage a hundred-yard-dash in. I contemplated making one. Ever since the Army, big institutions depressed me: channels, red tape, protocol, buck-passing, hurry up and wait. Only now and then you met a man with enough gumption to keep the big machine from bogging down of its own weight.

The door with Dr. Brockley's name above it was standing open. He came around from behind his desk, a middle-sized, middle-aged man in a gray herringbone suit, and gave me a quick hard hand.

"Mr. Archer? I happened to come in early this morning, so I can give you fifteen minutes. Then I'm due on the ward."

He placed me in a straight chair against the wall, brought me an ashtray, sat at his desk with his back to the window. He was quick in movement, very still in repose. His bald scalp and watchful eyes made him resemble a lizard waiting for a fly to expose itself.

"I understand you have a complaint against Carl Hallman. Perhaps you should understand that the hospital is not responsible for his actions. We're interested, but not responsible. He left here without permission."

"I know that. He told me."

"You're a friend of Hallman's?"

"I don't know him at all. He came to my house early this morning to try and get my help."

"What sort of help did he want?"

"It's a pretty involved story, having to do with his family. I think a lot of it was pure delusion. The main thing seems to be, he feels responsible for his father's death. He wants to get rid of the feeling. So he came to me. I happen to be a private detective. A friend of his recommended me to him."

When I named my profession, or sub-profession, the temperature went down. The doctor said frostily:

"If you're looking for family information, I can't give it to you."

"I'm not. I thought the best thing I could do for Hallman was bring him back here. I talked him into it, and we almost made it. Then he got excited and started throwing his weight around. As a matter of fact—" I'd been holding it back, because I was ashamed of it—"he took me by surprise and stole my car."

"It doesn't sound like him."

"Maybe I shouldn't say he stole it. He was upset, and I don't think he knew what he was doing. But he took it, and I want it back."

"Are you sure he took it?"

Another bureaucrat, I thought, with a noose of red tape up his sleeve. Another one of those. I said:

"I confess, Doctor. I never had a car. It was all a dream. The car was a sex symbol, see, and when it disappeared, it meant I'm entering the change of life."

He answered without a flicker of expression, smile or frown: "I mean, are you sure it wasn't the other one who stole your car? Another patient was with him when he took off last night. Didn't they stick together?"

"I only saw the one. Who was the other?"

Dr. Brockley lifted a manila folder out of his in-basket and studied its contents, or pretended to. "Normally," he said after a while, "we don't discuss our patients with outsiders. On the other hand, I'd like—" He closed the folder and slapped it down. "Let me put it this way. What do you intend to do about this alleged car theft? You want to see Hallman punished, naturally."

"Do I?"

"Don't you?"

"No."

"Why not?"

"I think he belongs in the hospital."

"What makes you think so?"

"He's flying, and he could be dangerous. He's a powerful boy. I don't want to be an alarmist, but he tried to throttle me."

"Really? You're not exaggerating?"

I showed him the marks on my neck. Dr. Brockley forgot himself for a second, and let his humanity show through, like a light behind a door. "Damn it, I'm sorry." But it was his patient he was sorry for. "Carl was doing so well these last few months—no acting out at all. What happened to set him off, do you know?"

"It may have been the idea of coming back here—this happened just up the road. The situation was sort of complicated. I let him talk too much, about his family, and then I made the mistake of arguing with him."

"Do you remember what about?"

"A fellow patient of his. Carl said he was a narcotics addict. He claimed the man gave him some suspicious information about a doctor he knew, a Dr. Grantland."

"I've met him. He's the Hallman family doctor. Incidentally, Grantland was instrumental in having Carl committed. It's natural that Carl would have feelings against him."

"He made some accusations. I don't think I'll repeat them, at least to another doctor."

"As you please." Brockley had resumed his poker face. "You say the source of the accusation was another patient, a narcotics addict?"

"That's right. I told Carl he should consider the source. He thought I was calling *him* a liar."

"What was the addict's name?"

"He wouldn't tell me."

Brockley said thoughtfully: "The man who escaped with him last night was a heroin addict. He's just another patient, of course—we treat them all alike—but he's quite a different kettle of fish from Carl Hallman. In spite of his disturbance, Carl's essentially a naïve and idealistic young man. Potentially a valuable man." The doctor was talking more to himself than to me. "I'd hate to think he's under Tom Rica's influence."

"Did you say Tom Rica?"

But the doctor had reached for his phone: "Miss Parish. This is Dr. Brockley. Tom Rica's folder, please— No, bring it to my office."

"I used to know a Tom Rica," I said when he put down the phone. "Let's see, he was eighteen about ten years ago, when he left Compton High. That would make him twenty-eight or -nine now. How old is Carl Hallman's friend?"

"Twenty-eight or -nine," Brockley said drily. "He looks a good deal older. Heroin has that effect, and the things that heroin leads to."

"This Rica has a record, eh?"

"Yes, he has. I didn't think he belonged here, but the authorities thought he could be rehabilitated. Maybe he can, at that. Maybe he can. We've had a few heroin cures. But he won't get cured wandering around the countryside."

There was a tap at the door. A young woman carrying a folder came in and handed it to Brockley. She was tall and generously made, with a fine sweep of bosom and the shoulders to support it. Her black hair was drawn back severely in a chignon. She had on a rather severely tailored dress which seemed intended to play down her femininity, without too much success.

"Miss Parish, this is Mr. Archer," Brockley said. "Mr. Archer ran into Carl Hallman this morning."

Her dark eyes lit with concern. "Where did you see him?"

"He came to my house."

"Is he all right?"

"It's hard to say."

"There's been a little trouble," Brockley put in. "Nothing too serious. I'll fill you in later if you like. I'm a bit rushed right now."

She took it as a reproof. "I'm sorry, Doctor."

"Nothing to be sorry about. I know you're interested in the case."

He opened the folder and began to scan it. Miss Parish went out rather hastily, bumping one hip on the doorframe. She had the kind of hips that are meant for child-bearing and associated activities. Brockley cleared his throat, and brought my attention back to him:

"Compton High School. Rica's your boy all right."

I WASN'T surprised, just disappointed. Tom had played his part in the postwar rebellion that turned so many boys against authority. But he had been one of the salvageable ones, I thought. I'd helped to get him probation after his first major conviction—car theft, as usual—taught him a little boxing and shooting, tried to teach him some of the other things a man should know. Well, at least he remembered my name.

"What happened to Tom?" I said.

"Who can say? He was only in a short time, and we hadn't got to him yet. Frankly, we don't spend much time on personal work with addicts. It's mostly up to them. Some of them make it, some don't." He looked down into the folder on his desk. "Rica has a history of trouble. We'll have to notify the police of his escape."

"What about Carl Hallman?"

"I've been in touch with his family. They're contacting Ostervelt, the sheriff in Purissima—he knows Carl. I'd rather handle it unofficially, if it's all right with you. Keep this car trouble off the books until Carl has a chance to think twice about it."

"You think he'll come to his senses and bring it back?"

"It wouldn't surprise me. We could at least give him a chance."

"He's not dangerous, in your opinion?"

"Everybody's dangerous, given the wrong circumstances. I can't predict individual behavior. I know that Carl got rough with you. Still, I'd be willing to take a chance on him. His hospital record is good. And there are other considerations. You know what happens when a patient goes out of here, with or without leave, and gets into any kind of trouble. The newspapers play it up, and then there's public pressure on us to go back to the snake-pit days—lock the loonies up and forget about them." Brockley's voice was bitter. He passed his hand over his mouth, pulling it to one side. "Are you willing to wait a bit, Mr. Archer? I can get you transportation back to town."

"I'd like a few questions answered first."

"I'm overdue on the ward now." He glanced at the watch on his wrist, then shrugged. "All right. Shoot away."

"Was Carl being kept here by his brother Jerry, after he needed it?"

"No. It was a staff matter, essentially my decision."

"Did he tell you he blamed himself for his father's death?"

"Many times. I'd say that guilt feeling was central in his illness. He also attached it to his mother's death. Her suicide was a great shock to him."

"She killed herself?"

"Yes, some years ago. Carl thought she did it because he broke her heart. It's typical of psychotic patients to blame themselves for everything that happens. Guilt is our main commodity here." He smiled. "We give it away."

"Hallman has a lot on his mind."

"He's been getting rid of it, gradually. And shock therapy helped. Some of my patients tell me that shock treatment satisfies their need for punishment. Maybe it does. We don't know for certain how it works."

"How crazy is he, can you tell me that?"

"He was manic-depressive, manic phase, when he came in. He isn't now, unless he's starting to go into a windup. Which I doubt."

"Is he likely to?"

"It depends on what happens to him." Brockley stood up, and came around the desk. He added, in a casual voice, but glancing sharply down at me: "You needn't feel that it's any responsibility of yours."

"I get your message. Lay off."

"For a while, anyway. Leave your telephone number with Miss Parish down the hall. If your car turns up, I'll get in touch with you."

Brockley let me out, and walked rapidly away. A few steps down the hall, I found a door lettered with Miss Parish's name and her title, Psychiatric Social Worker. She opened it when I knocked.

"I've been hoping you'd come by, Mr. Archer, is it? Please sit down."

Miss Parish indicated a straight chair by her desk. Apart from the filing cabinets, the chair and desk were about all the furniture the small office contained. It was barer than a nun's cell.

"Thanks, I won't take the time to sit down. The doctor asked me to leave my telephone number with you, in case our friend changes his mind and comes back."

I recited the number. She sat down at her desk and wrote it on a memo pad. Then she gave me a bright and piercing look which made me self-conscious. Tall women behind desks had always bothered me, anyway. It probably went back to the vice-principal of Wilson Junior High, who disapproved of the live bait I used to carry in the thermos bottle in my lunch pail, and other ingenious devices. Vice-Principal Trauma with Archer's Syndrome. The hospital atmosphere had me thinking that way.

"You're not a member of Mr. Hallman's immediate family, or a close friend." The statement lifted at the end into a question.

"I never saw him until today. I'm mainly interested in getting my car back."

"I don't understand. You mean he has your car?"

"He took it away from me." Since she seemed interested, I outlined the circumstances.

Her eyes darkened like thunderclouds. "I can't believe it."

"Brockley did."

"I'm sorry, I don't mean I doubt your word. It's simply—this eruption doesn't fit in with Carl's development. He's been making such wonderful strides with us—helping us look after the less competent ones— But of course you're not interested. You're naturally resentful about the loss of your car."

"Not so very. He's had a good deal of trouble. I can afford a little, if he had to pass it on."

She looked more friendly. "You sound as though you talked to him."

"He talked to me, quite a lot. I almost got him back here."

"Did he seem disturbed? Apart from the outburst of violence, I mean?"

"I've seen worse, but I'm no judge. He was pretty bitter about his family."

"Yes, I know. It was his father's death that set him off in the first place. The first few weeks he talked of nothing else. But the trouble had died down, at least I thought it had. Of course I'm not a psychiatrist. On the other hand, I've had a lot more to do with Carl than any of the psychiatrists." She added softly: "He's a sweet person, you know."

Under the circumstances, the sentiment seemed slightly sticky. I said: "He picked a funny way to show it."

Miss Parish had emotional equipment to match her splendid physical equipment. The thunderclouds came into her eyes again, with lightning. "He's not responsible!" she cried. "Can't you see that? You mustn't judge him."

"All right. I'll go along with that."

This seemed to calm her, though her brow stayed dark. "I can't imagine what happened to stir him up. Considering the distance he'd had to come back, he was the most promising patient on the ward. He was due for a P-card in a very few weeks. He'd probably have gone home in two or three months. Carl didn't have to run away, and he knew it."

"Remember he had another man with him. Tom Rica may have done some pretty good needling."

"Is Tom Rica with him now?"

"He wasn't when I saw Carl."

"That's good. I shouldn't say it about a patient, but Tom Rica is a poor risk. He's a heroin addict, and this isn't his first cure. Or his last, I'm afraid."

"I'm sorry to hear it. I knew him when he was a boy. He had his troubles even then, but he was a bright kid."

"It's queer that you should know Rica," she said with some suspicion. "Isn't that quite a coincidence?"

"No. Tom Rica sent Carl Hallman to me."

"They are together, then?"

"They left here together. Afterwards, they seem to have gone separate ways."

"Oh, I hope so. An addict looking for dope, and a vulnerable boy like Carl—they could make an explosive combination."

"Not a very likely combination," I said. "How did they happen to be buddies?"

"I wouldn't say they were buddies, exactly. They were committed from the same place, and Carl's been looking after Rica on the ward. We never have enough nurses and technicians to go around, so our better patients help to take care of the worse ones. Rica was in a bad way when he came in."

"How long ago was that?"

"A couple of weeks. He had severe withdrawal symptoms—couldn't eat, couldn't sleep. Carl was a positive saint with him: I watched them together. If I'd known how it was going to turn out, I'd have—" She broke off, clamping her teeth down on her lower lip.

"You like Carl," I said in a neutral tone.

The young woman colored, and answered rather sharply: "You would, too, if you knew him when he's himself."

Maybe I would, I thought, but not the way Miss Parish did. Carl Hallman was a handsome boy, and a handsome boy in trouble was a double threat to women, a triple threat if he needed mothering.

Not needing it, and none being offered, I left.

⪢⪢⪢⪢⪢
⪢⪢⪢⪢⪢ *chapter* 7
⪢⪢⪢⪢⪢

THE address which Carl had given me for his wife was near the highway in an older section of Purissima. The highway traffic thrummed invisibly like a damaged artery under the noon silence in the street. Most of the houses were frame cottages or stucco boxes built in the style of thirty years ago. A few were older, three-story mansions surviving from an era of elegance into an era of necessity.

Two-twenty was one of these. Its long closed face seemed abashed by the present. Its white wooden walls needed paint. The grass in the front yard had grown and withered, untouched by the human hand.

I asked the cab-driver to wait and knocked on the front door, which was surmounted by a fanlight of ruby-colored glass. I had to knock several times before I got an answer. Then the door was unlocked and opened, reluctantly and partially.

The woman who showed herself in the aperture had unlikely purplish red hair cut in bangs on her forehead and recently permanented. Blue eyes burned like gas-flames in her rather inert face.

Her mouth was crudely outlined in fresh lipstick, which I guessed she had just dabbed on as a concession to the outside world. The only other concession was a pink nylon robe from which her breasts threatened to overflow. I placed her age in the late forties. She couldn't be Mrs. Carl Hallman. At least I hoped she couldn't.

"Is Mrs. Hallman home?"

"No, she isn't here. I'm Mrs. Gley, her mother." She smiled meaninglessly. There was lipstick on her teeth, too, gleaming like new blood. "Is it something?"

"I'd like very much to see her."

"Is it about—him?"

"Mr. Hallman, you mean?"

She nodded.

"Well, I would like to talk to him."

"Talk to him! It needs more than talk to him. You might as well talk to a stone wall—beat your head bloody against it trying to change his ways." Though she seemed angry and afraid, she spoke in a low monotone. Her voice was borne on a heavy breath in which Sen-Sen struggled for dominance. You inhaled it as much as heard it.

"Is Mr. Hallman here?"

"No, thank God for small mercies. He hasn't been here. But I've been expecting him ever since she got that call from the hospital." Her gaze, which had swiveled past me to the street, returned to my face. "Is that your taxi?"

"Yes."

"Well, that's a relief. Are you from the hospital?"

"I just came from there."

I'd intended some misrepresentation, which she made me regret immediately:

"Why don't you keep them locked up better? You can't let crazymen run around loose. If you knew what my girl has suffered from that man—it's a terrible thing." She took the short easy step from motherly concern to self-concern: "Sometimes I think I'm the one who suffered most. The things I hoped and planned for that girl, and then she had to bring *that* one into the family. I begged and pleaded with her to stay home today. But no, she has to go to work, you'd think the office couldn't go on without her. She leaves me here by myself to cope."

She spread out her hands and pressed them into her bosom, the white flesh rising like dough between her fingers.

"It isn't fair. The world is cruel. You work and hope and plan, then everything goes to pieces. I didn't deserve it." A few easy tears ran down her cheeks. She found a ball of Kleenex in her sleeve and wiped her eyes. They shone, undimmed by her grief, with a remarkable intensity. I wondered what fuel fed them.

"I'm sorry, Mrs. Gley. I'm new on this case. My name is Archer. May I come in and talk to you?"

"Come in if you like. I don't know what *I* can tell you. Mildred ought to be home over the noon-hour, she promised she would."

She moved along the dim hallway, a middle-aged woman going to seed, but not entirely gone. There was something about the way she carried herself: old beauty and grace controlling her flesh, like an unforgotten discipline. She turned at a curtained archway behind which voices murmured.

"Please go in and sit down. I was just changing for lunch. I'll put something on."

She started up a flight of stairs which rose from the rear of the hallway. I went in through the curtains, and found myself in a twilit sitting-room with a lighted television screen. At first the people on the screen were unreal shadows. After I sat and watched them for a few minutes, they became realer than the room. The screen became a window into a brightly lighted place where life was being lived, where a beautiful actress couldn't decide between career and children and had to settle for both. The actual windows of the sitting-room were heavily blinded.

In the shifting light from the screen, I noticed an empty glass on the coffeetable beside me. It smelled of gin. Just to keep my hand in, I made a search for the bottle. It was stuffed behind the cushion of my chair, a half-empty Gordon's bottle, its contents transparent as tears. Feeling a little embarrassed, I returned it to its hiding place. The woman on the screen had had her baby, and held it up to her husband for his approval.

The front door opened and closed. Quick heels clicked down the hallway, and paused at the archway. I started to get up. A woman's voice said:

"Who—Carl? Is that you, Carl?"

Her voice was high. She looked very pale and dark-eyed in the light from the screen, almost like a projection from it. She fumbled behind the curtains for a lightswitch. A dim ceiling light came on over my head.

"Oh. Excuse me. I thought you were someone else."

She was young and small, with a fine small head, its modeling emphasized by a short boyish haircut. She had on a dark business suit which her body filled the way grapes fill their skins. She held a shiny black plastic bag, like a shield, in front of it.

"Mrs. Hallman?"

"Yes." Her look said: who are you, and what are you doing here?

I told her my name. "Your mother asked me to sit down for a minute."

"Where is Mother?" She tried to speak in an ordinary tone, but she looked at me suspiciously, as if I had Mother's body hidden in a closet.

"Upstairs."

"Are you a policeman?"

"No."

"I just wondered. She phoned me at the office about half an hour ago and said she was going to ask for police protection. I couldn't get away immediately."

She stopped abruptly, and looked around the room. Its furnishings would have been antiques if they'd ever possessed distinction. The carpet was threadbare, the wallpaper faded and stained brown in patches. The mohair sofa that matched the chair I'd sat in was ripped and spilling its guts. The mahogany veneer was peeling off the coffeetable which held the empty glass. It was no wonder Mrs. Gley preferred darkness and gin and television to the light of morning.

The girl went past me in a birdlike rush, snatched up the glass, and sniffed at it. "I thought so."

On the screen behind her a male announcer, not so very male, was telling women how to be odorless and beloved. The girl turned with the glass in her hand. For a second I thought she'd throw it at the screen. Instead she stooped and switched the television off. Its light faded slowly like a dream.

"Did Mother pour you a drink?"

"Not yet."

"Has anyone else been here?"

"Not that I know of. But your mother may have the right idea. I mean, about police protection."

She looked at me in silence for a minute. Her eyes were the same color as her mother's, and had the same intensity, almost tangible on my face. Her gaze dropped to the glass in her hand. Setting it down, she said under cover of the movement: "You know about Carl? Did Mother tell you?"

"I talked to Dr. Brockley at the hospital this morning. I had a run-in with your husband earlier. As a matter of fact he took my car." I told her about that.

She listened with her head bowed, biting one knuckle like a doleful child. But there was nothing childish about the look she gave me. It held a startled awareness, as if she'd had to grow up in a hurry, painfully. I had a feeling that she was the one who had suffered most in the family trouble. There was resignation in her posture, and in the undertones of her voice:

"I'm sorry. He never did anything like that before."

"I'm sorry, too."

"Why did you come here?"

I had several motives, some more obscure than others. I picked the easiest: "I want my car back. If I can handle it myself, without reporting it as a theft—"

"But you said yourself that we should call the police."

"For protection, yes. Your mother's frightened."

"Mother's very easily frightened. I'm not. Anyway, there's no basis for it. Carl's never hurt anyone, let alone Mother and me. He talks a lot sometimes—that's all it amounts to. I'm not afraid of him." She gave me a shrewd and very female glance. "Are you?"

Under the circumstances, I had to say I wasn't. I couldn't be sure, though. Perhaps that was my reason for coming there—the obscurest motive that underlay the others.

"I've always been able to handle Carl," she said. "I'd never have let them take him to the hospital, if I could have kept him here and looked after him myself. But somebody had to go to work." She frowned. "What can be keeping Mother? Excuse me for a minute."

She left the room and started up the stairs. The ringing of a telephone brought her down into the hallway again. From somewhere upstairs her mother called:

"Is that you, Mildred? The phone's ringing."

"Yes. I'll get it." I heard her lift the receiver. "This is Mildred. Zinnie? What do you want? . . . Are you sure? . . . No, I can't. I can't possibly. . . . I don't believe it. . . ." Then, on a rising note: "All *right*. I'll come."

The receiver dropped in its cradle. I went to the door and looked into the hallway. Mildred was leaning against the wall beside the telephone table. Her face was wan, her eyes shock-bright. Her gaze shifted to me, but it was so inward I don't think it took me in.

"Trouble?"

She nodded mutely and drew in a shuddering breath. It came out as a sigh:

"Carl's at the ranch now. One of the hands saw him. Jerry isn't there, and Zinnie's terrified."

"Where's Jerry?"

"I don't know. In town, probably. He follows the stock market every day until two, at least he used to."

"What's she so scared about?"

"Carl has a gun with him." Her voice was low and wretched.

"You're sure?"

"The man who saw him said so."

"Is he likely to use it?"

"No. I don't think so. It's the others I'm worried about—what they might do to Carl if there's any shooting."

"What others?"

"Jerry, and the sheriff and his deputies. They've always taken orders from the Hallmans. I've got to go and find Carl—talk to him, before Jerry gets back to the ranch."

But she was having a hard time getting under way. She stood stiff against the wall, hands knotted at the ends of their straight arms, immobilized by tension. When I touched her elbow, she shied:

"Yes?"

"I have a taxi waiting. I'll take you out there."

"No. Taxis cost money. We'll go in my car." She scooped up her bag and pressed it under her arm.

"Go where?" her mother cried from the top of the stairs. "Where are you going? You're not going to leave me alone."

Mrs. Gley came down in a rush. She had on a kind of tea gown whose draperies flew out behind her, like the tail of a blowzy comet.

Her body swayed softly and heavily against the newel post at the foot of the stairs. "You can't leave me alone," she repeated.

"I'm sorry, Mother. I have to go to the ranch. Carl's out there now, so there's nothing for you to worry about."

"Nothing to worry about, that's a good one. I've got my life to worry about, that's all. And your place is with your mother at this time."

"You're talking nonsense."

"Am I? When all I ask is a little love and sympathy from my own daughter?"

"You've had all I've got."

The younger woman turned and started for the door. Her mother followed her, a clumsy ghost trailing yellowing draperies and the powerful odor of Sen-Sen. Either her earlier drinks were catching up with her, or she had another bottle upstairs. She made her final plea, or threat:

"I'm drinking, Mildred."

"I know, Mother."

Mildred opened the door and went out.

"Don't you care?" her mother screamed after her.

Mrs. Gley turned to me as I passed her in the doorway. The light from the window over the door lent her face a rosy youthfulness. She looked like a naughty girl who was trying to decide whether or not to have a tantrum. I didn't wait to find out if she did.

›››››››››
››››››››› *chapter* 8
›››››››››

MILDRED HALLMAN'S car was an old black Buick convertible. It was parked behind my cab, wide of the curb. I paid off the cab-driver and got in. Mildred was sitting on the righthand side of the front seat.

"You drive, will you?" She said as we started: "Between Carl and Mother, I'm completely squeezed out. They both need a keeper, and in the end it always turns out to be me. No, don't think I'm feeling sorry for myself, because I'm not. It's nice to be needed."

She spoke with a kind of wilted gallantry. I looked at her. She'd leaned her head against the cracked leather seat, and closed her eyes. Without their light and depth in her face, she looked about thirteen. I caught myself up short, recognizing a feeling I'd had before. It started out as paternal sympathy but rapidly degenerated, if I let it. And Mildred had a husband.

"You're fond of your husband," I said.

She answered dreamily: "I'm crazy about him. I had a crush on him in high school, the first and only crush I ever had. Carl was a big wheel in those days. He barely knew I existed. I kept hoping, though." She paused, and added softly: "I'm still hoping."

I stopped for a red light, and turned right onto the highway which paralleled the waterfront. Gas fumes mixed with the odors of fish and underwater oil wells. To my left, beyond a row of motels and seafood restaurants, the sea lay low and flat and solid like blue tiling, swept clean and polished. Some white triangular sails stood upright on it.

We passed a small-boat harbor, gleaming white on blue, and a long pier draped with fishermen. Everything was as pretty as a post-card. The trouble with you, I said to myself: you're always turning over the postcards and reading the messages on the underside. Writ-ten in invisible ink, in blood, in tears, with a black border around them, with postage due, unsigned, or signed with a thumbprint.

Turning right again at the foot of the main street, we passed through an area of third-rate hotels, bars, pool halls. Stunned by sun and sherry, unemployed field hands and rumdums paraded like zom-bies on the noon pavements. A Mexican movie house marked the upper limits of the lower depths. Above it were stores and banks and office buildings, sidewalks bright with tourists, or natives who dressed like tourists.

The residential belt had widened since I'd been in Purissima last, and it was still spreading. New streets and housing tracts were climb-ing the coastal ridge and pushing up the canyons. The main street became a country blacktop which wound up over the ridge. On its far side a valley opened, broad and floored with rich irrigation green. A dozen miles across it, the green made inlets between the foothills and lapped at the bases of the mountains.

The girl beside me stirred. "You can see the house from here. It's off the road to the right, in the middle of the valley."

I made out a sprawling tile-roofed building floating low like a heavy red raft in the ridged green. As we went downhill, the house sank out of sight.

"I used to live in that house," Mildred said. "I promised myself I'd never go back to it. A building can soak up emotions, you know, so that after a while it has the same emotions as the people who live in it. They're in the cracks in the walls, the smokestains on the ceiling, the smells in the kitchen."

I suspected that she was dramatizing a little: there was some of her mother in her after all: but I kept still, hoping she'd go on talking.

"Greed and hate and snobbery," she said. "Everyone who lived in that house became greedy and hateful and snobbish. Except Carl. It's no wonder he couldn't take it. He's so completely different from the others." She turned toward me, the leather creaking under her. "I know what you're thinking—that Carl is crazy, or he was, and I'm twisting the facts around to suit myself. I'm not, though. Carl is good. It's often the very best people who crack up. And when he cracked, it was family pressure that did it to him."

"I gathered that, from what he said to me."

"Did he tell you about Jerry—constantly taunting him, trying to make him mad, then running to his father with tales of the trouble Carl made?"

"Why did he do that?"

"Greed," she said. "The well-known Hallman greed. Jerry wanted control of the ranch. Carl was due to inherit half of it. Jerry did everything he could to ruin Carl with his father, and Zinnie did, too. They were the ones who were really responsible for that last big quarrel, before the Senator died. Did Carl tell you about that?"

"Not very much."

"Well, Jerry and Zinnie started it. They got Carl talking about the Japanese, how much the family owed them for their land— I admit that Carl was hipped on the subject, but Jerry encouraged him to go on and on until he was really raving. I tried to stop it, but nobody listened to me. When Carl was completely wound up, Jerry went to the Senator and asked him to reason with Carl. You can imagine how much reasoning they did, when they got together. We could hear them shouting all over the house.

"The Senator had a heart attack that night. It's a terrible thing to say about a man, but Jerry was responsible for his father's death. He may even have planned it that way: he knew his father wasn't to be excited. I heard Dr. Grantland warn the family myself, more than once."

"What about Dr. Grantland?"

"In what way do you mean?"

"Carl thinks he's crooked," I hesitated, then decided she could hold it: "In fact, he made some pretty broad accusations."

"I think I've heard them. But go on."

"Conspiracy was one of them. Carl thought Grantland and his brother conspired to have him committed. But the doctor at the hospital says there's nothing to it."

"No," she said. "Carl needed hospital treatment. I signed the necessary papers. That was all aboveboard. Only, Jerry made me and Carl sign other papers at the same time, making him Carl's legal guardian. I didn't know what it meant. I thought it was just a part of the commitment. But it means that as long as Carl is ill, Jerry controls every penny of the estate."

Her voice had risen. She brought it under control and said more quietly: "I don't care about myself. I'd never go back there anyway. But Carl needs the money. He could get better treatment—the best psychiatrists in the country. It's the last thing Jerry wants, to see his brother cured. That would end the guardianship, you see."

"Does Carl know all this?"

"No, at least he's never heard it from me. He's mad enough at Jerry as it is."

"Your brother-in-law sounds charming."

"Yes indeed he is." Her voice was thin. "If it was just a question of saving Jerry, I wouldn't move a step in his direction. Not a step. But you know what will happen to Carl if he gets into any kind of trouble. He's already got more guilt than he can bear. It could set him back years, or make him permanent— No! I won't think about it. Nothing is going to happen."

She twisted in the seat away from me, as though I represented the things she feared. The road had become a green trench running through miles of orange trees. The individual rows of trees, slanting diagonally from the road, whirled and jumped backward in staccato movement. Mildred peered down the long empty vistas between them, looking for a man with straw-colored hair.

A large wooden sign, painted black on white, appeared at the road-side ahead: Hallman Citrus Ranch. I braked for the turn, made it on whining tires, and almost ran down a big old man in a sheriff's blouse. He moved away nimbly, then came heavily back to the side of the car. Under a wide-brimmed white hat, his face was flushed. Veins squirmed like broken purple worms under the skin of his nose. His eyes held the confident vacancy that comes from the exercise of other people's power.

"Watch where you're going, bud. Not that you're going anywhere, on this road. What do you think I'm here for, to get myself a tan?"

Mildred leaned across me, her breast live against my arm:

"Sheriff! Have you seen Carl?"

The old man leaned to peer in. His sun-wrinkles deepened and his mouth widened in a smile which left his eyes as vacant as before. "Why hello, Mrs. Hallman, I didn't see you at first. I must be going blind in my old age."

"Have you seen Carl?" she repeated.

He made a production out of answering her, marching around to her side of the car, carrying his belly in front of him like a gift. "Not personally, I haven't. We know he's on the ranch, though. Sam Yogan saw him to talk to, not much more than an hour ago."

"Was he rational?"

"Sam didn't say. Anyway, what would a Jap gardener know about it?"

"A gun was mentioned," I said.

The sheriff's mouth drooped at the corners. "Yeah, he's carrying a gun. I don't know where in hell he got hold of it."

"How heavy a gun?"

"Sam said not so heavy. But any gun is too big when a man is off his rocker."

Mildred let out a small cry.

"Don't worry, Mrs. Hallman. We got the place staked out. We'll pick him up." Tipping his hat back, he pushed his face in at her window. "You better get rid of your boyfriend before we do pick him up. Carl won't like it if you got a boyfriend, driving his car and all."

She looked from him to me, her mouth a thin line. "This is

Sheriff Ostervelt, Mr. Archer. I'm sorry I forgot my manners. Sheriff Ostervelt never had any to remember."

Ostervelt smirked. "Take a joke, eh?"

"Not from you," she said without looking at him.

"Still mad, eh? Give it time. Give it time."

He laid a thick hand on her shoulder. She took it in both of hers and flung it away from her. I started to get out of the car.

"Don't," she said. "He only wants trouble."

"Trouble? Not me," Ostervelt said. "I try to make a little joke. You don't think it's funny. Is that trouble, between friends?"

I said: "Mrs. Hallman's expected at the house. I said I'd drive her there. Much as I'd love to go on talking to you all afternoon."

"I'll take her to the house." Ostervelt gestured toward the black Mercury Special parked on the shoulder, and patted his holster. "The husband's lurking around in the groves, and I don't have the men to comb them for him. She might need protection."

"Protection is my business."

"What the hell does that mean?"

"I'm a private detective."

"What do you know? You got a license, maybe?"

"Yes. It's good statewide. Now do we go, or do we stay here and have some more repartee?"

"Sure," he said, "I'm stupid—just a stupid fool, and my jokes ain't funny. Only I got an official responsibility. So you better let me see that license you say you got."

Moving very slowly, the sheriff came around to my side of the car again. I slapped my photostat into his hand. He read it aloud, in an elocutionary voice, pausing to check the physical description against my appearance.

"Six-foot-two, one-ninety," he repeated. "A hunk of man. Love those beautiful blue eyes. Or are they gray, Mrs. Hallman? You'd know."

"Leave me alone." Her voice was barely audible.

"Sure. But I better drive you up to the house in person. Hollywood here has those beautiful powder-blue eyes, but it don't say here"—he flicked my photostat with his forefinger—"what his score is on a moving target."

I picked the black-and-white card out of his hand, released the

emergency brake, stepped on the gas. It wasn't politic. But enough
was enough.

>>>>>>>>>
>>>>>>>>> *chapter* 9
>>>>>>>>>

THE private road ran ruler-straight through the geo-
metric maze of the orange trees. Midway between the highway and
the house, it widened in front of several barnlike packing-sheds. The
fruit on the trees was unripe, and the red-painted sheds were empty
and deserted-looking. In a clearing behind them, a row of tumble-
down hutches, equally empty, provided shelter of a sort for migrant
pickers.

Nearly a mile further on, the main house stood back from the
road, half-shadowed by overarching oaks. Its brown adobe walls
looked as indigenous as the oaks. The red Ford station wagon and
the sheriff's patrol car on the curving gravel driveway seemed out of
place, or rather out of time. The thing that struck me most as I
parked in the driveway was a child's swing suspended by new rope
from a branch of one of the trees. No one had mentioned a child.

When I switched off the Buick's engine, the silence was almost ab-
solute. The house and its grounds were tranquil. Shadows lay soft as
peace in the deep veranda. It was hard to believe the other side of
the postcard.

The silence was broken by a screen door's percussion. A blonde
woman wearing black satin slacks and a white shirt came out on the
front veranda. She folded her arms over her breasts and stood as still
as a cat, watching us come up the walk.

"Zinnie," Mildred said under her breath. She raised her voice:
"Zinnie? Is everything all right?"

"Oh fine. Just lovely. I'm still waiting for Jerry to come home. You
didn't see him in town, did you?"

"I never see Jerry. You know that."

Mildred halted at the foot of the steps. There was a barrier of hostility, like a charged fence, between the two women. Zinnie, who was

at least ten years older, held her body in a compact defensive posture against the pressure of Mildred's eyes. Then she dropped her arms in a rather dramatic gesture which may have been meant for me.

"I hardly ever see him myself."

She laughed nervously. Her laugh was harsh and unpleasant, like her voice. It was easy for me to overlook the unpleasantness. She was a beautiful woman, and her green eyes were interested in me. The waist above her snug hips was the kind you can span with your two hands, and would probably like to.

"Who's your friend?" she purred.

Mildred introduced me.

"A private detective yet," Zinnie said. "The place is crawling with policemen already. But come on in. That sun is misery."

She held the door for us. Her other hand went to her face where the sun had parched the skin, then to her sleek hair. Her right breast rose elastically under the white silk shirt. A nice machine, I thought: pseudo-Hollywood, probably empty, certainly expensive, and not new; but a nice machine. She caught my look and didn't seem to mind. She switch-hipped along the hallway, to a large, cool living-room.

"I've been waiting for an excuse to have a drink. Mildred, you'll have ginger ale, I know. How's your mother, by the way?"

"Mother is fine. Thank you." Mildred's formality broke down suddenly. "Zinnie? Where is Carl now?"

Zinnie lifted her shoulders. "I wish I knew. He hasn't been heard from since Sam Yogan saw him. Ostervelt has several deputies out looking for him. The trouble is, Carl knows the ranch better than any of them."

"You said they promised not to shoot."

"Don't worry about that. They'll take him without any fireworks. That's where you come in, if and when he shows up."

"Yes." Mildred stood like a stranger in the middle of the floor. "Is there anything I can do now?"

"Not a thing. Relax. I need a drink if you don't. What about you, Mr. Archer?"

"Gibson, if it's available."

"That's handy, I'm a Gibson girl myself." She smiled brilliantly, too brilliantly for the circumstances. Zinnie seemed to be a trier, though, whatever else she was.

Her living-room bore the earmarks of a trier with a restless urge to be up to the minute in everything. Its bright new furniture was sectional, scattered around in cubes and oblongs and arcs. It sorted oddly with the dark oak floor and the heavily beamed ceiling. The adobe walls were hung with modern reproductions in limed oak frames. A row of book-club books occupied the mantel above the ancient stone fireplace. A free-form marble coffeetable held *Harper's Bazaar* and *Vogue* and a beautiful old silver handbell. It was a room in which an uneasy present struggled to overcome the persistent past.

Zinnie picked up the bell and shook it. Mildred jumped at the sound. She was sitting very tense on the edge of a sectional sofa. I sat down beside her, but she paid no attention to my presence. She turned to look out the window, toward the groves.

A tiny girl came into the room, pausing near the door at the sight of strangers. With light blond hair and delicate porcelain features, she was obviously Zinnie's daughter. The child was fussily dressed in a pale blue frock with a sash, and a matching blue ribbon in her hair. Her hand crept toward her mouth. The tiny fingernails were painted red.

"I was ringing for Juan, dear," Zinnie said.

"I want to ring for him, Mummy. Let me ring for Juan."

Though the child wasn't much more than three, she spoke very clearly and purely. She darted forward, reaching for the handbell. Zinnie let her ring it. Above its din, a white-jacketed Filipino said from the doorway:

"Missus?"

"A shaker of Gibsons, Juan. Oh, and ginger ale for Mildred."

"I want a Gibson, too," the little girl said.

"All right, darling." Zinnie turned to the houseboy: "A special cocktail for Martha."

He smiled comprehendingly, and disappeared.

"Say hello to your Aunt Mildred, Martha."

"Hello, Aunt Mildred."

"Hello, Martha. How are you?"

"I'm fine. How is Uncle Carl?"

"Uncle Carl is ill," Mildred said in a monotone.

"Isn't Uncle Carl coming? Mummy said he was coming. She said so on the telephone."

"No," her mother cut in. "You didn't understand what I said, dear. I was talking about somebody else. Uncle Carl is far away. He's living far away."

"Who is coming, Mummy?"

"Lots of people are coming. Daddy will be here soon. And Dr. Grantland. And Aunt Mildred is here."

The child looked up at her, her eyes clear and untroubled. She said: "I don't want Daddy to come. I don't like Daddy. I want Dr. Grantland to come. He will come and take us to a nice place."

"Not *us,* dear. You and Mrs. Hutchinson. Dr. Grantland will take you for a ride in his car, and you'll spend the day with Mrs. Hutchinson. Maybe all night, too. Won't that be fun?"

"Yes," the child answered gravely. "That will be fun."

"Now go and ask Mrs. Hutchinson to give you your lunch."

"I ate my lunch. I ate it all up. You said I could have a special cocktail."

"In the kitchen, dear. Juan will give you your cocktail in the kitchen."

"I don't want to go in the kitchen. I want to stay here, with people."

"No, you can't." Zinnie was getting edgy. "Now be a nice girl and do what you're told, or I'll tell Daddy about you. He won't like it."

"I don't care. I want to stay here and talk to the people."

"Some other time, Martha." She rose and hustled the little girl out of the room. A long wail ended with the closing of a door.

"She's a beautiful child."

Mildred turned to me. "Which one of them do you mean? Yes, Martha is pretty. And she's bright. But the way Zinnie is handling her —she treats her as if she were a doll."

Mildred was going to say more, but Zinnie returned, closely followed by the houseboy with the drinks. I drank mine in a hurry, and ate the onion by way of lunch.

"Have another, Mr. Archer." One drink had converted Zinnie's tension into vivacity, of a sort. "We've got the rest of the shaker to knock back between us. Unless we can persuade Mildred to climb down off her high wagon."

"You know where I stand on the subject." Mildred gripped her glass of ginger ale defensively. "I see you've had the room redone."

I said: "One's enough for me, thanks. What I'd like to do, if you don't object, is talk to the man who saw your brother-in-law. Sam something?"

"Sam Yogan. Of course, talk to Sam if you like."

"Is he around now?"

"I think so. Come on, I'll help you find him. Coming, Mildred?"

"I'd better stay here," Mildred said. "If Carl comes to the house, I want to be here to meet him."

"Aren't you afraid of him?"

"No, I'm not afraid of him. I love my husband. No doubt it's hard for you to understand that."

The hostility between the two women kept showing its sharp edges. Zinnie said:

"Well, I'm afraid of him. Why do you think I'm sending Martha to town? And I've got half a mind to go myself."

"With Dr. Grantland?"

Zinnie didn't answer. She rose abruptly, with a glance at me. I followed her through a dining-room furnished in massive old mahogany, into a sunlit kitchen gleaming with formica and chrome and tile. The houseboy turned from the sink, where he was washing dishes:

"Yes, Missus?"

"Is Sam around?"

"Before, he was talking to policeman."

"I know that. Where is he now?"

"Bunkhouse, greenhouse, I dunno." The houseboy shrugged. "I pay no attention to Sam Yogan."

"I know that, too."

Zinnie moved impatiently through a utility room to the back door. As soon as we stepped outside, a young man in a western hat raised his head from behind a pile of oak logs. He came around the woodpile, replacing his gun in its holster, swaggering slightly in his deputy's suntans.

"I'd stay inside if I was you, Mrs. Hallman. That way we can look after you better." He looked inquiringly at me.

"Mr. Archer is a private detective."

A peevish look crossed the young deputy's face, as though my presence threatened to spoil the game. I hoped it would. There were too many guns around.

"Any sign of Carl Hallman?" I asked him.

"You check in with the sheriff?"

"I checked in." Ostensibly to Zinnie, I said: "Didn't you say there wouldn't be any shooting? That the sheriff's men would take your brother-in-law without hurting him?"

"Yes. Sheriff Ostervelt promised to do his best."

"We can't guarantee nothing," the young deputy said. Even as he spoke, he was scanning the tree-shaded recesses of the back yard, and the dense green of the trees that stretched beyond. "We got a dangerous man to deal with. He bust out of a security ward last night, stole a car for his getaway, probably stole the gun he's carrying."

"How do you know he stole a car?"

"We found it, stashed in a tractor turnaround between here and the main road. Right near where the old Jap ran into him."

"Green Ford convertible?"

"Yeah. You seen it?"

"It's my car."

"No kidding? How'd he happen to steal your car?"

"He didn't exactly steal it. I'm laying no charges. Take it easy with him if you see him."

The deputy's face hardened obtusely. "I got my orders."

"What are they?"

"Fire if fired upon. And that's leaning way over backwards. You don't play footsie with a homicidal psycho, Mister."

He had a point: I'd tried to, and got my lumps. But you didn't shoot him, either.

"He isn't considered homicidal."

I glanced at Zinnie for confirmation. She didn't speak, or look in my direction. Her pretty head was cocked sideways in a strained listening attitude. The deputy said:

"You should talk to the sheriff about that."

"He didn't threaten Yogan, did he?"

"Maybe not. The Jap and him are old pals. Or maybe he did, and the Jap ain't telling us. We do know he's carrying a gun, and he knows how to use it."

"I'd like to talk to Yogan."

"If you think it'll do you any good. Last I saw of him he was in the bunkhouse."

He pointed between the oaks to an old adobe which stood on the edge of the groves. Behind us, the sound of an approaching car floated over the housetop.

"Excuse me, Mr. Carmichael," Zinnie said. "That must be my husband."

Walking quickly, she disappeared around the side of the house. Carmichael pulled his gun and trotted after her. I followed along, around the attached greenhouse which flanked the side of the house.

A silver-gray Jaguar stopped behind the Buick convertible in the driveway. Running across the lawn toward the sports car, under the towering sky, Zinnie looked like a little puppet, black and white and gold, jerked across green baize. The big man who got out of the car slowed her with a gesture of his hand. She looked back at me and the deputy, stumbling a little on her heels, and assumed an awkward noncommittal pose.

>>>>>>>>
>>>>>>>> *chapter* 10
>>>>>>>>

THE driver of the Jaguar had dressed himself to match it. He had on gray flannels, gray suede shoes, a gray silk shirt, a gray tie with a metallic sheen. In striking contrast, his face had the polished brown finish of hand-rubbed wood. Even at a distance, I could see he used it as an actor might. He was conscious of planes and angles, and the way his white teeth flashed when he smiled. He turned his full smile on Zinnie.

I said to the deputy: "That wouldn't be Jerry Hallman."

"Naw. It's some doctor from town."

"Grantland?"

"I guess that's his name." He squinted at me sideways. "What kind of detective work do you do? Divorce?"

"I have."

"Which one in the family hired you, anyway?"

I didn't want to go into that, so I gave him a wise look and drifted away. Dr. Grantland and Zinnie were climbing the front steps. As she passed him in the doorway, Zinnie looked up into his face. She inclined her body so that her breast touched his arm. He put the same arm around her shoulders, turned her away from him, and propelled her into the house.

Without going out of my way to make a lot of noise, I mounted the veranda and approached the screen door. A carefully modulated male voice was saying:

"You're acting like a wild woman. You don't have to be so conspicuous."

"I want to be. I want everyone to know."

"Including Jerry?"

"Especially him." Zinnie added illogically: "Anyway, he isn't here."

"He soon will be. I passed him on the way out. You should have seen the look he gave me."

"He hates anybody to pass him."

"No, there was more to it than that. Are you sure you haven't told him about us?"

"I wouldn't tell him the time of day."

"What's this about wanting everybody to know then?"

"I didn't mean anything. Except that I love you."

"Be quiet. Don't even say it. You could throw everything away, just when I've got it practically made."

"Tell me."

"I'll tell you afterwards. Or perhaps I won't tell you at all. It's working out, and that's all you need to know. Anyway, it will work out, if you can act like a sensible human being."

"Just tell me what to do, and I'll do it."

"Then remember who you are, and who I am. I'm thinking about Martha. You should be, too."

"Yes. I forget her sometimes, when I'm with you. Thank you for reminding me, Charlie."

"Not Charlie. Doctor. Call me doctor."

"Yes, Doctor." She made the word sound erotic. "Kiss me once, Doctor. It's been a long time."

Having won his point, he became bland. "If you insist, Mrs. Hallman."

She moaned. I walked to the end of the veranda, feeling a little let down because Zinnie's vivacity hadn't been for me. I lit a consolatory cigarette.

At the side of the house, childish laughter bubbled. I leaned on the railing and looked around the corner. Mildred and her niece were playing a game of catch with a tennisball. At least it was catch for Mildred, when Martha threw the ball anywhere near her. Mildred rolled the ball to the child, who scampered after it like a small utility infielder in fairy blue. For the first time since I'd met her, Mildred looked relaxed.

A gray-haired woman in a flowered dress was watching them from a chaise longue in the shade. She called out:

"Martha! You mustn't get overtired. And keep your dress clean."

Mildred turned on the older woman: "Let her get dirty if she likes."

But the spell of the game was broken. Smiling a perverse little smile, the child picked up the ball and threw it over the picket fence that surrounded the lawn. It bounced out of sight among the orange trees.

The woman on the chaise longue raised her voice again:

"Now look what you've done, you naughty girl—you've gone and lost the ball."

"Naughty girl," the child repeated shrilly, and began to chant: "Martha's a naughty girl, Martha's a naughty girl."

"You're not, you're a nice girl," Mildred said. "The ball isn't lost. I'll find it."

She started for the gate in the picket fence. I opened my mouth to warn her not to go into the trees. But something was going on in the driveway behind me. Car wheels crunched in the ground, and slid to a stop. I turned and saw that it was a new lavender Cadillac with gold trim.

The man who got out of the driver's seat was wearing fuzzy tweeds. His hair and eyes had the same coloring as Carl, but he was older, fatter, shorter. Instead of hospital pallor, his face was full of angry blood.

Zinnie came out on the veranda to meet him. Unfortunately her lipstick was smeared. Her eyes looked feverish.

"Jerry, thank God you're here!" The dramatic note sounded wrong, and she lowered her voice: "I've been worried sick. Where on earth have you been all day?"

He stumped up the steps and faced her, not quite as tall as she was on her heels. "I haven't been gone all day. I drove down to see Brockley at the hospital. Somebody had to give him the bawling-out he had coming to him. I told him what I thought of the loose way they run that place."

"Was that wise, dear?"

"It was some satisfaction, anyway. These bloody doctors! They take the public's money and—" He jerked a thumb toward Grantland's car: "Speaking of doctors, what he's doing here? Is somebody sick?"

"I thought you knew, about Carl. Didn't Ostie stop you at the road?"

"I saw his car there, he wasn't in it. What about Carl?"

"He's on the ranch, carrying a gun." Zinnie saw the shock on her husband's face, and repeated: "I thought you knew. I thought that's why you were staying away, because you're afraid of Carl."

"I'm not afraid of him," he said, on a rising note.

"You were, the day he left here. And you should be, after the things he said to you." She added, with unconscious cruelty, perhaps not entirely unconscious: "I believe he wants to kill you, Jerry."

His hands clutched his stomach, as though she'd struck him a physical blow there. They doubled into fists.

"You'd like that, wouldn't you? You and Charlie Grantland?"

The screen door rattled. Grantland came out on cue. He said with false joviality: "I *thought* I heard someone taking my name in vain. How are you, Mr. Hallman?"

Jerry Hallman ignored him. He said to his wife: "I asked you a simple question. What's he doing here?"

"I'll give you a simple answer. I had no man around I could trust to take Martha into town. So I called Dr. Grantland to chauffeur her. Martha is used to him."

Grantland had come up beside her. She turned and gave him a little smile, her smudged mouth doubling its meaning. Of the three, she and Grantland formed the paired unit. Her husband was the one who stood alone. As if he couldn't bear that loneliness, he turned on his heel, walked stiffly down the veranda steps, and disappeared through the front door of the greenhouse.

Grantland took a gray handkerchief out of his breast pocket and wiped Zinnie's mouth. The center of her body swayed toward him.

"Don't," he said urgently. "He knows already. You must have told him."

"I asked him for a divorce—you know that—and he's not a complete fool. Anyway, what does it matter?" She had the false assurance, or abandon, of a woman who has made a sexual commitment and swung her whole life from it like a trapeze. "Maybe Carl will kill him."

"Be quiet, Zin! Don't even think it—!"

His voice broke off. Her gaze had moved across me as he spoke, and telegraphed my presence to him. He turned on his toes like a dancer. The blood seeped out from underneath his tan. He might have been a beady-eyed old man with jaundice. Then he pulled himself together and smiled—a downward-turning smile but a confident one. It was unsettling to see a man's face change so rapidly and radically.

I threw away the butt of my cigarette, which seemed to have lasted for a long time, and smiled back at him. Felt from inside, like a rubber Halloween mask, my smile was a stiff grimace. Jerry Hallman relieved my embarrassment, if that is what I was feeling. He came hustling out of the greenhouse with a pair of shears in his hand, a dull blotched look on his face.

Zinnie saw him, and backed against the wall. "Charlie! Look out!"

Grantland turned to face Jerry as he came up the steps, a dumpy middle-aging man who couldn't stand loneliness. His eyes had a very solitary expression. The shears projected outward from the grip of his two hands, gleaming in the sun, like a double dagger.

"Yah, Charlie!" he said. "Look out! You think you can get away with my wife and my daughter both. You're taking nothing of mine."

"I had no such intention." Grantland stuttered over the words. "Mrs. Hallman telephoned—"

"Don't 'Mrs. Hallman' me. You don't call her that in town. Do you?" Standing at the top of the steps with his legs planted wide apart, Jerry Hallman opened and closed the shears. "Get out of here, you lousy cod. If you want to go on being a man, get off my property and stay off my property. That includes my wife."

Grantland had put on his old-man face. He backed away from the threatening edges and looked for support to Zinnie. Green-faced in the shadow, she stood still as a bas-relief against the wall. Her mouth worked, and managed to say:

"Stop it, Jerry. You're not making sense."

Jerry Hallman was at that trembling balance point in human rage where he might have alarmed himself into doing murder. It was time for someone to stop it. Shouldering Grantland out of my way, I walked up to Hallman and told him to put the shears down.

"Who do you think you're talking to?" he sputtered.

"You're Mr. Jerry Hallman, aren't you? I heard you were a smart man, Mr. Hallman."

He looked at me stubbornly. The whites of his eyes were yellowish from some internal complaint, bad digestion or bad conscience. Something deep in his head looked out through his eyes at me, gradually coming forward into light. Fear and shame, perhaps. His eyes seemed to be puzzled by dry pain. He turned and went down the steps and into the greenhouse, slamming the door behind him. Nobody followed him.

>>>>>>>>>
>>>>>>>>> *chapter* 11
>>>>>>>>>

VOICES rose on the far side of the house, as if another door had opened there. Female and excited, they sounded like chickens after a hawk has swooped. I ran down the steps and around the end of the veranda. Mildred came across the lawn toward me, holding the little girl's hand. Mrs. Hutchinson trailed behind them, her head turned at an angle toward the groves, her face as gray as her hair. The gate in the picket fence was open, but there was no one else in sight.

The child's voice rose high and penetrating. "Why did Uncle Carl run away?"

Mildred turned and bent over her. "It doesn't matter why. He likes to run."

"Is he mad at you, Aunt Mildred?"

"Not really, darling. He's just playing a game."

Mildred looked up and saw me. She shook her head curtly: I wasn't to say anything to frighten the child. Zinnie swept past me and lifted Martha in her arms. The deputy Carmichael was close behind her, unhitching his gun.

"What happened, Mrs. Hallman? Did you see him?"

She nodded, but waited to speak till Zinnie had carried the little girl out of hearing. Mildred's forehead was bright with sweat, and she was breathing rapidly. I noticed that she had the ball in her hand.

The gray-haired woman elbowed her way into the group. "I saw him, sneaking under the trees. Martha saw him, too."

Mildred turned on her. "He wasn't sneaking, Mrs. Hutchinson. He picked up the ball and brought it to me. He came right up to me." She displayed the ball, as if it was important evidence of her husband's gentleness.

Mrs. Hutchinson said: "I was never so terrified in my born days. I couldn't even open my mouth to let out a scream."

The deputy was getting impatient. "Hold it, ladies. I want a straight story, and fast. Did he threaten you, Mrs. Hallman—attack you in any way?"

"No."

"Did he say anything?"

"I did most of the talking. I tried to persuade Carl to come in and give himself up. When he wouldn't, I put my arms around him, to try and hold him. He was too strong for me. He broke away, and I ran after him. He wouldn't come back."

"Did he show his gun?"

"No." She looked down at Carmichael's gun. "Please, don't use your gun if you see my husband. I don't believe he's armed."

"Maybe not," Carmichael said noncommittally. "Where did all this happen?"

"I'll show you."

She turned and started toward the open gate, moving with a kind of dogged gallantry. It wasn't quite enough to hold her up. Suddenly she went to her knees and crumpled sideways on the lawn, a small dark-suited figure with spilled brown hair. The ball rolled out of her hand. Carmichael knelt beside her, shouting as if mere loudness could make her answer:

"Which way did he go?"

Mrs. Hutchinson waved her arm toward the groves. "Right through there, in the direction of town."

The young deputy got up and ran through the gateway in the picket fence. I ran after him, with some idea of trying to head off violence. The ground under the trees was adobe, soft and moist with cultivation. I never had gone well on a heavy track. The deputy was out of sight. After a while he was out of hearing, too. I slowed down and stopped, cursing my obsolescent legs.

It was purely a personal matter between me and my legs, because running couldn't accomplish anything, anyway. When I thought about it, I realized that a man who knew the country could hide for days on the great ranch. It would take hundreds of searchers to beat him out of the groves and canyons and creekbeds.

I went back the way I had come, following my own footmarks. Five of my walking steps, if I stretched my legs, equaled three of my running steps. I crossed other people's tracks, but had no way to identify them. Tracking wasn't my forte, except on asphalt.

After a long morning crowded with people under pressure, it was pleasant to be walking by myself in the green shade. Over my head, between the tops of the trees, a trickle of blue sky meandered. I let myself believe that there was no need to hurry, that trouble had been averted for the present. Carl had done no harm to anybody, after all.

Back-tracking on the morning, I walked slower and slower. Brockley would probably say that it was unconscious drag, that I didn't want to get back to the house. There seemed to be some truth in Mildred's idea that a house could make people hate each other. A house, or the money it stood for, or the cannibalistic family hungers it symbolized.

I'd run further than I'd realized, perhaps a third of a mile. Eventually the house loomed up through the trees. The yard was empty. Everything was remarkably still. One of the french doors was standing open. I went in. The dining-room had a curious atmosphere, unlived in and unlivable, like one of those three-walled rooms laid out in a museum behind silk rope: Provincial California Spanish, Pre-Atomic Era. The living-room, with its magazines and dirty glasses and Hollywood-Cubist furniture, had the same deserted quality.

I crossed the hallway and opened the door of a study lined with books and filing cabinets. The venetian blinds were drawn. The room had a musty smell. A dark oil portrait of a bald old man hung on one wall. His eyes peered through the dimness at me, out of a lean rapacious face. Senator Hallman, I presumed. I closed the study door on him.

I went through the house from front to back, and finally found two human beings in the kitchen. Mrs. Hutchinson was sitting at the kitchen table, with Martha on her knee. The elderly woman started at my voice. Her face had sharpened in the quarter-hour since I'd seen her. Her eyes were bleak and accusing.

"What happened next?" Martha said.

"Well, the little girl went to the nice old lady's house, and they had tea-cakes." Mrs. Hutchinson's eyes stayed on me, daring me to speak. "Tea-cakes and chocolate ice cream, and the old lady read the little girl a story."

"What was the little girl's name?"

"Martha, just like yours."

"She couldn't eat chocolate ice cream, 'cause of her algery."

"They had vanilla. We'll have vanilla, too, with strawberry jam on top."

"Is Mummy coming?"

"Not right away. She'll be coming later."

"Is Daddy coming? I don't want Daddy to come."

"Daddy won't—" Mrs. Hutchinson's voice broke off. "That's the end of the story, dear."

"I want another story."

"We don't have time." She set the child down. "Now run into the living-room and play."

"I want to go into the greenhouse." Martha ran to an inner door, and rattled the knob.

"No! Stay here! Come back here!"

Frightened by the woman's tone, Martha returned, dragging her feet.

"What's the matter?" I said, though I thought I knew. "Where is everybody?"

Mrs. Hutchinson gestured toward the door that Martha had tried to open. I heard a murmur of voices beyond it, like bees behind a wall. Mrs. Hutchinson rose heavily and beckoned me to her. Conscious of the child's unwavering gaze, I leaned close to the woman's mouth. She said:

"Mr. Hallman was ess aitch oh tee. He's dee ee ay dee."

"Don't spell! You mustn't spell!"

In a miniature fury, the child flung herself between us and struck the old woman on the hip. Mrs. Hutchinson drew her close. The child stood still with her face in the flowered lap, her tiny white arms embracing the twin pillars of the woman's legs.

I left them and went through the inner door. An unlit passageway lined with shelves ended in a flight of steps. I stumbled down them to a second door, which I opened.

The edge of the door struck softly against a pair of hind quarters. These happened to belong to Sheriff Ostervelt. He let out a little snort of angry surprise, and turned on me, his hand on his gun.

"Where do you think you're going?"

"Coming in."

"You're not invited. This is an official investigation."

I looked past him into the greenhouse. In the central aisle, between rows of massed cymbidiums, Mildred and Zinnie and Grantland were grouped around a body which lay face up. The face had been covered by a gray silk handkerchief, but I knew whose body it was. Jerry's fuzzy tweeds, his rotundity, his helplessness, gave him the air of a defunct teddy bear.

Zinnie stood above him, incongruously robed in ruffled white nylon. Without makeup, her face was almost as colorless as the robe. Mildred stood near her, looking down at the dirt floor. A little apart, Dr. Grantland leaned on one of the planters, controlled and watchful.

Zinnie's face worked stiffly: "Let him come in if he wants to, Ostie. We can probably use all the help we can get."

Ostervelt did as she said. He was almost meek about it. Which reminded me of the simple fact that Zinnie had just fallen heir to the Hallman ranch and whatever power went with it. Grantland didn't seem to need reminding. He leaned close to whisper in her ear, with something proprietary in the angle of his head.

She silenced him with a sidewise warning glance, and edged away from him. Acting on impulse—at least it looked like impulse from where I stood—Zinnie put her arm around Mildred and hugged her. Mildred made as if to pull away, then leaned on Zinnie and closed her eyes. Through the white-painted glass roof, daylight fell harsh and depthless on their faces, sistered by shock.

Ostervelt missed these things, which happened in a moment. He was fiddling with the lid of a steel box that stood on a workbench behind the door. Getting it open, he lifted out a piece of shingle to which a small gun was tied with twine.

"Okay, so you want to be a help. Take a look at this."

It was a small, short-barreled revolver, of about .25 caliber, probably of European make. The butt was sheathed in mother-of-pearl, and ornamented with silver filagree work. A woman's gun, not new: the silver was tarnished. I'd never seen it, or a gun like it, and I said so.

"Mrs. Hallman, Mrs. *Carl* Hallman, said you had some trouble with her husband this morning. He stole your car, is that right?"

"Yes, he took it."

"Under what circumstances?"

"I was driving him back to the hospital. He came to my house early this morning, with some idea I might be able to help him. I figured the best thing I could do for him was talk him into going back in. It didn't quite work."

"What happened?"

"He took me by surprise—overpowered me."

"What do you know?" Ostervelt smirked. "Did he pull this little gun on you?"

"No. He had no gun that I saw. I take it this is the gun that killed Hallman."

"You take it correct, mister. This is also the gun the brother had, according to Yogan's description of it. The doctor found it right beside the body. Two shells fired, two holes in the man's back. The doctor said he died instantly, that right, Doctor?"

"Within a few seconds, I'd say." Grantland was cool and professional. "There was no external bleeding. My guess is that one of the bullets pierced his heart. Of course it will take an autopsy to establish the exact cause of death."

"Did you discover the body, Doctor?"

"I did, as a matter of fact."

"I'm interested in matters of fact. What brought you out to the greenhouse?"

"The shots, of course."

"You heard them?"

"Very clearly. I was taking Martha's clothes out to the car."

Zinnie said wearily: "We all heard them. I thought at first that Jerry—" She broke off.

"Jerry what?" Ostervelt said.

"Nothing. Ostie? Do we have to go through this again—all this palaver? I'm very anxious to get Martha out of the house. God knows what this is doing to her. And wouldn't you accomplish more if you went out after Carl?"

"I got every free man in the department looking for him now. I can't leave until the deputy coroner gets here."

"Does that mean we have to wait?"

"Not right here, if it's getting you down. I think you ought to stick around the house, though."

"I've told you all I can," Grantland said. "And I have patients waiting. In addition to which, Mrs. Hallman has asked me to drive her daughter and her housekeeper into Purissima."

"All right. Go ahead, Doctor. Thanks for your help."

Grantland went out the back door. The two women came down the funereal aisle between the rows of flowers, bronze and green and blood-red. They walked with their arms around each other, and passed through the door that led toward the kitchen. Before the door closed, one of them broke into a storm of weeping.

The noise of grief is impersonal, and I couldn't be sure which one of them it was. But I thought it must have been Mildred. Her loss was the worst. It had been going on for a long time, and was continuing.

>>>>>>>>>>
>>>>>>>>>> *chapter* 12
>>>>>>>>>>

THE back door of the greenhouse opened, and two men came in. One was the eager young deputy who excelled at cross-country running. Carmichael's blouse was dark with sweat, and he was still breathing deeply. The other man was a Japanese of indeterminate age. When he saw the dead man on the floor, he stood still, with his head bowed, and took off his soiled cloth hat. His sparse gray hair stood erect on his scalp, like magnetized iron filings.

The deputy squatted and lifted the gray handkerchief over the dead man's face. His held breath came out.

"Take a good long look, Carmichael," the sheriff said. "You were supposed to be guarding this house and the people in it."

Carmichael stood up, his mouth tight. "I did my best."

"Then I'd hate to see your worst. Where in Christ's name did you go?"

"I went after Carl Hallman, lost him in the groves. He must of circled around and come back here. I ran into Sam Yogan back of the bunkhouse, and he told me he heard some shots."

"You heard the shots?"

The Japanese bobbed his head. "Yessir. Two shots." He had a mouthy old-country accent, and some trouble with his esses.

"Where were you when you heard them?"

"In the bunkhouse."

"Can you see the greenhouse from there?"

"Back door, you can."

"He must of left by the back door, Grantland was at the front, and the women came in the side here. You see him, going or coming?"

"Mr. Carl?"

"You know I mean him. Did you see him?"

"No sir. Nobody."

"Did you look?"

"Yessir. I looked out the door of the bunkhouse."

"But you didn't come and look in the greenhouse."

"No sir."

"Why?" The sheriff's anger, flaring and veering like fire in the wind, was turned on Yogan now. "Your boss was lying shot in here, and you didn't move a muscle."

"I looked out the door."

"But you didn't move a muscle to help him, or apprehend the killer."

"He was probably scared," Carmichael said. With the heat removed from him, he was relaxing into camaraderie.

Yogan gave the deputy a look of calm disdain. He extended his hands in front of his body, parallel and close together, as though he was measuring off the limits of his knowledge:

"I hear two guns—two shots. What does it mean? I see guns all morning. Shooting quail, maybe?"

"All right," the sheriff said heavily. "Let's get back to this morning. You told me Mr. Carl was a very good friend of yours, and that was the reason you weren't scared of him. Is that correct, Sam?"

"I guess so. Yessir."

"How good a friend, Sam? Would you let him shoot his brother and get away? Is that how good a friend?"

Yogan showed his front teeth in a smile which could have meant anything. His flat black eyes were opaque.

"Answer me, Sam."

Yogan said without altering his smile: "Very good friend."

"And Mr. Jerry? Was he a good friend?"

"Very good friend."

"Come off it, Sam. You don't like any of us, do you?"

Yogan grinned implacably, like a yellow skull.

Ostervelt raised his voice:

"Wipe the smile off, tombstone-teeth. You're not fooling anybody. You don't like me, and you don't like the Hallman family. Why the hell you came back here, I'll never know."

"I like the country," Sam Yogan said.

"Oh sure, you like the country. Did you think you could con the Senator into giving you your farm back?"

The old man didn't answer. He looked a little ashamed, not for himself. I gathered that he had been one of the Japanese farmers bought out by the Senator and relocated during the War. I gathered further that he made Ostervelt nervous, as though his presence was an accusation. An accusation which had to be reversed:

"You didn't shoot Mr. Jerry Hallman yourself, by any chance?"

Yogan's smile brightened into scorn.

Ostervelt moved to the workbench and picked up the shingle with the pearl-handled gun attached to it. "Come here, Sam."

Yogan stayed immobile.

"Come here, I said. I won't hurt you. I ought to kick those big white teeth down your dirty yellow throat, but I'm not gonna. Come here."

"You heard the sheriff," Carmichael said, and gave the small man a push.

Yogan came one step forward, and stood still. By sheer patience, his slight figure had become the central object in the room. Having nothing better to do, I went and stood beside him. He smelled faintly of fish and earth. After a while the sheriff came to him.

"Is this the gun, Sam?"

Yogan drew in his breath in a little hiss of surprise. He took the shingle and examined the gun minutely, from several angles.

"You don't have to eat it." Ostervelt snatched it away. "Is this the gun Mr. Carl had?"

"Yessir. I think so."

"Did he pull it on you? Threaten you with it?"

"No sir."

"Then how'd you happen to see it?"

"Mr. Carl showed it to me."

"He just walked up to you and showed you the gun?"

"Yessir."

"Did he say anything?"

"Yessir. He said, hello Sam, how are you, nice to see you. Very polite. Also, where is my brother? I said he went to town."

"Anything about the gun, I mean."

"Said did I recognize it. I said, yes."

"You recognized it?"

"Yessir. It was Mrs. Hallman's gun."

"Which Mrs. Hallman?"

"Old lady Mrs. Hallman, Senator's wife."

"This gun belonged to her?"

"Yessir. She used to bring it out to the back garden, shoot at the blackbirds. I said she wanted a better one, a shotgun. No, she said, she didn't want to hit them. Let them live."

"That must of been a long time ago."

"Yessir, ten-twelve years. When I came back here on the ranch, put in her garden for her."

"What happened to the gun?"

"I dunno."

"Did Carl tell you how *he* got it?"

"No sir. I didn't ask."

"You're a close-mouthed s.o.b., Sam. You know what that means?"

"Yessir."

"Why didn't you tell me all this this morning?"

"You didn't ask me."

The sheriff looked up at the glass roof, as if to ask for comfort and help in his deep tribulations. The only apparent result was the arrival of a moon-faced young man wearing shiny rimless spectacles and a shiny blue suit. I needed no intuition to tab him as the deputy coroner. He carried a black medical bag, and the wary good humor of men whose calling is death.

Surveying the situation from the doorway, he raised his hand to the sheriff and made a beeline for the body. A sheriff's captain with a tripod camera followed close on his heels. The sheriff joined them, issuing a steady flux of orders.

Sam Yogan bowed slightly to me, his forehead corrugated, his eyes bland. He picked up a watering can, filled it at a tin sink in the corner, and moved with it among the cymbidiums. Disregarding the flashbulbs, he was remote as a gardener bent in ritual over flowers in a print.

>>>>>>>>
>>>>>>>> *chapter* 13
>>>>>>>>

I WALKED around to the front of the house and rapped on the screen door. Zinnie answered. She had changed to a black dress without ornament of any kind. Framed in the doorway, she looked like a posed portrait of a young widow, carefully painted in two dimensions. The third dimension was in her eyes, which had green fire in their depths.

"Are you still here?"

"I seem to be."

"Come in if you like."

I followed her into the living-room, noticing how corseted her movements had become. The room had altered, too, though there was no change in its physical arrangement. The murder in the greenhouse had killed something in the house. The bright furnishings looked cheap and out of place in the old room, as if somebody had tried to set up modern housekeeping in an ancestral cave.

"Sit down if you like."

"Am I wearing out my welcome?"

"Everybody is," she said, a little obscurely. "I don't even feel at home here myself. Come to think of it, maybe I never did. Well, it's a little late to go into that now."

"Or a little early. No doubt you'll be selling."

"Jerry was planning to sell out himself. The papers are practically all drawn up."

"That makes it convenient."

Facing me in front of the dead hearth, she looked into my eyes for a long minute. Being a two-way experience, it wasn't unpleasant at all. The pain she'd just been through, or something else, had wiped out a certain crudity in her good looks and left them pretty dazzling. I hoped it wasn't the thought of a lot of new money shining in her head.

"You don't like me," she said.

"I hardly know you."

"Don't worry, you never will."

"There goes another bubble, iridescent but ephemeral."

"I don't think I like you, either. That's quite a spiel you have, for a cheap private detective. Where do you come from, Los Angeles?"

"Yep. How do you know I'm cheap?"

"Mildred couldn't afford you if you weren't."

"Unlike you, eh? I could raise my prices."

"I bet you could. And I was wondering when we were going to get around to that. It didn't take long, did it?"

"Get around to what?"

"What everybody wants. Money. The *other* thing that everybody wants." She turned, handling her body contemptuously and provocatively, identifying the first thing. "You might as well sit down and we'll talk about it."

"It will be a pleasure."

I sat on the end of a white *bouclé* oblong, and she perched tightly on the other end, with her beautiful legs crossed in front of her. "What I ought to do is tell Ostie to throw you the hell out of here."

"For any particular reason. Or just on general principles?"

"For attempted blackmail. Isn't blackmail the idea?"

"It never crossed my mind. Until now."

"Don't kid me. I know your type. Maybe you like to wrap it up in different words. I pay you a retainer to protect my interests or something like that. It's still blackmail, no matter how you wrap it."

"Or baloney, no matter how you slice it. But go on. It's a long time since anybody offered me some free money. Or is this only a daydream?"

She sneered, not very sophisticatedly. "How dare you try to be funny, with my husband not yet cold in his grave?"

"He isn't in it yet. And you can do better than that, Zinnie. Try another take."

"Have you no respect for a woman's emotions—no respect for anything?"

"Show me some real ones. You have them."

"What do you know about it?"

"I'd have to be blind and deaf not to. You go around shooting them off like fireworks."

She was silent. Her face was unnaturally calm, except for the deep dimension of the eyes. "You mean that scene on the front porch, no doubt. It didn't mean a thing. Not a thing." She sounded like a child repeating a lesson. "I was frightened and upset, and Dr. Grantland is an old friend of the family. Naturally I turned to him in trouble. You'd think even Jerry would understand that. But he's always been irrationally jealous. I can't even look at a man."

She sneaked a look at me to see if I believed her. Our eyes met.

"You can now."

"I tell you I'm not in the least interested in Dr. Grantland. Or anybody else."

"You're young to retire."

Her eyes narrowed rather prettily, like a cat's. Like a cat, she was kind of smart, but too self-centered to be really smart. "You're terribly cynical, aren't you? I hate cynical men."

"Let's stop playing games, Zinnie. You're crazy about Grantland. He's crazy about you. I hope."

"What do you mean, you hope?" she said, laying my last doubt to rest.

"I hope Charlie is crazy about you."

"He is. I mean, he would be, if I let him. What makes you think he isn't?"

"What makes you think it?"

She put her hands over her ears and made a monkey face. Even then, she couldn't look ugly. She had such good bones, her skeleton would have been an ornament in any closet.

"All this talky-talk," she said. "I get mixed up. Could we come down to cases? That business on the porch, I know it looks bad. I don't know how much you heard?"

I put on my omniscient expression. She was still coming to me, pressed by a fear that made her indiscreet.

"Whatever you heard, it doesn't mean I'm glad that Jerry is dead. I'm sorry he's dead." She sounded surprised. "I felt *sorry* for the poor guy when he was lying there. It wasn't his fault he didn't have it— that we couldn't make it together— Anyway, I had nothing to do with his death, and neither did Charlie."

"Who said you did?"

"Some people would say it, if they knew about that silly fuss on the porch. Mildred might."

"Where is Mildred now, by the way?"

"Lying down. I talked her into taking some rest before she goes back to town. She's emotionally exhausted."

"That was nice of you."

"Oh, I'm not a total all-round bitch. And I don't blame her for what her husband did."

"*If* he did." With nothing much to go on, I threw that in to test her reaction.

She took it personally, almost as an insult. "Is there any doubt he did it?"

"There always is, until it's proved in court."

"But he hated Jerry. He had the gun. He came here to kill Jerry, and we know he was here."

"We know he was here, all right. Maybe he still is. The rest is your version. I'd kind of like to hear his, before we find him guilty and execute him on the spot."

"Who said anything about executing him? They don't execute crazy people."

"They do, though. More than half the people who go to the gas-chamber in this state are mentally disturbed—medically insane, if not legally."

"But they'd never convict Carl. Look what happened last time."

"What did happen last time?"

She put the back of her hand to her mouth and looked at me over it.

"You mean the Senator's death, don't you?" I was frankly fishing, fishing in the deep green of her eyes.

She couldn't resist the dramatic thing. "I mean the Senator's murder. Carl murdered him. Everybody knows it, and they didn't do a thing to him except send him away."

"The way I heard it, it was an accident."

"You heard it wrong then. Carl pushed him down in the bathtub and held him until he drowned."

"How do you know?"

"He confessed the very next day."

"To you?"

"To Sheriff Ostervelt."

"Ostervelt told you this?"

"Jerry told me. He talked the sheriff out of laying charges. He wanted to protect the family name."

"Is that all he was trying to protect?"

"I don't know what you mean by that. Why did Mildred bring you out here, anyway?"

"For the ride. My main idea was to get my car back."

"When you get it, will you be satisfied?"

"I doubt it. I've never been yet."

"You mean you're going to poke around and twist the facts and try to prove that Carl didn't do—what he did do?"

"I'm interested in facts, as I told Dr. Grantland."

"What's he got to do with it?"

"I'd like an answer to that. Maybe you can tell me."

"I know he didn't shoot Jerry. The idea is ridiculous."

"Perhaps. It was your idea. But let's kick it around a little. If Yogan's telling the truth, Carl had the pearl-handled gun, or one like it. We don't know for certain that it killed your husband. We won't until we get ballistic evidence."

"But Charlie found it in the greenhouse, right beside the—poor Jerry."

"Charlie could have planted it. Or he could have fired it himself. That would make it easy for him to find."

"You're making this up."

But she was frightened. She didn't seem to know for sure that it hadn't happened that way.

"Did Ostervelt show you the gun?"

"I saw it."

"Did you ever see it before?"

"No." Her answer was emphatic and quick.

"Did you know it belonged to your mother-in-law?"

"No." But Zinnie asked no questions, showed no surprise, and took my word for it.

"Did you know she had a gun?"

"No. Yes. I guess I did. But I never saw it."

"I heard your mother-in-law committed suicide. Is that right?"

"Yes. Poor Alicia walked into the ocean, about three years ago."

"Why would she commit suicide?"

"Alicia had had a lot of illness."

"Mental?"

"I suppose you'd call it that. The menopause hit her very hard. She never came back, entirely. She was practically a hermit the last few years. She lived in the east wing by herself, with Mrs. Hutchinson to look after her. These things seem to run in the family."

"Something does. Do you know what happened to her gun?"

"Evidently Carl got hold of it, some way. Maybe she gave it to him before she died."

"And he's been carrying it all these years?"

"He could have hid it right here on the ranch. Why ask me? I don't know anything about it."

"Or who fired it in the greenhouse?"

"You know what I think about that. What I *know*."

"I believe you said you heard the shots."

"Yes. I heard them."

"Where were you, at the time?"

"In my bathroom. I'd just finished taking a shower." With never-say-die eroticism, she tried to set up a diversion: "If you want proof of that, examine me. I'm clean."

"Some other time. Stay clean till then. Is that the same bathroom your father-in-law was murdered in?"

"No. He had his own bathroom, opening off his bedroom. I wish you wouldn't use that word murder. I didn't mean to tell you that. I said it in confidence."

"I didn't realize that. Would you mind showing me that bathroom? I'd like to see how it was done."

"I don't know how it was done."

"You did a minute ago."

Zinnie took time out to think. Thinking seemed to come hard to her. "I only know what people tell me," she said.

"Who told you that Carl pushed his father down in the bathtub?"

"Charlie did, and he ought to know. He was the old man's doctor."

"Did he examine him after death?"

"Yes, he did."

"Then he must have known that the Senator didn't die of a heart attack."

"I told you that. Carl killed him."

"And Grantland knew it?"

"Of course."

"You realize what you've just said, Mrs. Hallman? Your good friends Sheriff Ostervelt and Dr. Grantland conspired to cover up a murder."

"No!" She flung the thought away from her with both hands. "I didn't mean it that way."

"How did you mean it?"

"I don't really know anything about it. I was lying."

"But now you're telling the truth."

"You've got me all twisted up. Forget what I said, eh?"

"How can I?"

"What are you looking for? Money? You want a new car?"

"I'm sort of attached to the old one. We'll get along better if you stop assuming I can be bought. It's been tried by experts."

She rose and stood over me, looking down in mingled fear and hatred. Making a great convulsive effort, she swallowed both. In the same effort, she changed her approach, and practically changed her personality. Her shoulders and breasts slumped, her belly arched forward, one of her hips tilted up. Even her eyes took on a melting-iceberg look.

"We *could* get along, quite nicely."

"Could we?"

"You wouldn't want to make trouble for little old me. Why don't you make us a shakerful of Gibsons instead? We'll talk it over?"

"Charlie wouldn't like it. And your husband's not yet cold in his grave, remember?"

There was a greenhouse smell in the room, the smell of flowers and earth and trapped heat. I got up facing her. She placed her hands on my shoulders and let her body come forward until it rested lightly against me. It moved in small intricate ways.

"Come on. What's the matter? Are you scared? I'm not. And I'm very good at it, even if I am out of practice."

In a way, I was scared. She was a hard blonde beauty fighting the world with two weapons, money and sex. Both of them had turned in her hands and scarred her. The scars were invisible, but I could sense the dead tissue. I wanted no part of her.

She exploded against me hissing like an angry cat, fled across the room to one of the deep windows. Her clenched hand jerked spasmodically at the curtains, like somebody signaling a train to stop.

Footsteps whispered on the floor behind me. It was Mildred, small and waiflike in her stocking feet.

"What on earth's the matter?"

Zinnie glared at her across the room. Except for her thin red lips and narrow green eyes, her face was carved from chalk. In one of those instinctive female shifts that are always at least partly real, Zinnie released her fury on her sister-in-law:

"So there you are—spying on me again. I'm sick of your spying, talking behind my back, throwing mud at Charlie Grantland, just because you wanted him yourself—"

"That's nonsense," Mildred said in a low voice. "I've never spied on you. As for Dr. Grantland, I barely know him."

"No, but you'd like to, wouldn't you? Only you know that you can't have him. So you'd like to see him destroyed, wouldn't you? You hired this man to ruin him."

"I did no such thing. You're upset, Zinnie. *You* should lie down and have a rest."

"I should, eh? So you can carry on your machinations without any interference?"

Zinnie crossed the room in an unsteady rush. I stayed between her and Mildred.

"Mildred didn't hire me," I said. "I have no instructions from her. You're way off the beam, Mrs. Hallman."

"You lie!" She screamed across me at Mildred: "You dirty little sneak, you can get out of my house. Keep your maniac husband away from here or by God I'll have him shot down. Take your bully-boy along with you. Go on, get out, both of you."

"I'll be glad to."

Mildred turned to the door in weary resignation, and I went out after her. I hadn't expected the armistice to last.

>>>>>>>>>
>>>>>>>>> *chapter* 14
>>>>>>>>>

I WAITED for Mildred on the front veranda. There were several more cars in the driveway. One of them was my Ford convertible, gray with dust but looking none the worse for wear. It was parked behind a black panel truck with county markings.

A deputy I hadn't seen before was in the front seat of another county car, monitoring a turned-up radio. The rest of the sheriff's men were still in the greenhouse. Their shadows moved on its translucent walls.

"Attention all units," the huge voice of the radio said. "Be on the lookout for following subject wanted as suspect in murder which occurred at Hallman ranch in Buena Vista Valley approximately one hour ago: Carl Hallman, white, male, twenty-four, six-foot-three, two hundred pounds, blond hair, blue eyes, pale complexion, wearing blue cotton workshirt and trousers. Suspect may be armed and is considered dangerous. When last seen he was traveling across country on foot."

Mildred came out, freshly groomed and looking fairly brisk in spite of her wilted-violet eyes. Her head moved in a small gesture of relief as the screen door slammed behind her.

"Where do you plan to go?" I asked her.

"Home. It's too late to think of going back to work. I have to see to Mother, anyway."

"Your husband may turn up there. Have you thought of that possibility?"

"Naturally. I hope he does."

"If he does, will you let me know?"

She gave me a clear cold look. "That depends."

"I know what you mean. Maybe I better make it plain that I'm in your husband's corner. I'd like to get to him before the sheriff does.

Ostervelt seems to have his mind made up about this case. I haven't. I think there should be further investigation."

"You want me to pay you, is that it?"

"Forget about that for now. Let's say I like the old-fashioned idea of presumption of innocence."

She took a step toward me, her eyes brightening. Her hand rested lightly on my arm. "You don't believe he shot Jerry, either."

"I don't want to build up your hopes with nothing much to go on. I'm keeping an open mind until we have more information. You heard the shots that killed Jerry?"

"Yes."

"Where were you at the time? And where were the others?"

"I don't know about the others. I was with Martha on the other side of the house. The child seemed to sense what had happened, and I had a hard time calming her. I didn't notice what other people were doing."

"Was Ostervelt anywhere around the house?"

"I didn't see him if he was."

"Was Carl?"

"The last I saw of Carl was in the grove there."

"Which way did he go when he left you?"

"Toward town, at least in that general direction."

"What was his attitude when you talked to him?"

"He was upset. I begged him to turn himself in, but he seemed frightened."

"Emotionally disturbed?"

"It's hard to say. I've seen him much worse."

"Did he show any signs of being dangerous?"

"Certainly not to me. He never has. He was a little rough when I tried to hold him, that's all."

"Has he often been violent?"

"No. I didn't say he was violent. He simply didn't want to be held. He pushed me away from him."

"Did he say why?"

"He said something about following his own road. I didn't have time to ask him what he meant."

"Do you have any idea what he meant?"

"No." But her eyes were wide and dark with possibility. "I'm certain, though, he didn't mean anything like shooting his brother."

"There's another question that needs answering," I said. "I hate to throw it at you now."

She squared her slender shoulders. "Go ahead. I'll answer it if I can."

"I've been told your husband killed his father. Deliberately drowned him in the bathtub. Have you heard that?"

"Yes. I've heard that."

"From Carl?"

"Not from him, no."

"Do you believe it?"

She took a long time to answer. "I don't know. It was just after Carl was hospitalized—the same day. When a tragedy cuts across your life like that, you don't know what to believe. The world actually seemed to fly apart. I could recognize the pieces, but all the patterns were unfamiliar, the meanings were different. They still are. It's an awful thing for a human being to admit, but I don't know *what* I believe. I'm waiting. I've been waiting for six months to find out where I stand in the world, what sort of a life I can count on."

"You haven't really answered my question."

"I would if I could. I've been trying to explain why I can't. The circumstances were so queer, and awful." The thought of them, whatever they were, pinched her face like cold.

"Who told you about this alleged confession?"

"Sheriff Ostervelt did. I thought at the time he was lying, for reasons of his own. Perhaps I was rationalizing, simply because I couldn't face the truth—I don't know."

Before she trailed off into further self-doubts, I said: "What reasons would he have for lying to you?"

"I can tell you one. It isn't very modest to say it, but he's been interested in me for quite a long time. He was always hanging around the ranch, theoretically to see the Senator, but looking for excuses to talk to me. I knew what he wanted; he was about as subtle as an old boar. The day we took Carl to the hospital, Ostervelt made it very clear, and very ugly." She shut her eyes for a second. A faint dew had gathered on her eyelids, and at her temples. "So ugly that I'm afraid I can't talk about it."

"I get the general idea."

But she went on, in a chilly trance of memory which seemed to negate the place and time: "He was to drive Carl to the hospital that morning, and naturally I wanted to go along. I wanted to be with Carl until the last possible minute before the doors closed on him. You don't know how a woman feels when her husband's being taken away like that, perhaps forever. I was afraid it was forever. Carl didn't say a word on the way. For days before he'd been talking constantly, about everything under the sun—the plans he had for the ranch, our life together, philosophy, social justice, and the brotherhood of man. Suddenly it was all over. Everything was over. He sat in the car, between me and the sheriff, as still as a dead man.

"He didn't even kiss me good-by at the admissions door. I'll never forget what he did do. There was a little tree growing beside the steps. Carl picked one of the leaves and folded it in his hand and carried it into the hospital with him.

"I didn't go in. I couldn't bear to, that day, though I've been there often enough since. I waited outside in the sheriff's car. I remember thinking that this was the end of the line, that nothing worse could ever happen to me. I was wrong.

"On the way back, Ostervelt began to act as if he owned me. I didn't give him any encouragement; I never had. In fact, I told him what I thought of him.

"It was then he got really nasty. He told me I'd better be careful what I said. That Carl had confessed the murder of his father, and he was the only one who knew. He'd keep it quiet if I'd be nice to him. Otherwise there'd be a trial, he said. Even if Carl wasn't convicted we'd be given the kind of publicity that people can't live through." Her voice sank despairingly. "The kind of publicity we're going to have to live through now."

Mildred turned and looked out across the green country as if it were a wasteland. She said, with her face averted:

"I didn't give in to him. But I was afraid to reject him as flatly as he deserved. I put him off with some sort of a vague promise, that we might get together sometime in the future. I haven't kept the promise, needless to say, and I never will." She said it calmly enough, but her shoulders were trembling. I could see the rim of one of her ears, between silky strands of hair. It was red with shame or anger. "The horrible old man hasn't forgiven me for that. I've lived in fear for the last six months, that he'd take action against Carl—drag him back to stand trial."

"He didn't, though," I said, "which means that the confession was probably a phony. Tell me one thing, could it have happened the way Ostervelt claimed? I mean, did your husband have the opportunity?"

"I'm afraid the answer is yes. He was roaming around the house most of the night, after the quarrel with his father. I couldn't keep him in bed."

"Did you ask him about it afterwards?"

"At the hospital? No, I didn't. They warned me not to bring up disturbing subjects. And I was glad enough to let sleeping dogs lie. If it was true, I felt better not knowing than knowing. There's a limit to what a person can bear to know."

She shuddered, in the chill of memory.

The front door of the greenhouse was flung open suddenly. Carmichael backed out, bent over the handles of a covered stretcher. Under the cover, the dead man huddled lumpily. The other end of the stretcher was supported by the deputy coroner. They moved awkwardly along the flagstone path toward the black panel truck. Against the sweep of the valley and the mountains standing like monuments in the sunlight, the two upright men and the prostrate man seemed equally small and transitory. The living men hoisted the dead man into the back of the truck and slammed the double doors. Mildred jumped at the noise.

"I'm terribly edgy, I'd better get out of here. I shouldn't have gone into—all that. You're the only person I've ever told."

"It's safe with me."

"Thank you. For everything, I mean. You're the only one who's given me a ray of hope."

She raised her hand in good-by and went down the steps into sunlight which gilded her head. Ostervelt's senescent passion for her was easy to understand. It wasn't just that she was young and pretty, and round in the right places. She had something more provocative than sex: the intense grave innocence of a serious child, and a loneliness that made her seem vulnerable.

I watched the old Buick out of sight and caught myself on the edge of a sudden hot dream. Mildred's husband might not live forever. His chances of surviving the day were not much better than even. If her husband failed to survive, Mildred would need a man to look after her.

I gave myself a mental kick in the teeth. That kind of thinking put me on Ostervelt's level. Which for some reason made me angrier at Ostervelt.

THE deputy coroner had lit a cigar and was leaning against the side of the panel truck, smoking it. I strolled over and took a look at my car. Nothing seemed to be missing. Even the key was in the ignition. The additional mileage added up, so far as I could estimate, to the distance from the hospital to Purissima to the ranch.

"Nice day," the deputy coroner said.

"Nice enough."

"Too bad Mr. Hallman isn't alive to enjoy it. He was in pretty good shape, too, judging from a superficial examination. I'll be interested in what his organs have to say."

"You're not suggesting he died of natural causes."

"Oh, no. It's merely a little game I play with myself to keep the interest up." He grinned, and the sunlight glinted on his spectacles in cold mirth. "Not every doctor gets a chance to know his patients inside and out."

"You're the coroner, aren't you?"

"Deputy coroner. Ostervelt's the coroner—he wears two hats. Actually I do, too. I'm pathologist at the Purissima Hospital. Name's Lawson."

"Archer." We shook hands.

"You from one of the L.A. papers? I just got finished talking to the local man."

"I'm a private investigator, employed by a member of the family. I was wondering about your findings."

"Haven't got any yet. I know there're two bullets in him because they went in and didn't come out. I'll get 'em when I do the autopsy."

"When will that be?"

"Tonight. Ostervelt wants it quick. I ought to have it wrapped up by midnight, sooner maybe."

"What happens to the slugs after you remove them?"

"I turn 'em over to the sheriff's ballistics man."

"Is he any good?"

"Oh, yeah, Durkin's a pretty fair technician. If it gets too tough, we send the work up to the L.A. Police Lab, or to Sacramento. But this isn't a case where the physical evidence counts for much. We pretty well know who did it. Once they catch him, he shouldn't be hard to get a story out of. Ostervelt may not bother doing anything with the slugs. He's a pretty easy-going guy. You get that way after twenty-five or thirty years in office."

"Worked for him long?"

"Four-five years. Five." He added, a little defensively: "Purissima's a nice place to live. The wife won't leave it. Who can blame her?"

"Not me. I wouldn't mind settling here myself."

"Talk to Ostervelt, why don't you? He's understaffed—always looking for men. You have any police experience?"

"A few years back. I got tired of living on a cop's salary. Among other things."

"There are always ways of padding it out."

Not knowing how he meant me to take that, I looked into his face. He was sizing me up, too. I said:

"That was one of the other things I got tired of. But you wouldn't think there'd be much of that in this county."

"More than you think, brother, more than you think. We won't go into that, though." He took a bite out of the tip of his cigar and spat it into the gravel. "You say you're working for the Hallman family?"

I nodded.

"Ever been in Purissima before?"

"Over the years, I have."

He looked at me with curiosity. "Are you one of the detectives the Senator brought in when his wife drowned?"

"No."

"I just wondered. I spent several hours with one of them—a smart old bulldog named Scott. You wouldn't happen to know him? He's from L.A. Glenn Scott?"

"I know Scott. He's one of the old masters in the field. Or he was until he retired."

"My impression exactly. He knew more about pathology than most medical students. I never had a more interesting conversation."

"What about?"

"Causes of death," he said brightly. "Drowning and asphyxiation and so on. Fortunately I'd done a thorough post-mortem. I was able to establish that she died by drowning; she had sand and fragments of kelp in her bronchial tubes, and the indicated saline solution in her lungs."

"There wasn't any doubt of it, was there?"

"Not after I got through. Scott was completely satisfied. Of course I couldn't entirely rule out the possibility of murder, but there were no positive indications. It's almost certain that the contusions were inflicted after death."

"Contusions?" I prompted softly.

"Yeah, the contusions on the back and head. You often get them in drownings along this coast, with the rocks and the heavy surf. I've seen some cadavers that were absolutely macerated, poor things. At least they got Mrs. Hallman before that happened to her. But she was bad enough. They ought to print a few of my pictures in the papers. There wouldn't be so many suicides walking into the water. Not so many women, anyway, and most of them *are* women."

"Is that what Mrs. Hallman did, walk into the water?"

"Probably. Or else she jumped from the pier. Of course there's always an outside chance that she fell, and that's how she got the contusions. The Coroner's Jury called it an accident, but that was mainly to spare the family's feelings. Elderly women don't normally go down to the ocean at night and accidentally fall in."

"They don't normally commit suicide, either."

"True enough, only Mrs. Hallman wasn't what you'd call exactly normal. Scott talked to her doctor after it happened and he said she'd been having emotional trouble. It's not fashionable these days to talk about hereditary insanity, but you can't help noticing certain family tie-ups. This one in the Hallman family, for instance. It isn't pure chance when a woman subject to depression has a son with a manic-depressive psychosis."

"Mother had blue genes, eh?"

"Ouch."

"Who was her doctor?"

"G.P. in town named Grantland."

"I know him slightly," I said. "He was out here today. He seems like a good man."

"Uh-huh." In the light of the medical code that inhibits doctors from criticizing each other, his grunt was eloquent.

"You don't think so?"

"Hell, it's not for me to second-guess another doctor. I'm not one of these medical hotshots with the big income and the bedside manner. I'm purely and simply a lab man. I did think at the time he should have referred Mrs. Hallman to a psychiatrist. Might have saved her life. After all, he knew she was suicidal."

"How do you know that?"

"He told Scott. Until he did, Scott thought it could be murder, in spite of the physical evidence. But when he found out she'd tried to shoot herself—well, it all fitted into a pattern."

"When did she try to shoot herself?"

"A week or two before she drowned, I think." Lawson stiffened perceptibly, as if he realized that he'd been talking very freely. "Understand me, I'm not accusing Grantland of negligence or anything like that. A doctor has to use his own judgment. Personally I'd be helpless if I had to handle one of these—"

He noticed that I wasn't listening, and peered into my face with professional solicitude. "What's the trouble, fellow? You got a cramp?"

"No trouble." At least no trouble I wanted to put into words. It was the Hallman family that really had trouble: father and mother dead under dubious circumstances, one son shot, the second being hunted. And at each high point of trouble, Grantland cropped up. I said:

"Do you know what happened to the gun?"

"What gun?"

"The one she tried to shoot herself with."

"I'm afraid I don't know. Maybe Grantland would."

"Maybe he would."

Lawson tapped the lengthening ash from his cigar. It splattered silently on the gravel between us. He drew on the cigar, its glowing end pale salmon in the sun, and blew out a cloud of smoke. The smoke ascended lazily, almost straight up in the still air, and drifted over my head toward the house.

"Or Ostervelt," he said. "I wonder what's keeping Ostervelt. I suppose he's trying to make an impression on Slovekin."

"Slovekin?"

"The police reporter from the Purissima paper. He's talking to Ostervelt in the greenhouse. Ostervelt loves to talk."

Ostervelt wasn't the only one, I thought. In fifteen or twenty minutes, a third of a cigar length, Lawson had given me more information than I knew what to do with.

"Speaking of causes of death," I said, "did you do the autopsy on Senator Hallman?"

"There wasn't any," he said.

"You mean no autopsy was ordered?"

"That's right, there was no question about cause of death. The old man had a heart history. He'd been under a doctor's care practically from day to day."

"Grantland again?"

"Yes. It was his opinion the Senator died of heart failure, and I saw no reason to question it. Neither did Ostervelt."

"Then there was no indication of drowning?"

"Drowning?" He looked at me sharply. "You're thinking about his wife, aren't you?"

His surprise seemed real, and I had no reason to doubt his honesty. He wore the glazed suit and frayed shirt of a man who lived on his salary.

"I must have got my signals switched," I said.

"It's understandable. He did die in the bathtub. But not of drowning."

"Did you examine the body?"

"It wasn't necessary."

"Who said it wasn't necessary?"

"The family, the family doctor, Sheriff Ostervelt, everybody concerned. I'm saying it now," he added with some spirit.

"What happened to the body?"

"The family had it cremated." He thought about this for a moment, behind his glasses. "Listen, if you're thinking that there was foul play involved, you're absolutely wrong. He died of heart failure, in a locked bathroom. They had to break in to get to him." Then, perhaps to put his own doubts to rest: "I'll show you where it happened, if you like."

"I would like."

Lawson pressed out his cigar against the sole of his shoe, and dropped the smelly butt in his side pocket. He led me through the house to a large rear bedroom. With blinds drawn, dust covers on the bed and the other furniture, the room had a ghostly air.

We went into the adjoining bathroom. It contained a six-foot tub supported on cast-iron feet. Lawson switched on the lofty ceiling fixture above it.

"The poor old man was lying in here," he said. "They had to force the window to get to him." He indicated the single window high above the basin.

"Who had to force the window?"

"The family. His two sons, I believe. The body was in the bathtub most of the night."

I examined the door. It was thick and made of oak. The lock was the old-fashioned kind that has to be turned with a key. The key was in the keyhole.

I turned it back and forth several times, then pulled it out and looked at it. The heavy, tarnished key told me nothing in particular. Either Lawson was misinformed, or the Senator had died alone. Or I had a locked-room mystery to go with the other mysteries in the house.

I tried a skeleton key on the door, and after a little jiggling around, it worked. I turned to Lawson. "Was the key in the lock when they found him?"

"I couldn't say, really. I wasn't here. Maybe Ostervelt could tell you."

>>>>>>>>>
>>>>>>>>> *chapter* 16
>>>>>>>>>

WE ran into Ostervelt in the front hallway, ran into him almost literally as he came out of the living-room. He pushed between us, his belly projecting like a football concealed in his clothes. His jowls became convulsive:

"What goes on?"

"Mr. Archer wanted to see the Senator's bathroom," Lawson said. "You remember the morning they found him, Chief. Was the key in the lock?"

"What lock, for Christ sake?"

"The lock on the bathroom door."

"I don't know." Ostervelt's head jerked as he hammered out the words: "I'll tell you what I do know, Lawson. You don't talk official business to strangers. How many times do we have to go into that?"

Lawson removed his glasses and wiped them with the inside of his tie. Without them, his face looked unformed and vulnerable. But he had guts and some professional poise:

"Mr. Archer isn't a stranger, exactly. He's employed by the Hallman family."

"To do what? Pick your brains, if you have any?"

"You can't talk to me like that."

"What do you think you're going to do about it? Resign?"

Lawson turned on his heel, stiffly, and walked out. Ostervelt called after him:

"Go ahead and resign. I accept your resignation."

Feeling some compunction, since I had been picking Lawson's brains, I said to Ostervelt:

"Lay off him. What's the beef?"

"The beef is you. Mrs. Hallman said you asked her for money, made a pass at her."

"Did she rip her dress open at the neck? They usually rip their dresses open at the neck."

"It's no joke. I could put you in jail."

"What are you waiting for? The suit for false arrest will make my fortune."

"Don't get flip with me." Under his anger, Ostervelt seemed to be badly shaken. His little eyes were dirty with dismay. He took out his gun to make himself feel better.

"Put it away," I said. "It takes more than a Colt revolver to change a Keystone cop into an officer."

Ostervelt raised the Colt and laid it raking and burning across the side of my head. The ceiling slanted, then rose away from me as I went down. As I got up, a thin young man in a brown corduroy jacket appeared in the doorway. Ostervelt started to raise the gun for another blow. The thin young man took hold of his arm and almost ascended with it.

Ostervelt said: "I'll cut him to pieces. Get away from me, Slovekin."

Slovekin held onto his arm. I held onto my impulse to hit an old man. Slovekin said:

"Wait a minute, Sheriff. Who is this man, anyway?"

"A crooked private dick from Hollywood."

"Are you arresting him?"

"You're damn right I'm arresting him."

"What for? Is he connected with this case?"

Ostervelt shook him off. "That's between him and I. You stay out of it, Slovekin."

"How can I, when I'm assigned to it? I'm just doing my job, the same as you are, Sheriff." The black eyes in Slovekin's sharp young face glittered with irony. "I can't do my job if you give me no information. I have to fall back on reporting what I see. I see a public official beating a man with a gun, naturally I'm interested."

"Don't try to blackmail me, you little twerp."

Slovekin stayed cool and smiling. "You want me to deliver that message to Mr. Spaulding? Mr. Spaulding's always looking for a good local topic for an editorial. This could be just what he needs."

"Screw Spaulding. You know what you can do with that rag you work for, too."

"That's pretty language from the top law-enforcement official in the county. An elected official, at that. I suppose you don't mind if I quote you." Slovekin produced a notebook from a side pocket.

Ostervelt's face tried various colors and settled for a kind of mottled purple. He put his gun away. "Okay, Slovekin. What else do you want to know?" His voice was a rough whisper.

"Is this man a suspect? I thought Carl Hallman was the only one."

"He is, and we'll have him in twenty-four hours. Dead or alive. You can quote me on that."

I said to Slovekin: "You're a newspaperman, are you?"

"I try to be." He looked at me quizzically, as if he wondered what I was trying to be.

"I'd like to talk to you about this murder. The sheriff's got Hall-man convicted already, but there are certain discrepancies—"

"The hell there are!" Ostervelt said.

Slovekin whipped out a pencil and opened his notebook. "Clue me in."

"Not now. I need more time to pin them down."

"He's bluffing," Ostervelt said. "He's just trying to make me look bad. He's one of these jokers, tries to make a hero out of himself."

Disregarding him, I said to Slovekin: "Where can I get in touch with you, tomorrow, say?"

"You're not going to be here tomorrow," Ostervelt put in. "I want you out of this county in one hour, or else."

Slovekin said mildly: "I thought you were arresting him."

Ostervelt was getting frantic. He began to yammer: "Don't get too cocky, Mr. Slovekin. Bigger men than you thought they could cross me, and lost their jobs."

"Oh, come off it, Sheriff. Do you go to movies much?" Slovekin unwrapped a piece of gum, put it in his mouth, and began to chew it. He said to me: "You can reach me through the paper any time— Purissima *Record*."

"You think so, eh?" Ostervelt said. "After today you won't be working there."

"Phone 6328," Slovekin said. "If I'm not there, talk to Spaulding. He's the editor."

"I can go higher than Spaulding, if I have to."

"Take it to the Supreme Court, Sheriff." Slovekin's chewing face had an expression of pained superiority which made him look like an intellectual camel. "I'd certainly like to get what you have now. Spaulding's holding the city edition for this story."

"I'd like to give it to you, but it hasn't jelled."

"You see?" Ostervelt said. "He's got nothing to back it up. He's only trying to make trouble. You're crazy if you take his word against mine. Christ, he may even be in cahoots with the psycho. He let Hallman use his car, remember."

"It's getting pretty noisy in here," I said to Slovekin, and moved toward the door.

He followed me outside to my car. "What you said about the evidence—you weren't kidding?"

"No. I think there's a good chance that Hallman's getting the dirty end of the stick."

"I hope you're right. I rather like the guy, or used to before he got sick."

"You know Carl, do you?"

"Ever since high school. I've known Ostervelt for quite a long time, too. But this is no time to go into Ostervelt." He leaned on the car window, smelling of Dentyne chewing gum. "Do you have another suspect in mind?"

"Several."

"Like that, eh?"

"Like that. Thanks for the assist."

"Don't mention it." His black gaze shifted to the side of my head. "Did you know you've got a torn ear? You should see a doctor."

"I intend to."

>>>>>>>>>
>>>>>>>>> *chapter* 17
>>>>>>>>>

I DROVE into Purissima and checked in at a waterfront motel named the Hacienda. Not being on expense account and having forty-odd dollars in my wallet to tide me over until I qualified for the old-age pension, I picked the cheapest one I could find with telephones in the rooms. The room I paid eight dollars for in advance contained a bed and a chair and a limed-oak veneer chest of drawers, as well as a telephone. The window overlooked a parking lot.

The room surprised me into a sharp feeling of pain and loss. The pain wasn't for Carl Hallman, though his fugitive image continually crossed my mind. Perhaps the pain was for myself; the loss was of a self I had once imagined.

Peering out through the slats of the dusty blind, I felt like a criminal hiding out from the law. I didn't like the feeling, so I clowned it away. All I needed was a suitcase full of hot money and an ash-blonde moll whining for mink and diamonds. The closest thing to an ash-blonde moll I knew was Zinnie, and Zinnie appeared to be somebody else's moll.

I was kind of glad that Zinnie wasn't my moll. It was a small room, and the printed notice under the glass top of the chest of drawers said that the room rented for fourteen dollars double. Check-out time was twelve noon. Lighting an ash-blond cigarette, I calculated that I had about twenty-four hours to wrap up the case. I wasn't going to pay for another day out of my own pocket. That would be criminal.

Try listening to yourself sometime, alone in a transient room in a strange town. The worst is when you draw a blank, and the ash-blonde ghosts of the past carry on long twittering long-distance calls with your inner ear, and there's no way to hang up.

Before I made a long-distance call of my own, I went into the bathroom and examined my head in the mirror over the sink. It looked worse than it felt. One ear was cut, and half full of drying blood. There were abrasions on temple and cheek. One eye was slightly blackened, and made me appear more dissipated than I was. When I smiled at a thought that struck me, the effect was pretty grim.

The thought that struck me sent me back to the bedroom. I sat down on the edge of the bed and looked up Zinnie's doctor friend in the local directory. Grantland maintained an office on upper Main Street and a residence on Seaview Road. I made a note of the addresses and telephone numbers, and called his office number. The girl who answered gave me, after some persuasion, an emergency appointment for five-thirty, the end of office hours.

If I hurried, and if Glenn Scott was at home, I should have time to see him and get back for my appointment with Grantland. Glenn had retired to an avocado ranch in the Malibu hinterland. I'd driven up two or three times in the last two years to play chess with him. He always beat me at chess, but his whisky was good. Also, I happened to like him. He was one of the few survivors of the Hollywood rat race who knew how to enjoy a little money without hitting other people over the head with it.

I thought as I put through the call to his house that money happened to Glenn the way poverty happened to a lot of others. He'd worked hard all his life, of course, but he'd never knocked himself

out for money. He used to say that he'd never tried to sell himself
for fear that somebody might be tempted to buy him.

The maid who'd been with the Scotts for twenty years answered
the telephone. Mr. Scott was outside watering his trees. Far as she
knew, he'd be there all afternoon, and he'd be glad to see me, far as
she knew.

I found him about a half-hour later, wielding a hose on the side of
a sunburnt hill. The rocky barrenness of the hillside was accentuated
by the rows of scrawny young avocado trees. Glenn's jeep was at the
side of the road. Turning and parking behind it, I could look down
on the gravel roof of his cantilevered redwood house, and further
down on the long white curve of the beach rimming the sea. I felt a
twinge of envy as I crossed the field toward him. It seemed to me
that Glenn had everything worth having: a place in the sun, wife
and family, enough money to live on.

Glenn gave me a smile that made me ashamed of my thoughts.
His keen gray eyes were almost lost in his sun-wrinkles. His wide-
brimmed straw hat and stained khaki coveralls completed his resemblance to a veteran farmhand. I said:

"Hi, farmer."

"You like my protective coloration, eh?" He turned off the water
and began to coil the hose. "How you been, Lew? Still brawling, I
see."

"I ran into a door. You're looking well."

"Yeah, the life suits me. When I get bored, Belle and I go in to
the Strip for dinner and take a quick look around and beat it the
hell back home."

"How is Belle?"

"Oh, she's fine. Right now she's in Santa Monica with the kids.
Belle had her first grandson last week, with a little help from the
daughter-in-law. Seven and a half pounds, built like a middleweight,
they're going to call him Glenn. But you didn't make a special trip to
ask me about my family."

"Somebody else's family. You had a case in Purissima about three
years ago. Elderly woman committed suicide by drowning. Husband
suspected murder, called you in to check."

"Uh-huh. I wouldn't call Mrs. Hallman elderly. She was probably
in her early fifties. Hell, I'm older than that myself, and I'm not elderly."

"Okay, grandpa," I said with subtle flattery. "Are you willing to answer a couple of questions about the Hallman case?"

"Why?"

"It seems to be kind of reopening itself."

"You mean it was homicide?"

"I wouldn't go that far. Not yet. But the woman's son was murdered this afternoon."

"Which son? She had two."

"The older one. His younger brother escaped from a mental ward last night, and he's prime suspect. He was at the ranch shortly before the shooting—"

"Jesus," Glenn breathed. "The old man was right."

I waited, with no result, and finally said: "Right about what?"

"Let's skip that, Lew. I know he's dead now, but it's still a confidential case."

"I get no answers, eh?"

"You can ask the questions, I'll use my judgment about answering 'em. First, though, who are you representing in Purissima?"

"The younger son. Carl."

"The psycho?"

"Should I give my clients a Rorschach before I take them on?"

"I didn't mean that. He hire you to clear him?"

"No, it's my own idea."

"Hey, you're not off on one of your crusades."

"Hardly," I said with more hope than I felt. "If my hunch pans out, I'll get paid for my time. There's a million or two in the family."

"More like five million. I get it. You're on a contingency basis."

"Call it that. Do I get to ask you any questions?"

"Go ahead. Ask them." He leaned against a boulder and looked inscrutable.

"You've answered the main one already. That drowning could have been homicide."

"Yeah. I finally ruled it out at the time because there were no positive indications—nothing you could take to court, I mean. Also on account of the lady's background. She was unstable, been on barbiturates for years. Her doctor wouldn't admit she was hooked on them, but that was the picture I got. In addition to which, she'd attempted suicide before. Tried to shoot herself right in the doctor's office, a few days before she drowned."

"Who told you this?"

"The doctor told me himself, and he wasn't lying. She wanted a bigger prescription from him. When he wouldn't give it to her, she pulled a little pearl-handled revolver out of her purse and pointed it at her head. He knocked it up just in time, and the slug went into the ceiling. He showed me the hole it made."

"What happened to the gun?"

"Naturally he took it away from her. I think he told me he threw it into the sea."

"That's a funny way to handle it."

"Not so funny, under the circumstances. She begged him not to tell her husband about the attempt. The old man was always threatening to stash her away in a snake-pit. The doctor covered for her."

"You get any confirmation of this?"

"How could I? It was strictly between him and her." He added with a trace of irritation: "The guy didn't have to tell me anything. He was sticking his neck out, telling me what he did. Speaking of necks, mine is out a mile right now."

"Then you might as well stick it out some more. What do you think of the local law?"

"In Purissima? They have a good police force. Under-manned, like most, but one of the better small-city departments, I'd say."

"I was thinking more of the county department."

"Ostervelt, you mean? We got along. He co-operated fine." Glenn smiled briefly. "Naturally he co-operated. Senator Hallman swung a lot of votes."

"Is Ostervelt honest?"

"I never saw any evidence that he wasn't. Maybe some graft crept in here and there. He isn't as young as he used to be, and I heard a rumor or two. Nothing big, you understand. Senator Hallman wouldn't stand for it. Why?"

"Just checking." Very tentatively, I said: "I don't suppose I could get a peek at your report on the case?"

"Not even if I had one. You know the law as well as I do."

"You didn't keep a copy?"

"I didn't make a written report. The old man wanted it word-of-mouth, and that was the way I gave it to him. I can tell you what I said in one word. Suicide." He paused. "But maybe I was wrong, Lew."

"Do you think you were wrong?"

"Maybe I was. If I did make a mistake, like La Guardia said, it was a beaut: they don't come often like that. I know I shouldn't admit it to an ex-competitor. On the other hand, you were never a very serious competitor. They went to you when they couldn't afford me." Scott was trying to carry it off lightly, but his face was heavy. "On the other hand, I wouldn't want you to climb way out on a limb, and get it sawed off from under you."

"So?"

"So take a piece of advice from an old pro who started in the rack —in the business, before you learned toilet control. You're wasting your time on this one."

"I don't think so. You gave me what I need."

"Then I better give you something you don't need, just so you won't get elated." Scott looked the opposite of elated. His voice dragged slower and slower. "Don't start to spend your piece of that five million until after you deposit the check. You know there's a little rule of law that says a murderer can't benefit from the estate of his victim."

"Are you trying to tell me Carl Hallman murdered his father?"

"I heard the old man died of natural causes. I didn't investigate his death. It looks as if somebody ought to."

"I intend to."

"Sure, but don't be surprised if you come up with an answer you don't like."

"Such as?"

"You said it a minute ago yourself."

"You've got some inside information?"

"Only what you told me, and what the old man told me when his lawyer sent for me. You know why he wanted me to make a confidential investigation of that drowning?"

"He didn't trust the local law."

"Maybe. The main reason was, he suspected his own son of knocking out the mother and throwing her in the water. And I'm beginning to think that's what actually happened."

I'd seen it coming from a long way off, but it hit me hard, with the weight of Glenn Scott's integrity behind it.

"Do you know what the Senator's suspicions were based on?"

"He didn't tell me much about that. I assumed he knew his own boy better than I did. I never even got to meet the boy. I talked to the rest of the family, though, and I gathered that he was very close to his mother. Too close for comfort, maybe."

"Close like Oedipus?"

"Could be. There was apronstring trouble, all right. The mother raised a hell of a stink when he went away to college. She was a clutcher, for sure, and not very stable, like I said. Could be he thought he had to kill her to get free. There've been cases like that. I'm only brainstorming, understand. You won't quote me."

"Not even to myself. Where was Carl when she died?"

"That's just the trouble, I don't know. He was going to school in Berkeley at the time, but he left there about a week before it happened. Dropped out of sight for maybe ten days, all told."

"What did he say he was doing?"

"I don't know. The Senator wouldn't even let me ask him. It wasn't a very satisfactory case to work on. As you'll discover."

"I already have."

>>>>>>>>>
>>>>>>>>> *chapter* 18
>>>>>>>>>

I PARKED on upper Main Street, in front of a flat-topped building made of pink stucco and glass brick. An imitation flagstone walk led through well-trimmed shrubbery to a door inset in one corner. A small bronze plate beside the door announced discreetly: J. Charles Grantland, M.D.

The waiting-room was empty, except for a lot of new-looking furniture. A fairly new-looking young woman popped up behind a bleached oak counter in the far corner beside an inner door. She had dark, thin good looks which needed a quick paint job.

"Mr. Archer?"

"Yes."

"I'm sorry, doctor's still busy. We're behind schedule today. Do you mind waiting a few minutes?"

I said I didn't mind. She took down my address.

"Were you in an accident, Mr. Archer?"

"You could call it that."

I sat in the chair nearest her, and took a folded newspaper out of my jacket pocket. I'd bought it on the street a few minutes earlier, from a Mexican newsboy crying murder. I spread it out on my knees, hoping that it might make a conversation piece.

The Hallman story had Eugene Slovekin's by-line under a banner heading: Brother Sought in Shooting. There was a three-column picture of the Hallman brothers in the middle of the page. The story began in a rather stilted atmospheric style which made me wonder if Slovekin had been embarrassed by the writing of it:

"In a tragedy which may parallel the ancient tragedy of Cain and Abel, violent death paid a furtive and shocking visit today to a well-known local family. Victim of the apparent slaying was Jeremiah Hallman, 34, prominent Buena Vista Valley rancher. His younger brother, Carl Hallman, 24, is being sought for questioning in the shooting. Mr. Hallman, son of the recently deceased Senator Hallman, was found dead at approximately one o'clock this afternoon by his family physician, Dr. Charles Grantland, in the conservatory of the Hallman estate.

"Mr. Hallman had been shot twice in the back, and apparently died within seconds of the shooting. A pearl-handled revolver, with two cartridges discharged, was found beside the body, lending a touch of fantastic mystery to the case. According to family servants the murder gun formerly belonged to the late Mrs. Alicia Hallman, mother of the victim.

"Sheriff Duane Ostervelt, who was on the scene within minutes of the shooting, stated that the murder weapon was known to be in the possession of Carl Hallman. Young Hallman was seen on the ranch immediately prior to the shooting. He escaped last night from the State Hospital, where he had been a patient for some months. According to members of the family, young Hallman has been a long-time victim of mental illness. An all-points search is being made for him, by the local sheriff's department and city and state police.

"Contacted by long-distance telephone, Dr. Brockley of the State Hospital staff said that young Hallman was suffering from manic-depressive psychosis when admitted to the hospital six months ago. According to Dr. Brockley, Hallman was not considered dangerous, and was thought to be 'well on the road to recovery.' Dr. Brockley expressed surprise and concern at the tragic outcome of Hallman's escape. He said that the local authorities were informed of the escape as soon as it occurred, and expressed the hope that the public would 'take a calm view of the situation. There is no violence in Hallman's hospital record,' Dr. Brockley said. 'He is a sick boy who needs medical care.'

"A similar view was expressed by Sheriff Ostervelt, who says that he is organizing a posse of a hundred or more local citizens to supplement the efforts of his department in the search. The public is asked to be on the lookout for Hallman. He is six feet three inches tall, of athletic build, blue-eyed, with light hair cut very short. When last seen he was wearing a blue work shirt and blue dungaree trousers. According to Sheriff Ostervelt, Hallman may be accompanied by Thomas Rica, alias Rickey, a fellow-escapee from . . ."

The story was continued on the second page. Before turning over, I took a close look at the picture of the two brothers. It was a stiffly posed portrait of the sort that photographers make to commemorate weddings. Both brothers wore boiled shirts and fixed smiles. Their resemblance was accentuated by this, and by the fact that Jerry hadn't grown fat when the picture was taken. The caption was simply: "The Hallman brothers (Carl on the right)."

The dark girl coughed insinuatingly. I looked up and saw her leaning far out over her counter, slightly cross-eyed with desire to break the silence.

"Terrible, isn't it? What makes it worse, I know him." She shivered, and hunched her thin shoulders up. "I talked to him just this morning."

"Who?"

"The murderer." She rolled the "r's" like an actress in melodrama.

"He telephoned here?"

"He *came* here, personally. He was standing right here in front of me." She pointed at the floor between us with a fingernail from which the red polish was flaking. "I didn't know him from Adam, but *I* could tell there was something funny. He had that wild look they have in their eyes." Her own look was slightly wild, in a girlish way, and she'd forgotten her receptionist's diction: "Jeeze, it bored right through me."

"It must have been a frightening experience."

"*You're* not kidding. Course I had no way of knowing he was going to shoot somebody, he only *looked* that way. 'Where's the doctor?' he said, just like that. I guess he thought he was Napoleon or something. Only he was dressed like any old bum. You'd never think he was a Senator's son. His brother used to come in here, and *he* was a real gentleman, always nicely dressed in the height of fashion—cashmere jackets and stuff. It's too bad about him. I feel sorry for his wife, too."

"You know her?"

"Oh yes, Mrs. Hallman, she comes in all the time for her sinuses." Her eyes took on the waiting birdlike expression of a woman naming another woman she happens not to like.

"Did you get rid of him all right?"

"The crazy-man? I tried to tell him doctor wasn't in, but he wouldn't take no for an answer. So I called out Dr. Grantland, *he* knows how to handle them, Dr. Grantland hasn't got a nerve in his body." The birdlike expression subtly changed to the look of adoration which very young receptionists reserve for their doctor-employers. " 'Hello, old man, what brings you here?' the doctor says, like they were buddy-buddy from way back. He put his arm around him, calm as anything, and off they went into the back room. I guess he got rid of him out the back way, 'cause that was the last I saw of him. Least I hope that's the last. Anyway, doctor told me not to worry about it, that things like that come up in every office."

"Have you worked here long?"

"Just three months. This is my first real job. I filled in for other girls before, when they went on vacation, but I considered this the real start of my career. Dr. Grantland is wonderful to work for. Most of his patients are the nicest people you'd ever want to meet."

As though to illustrate this boast, a fat woman wearing a small flat hat and a mink neckpiece emerged through the inner door. She was followed by Grantland, looking professional in a white smock. She had the vaguely frightened eyes of a hypochondriac, and she clutched a prescription slip in her chubby hand. Grantland escorted her to the front door and opened it, bowing her out. She turned to him on the threshold:

"Thank you so much, Doctor. I know I'll be able to sleep tonight."

GRANTLAND closed the door and saw me. The lingering smile on his face gave up the ghost entirely. Shoved by a gust of anger, he crossed the room toward me. His fists were clenched.

I rose to meet him. "Hello, Doctor."

"What are you doing here?"

"I have an appointment with you."

"Oh no you haven't." He was torn between anger and the need to be charming to his receptionist. "Did you make an appointment for this—this gentleman?"

"Why not?" I said, since she was speechless. "Are you retiring from practice?"

"Don't try to tell me you're here as a patient."

"You're the only doctor I know in town."

"You didn't tell me you knew Dr. Grantland," the receptionist said accusingly.

"I must have forgotten to."

"Very likely," Grantland said. "You can go now, Miss Cullen, unless you've made some more of these special appointments for me."

"He told me it was an emergency."

"I said you can go."

She went, with a backward look from the doorway. Grantland's face was trying various attitudes: outrage, dignified surprise, bewildered innocence.

"What are you trying to pull on me?"

"Not a thing. Look, if you don't want to treat me, I can find another doctor."

He weighed the advantages and disadvantages of this, and decided against it. "I don't do much in the surgical line, but I guess I can fix you up. What happened to you, anyway—did you run into Hallman again?" Zinnie had briefed him well, apparently.

"No. Did you?"

He let that go by. We went through a consulting-room furnished in mahogany and blue leather. There were sailing prints on the walls, and above the desk a medical diploma from a college in the middle west. Grantland switched on the lights in the next room and asked me to remove my coat. Washing his hands at the sink in the corner, he said over his shoulder:

"You can get up on the examination table if you like. I'm sorry my nurse has gone home—I didn't know I'd be wanting to use her."

I stretched out on the leatherette top of the metal table. Lying flat on the back wasn't a bad position for self-defense, if it came to that.

Grantland crossed the room briskly and leaned over me, turning on a surgical light that extended on retractable arms from the wall. "You get yourself gun-whipped?"

"Slightly. Not every doctor would recognize the marks."

"I interned at Hollywood Receiving. Did you report this to the police?"

"I didn't have to. Ostervelt did it to me."

"You're not a fugitive, for God's sake?"

"No, for God's sake."

"Were you resisting arrest?"

"The sheriff just lost his temper. He's a hot-headed old youth."

Grantland made no comment. He went to work cleaning my cuts with swabs dipped in alcohol. It hurt.

"I'm going to have to put some clamps in that ear. The other cut ought to heal itself. I'll simply put an adhesive bandage over it."

Grantland went on talking as he worked: "A regular surgeon could do a better job for you, especially a plastic surgeon. That's why I was a little surprised when you came to me. You're going to have a small scar, I'm afraid. But that's all right with me if it's all right with you." He pressed a series of clamps into my torn ear. "That ought to do it. You ought to have a doctor look at it in a day or two. Going to be in town long?"

"I don't know." I got up, and faced him across the table. "It could depend on you."

"Any doctor can do it," he said impatiently.

"You're the only one who can help me."

Grantland caught the implication, and glanced at his watch. "I'm late for an appointment now—"

"I'll make it as fast as I can. You saw a pearl-handled gun today. You didn't mention that you'd seen it before."

He was a very quick study. Without a second's hesitation, he said: "I like to be sure of my facts before I sound off. I'm a medical man, after all."

"What are your facts?"

"Ask your friend the sheriff. He knows them."

"Maybe. I'm asking you. You might as well tell a straight story. I've been in touch with Glenn Scott."

"Glenn who?" But he remembered. His gaze flickered sideways.

"The detective Senator Hallman hired to investigate the murder of his wife."

"Did you say murder?"

"It slipped out."

"You're mistaken. She committed suicide. If you talked to Scott, you know she was suicidal."

"Suicidal people can be murdered."

"No doubt, but what does that prove?" A womanish petulance tugged at his mouth, disrupting his false calm. "I'm sick and tired of being badgered about it, simply because she happened to be my patient. Why, I saved her life the week before she drowned. Did Scott bother to tell you that?"

"He told me what you told him. That she attempted suicide in this office."

"It was in my previous office. I moved last year."

"So you can't show me the bullethole in the ceiling."

"Good Lord, are you questioning that? I got that gun away from her at the risk of my own life."

"I don't question it. I wanted to hear it from you, though."

"Well, now you've heard it. I hope you're satisfied." He took off his smock and turned to hang it up.

"Why did she try to commit suicide in your office?"

He was very still for an instant, frozen in the act of placing the white garment on a hook. Between the shoulderblades and under the arms, his gray shirt was dark with sweat. It was the only indication that I was giving him a hard time. He said:

"She wanted something I wasn't prepared to give her. A massive dose of sleeping pills. When I refused, she pulled this little revolver out of her purse. It was touch and go whether she was going to shoot me or herself. Then she pointed it at her head. Fortunately I managed to reach her, and take the gun away." He turned with a bland and doleful look on his face.

"Was she on a barb kick?"

"You might call it that. I did my best to keep it under control."

"Why didn't you have her put in a safe place?"

"I miscalculated, I admit it. I don't pretend to be a psychiatrist. I didn't grasp the seriousness of her condition. We doctors make mistakes, you know, like everybody else."

He was watching me like a chess-player. But his sympathy gambit was a giveaway. Unless he had something important to cover up, he'd have ordered me out of his office long ago.

"What happened to the gun?" I said.

"I kept it. I intended to throw it away, but never got around to it."

"How did Carl Hallman get hold of it?"

"He lifted it out of my desk drawer." He added disarmingly: "I guess I was a damn fool to keep it there."

I'd been holding back my knowledge of Carl Hallman's visit to his office. It was disappointing to have the fact conceded. Grantland said with a faint sardonic smile:

"Didn't the sheriff tell you that Carl was here this morning? I telephoned him immediately. I also got in touch with the State Hospital."

"Why did he come here?"

Grantland turned his hands palms outward. "Who can say? He was obviously disturbed. He bawled me out for my part in having him committed, but his main animus was against his brother. Naturally I tried to talk him out of it."

"Naturally. Why didn't you hold on to him?"

"Don't think I didn't try to. I stepped into the dispensary for a minute to get him some thorazine. I thought it might calm him down. When I came back to the office, he was gone. He must have run out the back way here." Grantland indicated the back door of the examination room. "I heard a car start, but he was gone before I could catch him."

I walked over to the half-curtained window and looked out. Grantland's Jaguar was parked in the paved lot. Back of the lot, a dirt lane ran parallel with the street. I turned back to Grantland: "You say he took your gun?"

"Yes, but I didn't know it at the time. It wasn't exactly *my* gun, either. I'd practically forgotten it existed. I didn't even think of it till I found it in the greenhouse beside poor Jerry's body. Then I couldn't be sure it was the same one, I'm no expert on guns. So I waited until I got back here this afternoon, and had a chance to check the drawer of my desk. When I found it gone I got in touch with the sheriff's department right away—much as I hated to do it."

"Why did you hate to do it?"

"Because I'm fond of the boy. He used to be my patient. You'd hardly expect me to get a kick out of proving that he's a murderer."

"You've proved that, have you?"

"You're supposed to be a detective. Can you think of any other hypothesis?"

I could, but I kept it to myself. Grantland said:

"I can understand your feeling let down. Ostervelt told me you're representing poor Carl, but don't take it too hard, old man. They'll take his mental condition into account. I'll see to it personally that they do."

I wasn't as sad as I looked. Not that I was happy about the case. Every time I moved, I picked up another link in the evidence against my client. But this happened with such clockwork regularity that I was getting used to it and beginning to discount it. Besides, I was encouraged by the firm and lasting faith which I was developing in Dr. Grantland's lack of integrity.

>>>>>>>>
>>>>>>>> *chapter* 20
>>>>>>>>

TWILIGHT was thickening in the street outside. The white-walled buildings, fluorescent with last light, had taken on the beauty and mystery of a city in Africa or someplace else I'd never been. I nosed my car out into a break in the traffic, turned right at the next intersection, and parked a hundred feet short of the entrance to Grantland's back lane. I hadn't been there five minutes when his Jaguar came bumping along the lane. It arced out into the street on whining tires.

Grantland didn't know my car. I followed him fairly closely, two blocks south, then west on a boulevard that slanted toward the sea. I almost lost him when he made a left turn onto the highway on the tail end of a green light. I followed through on the yellow as it turned red.

From there the Jaguar was easy to keep in sight. It headed south on the highway through the outskirts where marginal operators purveyed chicken-fried steaks and salt-water taffy, Mexican basketry and redwood mementoes. The neon-cluttered sub-suburbs dropped behind. The highway snaked up and along brown bluffs which rose at a steep angle above the beach. The sea lay at their foot, a more somber reflection of the sky, still tinged at its far edge with the sun's red death.

About two miles out of town, as many minutes, the Jaguar's brakelights blazed. It heeled and turned onto a black top shelf overlooking the sea. There was one other car in the turnout, a red Cadillac with its nose against the guardrail. Before the next curve swept me out of sight, I saw Grantland's car pull up beside the Cadillac.

There was traffic behind me. I found another turnout a quarter of a mile further on. By the time I'd made my turn and got back to the first turnout, the Jaguar was gone and the Cadillac was going.

I caught a glimpse of the driver's face as he turned onto the highway. It gave me the kind of shock you might get from seeing the ghost of someone you'd once known. I'd known him ten years before, when he was a high-school athlete, a big boy, nice-looking, full of fermenting energy. The face behind the wheel of the Cadillac: yellow skin stretched over skull, smokily lit by black unfocused eyes: could have belonged to that boy's grandfather. I knew him, though. Tom Rica.

I turned once again and followed him south. He drove erratically, slowing on the straightaway and speeding up on the curves, using two of the four lanes. Once, at better than seventy, he left the road entirely, and veered onto the shoulder. The Cadillac skidded sideways in the gravel, headlights swinging out into gray emptiness. The bumper clipped the steel guardrail, and the Cadillac slewed wildly in the other direction. It regained the road and went on as if nothing had happened.

I stayed close behind, trying to think my way into Tom Rica's brain and along his damaged nerves and do his driving for him. I'd always felt an empathy for the boy. When he was eighteen and his unmaturing youth had begun to go rank, I'd tried to hold him straight, and even run some interference for him. An old cop had done it for me when I was a kid. I couldn't do it for Tom.

The memory of my failure was bitter and obscure, mixed with the ash-blonde memory of a woman I'd once been married to. I put both memories out of my mind.

Tom was steadying down to his driving. The big car held the road, and even stayed in one lane most of the time. The road straightened out, and began to climb. Just beyond the crest of the rise, a hundred feet or more above the invisible sea, a red neon sign flashed at the entrance to a private parking lot: Buenavista Inn.

The Cadillac turned in under the sign. I stopped before I got to it, and left my car on the shoulder of the road. The inn lay below, a pueblo affair with a dozen or more stucco cottages staggered along the shadowy terraces. About half of them had lights behind their blinds. There was a red neon Office sign above the door of the main building beside the parking lot.

Tom parked the Cadillac with several other cars, and left it with its lights burning. I kept the other cars between me and him. I didn't think he saw me, but he began to run toward the main building. He moved in a jerky knock-kneed fashion, like an old man trying to catch a bus which had already left.

The door under the red sign opened before he reached it. A big woman stepped out onto the platform of light projected from the doorway. Her hair was gold, her skin a darker gold. She wore a gold lamé gown with a slashed neckline. Even at a distance, she gave the impression of a shining hardness, as though she'd preserved her body from age by having it cast in metal. Her voice had a metallic carrying quality:

"Tommy! Where've you been?"

If he answered, I couldn't hear him. He stopped on his heels in front of her, feinted to the left, and tried to move past her on the right. The action was a sad parody of the broken-field running he'd once been pretty good at. Her flashing body blocked him in the doorway, and one of her round gold arms encircled his neck. He struggled weakly. She kissed him on the mouth, then looked out over his shoulder across the parking lot.

"You took my car, you naughty boy. And now you left the lights on. Get inside now, before somebody sees you."

She slapped him half-playfully, and released him. He scuttled into the lighted lobby. She marched across the parking lot, an unlikely figure of a woman with a broad serene brow, deep eyes, an ugly hungry tortured mouth, a faint pouch under her chin. She walked as if she owned the world, or had owned it once and lost it but remembered how it felt.

She switched off the lights of the car, removed the ignition key and pulled up her skirt to slip it into the top of her stocking. Her legs were heavy and shapely, with slender ankles. She slammed the door of the Cadillac and said out loud, in a tone of mingled anger and indulgence:

"Silly damn little fool."

She breathed and sighed, and noticed me in the middle of the sigh. Without changing the rhythm of her breathing, she smiled and nodded: "Hello there. What can I do for you?"

"You look as if you could do plenty."

"Kidder." But her smile widened, revealing bright gold inlays in its corners. "Nobody's interested in Maude any more. Except Maude. I'm very much interested in Maude."

"That's because you're Maude."

"You bet your sweet life I am. Who are you?"

I told her as I got out of my car, and added: "I'm looking for a friend."

"A new friend?"

"No, an old friend."

"One of my dolls?"

"Could be."

"Come on inside if you want to."

I followed her in. I'd hoped to find Tom Rica in the lobby, but he'd evidently gone through into the private part of the building.

The lobby was surprisingly well furnished with pastel leather chairs, potted palms. One end wall was covered with a photomural of Hollywood at night, which gave the effect of a picture window overlooking the city. The opposite wall was an actual window overlooking the sea.

Maude went around the curved teakwood counter across from the door. The inner door behind the counter was partly open. She closed it. She unlocked a drawer and took out a typewritten sheet, much interlined.

"I mayn't have her listed any more. My turnover is terrific. The girls get married."

"Good for them."

"But not so good for me. I've had a recruiting problem ever since the war. You'd think I was running a matrimonial bureau or something. Well, if she isn't with me any more I can always get you another one. It's early. What did you say her name was?"

"I didn't say. And it's not a her."

She gave me a slightly disappointed look. "You're in the wrong pew. I run a clean place, strictly from heterosex."

"Who said I had sex on my mind?"

"I thought everybody had," she said with a kind of habitual wiggle.

"All the time?"

She glanced at me from the hard gray surface of her deep-set eyes. "What happened to you?"

"A lot of things. I'm trying to sell the movie rights to my life. Somebody down here hates me."

"I mean your face."

"Oh, that."

"What are you stalling for? My God, don't tell me you're a lamster, too. The woods are crawling with them."

"Could you put me up if I was?"

She took it as the fact, with the gullibility of cynicism: "How hot are you?"

"Not very."

"That car outside belong to you?"

"It's mostly the bank's."

"My God, you robbed a bank?"

"They're robbing me. Ten per cent interest on the money I borrowed to buy the crate."

She leaned forward across the counter, her ringed hands flat on its top, her eyes hard-bright as the cut stones in the rings:

"What kind of a joker are you? If you're thinking of knocking me over, I warn you I got protection, plenty of it."

"Don't get hinky."

"I'm not hinky. I get a little irritated, is all, when a beat-up punk walks into my place and won't tell me what he wants." She moved quickly to a small switchboard at the end of the counter, picked up a headphone, and said over her shoulder: "So get to the point, brother."

"Tom Rica is the friend I'm looking for."

A ripple of nerves went through her. Then she stood heavy and solid again. Her eyes didn't shift, but their bright stare became more intense.

"Who sent you here?"

"I came on my own."

"I doubt that. Whoever it was gave you the wrong information." She put down the phone and returned to the counter. "Come to think of it, there was a boy named Rica worked here a while back. What did you say the first name was?"

"Tom."

"What do you want with him?"

"A chance to talk, that's all."

"What about?"

"Old times."

She struck the countertop with the front of her fist. "Cut the doubletalk, eh? You're no friend of his."

"Better than some he has. I hate to see him poison his brains with heroin. He used to be a smart boy."

"He still is," she said defensively. "It isn't his fault he was sick." In a sudden gesture of self-contempt, self-doubt, she tugged at the pouch of flesh under her chin, and went on worrying it. "Who are you, anyway? Are you from the hospital?"

"I'm a private detective investigating a murder."

"That shooting in the country?" For the first time she seemed afraid. "You can't tie Tom in with it."

"What makes you think I'm trying to?"

"You said you wanted to see him, didn't you? But you're not seeing him. He had nothing to do with that killer."

"They escaped together last night."

"That proves nothing. I got rid of that Hallman character soon as we hit the main road. Him I wanted no part of. I see enough of them in line of business. And Tom hasn't seen him since, or gone anywhere. He's been here all day. With me."

"So you helped them get away from the hospital."

"What if I did?"

"You weren't doing Hallman a favor. Or Tom, either."

"I beg to differ. They were torturing him. They cut him off cold turkey. He had nothing to eat for over a week. You ought to've seen him when I picked him up."

"So you put him back on horse."

"I did not. He begged me to get him some caps, but I wouldn't do it. It's the only one thing I wouldn't do for Tom. I did buy him some bottles of cough medicine with the codeine in it. I couldn't just sit there and watch him suffer, could I?"

"You want him to be a hype for the rest of his life? And die of it?"

"Don't say that."

"What are you trying to do to him?"

"Look after him."

"You think you're qualified?"

"I love the boy," she said. "I did what I could for him. Does that make me so lousy?"

"Nobody said you're lousy."

"Nobody has to say it. I tried to make him happy. I didn't have what it takes."

Fingering her heavy breasts, she looked down at herself in sorrow.

>>>>>>>>
>>>>>>>> *chapter* 21
>>>>>>>>

THE door behind her opened. Tom Rica leaned in the opening, with one frail shoulder propped against the doorframe. His sharp tweed jacket hung loosely on him.

"What's the trouble, Maudie?" His voice was thin and dry, denatured. His eyes were puddles of tar.

Maude resumed her smiling mask before she turned to him. "No trouble. Go back in."

She put her hands on his shoulders. He smiled past her at me, detachedly, pathetically, as if there was a thick glass wall between us. She shook him: "Did you get a needle? Is that where you were?"

"Wouldn't you like to know," he said in dull coquetry, using his hollow face as if it was young and charming.

"Where did you get it? Where did you get the money?"

"Who needs money, honey?"

"Answer me." Her shoulders bowed across him. She shook him so that his teeth clicked. "I want to know who gave you the stuff and how much you got and where the rest of it is."

He collapsed against the doorframe. "Lay off me, bag."

"That isn't a bad idea," I said, coming around the counter.

She whirled as if I'd stuck a knife in her back. "You stay out of this, brother. I'm warning you. I've taken enough from you, when all I want is to do what's right for my boy."

"You own him, do you?"

She yelled in a brass tenor: "Get out of my place."

Tom moved between us, like a vaudeville third man. "Don't talk like that to my old buddy." He peered at me through the glass wall. His eyes and speech were more focused, as though the first shock of the drug was passing off. "You still a do-gooder, old buddy? Myself, I'm a do-badder. Every day in every way I'm doing badder and badder, as dear old mother used to say."

"You talk too much," Maude said, laying a heavy arm across his shoulders. "Come in and lie down now."

He turned on her in a sudden spurt of viciousness. "Leave me be. I'm in good shape, having a nice reunion with my old buddy. You trying to break up my friendships?"

"I'm the only friend you got."

"Is that so? Let me tell you something. You'll have dirt in your eyes, and I'll be riding high, living the life of Riley. Who needs you?"

"You need me, Tom," she said, without assurance. "You were on your uppers when I took you in. If it wasn't for me you'd be in the pen. I got your charge reduced, and you know it, and it cost me plenty. So here you go right back on the same crazy kick. Don't you ever learn?"

"I learn, don't worry. All these years I been studying the angles, see, like an apprenticeship. I know the rackets like I know the back of my hand. I know where you stupid hustlers make your stupid mistakes. And I'm not making any. I got a racket of my own now, and it's as safe as houses." His mood had swung violently upward, in anger and elation.

"Houses with bars on the windows," the blonde woman said. "You stick your neck out again, and I can't cover for you."

"Nobody asked you to. I'm on my own now. Forget me."

He turned his back on her and went through the inner door. His body moved loosely and lightly, supported by invisible strings. I started to follow him. Maude turned her helpless anger on me:

"Stay out of there. You got no right in there."

I hesitated. She was a woman. I was in her house. With the toe of her shoe, Maude pressed a faintly worn spot in the carpet behind the counter:

"You better beat it out of here, I'm warning you."

"I think I'll stay for a while."

She folded her arms across her breasts and looked at me like a lioness. A short broad man in a plaid shirt opened the front door and came in quietly. His smile was wide and meaningless under a hammered-in nose. A leather blackjack, polished like a keepsake, swung from his hand.

"Dutch, take this one out," Maude said, standing away.

I went around the counter and took Dutch out instead. Perhaps bouncing drunks had spoiled him. Anyway, he was easy to hit. Between his wild swings, I hit him with a left to the head, a right cross to the jaw, a long left hook to the solar plexus which bent him over into my right coming up. He subsided. I picked up his blackjack and moved past Maude through the inner door. She didn't say a word.

I went through a living-room crowded with overstuffed furniture in a green-and-white jungle design from which eyes seemed to watch me, down a short hallway past a pink satin bedroom which reminded me of the inside of a coffin in disarray, to the open door of a bathroom. Tom's jacket lay across the lighted threshold like the headless torso of a man, flattened by the passage of some enormous engine.

Tom was sitting on the toilet seat with his left shirtsleeve rolled up and a hypodermic needle in his right hand. He was too busy looking for a vein to notice me. The veins he had already used and ruined writhed black up his arm from wrist to wasted biceps. Blue tattoo marks disguised the scars on his wrists.

I took the needle away from him. It was about a quarter full of clear liquid. Upturned in the bright bathroom light, his face set in hard wrinkles like a primitive mask used to conjure evil spirits, its eyeholes full of darkness.

"Give it back. I didn't get enough."

"Enough to kill yourself?"

"It keeps me alive. I almost died without it, there in the hospital. My brains were running out of my ears."

He made a sudden grab for the needle in my hand. I held it out of his reach.

"Go back to the hospital, Tom."

He swung his head slowly from side to side. "There's nothing for me there. Everything I want is on the outside."

"What do you want?"

"Kicks. Money and kicks. What else is there?"

"A hell of a lot."

"You've got it?" He sensed my hesitation, and looked up slyly. "Do-gooder ain't doing so good, eh? Don't go into the old look-to-the-future routine. It makes me puke. It always made me puke. So save it for the birds. *This* is my future, *now.*"

"You like it?"

"If you give me back my needle. It's all I need from you."

"Why don't you kick it, Tom? Use your guts for that. You're too young to go down the drain."

"Save it for the boy scouts, den-father. You want to know why I'm a hype? Because I got bored with double-mouthed bastards like you. You spout the old uplift line, but I never seen a one of you that believed in it for himself. While you're telling other people how to live, you're double-timing your wife and running after gash, drinking like a goddam fish and chasing any dirty nickel you can see."

There was enough truth in what he said to tie my tongue for a minute. The obscure pain of memory came back. It centered in an image in my mind: the face of the woman I had lost. I blotted the image out, telling myself that that was years ago. The important things had happened long ago.

Tom spoke to the doubt that must have showed in my face:

"Give me back my needle. What's to lose?"

"Not a chance."

"Come on," he wheedled. "The stuff is weak. The first shot didn't even give me a lift."

"Then you don't have so far to fall."

He beat his sharp knees with his fists. "Give me my needle, you hot-and-cold-running false-faced mother-lover. You'd steal the pennies off a dead man's eyes and sell his body for soap."

"Is that how you feel? Dead?"

"The hell I am. I'll show you. I can get more."

He got up and tried to push past me. He was frail and light as a scarecrow. I forced him back onto the seat, holding the needle carefully out of his reach.

"Where did you get it in the first place, Tom?"

"Would I tell you?"

"Maybe you don't have to."

"Then why ask?"

"What's this fine new racket of yours that you were warbling about?"

"Wouldn't you like to know."

"Pushing reefers to school kids?"

"You think I'm interested in peanuts?"

"Buying and selling old clothes?"

His ego couldn't stand to be downgraded. The insult blew it up like a balloon. "You think I'm kidding? I got a piece of the biggest racket in the world. Before I'm through I'll be buying and selling peanut-eaters like you."

"By saving green stamps, no doubt."

"By putting on the squeeze, jerk, where the money is. You get something on somebody, see, and you sell it back a little piece at a time. It's like an annuity."

"Or a death-warrant."

He looked at me imperviously. Dead men never die.

"The good doctor could be very bad medicine."

He grinned. "I got an antidote."

"What have you got on him, Tom?"

"Do I look crazy enough to tell you?"

"You told Carl Hallman."

"Did I? Maybe he thinks I did. I told him any little thing that came into my little pointed head."

"What were you trying to do to him?"

"Just stir him up a little. I had to get out of that ward. I couldn't make it alone."

"Why did you send Hallman to me?"

"Get him off my hands. He was in my way."

"You must have had a better reason than that."

"Sure. I'm a do-gooder." His wise grin turned malign. "I thought you could use the business."

"Carl Hallman's got a murder rap on his hands, did you know that?"

"I know it."

"If I thought you talked him into it—"

"What would you do? Slap my wrist, do-gooder?"

He looked at me through the glass wall with lazy curiosity, and added casually: "Anyway, he didn't shoot his brother. He told me so himself."

"Has he been here?"

"Sure he was here. He wanted Maude to hide him out. She wouldn't touch him with gloves on."

"How long ago was this?"

"A couple of hours, maybe. He took off for town when Maude and Dutch gave him the rush."

"Did he say where he was going in town?"

"No."

"He didn't shoot his brother, you say?"

"That's right, he told me that."

"Did you believe him?"

"I had to believe him, because I did it myself." Tom looked at me dead-pan. "I flew over there by helicopter, see. In my new supersonic helicopter with the synchronized death-ray gun."

"Turn off the stardrive, Tom. Tell me what really happened."

"Maybe I will, if you give me back my needle."

His eyes held a curious mixture of plea and threat. They looked expectantly at the bright instrument in my fist. I was tempted to let him have it, on the chance that he knew something I could use. A few more caps in those black veins wouldn't make any difference. Except to me.

I was sick of the whole business. I threw the needle into the square pink bathtub. It smashed to pieces.

Tom looked at me incredulously. "What did you do that for?"

Sudden fury shook him, too strong for his nerves to carry. It broke through into grief. He flung himself face down on the pink tile floor, sobbing in a voice like fabric tearing.

In the intervals of the noise he made, I heard other noises behind me. Maude was coming through the jungle-colored living-room. A gun gleamed dully blue in her white hand. The man called Dutch was a pace behind her. His grin was broken-toothed. I could see why my knuckles were sore.

"What goes on?" Maude cried. "What did you do to him?"

"Took his needle away. See for yourself."

She didn't seem to hear me. "Come out of there. Leave him alone." She pushed the gun toward my face.

"Let me at him. I'll clobber the bastard," the man behind her lisped in punchy eagerness.

An Argyle sock hung heavy and pendulous from his hand. It reminded me of the blackjack in my pocket. I backed out of the doorway to gain elbowroom, and swung the leather club over and down at Maude's wrist.

She hissed with pain. The gun clanked at her feet. Dutch went down on his hands and knees after it. I hit him on the back of the head with the blackjack, not too hard, just hard enough to stretch him on his face again. The heavy sock fell from his numb hand, some of its sand spilling out.

Maude was scrambling in the doorway for the gun. I pushed her back and picked it up and put it in my pocket. It was a medium-caliber revolver and it made a very heavy pocket. I put the blackjack in my other pocket so that I wouldn't walk lopsided.

Maude leaned on the wall outside the door, holding her right wrist in her left hand. "You're going to be sorry for this."

"I've heard that before."

"Not from me you haven't, or you wouldn't be running around making trouble for people. Don't think it's going to last. I got the top law in this county in my pocket."

"Tell me more," I said. "You have a lovely singing voice. Maybe I can arrange a personal appearance, in front of the Grand Jury."

Her ugly mouth said yah at me. Her left hand came out stiff, its carmine talons pointed at my eyes. It was more of a threat than attempt, but it made me despair of our relationship.

I left her and found a back way out. There were soft lights and loud noises in the cottages on the terraces, music, female laughter, money, kicks.

>>>>>>>>>
>>>>>>>>> *chapter* 22
>>>>>>>>>

I DROVE back toward Purissima, keeping a not very hopeful lookout for Carl Hallman. Just outside the city limits, where the highway dipped down from the bluffs toward the sea, I saw a huddle of cars on the shoulder. Two of the cars had red pulsating lights. Other lights were moving on the beach.

I parked across the highway and got the flashlight out of my dash compartment. Before I closed it, I relieved my pockets of the gun and the blackjack and locked them up. I descended a flight of concrete steps which slanted down to the beach. Near their foot, the vestiges of a small fire glowed. Beside it, a blanket was spread on the sand, weighted down by a picnic basket.

Most of the lights were far up the beach by now, bobbing and swerving like big slow fireflies. Between me and the dim thumping line of the surf, a dozen or so people were milling aimlessly. A man detached himself from the shadowy group and trotted toward me, soft-footed in the sand.

"Hey! That's my stuff. It belongs to me."

I flashed my light across him. He was a very young man in a gray sweatshirt with a college letter on the front of it. He moved as though he had won the letter playing football.

"What's the excitement about?" I said.

"I'm not excited. I just don't like people messing around with my stuff."

"Nobody's messing around with your stuff. I mean the excitement up the beach."

"The cops are after a guy."

"What guy is that?"

"The maniac—the one that shot his brother."

"Did you see him?"

"I hope to tell you. I was the one that raised the alarm. He walked right up to Marie when she was sitting here. Lord knows what would have happened if I hadn't been within reach." The boy arched his shoulders and stuck out his chest.

"What did happen?"

"Well, I went up to the car to get some cigarettes, and this guy came out of the dark and asked Marie for a sandwich. It wasn't just a sandwich that he wanted, she could tell. A sandwich was just the thin edge of the wedge. Marie let out a yell, and I came down the bank and threw a tackle at him. I could have held him, too, except that it was dark and I couldn't see what I was doing. He caught me a lucky blow in the face, and got away."

I turned my light on his face. His lower lip was swollen.

"Which way did he go?"

He pointed along the shore to the multicolored lights of the Purissima waterfront. "I would have run him down, only maybe he had confederates, so I couldn't leave Marie here by herself. We drove to the nearest gas station and I phoned in the alarm."

The onlookers on the beach had begun to straggle up the concrete steps. A highway patrolman approached us, the light from his flash stabbing at the pockmarked sand. The boy in the sweatshirt called out heartily:

"Anything else I can do?"

"Not right now there isn't. He got clean away, it looks like."

"Maybe he swam out to sea and went aboard a yacht and they'll put him ashore in Mexico. I heard the family is loaded."

"Maybe," the patrolman said drily. "You're sure you saw the man? Or have you been seeing too many movies?"

The boy retorted hotly: "You think I smacked myself in the mouth?"

"Sure it was the man we're looking for?"

"Of course. Big guy with light-colored hair in dungarees. Ask Marie. She had a real good look at him."

"Where is your girlfriend now?"

"Somebody took her home, she was pretty upset."

"I guess we better have her story. Show me where she lives, eh?"

"I'll be glad to."

While the young man was dousing the fire with sand and collecting his belongings, another car stopped on the roadside above us. It was an old black convertible which looked familiar. Mildred got out and started down the steps. She came so blindly and precipitously that I was afraid she'd fall and plunge headlong. I caught her at the foot of the steps with one arm around her waist.

"Let me go!"

I let her go. She recognized me then, and returned to her mind's single track: "Is Carl here? Have you seen him?"

"No—"

She turned to the patrolman: "Has my husband been here?"

"You Mrs. Hallman?"

"Yes. The radio said my husband was seen on Pelican Beach."

"He's been and gone, ma'am."

"Gone where?"

"That's what we'd like to know. Do you have any ideas on the subject?"

"No. I haven't."

"Has he got any close friends in Purissima—somebody he might go to?"

Mildred hesitated. The faces of curious onlookers strained out of the darkness toward her. The boy in the sweatshirt was breathing on the back of her neck. He spoke as if she were deaf or dead:

"This is the guy's *wife*."

The patrolman looked disgusted. "Break it up, eh? Move along there now." He turned back to Mildred: "Any ideas, ma'am?"

"I'm sorry—it's hard for me to think. Carl had lots of friends in high school. They all dropped away. He didn't see anyone the last year or so." Her voice trailed off. She seemed confused by the lights and the people.

I said, as stuffily as possible: "Mrs. Hallman came here to look for her husband. She doesn't have to answer questions."

The patrolman's light came up to my face. "Who are you?"

"A friend of the family. I'm going to take her home."

"All right. Take her home. She shouldn't be running around by herself, anyway."

With a hand under her elbow, I propelled Mildred up the steps and across the highway. Her face was an oval blur in the dark interior of my car, so pale that it seemed luminous.

"Where are you taking me?"

"Home, as I said. Is it far from here?"

"A couple of miles. I have my own car, thank you, and I'm perfectly fit to drive it. After all, I drove it here."

"Don't you think it's time you relaxed?"

"With Carl still being hunted? How can I? Anyway, I've been home all day. You said he might come to the house, but he never did."

Exhaustion or disappointment overcame her. She sat inertly, propped doll-like in the seat. Headlights went by in the road like brilliant forlorn hopes rushing out of darkness into darkness.

"He may be on his way there now," I said. "He's hungry, and he must be bone-tired. He's been on the run for a night and a day." And another night was beginning.

Her hand moved from her mouth to my arm. "How do you know he's hungry?"

"He asked a girl on the beach for a sandwich. Before that he went to a friend, looking for shelter. Friend may be the wrong word. Did Carl ever mention Tom Rica to you?"

"Rica? Isn't that the fellow who escaped with him? His name was in the paper."

"That's right. Do you know anything else about him?"

"Just from what Carl said."

"When was that?"

"The last time I saw him, in the hospital. He told me how this Rica man had suffered in the ward. Carl was trying to make it easier for him. He said that Rica was a heroin addict."

"Did he tell you anything more about him?"

"Not that I remember. Why?"

"Rica saw Carl, not more than a couple of hours ago. If Rica can be believed. He's staying with a woman named Maude, at a place called the Buenavista Inn, just a few miles down the highway. Carl went there looking for a place to hole up."

"I don't understand," Mildred said. "Why would Carl go to a woman like that for help?"

"You know Maude, do you?"

"Certainly not. But everybody in town knows what goes on at that so-called Inn." Mildred looked at me with a kind of terror. "Is Carl mixed up with those people?"

"It doesn't follow. A man on the run will take any out he can think of."

The words didn't sound the way I'd meant them to. Her head went down under the weight of the heavy image they made. She sighed again.

It was hard to listen to. I put my arm around her. She held herself stiff and silent against my shoulder.

"Relax. This isn't a pass."

I didn't think it was. Possibly Mildred knew better. She pulled herself away from me and got out of my car in a single flurry of movement.

Most of the cars across the highway had left as we sat talking. The road was empty except for a heavy truck highballing down the hill from the south. Mildred stood at the edge of the pavement, silhouetted by its approaching lights.

The situation went to pieces, and came together in the rigid formal clarity of a photographed explosion. Mildred was on the pavement, walking head down in the truck's bright path. It bore down on her as tall as a house, braying and squealing. I saw its driver's lantern-slide face high above the road, and Mildred in the road in front of the giant tires.

The truck stopped a few feet short of her. In the sudden vacuum of sound, I could hear the sea mumbling and spitting like a beast under the bank. The truck-driver leaned from his cab and yelled at Mildred in relief and indignation:

"Damn fool woman! Watch where you're going. You damn near got yourself killed."

Mildred paid no attention to him. She climbed into the Buick, waited until the truck was out of the way, and made a sweeping turn in front of me. I was bothered by the way she handled herself and the car. She moved and drove obliviously, like someone alone in black space.

My quasi-paternal instinct followed her home; I went along for the ride. She made it safely, and left the black convertible at the curb. When I pulled in behind it, she stopped in the middle of the sidewalk:

"What are you trying to do?"

"Seeing Millie home."

Her response was flat. "Well, I'm home."

The old house leaned like a tombstone on the night. But there were lights inside, behind cracked blinds, and the sound of a broken soprano voice. I got out and followed Mildred up the walk:

"You almost got yourself run over."

"Did I?" She turned at the top of the veranda steps. "I don't need a keeper, thank you. In fact, all I want is to be let alone."

"The deep tangled wildwood," the lost and strident voice sang from the house. "And all the loved songs that my infancy knew."

"Is your mother all right, Mildred?"

"Mother's just dandy, thank you. She's been drinking all day." She looked up and down the dark street and said in a different voice: "Even the crummy people who live on this street look down their noses at us. I can't put up a front any more. I'd simply like to crawl into a hole and die."

"You need some rest."

"How can I get any rest? With all this trouble on my shoulders? And that?"

Cast by the light from one of the front windows, her shadow lay broken on the steps. She gestured toward the window. Behind it her mother had finished her song and was playing some closing bars on a badly tuned piano.

"Anyway," Mildred said, "I have to go to work tomorrow morning. I can't miss another half day."

"Who do you work for, Simon Legree?"

"I don't mean that. Mr. Haines is very nice. It's just, if I go off schedule, I'm afraid I'll never get back on."

She fumbled in her black plastic bag for her key. The doorknob turned before she touched it. The outside light came on over our heads. Mrs. Gley opened the door, smiling muzzily:

"Bring your friend in, dear. I've said it before and I'll say it again. Your mother's always pleased and proud to entertain your friends."

Mrs. Gley didn't seem to recognize me; I was part of the indiscriminate past blurred out by the long day's drinking. She was glad to see me anyway.

"Bring your friend in, Mildred. I'll pour him a drink. A young man likes to be entertained; that's something you've got to learn. You've wasted too much of your youth on that good-for-nothing husband—"

"Stop making a fool of yourself," Mildred said coldly.

"I am not making a fool of myself. I am expressing the feelings of my womanly heart. Isn't that so?" she appealed to me. "You'll come in and have a drink with me, won't you?"

"Be glad to."

"And I'll be glad to have you."

Mrs. Gley spread her arms out in a welcoming gesture, and toppled toward me. I caught her under the arms. She giggled against my shirt front. With Mildred's help, I walked her into the sitting-room. She was awkward to handle in her draperies, like a loosely shrouded corpse.

But she managed to sit upright on the sofa and say in gracious tones:

"Excuse me. I was overcome by dizziness for a moment. The shock of the night air, you know."

Like someone struck by a bullet, invisible and inaudible, she fell softly sideways. Very soon, she began to snore.

Mildred straightened out her mother's legs, smoothed her purplish red hair and put a cushion under her head. She took off her own cloth coat and covered the lower part of her mother's body. She did these things with neutral efficiency, without tenderness and without anger, as though she'd done them many times before and expected to do them many times again.

In the same neutral way, like an older woman speaking to a

younger, she said: "Poor mother, have sweet dreams. Or no dreams. I wish you no dreams at all."

"Can I help to get her upstairs?" I said.

"She can sleep here. She often has. This happens two or three times a week. We're used to it."

Mildred sat at her mother's feet and looked around the room as if to memorize its shabby contents. She stared at the empty eye of the television set. The empty eye stared back at her. She looked down at her mother's sleeping face. My feeling that their ages were reversed was stronger when she spoke again:

"Poor redhead. She used to be a genuine redhead, too. I give her money to have it dyed. But she prefers to dye it herself, and save the money for drinking. I can't really blame her. She's tired. She ran a boarding-house for fourteen years and then she got tired."

"Is your mother a widow?"

"I don't know." She raised her eyes to my face. "It hardly matters. My father took off when I was seven years old. He had a wonderful chance to buy a ranch in Nevada for very little down. Father was always getting those wonderful chances, but this was the one that was really going to pay off. He was supposed to come back for us in three weeks or a month, when everything was settled. He never did come back. I heard from him just once. He sent me a present for my eighth birthday, a ten-dollar gold piece from Reno. There was a little note along with it, that I wasn't to spend it. I was to keep it as a token of his love. I didn't spend it, either. Mother did."

If Mildred felt resentment, she didn't show it. She sat for a time, silent and still. Then she twitched her slender shoulders, as though to shake off the dead hand of the past:

"I don't know how I got off on the subject of Father. Anyway, it doesn't matter." She changed the subject abruptly: "This man Rica, at the Buenavista Inn, what kind of a person is he?"

"Pretty dilapidated. There's not much left but hunger. He's been on dope for years. As a witness he may be useless."

"As a witness?"

"He said that Carl told him he didn't shoot Jerry."

Faint color rose in her face, and her eyes brightened. "Why didn't you tell *me* that?"

"You didn't give me a chance to. You seemed to have a rendezvous with a truck."

Her color deepened. "I admit I had a bad reaction. You oughtn't to have put your arm around me."

"I meant it in a friendly way."

"I know. It just reminded me of something. We were talking about those people at the Inn."

"I thought you didn't know them."

"I don't know them. I don't want to know them." She hesitated. "But don't you think you should inform the police about what that man said?"

"I haven't made up my mind."

"Did you believe what he said?"

"With reservations. I never did think that Carl shot his brother. But my opinion isn't based on Rica's testimony. He's a dreamtalker."

"What is it based on?"

"It's hard to say. I had a strange feeling about the events at the ranch today. They had an unreal quality. Does that fit in with anything you noticed?"

"I think so, but I couldn't pin it down. What do you mean, exactly?"

"If I could say exactly, I'd know what happened out there. I don't know what happened, not yet. Some of the things I saw with my own eyes seemed as if they'd been staged for my benefit. Your husband's movements don't make sense to me, and neither do some of the others. That includes the sheriff."

"It doesn't mean Carl is guilty."

"That's just my point. He did his best to try and prove that he was, but I'm not convinced. You're familiar with the situation, the people involved. And if Carl didn't shoot Jerry, somebody else did. Who had a motive?"

"Zinnie had, of course. Only the idea of Zinnie is impossible. Women like Zinnie don't shoot people."

"Sometimes they do if the people are their husbands, and if they have strong enough motives. Love and money are a strong combination."

"You know about her and Dr. Grantland? Yes, of course, you must. She's pretty obvious."

"How long has it been going on?"

"Not long, I'm sure of that. Whatever there is between them

started after I left the ranch. I heard rumors downtown. One of my best friends is a legal secretary. She told me two or three months ago that Zinnie wanted a divorce from Jerry. He wasn't willing to give it to her, though. He threatened to fight her for Martha, and apparently she dropped the whole idea. Zinnie would never do anything that would lose her Martha."

"Shooting Jerry wouldn't lose her Martha," I said, "unless she was caught."

"You're not suggesting that Zinnie did shoot him? I simply don't believe it."

I didn't believe it, either. I didn't disbelieve it. I held it in my mind and turned it around to see how it looked. It looked as ugly as sin.

"Where's Zinnie now, do you know?"

"I haven't seen her since I left the ranch."

"What about Martha?"

"I suppose she's with Mrs. Hutchinson. She spends a lot of her life with Mrs. Hutchinson." Mildred added in a lower tone: "If I had a little girl like Martha, I'd stay with her and look after her myself. Only I haven't."

Her eyes brightened with tears. I realized for the first time what her barren broken marriage meant to her.

The telephone rang like an alarm clock in the hall. Mildred went to answer it.

"This is Mildred Hallman speaking." Her voice went higher. "No! I don't want to see you. You have no right to harass me. . . . Of course he hasn't. I don't need anyone to protect me."

I heard her hang up, but she didn't come back to the sitting-room. Instead she went into the front of the house. I found her in a room off the hallway, standing in the dark by the window.

"What's the trouble?"

She didn't answer. I found the light switch by the door, and pressed it. A single bulb winked on in the old brass chandelier. Against the opposite wall, an ancient piano grinned at me with all its yellow keys. An empty gin bottle stood on top of it.

"Was that Sheriff Ostervelt on the telephone?"

"How did you know?"

"The way you react to him. The Ostervelt reaction."

"I hate him," she said. "I don't like her, either. Ever since Carl's been in the hospital, she's been acting more and more as if she owns him."

"I seem to have lost the thread. Who are we talking about?"

"A woman called Rose Parish, a social worker at the State Hospital. She's with Sheriff Ostervelt, and they both want to come here. I don't want to see them. They're people-eaters."

"What does that mean?"

"They're people who live on other people's troubles. I hope I headed them off. I've had enough bites taken out of me."

"I think you're wrong about Miss Parish."

"You know her?"

"I met her this morning, at the hospital. She seemed very sympathetic to your husband's case."

"Then what's she doing with Sheriff Ostervelt?"

"Probably straightening him out, if I know Miss Parish."

"He can use some straightening out. If he comes here, I won't let him in."

"Are you afraid of him?"

"I suppose I am. No. I hate him too much to be afraid of him. He did a dreadful thing to me."

"You mean the day you took Carl to the hospital?"

Mildred nodded. Pale and heavy-eyed, she looked as if her youth had run out through the unstopped wound of that day.

"I'd better tell you what actually happened. He tried to make me his—his whore. He tried to take me to Buenavista Inn."

"That same day?"

"Yes, on the way back from the hospital. He'd already made three or four stops, and every time he came back to the car he was drunker and more obnoxious. Finally I asked him to let me off at the nearest bus station. We were in Buena Vista by then, just a little way from home, but I couldn't put up with him any longer.

"I was forced to, however. Instead of taking me to the bus station, he drove out the highway to the Inn, and parked above it. The owner was a friend of his, he said—a wonderful woman, very broadminded. If I wanted to stay there with her, she'd give me a suite to myself, and it wouldn't cost me a cent. I could take a week's vacation, or a month's—as long as I liked—and he would come and keep me company at night.

"He said he'd had this in mind for a long time, ever since his wife passed away, before that. Now that Carl was out of the way, he and I could get together at last. You should have heard him, trying to be romantic. The great lover. Leaning across me with his bald head, sweating and breathing hard and smelling of liquor."

Anger clenched in my stomach like a fist. "Did he try to use force on you?"

"He tried to kiss me. I was able to handle him, though, when he saw how I felt about him. He didn't assault me, not physically, if that's what you're getting at. But he treated me as if I—as if a woman whose husband was sick was fair game for anybody."

"What about Carl's alleged confession? Did he try to use it to make you do what he wanted?"

"Yes, he did. Only please don't do anything about it. The situation is bad enough already."

"It could get worse for him. Abuse of office cuts two ways."

"You mustn't talk like that. It will only make things worse for Carl."

A car purred somewhere out of sight. Then its headlights entered the street.

"Turn off the light," Mildred whispered, "I have a feeling it's them."

I pressed the switch and crossed to the window where she stood. A black Mercury Special pulled in to the curb behind my convertible. Ostervelt and Miss Parish got out of the back seat. Mildred pulled down the blind and turned to me:

"Will you talk to them? I don't want to see them."

"I don't blame you for not wanting to see Ostervelt. You ought to talk to Miss Parish, though. She's definitely on our side."

"I'll talk to her if I have to. But she'll have to give me a chance to change my clothes."

Their footsteps were on the porch. As I went to answer the door, I heard Mildred running up the stairs behind me.

MISS PARISH and the sheriff were standing in uncomfortable relation to each other. I guessed they'd had an argument. She looked official and rather imposing in a plain blue coat and hat. Ostervelt's face was shadowed by his wide hatbrim, but I got the impression that he was feeling subdued. If there had been an argument, he'd lost.

"What are you doing here?" He spoke without force, like an old actor who has lost faith in his part.

"I've been holding Mrs. Hallman's hand. Hello, Miss Parish."

"Hello." Her smile was warm. "How *is* Mrs. Hallman?"

"Yeah," Ostervelt said. "How is she? She sounded kind of upset on the telephone. Did something happen?"

"Mrs. Hallman doesn't want to see you unless it's necessary."

"Hell, I'm just interested in her personal safety." He looked sideways at Miss Parish and added for her benefit, in an injured-innocent tone: "What's Mildred got against me?"

I stepped outside and shut the door behind me. "Are you sure you want an answer?"

I couldn't keep the heat out of my voice. In reflex, Ostervelt put his hand on his gun-butt.

"Good heavens!" Miss Parish said with a forced little laugh. "Haven't we got enough trouble, gentlemen?"

"I want to know what he means by that. He's been needling me all day. I don't have to take that stuff from any keyhole cop." Ostervelt sounded almost querulous. "Not in my own county I don't."

"You ought to be ashamed of yourself, Mr. Archer." She stepped between us, turning her back on me and her full maternal charm on Ostervelt. "Why don't you wait for me in the car, Sheriff? I'll talk to Mrs. Hallman if she'll let me. It's obvious that her husband hasn't been here. That's all you wanted to know, isn't it?"

"Yeah, but—" He glared at me over her shoulder. "I didn't like that crack."

"You weren't intended to. Make something out of it."

The situation was boiling up again. Miss Parish poured cool words on it: "I didn't hear any crack. Both you men are under a strain. It's no excuse for acting like boys with a chip on your shoulder." She touched Ostervelt's shoulder, and let her hand linger there. "You will go and wait in the car, won't you? I'll only be a few minutes."

With a kind of caressing firmness, she turned Ostervelt around and gave him a gentle push toward the street. He took it, and he went. She gave me a bright, warm look.

"How did you get him eating out of your hand?"

"Oh, that's my little secret. Actually, something came up."

"What came up?"

She smiled. "I did. Dr. Brockley couldn't make it; he had an important meeting. So he sent me instead. I asked him to."

"To check up on Ostervelt?"

"I have no official right to do anything like that." The door of the Mercury slammed in the street. "We'd better go inside, don't you think? He'll know we're talking about him."

"Let him."

"You men. Sometimes I feel as though the whole world were a mental hospital. It's certainly a safe enough assumption to act on."

After the day I'd put in, I wasn't inclined to argue.

I opened the door and held it for her. She faced me in the lighted hallway.

"I didn't expect to find you here."

"I got involved."

"I understand you have your car back."

"Yes." But she wasn't interested in my car. "If you're asking the question I think you are, I'm working for your friend Carl. I don't believe he killed his brother, or anybody else."

"Really?" Her bosom rose under her coat. She unbuttoned the coat to give it the room it needed. "I just got finished telling Sheriff Ostervelt the same thing."

"Did he buy it?"

"I'm afraid not. The circumstances are very much against Carl, aren't they? I did manage to cool the old man off a bit."

"How did you manage that?"

"It's official business. Confidential."

"Having to do with Carl?"

"Indirectly. The man he escaped with, Tom Rica. I really can't give you any more information, Mr. Archer."

"Let me guess. If I'm right, I know it already. If I'm wrong, there's no harm done. Ostervelt got Rica off with a state-hospital commitment when under the law he should have been sent to the pen."

Miss Parish didn't say I was wrong. She didn't say anything.

I ushered her into the front room. Her dark awareness took it in at a glance, staying on the empty bottle on top of the piano. There was a family photograph beside it, in a tarnished silver frame, and a broken pink conch shell.

Miss Parish picked up the bottle and sniffed it and set it down with a rap. She looked suspiciously toward the door. Her bold profile and mannish hat reminded me of a female operative in a spy movie.

"Where's the little wife?" she whispered.

"Upstairs, changing her clothes."

"Is she a drinker?"

"Never touches the stuff. Her mother drinks for both of them."

"I see."

Miss Parish leaned forward to examine the photograph. I looked at it over her shoulder. A smiling man in shirtsleeves and wide suspenders stood under a palm tree with a strikingly pretty woman. The woman held a long-dressed child on her arm. The picture had been amateurishly tinted by hand. The tree was green, the woman's bobbed hair was red, the flowers in her dress were red. All the colors were fading.

"Is this the mother-in-law?"

"Apparently."

"Where is she now?"

"Dreamland. She passed out."

"Alcoholic?"

"Mrs. Gley is working at it."

"What about the father?"

"He dropped away long ago. He may be dead."

"I'm surprised," Miss Parish murmured. "I understood Carl came from quite a wealthy—quite a good background."

"Wealthy, anyway. His wife doesn't."

"So I gather." Miss Parish looked around the mortuary room where the past refused to live or die. "It helps to fill in the picture."

"What picture?" Her patronizing attitude irked me.

"My understanding of Carl and his problems. The type of family a sick man marries into can be very significant. A person who feels socially inadequate, as sick people do, will often lower himself in the social scale, deliberately declass himself."

"Don't jump to conclusions too fast. You should take a look at his own family."

"Carl's told me a great deal about them. You know, when a person breaks down, he doesn't do it all by himself. It's something that happens to whole families. The terrible thing is when one member cracks up, the rest so often make a scapegoat out of him. They think they can solve their own problems by rejecting the sick one—locking him up and forgetting him."

"That applies to the Hallmans," I said. "It doesn't apply to Carl's wife. I think her mother would like to see him put away for good, but she doesn't count for much."

"I know, I mustn't let myself be unfair to the wife. She seems to be quite a decent little creature. I have to admit she stayed with it when the going was rough. She came to see Carl every week, never missed a Sunday. Which is more than you can say for a lot of them." Miss Parish cocked her head, as if she could hear a playback of herself. She flushed slowly. "Good heavens, listen to me. It's such a temptation to identify with the patients and blame the relatives for everything. It's one of our worst occupational hazards."

She sat down on the piano stool and took out a cigarette, which I lit for her. Twin lights burned deep in her eyes. I could sense her emotions burning behind her professional front, like walled atomic fires. They didn't burn for me, though.

Just to have something burning for me, I lit a cigarette of my own. Miss Parish jumped at the snap of the lighter; she had nerves, too. She turned on the stool to look up at me:

"I know I identify with my patients. Especially Carl. I can't help it."

"Isn't that doing it the hard way? If I went through the wringer every time one of my clients does—" I lost interest in the sentence, and let it drop. I had my own identification with the hunted man.

"I don't *care* about myself." Miss Parish crushed out her cigarette rather savagely, and moved to the doorway. "Carl is in serious jeopardy, isn't he?"

"It could be worse."

"It may be worse than you think. I talked to several people at the courthouse. They're raking up those other deaths in his family. He did a lot of talking, you know, at the time he was committed. Completely irrational talking. You don't take what a disturbed person says at its face value. But a lot of men in law enforcement don't understand that."

"Did the sheriff tell you about Carl's alleged confession?"

"He hinted around about it. I'm afraid he gives it a lot of weight. As if it proved anything."

"You sound as if you've heard it all before."

"Of course I have. When Carl was admitted six months ago he had himself convinced that he was the criminal of the century. He accused himself of killing both his parents."

"His mother, too?"

"I think his guilt-feelings originated with her suicide. She drowned herself several years ago."

"I knew that. But I don't understand why he'd blame himself."

"It's a typical reaction in depressed patients to blame themselves for everything bad that happens. Particularly the death of people they love. Carl was devoted to his mother, deeply dependent on her. At the same time he was trying to break away and have a life of his own. She probably killed herself for reasons that had no connection with Carl. But he saw her death as a direct result of his disloyalty to her, what he thought of as disloyalty. He felt as though his efforts to cut the umbilical cord had actually killed her. From there it was only a step to thinking that he was a murderer."

It was tempting doctrine, that Carl's guilt was compounded of words and fantasies, the stuff of childhood nightmares. It promised to solve so many problems that I was suspicious of it.

"Would a theory like that stand up in court?"

"It isn't theory, it's fact. Whether or not it was accepted as fact would depend on the human element: the judge, the jury, the quality of the expert witnesses. But there's no reason why it should ever come to court." Her eyes were watchful, ready to be angry with me.

"I'd still like to get my hands on firm evidence that he didn't do these crimes, that somebody else did. It's the only certain way to prove that his confession was a phony."

"But it definitely was. We know his mother was a suicide. His father died of natural causes, or possibly by accident. The story Carl told about that was pure fantasy, right out of the textbook."

"I haven't read the textbook."

"He said that he broke into his father's bathroom when the old man was in the tub, knocked him unconscious, and held him under water until he was dead."

"Do you know for a fact that it didn't happen that way?"

"Yes," she said. "I do. I have the word of the best possible witness, Carl himself. He knows now that he had no direct connection with his father's death. He told me that several weeks ago. He's developed remarkable insight into his guilt-feelings, and his reasons for confessing something he didn't do. He knows now that he wanted to punish himself for his father-killing fantasies. Every boy has the Oedipus fantasies, but they seldom come out so strongly, except in psychotic breakthrough.

"Carl had a breakthrough the morning he and his brother found their father in the bathtub. The night before, he'd had a serious argument with his father. Carl was very angry, murderously angry. When his father actually did die, he felt like a murderer. The guilt of his mother's death came up from the unconscious and reinforced this new guilt. His mind invented a story to explain his terrible guilt-feelings, and somehow deal with them."

"Carl told you all this?" It sounded very complicated and tenuous.

"We worked it out together," she said softly and gravely. "I don't mean to take credit to myself. Dr. Brockley directed the therapy. Carl simply happened to do his talking-out to me."

Her face was warm and bright again, with the pride a woman can take in being a woman, exerting peaceful power. It was hard to hold on to my skepticism, which seemed almost like an insult to her calm assurance.

"How can you tell the difference between true confessions and fantasies?"

"That's where training and experience come in. You get a feeling for unreality. It's partly in the tone, and partly in the content. Often you can tell by the very enormity of the fantasy, the patient's complete insistence on his guilt. You wouldn't believe the crimes I've had confessed to me. I've talked to a Jack the Ripper, a man who claimed he shot Lincoln, several who killed Christ himself. All these people feel they've done evil—we all do in some degree—and unconsciously they want to punish themselves for the worst possible crimes. As the patient gets better, and he can face his actual problems, the need for punishment and the guilty fantasies disappear together. Carl's faded out that way."

"And you never make a mistake about these fantasies?"

"I don't claim that. There's no mistake about Carl's. He got over them, and that's proof positive that they were illusory."

"I hope he got over them. This morning when I talked to him, he was still hung up on his father's death. In fact, he wanted to hire me to prove that somebody else murdered his father. I guess that's some improvement over thinking he did it himself."

Miss Parish shook her head. She brushed past me and moved to the window, stood there with her thumbnail between her teeth. Her shadow on the blind was like an enlarged image of a worried child. I sensed the doubts and fears that had kept her single and turned her love toward the sick.

"He's had a setback," she said bitterly. "He should never have left the hospital so soon. He wasn't ready to face these dreadful things."

I laid my hand on one of her bowed shoulders. "Don't let it get *you* down. He's depending on people like you to help him out of it." Whether or not he's guilty, the words ran on unspoken in my head.

I looked out past the edge of the blind. The Mercury was still in the street. I could hear the squawk of its radio faintly through the glass.

"I'd do anything for Carl," Miss Parish said close to my ear. "I suppose that's no secret to you."

I didn't answer her. I was reluctant to encourage her intimacy. Miss Parish alternated between being too personal and too official. And Mildred was a long time coming down.

I went to the piano and picked out a one-finger tune. I quit when I recognized it: "Sentimental Journey." I took the conch shell and set it to my ear. Its susurrus sounded less like the sea than the labored breathing of a tiring runner. No doubt I heard what I was listening for.

I saw the reason for Mildred's delay when she appeared finally. She'd brushed her hair shining, changed to a black jersey dress which molded her figure and challenged comparison with it, changed to heels which added three inches to her height. She stood in the doorway, holding out both her hands. Her smile was forced and brilliant:

"I'm so glad to see you, Miss Parish. Forgive me for keeping you waiting. I know how precious your time must be, with all your nursing duties."

"I'm not a nurse." Miss Parish was upset. For a moment she looked quite ugly, with her black brows pulled down and her lower lip pushed out.

"I'm sorry, did I make a mistake? I thought Carl mentioned you as one of his nurses. He has mentioned you, you know."

Miss Parish rose rather awkwardly to the occasion. I gathered that the two young women had crossed swords or needles before. "It doesn't matter, dear. I know you've had a bad day."

"You're so sympathetic, Rose. Carl thinks so, too. You don't mind if I call you Rose? I've felt so close to you, through Carl."

"I *want* you to call me Rose. I'd love nothing better than for you to regard me as a big sister, somebody you can lean on."

Like other forthright people, Miss Parish got very phony when she got phony at all. I guessed that she'd come with some notion of mothering Mildred, the next best thing to mothering Mildred's husband. Clumsily, she tried to embrace the smaller woman. Mildred evaded her:

"Won't you sit down? I'll make you a cup of tea."

"Oh, no thanks."

"You must take something. You've come such a long way. Let me get you something to eat."

"Oh, no."

"Why not?" Mildred stared frankly at the other woman's body. "Are you dieting?"

"No. Perhaps I ought to." Large and outwitted and rebuffed, Miss Parish sank into a chair. Its springs creaked satirically under her weight. She tried to look small. "Perhaps, if I could have a drink?"

"I'm sorry." Mildred glanced at the bottle on the piano, and met the issue head-on. "There's nothing in the house. My mother happens to drink too much. I try to keep it unavailable. I don't always succeed, as you doubtless know. You hospital workers keep close tabs on the patients' relatives, don't you?"

"Oh, no," Miss Parish said. "We don't have the staff—"

"What a pity. But I can't complain. You've made an exception for me. I think it's marvelous of you. It makes me feel so looked-after."

"I'm sorry you feel that way. I just came by to help in any way I could."

"How thoughtful of you. I hate to disappoint you. My husband is not here."

Miss Parish was being badly mauled. Although in a way she'd asked for it, I felt sorry for her.

"About that drink," I said with faked cheerfulness. "I could use a drink, too. What do you say we surge out and find one, Rose?"

She looked up gratefully, from the detailed study she had been making of her fingernails. I noticed that they had been bitten short. Mildred said:

"Please don't rush away. I could have a bottle sent in from the liquor store. Perhaps my mother will join you. We could have a party."

"Lay off," I said to her under my breath.

She answered with her brilliant smile: "I hate to appear inhospitable."

The situation was getting nowhere except on my nerves. It was terminated abruptly by a scuffle of feet on the porch, a knock on the door. The two women followed me to the door. It was Carmichael, the sheriff's deputy. Behind him in the street, the sheriff's car was pulling away from the curb.

"What is it?" Mildred said.

"We just got a radio report from the Highway Patrol. A man answering your husband's description was sighted at the Red Barn drive-in. Sheriff Ostervelt thought you ought to be warned. Apparently he's headed in this direction."

"I'm glad if he is," Mildred said.

Carmichael gave her an astonished look. "Just the same, I'll keep guard on the house. Inside if you want."

"It isn't necessary. I'm not afraid of my husband."

"Neither am I," Miss Parish said behind her. "I know the man thoroughly. He isn't dangerous."

"A lot of people think different, ma'am."

"I know Sheriff Ostervelt thinks different. What orders did he give you, concerning the use of your gun?"

"I use my own discretion if Hallman shows. Naturally I'm not going to shoot him if I don't have to."

"You'd be wise to stick to that, Mr. Carmichael." Miss Parish's voice had regained its authority. "Mr. Hallman is a suspect, not a convict. You don't want to do something that you'll regret to the end of your days."

"She's right," I said. "Take him without gunfire if you can. He's a sick man, remember."

Carmichael's mouth set stubbornly. I'd seen that expression on his face before, in the Hallman greenhouse. "His brother Jerry is sicker. We don't want any more killings."

"That's my point exactly."

Carmichael turned away, refusing to argue further. "Anyway," he said from the steps, "I'm keeping guard on the house. Even if you don't see me, I'll be within call."

The low augh of a distant siren rose to an ee. Mildred shut the door on the sound, the voice of the treacherous night. Behind her freshly painted mask her face was haggard.

"They want to kill him, don't they?"

"Nonsense," Miss Parish said in her heartiest voice.

"I think we should try to get to him first," I said.

Mildred leaned on the door. "I wonder—it's barely possible he's trying to reach Mrs. Hutchinson's house. She lives directly across the highway from the Red Barn."

"Who on earth is Mrs. Hutchinson?" Miss Parish said.

"My sister-in-law's housekeeper. She has Zinnie's little girl with her."

"Why don't you phone Mrs. Hutchinson?"

"She has no phone, or I'd have been in touch long ago. I've been worried about Martha. Mrs. Hutchinson means well, but she's an old woman."

Miss Parish gave her a swift, dark look. "You don't seriously think there's any danger to the child?"

"I don't know."

None of us knew. On a deeper level than I'd been willing to recognize till now, I experienced fear. Fear of the treacherous darkness around us and inside of us, fear of the blind destruction that had wiped out most of a family and threatened the rest.

"We could easily check on Martha," I said, "or have the police check."

"Let's keep them out of it for now," Miss Parish said. "What's this Mrs. Hutchinson's address?"

"Fourteen Chestnut Street. It's a little white frame cottage between Elmwood and the highway." Mildred opened the door and pointed down the street. "I can easily show you."

"No. You better stay here, dear."

Rose Parish's face was dismal. She was afraid, too.

>>>>>>>>>
>>>>>>>>> *chapter* 26
>>>>>>>>>

MRS. HUTCHINSON's cottage was the third of three similar houses built on narrow lots between Elmwood and the highway. Only one side of the short block was built up. The other side was vacant ground overgrown with scrub oaks. A dry creek, brimming with darkness, cut along the back of the empty lots. Beyond the continuous chain-lightning of the highway headlights, I could see the neon outline of the Red Barn, with cars clustered around it.

A softer light shone through lace curtains in Mrs. Hutchinson's front window. When I knocked on the door, a heavy shadow moved across the light. The old woman spoke through the closed door:

"Who is that?"

"Archer. We talked this morning at the Hallman ranch."

She opened the door cautiously and peered out. "What do you want?"

"Is Martha with you?"

"Sure she is. I put her to bed in my room. It looks like she's spending the night."

"Has anyone else been here?"

"The child's mother was in and out. She didn't waste much time on us, I can tell you. Mrs. Hallman has more important things on her mind than her little orphan daughter. But don't let me get started on that or I'll keep you standing on the steps all night." She glanced inquiringly at Rose Parish. With the excessive respect for privacy of her class, she had avoided noticing her till now.

"This is Miss Parish, from the State Hospital."

"Pleased to meet you, I'm sure. You folks come inside, if you want. I'll ask you to be as quiet as you can. Martha isn't asleep yet. The poor child's all keyed up."

The door opened directly into the front room. The room was small and neat, warmed by rag rugs on the floor, an afghan on the couch. Embroidered mottoes on the plasterboard walls went with the character lines in the old woman's face. A piece of wool with knitting needles in it lay on the arm of a chair. She picked it up and hid it in a drawer, as if it was evidence of criminal negligence in her housekeeping.

"Sit down, if you can find a place to sit. Did you say you were from the State Hospital? They offered me a job there once, but I always liked private work better."

Rose Parish sat beside me on the couch. "Are you a nurse, Mrs. Hutchinson?"

"A special nurse. I started to train for an R.N. but I never got my cap. Hutchinson wouldn't wait. Would you be an R.N., Miss?"

"I'm a psychiatric social worker. I suppose that makes me a sort of nurse. Carl Hallman was one of my patients."

"You wanted to ask me about him? Is that it? I say it's a crying shame what happened to that boy. He used to be as nice as you could want. There in that house, I watched him change right in front of my eyes. I could see his mother's trouble coming out in him like a family curse, and not one of them made a move to help him until it was too late."

"Did you know his mother?" I said.

"Know her? I nursed her for over a year. Waited on her hand and foot, day and night. I should say I did know her. She was the saddest woman you ever want to see, specially toward the end there. She got the idea in her head that nobody loved her, nobody ever *did* love her. Her husband didn't love her, her family didn't love her, even her poor dead parents didn't love her when they were alive. It became worse when Carl went away to school. He was always her special darling, and she depended on him. After he left home, she acted like there was nothing for her in life except those pills she took."

"What kind of pills?" Rose Parish said. "Barbiturates?"

"Them, or anything else she could get her hands on. She was addicted for many years. I guess she ran through every doctor in town, the old ones and then the new ones, ending up with Dr. Grantland. It isn't for me to second-guess a doctor, but I used to think those pills he let her have were her main trouble. I got up my nerve and told him so, one day toward the end. He said that he was trying to limit her, but Mrs. Hallman would be worse off without them."

"I doubt that," Rose Parish said. "He should have committed her; he might have saved her life."

"Did the question ever come up, Mrs. Hutchinson?"

"Between me and her it did, when the doctor first sent me out there to look after her. I had to use *some* kind of leverage on her. She was a sad, spoiled woman, spoiled rotten all ler life. She was always hiding her pills on me, and taking more than her dosage. When I bawled her out for it, she pulled out that little gun she kept under her pillow. I told her she'd have to give up those shenanigans, or the doctor would have to commit her. She said he better not. She said if he tried it on her, she'd kill herself and ruin him. As for me, I'd never get another job in this town. Oh, she could be a black devil when she was on the rampage."

Breathing heavily with remembered anger, Mrs. Hutchinson looked up at the wall above her armchair. An embroidered motto there exhorted Christian charity. It calmed her visibly. She said:

"I don't mean she was like that all the time, just when she had a spell. Most of the time she wasn't a bad sort of lady to have to deal with. I've dealt with worse. It's a pity what had to happen to her. And not only her. You young people don't read the Bible any more. I know that. There's a line from the Word keeps running in my head since all this trouble today. 'The fathers have eaten sour grapes, and the children's teeth are set on edge.' "

"Right out of Freud," Rose Parish said in a knowing undertone.

I thought she was putting the cart in front of the horse, but I didn't bother arguing. The Old Testament words reverberated in my mind. I cut their echo short, and brought Mrs. Hutchinson back to the line of questioning I'd stumbled upon:

"It's funny they'd let Mrs. Hallman have a gun."

"All the ranch women have them, or used to have. It was a hangover from the old days when there were a lot of hoboes and outlaws wandering around in the west. Mrs. Hallman told me once her father sent her that gun, all the way from the old country—he was a great traveler. She took a pride in it, the way another kind of woman would take pride in a piece of jewelry. It was something like a gewgaw at that—a short-barreled little thing with a pearl handle set in filigree work. She used to spend a lot of time cleaning and polishing it. I remember the fuss she made when the Senator wanted to take it away from her."

"I'm surprised he didn't," Rose Parish said. "We don't even permit nailfiles or bottles on our closed wards."

"I know that, and I told the Senator it was a danger to her. He was a hard man to understand in some ways. He couldn't really admit to himself that there was anything the matter with her mind. It was the same with his son later. He believed that their troubles were just notions, that all they wanted was to attract some attention to themselves. He let her keep that gun in her room, and the box of shells that went with it, right up to the day of her death. You'd almost think," she added with the casual insight of the old, "you'd almost think he wanted her to do herself a harm. Or somebody else."

"Somebody else?" I said.

Mrs. Hutchinson reddened and veiled her eyes. "I didn't mean anything, I was only talking."

"You said Mrs. Hallman had that gun right up to the day of her death. Do you know that for a fact?"

"Did I say that? I didn't mean it that way."

There was a breathing silence.

"How did you mean it?"

"I wasn't trying to pin down any exact time. What I said was in a general manner of speaking."

"*Did* she have it on the day of her death?"

"I can't remember. It was a long time ago—more than three years. It doesn't matter, anyway." Her statement had the force of a question. Her gray head turned toward me, the skin of her neck stretched in diagonal folds like recalcitrant material being twisted under great pressure.

"Do you know what happened to Mrs. Hallman's gun?"

"I never was told, no. For all I know it's safe at the bottom of the ocean."

"Mrs. Hallman had it the night she drowned herself?"

"I didn't say that. I don't know."

"Did she drown herself?"

"Sure she did. But I couldn't swear to it. I didn't see her jump in." Her pale gaze was still on me, cold and watchful under slack folded lids. "What is it that's so important about her gun? Do you know where it is?"

"Don't you?"

The strain was making her irritable. "I wouldn't be asking you if I knew all about it, would I?"

"The gun is in an evidence case in the sheriff's office. It was used to shoot Jerry Hallman today. It's strange you don't know that, Mrs. Hutchinson."

"How would *I* know what they shot him with?" But the color of confusion had deepened in her face. Its vessels were purplish and congested with the hot shame of an unpracticed barefaced liar. "I didn't even hear the shot, let alone see it happen."

"There were two shots."

"That's news to me. I didn't hear either one of them. I was in the front room with Martha, and she was playing with that silver bell of her mother's. It drowned out everything."

The old woman sat in a listening attitude, screwing up her face as if she was hearing the shots now, after a long delay. I was certain that she was lying. Apart from the evidence of her face, there was at least one discrepancy in her story. I scanned back across the rush and welter of the day, trying to pin it down, but without success. Too many words had been spilled. The sense of discrepancy persisted in my mind, a gap in the known through which the darkness threatened, like sea behind a dike.

Mrs. Hutchinson shuffled her slippered feet in token flight. "Are you trying to tell me I shot him?"

"I made no such accusation. I have to make one, though. You're hiding something."

"Me hide something? Why should I do that?"

"It's the question I'm asking myself. Perhaps you're protecting a friend, or think you are."

"My friends don't get into that kind of trouble," she said angrily.

"Speaking of friends, have you known Dr. Grantland long?"

"Long enough. That doesn't mean we're friends." She corrected herself hastily: "A special nurse doesn't consider herself friends with her doctors, not if she knows her place."

"I gather he got you your job with the Hallmans."

"He recommended me."

"And he drove you into town today, shortly after the shooting."

"He wasn't doing it for me. He was doing it for *her*."

"I know that. Did he mention the shooting to you?"

"I guess he did. Yes. He mentioned it, said it was a terrible thing."

"Did he mention the gun that was used?"

She hesitated before answering. The color left her face. Otherwise she was completely immobile, concentrating on what she would say and its possible implications. "No. Martha was with us, and all. He didn't say anything about the gun."

"It still seems queer to me. Grantland saw the gun. He told me himself that he recognized it, but wasn't certain of the identification. He must have known that you were familiar with it."

"I'm no expert on guns."

"You gave me a good description of it just now. In fact, you probably knew it as well as anyone alive. But Grantland didn't say a word to you about it, ask you a single question. Or did he?"

There was another pause. "No. He didn't say a word."

"Have you seen Dr. Grantland since this afternoon?"

"What if I have?" she answered stolidly.

"Has Grantland been here tonight?"

"What if he was? Him coming here had nothing to do with me."

"Who did it have to do with? Zinnie?"

Rose Parish stirred on the couch beside me, nudging my knee with hers. She made a small coughing noise of distress. This encouraged Mrs. Hutchinson, as perhaps it was intended to. I could practically see her resistance solidifying. She sat like a monument in flowered silk:

"You're trying to make me talk myself out of a job. I'm too old to get another job. I've got too much property to qualify for the pension, and not enough to live on." After a pause, she said: "No! I'm falsifying myself. I could always get along someway. It's Martha that keeps me on the job. If it wasn't for her, I would have quit that house long ago."

"Why?"

"It's a bad-luck house, that's why. It brings bad luck to everybody who goes there. Yes, and I'd be happy to see it burn to the ground like Sodom. That may sound like a terrible thing for a Christian woman to say. No loss of life; I wouldn't wish that on them; there's been loss of life enough. I'd just like to see that house destroyed, and that family scattered forevermore."

I thought without saying it that Mrs. Hutchinson was getting her awesome wish.

"What are you leading up to?" I said. "I know the doctor and Zinnie Hallman are interested in each other. Is that the fact you're trying to keep from spilling? Or is there more?"

She weighed me in the balance of her eyes. "Just who are you, Mister?"

"I'm a private detective—"

"I know that much. Who're you detecting for? And who against?"

"Carl Hallman asked me to help him."

"Carl did? How could that be?"

I explained briefly how it could be. "He was seen in your neighborhood tonight. It's why Miss Parish and I came here to your house, to head off any possible trouble."

"You think he might try and do something to the child?"

"It occurred to us as a possibility," Rose Parish said. "I wouldn't worry about it. We probably went off half-cocked. I honestly don't believe that Carl would harm anyone."

"What about his brother?"

"I don't believe he shot his brother." She exchanged glances with me. "Neither of us believes it."

"I thought, from the paper and all, they had it pinned on him good."

"It nearly always looks like that when they're hunting a suspect," I said.

"You mean it isn't true?"

"It doesn't have to be."

"Somebody else did it?"

Her question hung unanswered in the room. An inner door at the far end was opening slowly, softly. Martha slipped in through the narrow aperture. Elfin in blue sleepers, she scampered into the middle of the room, stood and looked at us with enormous eyes.

Mrs. Hutchinson said: "Go back to bed, you minx."

"I won't. I'm not sleepy."

"Come on, I'll tuck you in."

The old woman rose ponderously and made a grab for the child, who evaded her.

"I want Mommy to tuck me in. I want my Mommy."

In the middle of her complaint, Martha stopped in front of Rose Parish. A reaching innocence, like an invisible antenna, stretched upward from her face to the woman's face, and was met by a similar reaching innocence. Rose opened her arms. Martha climbed into them.

"You're bothering the lady," Mrs. Hutchinson said.

"She's no bother, are you, honey?"

The child was quiet against her breast. We sat in silence for a bit. The tick of thought continued like a tiny stitching in my consciousness or just below it, trying to piece together the rags and bloody tatters of the day. My thoughts threatened the child, the innocent one, perhaps the only one who was perfectly innocent. It wasn't fair that her milk teeth should be set on edge.

>>>>>>>>>
>>>>>>>>> *chapter* 27
>>>>>>>>>

NOISES from outside, random voices and the scrape of boots, pulled me out of my thoughts and to the door. A guerrilla formation of men carrying rifles and shotguns went by in the street.

A second, smaller group was fanning out across the vacant lots toward the creekbed, probing the tree-clotted darkness with their flashlights.

The man directing the second group wore some kind of uniform. I saw when I got close to him that he was a city police sergeant.

"What's up, Sergeant?"

"Manhunt. We got a lunatic at large in case you don't know it."

"I know it."

"If you're with the posse, you're supposed to be searching farther up the creek."

"I'm a private detective working on this case. What makes you think that Hallman's on this side of the highway?"

"The carhop at the Barn says he came through the culvert. He came up the creek from the beach, and the chances are he's following it right on up. He may be long gone by now, though. She was slow in passing the word to us."

"Where does the creekbed lead to?"

"Across town." He pointed east with his flashlight. "All the way to the mountains, if you stay with it. But he won't get that far, not with seventy riflemen tracking him."

"If he's gone off across town, why search around here?"

"We can't take chances with him. He may be lying doggo. We don't have the trained men to go through all the houses and yards, so we're concentrating on the creek." His light came up to my face for a second. "You want to pitch in and help?"

"Not right now." With seventy hunters after a single buck, conditions would be crowded. "I left my red hat home."

"Then you're taking up my time, fellow."

The sergeant moved off among the trees. I walked to the end of the block and crossed the highway, six lanes wide at this point.

The Red Barn was a many-windowed building which stood in the center of a blacktop lot on the corner. Its squat pentagonal structure was accentuated by neon tubing along the eaves and corners. Inside this brilliant red cage, a tall-hatted short-order cook kept several waitresses running between his counter and the cars in the lot. The waitresses wore red uniforms and little red caps which made them look like bellhops in skirts. The blended odors of gasoline fumes and frying grease changed in my nostrils to a foolish old hot-rod sorrow, nostalgia for other drive-ins along roads I knew in prewar places before people started dying on me.

It seemed that my life had dwindled down to a series of one-night stands in desolate places. Watch it, I said to myself; self-pity is the last refuge of little minds and aging professional hardnoses. I knew the desolation was my own. Brightness had fallen from my interior air.

A boy and a girl in a hand-painted lavender Chevrolet coupé made me feel better, for some reason. They were sitting close, like a body with two ducktailed heads, taking alternate sips of malted milk from the same straw, germ-free with love. Near them in a rusty Hudson a man in a workshirt, his dark and hefty wife, three or four children whose eyes were brilliant and bleary with drive-in-movie memories, were eating mustard-dripping hot dogs with the rapt solemnity of communicants.

Among the half-dozen other cars, one in particular interested me. It was a fairly new Plymouth two-door with Purissima *Record* lettered across the door. I walked over for a closer look.

A molded prewar Ford with a shackled rear end and too much engine came off the highway on banshee tires and pulled up beside the Plymouth. The two boys in the front seat looked me over with bold and planless eyes and forgot about me. I was a pedestrian, earthborne. While they were waiting for a carhop, they occupied themselves with combing and rearranging their elaborate hair-structures. This process took a long time, and continued after one of the waitresses came up to the side of their car. She was a little blonde, pert-breasted in her tight uniform.

"Drive much?" she said to the boys. "I saw you come into the lot. You want to kill it before it multiplies."

"A lecture," the boy at the wheel said.

The other boy leaned toward her. "It said on the radio Gwen saw the killer."

"That's right, she's talking to the reporter now."

"Did he pull a gun on her?"

"Nothing like that. She didn't even know he *was* the killer."

"What did he *do?*" the driver said. He sounded very eager, as if he was seeking some remarkable example to emulate.

"Nothing. He was poking around in the garbage pails. When he saw her, he took off. Listen, kids, I'm busy. What'll it be?"

"You got a big George, George?" the driver asked his passenger.

"Yeah, I'm loaded. We'll have the usual, barbecued baby and double martinis. On second thought, make it a couple of cokes."

"Sure, kids, have yourselves a blast." She came around the Plymouth to me. "What can I do for you, sir?"

I realized I was hungry. "Bring me a hamburger, please."

"Deluxe, Stackburger, or Monarch? Monarchburger is the seventy-five-center. It's bigger, and you get free potatoes with it."

"Free potatoes sounds good."

"You can eat it inside if you want."

"Is Gwen inside? I want to talk to her."

"I wondered if you were plainclothes. Gwen's out behind with Gene Slovekin from the paper. He wanted to take her picture."

She indicated an open gate in the grapestake fence that surrounded the rear of the lot. There were several forty-gallon cans beside the gate. I looked into the nearest one. It was half full of a greasy tangle of food and other waste. Carl Hallman was hard-pressed.

On the other side of the gate, a footpath led along the bank of the creek. The dry bed of the creek was lined with concrete here, and narrowed down to a culvert which ran under the highway. This was high enough for a man to walk upright through it.

Slovekin and the carhop were coming back along the path toward me. She was thirtyish and plump; her body looked like a ripe tomato in her red uniform. Slovekin was carrying a camera with a flashbulb attachment. His tie was twisted, and he walked as if he was tired. I waited for them beside the gate.

"Hello, Slovekin."

"Hello, Archer. This is a mad scramble."

The carhop turned to him. "If you're finished with me, Mr. Slovekin, I got to get back to work. The manager'll be docking me, and I got a kid in school."

"I was hoping to ask you a couple of questions," I said.

"Gee, I dunno about that."

"I'll fill you in," Slovekin said, "if it doesn't take too long. Thanks, Gwen."

"You're more than welcome. Remember you promised I could have a print. I haven't had my picture taken since God made little green apples."

She touched the side of her face, delicately, hopefully, and hustled into the building on undulating hips. Slovekin deposited the camera in the back seat of his press car. We got into the front.

"Did she see Hallman enter the culvert?"

"Not actually," Slovekin said. "She made no attempt to follow him. She thought he was just a bum from the jungle on the other side of the tracks. Gwen didn't catch onto who he was until the police got here and asked some questions. They came up the creekbed from the beach, incidentally, so he couldn't have gone that way."

"What was his condition?"

"Gwen's observations aren't worth much. She's a nice girl, but not very bright. Now that she knows who he is, he was seven feet tall with horns and illuminated revolving eyeballs." Slovekin moved restlessly, turning the key in the ignition. "That's about all there is here. Can I drop you anywhere? I'm supposed to cover the movements of the sheriff's posse." His intonation satirized the phrase.

"Wear your bulletproof vest. Turning seventy hunters loose in a town is asking for double trouble."

"I agree. So does Spaulding, my editor. But we report the news, we don't make it. You got any for me, by any chance?"

"Can I talk off the record?"

"I'd rather have it on. It's getting late, and I don't mean late at night. We've never had a lynching in Purissima, but it could happen here. There's something about insanity, it frightens people, makes *them* irrational, too. Their worst aggressions start popping out."

"You sound like an expert in mob psychology," I said.

"I sort of am. It runs in the family. My father was an Austrian Jew. He got out of Vienna one jump ahead of the storm troopers. I also inherited a prejudice in favor of the underdog. So if you know something that will let Hallman off the hook, you better spill it. I can have it on the radio in ten minutes."

"He didn't do it."

"Do you know he didn't for certain?"

"Not quite. I'd stake my reputation on it, but I have to do better than that. Hallman's being used as a patsy, and a lot of planning went into it."

"Who's behind it?"

"There's more than one possibility. I can't give you any names."

"Not even off the record?"

"What would be the use? I haven't got enough to prove a case. I don't have access to the physical evidence, and I can't depend on the official interpretation of it."

"You mean it's been manipulated?"

"Psychologically speaking, anyway. There may have been some actual tampering. I don't know for sure that the gun that was found in the greenhouse fired the slugs in Jerry Hallman."

"The sheriff's men think so."

"Have they run ballistics tests?"

"Apparently. The fact that it was his mother's gun has generated a lot of heat downtown. They're going into ancient history. The rumor's running around that Hallman killed his mother, too, and possibly his father, and the family money got him off and hushed it up." He gave me a quick, sharp look. "Could there be anything in that?"

"You sound as if you're buying it yourself."

"I wouldn't say that, but I know some things it could jibe with. I went to see the Senator last spring, just a few days before he died." He paused to organize his thoughts, and went on more slowly. "I had dug up certain facts about a certain county official whose re-election was coming up in May. Spaulding thought the Senator ought to know these facts, because he'd been supporting this certain official for a good many years. So had the paper, as a matter of fact. The paper generally went along with Senator Hallman's ideas on county government. Spaulding didn't want to change that policy without checking with Senator Hallman. He was a big minority stockholder in the paper, and you might say the local elder statesman."

"If you're trying to say he was county boss and Ostervelt was one of his boys, why beat around the bush?"

"It wasn't quite that simple, but that's the general picture. All right, so you know." Slovekin was young and full of desire, and his tone became competitive: "What you don't know is the nature of my facts. I won't go into detail, but I was in a position to prove that Ostervelt had been taking regular payoff money from houses of prostitution. I showed Senator Hallman my affidavits. He was an old man, and he was shocked. I was afraid for a while that he might have a heart attack then and there. When he calmed down, he said he needed time to think about the problem, perhaps talk it over with

Ostervelt himself. I was to come back in a week. Unfortunately, he died before the week was up."

"All very interesting. Only I don't see how it fits in with the idea that Carl killed him."

"It depends on how you look at it. Say Carl did it and Ostervelt pinned it on him, but kept the evidence to himself. It would give Ostervelt all the leverage he needed to keep the Hallman family in line. It would also explain what happened afterwards. Jerry Hallman went to a lot of trouble to quash our investigation. He also threw all his weight behind Ostervelt's re-election."

"He might have done that for any number of reasons."

"Name one."

"Say he killed his father himself, and Ostervelt knew it."

"You don't believe that," Slovekin stated.

He looked around nervously. The little blonde ankled up to the side of the car with my Monarchburger. I said, when she was out of hearing:

"This is supposed to be a progressive county. How does Ostervelt keep his hold on it?"

"He's been in office a long time, and, as you know, he's got good political backing, at least until now. He knows where the bodies are buried. You might say he's buried a couple of them himself."

"Buried them himself?"

"I was speaking more or less figuratively." Slovekin's voice had sunk to a worried whisper. "He's shot down one or two escaping prisoners—shootings that a lot of the townspeople didn't think were strictly necessary. The reason I mention it—I wouldn't want to see *you* end up with a hole in the back."

"That's a hell of a thought, when I'm eating a sandwich."

"I wish you'd take me seriously, Archer. I didn't like what happened between you this afternoon."

"Neither did I."

Slovekin leaned toward me. "Those names you have in mind that you won't give me—is Ostervelt one of them?"

"He is now. You can write it down in your little black book."

"I already have, long ago."

I WAITED for the green light and walked back across the highway. Chestnut Street was empty again, except for my car at the curb, and another car diagonally across from it near the corner of Elmwood. It hadn't been there before, or I would have noticed it.

It was a new red station wagon very like the one I had seen in the drive of the Hallman ranch-house. I went up the street and looked in at the open window on the driver's side. The key was in the ignition. The registration slip on the steering-post had Jerry Hallman's name on it.

Evidently Zinnie had come back to tuck her baby in. I glanced across the roof of the wagon toward Mrs. Hutchinson's cottage. Her light shone steadily through the lace-veiled windows. Everything seemed peaceful and as it should be. Yet a sense of disaster came down on me like a ponderous booby trap.

Perhaps I'd glimpsed and guessed the meaning of the blanket-covered shape on the floor at the rear of the wagon. I opened the back door and pulled the blanket away. So white that it seemed luminous, a woman's body lay huddled in the shadow.

I turned on the ceiling light and Zinnie jumped to my vision. Her head was twisted toward me, glaring at me open-eyed. Her grin of fear and pain had been fixed in the rictus of death. There were bloody slits in one of her breasts and in her abdomen. I touched the unwounded breast, expecting a marble coldness. The body was still warm, but unmistakably dead. I drew the blanket over it again, as if that would do any good.

Darkness flooded my mind for an instant, whirling like black water in which three bodies turned unburied. Four. I lost my Monarchburger in the gutter. Sweating cold, I looked up and down the street. Across the corner of the vacant lot, a concrete bridge carried Elmwood Street over the creekbed. Further up the creek, around a bend, I could see the moving lights of the sergeant and his men.

I could tell them what I had found, or I could keep silent. Slovekin's talk of lynching was fresh in my thought. Under it I had an urge to join the hunt, run Hallman down and kill him. Because I distrusted that urge, I made a decision which probably cost a life. Perhaps it saved another.

I closed the door, left the wagon as it stood, and went back to Mrs. Hutchinson's house. The sight of me seemed to depress her, but she invited me in. Before I stepped inside, I pointed out the red wagon:

"Isn't that Mrs. Hallman's car?"

"I believe so. I couldn't swear to it. She drives one like it."

"Was she driving it tonight?"

The old woman hesitated. "She was in it."

"You mean someone else was driving?"

She hesitated again, but she seemed to sense my urgency.

When her words finally came, they sounded as if an inner dam had burst, releasing waves of righteous indignation:

"I've worked in big houses, with all sorts of people, and I learned long ago to hold my tongue. I've done it for the Hallmans, and I'd go on doing it, but there's a limit, and I've reached mine. When a brand-new widow goes out on the town the same night her husband was killed—"

"Was Dr. Grantland driving the car? This is important, Mrs. Hutchinson."

"You don't have to tell me that. It's a crying shame. Away they go, as gay as you please, and the devil take the hindmost. I never did think much of her, but I used to consider him a fine young doctor."

"What time were they here?"

"It was Martha's suppertime, round about six-fifteen or six-thirty. I know she spoiled the child's evening meal, running in and out like that."

"Did Grantland come in with her?"

"Yes, he came in."

"Did he say anything? Do anything?"

Her face closed up on me. She said: "It's chilly out here. Come in if you want to talk."

There was nobody else in the living-room. Rose Parish's coat lay on the couch. I could hear her behind the wall, singing a lullaby to the child.

"I'm glad for a little help with that one. I get tired," the old woman said. "Your friend seems to be a good hand with children. Does she have any of her own?"

"Miss Parish isn't married, that I know of."

"That's too bad. I was married myself for nearly forty years, but I never had one of my own either. I never had the good fortune. It was a waste of me." The wave of her indignation rose again: "You'd think that those that had would look after their own flesh and bone."

I seated myself in a chair by the window where I could watch the station wagon. Mrs. Hutchinson sat opposite me:

"Is *she* out there?"

"I want to keep an eye on her car."

"What did you mean, did Dr. Grantland say anything?"

"How did he act toward Zinnie?"

"Same as usual. Putting on the same old act, as if he wasn't interested in her, just doing his doctor's duty. As if I didn't know all about them long ago. I guess he thinks I'm old and senile, but I've got my eyes and my good ears. I've watched that woman playing him like a big stupid fish, ever since the Senator died. She's landing him, too, and he acts like he's grateful to her for slipping the gaff to him. I thought he had more sense than to go for a woman like that, just because she's come into a wad of money."

With my eye on the painted red wagon in which her body lay, I felt an obscure need to defend Zinnie:

"She didn't seem like a bad sort of woman to me."

"You talk about her like she was dead," Mrs. Hutchinson said. "Naturally you wouldn't see through her, you're a man. But I used to watch her like the flies on the wall. She came from nothing, did you know that? Mr. Jerry picked her up in a nightclub in Los Angeles, he said so in one of the arguments they had. They had a lot of arguments. She was a driving hungry woman, always hungry for something she didn't have. And when she got it, she wasn't satisfied. An unsatisfied wife is a terrible thing in this life.

"She turned against her husband after the child was born, and then she went to work to turn the child against him. She even had the brass to ask me to be a divorce-court witness for her, so's she could keep Martha. She wanted me to say that her husband treated her cruel. It would have been a lie, and I told her so. It's true they didn't get along, but he never raised a hand to her. He suffered in silence. He went to his death in silence."

"When did she ask you to testify?"

"Three-four months ago, when she thought that a divorce was what she wanted."

"So she could marry Grantland?"

"She didn't admit it outright, but that was the idea. I was surprised, surprised and ashamed for him, that he would fall for her and her shabby goods. I could have saved my feelings. They make a pair. He's no better than she is. He may be a lot worse."

"What makes you say so?"

"I *hate* to say it. I remember him when he first moved to town, an up-and-coming young doctor. There was nothing he wouldn't do for his patients. He told me once it was the great dream of his life to be a doctor. His family lost their money in the depression, and he put himself through medical school by working in a garage. He went through the college of hard knocks as well as medical college, and it taught him something. In those early days, six-eight years ago, when his patients couldn't pay him he went right on caring for them. That was before he got his big ideas."

"What happened, did he get a whiff of money?"

"More than that happened to him. Looking back, I can see that the big change in him started about three years ago. He seemed to lose interest in his medical practice. I've seen the same thing with a few other doctors, something runs down in them and something else starts up, and they go all out for the money. All of a sudden they're nothing more than pill-pushers, some of them living on their own pills."

"What happened to Dr. Grantland three years ago?"

"I don't know for sure. I can tell you it happened to more people than him, though. Something happened to me, if you want the truth."

"I do want the truth. I think you've been lying to me."

Her head jerked up as if I'd tightened a rope. She narrowed her eyes. They watched me with a faded kind of guile. I said:

"If you know something important about Alicia Hallman's death, it's your duty to bring it out."

"I've got a duty to myself, too. This thing I've kept locked up in my breast—it don't make me look good."

"You could look worse, if you let an innocent man take the blame for murder. Those men that went by in the street are after him. If you hold back until they find him and shoot him down, it's going to be too late. Too late for Carl Hallman and too late for you."

Her glance followed mine out to the street. Except for my car and Zinnie's, it was still empty. Like the street's reflection, her eyes grew dark with distant lights in them. Her mouth opened, and shut in a grim line.

"You can't sit and hold back the truth while a whole family dies off, or is killed off. You call yourself a good woman—"

"Not any more, I don't."

Mrs. Hutchinson lowered her head and looked down at her hands in her lap. On their backs the branched blue veins showed through the skin. They swelled as her fingers retracted into two clenched fists. Her voice came out half-choked, as though the moral noose had tightened on her:

"I'm a wicked woman. I did lie about that gun. Dr. Grantland brought it up on the way into town today. He brought it up again to-night when she was with the child."

"What did he say to you?"

"He said if anybody asked me about that gun, that I was to stick to my original story. Otherwise I'd be in a peck of trouble. Which I am."

"You're in less trouble than you were a minute ago. What was your original story?"

"The one he told me to tell. That she didn't have the gun the night she died. That I hadn't seen it for at least a week, or the box of shells, either."

"What happened to the shells?"

"He took them. I was to say that he took the gun and the shells away from her for her own protection."

"When did he feed you this story?"

"That very same night when he came out to the ranch."

"It was his story. Why did you buy it from him?"

"I was afraid," she said. "That night when she didn't come home and didn't come home, I was afraid she'd done herself a harm, and I'd be blamed."

"Who would blame you?"

"Everybody would. They'd say I was too old to go on nursing."

The blue-veined hands opened and shut on her thighs. "I blamed myself. It was my fault. I should have stayed with her every minute, I shouldn't have let her go out. She'd had a phone call from Berkeley the evening before, something about her son, and she was upset all day. Talking about killing herself because her family deserted her and nobody loved her. She blamed it all on the Doomsters."

"The what?"

"The Doomsters. She was always talking about those Doomsters of hers. She believed her life was ruled by evil fates like, and they had killed all the love in the world the day that she was born. It was true, in a way, I guess. Nobody did love her. I was getting pretty sick of her myself. I thought if she did die it would be a relief to her and a good riddance. I took it upon myself to make that judgment which no human being has a right to do."

Her eyes seemed to focus inward, on an image in her memory. She blinked, as though the image lay under brilliant light:

"I remember the very minute I made that judgment and washed my hands of her. I walked into her room with her dinner tray, and there she was in her mink coat in front of the full-length mirror. She was loading the gun and talking to herself, about how her father abandoned her—he didn't, he just died, but she took it personally—and how her children were running out on her. She pointed the gun at herself in the mirror, and I remember thinking she ought to turn it around and put an end to herself instead of just talking about it. I didn't blame her son for running away. She was a burden on him, and on the whole family.

"I know that's no excuse for me," she added stonily. "A wicked thought is a wicked act, and it leads to wicked acts. I heard her sneak out a few minutes later, when I was making her coffee in the kitchen. I heard the car drive up and I heard it drive away. I didn't lift a finger to stop her. I just let her go, and sat there drinking coffee with the evil wish in my heart."

"Who was driving the car?"

"Sam Yogan. I didn't see him go but he was back in less than an hour. He said he dropped her off at the wharf, which was where she wanted to go. Even then, I didn't phone the police."

"Did Yogan often drive her into town?"

"She didn't go very often, but Sam did a lot of her driving for her.

He's a good driver, and she liked him. He was about the only man she ever liked. Anyway, he was the only one available that night."

"Where were the rest of the family?"

"Away. The Senator and Jerry had gone to Berkeley, to try and find out where Carl was. Zinnie was staying with some friends in town here. Martha was only a few months old at the time."

"Where was Carl?"

"Nobody knew. He kind of disappeared for a while. It turned out afterwards he was in the desert all the time, over in Death Valley. At least that was his story."

"He could have been here in town?"

"He could have been, for all I know. He didn't report in to me, or anybody else for that matter. Carl didn't show up until after they found his mother in the sea."

"When did they find her?"

"Next day."

"Did Grantland come to see you before they found her?"

"Long before. He got to the ranch around midnight. I was still awake, I couldn't sleep."

"And Mrs. Hallman had left the house around dinner time?"

"Yes, around seven o'clock. She always ate at seven. That night she didn't eat, though."

"Had Grantland seen her between dinner time and midnight?"

"Not that I know of. I took it for granted he was looking for her. I never thought to ask him. I was so full of myself, and the guilt I felt. I just spilled out everything about her and the gun and me letting her go without a by-your-leave, and my wicked thoughts. Dr. Grantland said I was overexhausted, and blaming myself too much. She'd probably turn up all right. But if she didn't I was to say that I didn't know anything about any gun. That she just slipped out on me, and I took it for granted she went to town for something, maybe to see her grandchild, I didn't know what. I wasn't to mention him coming out here either. That way, they'd be more likely to believe me. Anyway, I did what Dr. Grantland said. He was a doctor. I'm only a special nurse. I don't pretend to be smart."

She let her face fall into slack and stupid folds, as if to relieve herself of responsibility. I couldn't blame her too much. She was an old woman, worn out by her ordeal of conscience, and it was getting late.

ROSE PARISH came quietly into the room. She looked radiant and slightly disorganized.

"I finally got her to sleep. Goodness, it's past eleven. I didn't mean to keep you waiting so long."

"It's all right. You didn't keep me waiting."

I spent most of my working time waiting, talking and waiting. Talking to ordinary people in ordinary neighborhoods about ordinary things, waiting for truth to come up to the surface. I'd caught a glimpse of it just now, and it must have showed in my eyes.

Rose glanced from me to Mrs. Hutchinson. "Has something happened?"

"I talked his arm off, that's what happened." The old woman's face had resumed its peculiar closed look. "Thank you for helping out with the child. You ought to have some of your own to look after."

Rose flushed with pleasure, then shook her head quite sharply, as if to punish herself for the happy thought. "I'd settle for Martha any day. She's a little angel."

"Sometimes," Mrs. Hutchinson said.

A rattle in the street drew my attention back to the window. An old gray pickup had come off the highway. It slowed down as it passed the house, and stopped abreast of the station wagon. A slight, wiry figure got out of the truck on the righthand side and walked around the back of it to the wagon. I recognized Sam Yogan by his quick unhurried movements.

The truck was rattling away on Elmwood by the time I reached the wagon. Yogan was behind the wheel, trying to start it. It wouldn't start for him.

"Where are you going, Sam?"

He looked up and smiled when he saw me. "Back to the ranch. Hello."

He turned the motor over again, but it refused to catch. It sounded as though it was out of gas.

"Leave it, Sam. Get out and leave it."

His smile widened and became resistant. "No, sir. Mrs. Hallman says take it back to the ranch."

"Did she tell you herself?"

"No, sir. Garageman phoned Juan, Juan told me."

"Garageman?"

"Yessir. He said Mrs. Hallman said to pick up the car on Chestnut Street."

"How long ago did he call?"

"Not so long. Garageman says hurry up. Juan brought me in right away."

He tried the motor again, without success. I reached across him and removed the ignition key.

"You might as well get out, Sam. The fuel line's probably cut."

He got out and started for the front of the hood. "I fix it, eh?"

"No. Come here."

I opened the back door and showed him Zinnie Hallman. I watched his face. There was nothing there but an imperturbable sorrow. If he had guilty knowledge, it was hidden beyond my reach. I didn't believe he had.

"Do you know who killed her?"

His black eyes looked up from under his corrugated forehead. "No, sir."

"It looks like whoever did it tried to blame it on you. Doesn't that make you mad?"

"No, sir."

"Don't you have any idea who it was?"

"No, sir."

"Do you remember the night old Mrs. Hallman died?"

He nodded.

"You let her off on the wharf, I believe."

"The street in front of the wharf."

"What was she doing there?"

"Said she had to meet somebody."

"Did she say who?"

"No, sir. She told me go away, don't wait. She didn't want me to see, maybe."

"Did she have her gun?"

"I dunno."

"Did she mention Dr. Grantland?"

"I don't think."

"Did Dr. Grantland ever ask you about that night?"

"No, sir."

"Or give you a story to tell?"

"No, sir." He gestured awkwardly toward the body. "We ought to tell the police."

"You're right. You go and tell them, Sam."

He nodded solemnly. I handed him the key to the wagon and showed him where to find the sergeant's party. As I was starting my own car, Rose came out of the house and got in beside me. I turned onto Elmwood, bumped over the bridge, and accelerated. The arching trees passed over us with a whoosh, like giant dark birds.

"You're in an awful hurry," she said. "Or do you always drive like this?"

"Only when I'm frustrated."

"I'm afraid I can't help you with that. Did I do something to make you angry?"

"No."

"Something *has* happened, hasn't it?"

"Something is going to. Where do you want to be dropped off?"

"I don't want to be."

"There may be trouble. I think I can promise it."

"I didn't come to Purissima with the idea of avoiding trouble. I didn't come to get killed in an auto accident, either."

The lights at the main-street intersection were flashing red. I braked to a hard stop. Rose Parish didn't go with the mood I was in. "Get out."

"I will not."

"Stop asking questions then." I turned east toward the hills.

"I will not. Is it something about Carl?"

"Yes. Now hold the thought."

It was an early-to-bed town. There was practically no traffic. A few drunks drifted and argued on the pavement in front of the bars. Two night-blooming tarts or their mothers minced purposefully toward nothing in particular. A youth on a stepladder was removing the lettering from the shabby marquee of the Mexican movie house. AMOR was the only word that was left. He started to take that down.

In the upper reaches of the main street there was no one on foot at all. The only human being in sight was the attendant of an all-night gas station. I pulled in to the curb just below Grantland's office. A light shone dimly inside, behind the glass bricks. I started to get out. Some kind of animal emerged from the shrubbery and crawled toward me onto the sidewalk.

It was a human kind of animal, a man on his hands and knees. His hands left a track of blood, black as oil drippings under my headlights. His arms gave away and he fell on his side. His face was the dirty gray of the pavement. Rica again.

Rose went to her knees beside him. She gathered his head and shoulders into her lap.

"Get him an ambulance. I think he's cut his wrists."

Rica struggled feebly in her arms. "Cut my wrists hell. You think I'm one of your psychos?"

His red hands struck at her. Blood daubed her face and smeared the front of her coat. She held him, talking softly in the voice she used for Martha:

"Poor man, you hurt yourself. How did you hurt yourself?"

"There was wire in the window-glass. I shouldn't have tried to bust it with my hands."

"Why did you want to bust it?"

"I didn't want to. He made me. He gave me a shot in the back office and said he'd be back in a minute. He never did come back. He turned the key on me."

I squatted beside him. "Grantland locked you up?"

"Yeah, and the bastard's going to pay for it." Rica's eyes swiveled toward me, heavy and occulted like ball bearings dusted with graphite. "I'm going to lock him up in San Quentin death row."

"How are you going to do that?"

"He killed an old lady, see, and I'm a witness to it. I'll stand up in any court and swear to it. You ought to've seen his office after he did it. It was a slaughterhouse, with that poor old lady lying there in the blood. And he's a dirty butcher."

"Hush now," Rose said. "Be quiet now. Take it easy."

"Don't tell him that. Do you know who she was, Tom?"

"I found out. It was old lady Hallman. He beat her to death and tossed her in the drink. And I'm the one that's gonna see him gassed for it."

"What were you doing there?"

His face became inert. "I don't remember."

Rose gave me a look of pure hatred. "I forbid you to question him. He's half out of his mind. God knows how much drug he's had, or how much blood he's lost."

"I want his story now."

"You can get it tomorrow."

"He won't be talking tomorrow. Tom, what were you doing in Grantland's office that night?"

"Nothing. I was cruising. I needed a cap, so I just dropped by to see if I could con him out of one. I heard this shot, and then this dame came out. She was dripping blood."

Tom peered at his own hands. His eyes rolled up and went blind. His head rolled loosely sideways.

I shouted in his ear: "What dame? Can you describe her?"

Rose cradled his head in her arms protectively. "We have to get him to a hospital. I believe he's had a massive overdose. Do you want him to die?"

It was the last thing I wanted. I drove back to the all-night station and asked the attendant to call an ambulance.

He was a bright-looking boy in a leather windbreaker. "Where's the accident?"

"Up the street. There's an injured man on the sidewalk in front of Dr. Grantland's office."

"It isn't Dr. Grantland?"

"No."

"I just wondered. He came in a while ago. Buys his gas from us."

The boy made the call and came out again. "They ought to be here pretty quick. Anything else I can do?"

"Did you say Dr. Grantland was here tonight?"

"Sure thing." He looked at the watch on his wrist. "Not more than thirty minutes ago. Seemed to be in a hurry."

"What did he stop for?"

"Gas. Cleaning gas, not the regular kind. He spilt something on his rug. Gravy, I think he said. It must've been a mess. He was real upset about it. The doc just got finished building himself a nice new house with wall-to-wall carpeting."

"Let's see, that's on Seaview."

"Yeah." He pointed up the street toward the ridge. "It runs off the boulevard to the left. You'll see his name on the mailbox if you want to talk to him. Was he involved in the accident?"

"Could be."

Rose Parish was still on the sidewalk with Tom Rica in her arms. She looked up as I went by, but I didn't stop. Rose threatened something in me which I wanted to keep intact at least a little longer. As long as it would take to make Grantland pay with everything he had.

>>>>>>>>>
>>>>>>>>> *chapter* 30
>>>>>>>>>

His house stood on a terraced lot near the crest of the ridge. It was a fairly extensive layout for a bachelor, a modern redwood with wide expanses of glass and many lights inside, as though to demonstrate that its owner had nothing to hide. His Jaguar was in the slanting driveway.

I turned and stopped in the woven shadow of a pepper tree. Before I left my car, I took Maude's gun out of the dash compartment. It was a .32 caliber automatic with a full clip and an extra shell in the chamber, ready to fire. I walked down Grantland's driveway very quietly, with my hand in my heavy pocket.

The front door was slightly ajar. A rasping radio voice came from somewhere inside the house. I recognized the rhythmic monotonous clarity of police signals. Grantland had his radio tuned to the CHP dispatching station.

Under cover of the sound, I moved along the margin of the narrow light that fell across the doorstep. A man's legs and feet, toes down, were visible through the opening. My heart skipped a beat when I saw them, another beat when one of the legs moved. I kicked the door wide open and went in.

Grantland was on his knees with a red-stained cloth in his hand. There were deeper stains in the carpet which he had been scrubbing.

He whirled like an animal attacked from the rear. The gun in my hand froze him in mid-action.

He opened his mouth wide as if he was going to scream at the top of his lungs. No sound came from him. He closed his mouth. The muscles dimpled along the line of his jaw. He said between his teeth:

"Get out of here."

I closed the door behind me. The hallway was full of the smell of gasoline. Beside a telephone table against the opposite wall, a gallon can stood open. Spots of undried gasoline ran the length of the hallway.

"Did she bleed a lot?" I said.

He got up slowly, watching the gun in my hand. I patted his flanks. He was unarmed. He backed against the wall and leaned there chin down, folding his arms across his chest, like a man on a cold night.

"Why did you kill her?"

"I don't know what you're talking about."

"It's a little late for that gambit. Your girl's dead. You're a dead pigeon yourself. But they can always use good hospital orderlies in the pen. Maybe you'll get some consideration if you talk."

"Who do you think you are? God?"

"I think maybe you did, Grantland. The big dream is over now. The best you have to hope for is a little consideration from a jury."

He looked down at the spotted carpet under his feet. "Why would I kill Zinnie? I loved her."

"Sure you did. You fell in love with her as soon as she got within one death of five million dollars. Only now she's one death past it, no good to you, no good to anybody."

"Do you have to grind my nose in it?" His voice was dull with the after-boredom of shock.

I felt a flicker of sympathy for him, which I repressed. "Come off it. If you didn't cut her yourself, you're covering for the ripper."

"No. I swear I'm not. I don't know who it was. I wasn't here when it happened."

"But Zinnie was?"

"Yes, she was. She was tired and ill, so I put her to bed in my room. I had an emergency patient, and had to leave the house." His face was coming to life as he talked, as though he saw an opening that he could slip through. "When I returned, she was gone. I was frantic. All I could think of was getting rid of the blood."

"Show me the bedroom."

Reluctantly, he detached himself from the support of the wall. I followed him through the door at the end of the hallway, into the lighted bedroom. The bed had been stripped. The bloody bed-clothes, sheets and electric blanket, lay in the middle of the floor with a heap of women's clothes on top of them.

"What were you going to do with these? Burn them?"

"I guess so," he said with a wretched sidewise look. "There was nothing between us, you understand. My part in all this was per-fectly innocent. But I knew what would happen if I didn't get rid of the traces. I'd be blamed."

"And you wanted someone else to be blamed, as usual. So you bundled her body into her station wagon and left it in the lower town, near where Carl Hallman was seen. You kept track of his movements by tuning in the police band. In case he wasn't available for the rap, you phoned the ranch and brought Zinnie's servants in, as secondary patsies."

Grantland's face took on its jaundiced look. He sat on the edge of the mattress with his head down. "You've been keeping track of my movements, have you?"

"It's time somebody did. Who was the emergency patient who called you out tonight?"

"It doesn't matter. Nobody you know."

"You're wrong again. It matters, and I've known Tom Rica for a good many years. You gave him an overdose of heroin and left him to die."

Grantland sat in silence. "I gave him what he asked for."

"Sure. You're very generous. He wanted a little death. You gave him the whole works."

Grantland began to speak rapidly, surrounding himself with a pro-tective screen of words:

"I must have made a mistake in the dosage. I didn't know how much he was used to. He was in a bad way, and I had to give him something for temporary relief. I intended to have him moved to the hospital. I see now I shouldn't have left him without an attendant.

Apparently he was worse off than I realized. These addicts are unpredictable."

"Lucky for you they are."

"Lucky?"

"Rica isn't quite dead. He was even able to do some talking before he lost consciousness."

"Don't believe him. He's a pathological liar, and he's got a grudge against me. I wouldn't provide him with drugs—"

"Wouldn't you? I thought that's what you were doing, and I've been wondering why. I've also been wondering what happened in your office three years ago."

"When?" He was hedging for time, time to build a story with escape hatches, underground passages, somewhere, anywhere to hide.

"You know when. How did Alicia Hallman die?"

He took a deep breath. "This will come as a surprise to you. Alicia died by accident. If anyone was culpable, it was her son Jerry who was. He'd made a special night appointment for her, and drove her to my office himself. She was terribly upset about something, and she wanted drugs to calm her nerves. I wouldn't prescribe any for her. She pulled a gun out of her purse and tried to shoot me with it. Jerry heard the shot. He rushed in from the waiting-room and grappled with her. She fell and struck her head on the radiator. She was mortally hurt. Jerry begged me to keep it quiet, to protect him and his mother's name and save the family from scandal. I did what I could to shield them. They were my friends as well as my patients."

He lowered his head, the serviceable martyr.

"It's a pretty good story. Are you sure it wasn't rehearsed?"

He looked up sharply. His eyes met mine for an instant. There were red fiery points in their centers. They veered away past me to the window and I glanced over my shoulder. The window framed only the half-lit sky above the city.

"Is that the story you told Carl this morning?"

"It is, as a matter of fact. Carl wanted the truth. I felt I had no right to keep it from him. It had been a load on my conscience for three years."

"I know how conscientious you are, Doctor. You got your hooks into a sick man, told him a lying story about his mother's death, gave him a gun and sicked him on his brother and turned him loose."

"It wasn't like that. He asked to see the gun. It was evidence of the truth. I suppose I'd kept it with that in mind. I brought it out of the safe and showed it to him."

"You kept it with murder in mind. You had it loaded, ready for him, didn't you?"

"That simply isn't so. Even if it were, you could never prove it. Never. He grabbed the gun and ran. I was helpless to stop him."

"Why did you lie to him about his mother's death?"

"It wasn't a lie."

"Don't contradict me, brother." I wagged the gun to remind him of it. "It wasn't Jerry who drove his mother into town. It was Sam Yogan. It wasn't Jerry who beat her to death. He was in Berkeley with his father. You wouldn't stick your neck out for Jerry, anyway. I can only think of two people you'd take that risk for—yourself, or Zinnie. Was Zinnie in your office with Alicia?"

He looked at me with flaring eyes, as if his brains were burning in his skull. "Go on. This is very interesting."

"Tom Rica saw a woman come out of there dripping blood. Was Zinnie wounded by Alicia's shot?"

"It's your story," he said.

"All right. I think it was Zinnie. She panicked and ran. You stayed behind and disposed of her mother-in-law's body. Your only motive was self-protection, but Zinnie wouldn't think of that, with the fear and guilt she had on her mind. She wouldn't stop to think that when you pushed that body into the ocean, you were converting justifiable manslaughter into murder—making a murderer out of your true love. No doubt she was grateful to you.

"Of course she wasn't your true love at the time. She wasn't rich enough yet. You wouldn't want her, or any woman, without money. Sooner or later, though, when the Senator died, Zinnie and her husband were due to come into a lot of money. But the years dragged on, and the old man's heart kept beating, and you got impatient, tired of sweating it out, living modestly on the profits from pills while other people had millions.

"The Senator needed a little help, a little send-off. You were his doctor, and you could easily have done it for him yourself, but that's not the way you operate. Better to let somebody else take the risks. Not too many risks, of course—Zinnie was going to be worth money to you. You helped her to set the psychological stage, so that Carl would be the obvious suspect. Shifting the blame onto Carl served a double purpose. It choked off any real investigation, and it got Carl and Mildred out of the picture. You wanted the Hallman money all to yourself.

"Once the Senator was gone, there was only one hurdle left between you and the money. Zinnie wanted to take it the easy way in a divorce settlement, but her child got in the way of a divorce. I imagine you did, too. You had one death to go, for the whole five million less taxes and a wife who would have to take orders the rest of her life. That death occurred today, and you've practically admitted that you set it up."

"I admitted nothing. I gave you practical proof that Carl Hallman killed his brother. The chances are he killed Zinnie, too. He could have made it across town in a stolen car."

"How long ago was Zinnie killed?"

"I'd say about four hours."

"You're a liar. Her body was warm when I found it, less than an hour ago."

"You must have been mistaken. You may not think much of me, but I am a qualified doctor. I left her before eight, and she must have died soon after. It's midnight now."

"What have you been doing since then?"

Grantland hesitated. "I couldn't move for a long time after I found her. I simply lay on the bed beside her."

"You say you found her in bed?"

"I did find her in bed."

"How did the blood get in the hall?"

"When I was carrying her out." He shuddered. "Can't you see that I'm telling you the truth? Carl must have come in and found her asleep. Perhaps he was looking for me. After all, I'm the doctor who committed him. Perhaps he killed her to get back at me. I left the door unlocked, like an idiot."

"You wouldn't have been setting her up for him? Or would you?"

"What do you think I am?"

It was a hard question. Grantland was staring down at Zinnie's clothes, his face distorted by magnetic lines of grief. I'd known murderers who killed their lovers and grieved for them. Most of them were half-hearted broken-minded men. They killed and cried and tore their prison blankets and twisted their blankets into nooses. I doubted that Grantland fitted the pattern, but it was possible.

"I think you're basically a fool," I said, "like any other man who tries to beat the ordinary human averages. I think you're a dangerous fool, because you're frightened. You proved that when you tried to silence Rica. Did you try to silence Zinnie, too, with a knife?"

"I refuse to answer such questions."

He rose jerkily and moved to the window. I stayed close to him, with the gun between us. For a moment we stood looking down the long slope of the city. Its after-midnight lights were scattered on the hillsides, like the last sparks of a firefall.

"I really loved Zinnie. I wouldn't harm her," he said.

"I admit it doesn't seem likely. You wouldn't kill the golden goose just when she was going to lay for you. Six months from now, or a year, when she'd had time to marry you and write a will in your favor, you might have started thinking of new angles."

He turned on me fiercely. "I don't have to listen to any more of this."

"That's right. You don't. I'm as sick of it as you are. Let's go, Grantland."

"I'm not going anywhere."

"Then we'll tell them to come and get you. It will be rough while it lasts, but it won't last long. You'll be signing a statement by morning."

Grantland hung back. I prodded him along the hallway to the telephone.

"You do the telephoning, Doctor."

He balked again. "Listen. There doesn't have to be any telephoning. Even if your hypothesis were correct, which it isn't, there's no real evidence against me. My hands are clean."

His eyes were still burning with fierce and unquenched light. I thought it was a light that burned from darkness, a blind arrogance masking fear and despair. Behind his several shifting masks, I caught a glimpse of the unknown dispossessed, the hungry operator who sat in Grantland's central darkness and manipulated the shadow play of his life. I struck at the shape in the darkness.

"Your hands are dirty. You don't keep your hands clean by betraying your patients and inciting them to murder. You're a dirty doctor, dirtier than any of your victims. Your hands would be cleaner if you'd taken that gun and used it on Hallman yourself. But you haven't the guts to live your own life. You want other people to do it for you, do your living, do your killing, do your dying."

He twisted and turned. His face changed like smoke and set in a new smiling mask. "You're a smart man. That hypothesis of yours, about Alicia's death—it wasn't the way it happened, but you hit fairly close in a couple of places."

"Straighten me out."

"If I do, will you let me go? All I need is a few hours to get to Mexico. I haven't committed any extraditable offense, and I have a couple of thousand—"

"Save it. You'll need it for lawyers. This is it, Grantland." I gestured with the gun in my hand. "Pick up the telephone and call the police."

His shoulders slumped. He lifted the receiver and started to dial. I ought to have distrusted his hangdog look.

He kicked sideways and upset the gasoline can. Its contents spouted across the carpet, across my feet.

"I wouldn't use that gun," he said. "You'd be setting off a bomb."

I struck at his head with the automatic. He was a millisecond ahead of me. He swung the base of the telephone by its cord and brought it down like a sledge on top of my head.

I got the message. Over and out.

>>>>>>>>>
>>>>>>>>> *chapter* 31
>>>>>>>>>

I CAME to crawling across the floor of a room I'd never seen. It was a long, dim room which smelled like a gas station. I was crawling toward a window at the far end, as fast as my cold and sluggish legs would push me along.

Behind me, a clipped voice was saying that Carl Hallman was still at large, and was wanted for questioning in a second murder. I looked back over my shoulder. Time and space came together, threaded by the voice from Grantland's radio. I could see the doorway into the lighted hall from which my instincts had dragged me.

There was a puff of noise beyond the doorway, a puff of color. Flames entered the room like dancers, orange-colored and whirring. I got my feet under me and my hands on a chair, carried it to the window and smashed the glass out of the frame.

Air poured in over me. The dancing flames behind me began to sing. They postured and beckoned when I looked at them, and reached for my cold wet legs, offering to warm them. My dull brain put several facts together, like a boy playing with blocks on the burning deck, and realized that my legs were gasoline-soaked.

I went over the jagged sill, fell further than I expected to, struck the earth full length and lay whooping for breath. The fire bit into my legs like a rabid fox.

I was still going on instinct. All instinct said was, Run. The fire ran with me, snapping. The providence that suffers fools and cushions drunks and tempers the wind to shorn lambs and softening hardheads rescued me from the final barbecue. I ran blind into the rim of a goldfish pond and fell down in the water. My legs Suzette sizzled and went out.

I reclined in the shallow, smelly blessed water and looked back at Grantland's house. Flames blossomed in the window I had broken and grew up to the eaves like quick yellow hollyhocks. Orange and yellow lights appeared behind other windows. Tendrils of smoke thrust delicately through the shake roof.

In no time at all, the house was a box of brilliant jumping lights. Breaking windows tinkled distinctly. Trellised vines of flame climbed along the walls. Little flame salamanders ran up the roof, leaving bright zigzag trails.

Above the central furnace roar, I heard a car engine start. Skidding in the slime at the bottom of the pool, I got to my feet and ran toward the house. The sirens were whining in the city again. It was a night of sirens.

Radiating heat kept me at a distance from the house. I waded through flowerbeds and climbed over a masonry wall. I was in time to see Grantland gun his Jaguar out of the driveway, its twin exhausts tracing parallel curves on the air.

I ran to my car. Below, the Jaguar was dropping down the hill like a bird. I could see its lights on the curves, and further down the red shrieking lights of a fire truck. Grantland had to stop to let it pass, or I'd have lost him for good.

He crossed to a boulevard running parallel with the main street, and followed it straight through town. I thought he was on his way to the highway and Mexico, until he turned left on Elmwood, and again left. When I took the second turn, into Grant Street, the Jaguar was halfway up the block with one door hanging open. Grantland was on the front porch of Mrs. Gley's house.

The rest of it happened in ten or twelve seconds, but each of the seconds was divided into marijuana fractions. Grantland shot out the lock of the door. It took three shots to do it. He pushed through into the hallway. By that time I was braking in front of the house, and could see the whole length of the hallway to the stairs. Carl Hallman came down them.

Grantland fired twice. The bullets slowed Carl to a walk. He came on staggering, as if the knife in his lifted hand was holding him up. Grantland fired again. Carl stopped in his tracks, his arms hanging loose, came on in a spraddling shuffle.

I started to run up the walk. Now Mildred was at the foot of the stairs, clinging to the newel post. Her mouth was open, and she was screaming something. The scream was punctuated by Grantland's final shot.

Carl fell in two movements, to his knees, then forehead down on the floor. Grantland aimed across him. The gun clicked twice in his hand. It held only seven shells. Mildred shuddered under imaginary bullets.

Carl rose from the floor with a Lazarus grin, bright badges of blood on his chest. His knife was lost. He looked blind. Bare-handed he threw himself at Grantland, fell short, lay prone and still in final despair.

My feet were loud on the veranda boards. I got my hands on Grantland before he could turn, circled his neck with my arm and bent him over backwards. He was slippery and strong. He bucked and twisted and broke my hold with the hammering butt of the gun.

Grantland moved away crabwise along the wall. His face was bare as bone, a wet yellow skull from which the flesh had been dissolved away. His eyes were dark and empty like the eye of the empty gun that he was still clutching.

A door opened behind me. The hallway reverberated with the roar of another gun. A bullet creased the plaster close above Grantland's

head and sprinkled it with dust. It was Ostervelt, in the half-shadow
under the stairs:

"Out of the way, Archer. You, Doctor, stand still, and drop it. I'll
shoot to kill you this time."

Perhaps in his central darkness Grantland yearned for death. He
threw the useless gun at Ostervelt, jumped across Carl's body, took
off from the veranda and seemed to run in air.

Ostervelt moved to the doorway and sent three bullets after him
in rapid fire, faster than any man runs. They must have been very
heavy. Grantland was pushed and hustled along by their blows, until
his legs were no longer under him. I think he was dead before he
struck the road.

"He oughtn't to have ran," Ostervelt said. "I'm a sharpshooter. I
still don't like to kill a man. It's too damn easy to wipe one out and
too damn hard to grow one." He looked down at his Colt .45 with a
kind of shamed awe, and replaced it in its holster.

I liked the sheriff better for saying that, though I didn't let it run
away with me. He was looking out toward the street where Grantland's body lay. People from the other houses had already begun to
converge on him. Carmichael appeared from somewhere and kept
them off.

Ostervelt turned to me. "How in hell did you get here? You look
like you swam through a swamp."

"I followed Grantland from his house. He just got finished setting
fire to it."

"Was he off his rocker, too?" Ostervelt sounded ready to believe
anything.

"Maybe he was in a way. His girlfriend was murdered."

"I know that. What's the rest of the story? Hallman knocked off
his girl, so Grantland knocked Hallman off?"

"Something like that."

"You got another theory?"

"I'm working on one. How long have you been here?"

"Couple of hours, off and on."

"In the house?"

"Out back, mostly. I came in through the kitchen when I heard
the gunfire. I just relieved Carmichael at the back. He's been keeping
guard on the house for more than four hours. According to him
nobody came in or went out."

"Does that mean Hallman's been in the house all this time?"

"It sure looks like it. Why?"

"Zinnie's body was warm when I found her."

"What time was that?"

"Shortly before eleven. It's a cold night for September. If she was killed before eight, you'd expect her to lose some heat."

"That's pretty thin reasoning. Anyway, she's refrigerated now. Why in hell didn't you report what you found when you found it?"

I didn't answer him. It was no time for argument. To myself, I had to admit that I was still committed to Carl Hallman. Mental case or not, I couldn't imagine a man of his courage shooting his brother in the back or cutting a defenseless woman.

Carl was still alive. His breathing was audible. Mildred was kneeling beside him in a white slip. She'd turned his head to one side and supported it on one of his limp arms. His breath bubbled and sighed.

"Better not move him any more. I'll radio for an ambulance." Ostervelt went out.

Mildred didn't seem to have heard him. I had to speak twice before she paid any attention. She looked up through the veil of hair that had fallen over her face:

"Don't look at me."

She pushed her hair back and covered the upper parts of her breasts with her hands. Her arms and shoulders were rough with gooseflesh.

"How long has Carl been here in the house?"

"I don't know. Hours. He's been asleep in my room."

"You knew he was here?"

"Of course. I've been with him." She touched his shoulder, very lightly, like a child fingering a forbidden object. "He came to the house when you and Miss Parish were here. While I was changing my clothes. He threw a stick at my window and came up the back stairs. That's why I had to get rid of you."

"You should have taken us into your confidence."

"Not *her*. That Parish woman hates me. She's been trying to take Carl away from me."

"Nonsense," though I suspected it wasn't entirely nonsense. "You should have told us. You might have saved his life."

"He isn't going to die. They won't let him die."

She hid her face against his inert shoulder. Her mother was watching us from the curtained doorway below the stairs. Mrs. Gley looked like the wreck of dreams. She turned away, and disappeared into the back recesses of the house.

I went outside, looking for Carmichael. The street was filling up with people now. Rifles glinted among them, but there was no real menace in the crowd. Carmichael was having no trouble keeping them away from the house.

I talked to him for a minute. He confirmed the fact that he had been watching the house from various positions since eight o'clock. He couldn't be absolutely sure, but he was reasonably sure, that no one had entered or left it in that time. Our conversation was broken up by the ambulance's arrival.

I watched two orderlies roll Carl Hallman into a wire basket. He had a leg wound, at least one chest wound, and one wound in the abdomen. That was bad, but not so finally bad as it would have been in the days before antibiotics. Carl was a durable boy; he was still breathing when they carried him out.

I looked around for the knife that had dropped from his hand. It wasn't there any longer. Perhaps the sheriff had picked it up. From what I had seen of it at a distance, it was a medium-sized kitchen knife, the kind that women use for paring or chopping. It could also have been used for stabbing Zinnie, though I still didn't see how.

>>>>>>>>>
>>>>>>>>> *chapter* 32
>>>>>>>>>

I FOUND Mrs. Gley in the dim, old mildew-smelling kitchen. She was barricaded behind an enamel-topped table under a hanging bulb, making a last stand against sobriety. I smelled vanilla extract when I approached her. She clutched a small brown bottle to her breast, like an only child which I was threatening to kidnap.

"Vanilla will make you sick."

"It never has yet. Do you expect a woman to face these tragedies without a drink?"

"As a matter of fact, I could use a drink myself."

"There isn't enough for me!" She remembered her manners then: "I'm sorry, I ran out of liquor way back when. You *look* as if you could use a drink."

"Forget it." I noticed a bowl of apples on the worn woodstone sink behind her. "Mind if I peel myself an apple?"

"Please do," she said very politely. "I'll get you my paring knife."

She got up and rummaged in a drawer beside the sink. "Dunno what happened to my paring knife," she muttered, and turned around with a butcher knife in her hand. "Will this do?"

"I'll just eat it in the skin."

"They say you get more vitamins."

She resumed her seat at the table. I sat across from her on a straight-backed chair, and bit into my apple. "Has Carl been in the kitchen tonight?"

"I guess he must have been. He always used to come through here and up the back stairs." She pointed toward a half-open door in the corner of the room. Behind it, bare wooden risers mounted steeply.

"Has he come in this way before?"

"I hope to tell you he has. That boy has been preying on my little girl for more years than I care to count. He cast a spell on her with his looks and his talk. I'm glad he's finally got what's coming to him. Why, when she was a little slip of a thing in high school, he used to sneak in through my kitchen and up to her room."

"How do you know?"

"I've got eyes in my head, haven't I? I was keeping boarders then, and I was ashamed they'd find out about the carryings-on in her room. I tried to reason with her time and again, but she was under his spell. What could I do with my girl going wrong and no man to back me up in it? When I locked her up, she ran away, and I had to get the sheriff to bring her back. Finally she ran away for good, went off to Berkeley and left me all alone. Her own mother."

Her own mother set the brown bottle to her mouth and swallowed a slug of vanilla extract. She thrust her haggard face toward me across the table:

"But she learned her lesson, let me tell you. When a girl gets into trouble, she finds out that she can't do without her mother. I'd like to know where she would have been after she lost her baby, without me to look after her. I nursed her like a saint."

"Was this since her marriage?"

"It was not. He got her into trouble, and he wasn't man enough to stay around and help her out of it. He couldn't stand up to his family and face his responsibility. My girl wasn't good enough for him and his mucky-muck folks. So look what *he* turned out to be."

I took another bite of my apple. It tasted like ashes. I got up and dropped the apple into the garbage container in the sink. Mrs. Gley depressed me. Her mind veered fuzzily, like a moth distracted by shifting lights, across the fibrous surface of the past, never quite making contact with its meaning.

Voices floated back from the front of the house, too far away for me to make out the words. I went into the corridor, which darkened as I shut the door behind me. I stayed in the shadow.

Mildred was talking to Ostervelt and two middle-aged men in business suits. They had the indescribable, unmistakable look of harness bulls who had made it into plain clothes but would always feel a little uncomfortable in them. One of them was saying:

"I can't figure out what this doctor had against him. Do you have any ideas on the subject, ma'am?"

"I'm afraid not." I couldn't see Mildred's face, but she had changed to the clothes in which she'd met Rose Parish.

"Did Carl kill his sister-in-law tonight?" Ostervelt said.

"He couldn't have. Carl came directly here from the beach. He was here with me all evening. I know I did wrong in hiding him. I'm willing to take the consequences."

"It ain't legal," the second detective said, "but I hope my wife would do the same for me. Did he mention the shooting of his brother Jerry?"

"No. We've been over that. I didn't even bring the subject up. He was dog-tired when he dragged himself in. He must have run all the way from Pelican Beach. I gave him something to eat and drink, and he went right off to sleep. Frankly, gentlemen, I'm tired, too. Can't the rest of this wait till morning?"

The detectives and the sheriff looked at each other and came to a silent agreement. "Yeah, we'll let it ride for now," the first detective said. "Under the circumstances. Thanks for your co-operation, Mrs. Hallman. You have our sympathy."

Ostervelt lingered behind after they left to offer Mildred his own brand of sympathy. It took the form of a heavy pass. One of his hands held her waist. The other stroked her body from breast to thigh. She stood and endured it.

Anger stung my eyes and made me clench my fists. I hadn't been so mad since the day I took the strap away from my father. But something held me still and quiet. I'd been wearing my anger like blinders, letting it be exploited, and exploiting it for my own unacknowledged purposes. I acknowledged now that my anger against the sheriff was the expression of a deeper anger against myself. In plain terms, he was doing what I had wanted to be doing.

"Don't be so standoffish," he was saying. "You were nice to Dr. Grantland; why can't you be nice to me?"

"I don't know what you're talking about."

"Sure you do. You're not as hard to get as you pretend to be. So why play dumb with Uncle Ostie? My yen for you goes back a long ways, kid. Ever since you were a filly in high school giving your old lady a hard time. Remember?"

Her body stiffened in his hands. "How could I forget?"

Her voice was thin and sharp, but his aging lust converted it into music. He took what she said for romantic encouragement.

"I haven't forgotten, either, baby," he said, huskily. "And things are different now, now that I'm not married any more. I can make you an offer on the up-and-up."

"*I'm* still married."

"Maybe, if he lives. Even if he does live, you can get it annulled. Carl's going to be locked up for the rest of his life. I got him off easy the first time. This time he goes to the Hospital for the Criminally Insane."

"No!"

"Yes. You been doing your best to cover for him, but you know as well as I do he knocked off his brother and sister-in-law. It's time for you to cut your losses, kid, think of your own future."

"I have no future."

"I'm here to tell you you have. I can be a lot of help to you. One hand washes the other. There's no legal proof he killed his father, without me there never will be. It's a closed case. That means you can get your share of the inheritance. Your life is just beginning, baby, and I'm a part of it, built right into it."

His hands busied themselves with her. She stood quiescent, keeping her face away from his. "You always wanted me, didn't you?"

There was despair in her voice, but he heard only the words. "More than ever now. There's plenty of shots in the old locker. I'm planning to retire next year, after we settle the case and the estate. You and me, we can go anywhere we like, do anything we want."

"Is this why you shot Grantland?"

"One of the reasons. He had it coming, anyway. I'm pretty sure he masterminded Jerry's murder, if that's any comfort to you—talked Carl into doing it. But it makes a better case without Grantland in it. This way there's no danger that the Senator's death will have to be dragged in. Or the thing between you and Grantland."

Mildred lifted her face. "That was years ago, before my marriage. How did you know about it?"

"Zinnie told me this afternoon. He told Zinnie."

"He always was a rat. I'm glad you shot him."

"Sure you are. Uncle Ostie knows best."

She let him have her mouth. He seemed to devour it. She hung limp in his arms until he released her.

"I know you're tired tonight, honey. We'll leave it lay for now. Just don't do any talking, except to me. Remember we got a couple of million bucks at stake. Are you with me?"

"You know I am, Ostie." Her voice was dead.

He lifted his hand to her and went out. She wedged a newspaper between the splintered door and the doorframe. Coming back toward the stairs, her movements were awkward and mechanical, as though her body was a walking doll run by remote control. Her eyes were like blue china, without sight, and as her heels tapped up the stairs I thought of a blind person in a ruined house tapping up a staircase that ended in nothing.

In the kitchen, Mrs. Gley was subsiding lower and lower on her bones. Her chin was propped on her arms now. The brown bottle lay empty at her elbow.

"I was thinking you deserted me," she said with elocutionary carefulness. "Everybody else has."

The blind footsteps tapped across the ceiling. Mrs. Gley cocked her head like a molting red parrot. "Izzat Mildred?"

"Yes."

"She ought to go to bed. Keep up her strength. She's never been the same since she lost that child of grief."

"How long ago did she lose it?"

"Three years, more or less."

"Did she have a doctor to look after her?"

"Sure she did. It was this same Dr. Grantland, poor fellow. It's a shame what had to happen to him. He treated her real nice, never even sent her a bill. That was before she got married, of course. Long before. I told her at the time, here was her chance to break off with that Carl and make a decent connection. A rising young doctor, and all. But she never listened to me. It had to be Carl Hallman or nothing. So now it's nothing. They're both gone."

"Carl isn't dead yet."

"He might as well be. I might as well be, too. My life is nothing but disappointment and trouble. I brought my girl up to associate with nice people, marry a fine young man. But no, she had to have him. She had to marry into trouble and sickness and death." Her drunken self-pity rose in her throat like vomit. "She did it to spite me, that's what she did. She's trying to kill me with all this trouble that she brought into my house. I used to keep a nice house, but Mildred broke my spirit. She never gave me the love that a daughter owes her mother. Mooning all the time over her no-good father— you'd think *she* was the one that married him and lost him."

Her anger wouldn't come in spite of the invocation. She looked in fear at the ceiling, blinking against the light from the naked bulb. The fear in her drained parrot's eyes refused to dissolve. It deepened into terror.

"I'm not a good mother, either," she said. "I never have been any good to her. I've been a living drag on her all these years, and may God forgive me."

She slumped forward across the table, as if the entire weight of the night had fallen on her. Her harsh red hair spilled on the white tabletop. I stood and looked at her without seeing her. A pit or tunnel had opened in my mind, three years deep or long. Under white light at the bottom of it, fresh and vivid as a hallucination, I could see the red spillage where life had died and murder had been born.

I was in a stretched state of nerves where hidden things are coming clear and ordinary things are hidden. I thought of the electric blanket on the floor of Grantland's bedroom. I didn't hear Mildred's quiet feet till she was half-way down the back stairs. I met her at the foot of them.

Her whole body jerked when she saw me. She brought it under control, and tried to smile:

"I didn't know you were still here."

"I've been talking to your mother. She seems to have passed out again."

"Poor mother. Poor everybody." She shut her eyes against the sight of the kitchen and its raddled occupant. She brushed her blue-veined eyelids with the fingertips of one hand. Her other hand was hidden in the folds of her skirt. "I suppose I should put her to bed."

"I have to talk to you first."

"What on earth about? It's terribly late."

"About poor everybody. How did Grantland know that Carl was here?"

"He didn't. He couldn't have."

"I think you're telling the truth for once. He didn't know Carl was here. He came here to kill you, but Carl was in his way. By the time he got to you, the gun was empty."

She stood silent.

"Why did Grantland want to kill you, Mildred?"

She moistened her dry lips with the tip of her tongue. "I don't know."

"I think I do. The reasons he had wouldn't drive an ordinary man to murder. But Grantland was frightened as well as angry. Desperate. He had to silence you, and he wanted to get back at you. Zinnie meant more to him than money."

"What's Zinnie got to do with me?"

"You stabbed her to death with your mother's paring knife. I didn't see at first how it was possible. Zinnie's body was warm when I found her. You were here under police surveillance. The timing didn't fit, until I realized that her body was kept warm under an electric blanket in Grantland's bed. You killed her before you drove to Pelican Beach. You heard over Grantland's radio that Carl was seen there. Isn't that true?"

"Why would I do a thing like that?" she whispered.

The question wasn't entirely rhetorical. Mildred looked as if she earnestly desired an answer. Like an independent entity, her hidden fist jumped up from the folds of her skirt to supply an answer. A pointed blade projected downward from it. She drove it against her breast.

Even her final intention was divided. The knife turned in her hand, and only tore her blouse. I had it away from her before she could do more damage.

"Give it back to me. Please."

"I can't do that." I was looking at the knife. Its blade was etched with dry brown stains.

"Then kill me. Quickly. I have to die anyway. I've known it now for years."

"You have to live. They don't gas women any more."

"Not even women like me? I couldn't bear to live. Please kill me. I know you hate me."

She tore her blouse gaping and offered her breast to me in desperate seduction. It was like a virgin's, unsunned, the color of pearl.

"I'm sorry for you, Mildred."

My voice sounded strange; it had broken through into a tone that was new to me, deep as the sorrow I felt. It had nothing to do with sex, or with the possessive pity that changed to sex when the wind blew from the south. She was a human being with more grief on her young mind than it was able to bear.

>>>>>>>>>
>>>>>>>>> *chapter* 33
>>>>>>>>>

MRS. GLEY groaned in her sleep. Mildred ran up the stairs away from both of us. I went up after her, across a drab brown hallway, into a room where she was struggling to raise the window.

It wasn't a woman's room, or anybody's room. It was more like an unused guestroom where unwanted things were kept: old books and pictures, an old iron double bed, a decaying rug. I felt a strange proprietary embarrassment, like a pawnbroker who's lent money on somebody else's possessions, sight unseen.

The window resisted her efforts. I saw her watching me in its dark mirror. Her own reflected face was like a ghost's peering from outer darkness.

"Go away and leave me alone."

"A lot of people have. Maybe that's the trouble. Come away from the window, eh?"

She moved back into the room and stood by the bed. There was a soiled depression in the cheap chenille spread where I guessed Carl had been lying. She sat on the edge of the iron bed.

"I don't want any of your phony sympathy. People always want to be paid for it. What do you want from me? Sex? Money? Or just to see me suffer?"

I didn't know how to answer her.

"Or do you simply want to hear me say it? Listen then, I'm a murderer. I murdered four people."

She sat and looked at the faded flowers in the wallpaper. I thought that it was a place where dreams could grow rank without much competition from the actual.

"What did you want, Mildred?"

She put a name to one of the dreams. "Money. That was what set him off from everyone—the thing that made him so handsome to me, so—shining."

"Do you mean Carl?"

"Yes. Carl." Her hand moved behind her to the depression in the spread. She leaned on it. "Even tonight, when he was lying here, all dirty and stinking, I felt so happy with him. So rich. Mother used to say I talked like a whore, but I was never a whore. I never took money from him. I gave myself to him because he needed me. The books said he had to have sex. So I used to let him come up here to the room."

"What books are you talking about?"

"The books he used to read. We read them together. Carl was afraid of going homosexual. That's why I used to pretend to be excited with him. I never really was, though, with him or any man."

"How many men were there?"

"Only three," she said, "and one of them only once."

"Ostervelt?"

She made an ugly face. "I don't want to talk about him. It was different with Carl. I'd be glad for him, but then the gladness would split off from my body. I'd be in two parts, a hot part and a cold part, and the cold part would rise up like a spirit. Then I'd imagine that I was in bed with a golden man. He was putting gold in my purse, and I'd invest it and make a profit and reinvest. Then I'd feel rich and real, and the spirit would stop watching me. It was just a game I played with myself. I never told Carl about it; Carl never really knew me. Nobody ever knew me."

She spoke with the desperate pride of loneliness and lostness. Then hurried on, as though some final disaster was about to fall, and I was her one chance to be known:

"I thought if we could get married, and I was Mrs. Carl Hallman, then I'd feel rich and solid all the time. When he went away to the university I followed him. No other girl was going to get him from me. I went to business college and found a job in Oakland. I rented an apartment of my own where he could visit me. I used to make supper for him, and help him with his studies. It was almost like being married.

"Carl wanted to make it legal, too, but his parents couldn't see it, especially his mother. She couldn't see *me*. It made me mad, the way she talked about me to Carl. You'd think I was human garbage. That was when I decided to stop taking precautions.

"It took me over a year to get our baby started. I wasn't in very good health. I don't remember very much about that time. I know I went on working in the office. They even gave me a raise. But it was the nights I lived for, not so much the times with Carl—the times after he left when I would lie awake and think about the child I was going to have. I knew that he would have to be a boy. We'd call him Carl, and bring him up just right. I'd do everything for him myself, dress him and feed him his vitamins and keep him away from bad influences, such as his grandmother. Both his grandmothers.

"After Zinnie had Martha, I thought about him all the time and I became pregnant at last. I waited two months to be sure, and then I told Carl. He was frightened, he couldn't hide it. He didn't want our baby. Mainly, he was afraid of what his mother would do. She was far gone by that time, ready to do anything to have her way. When Carl first told her about me, long before, she said she'd rather kill herself than let him marry me.

"She still had him hypnotized. I have a nasty tongue, and I told him so. I told him that he was the daring young man on the umbilical cord, but it was a hangman's noose. We had a battle. He smashed my new set of dishes in the sink. I was afraid he was going to smash me, too. Perhaps that's why he ran away. I didn't see him for days, or hear from him.

"His landlady said he'd gone home. I waited as long as I could stand it before I phoned the ranch. His mother said he hadn't been there. I thought she was lying to me, trying to get rid of me. So I told her I was pregnant, and Carl would have to marry me. She called me a liar, and other things, and then she hung up on me.

"That was a little after seven o'clock on a Friday night. I'd waited for the night rates before I phoned. I sat and watched night come on. She wouldn't let Carl come back to me, ever. I could see part of the Bay from my window, and the long ramp where the cars climbed towards the Bridge, the mud flats under it, and the water like blue misery. I thought that the place for me was in the water. And I'd have done it, too. She shouldn't have stopped me."

I had been standing over her all this time. She looked up and pushed me away with her hands, not touching me. Her movements were slow and gingerly, as if any sudden gesture might upset a delicate balance, in the room or in her, and let the whole thing collapse.

I placed a straight chair by the bed and straddled it, resting my arms on the back. It gave me a queer bedside feeling, like a quack doctor, without a bedside manner:

"Who stopped you, Mildred?"

"Carl's mother did. She should have let me kill myself and be done with it. It doesn't lessen my guilt, I know that, but Alicia brought what happened on herself. She phoned me back while I was sitting there, and told me that she was sorry for what she'd said. Could I forgive her? She'd thought the whole thing over and wanted to talk to me, help me, see that I was looked after. I believed that she'd come to her senses, that my baby would bring us all together and we'd be a happy family.

"She made an appointment for me to meet her on the Purissima wharf next evening. She said she wanted to get to know me, just the two of us. I drove down Saturday, and she was waiting in the parking lot when I got there. I'd never met her face to face before. She was a big woman, wearing mink, very tall and impressive. Her eyes shone like a cat, and her voice buzzed. I think she must have been high on some kind of drug. I didn't know it then. I was so pleased that we were coming together. I was proud to have her sitting in my old clunk in a mink coat.

"But she wasn't there to do me any favors. She started out all right, very sympathetic. It was a dirty trick Carl played on me, running out like that. The worst of it was, she had her doubts that he would ever come back. Even if he did, he'd be no bargain as a husband or a father. Carl was hopelessly unstable. She was his mother, and she ought to know. It ran in the family. Her own father had died in a sanitarium, and Carl took after him.

"Even without an ancestral curse hanging over you—that was what she called it—it was a hideous world, a crime to bring children into it. She quoted a poem to me:

> 'Sleep the long sleep;
> The Doomsters heap
> Travails and teens around us here . . .'

I don't know who wrote it, but I've never been able to get those lines out of my head.

"She said it was written to an unborn child. Teens meant heartaches and troubles, and that was all any child had to look forward to in this life. The Doomsters saw to that. She talked about those Doomsters of hers as if they really existed. We were sitting looking out over the sea, and I almost thought I could see them walking up out of the black water and looming across the stars. Monsters with human faces.

"Alicia Hallman was a monster herself, and I knew it. Yet everything she said had some truth to it. There was no way to argue except from the way I felt, about my baby. It was hard to keep my feeling warm through all the talk. I didn't have sense enough to leave her, or shut my ears. I even caught myself nodding and agreeing with her, partly. Why go to all the trouble of having a child if he was going to live in grief, cut off from the stars. Or if his daddy was never coming back.

"She almost had me hypnotized with that buzzing voice of hers, like violins out of tune. I went along with her to Dr. Grantland's office. The same part of me that agreed with her knew that I was going to lose my baby there. At the last minute, when I was on the table and it was too late, I tried to stop it. I screamed and fought against him. She came into the room with that gun of hers and told me to lie down and be quiet, or she'd kill me on the spot. Dr. Grantland didn't want to go through with it. She said if he didn't she'd run him out of his practice. He put a needle in me.

"When I came back from the anesthetic, I could see her cat eyes watching me. I had only the one thought, she had killed my baby. I must have picked up a bottle. I remember smashing it over her head. Before that, she must have tried to shoot me. I heard a gun go off, I didn't see it.

"Anyway, I killed her. I don't remember driving home, but I must have. I was still drunk on pentothal; I hardly knew what I was doing. Mother put me to bed and did what she could for me, which wasn't much. I couldn't go to sleep. I couldn't understand why the police didn't come and get me. Next day, Sunday, I went back to the doctor. He frightened me, but I was even more frightened not to go.

"He was gentle with me. I was surprised how gentle. I almost loved him when he told me what he'd done for me, making it look like a suicide. They'd already recovered her body from the sea, and nobody even asked me a question about it. Carl came back on Monday. We went to the funeral together. It was a closed-coffin funeral, and I could nearly believe that the official story of suicide was true, that the rest was just a bad dream.

"Carl thought she'd drowned herself. He took it better than I expected, but it had a strange effect on him. He said he'd been in the desert for almost a week, thinking and praying for guidance. He was coming back from Death Valley when a highway patrolman stopped him and told him his family was looking for him, and why. That was on Sunday, just before sunset.

"Carl said he looked up at the Sierra, and saw an unearthly light behind it in the west toward Purissima. It streamed, like milk, from the heavens, and it made him realize that life was a precious gift which had to be justified. He saw an Indian herding sheep on the hillside, and took it for a sign. He decided then and there to study medicine and devote his life to healing, perhaps on the Indian reservations, or in Africa like Schweitzer.

"I was carried away myself. That glorious light of Carl's seemed like an answer to the darkness I'd been in since Saturday night. I told Carl I'd go along with him if he still wanted me. Carl said that he would need a worthy helpmeet, but we couldn't get married yet. He wasn't twenty-one. It was too soon after his mother's death. His father was opposed to early marriages, anyway, and we mustn't do anything to upset an old man with a heart condition. In the meantime we should live as friends, as brother and sister, to prepare ourselves for the sacrament of marriage.

"Carl was becoming more and more idealistic. He took up theology that fall, on top of his premed courses. My own little spurt of idealism, or whatever you want to call it, didn't last very long. Dr. Grantland came to see me one day that summer. He said that he was a businessman, and he understood that I was a businesswoman. He certainly hoped I was. Because if I played my cards right, with him kibitzing for me, I would be worth a lot of money with very little effort.

"Dr. Grantland had changed, too. He was very smiley and businesslike, but he didn't look like a doctor any more. He didn't talk like one—more like a ventriloquist's dummy moving his lips in time to somebody else's lines. He told me the Senator's heart and arteries were deteriorating, he was due to die before long. When he did, Carl and Jerry would divide the estate between them. If I was married to Carl, I'd be in a position to repay my friends for any help they'd given me.

"He considered us good friends, but it would sort of set the seal on our friendship if we went to bed together. He'd been told that he was very good in bed. I let him. It made no difference to me, one way or the other. I even liked being with him, in a way. He was the only one who knew about me. When I was in Purissima after that, I used to go and visit him in his office. Until I married Carl, I mean. I quit seeing Grantland then. It wouldn't have been right.

"Carl was twenty-one on the fourteenth of March, and we were married in Oakland three days later. He moved into the apartment with me, but he thought we should make up for our earlier sins by living in chastity for another year. Carl was so tense about it that I was afraid to argue with him. He was pale, and bright in the eyes. Sometimes he wouldn't talk for days at a time, and then the floodgates would open and he'd talk all night.

"He'd begun to fail in his studies, but he was full of ideas. We used to discuss reality, appearance and reality. I always thought appearance was the front you put on for people, and reality was how you really felt. Reality was death and blood and the curse. Reality was hell. Carl told me I had it all wrong, that pain and evil were only appearances. Goodness was reality, and he would prove it to me in his life. Now that he'd discovered Christian existentialism, he saw quite clearly that suffering was only a test, a fire that purified. That was the reason we couldn't sleep together. It was for the good of our souls.

"Carl had begun to lose a lot of weight. He got so nervous that spring, he couldn't sit still to work. Sometimes I'd hear him walking in the living-room all night. I thought if I could get him to come to bed with me, it would help him to get some sleep, settle him down. I had some pretty weird ideas of my own. I paraded around in floozie nightgowns, and drenched myself with perfume, and did my best to seduce him. My own husband. One night in May, I served him a candlelight dinner with wine and got him drunk enough.

"It didn't work, not for either of us. The spirit rose up from me and floated over the bed. I looked down and watched Carl using my body. And I hated him. He didn't love *me*. He didn't want to know *me*. I thought that we were both dead, and our corpses were in bed together. Zombies. Our two spirits never met.

"Carl was still in bed when I came home the next night. He hadn't been to his classes, hadn't moved all day. I thought at first he was sick, physically sick, and I called a doctor. Carl told him that the light of heaven had gone out. He had done it himself by putting out the light in his own mind. Now there was nothing in his head but darkness.

"Dr. Levin took me into the next room and told me that Carl was mentally disturbed. He should probably be committed. I telephoned Carl's father, and Dr. Levin talked to him, too. The Senator said that the idea of commitment was absurd. Carl had simply been hitting the books too hard, and what he needed was some good, hard down-to-earth work.

"Carl's father came and took him home the next day. I gave up my apartment and my job, and a few days later I followed them. I should have stayed where I was, but I wanted to be with Carl. I didn't trust his family. And I had a sneaking desire, even under the circumstances, to live on the ranch and be Mrs. Carl Hallman in Purissima. Well, I was, but it was worse than I expected. His family didn't like me. They blamed me for Carl's condition. A *good* wife would have been able to keep him healthy and wealthy and wise.

"The only person there who really liked me was Zinnie's baby. I used to play a game pretending that Martha was *my* baby. That was how I got through those two years. I'd pretend that I was alone with her in the big house. The others had all gone away, or else they'd

died, and I was Martha's mother, doing for her all by myself, bringing her up just right, without any nasty influences. We did have
good times, too. Sometimes I really believed that the nightmare in
the doctor's office hadn't happened at all. Martha was there to prove
it, my own baby, going on two.

"But Dr. Grantland was often there to remind me that it had happened. He was looking after Carl and his father, both. The Senator
liked him because he didn't charge much or make expensive suggestions, such as hospitals or psychiatric treatment. Carl's father was
quite a money-saver. We had margarine on the table instead of butter,
and nothing but the culled oranges for our own use. I was even expected to pay board, until my money ran out. I didn't have a new
dress for nearly two years. Maybe if I had, I wouldn't have killed
him."

Mildred said that quietly, without any change in tone, without apparent feeling. Her face was expressionless. Only her forefinger
moved on her skirted knee, tracing a small pattern: a circle and then
a cross inside of the circle; as though she was trying to exorcise bad
thoughts.

"I certainly wouldn't have killed him if he'd died when he was
supposed to. Dr. Grantland had said a year, but the year went by,
then most of another year. I wasn't the only one waiting. Jerry and
Zinnie were waiting just as hard. They did their best to stir up trouble
between Carl and his father, which wasn't hard to do. Carl was a little better, but still depressed and surly. He wasn't getting along with
his father, and the old man kept threatening to change his will.

"One night Jerry baited Carl into a terrible argument about the
Japanese people who used to own part of the valley. The Senator
jumped into it, of course, as he was supposed to. Carl told him he
didn't want any part of the ranch. If he ever did inherit any share of
it, he'd give it back to the people who'd been sold up. I never saw
the old man so angry. He said Carl was in no danger of inheriting
anything. This time he meant it, too. He asked Jerry to make an appointment with his lawyer in the morning.

"I telephoned Dr. Grantland and he came out, ostensibly to see
the Senator. Afterwards I talked to him outside. He took a very dim
view. It wasn't that he was greedy, but he was thousands of dollars
out of pocket. It was the first time he told me about the other man,

this Rickey or Rica who'd been blackmailing him ever since Alicia's death. The same man who escaped with Carl last night."

"Grantland had never mentioned him to you?"

"No, he said he'd been trying to protect me. But now he was just about bled white, and something had to be done. He didn't tell me outright that I had to kill the Senator. I didn't have to be told. I didn't even have to think about it. I simply let myself forget who I was, and went through the whole thing like clockwork."

Her forefinger was active on her knee, repeating the symbol of the cross in the circle. She said, as if in answer to a question:

"You'd think I'd been planning it for years, all my life, ever since—"

She broke off, and covered the invisible device on her knee with her whole hand. She rose like a sleepwalker and went to the window. An oak tree in the backyard was outlined like a black paper cutout against the whitening sky.

"Ever since what?" I said to her still back.

"I was just remembering. When my father went away, afterwards, I used to think of funny things when I was in bed before I went to sleep. I wanted to track him down, and find him, and—"

"Kill him?"

"Oh no!" she cried. "I wanted to tell him how much we missed him and bring him back to Mother, so that we could be a happy family again. But if he wouldn't come—"

"What if he wouldn't come?"

"I don't want to talk about it. I don't remember." She struck the window where her reflection had been, not quite hard enough to break it.

>>>>>>>>
>>>>>>>> *chapter* 34
>>>>>>>>

DAWN was coming on over the trees, like fluorescent lights in an operating room. Mildred turned away from the white agony of the light. Her outburst of feeling had passed, leaving her face smooth and her voice unshaken. Only her eyes had changed. They were heavy, and the color of ripe plums.

"It wasn't like the first time. This time I felt nothing. It's strange to kill someone and have no feeling about it. I wasn't even afraid while I was waiting for him in his bathroom closet. He always took a warm bath at night to help him sleep. I had an old ball-peen hammer I'd found on Jerry's workbench in the greenhouse. When he was in the bathtub, I slipped out of the closet and hit him on the back of the head with the hammer. I held his face under the water until the bubbles stopped.

"It only took a few seconds. I unlocked the bathroom door and locked it again on the outside and wiped the key and pushed it back under the door. Then I put the hammer where I found it, with Jerry's things. I hoped it would be taken for an accident, but if it wasn't I wanted Jerry to be blamed. It was really his fault, egging Carl on to quarrel with his father.

"But Carl was the one they blamed, as you well know. He seemed to *want* to be blamed. I think for a while he convinced himself that he had actually done it, and everyone else went along with it. The sheriff didn't even investigate."

"Was he protecting you?"

"No. If he was, he didn't know it. Jerry made some kind of a deal with him to save the county money and save the family's face. He didn't want a murder trial in his distinguished family. Neither did I. I didn't try to interfere when Jerry arranged to send Carl to the hospital. I signed the papers without a word.

"Jerry knew what he was doing. He was trained in the law, and he arranged it so that he was Carl's legal guardian. It meant that he controlled everything. I had no rights at all, as far as the family estate was concerned. The day after Carl was committed, Jerry hinted politely that I might as well move out. I believe that Jerry suspected me, but he was a cagey individual. It suited him better to blame it all on Carl, and keep his own cards face down.

"Dr. Grantland turned against me, too. He said he was through with me, after the mess I'd made of things. He said that he was through protecting me. For all he cared, the man he'd been paying off could go to the police and tell them all about me. And I mustn't think that I could get back at him by talking him into trouble. It would be my word against his, and I was as schitzy as hell, and he could prove it. He slapped me and ordered me out of his house. He said if I didn't like it, he'd call the police right then.

"I've spent the last six months waiting for them," she said. "Waiting for the knock on the door. Some nights I'd wish for them to come, *will* them to come, and get it over with. Some nights I wouldn't care one way or the other. Some nights—they were the worst—I'd lie burning up with cold and watch the clock and count its ticks, one by one, all night. The clock would tick like doom, louder and louder, like doomsters knocking on the door and clumping up the stairs.

"I got so I was afraid to go to sleep at night. I haven't slept for the last four nights, since I found out about Carl's friend on the ward. It was this man, Rica, the one who knew all about me. I could imagine him telling Carl. Carl would turn against me. There's be nobody left in the world who even liked me. When they phoned me yesterday morning that Carl had escaped with him, I knew that this had to be it." She looked at me quite calmly. "You know the rest. You were here."

"I saw it from the outside."

"That's all there was, the outside. There wasn't any inside, at least for me. It was like a ritual which I made up as I went along. Every step I took had a meaning at the time, but I can't remember any of the meanings now."

"Tell me what you did, from the time that you decided to kill Jerry."

"It decided itself," she said. "I had no decision to make, no choice. Dr. Grantland phoned me at the office a little while before you got to town. It was the first I'd heard from him in six months. He said that Carl had got hold of a loaded gun. If Carl shot Jerry with it, it would solve a lot of problems. Money would be available, in case this man Rica tried to make more trouble for us. Also, Grantland would be able to use his influence with Zinnie to head off investigation of the other deaths. I'd even have a chance at my share of the property. If Carl didn't shoot Jerry, the whole thing would blow up in our faces.

"Well, Carl had no intention of shooting anybody. I found that out when I talked to him in the orange grove. The gun he had was his mother's gun, which Dr. Grantland had given him. Carl wanted to ask Jerry some questions about it—about her death. Apparently Grantland told him that Jerry killed her.

"I didn't know for certain that Jerry suspected me, but I was afraid of what he would say to Carl. This was on top of all the other reasons I had to kill him, all the little snubs and sneers I'd had to take from him. I said I'd talk to Jerry instead, and I persuaded Carl to hand over the gun to me. If he was found armed, they might shoot him without asking questions. I told him to stay out of sight, and come here after dark if he could make it. That I would hide him.

"I hid the gun away, inside my girdle—it hurt so much I fainted, there on the lawn. When I was alone, I switched it to my bag. Later, when Jerry was alone, I went into the greenhouse and shot him twice in the back. I wiped the gun and left it there beside him. I had no more use for it."

She sighed, with the deep bone-tiredness that takes years to come to. Even the engine of her guilt was running down. But there was one more death in her cycle of killings.

And still the questions kept rising behind my teeth, always the questions, with the taste of their answers, salt as sea or tears, bitter as iron or fear, sweet-sour as folding money that has passed through many hands:

"Why did you kill Zinnie? Did you actually believe that you could get away with it, collect the money and live happily ever after?"

"I never thought of the money," she said, "or Zinnie, for that matter. I went there to see Dr. Grantland."

"You took a knife along."

"For him," she said. "I was thinking about him when I took that knife out of the drawer. Zinnie happened to be the one who was there. I killed her, I hardly know why. I felt ashamed for her, lying naked like that in his bed. It was almost like killing myself. Then I heard the radio going in the front room. It said that Carl had been seen at Pelican Beach.

"It seemed like a special message intended for me. I thought that there was hope for us yet, if only I could reach Carl. We could go away together and start a new life, in Africa or on the Indian reservations. It sounds ridiculous now, but that's what I thought on the way down to Pelican Beach. That somehow everything could be made good yet."

"So you walked in front of a truck."

"Yes. Suddenly I saw what I had done. Especially to Carl. It was my fault he was being hunted like a murderer. I was the murderer. I saw what I was, and I wanted to put an end to myself before I killed more people."

"What people are you talking about?"

Averting her face, she stared fixedly at the rumpled pillow at the head of the bed.

"Were you planning to kill Carl? Is that why you sent us away to Mrs. Hutchinson's, when he was already here?"

"No. It was Martha I was thinking about. I didn't want anything to happen to Martha."

"Who would hurt her if you didn't?"

"I was afraid I would," she said miserably. "It was one of the thoughts that came to me, that Martha had to be killed. Otherwise the whole thing made no sense."

"And Carl too? Did he have to be killed?"

"I thought I could do it," she said. "I stood over him with the knife in my hand for a long time while he was sleeping. I could say that I killed him in self-defense, and that he confessed all the murders before he died. I could get the house and the money all to myself, and pay off Dr. Grantland. Nobody else would suspect me.

"But I couldn't go through with it," she said. "I dropped the knife on the floor. I couldn't hurt Carl, or Martha. I wanted them to live. It made the whole thing meaningless, didn't it?"

"You're wrong. The fact that you didn't kill them is the only meaning left."

"What difference does it make? From the night I killed Alicia and my baby, every day I've lived has been a crime against nature. There isn't a person on the face of the earth who wouldn't hate me if they knew about me."

Her face was contorted. I thought she was trying not to cry. Then I thought she was trying to cry.

"I don't hate you, Mildred. On the contrary."

I was an ex-cop, and the words came hard. I had to say them, though, if I didn't want to be stuck for the rest of my life with the old black-and-white picture, the idea that there were just good people and bad people, and everything would be hunky-dory if the good people locked up the bad ones or wiped them out with small personalized nuclear weapons.

It was a very comforting idea, and bracing to the ego. For years I'd been using it to justify my own activities, fighting fire with fire and violence with violence, running on fool's errands while the people died: a slightly earthbound Tarzan in a slightly paranoid jungle. Landscape with figure of a hairless ape.

It was time I traded the picture in on one that included a few of the finer shades. Mildred was as guilty as a girl could be, but she wasn't the only one. An alternating current of guilt ran between her and all of us involved with her. Grantland and Rica, Ostervelt, and me. The redheaded woman who drank time under the table. The father who had deserted the household and died for it symbolically in the Senator's bathtub. Even the Hallman family, the four victims, had been in a sense the victimizers, too. The current of guilt flowed in a closed circuit if you traced it far enough.

Thinking of Alicia Hallman and her open-ended legacy of death, I was almost ready to believe in her doomsters. If they didn't exist in the actual world they rose from the depths of every man's inner sea, gentle as night dreams, with the back-breaking force of tidal waves. Perhaps they existed in the sense that men and women were their own doomsters, the secret authors of their own destruction. You had to be very careful what you dreamed.

The wave of night had passed through Mildred and left her cold and shaking. I held her in my arms for a little while. The light outside the window had turned to morning. The green tree-branches moved in it. Wind blew through the leaves.

>>>>>>>>>
>>>>>>>>> *chapter* 35
>>>>>>>>>

I TALKED to Rose Parish at breakfast, in the cafeteria of the local hospital. Mildred was in another part of the same building, under city police guard and under sedation. Rose and I had insisted on these things, and got our way. There would be time enough for further interrogations, statements, prosecution and defense, for all the awesome ritual of the law matching the awesome ritual of her murders.

Carl had survived a two-hour operation, and wasn't out from under the anesthetic. His prognosis was fair. Tom Rica was definitely going to live. He was resting in the men's security ward after a night of walking. I wasn't sure that Rose and the others who had helped to walk him, had done him any great favor.

Rose listened to me in silence, tearing her toast into small pieces and neglecting her eggs. The night had left bruises around her eyes, which somehow improved her looks.

"Poor girl," she said, when I finished. "What will happen to her?"

"It's a psychological question as much as a legal question. You're the psychologist."

"Not much of a one, I'm afraid."

"Don't underestimate yourself. You really called the shots last night. When I was talking to Mildred, I remembered what you said about whole families breaking down together, but putting it off onto the weakest one. The scapegoat. Carl was the one you had in mind. In a way, though, Mildred is another."

"I know. I've watched her, at the hospital, and again last night. I couldn't miss her mask, her coldness, her not-being-there. But I didn't have the courage to admit to myself that she was ill, let alone speak out about it." She bowed her head over her uneaten breakfast, maltreating a fragment of toast between her fingers. "I'm a coward and a fraud."

"I don't understand why you say that."

"I was jealous of her, that's why. I was afraid I was projecting my own wish onto her, that all I wanted was to get her out of the way."

"Because you're in love with Carl?"

"Am I so obvious?"

"Very honest, anyway."

In some incredible reserve of innocence, she found the energy to blush. "I'm a complete fake. The worst of it is, I intend to go right on being one. I don't care if he is my patient, and married to boot. I don't care if he's ill or an invalid or anything else. I don't care if I have to wait ten years for him."

Her voice vibrated through the cafeteria. Its drab utilitarian spaces were filling up with white-coated interns, orderlies, nurses. Several of them turned to look, startled by the rare vibration of passion.

Rose lowered her voice. "You won't misunderstand me. I expect to have to wait for Carl, and in the meantime I'm not forgetting his wife. I'll do everything I can for her."

"Do you think an insanity plea could be made to stick?"

"I doubt it. It depends on how sick she is. I'd guess, from what I've observed and what you tell me, that she's borderline schizophrenic. Probably she's been in-and-out for several years. This crisis may bring her completely out of it. I've seen it happen to patients, and she must have considerable ego strength to have held herself together for so long. But the crisis could push her back into very deep withdrawal. Either way, there's no way out for her. The most we can do is see that she gets decent treatment. Which I intend to do."

"You're a good woman."

She writhed under the compliment. "I wish I were. At least I used to wish it. Since I've been doing hospital work, I've pretty well got over thinking in terms of good and bad. Those categories often do more harm than—well, good. We use them to torment ourselves, and hate ourselves because we can't live up to them. Before we know it, we're turning our hatred against other people, especially the unlucky ones, the weak ones who can't fight back. We think we have to punish somebody for the human mess we're in, so we single out the scapegoats and call them evil. And Christian love and virtue go down the drain." She poked with a spoon at the cold brown dregs of coffee in her cup. "Am I making any sense, or do I just sound softheaded?"

"Both. You sound soft-headed, and you make sense to me. I've started to think along some of the same lines."

Specifically, I was thinking about Tom Rica: the hopeful boy he had been, and the man he had become, hopeless and old in his twenties. I vaguely remembered a time in between, when hope and despair had been fighting for him, and he'd come to me for help. The rest of it was veiled in an old alcoholic haze, but I knew it was ugly.

"It's going to be a long time," Rose was saying, "before people really know that we're members of one another. I'm afraid they're going to be terribly hard on Mildred. If only there were some mitigation, or if there weren't so many. She killed so many."

"There were mitigating circumstances in the first one—the one that started her off. A judge trying it by himself would probably call it justifiable homicide. In fact, I'm not even sure she did it."

"Really?"

"You heard what Tom Rica said. He blamed that death on Grantland. Did he add anything to that in the course of the night?"

"No. I didn't press him."

"Did he do any talking at all?"

"Some." Rose wouldn't meet my eyes.

"What did he say?"

"It's all rather vague. After all, I wasn't taking notes."

"Listen, Rose. There's no point in trying to cover up for Tom, not at this late date. He's been blackmailing Grantland for years. He broke out of the hospital with the idea of converting it into a big-time operation. Carl probably convinced him that Grantland had something to do with his father's death, as well as his mother's, and that there was a lot of money involved. Tom persuaded Carl to come over the wall with him. His idea was to pile more pressure on Grantland. In case Carl couldn't boil up enough trouble by himself, Tom sent him to me."

"I know."

"Did Tom tell you?"

"If you really want to know, he told me a lot of things. Have you stopped to wonder why he picked on you?"

"We used to know each other. I guess my name stuck in his head."

"More than your name stuck. When he was a boy in high school, you were his hero. And then you stopped being." She reached across the littered table and touched the back of my hand. "I don't mean to hurt you, Archer. Stop me if I am."

"Go ahead. I didn't know I was important to Tom." But I was lying. I knew. You always know. On the firing range, in the gym, he even used to imitate my mistakes.

"He seems to have thought of you as a kind of foster-father. Then your wife divorced you, and there were some things in the newspapers, he didn't say what they were."

"They were the usual. Or a little worse than the usual."

"I am hurting you," she said. "This sounds like an accusation, but it isn't. Tom hasn't forgotten what you did for him before your private trouble interfered. Perhaps it was unconscious on his part, but I believe he sent Carl to you in the hope that you could help him."

"Which one? Tom or Carl?"

"Both of them."

"If he thought that, how wrong he was."

"I disagree. You've done what you can. It's all that's expected of anyone. You helped to save Carl's life. I know you'll do what you can for Tom, too. It's why I wanted you to know what he said, before you talk to him."

Her approval embarrassed me. I knew how far I had fallen short. "I'd like to talk to him now."

The security ward occupied one end of a wing on the second floor. The policeman guarding the steel-sheathed door greeted Rose like an old friend, and let us through. The morning light was filtered through a heavy wire mesh screen over the single window of Tom's cubicle.

He lay like a forked stick under the sheet, his arms inert outside it. Flesh-colored tape bound his hands and wrists. Except where the beard darkened it, his face was much paler than the tape. He bared his teeth in a downward grin:

"I hear you had a rough night, Archer. You were asking for it."

"I hear you had a rougher one."

"Tell me I asked for it. Cheer me up."

"Are you feeling better?" Rose asked him.

He answered with bitter satisfaction: "I'm feeling worse. And I'm going to feel worse yet."

"You've been through the worst already," I said. "Why don't you kick it permanently?"

"It's easy to say."

"You almost had it made when you were with us," Rose said. "If I could arrange a few months in a federal hospital—"

"Save your trouble. I'd go right back on. It's my meat and drink. When I kick it there's nothing left, I know that now."

"How long have you been on heroin?"

"Five or six hundred years." He added, in a different, younger voice: "Right after I left high school. This broad I met in Vegas—" His voice sank out of hearing in his throat. He twitched restlessly, and rolled his head on the pillow, away from Rose and me and memory. "We won't go into it."

Rose moved to the door. "I'll go and see how Carl is."

I said, when the door had closed behind her: "Was it Maude who got you started on horse, Tom?"

"Naw, she's death on the stuff. She was the one that made me go to the hospital. She could have sprung me clean."

"I hear you saying it."

"It's the truth. She got my charge reduced from possession so they'd send me up for treatment."

"How could she do that?"

"She's got a lot of friends. She does them favors, they do her favors."

"Is the sheriff one of her friends?"

He changed the subject. "I was going to tell you about this kid in Vegas. She was just a kid my own age, but she was main-lining already. I met her at this aluminus party where they wanted me to play football for their college. The old boys had a lot of drinks, and we young people had some, and then they wanted me to put on a show with this kid. They kept chunking silver dollars at us when we were doing it. We collected so many silver dollars I had a hard time carrying them up to her room. I was strong in those days, too."

"I remember you were."

"Damn them!" he said in weak fury. "They made a monkey out of me. I let them do it to me, for a couple of hundred lousy silver dollars. I told them what they could do with their football scholarship. I didn't want to go to college anyway. Too much like work."

"What's the matter with work?"

"Only suckers work. And you can pin it in your hat Tom Rica is no sucker. You want to know who finally cured me of suckering for all that uplift crap? You did, and I thank you for it."

"When did all this happen?"

"Don't you kid me, you remember that day I came to your office. I thought if I could talk—but we won't go into that. You wanted no part of me. I wanted no part of you. I knew which side I was on from there on out."

He sat up in bed and bared his arm as if the marks of the needle were battle scars; which I had inflicted on him: "The day you gave me the old rush, I made up my mind I'd rather be an honest junkie than a double-talking hypocrite. When they grabbed me this last time, I was main-lining two-three times a day. And liking it," he said, in lost defiance. "If I had my life to live over, I wouldn't change a thing."

I'd begun to feel restless, and a little nauseated. The alcoholic haze was lifting from the half-forgotten afternoon when Tom had come to my office for help, and gone away without it.

"What did you come to see me about, Tom?"

He was silent for quite a while. "You really want to know?"

"Very much."

"All right, I had a problem. Matter of fact, I had a couple of problems. One of them was the heroin. I wasn't all the way gone on it yet, but I was close to gone. I figured maybe you could tell me what to do about it, where I could get treatment. Well, you told me where to go."

I sat and let it sink in. His eyes never left my face. I said, when I got my voice back:

"What was the other problem you had?"

"They were the same problem, in a way. I was getting the stuff from Grantland, all I wanted. I hear the good doctor got his last night, by the way." He tried to say it casually but his eyes were wide with the question.

"Grantland's in the basement in a cold drawer."

"He earned it. He killed an old lady, one of his own patients. I told you that last night, didn't I? Or was it just a part of the dream I had?"

"You told me, all right, but it was just part of the dream. A girl named Mildred Hallman killed the old lady. Grantland was only an accessory after the fact."

"If he told you that, he's a liar."

"He wasn't the only one who told me that."

"They're all liars! The old lady was hurt, sure, but she was still alive when Grantland dropped her off the dock. She even tried to—" Tom put his hand over his mouth. His eyes roved round the walls and into the corners like a trapped animal's. He lay back and pulled the sheet up to his chin.

"What did she try to do, Tom? Get away?"

A darkness crossed his eyes like the shadow of a wing. "We won't talk about it."

"I think you want to."

"Not any more. I tried to tell you about her over three years ago.

It's too late now. I don't see any good reason to talk myself into more trouble. How would it help *her?* She's dead and gone."

"It could help the girl who thinks she murdered her. She's in worse trouble than you are. A lot worse. And she's got a lot more guilt. You could take some of it away from her."

"Be a hero, eh? Make the home folks proud of me. The old man always wanted me to be a hero." Tom couldn't sustain his sardonic bitterness. "If I admit I was on the dock, does that make me what you call accessory?"

"It depends on what you did. They're not so likely to press it if you volunteer the information. Did you help Grantland push her in?"

"Hell no, I argued with him when I saw she was still alive. I admit I didn't argue very much. I needed a fix, and he promised me one if I'd help him."

"How did you help him?"

"I helped him carry her out of his office and put her in his car. And I drove the car. He was too jittery to drive for himself. I did argue with him, though."

"Why did he drown her, do you know?"

"He said he couldn't afford to let her live. That if it came out, what happened that night, it would knock him right out of business. I figured if it was that important, I should start a little business of my own."

"Blackmailing Grantland for drugs?"

"You'll never prove it. He's dead. And I'm not talking for the record."

"You're still alive. You'll talk."

"Am I? Will I?"

"You're a better man than you think you are. You think it's the monkey that's killing you. I say you can train the monkey, chain him up and put him in the goddam zoo where he belongs. I say it's that old lady that's been weighing you down."

His thin chest rose and fell with his breathing. He fingered it under the sheet, as if he could feel a palpable weight there.

"Christ," he said. "She floated in the water for a while. Her clothes held her up. She was trying to *swim*. That was the hell of it that I couldn't forget."

"And that's why you came to see me?"

"Yeah, but it all went down the drain with the bathwater. You wouldn't listen. I was scared to go to the law. And I got greedy, let's face it. When I bumped into Carl in the hospital, and he filled me in on the family, I got greedy as hell. He said there was five million bucks there, and Grantland was knocking them off to get his hands on it. I thought here was my big chance for real."

"You were wrong. This is your real chance now. And you're taking it."

"Come again. You lost me somewhere."

But he knew what I meant. He lay and looked up at the ceiling as if there might just possibly be sky beyond it. And stars at night. Like any man with life left in him, he wanted to find a use for himself.

"Okay, Archer. I'm willing to make a statement. What have I got to lose?" He freed his arms from the sheet, grinning derisively, and flapped them like a small boy playing airman. "Bring on the D.A. Just keep Ostervelt out of it if you can, will you? He won't like all I got to say."

"Don't worry about him. He's on his way out."

"I guess it's Maude I'm worried about." His mood swung down with a hype's lability, but not as far down as it had been. "Jesus, I'm a no-good son. When I think of the real chances I had, and the dirty trouble I stirred up for the people that treated me good. I don't want Maude to be burned."

"I think she can look after herself."

"Better than I can, eh? If you see Carl, tell him I'm sorry, will you? He treated me like a brother when I was in convulsions, spouting like a whale from every hole in my head. And I got more holes than most, don't think I don't know it. Pass the word to Archer when you see him?"

"What word?"

"Sorry." It cost him an effort to say it directly.

"Double it, Tom."

"Forget it." He was getting expansive again. "This being Old Home Week, you might as well tell the Parish broad I'm sorry for brushing *her* off. She's a pretty good broad, you know?"

"The best."

"You ever think of getting married again?"

"Not to her. She's got a waiting list."

"Too bad for you."

Tom yawned and closed his eyes. He was asleep in a minute. The guard let me out and told me how to reach the post-operative ward. On the way there, I walked through the day in the past when this story should have begun for me, but didn't.

It was a hot day in late spring, three years and a summer before. The Strip fluttered like tinsel in the heat-waves rising from the pavements. I'd had five or six Gibsons with lunch, and I was feeling sweaty and cynical. My latest attempt to effect a reconciliation with Sue had just failed. By way of compensation, I'd made a date to go to the beach with a younger blonde who had some fairly expensive connections. If she liked me well enough, she could get me a guest membership in a good beach club.

When Tom walked in, my first and final thought was to get him out. I didn't want the blonde to find him in my office, with his special haircut and his Main Street jacket, his blank smile and his sniff and the liquid pain in the holes he was using for eyes. I gave him a cheap word or two, and the walking handshake that terminates at the door.

There was more to it than that. There always is. Tom had failed me before, when he dropped out of the boys' club I was interested in. He hadn't wanted to be helped the way I wanted to help him, the way that helped me. My vanity hadn't forgiven him, for stealing his first car.

There was more to it than that. I'd been a street boy in my time, gang-fighter, thief, poolroom lawyer. It was a fact I didn't like to remember. It didn't fit in with the slick Polaroid picture I had of myself as the rising young man of mystery who frequented beach clubs in the company of starlets. Who groped for a fallen brightness in private white sand, private white bodies, expensive peroxide hair.

When Tom stood in my office with the lost look on him, the years blew away like torn pieces of newspaper. I saw myself when I was a frightened junior-grade hood in Long Beach, kicking the world in the shins because it wouldn't dance for me. I brushed him off.

It isn't possible to brush people off, let alone yourself. They wait for you in time, which is also a closed circuit. Years later on a mental-hospital ward, Tom had a big colored dream and cast me for a part in it, which I was still playing out. I felt like a dog in his vomit.

I stopped and leaned on a white wall and lit a cigarette. When you looked at the whole picture, there was a certain beauty in it, or justice. But I didn't care to look at it for long. The circuit of guilty time was too much like a snake with its tail in its mouth, consuming itself. If you looked too long, there'd be nothing left of it, or you. We were all guilty. We had to learn to live with it.

Rose met me with a smile at the door of Carl's private room. She held up her right hand and brought the thumb and forefinger together in a closed circle. I smiled and nodded in response to her good news, but it took a while to penetrate to my inner ear. Where the ash-blond ghosts were twittering, and the hype dream beat with persistent violence, like colored music, trying to drown them out.

It was time I traded that in, too, on a new dream of my own. Rose Parish had hers. Her face was alive with it, her body leaned softly on it. But whatever came of her dream for better or worse belonged to her and Carl. I had no part in it, and wanted none. No Visitors, the sign on the door said.

For once in my life I had nothing and wanted nothing. Then the thought of Sue fell through me like a feather in a vacuum. My mind picked it up and ran with it and took flight. I wondered where she was, what she was doing, whether she'd aged much as she lay in ambush in time, or changed the color of her bright head.

THE
ZEBRA-STRIPED
HEARSE

>>>>>>>>>
>>>>>>>>> *chapter* 1
>>>>>>>>>

SHE WAS WAITING at the office door when I got back from my morning coffee break. The women I usually ran into in the rather dingy upstairs corridor were the aspiring hopeless girls who depended on the modeling agency next door. This one was different.

She had the kind of style that didn't go on with her make-up, and she was about my age. As a man gets older, if he knows what is good for him, the women he likes are getting older, too. The trouble is that most of them are married.

"I'm Mrs. Blackwell," she said. "You must be Mr. Archer."

I acknowledged that I was.

"My husband has an appointment with you in half an hour or so." She consulted a wrist watch on which diamonds sparkled. "Thirty-five minutes, to be precise. I've been waiting for some time."

"I'm sorry, I didn't anticipate the pleasure. Colonel Blackwell is the only appointment I have scheduled this morning."

"Good. Then we can talk."

She wasn't using her charm on me, exactly. The charm was merely there. I unlocked the outer door and led her across the waiting room, through the door marked Private, into my inner office, where I placed a chair for her.

She sat upright with her black leather bag under her elbow, touching as little of the chair as possible. Her gaze went to the mug shots on the wall, the faces you see in bad dreams and too often on waking. They seemed to trouble her. Perhaps they brought home to her where she was and who I was and what I did for a living.

I was thinking I liked her face. Her dark eyes were intelligent, and capable of warmth. There was a touch of sadness on her mouth. It was a face that had known suffering, and seemed to be renewing the acquaintance.

I said in an exploratory way: " 'Abandon hope all ye who enter here.' "

She colored slightly. "You're quick at catching moods. Or is that a stock line?"

"I've used it before."

"So has Dante." She paused, and her voice changed in tone and rhythm: "I suppose I've placed myself in a rather anomalous position, coming here. You mustn't imagine my husband and I are at odds. We're not, basically. But it's such a destructive thing he proposes to do."

"He wasn't very specific on the telephone. Is it divorce he has on his mind?"

"Heavens, no. There's no trouble of that sort in our marriage." Perhaps she was protesting a little too vehemently. "It's my husband's daughter I'm concerned—that we're both concerned about."

"Your stepdaughter?"

"Yes, though I dislike that word. I have tried to be something better than the proverbial stepmother. But I got to Harriet very late in the day. She was deprived of her own mother when she was only a child."

"Her mother died?"

"Pauline is still very much alive. But she divorced Mark years ago, when Harriet was eleven or twelve. Divorce can be terribly hard on a little girl, especially when she's approaching puberty. There hasn't been much I could do to make Harriet feel easier in the world. She's a grown woman, after all, and she's naturally suspicious of me."

"Why?"

"It's in the nature of things, when a man marries for the second time. Harriet and her father have always been close. I used to be able to communicate with her better before I married him." She stirred uneasily, and shifted her attention from herself to me. "Do you have any children, Mr. Archer?"

"No."

"Have you ever been married?"

"I have, but I don't quite see the relevance. You didn't come here to discuss my private life. You haven't made it clear why you did come, and your husband will be turning up shortly."

She looked at her watch and rose, I think without intending to. The tension in her simply levitated her out of the chair.

I offered her a cigarette, which she refused, and lit one for myself. "Am I wrong in thinking you're a little afraid of him?"

"You're completely wrong," she said in a definite voice, but she seemed to have some difficulty in continuing. "The thing I'm afraid of is letting him down. Mark needs to be able to trust me. I don't want to do anything behind his back."

"But here you are."

"Here I am." She relapsed into the chair.

"Which brings us back to the question of why."

"I'll be frank with you, Mr. Archer. I don't like Mark's battle plan"—she made the phrase sound ironic—"and I've told him so. I've done some social work, and I have some conception of what it means to be a young woman in the contemporary world. I believe it's best to let nature take its course. Let Harriet marry the man, if her heart is set on him. But Mark can't see it my way at all. He's fiercely opposed to the marriage, and determined to do something drastic."

"And I'm the something drastic."

"You're one version of it. Guns and horsewhips have also been mentioned. Not," she added quickly, "that I take everything he says seriously."

"I always take gun talk seriously. What do you want me to do?"

Her gaze had returned to the pin-ups on the wall. Killers, embezzlers, bigamists, and con men looked at her with unabashed eyes. She shifted her bag to her lap.

"Well, I can hardly ask you to turn him down. It would do no good, anyway. He'd simply find another detective and set him loose on Harriet and—her friend. All I really hoped to do was prepare you for the situation. You'll get a very one-sided view of it from Mark."

"I've gotten a very vague one from you, so far."

"I'll try to do better," she said with a small tight smile. "About five weeks ago Harriet went to Mexico. Her announced intentions were to visit her mother—Pauline lives on Lake Chapala—and to do some painting. But the fact is that she's not on very good terms with her mother, and her talent as a painter will never set the world on fire. I think she went to Lake Chapala deliberately to find a man.

"Any man. If that sounds cynical, let me add that I might have done the same thing myself, under the circumstances."

"What circumstances?"

"I mean her father's second marriage, to me. It's been quite apparent that Harriet hasn't been happy living with us. Fortunately for her, for all of us, her little Mexican expedition was successful. She found a friend, and brought him back alive."

"Does this live one have a name?"

"His name is Burke Damis. He's a young painter. While he's no great social prize—my husband tends to overrate the social—he is quite personable. He has no money, which is another of Mark's objections to him, but he does have artistic talent—a great deal more talent than Harriet possesses, as she knows. And, after all, she'll have money enough for both of them. With his talent and—virility, and her money and devotion, I'd say they had the makings of a marriage."

"She'll have money?"

"Quite a lot of money, and quite soon. One of her aunts left her a substantial trust fund. Harriet comes into it when she's twenty-five."

"How old is she now?"

"Twenty-four. Old enough to know her own mind and live her own life and get out from under Mark's domination—" She paused, as if the strength of her feeling had carried her too far.

I prompted her: "Domination is a strong word."

"It slipped out. I don't mean to malign my husband behind his back. He's a good man, according to his lights, but like other men he's capable of emotional foolishness. This isn't the first affair of Harriet's he's tried to break up. He's always succeeded before. If he succeeds this time, we could end up with a very sad girl on our hands." Her face was alive with passionate identification.

"You really care about Harriet, Mrs. Blackwell."

"I care about all three of us. It isn't good for her to live in her father's shadow. It isn't good for me to sit and watch it—I'm not the sitting and watching type—and it will become less good if it goes on. Harriet is so vulnerable, really, and Mark is such a powerful personality."

As if to illustrate this remark, a large masculine voice was raised in the outer room. I recognized it from Blackwell's telephone call. He said through the translucent glass door: "Isobel, are you in there?"

She jumped as if lightning had struck her, not for the first time. Then she tried to make herself small.

"Is there a back way out?" she whispered.

"I'm afraid not. Shall I get rid of him?"

"No. It would only lead to further trouble."

Her husband was fumbling at the door, his featureless shadow moving on the glass. "I wondered what you were up to when I saw your car in the parking lot. Isobel?"

She didn't answer him. She moved to the window and looked out through the slatted blind over Sunset Boulevard. She was very slim and tense against the striated light. I suppose my protective instinct was aroused. I opened the door a foot or so and slid out into the waiting room and closed the door behind me.

It was my first meeting with Colonel Blackwell. His phone call the day before had been our only contact. I'd looked him up afterward and learned that he was a Regular Army officer who had retired soon after the war from an undistinguished career.

He was a fairly big man who had begun to lose his battle with age. His brown outdoorsman's face made his white hair seem premature. He held himself with ramrod dignity. But his body had started to dwindle. His Shetland jacket hung loose around the shoulders; the collar of his shirt was noticeably large for his corded neck.

His eyebrows were his most conspicuous feature, and they gave him the air of an early Roman emperor. Black in contrast with his hair, they merged in a single eyebrow which edged his forehead like an iron rim. Under it, his eyes were unexpectedly confused.

He tried to shout down his own confusion: "I want to know what's going on in there. My wife is in there, isn't she?"

I gave him a vacant stare. "Your wife? Do I know you?"

"I'm Colonel Blackwell. We spoke on the telephone yesterday."

"I see. Do you have any identification?"

"I don't need identification! I vouch for myself!"

He sounded as though a yelling demon, perhaps the tormented ghost of a master sergeant, had taken possession of him. His tanned face turned red, then lavender.

I said at the purple end of the yell: "Are you really Colonel Blackwell? The way you came bulling in here, I thought you were a crank. We get a lot of cranks."

A woman with very tall pink hair looked in from the corridor, knotting her imitation pearls in her fist. It was Miss Ditmar, who ran the modeling agency:

"Is it all right?"

"Everything's under control," I said. "We were just having a yelling contest. This gentleman won."

Colonel Blackwell couldn't bear to be talked about in this fashion. He turned his back on me and stood with his face to the wall, like a plebe being braced. Miss Ditmar waved her hand benevolently and departed under her hive of hair, trailing a smog of perfume.

The door to the inner office was open now. Mrs. Blackwell had recovered her composure, which was mainly what I'd had in mind.

"Was that a mirage?" she said.

"That was Miss Ditmar in the next office. She was alarmed by the noise. She's very nervous about me all the time."

"I really must apologize," Mrs. Blackwell said with a glance at her husband, "for both of us. I shouldn't have come here. It's put you very much in the middle."

"I've been in the middle before. I rather enjoy it."

"You're very nice."

Like a man being rotated by invisible torque, Blackwell turned and let us see his face. The anger had drained out of it and left it open. His eyes had a hurt expression, as though his young wife had rejected him by complimenting me. He tried to cover this with a wide painful smile.

"Shall we start over, in a lower key?"

"A lower key would suit me, Colonel."

"Fine."

It did something for him to be called by his rank. He made an abrupt horizontal gesture which implied that he was in charge of himself and the situation. He cast an appraising glance around my waiting room as if he was thinking of having it redecorated. With a similar glance at me, he said: "I'll join you shortly in your office. First I'll put Mrs. Blackwell in her car."

"It isn't necessary, Mark. I can find my way—"

"I insist."

He offered her his elbow. She trudged out holding onto it. Though he was the big one and the loud one, I had the impression that she was supporting him.

Through the venetian blind I watched them emerge from the

street entrance onto the sidewalk. They walked very formally together, like people on their way to a funeral.

I liked Isobel Blackwell, but I was sort of hoping her husband wouldn't come back.

>>>>>>>>>
>>>>>>>>> *chapter* 2
>>>>>>>>>

HE CAME BACK, though, wearing a purged expression which failed to tell me what had been purged, or who. I took the hand he offered me across my desk, but I went on disliking him.

He was sensitive to this—a surprising thing in a man of his temper and background—and made an oblique attempt to get around it: "You don't know the pressures I live under. The combined forces of the females in my life—" He paused, and decided not to finish the sentence.

"Mrs. Blackwell was telling me about some of the pressures."

"So she said. I suppose she meant no harm in coming here. But dammit, if a man's wife won't go through channels," he said obscurely, "who will?"

"I understand the two of you disagree about your prospective son-in-law."

"Burke Damis is not my prospective son-in-law. I have no intention of letting the marriage go through."

"Why not?"

He glared down at me, moving his tongue around under his lips as if he had foreign objects between his teeth. "My wife has the standard female illusion that all marriages are made in heaven. Apparently she's infected you with it."

"I asked a simple question, about this particular marriage. Won't you sit down, Colonel?"

He sat stiffly in the chair his wife had occupied. "The man's a fortune-hunter, or worse. I suspect he's one of those confidence men who make a career of marrying silly women."

"Do you have any evidence along those lines?"

"The evidence is on his face, in his manner, in the nature of his relationship with my daughter. He's the kind of man who would make her miserable, and that's putting it gently."

Concern for her had broken through into his voice and changed its self-conscious tone. He wasn't the stuffed shirt I had taken him for, or at least the stuffing had its human elements.

"What about their relationship?"

He hitched his chair forward. "It's completely unilateral. Harriet is offering him everything—her money, her love, her not inconsiderable attractions. Damis offers nothing. He *is* nothing—a man from nowhere, a man from Mars. He pretends to be a serious painter, but I know something about painting and I wouldn't hire him to paint the side of a barn. Nobody's ever heard of him, and I've made inquiries."

"How extensive?"

"I asked a fellow at the art museum. He's an authority on contemporary American painters. The name Burke Damis meant nothing to him."

"The woods are full of contemporary American painters, and there are always new ones coming up."

"Yes, and a lot of them are fakes and impostors. We're dealing with one here, with this Burke Damis. I believe the name's an alias, one he picked out of a hat."

"What makes you think so?"

"The point is, he's given me no reason to think otherwise. I tried to question him about his background. His answers were evasive. When I asked him where he came from, he said Guadalajara, Mexico. He's obviously not Mexican and he admitted having been born in the States, but he wouldn't say where. He wouldn't tell me who his father was or what he'd done for a living or if he had any relatives extant. When I pressed him on it, he claimed to be an orphan."

"Maybe he is. Poor boys can be sensitive, especially under crossexamination."

"He's no boy, and I didn't cross-examine him, and he's got the sensitivity of a wild pig."

"I seem to have struck out, Colonel."

He sat back in his chair, unsmiling, and ran his hand over his head. He was careful not to dislodge the wave in his meticulously brushed white hair.

"You make it very clear that you think I'm taking the wrong approach to this problem. I assure you I am not. I don't know how much my wife told you, or how much of what she told you was true —objectively true. The fact remains that my daughter, whom I love dearly, is a fool about men."

"Mrs. Blackwell did mention," I said carefully, "that a similar situation had come up before."

"Several times. Harriet has a great desire to get married. Unfortunately she combines it with a genius for picking the wrong man. Don't misunderstand me, I'm not opposed to marriage. I want my daughter to get married—to the right man, at the proper time. But this idea of rushing into it with a fellow she barely knows—"

"Exactly how long has she known Damis?"

"No more than a month. She picked up with him in Ajijic, on Lake Chapala. I've visited Mexico myself, and I know what kind of floaters you can get involved with if you're not careful. It's no place for an unattached young woman. I realize now I shouldn't have let her go down there."

"Could you have stopped her?"

A shadow stained his eyes. "The fact is I didn't try. She'd had an unhappy winter, and I could see she needed a change. I was under the impression she would stay with her mother, my former wife, who lives in Ajijic. I should have known better than to depend on Pauline. I naturally supposed she'd surround her with the appropriate social safeguards. Instead she simply turned her loose on the town."

"Forgive my bluntness, but you talk about your daughter as though she wasn't responsible. She isn't mentally retarded?"

"Far from it. Harriet is a normal young woman with more than her share of intelligence. To a great extent," he said, as if this settled the matter, "I educated her myself. After Pauline saw fit to abandon us, I was both father and mother to my girl. It grieves me to say no to her on this marriage. She's pinned her hopes of heaven to it. But it wouldn't last six months.

"Or rather it would last six months—just long enough for him to get his hands on her money." He propped his head on his fist and peered at me sideways, one of his eyes half closed by the pressure of his hand. "My wife doubtless told you that there is money involved?"

"She didn't say how much."

"My late sister Ada set up a half-million-dollar trust fund for Harriet. She'll come into active control of the money on her next birthday. And she'll have at least as much again when I—pass away."

The thought of his own death saddened him. His sadness changed perceptibly to anger. He leaned forward and struck the top of my desk so hard that the pen-set hopped. "No thief is going to get his paws on it!"

"You're very certain in your mind that Burke Damis is one."

"I know men, Mr. Archer."

"Tell me about the other men Harriet wanted to marry. It may help me to understand the pattern of her behavior." And the pattern of her father's.

"They're rather painful to contemplate. However. One was a man in his forties with two wrecked marriages behind him, and several children. Then there was a person who called himself a folk singer. He was a bearded nonentity. Another was an interior decorator in Beverly Hills—a nancy-boy if I ever saw one. All of them were after her money. When I confronted them with the fact, they bowed out more or less gracefully."

"What did Harriet do?"

"She came around. She sees them now as I saw them from the beginning. If we can keep her from doing something rash, she'll see through Damis eventually, just as I do."

"It must be nice to have X-ray eyes."

He gave me a long black look from under his formidable eyebrow. "I resent that remark. You're not only personally insulting but you seem decidedly lukewarm about my problem. Apparently my wife really got to you."

"Your wife is a very charming woman, and possibly a wise one."

"Possibly, in some situations. But Damis has her hoodwinked—she's only a woman after all. I'm surprised that you should be taken in, however. I was told that you run one of the best one-man operations in Los Angeles County."

"Who told you that?"

"Peter Colton, of the D.A.'s office. He assured me I couldn't find a better man. But I must say you don't exhibit much of the bloodhound spirit."

"You may have enough of it for both of us."

"What is that supposed to mean?"

"You've got the case all wrapped up and tied with a noose before

I've started on it. But you haven't given me any concrete evidence."

"Getting the evidence is your job."

"If it's there. I'm not going to cook up evidence, or select it to confirm you in your prejudices. I'm willing to investigate Damis on the understanding that the chips fall where they fall."

He threw his Roman-emperor look around my office. It bounced off the drab green filing cabinet with the dents in it, riffled the flaking slats of the venetian blind, and found the ugly pin-ups on the wall all guilty as charged.

"You feel you can afford to lay down terms to your prospective clients?"

"Certain terms are always implied. Sometimes I have to spell them out. I have a license to lose, and a reputation."

His face had entered the color cycle again, starting with pink. "If you consider me a threat to your reputation—"

"I didn't say that. I said I had one. I intend to keep it."

He tried to stare me down. He used his face like an actor, making his brow horrendous, converting his eyes into flinty arrowheads pointed at me between slitted lids. But he grew tired of the game. He wanted my help.

"Of course," he said in a reasonable tone, "I had nothing in mind but a fair, unprejudiced investigation. If you got any other impression, you misread me. You realize my daughter is very dear to me."

"I can use a few more facts about her. How long has she been back from Mexico?"

"Just a week."

"This is the seventeenth of July. Does that mean she returned on the tenth?"

"Let me see. It was a Monday. Yes, she flew back on Monday, July tenth. I met them at the airport around lunchtime."

"Damis was with her?"

"He was very much with her. It's what all the trouble is about."

"Just what kind of trouble has there been?"

"Nothing overt, yet. We've had some—ah—discussions in the family. Harriet has been quite obstinate, and Isobel, as you know, is on the side of the lovebirds."

"You've talked to Damis?"

"I have, on two occasions. The three of us had lunch at the airport last Monday. He did a good deal of talking, about theories of painting and the like. Harriet sat there enthralled. I was not impressed.

"But it was the second time we met that I really began to smell a rat. He came to dinner Saturday night. Harriet had already confided to me that they were planning marriage, so I made an occasion to talk to him alone. It was then he gave me all those evasive answers. On one point at least he wasn't evasive. He admitted that he didn't have a dime. At the same time he was ogling around my house as if he already owned it. I told him that would happen only over my dead body."

"You told him that?"

"Later," he said. "After dinner. He'd made himself highly obnoxious at the table. I mentioned that the Blackwell family name embodies three centuries of tradition, going back to the early days of the Massachusetts colony. Damis seemed to think it was funny. He made a satiric remark about the Colonial Dames—my mother was one, as it happens—and announced that he was bored by such traditions. I said in that case he would certainly be bored as my son-in-law, and he agreed.

"But later I surprised the fellow in my bedroom. He was actually fingering through my wardrobe. I asked him what he thought he was doing there. He answered flippantly that he was making a study of how the other half lives. I said that he would never find out, not at my expense or the expense of any member of my family. I invited him to leave my house and while he was at it to vacate my other house which he is occupying. But Harriet came rushing in and made me countermand—withdraw the suggestion."

"Damis is living in a house that belongs to you?"

"Temporarily. Harriet talked me into it the first day. He needed a place to paint, she said, and I agreed to let him use the beach house."

"And he's still there?"

"I assume he is. They're not even married, and he's already scrounging on us. I tell you, the man's an operator."

"He doesn't sound like a very smooth one to me. I've known a few painters. The young unrecognized ones have a special feeling about accepting things from other people. They live off the country while they do their work. All most of them want is a north light and enough money to buy paints and eat."

"That's another thing," he said. "Harriet's given him money. I happened to glance through her checkbook yesterday, shortly after I phoned you." He hesitated. "I don't normally pry, but when it's a question of protecting her—"

"Just what are you trying to protect her from?"

"Disaster." His voice sank ominously. "Complete and utter personal disaster. I've had some experience of the world, and I know what can come of marrying the wrong person."

I waited for him to explain this, wondering if he meant his first wife. But he failed to satisfy my curiosity. He said: "Young people never seem to learn from their parents' experience. It's a tragic waste. I've talked to Harriet until I was blue in the face. But the fellow's got her completely under his thumb. She told me Saturday night that if it came to a showdown between me and Damis, she would go with him. Even if I disinherited her."

"The subject of disinheritance came up?"

"I brought it up. Unfortunately I have no ultimate control over the money she has coming from her aunt. Ada would have been well advised to leave the money permanently in my keeping."

This struck me as a doubtful proposition. Blackwell was a sad and troubled man, hardly competent to play God with anybody's life. But the sadder and more troubled they were, the more they yearned for omnipotence. The really troubled ones believed they had it.

"Speaking of money," I said.

We discussed my fee, and he gave me two hundred dollars' advance and the addresses of his houses in Bel Air and Malibu. He gave me something else I hadn't thought of asking for: a key to the beach house, which he detached from his key ring.

⋙⋙⋙
⋙⋙⋙ *chapter* 3
⋙⋙⋙

IT WAS IN a small isolated settlement north of Malibu. Far down below the highway under the slanting brown bluffs, twelve or fifteen houses huddled together as if for protection against the sea. It was calm enough this morning, at low tide, but the overcast made it grey and menacing.

I turned left off the highway and down an old switchback blacktop to a dead end. Other cars were parked here against a white rail which guarded the final drop to the beach. One of them, a new green Buick Special, was registered to Harriet Blackwell.

A wooden gangway ran from the parking area along the rear of the houses. The ocean glinted dully through the narrow spaces between them. I found the one I was looking for, a grey frame house with a peaked roof, and knocked on the heavy weathered door.

A man's voice grunted at me from inside. I knocked again, and his grudging footsteps padded across the floorboards.

"Who is it?" he said through the door.

"My name is Archer. I was sent to look at the house."

He opened the door. "What's the matter with the house?"

"Nothing, I hope. I'm thinking of renting it."

"The old man sent you out here, eh?"

"Old man?"

"Colonel Blackwell." He pronounced the name very distinctly, as if it was a bad word he didn't want me to miss.

"I wouldn't know about him. A real-estate office in Malibu put me onto this place. They didn't say it was occupied."

"They wouldn't. They're bugging me."

He stood squarely in the doorway, a young man with a ridged washboard stomach and pectorals like breastplates visible under his T-shirt. His black hair, wet or oily, drooped across his forehead and gave him a low-browed appearance. His dark blue eyes were emotional and a bit sullen. They had a potential thrust which he wasn't using on me.

The over-all effect of his face was that of a boy trying not to be aware of his good looks. Boy wasn't quite the word. I placed his age around thirty, a fairly experienced thirty.

He had wet paint on his fingers. His face, even his bare feet, had spots of paint on them. His jeans were mottled and stiff with dried paint.

"I guess he has a right, if it comes down to that. I'm moving out any day." He looked down at his hands, flexing his colored fingers. "I'm only staying on until I finish the painting."

"You're painting the house?"

He gave me a faintly contemptuous look. "I'm painting a picture, *amigo*."

"I see. You're an artist."

"I work at the trade. You might as well come in and look around, since you're here. What did you say your name was?"

"Archer. You're very kind."

"Beggars can't be choosers." He seemed to be reminding himself of the fact.

Stepping to one side, he let me into the main room. Except for the kitchen partitioned off in the corner to my left, this room took up the whole top floor of the house. It was spacious and lofty, with a raftered ceiling and a pegged oak floor that had been recently polished. The furniture was made of rattan and beige-colored leather. To my right as I went in, a carpeted flight of steps with a wrought iron railing descended to the lower floor. A red brick fireplace faced it across the room.

At the far end, the ocean end, on the inside of the sliding glass doors, an easel with a stretched canvas on it stood on a paint-splashed tarpaulin.

"It's a nice house," the young man said. "How much rent do they want from you?"

"Five hundred for the month of August."

He whistled.

"Isn't that what you've been paying?"

"I've been paying nothing. *Nada.* I'm a guest of the owner." His sudden wry grin persisted, changing almost imperceptibly to a look of pain. "If you'll excuse me, I'll get back to work. Take your time, you won't disturb me."

He walked the length of the room, moving with careful eagerness like an animal stalking prey, and planted himself in front of the easel. I was a little embarrassed by his casual hospitality. I'd expected something different: another yelling match, or even a show of violence. I could feel the tension in him, as it was, but he was holding it.

A kind of screaming silence radiated from the place where he stood. He was glaring at the canvas as if he was thinking of destroying it. Stooping quickly, he picked up a traylike palette, squizzled a brush in a tangle of color, and with his shoulder muscles bunched, stabbed at the canvas daintily with the brush.

I went through the swinging doors into the kitchen. The gas stove, the refrigerator, the stainless steel sink were all sparkling clean. I inspected the cupboards, which were well stocked with cans of everything from baked beans to truffles. It looked as though Harriet had been playing house, for keeps.

I crossed to the stairway. The man in front of the easel said: "Augh!" He wasn't talking to me. He was talking to his canvas. Stepping softly, I went down the stairs. At their foot a narrow door opened onto outside steps which led down to the beach.

There were two bedrooms, a large one in front and a smaller one in the rear, with a bathroom between them. There was nothing in the rear bedroom but a pair of twin beds with bare mattresses and pillows. The bathroom contained a pink washbowl and a pink tub with a shower curtain. A worn leather shaving kit with the initials B.C. stamped on it in gold lay on the back of the washbowl. I unzipped it. The razor was still wet from recent use.

The master bedroom in front, like the room above it, had sliding glass doors which opened onto a balcony. The single king-sized bed was covered with a yellow chenille spread on which women's clothes had been carefully folded: a plaid skirt, a cashmere sweater, underthings. A snakeskin purse with an ornate gold-filled clasp that looked Mexican lay on top of the chest of drawers. I opened it and found a red leather wallet which held several large and small bills and Harriet Blackwell's driving license.

I looked behind the louvered doors of the closet. There were no women's clothes hanging in it, and very few men's. The single lonesome suit was a grey lightweight worsted number which bore the label of a tailor on Calle Juares in Guadalajara. The slacks and jacket beside it had been bought at a chain department store in Los Angeles, and so had the new black shoes on the rack underneath. In the corner of the closet was a scuffed brown Samsonite suitcase with a Mexicana Airlines tag tied to the handle.

The suitcase was locked. I hefted it. It seemed to have nothing inside.

The door at the foot of the stairs opened behind me. A blonde girl wearing a white bathing suit and dark harlequin glasses came in. She failed to see me till she was in the room with me.

"Who are you?" she said in a startled voice.

I was a little startled myself. She was a lot of girl. Though she was wearing flat beach sandals, her hidden eyes were almost on a level with my own. Smiling into the dark glasses, I gave her my apologies and my story.

"Father's never rented the beach house before."

"He seems to have changed his mind."

"Yes, and I know why." Her voice was high and small for so large a girl.

"Why?"

"It doesn't concern you."

She whipped off her glasses, revealing a black scowl, and something else. I saw why her father couldn't believe that any man would love her truly or permanently. She looked a little too much like him.

She seemed to know this; perhaps the knowledge never left her thoughts. Her silver-tipped fingers went to her brow and smoothed away the scowl. They couldn't smooth away the harsh bone that rose in a ridge above her eyes and made her not pretty.

I apologized a second time for invading her privacy, and for the unspoken fact that she was not pretty, and went upstairs. Her fiancé, if that is what he was, was using a palette knife to apply cobalt blue to his canvas. He was sweating and oblivious.

I stood behind him and watched him work on his picture. It was one of those paintings concerning which only the painter could tell when it was finished. I had never seen anything quite like it: a cloudy mass like a dark thought in which some areas of brighter color stood out like hope or fear. It must have been very good or very bad, because it gave me a *frisson*.

He threw down his knife and stood back jostling me. His gymnasium smell was mixed with the sweeter smell of the oils. He turned with a black intensity in his eyes. It faded as I watched.

"Sorry, I didn't know you were there. Have you finished looking around?"

"Enough for now."

"Like the place?"

"Very much. When did you say you were moving?"

"I don't know. It depends." A troubled expression had taken the place of the singleness that was his working look. "You don't want it before August, anyway."

"I might."

The girl spoke from the head of the stairs in a carrying voice: "Mr. Damis will be out of here by the end of the week."

He turned to her with his wry, self-mocking smile. "Is that an order, Missy Colonel?"

"Of course not, darling. I never give orders. But you know what our plans are."

"I know what they're supposed to be."

She came toward him in a flurried rush, her plaid skirt swinging, the way a child moves in on a loved adult. "You can't mean you've changed your mind again?"

He lowered his head, and shook it. The troubled expression had spread from his eyes to his mouth.

"Sorry, kid, I have a hard time making decisions, especially now that I'm working. But nothing's changed."

"That's wonderful. You make me happy."

"You're easily made happy."

"You know I love you."

She had forgotten me, or didn't care. She tried to put her arms around him. He pushed her back with the heels of his hands, holding his fingers away from her sweater.

"Don't touch me, I'm dirty."

"I like you dirty."

"Silly kid," he said without much indulgence.

"I like you, love you, eat-you-up, you dirty."

She leaned toward him, taller in her heels than he was, and kissed him on the mouth. He stood and absorbed her passion, his hands held away from her body. He was looking past her at me. His eyes were wide open and rather sad.

>>>>>>>>
>>>>>>>> *chapter* 4
>>>>>>>>

HE SAID WHEN she released him: "Is there anything else, Mr. Archer?"

"No. Thanks. I'll check back with you later."

"If you insist."

Harriet Blackwell gave me a peculiar look. "Your name is Archer?"

I acknowledged that it was. She turned her back on me, in a movement that reminded me of her father, and stood looking out over the grey sea. Like a man stepping under a bell jar which muffled sound and feeling, Damis had already returned to his painting.

I let myself out, wondering if it had been a good idea to put in a personal appearance at the beach house. I found out in a moment that it hadn't been. Before I reached my car, Harriet came running after me, her heels rat-tat-tatting on the wooden gangway.

"You came here to spy on us, didn't you?"

She took hold of my arm and shook it. Her snakeskin bag fell to the ground between us. I picked it up and handed it to her as a peace offering. She snatched it out of my hand.

"What are you trying to do to me? What did I ever do to you?"

"Not a thing, Miss Blackwell. And I'm not trying to do anything to you."

"That's a lie. Father hired you to break it up between me and Burke. I heard him talk to you yesterday, on the telephone."

"You don't have very good security at your house."

"I have a right to protect myself, when people connive against me."

"Your father thinks he's protecting you."

"Oh, certainly. By trying to destroy the only happiness I'll ever know or want." There was a lilt of hysteria in her voice. "Father pretends to love me, but I believe in his secret heart of hearts he wishes me ill. He *wants* me to be lonely and miserable."

"That's not very sensible talk."

She shifted her mood abruptly. "But what you're doing is very sensible, I suppose. Sneaking around other people's houses pretending to be something different from what you are."

"It wasn't a good idea."

"So you admit it."

"I should have gone about it in a different way."

"You're *cynical*." She curled her lips at me youngly. "I don't know how you can bear to live with yourself."

"I was trying to do a job. I bungled it. Let's start over."

"I have nothing to say to you whatever."

"I have something to say to you, Miss Blackwell. Are you willing to sit in the car and listen to me?"

"You can say it right out here."

"I don't want interruptions," I said, looking back toward the beach house.

"You don't have to be afraid of Burke. I didn't tell him who you are. I don't like to upset him when he's working."

She sounded very much like a young wife, or almost-wife. I made a comment on this. It seemed to please her.

"I love him. It's no secret. You can write it down in your little black book and make a full report of it to Father. I love Burke, and I'm going to marry him."

"When?"

"Very soon now." She hid her secret behind a hushed mysterious look. Perhaps she wasn't sure she had a secret to hide. "I wouldn't dream of telling you when or where. Father would call out the National Guard, at least."

"Are you getting married to please yourself or spite your father?"

She looked at me uncomprehendingly. I had no doubt it was a relevant question, but she didn't seem to have an answer to it.

"Let's forget about Father," I said.

"How can I? There's nothing he wouldn't do to stop us. He said so himself."

"I'm not here to stop your marriage, Miss Blackwell."

"Then what are you trying to do?"

"Find out what I can about your friend's background."

"So Father can use it against him."

"That's assuming there's something that can be used."

"Isn't that your assumption?"

"No. I made it clear to Colonel Blackwell that I wouldn't go along with a smear attempt, or provide the material for any kind of moral blackmail. I want to make it clear to you."

"And I'm supposed to believe you?"

"Why not? I have nothing against your friend, or against you. If you'd co-operate—"

"Oh, very likely." She looked at me as though I'd made an obscene suggestion. "You're a brash man, aren't you?"

"I'm trying to make the best of a bad job. If you'd co-operate we might be able to get it over with in a hurry. It's not the kind of a job I like."

"You didn't have to take it. I suppose you took it because you needed the money." There was a note of patronage in her voice, the moral superiority of the rich who never have to do anything for money. "How much money is Father paying you?"

"A hundred a day."

"I'll give you five hundred, five days' pay, if you'll simply go away and forget about us."

She took out her red wallet and brandished it.

"I couldn't do that, Miss Blackwell. Besides, it wouldn't do you any good. He'd go and hire himself another detective. And if you think I'm trouble, you should take a look at some of my colleagues."

She leaned on the white guard rail and studied me in silence. Behind her the summer tide had begun to turn. The rising surge slid up the beach, and sanderlings skimmed along its wavering edges. She said to an invisible confidant located somewhere between me and the birds: "Can the man be honest?"

"I can and am. I can, therefore I am."

No smile. She never smiled. "I still don't know what I'm going to do about you. You realize this situation is impossible."

"It doesn't have to be. Don't you have any interest in your fiancé's background?"

"I know all I need to know."

"And what is that?"

"He's a sweet man, and a brilliant one, and he's had a very rough time. Now that he's painting again, there's no limit to what he can accomplish. I want to help him develop his potential."

"Where did he study painting?"

"I've never asked him."

"How long have you known him?"

"Long enough."

"How long?"

"Three or four weeks."

"And that's long enough to make up your mind to marry him?"

"I have a right to marry whom I please. I'm not a child, and neither is Burke."

"I realize *he* isn't."

"I'm twenty-four," she said defensively. "I'm going to be twenty-five in December."

"At which time you come into money."

"Father's briefed you very thoroughly, hasn't he? But there are probably a few things he left out. Burke doesn't care about money, he despises it. We're going to Europe or South America and live very simply, and he will do his work and I will help him and that will be our life." There were stars in her eyes, dim and a long way off. "If I thought the money would prevent me from marrying the man I love, I'd *give* it away."

"Would Burke like that?"

"He'd love it."

"Have you discussed it with him?"

"We've discussed everything. We're very frank with each other."

"Then you can tell me where he comes from and so on."

There was another silence. She moved restlessly against the guard rail as though I had backed her into a corner. The chancy stars in her eyes had dimmed out. In spite of her protestations, she was a worried girl. I guessed that she was mainlining on euphoria, which can be as destructive as any drug.

"Burke doesn't like to talk about the past. It makes him unhappy."

"Because he's an orphan?"

"That's part of it, I think."

"He must be thirty. A man stops being an orphan at twenty-one. What's he been doing since he gave up being a full-time orphan?"

"All he's ever done is paint."

"In Mexico?"

"Part of the time."

"How long had he been in Mexico when you met him?"

"I don't know. A long time."

"Why did he go to Mexico?"

"To paint."

We were going around in circles, concentric circles which contained nothing but a blank. I said: "We've been talking for some time now, and you haven't told me anything that would help to check your friend out."

"What do you expect? I haven't pried into his affairs. I'm not a detective."

"I'm supposed to be," I said ruefully, "but you're making me look like a slob."

"That could be because you are a slob. You could always give up and go away. Go back to Father and tell him you're a failure."

Her needle failed to strike a central nerve, but I reacted to it. "Look here, Miss Blackwell. I sympathize with your natural desire to break away from your family ties and make a life of your own. But you don't want to jump blindly in the opposite direction—"

"You sound exactly like Father. I'm sick of people breathing in my face, telling me what to do and what not to do. You can go back and tell him that."

She was getting terribly restless. I knew I couldn't hold her very much longer. Her body mimed impatience in its awkward gangling attitude, half sitting on the rail, with one foot kicking out spasmodically. It was a fine big body, I thought, not meant for spinsterhood. I had serious doubts that Harriet and her fine big body and her fine big wad of money were meant for Burke Damis, either. The little love scene I'd witnessed between them had been completely one-sided.

Her face had darkened. She turned it away from me. "Why are you looking at me like that?"

"I'm trying to understand you."

"Don't bother. There's nothing to understand. I'm a very simple person."

"I was thinking that, too."

"You make it sound like an insult."

"No. I doubt that your friend Burke is quite so simple. That isn't an insult, either."

"What is it?"

"Call it a warning. If you were my daughter, and you're young enough to be, I'd hate to see you fling yourself into this thing in a frantic hurry—merely because your father is against it."

"That isn't my reason. It's a positive thing."

"Whatever your reasons are, you could find yourself in water over your head."

She looked out past the kelp beds where the ocean went dark and deep and the sharks lived out of sight.

" 'Hang your clothes on a hickory limb,' " she quoted, " 'but don't go near the water.' I've heard that before."

"You could even keep your clothes on."

She gave me another of her looks, her black Blackwell looks. "How dare you speak to me in that way?"

"The words came out. I let them."

"You're an insufferable man."

"While I'm being insufferable, you may be able to clear up a small discrepancy for me. I noticed that the shaving kit in the bathroom has the initials B.C. on it. Those initials don't go with the name Burke Damis."

"I never noticed it."

"Don't you find it interesting?"

"No." But the blood had drained out of her face and left it sallow. "I imagine it belonged to some previous guest. A lot of different people have used the beach house."

"Name one with the initials B.C."

"Bill Campbell," she said quickly.

"Bill Campbell's initials would be W.C. Who is Bill Campbell, by the way?"

"A friend of Father's. I don't know if he ever used the beach house or not."

"Or if he ever existed?"

I'd pressed too hard, and lost her. She dismounted from the rail, smoothing down her skirt, and started away from me toward the beach house. I watched her go. No doubt she was a simple person, as she said, but I couldn't fathom her.

>>>>>>>>>
>>>>>>>>> *chapter* 5
>>>>>>>>>

I DROVE BACK up to the highway. Diagonally across the intersection, a large fading sign painted on the side of a roadside diner advertised Jumbo Shrimp. I could smell grease before I got out of the car.

The stout woman behind the counter looked as though she had spent her life waiting, but not for me. I sat in a booth by the front window, partly obscured by an unlit neon beer sign. She brought me a knife and fork, a glass of water, and a paper napkin. I was the only customer in the place.

"You want the shrimp special?"

"I'll just have coffee, thanks."

"That will cost you twenty cents," she said severely, "without the food to go with it."

She picked up the knife and fork and the paper napkin. I sat and nursed the coffee, keeping an eye on the blacktop road that led up from the beach.

The overcast was burning off. A sun like a small watery moon appeared behind it. The muffled horizon gradually cleared, and the sea changed from grey to greyish blue. The surf had begun to thump so hard I could hear it.

Two or three cars had come up from the cluster of beach houses, but there had been no sign of Harriet's green Buick. I started in on my second cup of coffee. Refills were only ten cents.

A zebra-striped hearse with a broken headlight came in off the highway. It disgorged, from front and rear, four boys and two girls who all looked like siblings. Their hair, bleached by sun and peroxide, was long on the boys and short on the girls so that it was almost uniform. They wore blue sweatshirts over bathing suits. Their faces were brown and closed.

They came in and sat in a row at the counter, ordered six beers, drank them with hero sandwiches which the girls made out of French loaves and other provisions brought in in paper bags. They ate quietly and voraciously. From time to time, between bites, the largest boy, who carried himself like their leader, made a remark about big surf. He might have been talking about a tribal deity.

They rose in unison like a platoon, and marched out to their hearse. Two of the boys got into the front seat. The rest of them sat in the back beside the surfboards. One of the girls, the pretty one, made a face at me through the side window. For no good reason, I made a face back at her. The hearse turned down the blacktop toward the beach.

"Beach bums," the woman behind the counter said.

She wasn't talking to me. Having nursed two coffees for an hour, I may have been included in her epithet. The coffee, or the waiting,

was beginning to make me nervous. I ordered a therapeutic beer and
turned back to the window.

The woman went on talking to herself. "You'd think they'd have
more respect, painting a hearse in stripes like that. They got no respect for the living or the dead. How they expect me to make a living, bringing in their own food? *I* don't know what the world is
coming to."

Harriet's car appeared, coming out of a tight curve, halfway up the
slope. I saw when it reached the highway that she was driving and
that her friend was in the seat beside her. He was wearing his grey
suit, with a shirt and tie, and he bore a curious resemblance to those
blank-faced dummies you see in the windows of men's clothing
stores. They turned south, toward Los Angeles.

I followed them down the highway. Malibu slowed them, and I
was close on their tail as they passed through the shabby fringes of
Pacific Palisades. They made a left turn onto Sunset. The light had
changed when I reached the corner. By the time it changed in my
favor, the Buick was far out of sight. I tried to make up the minutes
I had lost, but the squealing curves of the Boulevard kept my speed
down.

I remembered that the Blackwells lived in the hills off Sunset. On
the chance that Harriet was on her way home, I turned in through
the baronial gates of Bel Air. But I couldn't find the Blackwell
house, and had to go back to the hotel to ask directions.

It was visible from the door of the hotel bar. The white-coated
barman pointed it out to me: a graceful Spanish mansion which
stood at the top of the terraced slope. I gave the barman a dollar of
Blackwell's money and asked him if he knew the Colonel.

"I wouldn't say I *know* him. He isn't one of your talkative
drinkers."

"What kind of a drinker is he?"

"The silent type. My favorite type."

I went back to my car and up the winding road to the hilltop
house. The rose garden in front of it was contained like a conflagra-
tion by a clipped boxwood hedge. Harriet's Buick was standing in
the semicircular gravel drive.

I could see her father's white head over the roof of the car. His
voice carried all the way out to the road. I caught isolated words like
sneak and scrounger.

When I got nearer I could see that Blackwell was carrying a double-barreled shotgun at the hip. Burke Damis got out of the car and spoke to him. I didn't hear what he said, but the muzzle of the shotgun came up to the level of his chest. Damis reached for it.

The older man fell back a step. The level gun rested firmly at his shoulder. Damis took a step forward, thrusting out his chest as if he welcomed the threat of the gun.

"Go ahead and shoot me. It would fix you at least."

"I warn you, you can press me so far and no farther."

Damis laughed. "You ain't seen nothing yet, old man."

These things were being said as I climbed out of my car and walked toward them, slowly. I was afraid of jarring the precarious balance of the scene. It was very still on the hilltop. I could hear the sound of their breathing and other things besides: my feet crunching in the gravel, the low call of a mourning dove from the television antenna on the roof.

Neither Blackwell nor Damis looked at me as I came up beside them. They weren't in physical contact, but their faces were contorted as though their hands had death grips on each other. The double muzzle of the shotgun dominated the scene like a pair of empty insane eyes.

"There's a dove on the roof," I said conversationally. "If you feel like shooting something, Colonel, why don't you take a shot at it? Or is there a law against it in these parts? I seem to remember something about a law."

He turned to me with a grimace of rage stamped in the muscles of his face. The gun swung with his movement. I took hold of the double barrel and forced it up toward the unoffending sky. I lifted it out of Blackwell's hands, and broke open the breach. There was a shell in each chamber. I tore a fingernail unloading them.

"Give me back my shotgun," he said.

I gave it to him empty. "Shooting never solved a thing. Didn't you learn that in the war?"

"The fellow insulted me."

"The way I heard it, insults were traveling in both directions."

"But you didn't hear what he said. He made a filthy accusation."

"So you want big black filthy headlines, and a nice long filthy trial in Superior Court."

"The filthier the better," Damis said.

I turned on him. "Shut up."

His eyes were somber and steady. "You can't shut me up. Neither can he."

"He almost did, boy. Twelve-gauge shotgun wounds at this range ruin you for keeps."

"Tell *him*. I couldn't care less."

Damis looked as though he didn't care, for himself or anyone. But he seemed to feel exposed under my eyes. He got into the passenger's seat of Harriet's car and pulled the door shut. The action, all his actions, had something bold about them and something secretive.

Blackwell turned toward the house and I went along. The veranda was brilliant with fuchsias growing out of hanging redwood tubs. To my slightly jittered vision, they resembled overflowing buckets of blood.

"You came near committing murder, Colonel. You should keep your guns unloaded and locked up."

"I do."

"Maybe you ought to throw the key away."

He looked down at the gun in his hands as if he didn't remember how it had got there. Sudden pockets had formed under his eyes.

"What led up to this?" I said.

"You know the long-term part of it. He's been moving in on me and my household, robbing me of my most precious possession—"

"A daughter isn't exactly a possession."

"I have to look out for her. Someone has to. She announced a few minutes ago that she was going away to marry the fellow. I tried to reason with her. She accused me of being a little Hitler who had hired a private Gestapo. That accusation hurt, from my own daughter, but the fellow"—he shot an angry glance toward the car—"the fellow made a worse one."

"What did he say?"

"I wouldn't repeat it, to anyone. He made a filthy allegation about me. Of course there's nothing to it. I've always been upright in my dealings with others, especially my own daughter."

"I don't doubt that. I'm trying to find out what kind of thinking goes on in Damis's head."

"He's a mixed-up young man," Blackwell said. "I believe he's dangerous."

That made two of them, in my opinion.

A screen door slammed, and Harriet appeared behind the hanging red and purple fuchsias. She had changed to a light sharkskin suit and a hat with a little grey veil fluttering from it. The little veil bothered me, perhaps because it short-circuited the distance between brides and widows. She was carrying a blue hatbox and a heavy blue case.

Her father met her on the steps and reached for the blue case. "Let me help with that, dear."

She swung it away from him. "I can handle it myself, thank you."

"Is that all you have to say to me?"

"Everything's been said. We know what you think of us. Burke and I are going away where you won't be tempted to—harass us." Her cold young eyes rested on me, and then on the shotgun in her father's hand. "I don't even feel physically safe."

"The gun's empty," I said. "Nobody got hurt and nobody's going to. I wish you'd reconsider this move, Miss Blackwell. Give it a day's thought, anyway."

She wouldn't speak directly to me. "Call off your dogs," she said to Blackwell. "Burke and I are going to be married and you have no right to stop us. There must be legal limits to what even a *father* can do."

"But won't you listen to me, dear? I have no desire to do anything—"

"Stop doing it then."

I'd been surprised by his quiet reasonableness. He didn't have the self-control to sustain it. The sudden yelling demon took possession of him again. "You've made your choice, I wash my hands of you. Go off with your filthy little miracle man and roll in the mire with him. I won't lift a finger to rescue you."

She said from the height of her pale cold anger: "You're talking foolishly, Father. What is the matter with you?"

She strode on to the car, swinging her bags like clumsy weapons. Damis took them from her and put them in the trunk, beside his own suitcase.

Isobel Blackwell had come out of the house and down the veranda steps. As she passed between me and her husband, she pressed his shoulder in sympathy and perhaps in admonition. She went up to Harriet.

"I wish you wouldn't do this to your father."

"I'm not doing anything *to* him."

"He feels it that way. He loves you, you know."

"I don't love him."

"I'm sure you'll regret saying that, Harriet. When you do, please let him know."

"Why should I bother? He has you."

Isobel shrugged, as though the possession of herself was no great boon to anyone. "You're more important to him than I am. You could break his heart."

"He's going to have to get over it then. I'm sorry if you feel badly." In a quick uprush of feeling, Harriet embraced the older woman. "You've been the best to me—better than I deserve."

Isobel patted her back, looking past her at Damis. He had been watching the two of them like a spectator at a game on which he had placed a moderate bet.

"I hope you'll take good care of her, Mr. Damis."

"I can try."

"Where are you taking her?"

"Away from here."

"That isn't very informative."

"It wasn't intended to be. This is a big country, also a free one. Let's go, Harriet."

She disengaged herself from her stepmother and got into the driver's seat of her car. Damis climbed in beside her. I made a note of the license number as they drove away. Neither of them looked back.

Blackwell approached us, walking rather uncertainly in the gravel. His body seemed to have shrunk some more in his clothes, while his large face had grown larger.

"You let them go," he said accusingly.

"I had nothing to stop them with. I can't use force."

"You should have followed them."

"What for? You said you'd washed your hands of them."

His wife spoke up: "Perhaps it would be better if you did that, Mark. You can't go on in this fashion, letting the situation drive you crazy. You might as well accept it."

"I refuse to accept it, and it's not driving me crazy. I've never been saner in my life. I resent the implication that I'm not."

The ranting rhythm was taking over his voice again. She laid her gentle admonishing hand on his arm.

"Come into the house. You need to relax, after all you've been through."

"Leave me alone." He flung her hand off and said to me: "I want Damis put in jail, do you hear me?"

"To do that, you'd have to prove that he's committed a jailable offense."

"What about taking a girl across a state line for immoral purposes?"

"Has he done that?"

"He transported my daughter from Mexico—"

"But marriage isn't considered an immoral purpose under the law." Isobel Blackwell tittered unexpectedly.

He turned on her. "You think it's funny, do you?"

"Not particularly. But it's better to laugh than to weep. And better to marry than to burn. I'm quoting your own words to me, remember?"

Her tone was serious, but there was irony in it. Blackwell stalked toward the house, picking up his shotgun on the way. He slammed the front door so violently that the dove flew up with whistling wings from the television antenna. Isobel Blackwell spread her arms as though a larger bird had escaped from them.

"What am I going to do with him?"

"Give him a tranquilizer."

"Mark has been *eating* tranquilizers all week. It doesn't seem to help his nerves. If he goes on at this rate, I'm afraid he'll shake himself to pieces."

"It's other people I'm worried about."

"You mean the young man—Damis?"

"I mean anyone who crosses him."

She touched me lightly on the arm. "You don't think he's capable of doing actual harm to anyone?"

"You know him better than I do."

"I thought I knew Mark very well indeed. But he's changed in the last year. He's always been a gentle man. I never thought he belonged in the military profession. The Army came to agree with me, as it happened. They retired him after the war, very much against his will. His first wife, Pauline, divorced him about the same time."

"Why, if you don't mind my asking?"

"You'd have to ask her. She went to Nevada one day and got a divorce and married another man—a retired dentist named Keith Hatchen. They've lived in Mexico ever since. I suppose Pauline and her dentist have a right to whatever happiness they can muster. But it left poor Mark with nothing to fill his life but his guns and his sports and the Blackwell family history which he has been trying to write for lo these many years."

"And Harriet," I said.

"And Harriet."

"I'm beginning to get the picture. You say he's changed in the past year. Has anything special happened, besides Harriet's taking up with Damis?"

"Mark took up with me last fall," she said with a one-sided smile.

"You don't strike me as a malign influence."

"Thank you. I'm not."

"I had the impression that you'd been married longer than that." It was partly a question and partly an expression of sympathy.

"Did you now? Of course I've been married before. And I've known Mark and Harriet for a great many years, practically since she was a babe in arms. You see, my late husband was very close to Mark. Ronald was related to the Blackwells."

"Then you probably know a lot of things you haven't told me," I said.

"Every woman does. Isn't that your experience, Mr. Archer?"

I liked her dry wit, even if it was cutting me off from further information. I made a gesture that took in the big house and the roses and the gap in the boxwood hedge where Harriet's car had last been seen.

"Do you think I should go on with this?"

She answered deliberately: "Perhaps you had better. Mark certainly needs another man to guide his hand and advise him—not that he's terribly good at taking advice. I liked the way you handled this crisis just now. It could have erupted into something terrible."

"I wish your husband realized that."

"He does. I'm sure he does, though he won't admit it." Her dark eyes were full of feeling. "You've done us all a good turn, Mr.

Archer, and you'll do us another by staying with us in this. Find out what you can about Damis. If you can give him a clean bill of health, morally speaking, it should do a lot to reconcile Mark to the marriage."

"You're not suggesting a whitewash job on Damis?"

"Of course not. I'm interested in the truth, whatever it may turn out to be. We are all. Now if you'll excuse me I think I'd better go in and look after my husband. Holding his hand seems to be my function in life these days."

She wasn't complaining, exactly, but I detected a note of resignation. As she turned away, very slim in her linen sheath, I caught myself trying to estimate her age. If she had known the Blackwells since Harriet was a baby, and had come to know them through her first husband, she must have married him more than twenty years ago. Which suggested that she was over forty.

Well, so was I.

>>>>>>>>>
>>>>>>>>> *chapter* 6
>>>>>>>>>

I USED BLACKWELL'S KEY to let myself into the beach house. Nothing had changed in the big upstairs room, except that there were black paper ashes in the fireplace. They crumbled when I tried to pick them up on the fire shovel. The painting hung on its easel, still gleaming wet in places. In the light that slanted through the glass doors, the spot of cobalt blue which Damis had added last glared at me like any eye.

I backed away from the picture, trying to understand it, and went down the stairs to the master bedroom. The louvered doors of the closet were swinging open. It had been cleared out. There was nothing in the chest of drawers, nothing in the bathroom but some clean towels. The back bedroom was empty.

I moved back into the front bedroom and went through it carefully. The wastebasket had been emptied, which probably accounted for the burned paper in the upstairs fireplace. Damis had gone to a lot of trouble to cover his traces.

But he had overlooked one piece of paper. It was jammed between the sliding glass door and its frame, evidently to keep the door from rattling. It was thick and yellowish paper, folded small. When I unfolded it, I recognized it as one of those envelopes that airlines give their passengers to keep their tickets in.

This was a Mexicana Airlines envelope, with flight instructions typed inside the flap. Mr. Q. R. Simpson, the instructions said, was to leave the Guadalajara airport at 8:40 A.M. on July 10 and arrive at Los Angeles International at 1:30 P.M. the same day.

I messed around in the bedroom some more, discovered only some dust mice under the bed, and went upstairs. The painting drew me back to it. It affected me differently each time. This time I saw, or thought I saw, that it was powerful and ugly—an assault of dark forces on the vision. Perhaps I was reading my fantasy into it, but it seemed to me that its darkness was the ultimate darkness of death.

I had an impulse to take it along and find an expert to show it to. If Damis was a known artist, his style should be recognizable. But I couldn't move the thing. The oils were still wet and would smear.

I went out to the car to get my camera. The zebra-striped hearse was standing empty beside it. The sky had cleared, and a few sunbathers were lying around in the sand like bodies after a catastrophe. Beyond the surf line the six surfers waited in prayerful attitudes on their boards.

A big wave rose toward them. Five of the surfers rode it in, like statues on a traveling blue hillside. The sixth was less skillful. The wave collapsed on her. She lost her board and swam in after it.

Instead of taking it out to sea again, she carried it up the beach on her head. She left it on the sand above the tide line and climbed the rocky bank to the parking space. She had the bust and shoulders of a young Amazon, but she was shivering and close to tears.

It was the girl who had made the face at me, which gave us something in common. I said: "You took quite a spill."

She looked at me as if she had never seen me before, almost as if she wasn't seeing me now. I was a member of another tribe or species. Her eyes were wet and wild, like the eyes of sea lions.

She got a man's topcoat out of the back of the hearse and put it on. It was good brown tweed which looked expensive, but there were wavy white salt marks on it, as if it had been immersed in the sea. Her fingers trembled on the brown leather buttons. One of the buttons, the top one, was missing. She turned up the collar around the back of her head where the wet hair clung like a golden helmet.

"If you're cold I have a heater in my car."

"Blah," she said, and turned her tweed back on me.

I loaded the camera with color film and took some careful shots of Damis's painting. On my way to the airport I dropped the film off with a photographer friend in Santa Monica. He promised to get it developed in a hurry.

The very polite young man at the Mexicana desk did a few minutes' research and came up with the information that Q. R. Simpson had indeed been on the July 10 flight from Guadalajara. So had Harriet Blackwell. Burke Damis hadn't.

My tentative conclusion, which I kept to myself, was that Damis had entered the United States under the name of Simpson. Since he couldn't leave Mexico without a nontransferable tourist card or enter this country without proof of citizenship, the chances were that Q. R. Simpson was Damis's real name.

The polite young Mexican told me further that the crew of the July 10 flight had flown in from Mexico again early this afternoon. The pilot and copilot were in the office now, but they wouldn't know anything about the passengers. The steward and stewardess, who would, had already gone for the day. They were due to fly out again tomorrow morning. If I came out to the airport before flight time, perhaps they would have a few minutes to talk to me about my friend Señor Simpson.

Exhilarated by his Latin courtesy, I walked back to the Immigration and Customs shed. The officers on duty took turns looking at my license as if it was something I'd found in a box of breakfast cereal.

Feeling the need to check in with some friendly authority, I drove downtown. Peter Colton was in his cubicle in the District Attorney's office, behind a door that said Chief Criminal Investigator.

Peter had grown old in law enforcement. The grooves of discipline and thought were like saber scars in his cheeks. His triangular eyes glinted at me over half-glasses which had slid down his large aggressive nose.

He finished reading a multigraphed sheet, initialed it, and scaled it into his out-basket.

"Sit down, Lew. How's it going?"

"All right. I dropped by to thank you for recommending me to Colonel Blackwell."

He regarded me quizzically. "You don't sound very grateful. Is Blackie giving you a bad time?"

"Something is. He handed me a peculiar case. I don't know whether it's a case or not. It may be only Blackwell's imagination."

"He never struck me as the imaginative type."

"Known him long?"

"I served under him, for my sins, in Bavaria just after the war. He was in Military Government, and I was in charge of a plain-clothes section of Military Police."

"What was he like to work for?"

"Tough," Colton said, and added reflectively: "Blackie liked command, too much. He didn't get enough of it during the fighting. Some friend in Washington, or some enemy, kept him in the rear echelons. I don't know whether it was for Blackie's own protection or the protection of the troops. He was bitter about it, and it made him hard on his men. But he's a bit of an ass, and we didn't take him too seriously."

"In what way was he hard on his men?"

"All the ways he could think of. He went in for enforcement of petty rules. He was very keen on the anti-fraternization policy. My men had murder and rape and black-marketeering to contend with. But Blackie expected us to spend our nights patrolling the cabarets suppressing fraternization. It drove him crazy to think of all the fraternization that was going on between innocent American youths and man-eating *Fräuleins*."

"Is he some kind of a sex nut?"

"I wouldn't put it that strongly." But Colton's grin was wolfish. "He's a Puritan, from a long line of Puritans. What made it worse, he was having fraternization problems in his own family. His wife was interested in various other men. I heard later she divorced him."

"What sort of a woman is she?"

"Quite a dish, in those days, but I never knew her up close. Does it matter?"

"It could. Her daughter Harriet went to Mexico to visit her a few weeks ago and made a bad connection. At least it doesn't look too promising. He's a painter named Burke Damis, or possibly Q. R. Simpson. She brought him back here with her, intends to marry him. Blackwell thinks the man is trying to take her for her money. He hired me to investigate that angle, or anything else that I can find on Damis."

"Or possibly Q. R. Simpson, you said. Is Damis using an alias?"

"I haven't confirmed it. I'm fairly sure he entered the country a week ago under the Q. R. Simpson name. It may be his real name, since it isn't a likely alias."

"And you want me to check it out."

"That would be nice."

Colton picked up his ball-point pen and jabbed with it in my direction. "You know I can't spend public time and money on a private deal like this."

"Even for an old friend?"

"Blackwell's no friend of mine. I recommended you to get him out of my hair in one quick easy motion."

"I was referring to myself," I said, "no doubt presumptuously. A simple query to the State Bureau of Criminal Investigation wouldn't take much time, and it might save trouble in the long run. You always say you're more interested in preventing crime than punishing it."

"What crime do you have in mind?"

"Murder for profit is a possibility. I don't say it's probable. I'm mainly concerned with saving a naïve young woman from a lot of potential grief."

"And saving yourself a lot of potential legwork."

"I'm doing my own legwork as usual. But I could knock on every door from here to San Luis Obispo and it wouldn't tell me what I need to know."

"What, exactly, is that?"

"Whether Q. R. Simpson, or Burke Damis, has a record."

Colton wrote the names on a memo pad. I'd succeeded in arousing his curiosity.

"I suppose I could check with Sacramento." He glanced at the clock on the wall. It was nearly four. "If the circuits aren't too loaded, we might get an answer before we close up for the night. You want to wait outside?"

I read a law-enforcement trade journal in the anteroom, all the way through to the advertisements. Police recruits were being offered as much as four hundred and fifty dollars a month in certain localities.

Peter Colton opened his door at five o'clock on the nose and beckoned me into his office. A teletype flimsy rustled in his hand.

"Nothing on Burke Damis," he said. "Quincy Ralph Simpson is another story: he's on the Missing Persons list, has been for a couple of weeks. According to his wife, he's been gone much longer than that."

"His wife?"

"She's the one who reported him missing. She lives up north, in San Mateo County."

>>>>>>>>>
>>>>>>>>> *chapter* 7
>>>>>>>>>

IT WAS CLEAR late twilight when the jet dropped down over the Peninsula. The lights of its cities were scattered like a broken necklace along the dark rim of the Bay. At its tip stood San Francisco, remote and brilliant as a city of the mind, hawsered to reality by her two great bridges—if Marin and Berkeley were reality.

I took a cab to Redwood City. The deputy on duty on the ground floor of the Hall of Justice was a young man with red chipmunk cheeks and eyes that were neither bright nor stupid. He looked me over noncommittally, waiting to see if I was a citizen or one of the others.

I showed him my license and told him I was interested in a man named Quincy Ralph Simpson. "The Los Angeles D.A.'s office says you reported him missing about two weeks ago."

He said after a ruminative pause: "Have you spotted him?"

"I may have."

"Where?"

"In the Los Angeles area. Do you have a picture of Simpson?"

"I'll see." He went into the back of the office, rummaged through a drawerful of bulletins and circulars, and came back empty-handed. "I can't find any, sorry. But I can tell you what he looks like. Medium height, about five-nine or -ten; medium build, one-sixty-five or so; black hair; I don't know the color of his eyes; no visible scars or other distinguishing marks."

"Age?"

"About my age. I'm twenty-nine. Is he your man?"

"It's possible." Just barely possible. "Is Simpson wanted for anything?"

"Non-support, maybe, but I don't know of any complaint. What makes you think he's wanted?"

"The fact that you can describe him."

"I know him. That is, I've seen him around here."

"Doing what?"

He leaned on the counter with a kind of confidential hostility. "I'm not supposed to talk about what I see around here, friend. You want to know anything about that, you'll have to take it up with the boys upstairs."

"Is Captain Royal upstairs?"

"The Captain's off duty. I wouldn't want to disturb him at home. You know him well?"

"We worked together on a case."

"What case was that?"

"I'm not supposed to talk about it, friend. Can you give me Mrs. Simpson's address?"

He reached under the counter and produced a phone book which he pushed in my direction. Q. R. Simpson was listed, at 2160 Marvista Drive. My taxi driver told me that this was in a tract on the far side of Skyline, toward Luna Bay: a five-dollar run.

We drove through darkening hills and eventually turned off the road past a tattered billboard which announced: "No Down Payment. No Closing Costs." The tract houses were new and small and all alike and already declining into slums. Zigzagging through the grid of streets like motorized rats in a maze, we found the address we were looking for.

It stood between two empty houses, and had a rather abandoned air itself. The tiny plot of grass in front of it looked brown and withered in the headlights. A 1952 Ford convertible with the back window torn out was parked in the carport.

I asked the driver to wait, and rang the doorbell. A young woman answered. The door was warped, and she had some trouble opening it all the way.

She was a striking brunette, very thin and tense, with a red slash of mouth and hungry dark eyes. She had on a short black tight dress which revealed her slender knees and only half concealed her various other attractions.

She was aware of these. "This isn't free show night. What is it you want?"

"If you're Mrs. Simpson, I'd like to talk about your husband."

"Go ahead and talk about him. I'm listening." She cocked her head in an angry parody of interest.

"You reported him missing."

"Yes, I reported him missing. I haven't set eyes on him for two whole months. And that suits me just fine. Who needs him?" Her voice was rough with grief and resentment. She was looking past me across the scraggy untended lawn. "Who's that in the taxi?"

"Just the driver. I asked him to wait for me."

"I thought it might be Ralph," she said in a different tone, "afraid to come in the house and all."

"It isn't Ralph. You say he's been gone a couple of months, but you only reported him missing two weeks ago."

"I gave him all the leeway I could. He's taken off before, but never for this long. Mr. Haley at the motel said I ought to clue in the cops. I had to go back to work at the motel. Even with that I can't keep up the house payments without some help from Ralph. But a lot of good it did telling the cops. They don't do much unless you can prove foul play or something." She wrinkled her expressive upper lip. "Are you one?"

"I'm a private detective." I told her my name. "I ran into a man today who could be your missing husband. May I come in?"

"I guess so."

She moved sideways into her living room, glancing around as if to see it through a visitor's eyes. It was tiny and clean and poor, furnished with the kind of cheap plastic pieces that you're still paying installments on when they disintegrate. She turned up the three-way lamp and invited me to sit at one end of the chesterfield. She sat at the other end, hunched forward, her sharp elbows resting on her knees.

"So where did you see him?"

"Malibu."

I wasn't paying much attention to what I said. There was a framed oil painting on the wall above the television set. Though it was recognizable as a portrait of Mrs. Simpson, it looked amateurish to me. I went over and examined it more closely.

"That's supposed to be me," she said behind me.

"It's not a bad likeness. Did your husband do it?"

"Yeah. It's a hobby he has. He wanted to take it up seriously at one time but a man he knew, a real painter, told him he wasn't good enough. That's the story of his life, hopeful beginnings and nothing endings. So now he's living the life of Riley in Malibu while I stay here and work my fingers to the bone. What's he doing, beach-combing?"

I didn't answer her question right away. A dog-eared paperback entitled *The Art of Detection* lay on top of the television set. It was the only book I could see in the room. I picked it up and riffled through the pages. Many of them were heavily underlined; some of them were illustrated with bad cartoons penciled in the margins.

"That was another one of Ralph's big deals," she said. "He was going to be a great detective and put us on easy street. Naturally he didn't get to first base. He never got to first base with any of his big wheels and deals. A man he knows on the cops told him with his record—" She covered her mouth with her hand.

I laid the book down. "Ralph has a record?"

"Not really. That was just a manner of speaking." Her eyes had hardened defensively. "You didn't tell me what he was doing in Malibu."

"I'm not even certain it was your husband I saw there."

"What did he look like?"

I described Burke Damis, and thought I caught the light of recognition in her eyes. But she said definitely: "It isn't him."

"I'd like to be sure about that. Do you have a photograph of Ralph?"

"No. He never had his picture taken."

"Not even a wedding picture?"

"We had one taken, but Ralph never got around to picking up the copies. We were married in Reno, see, and he couldn't hold on to the twenty dollars long enough. He can't keep away from the tables when he's in Reno."

"Does he spend much time in Reno?"

"All the time he can get away from work. I used to go along with him, I used to think it was fun. I had another think coming. It's the reason we never been able to save a nickel."

I moved across the room and sat beside her. "What does Ralph do for a living, Mrs. Simpson?"

"Anything he can get. He never finished high school, and that makes it tough. He's a pretty good short-order cook, but he hated the hours. Same with bartending, which he did for a while. He's had some good-paying houseboy jobs around the Peninsula. But he's too proud for that kind of work. He hates to take orders from people. Maybe," she added bitterly, "he's too proud for any kind of work, and that's why he ran out on me."

"How long ago did he leave?"

"Two months ago, I told you that. He left here on the night of May eighteen. He just got back from Nevada that same day, and he took right off for Los Angeles. I think he only came home to try and talk me out of the car. But I told him he wasn't going to leave me marooned without a car. So he finally broke down and took a bus. I drove him down to the bus station."

"What was he planning to do in Los Angeles?"

"I don't know. He told me this story, when he was trying to talk me out of the car, but I didn't believe it. He said he was doing undercover work. I heard the same story from him before, when he was working in a drive-in on Camino Real. He claimed the cops were paying him to give them tips."

"Tips about what?"

"Kids smoking reefers, stuff like that. I didn't know whether to believe him or not. I thought maybe he was just talking to make himself feel important. He always wanted to be a cop himself."

"But his record wouldn't let him."

"He has no record."

"You said he had."

"You must have been hearing things. Anyway, I'm getting tired. I've had enough of this."

She rose in a sudden thrust of energy and stood by the door, inviting me to leave. I stayed where I was on the plastic chesterfield.

"You might as well leave," she said. "It isn't Ralph you saw in Malibu."

"I'm not so sure of that."

"You can take my word."

"All right, I take your word." It doesn't pay to argue with a source of information. "But I'm still interested in Ralph. Aren't you?"

"Naturally I am. I'm married to him. At least I'm supposed to be married to him. But I got a funny feeling, here." Her left hand moved up her body to her breast. "I got a feeling he traded me in on a new model, and *that's* the undercover work."

"Do you know who the other woman might be?"

"No. I just got a feeling. Why would a man go away and not come back?"

I could think of various answers to that, but I didn't see much point in spelling them out. "When Ralph took the bus south, did he say anything about going to Mexico?"

"Not to me he didn't."

"Has he ever been there?"

"I don't think so. He would of told me if he had."

"Did he ever talk about leaving the country?"

"Not lately. He used to talk about going back to Japan someday. He spent some time there in the Korean War. Wait a minute, though. He took his birth certificate with him, I think. That could mean he was planning to leave the States, couldn't it?"

"It could. He took his birth certificate to Los Angeles?"

"I guess he did, but it was a couple of weeks before that he had me looking for it. It took me hours to find it. He wanted to take it along to Nevada with him. He said he needed it to apply for a job."

"What kind of a job?"

"He didn't say. He was probably stringing me, anyway." She moved restlessly and stood over me. "You think he left the country?"

Before I could answer her, a telephone rang in another part of the house. She stiffened, and walked quickly out of the room. I heard her voice: "This is Vicky Simpson speaking."

There was a long pause.

"I don't believe it," she said.

Another pause.

"It can't be him," she said. "He can't be dead."

I followed the fading sound of her voice into the kitchen. She was

leaning on the yellow formica breakfast bar, holding the receiver
away from her head as if it was a dangerous yellow bird. The pupils
of her eyes had expanded and made her look blind.

"Who is it, Mrs. Simpson?"

Her lips moved, groping for words. "A caw—a policeman down
south. He says Ralph is dead. He can't be."

"Let me talk to the man."

She handed me the receiver. I said into the mouthpiece: "This is
Lew Archer. I'm a licensed private detective working in co-operation
with the Los Angeles District Attorney's office."

"We had a query from them this evening." The man's voice was
slow and uncertain. "We had this body on our hands, unidentified.
Their chief investigator called—fellow named Colton, maybe you
know him."

"I know him. Who am I talking to?"

"Leonard, Sergeant Wesley Leonard. I do the identification work
for the sheriff's department here in Citrus County. We use the L.A.
facilities all the time, and we had already asked for their help on this
body. Mr. Colton wanted to know if maybe it was this certain Ralph
Simpson who is missing. We must have mislaid the original missing
report," he added apologetically, "or maybe we never got it in the
first place."

"It happens all the time."

"Yeah. Anyway, we're trying to get a positive identification.
What's the chances of Mrs. Simpson coming down here?"

"Pretty good, I think. Does the body fit the description?"

"It fits all right. Height and weight and coloring and estimated
age, all the same."

"How did he die?"

"That's a little hard to say. He got pretty banged up when the
bulldozer rooted him out."

"A bulldozer rooted him out?"

"I'll explain. They're putting in this new freeway at the west end
of town. Quite a few houses got condemned to the state, they were
standing vacant you know, and this poor guy was buried in back of
one of them. He wasn't buried very deep. A 'dozer snagged him and
brought him up when they razed the houses last week."

"How long dead?"

"A couple of months, the doc thinks. It's been dry, and he's in pretty fair condition. The important thing is who he is. How soon can Mrs. Simpson get down here?"

"Tonight, if I can get her on a plane."

"Swell. Ask for me at the courthouse in Citrus Junction. Sergeant Wesley Leonard."

She said when I hung up: "Oh no you don't, I'm staying here."

She retreated across the kitchen, shocked and stumbling, and stood in a corner beside the refrigerator.

"Ralph may be dead, Vicky."

"I don't believe it. I don't want to see him if he is."

"Somebody has to identify him."

"*You* identify him."

"I don't know him. You do."

Her mascara had started to dissolve. She dashed murky tears from her eyes. "I don't *want* to see him dead. I never saw anybody dead before."

"Dead people won't hurt you. It's the live ones that hurt you."

I touched her goosefleshed arm. She jerked it away from me.

"You'll feel better if you have a drink," I said. "Do you have anything to drink in the house?"

"I don't drink."

I opened a cupboard and found a glass and filled it at the tap. Some of it spilled down her chin. She scrubbed at it angrily with a dish towel.

"I don't want to go. It'll only make me sick."

But after a while she agreed to get ready while I phoned the coastal airlines. There was room for us on a ten-thirty flight to Los Angeles. By midnight we were approaching Citrus Junction in the car I had left at International Airport.

The road was walled on each side by thick orange groves. It emerged into a desolate area rimmed with houses, where highway construction had been under way. Earth movers hulked in the darkness like sleeping saurians.

The road became the main street of the town. It was a back-country town, in spite of its proximity to Los Angeles. Everything was closed for the night, except for a couple of bars. A few men in working clothes wandered along the empty pavements, staggering under the twin burdens of alcohol and loneliness.

"I don't like it here," Vicky said. "It looks like hicksville."

"You won't have to stay long."

"How long? I'm stony until payday."

"The police will probably make arrangements for you. Let's wait and see how it falls."

The metal cupola of the courthouse swelled like a tarnished bubble under the stars. The building's dark interior smelled mustily of human lives, like the inside of an old trunk. I found the duty deputy in an office on the first floor. He told me that Sergeant Leonard was at the mortuary, just around the corner.

It was a three-storied white colonial building with a sign on the lawn in front of it: "Norton's Funeral Parlors." Vicky hung back when we got out of the car. I took her arm and walked her down a hall through the odor of carnations to a lighted doorway at the end of the hall and through it into the odor of formaldehyde.

She dragged on my arm. "I can't go through with it."

"You have to. It may not be Ralph."

"Then what am I doing here?"

"It may be Ralph."

She looked wildly around the room. It was bare except for a grey coffin standing on trestles against the wall.

"Is he in that?"

"No. Get yourself under control, Vicky. It will only take a minute and then it will be over."

"But what am I going to do afterward?"

It was a question I couldn't attempt to answer. A further door opened, and a deputy with sergeant's stripes on his arm came through toward us. He was a middle-aged man with a belly overlapping his gunbelt, and slow friendly eyes that went with his voice on the telephone.

"I'm Leonard."

"Archer. This is Mrs. Simpson."

He bowed with exaggerated courtliness. "I'm pleased to know you, ma'am. It was good of you to make the journey."

"I had to, I guess. Where is he?"

"The doctor's working on him."

"You mean he's still *alive?*"

"He's long dead, ma'am. I'm sorry. Dr. White is working on his internal organs, trying to find out what killed him."

She started to sit down on the floor. I caught her under the arms.

Leonard and I helped her into an adjoining room where a night light burned and the smell of carnations was strong. She half lay on an upholstered settee, with her spike heels tucked under her.

"If you don't mind waiting a little, ma'am, Doc White will get him ready for your inspection." Leonard's voice had taken on unctuous intonations from the surroundings. He hovered over her. "Maybe I could get you a drink. What would you like to drink?"

"Embalming fluid."

He made a shocked noise at the back of his palate.

"Just go away and leave me alone. I'm all right."

I followed Leonard into the autopsy room. The dead man lay on an enameled table. I won't describe him. His time in the earth, and on the table, had altered him for the worse. He bore no great resemblance to Burke Damis, and never had.

Dr. White was closing a butterfly incision in the body. His rubber-gloved hands looked like artificial hands. He was a bald-headed man with hound jowls drooping from under a tobacco-stained mustache. He had a burning cigarette in his mouth, and wagged his head slowly from side to side to keep the smoke out of his eyes. The smoke coiled and drifted in the brilliant overhead light.

I waited until he had finished what he was doing and had drawn a rubberized sheet up to the dead man's chin.

"What did you find out, Doctor?"

"Heart puncture, in the left ventricle. Looks like an icepick wound." He stripped off his rubber gloves and moved to the sink, saying above the noise of running water: "Those contusions on the head were inflicted after death, in my opinion—a long time after death."

"By the bulldozer?"

"I assume so."

"Just when was he dug up?"

"Friday, wasn't it, Wesley?"

The Sergeant nodded. "Friday afternoon."

"Did you make a preliminary examination then?"

Dr. White turned from the sink, drying his hands and arms. "None was ordered. The D.A. and the Sheriff, who's also Coroner, are both in Sacramento at a convention."

"Besides," Leonard put in, eager to save face, "the icepick wound didn't show from the outside hardly at all. It was just a little nick under the left breast."

It wasn't for me to tell them their business. I wanted co-operation. "Did you find the icepick?"

Leonard spread his hands loosely. "You couldn't find anything out there after the 'dozers went through. Maybe you saw the mess on your way into town?"

"I saw it. Are you ready for Mrs. Simpson now?"

I was talking to the doctor and the Sergeant, but the question hung in the air as though it belonged to the dead man on the table. I even had a feeling that he might answer me. The room was getting me down.

I brought Vicky Simpson into it. The time by herself had calmed her. She had strength enough to walk across the room and stand by the table and look down at the ruined head for a minute, for minutes on end.

"It's him. It's Ralph."

She proved it by stroking his dusty hair.

She looked up at Leonard. "What happened to him?"

"He was icepicked, ma'am, a couple of months ago."

"You mean he's been dead all this time?"

"A couple of months."

The two months of waiting seemed to rush across her eyes like dizzy film. She turned blindly. I took her back to the room where the night light burned.

"Do you know who killed him, Vicky?"

"How would I know? I've never even been in Citrus Junction—is that what they call this hole?"

"You mentioned that Ralph was paid by the police to gather information."

"That's what he said. I don't know if it was true or not. Anyway, it was a long time ago."

"Did Ralph have criminal connections?"

"No. He wasn't that kind of a man."

"You said he had a record."

She shook her head.

"You might as well tell me, Vicky. It can't hurt him now."

"It didn't amount to anything," she said. "He was just a kid. He got in with a bad crowd in high school and they got caught smoking reefers one time and they all got sent to Juvie. That was all the record Ralph had."

"You're certain?"

"I'm not lying."

"Did he ever speak of a man named Burke Damis?"

"Burke Damis?"

"Damis is the man I met in Malibu, the one I described to you. He's an artist, a painter, who apparently has been using your husband's name."

"Why would he do that?"

"Perhaps because he's ashamed of his own name. I believe he used Ralph's name to cross the border from Mexico last week. You're sure the name Burke Damis rings no bell?"

"I'm sure."

"And you don't recognize the description?"

"No. At this point I wouldn't recognize my own brother if he walked in the door. Aren't you ever going to leave me alone?"

Leonard came into the room. I suspected that he had been listening outside the door, and chose this moment to break up the interview. He was a kind man, and he said that he and his wife would look after Vicky for the balance of the night.

I drove him to Los Angeles, home to a hot shower and a cold drink and a dark bed.

>>>>>>>>>
>>>>>>>>> *chapter* 8
>>>>>>>>>

I HAD A DREAM which I'd been dreaming in variant forms for as long as I could remember. I was back in high school, in my senior year. The girl at the next desk smiled at me snootily.

"Poor Lew. You'll fail the exams."

I had to admit to myself that this was likely. The finals loomed up ahead like the impossible slopes of purgatory, guarded by men with books I hadn't read.

"*I'm* going to college," she said. "What are you going to do?"

I had no idea. I knew with a part of my dreaming mind that I was a grown man in my forties. There wasn't anything more that high school could do to me. Yet here I was, back in Mr. Merritt's classroom, dreading the finals and wondering what I would do when I had failed them.

"You'll have to learn a trade," the snooty one said.

So far it was more or less the dream I had always had. Then something different happened. I said to the girl, rather snootily: "I have a trade, kiddo. I'm a detective. You'll be reading about me in the papers."

I woke up with a warm feeling in my chest and the small birds peeping outside the pale grey rectangle of the window. The dream had never ended this way before. Did it mean that I had made it? That didn't seem likely. You went on making it, or trying to, all your life—working your way up the same old terraced slopes with different street names on them.

The Blackwell case came back on my mind, muffling the bird sounds and draining the last of the warm feeling from my chest. There were two cases, really. One belonged to me and one belonged to the authorities, but they were connected. The link between them was small but definite: the airline envelope with Q. R. Simpson's name on it which Burke Damis, or possibly someone else, had left in the beach house. I wanted to explore the connection further, without too much interference from the police. The possibility existed that Damis had come by the envelope, or even used the name, quite innocently.

It was broad daylight and the birds had finished their matins when I went back to sleep. I slept late into the morning. Perhaps I was hoping for another good dream. More likely I was fixing my schedule so that I wouldn't have time to report in to Peter Colton.

I had become a great frequenter of airports. Before I set out this time, I dug my birth certificate out of the strongbox in the bedroom closet. I had no definite plan to use it. I just thought it would be nice to have along.

The polite young man at the Mexicana desk greeted me like a long-lost brother. The crew I was interested in had already checked in for their flight, and the steward and stewardess had gone up to the restaurant for coffee. He was tall and dark; she was short and plump and pretty, with red hair. They both had on Mexicana uniforms, and I surely couldn't miss them.

I picked them out in the murmurous cavern of the restaurant, hunched over coffee cups at one of the long counters. The girl had an empty stool beside her, and I slid onto it. She was certainly pretty, though the red hair that curled from under her overseas-type cap had been dyed. She had melting dark eyes and a stung-cherry mouth. Like American airline hostesses, she had on enough make-up to go on the stage.

She was talking in Spanish with the steward, and I waited for a pause in their conversation.

"Miss Gomez?"

"Yessir, what can I do for you?" she said in a pleasantly accented voice.

"I'm looking for a little information. A week ago yesterday, a man and woman I know took your flight from Guadalajara to Los Angeles. That was Monday, July the tenth. You may remember them, or one of them. The woman is quite tall, about your age, blonde. She often wears dark glasses, and she probably had on expensive clothes. Her name is Harriet Blackwell."

She nodded her head emphatically. "I remember Miss Blackwell, yes—a very nice lady. The lady across from her was sick—we had some rough air out of Mazatlán—and she took care of the sick lady's baby for her." She said to the steward beside her: "You remember the tall lady who was so nice with the baby?"

"Sí."

"Is Miss Blackwell all right?" she asked me solicitously.

"I think so. Why do you ask?"

"I thought of her afterward, after we landed. And now you are inquiring about her."

"What did you think about her after you landed?"

"I thought—do you speak Spanish? I express myself better in Spanish."

"Your English is ten times better than my Spanish will ever be."

"Gracias, señor." She gave me a full dazzling smile. "Well, I saw her after we landed, going through Customs. She looked very—excited. I thought she was going to faint. I approached her and inquired if she was all right. The man with her said that she was all right. He didn't like—he didn't want me asking questions, so I went away."

"Can you describe the man?"

"Yes." She described Burke Damis. "A very beautiful young man," she added with a trace of satire in her voice.

"What was his name?"

"I don't remember."

She turned to her companion and spoke in rapid Spanish. He shrugged. He didn't remember either.

"Who would know?"

"You, perhaps," she said pertly. "You said they were your friends."

"I said I knew them."

"I see. Are they in trouble?"

"That's an interesting question. What brings it up?"

"You," she said. "You look like trouble for them."

"For him, not for her. Did they sit together on the plane?"

"Yes. They embarked together at Guadalajara. I noticed them, I thought they were *recién casados*—honeymooners. But they had different names."

"What was his name?"

"I said I don't remember. If I can find the passenger list—"

"Try and do that, will you?"

"You are a policeman?"

"An investigator."

"I see. Where will I see you?"

"On the plane, if they have a seat for me." I looked at my watch. I had half an hour till flight time.

"We are never crowded in the middle of the week."

She turned out to be right. I bought a return ticket to Guadalajara from my courteous friend, leaving the date of my return open. At another desk in the same building I applied for a Mexican tourist card. The hurried clerk who took my application barely glanced at my birth certificate.

"I'll type up your card *pronto*. Your plane will take off soon."

In the time I had left, I made the necessary call to Colonel Blackwell. He picked up the pnone on the first ring, as if he had been waiting there beside it.

"Mark Blackwell speaking."

"This is Archer. Have you heard anything from Harriet?"

"No. I don't expect to." His voice rose shakily from the depths of depression. "You haven't either, I take it."

"No. I have been busy on the case. It took me to the Bay area last night."

"Is that where they've gone?"

"It's possible, but it's not why I went up there. To make a long story short, I stumbled on a murder which Damis may be involved in."

"A murder?" His voice sank almost out of hearing. He said in a rustling whisper: "You're not trying to tell me that Harriet has been murdered?"

"No. It's a man named Simpson, icepicked in Citrus Junction two months ago. I'm trying to trace his connection with Damis, and get a line on Damis's identity and background. The next logical step, as I see it, is to go back to the point where Harriet met him and work forward from there. If it's all right with you, I intend to fly down to Mexico."

There was a long silence on the line. Outside the telephone booth, I could hear my flight being announced over the loudspeakers.

"Are you there, Colonel?"

"I'm here. You're planning to go to Mexico, you say. When?"

"In about five minutes. It's going to cost you a couple of hundred dollars—"

"Money is no object. By all means go if you think it will help."

"I can't guarantee any results, but it's worth trying. Can you give me your ex-wife's address in Ajijic?"

"She doesn't have an address. But any member of the American community should be able to tell you where she lives. Pauline was never one to hide her light under a bushel."

"Her last name is Hatchen?"

"That is correct. Good luck." He sounded as though his own had run out.

The plane was barely half full. I had a window seat over the left wing. As the redheaded stewardess placed me in it, I noticed that she looked at me in a peculiar way.

The broken jigsaw of Los Angeles tilted and drifted backward into brownish smog. When the plane had leveled out at cruising altitude, the stewardess slipped into the empty seat beside me. She held a folded newspaper in the hand away from me. Under the make-up, her color wasn't good.

"I found the seating chart for July—July ten. The man with Miss Blackwell, his name was Simpson, Q. R. Simpson."

"I thought so."

"You thought so?" Her look was accusing. "Why didn't you tell me, then, that Señor Simpson is dead?"

"I wasn't aware of it." It was a half truth, or a half lie, according to which version of Simpson we were talking about. "How do you know he is, Miss Gomez?"

She held the morning *Times* under my nose, jabbing the late bulletins at the bottom of the front page with a chipped carmine fingernail.

"Slain Man Identified," one of the items said.

The body of Quincy R. Simpson, found icepicked in a shallow grave in Citrus Junction last Friday, was positively identified late last night by his widow. The victim, missing for the past two months, was a resident of San Mateo County. Police suspect a gang killing, according to Sergeant Wesley Leonard of the Citrus County Sheriff's office.

"You see," Miss Gomez insisted, "he is dead. Murdered."

"I see."

"You said you are an investigator. Are you investigating his murder?"

"It's beginning to look like it, isn't it?"

"And you suspect someone from Mexico?" she said in a nationalistic way.

"Someone from the United States."

This relieved her, but not for long. "Poor Miss Blackwell, she was so crazy about him. All the time, even when she was holding the lady's baby, she kept looking at him like"—she searched for a phrase —"like he was a saint."

"He was no saint."

"Was he a *rufian*—a gangster?"

"I doubt it."

"It says in the paper that it was a gang killing."

"Gangsters kill citizens, too."

She wrinkled her dark brows over this idea. The doubleness of the conversation was getting on my nerves; or perhaps it was the doubleness of my attitude toward Damis. In spite of the evidence tightening around him, I was trying to keep an open mind.

I was glad when the girl went to attend to her duties. She stayed away. When she passed me in the aisle, she carefully avoided meeting my eyes. I think she was afraid of the contagion I carried from Simpson's death.

We were flying over the sea within sight of land. The air was perfectly transparent. Baja California passed under the wing like the endless harsh shores of hell, its desolation unbroken by tree or house or human being.

As the sun declined, the shadows of the yellow hills lengthened into the dry valleys. The first green and brown checkerboard of cultivated fields came as a relief to the eye and the mind. The desolation didn't go on forever.

Miss Gomez unbent a little when she brought me my dinner. "Are you enjoying the flight, sir?"

I said yes.

We circled in over Mazatlán in a red sunset. The three rocky islands offshore jutted up angrily out of a streaked purple sea. A single freighter lay in the harbor with the fishing boats. At the other end of the town, beyond the airport where we landed, new apartment buildings stood along the sea like a miniature Copacabana.

We were herded into the terminal building, to have our tourist cards checked, it was explained. A boy was selling, or trying to sell, costumed puppets which he manipulated on a string. His bare arms were almost as thin as the wooden arms of his dolls.

The line of passengers moved forward slowly in steamy heat. I got my turn at the battered rostrumlike desk where a man in an open-necked white shirt presided. He had pockmarks on his face, and they gave special emphasis to his question: *"Certificado de vacunacion, señor?"*

I had none. No one had told me. That was a silly thing to say, but I said it. He leaned toward me not so much in anger as in sorrow.

"You must have the *vacunacion*. I cannot permit you to enter—"

"How do I get one?"

"They will vacunate you *ahora*, now, here."

He summoned an attendant in olive whipcord who escorted me to an office at the far end of the building. A dark and dumpy woman in white was waiting at the desk with a maternal smile. The white masonry wall behind her had jagged cracks in it.

"Vaccination?"

"I'm afraid so."

She took my name and home address on a filing card. "Don't worry, it won't hurt, I never hurt 'em. Jacket off and roll up your left sleeve, please."

She struck my arm smartly as the needle went in.

"You took it well," she said. "Some of them keel over."

"You speak good English."

"Why not? I was a nurse's aide in Fresno six years before I went into training. I got a married daughter in Los Angeles. You can roll down your sleeve now. You'll probably have a reaction by tomorrow."

I buttoned the cuff of my shirt and put on my jacket. "Do you give many of these impromptu vaccinations?"

"Two or three a day, at least, since the government clamped down. People are always forgetting their certificates, or else they didn't get the word in the first place. They process so many at the L.A. airport that they get careless."

I said, on the off-chance of learning something: "A man I know passed through here from L.A. some time in the last two months. I'm wondering if you had to vaccinate him."

"What does he look like?"

I described Burke Damis.

She twisted her mouth to one side. "I think I do remember him. He had big fat biceps, like yours. But he didn't like the needle. He tried to talk himself out of it."

"When was this?"

"I couldn't say exactly. A couple of months ago, like you said. I could look it up if you'll give me his name."

"Quincy Ralph Simpson."

She opened one of the desk drawers, went through a filing box of cards, and picked out one of them.

"*Here* it is, Simpson. I gave him his shot on May twenty."

It meant that Burke Damis had entered Mexico two days after the original Simpson left home for the last time. It probably meant that

Simpson had been murdered between May 18 and May 20, more likely than not by the man who had stolen his name.

"A very nice-appearing young man," the woman was saying. "We had a nice chat after we got the vaccination out of the way."

"Chat about what?"

"My daughter in Los Angeles. And he wanted to know if that was earthquake damage." She waved her hand toward the cracks in the masonry.

"I was asking myself the same thing."

"It was no earthquake. The hurricane did it. It practically tore out the whole end of the building. You'd never know it was built in the last ten years."

The man in the whipcord uniform came back. He had two more victims with him, a young couple who were explaining that they had been assured that these formalities could be taken care of when they got to Mexico City. The nurse smiled at them maternally.

>>>>>>>>>
>>>>>>>>> *chapter* 9
>>>>>>>>>

IT WAS RAINING HARD when we put down at Guadalajara, as if our descent had ruptured a membrane in the lower sky. In spite of the newspaper tent I held over my head, the short walk from the plane to the terminal pasted my clothes to my back.

I exchanged some damp dollars for some dry pesos and asked the cashier to get me an English-speaking taxi driver, if possible. The porter he dispatched reappeared with a man in a plastic raincoat who grinned at me from under his dripping mustache.

"Yessir, where you want to go?"

"Ajijic, if they have a hotel there."

"Yessir, they have a very nice *posada*."

He led me across the many-puddled parking lot to a fairly new Simca sedan. I climbed squishing into the front seat.

"Wet night."

"Yessir."

He drove me through it for half an hour, entertaining me with fragments of autobiography. Like the nurse who had vaccinated me in Mazatlán, he had learned his English in the Central Valley.

"I was a wetback," he said with some pride. "Three times I walked across the border. Two times they picked me up on the other side and hauled me back on a bus. The third time, I made it, all the way to Merced. I worked around Merced for four years, in the fields. You know Merced?"

"I know it. How were working conditions?"

"Not so good. But the pay, it was very good. I made enough to come back home and go into business." He slapped the wheel of his Simca.

We emerged from between steep black hills onto a lakeshore road. I caught pale glimpses of ruffled water. A herd of burros crossed the headlights and galloped away into darkness. Through the streaming windshield they looked like the grey and shrunken ghosts of horses.

Church towers, buttressed by other buildings, rose from the darkness ahead. The rain was letting up, and had stopped by the time we reached the village. Though it was past ten o'clock, children swarmed in the doorways. Their elders were promenading in the steep cobbled streets, which had drained already.

At the corner of the central square an old woman in a shawl had set up a wooden table on the sidewalk. She was serving some kind of stew out of a pot, and I caught a whiff of it as we went by. It had a heady pungency, an indescribable smell which aroused no memories; expectation, maybe, and a smattering of doubt. The smell of Mexico.

I felt closer to home when we reached the *posada*. The night clerk was a big middle-aged American named Stacy, and he was glad to see me. The pillared lobby of the place had a deserted air. Stacy and I and my driver, who was waiting for me just inside the entrance, were the only human beings within sight or sound.

Stacy fussed over me like somebody trying to give the impression that he was more than one person. "I can certainly fix you up, Mr. Archer. I can give you your choice of several nice private cottages."

"Any one of them will do. I think I'll only be staying one night."

He looked disappointed. "I'll send out the *mozo* for your luggage."

"I have no luggage."

"But you're all *wet*, man."

"I know. Luckily this is a drip-dry suit."

"You can't let it dry right on you." He clucked sympathetically. "Listen, you're about my size. I'll lend you some slacks and a sweater if you like. Unless you're thinking of going right to bed."

"I wasn't intending to. You're very kind."

"Anything for a fellow American," he said in a mocking tone which was half serious after all.

He took me through a wet garden to my cottage. It was clean and roomy; a fire was laid in the fireplace. He left me with instructions to use the bottled water, even for cleaning my teeth. I lit the fire and hung up my wet suit on a wall bracket above the mantel.

Stacy came back after a while with an armful of dry clothes. His large rubbery face was flushed with generosity and a meantime drink. The flannel slacks he gave me were big in the waist. I cinched them in with my belt and pulled on his blue turtleneck sweater. It had a big monogrammed "S" like a target over the heart, and it smelled of the kind of piny scent they foist off on men who want to smell masculine.

"You look very nice," Stacy declared.

He stood and watched me in wistful empathy. Perhaps he saw himself with ten pounds shifted from his waistline to his shoulders, and ten lost years regained. He got a bit flustered when I told him I was going out. He may have been looking forward to an intimate conversation by the fire: *And what is your philosophy of life?*

Keep moving, amigo.

Stacy knew where the Hatchens lived, and passed the word in rapid Spanish to my driver. We drove to a nameless street. The only sign at the corner had been painted on a wall by an amateur hand: *"Cristianismo sí, Comunismo no."* A church tower rose on the far side of the wall.

The Hatchens' gate was closed for the night. I knocked for some time before I got a response. My knocking wasn't the only sound in the neighborhood. Up the street a radio was going full blast; hoofs clip-clopped; a burro laughed grotesquely in the darkness; the bell in the church tower rang the three-quarter hour and then repeated it for those who were hard of hearing; a pig squealed.

A man opened the upper half of the wicket gate and flashed a bright light in my face. *"Quien es?* Are you American?"

"Yes. My name is Archer. You're Mr. Hatchen?"

"Dr. Hatchen. I don't know you, do I? Is there some trouble?"

"Nothing immediate. Back in the States, your wife's daughter, Harriet, has run off with a young man named Burke Damis whom you may know. I came here to investigate him for Colonel Blackwell. Are you and Mrs. Hatchen willing to talk to me?"

"I suppose we can't refuse. Come back in the morning, eh?"

"I may not be here in the morning. If you'll give me a little time tonight, I'll try to make it short."

"All right."

I paid off my driver as Hatchen was opening the lower gate. He led me up a brick walk through an enclosed garden. The flashlight beam jumped along in front of us across the uneven bricks. He was a thin aging man who walked with great strenuosity.

He paused under an outside light before we entered the house. "Just what do you mean when you say Harriet's run off with Damis?"

"She intends to marry him."

"Is that bad?"

"It depends on what I find out about him. I've already come across some dubious things."

"For instance?" He had a sharp wizened face in which the eyes were bright and quick.

"Apparently he came here under an alias."

"That's not unusual. The Chapala woods are full of people living incognito. But come in. My wife will be interested."

He turned on a light in a screened portico and directed me through it to a further room. A woman was sitting there on a couch in an attitude of conscious elegance. Masses of blondish hair were arranged precariously on her head. Her black formal gown accentuated the white puffiness of her shoulders. The classic lines of her chin and throat were a little blurred by time.

"This is Mr. Archer, Pauline. My wife," Hatchen said proudly.

She took my hand with the air of a displaced queen and held onto it in a subtle kind of Indian wrestling until I was sitting beside her on the couch.

"Sit down," she said unnecessarily. "To what do we owe the pleasure?"

"Mr. Archer is an emissary from dear old Mark."

"How fascinating. And what has dear old Mark been up to now?

Wait, don't tell me. Let me guess." She held a forefinger upright in front of her nose. "He's worried about Harriet."

"You're a good guesser, Mrs. Hatchen."

She smiled thinly. "It's the same old story. He's always brooded over her like a father hen."

"Mother hen," Hatchen said.

"*Father* hen."

"At any rate, she's run off and married that Damis chap," he said.

"I'm not surprised. I'm glad she had it in her. All Harriet ever needed was a little of her mother's spirit and fortitude. Speaking of spirits, Mr. Archer"—she waved her finger—"Keith and I were just about to have a nightcap. Won't you join us?"

Hatchen looked at her brightly. He was still on his feet in the middle of the room. "You've had your ration, dear one. You know what the doctor said."

"The doctor's in Guad and I'm here."

"I'm here, too."

"So be a sport and get us all a drink. You know what I like."

He shrugged and turned to me. "What will you have?"

"Whisky?"

"I can't recommend the whisky. The gin's okay."

"Gin and tonic will be fine."

He left the room with a nervous glance at his wife, as if she might be contemplating elopement. She turned the full panoply of her charm on me.

"I know you must think I'm a strange sort of mother, totally unconcerned with my daughter's welfare and so on. The fact is I'm a kind of refugee. I escaped from Mark and his ménage long long ago. I haven't even seen him for thirteen years, and for once that's a lucky number. I turned over a fresh page and started a new chapter—a chapter dedicated to love and freedom." Romanticism soughed in her voice like a loosely strung Aeolian harp.

"It isn't entirely clear to me why you left him."

She took the implied question as a matter of course. "The marriage was a mistake. We had really very little in common. I love movement and excitement, interesting people, people with a sense of life." She looked at me sideways. "You seem to be a man with a sense of life. I'm surprised that you should be a friend of Mark's. He used to spend his spare time doing research on the Blackwell gene-alogy."

"I didn't say I was friend of Mark's."

"But I understood he sent you here."

"I'm a private detective, Mrs. Hatchen. He hired me to look into Damis's background. I was hoping you could give me some assist-ance."

"I barely knew the fellow. Though I sensed from the beginning that Harriet was smitten with him."

"When was the beginning?"

"A few days after she got here. She came a little over a month ago. I was really glad to see her." She sounded surprised. "A little disap-pointed, perhaps, but glad."

"Why disappointed?"

"I had various reasons. I'd always sort of hoped that she'd outgrow her ugly-duckling phase, and she did to some extent, of course. After all she is my daughter." Her active forefinger went to her brow and moved down her nose to her mouth and chin, which she tilted up. "And I was disappointed that we didn't really have anything in com-mon. She didn't take to our friends or our way of life. We did our best to make her comfortable, but she moved out before the end of the first week."

"And moved in with Damis?"

"Harriet wouldn't do that. She's quite a conventional girl. She rented a studio down near the lake. I think he had one somewhere in the neighborhood. I have no doubt they spent a lot of time together. More power to them, I thought."

"Did you know Burke Damis before she met him?"

"No, and she didn't meet him in our *casa*. We'd seen him around, of course, but we'd never met him till Harriet introduced him. That was a few days after she got here, as I said."

"Where did you see him around?"

"At the *Cantina* mostly. I think that's where Harriet picked—where Harriet met him. A lot of arty young people hang out there, or used to."

"You saw him there before she met him?"

"Oh, yes, several times. He's rather conspicuously good-looking, don't you think?"

"Was he using the name Burke Damis?"

"I suppose so. You could always ask the *Cantina* people. It's just down the street."

"I'll do that. Before Harriet arrived, did Damis ever try to contact you?"

"Never. We didn't know him from Adam." Her eyes narrowed. "Is Mark trying to pin the blame on me for something?"

"No, but it occurred to me that Damis might have had her spotted before she got here."

"Spotted?"

"As a girl with money behind her."

"He didn't learn it from us, if that's what you're thinking."

"And there was nothing to show that he deliberately planned to meet her?"

"I doubt it. He picked her up in the *Cantina* and she was dazzled with gratitude, poor girl."

"Why do you say 'poor girl'?"

"I've always felt that way about Harriet. She had a rough deal, from both of us. I realize I appear to be a selfish woman, leaving her and Mark when she was just a child. But I had no choice if I wanted to save my soul."

I sat there wondering if she had saved it and waiting for her to elaborate. Her eyes had the hardness that comes from seeing too many changes and not being changed by them.

"To make a long story short, and a sordid one, I moved into the Tahoe house and got a Reno divorce. I didn't want to do it. It broke my heart to turn my back on Harriet. But she was very much her father's daughter. There was nothing I could do to break that up, short of murder. And don't think I haven't contemplated murder. But a Nevada divorce seemed more civilized. Keith"—she gestured toward the kitchen, where ice was being picked—"Keith was in Nevada on the same errand. What's keeping him out there so long?"

"He may be giving us a chance to talk."

"Yes, he's a very thoughtful man. I've been very happy with Keith, don't think I haven't." There was a hint of defiance in her voice. "On the other hand, don't think I haven't felt guilty about my daughter. When she visited us last month the old guilt feelings came back. It was so obvious that she wanted—that she needed something from me. Something I couldn't give, and if I could, she couldn't have taken it. She still blamed me for deserting her, as she put it. I tried to explain, but she wouldn't listen to any criticism of her father. He's always dominated her every thought. She went into hysterics, and so did I, I suppose. We quarreled, and she moved out on *me*."

"It looks as though that made her ripe for Damis. I've known other men like him. They prey on girls and women who step outside the protection of their families."

"You make him sound like a very devious type."

"He's devious. Does the name Q. R. Simpson mean anything to you? Quincy Ralph Simpson?"

She shook her head and her hairdo slipped. It made her entire personality seem held in place by pins. "Should I know the name?"

"I didn't really expect you to."

"What name?" her husband said from the doorway. He came in carrying a hammered brass tray with three pale drinks placed geometrically on it.

"The name that Burke Damis used to cross the border, coming and going. Quincy Ralph Simpson."

"I've never heard it."

"You will if you take the California papers."

"But we don't." He passed the drinks around with a flourish. "We are happy fugitives from the California papers, and from nuclear bombs and income taxes—"

"And the high cost of liquor," his wife chimed in like the other half of a vaudeville team.

"This gin costs me forty American cents a liter," he said, "and I don't believe you can top it at any price. Well, *salud*." He lifted his glass.

I drank from mine. The gin was all right, but it failed to warm me. There was something cold and lost about the room and the people in it. They had roosted like migrant birds that had lost their homing instincts, caught in a dream of perpetual static flight. Or so it seemed through the bottom of my glass.

I set it down and got up. Hatchen rose, too.

"What was that about this man Simpson and the newspapers?"

"Simpson was stabbed with an icepick a couple of months ago. His body was found last week."

"And you say Damis was using his name?"

"Yes."

"Is he suspected of Simpson's murder?"

"Yes. By me."

"Poor Harriet," Mrs. Hatchen said over her drink.

>>>>>>>>>
>>>>>>>>> *chapter* 10
>>>>>>>>>

THE *Cantina* had several interconnected public rooms, and looked as though it had once been a private house. At eleven-thirty on this Tuesday night it had just about reverted to privacy. A single drinker, a big man with streaked yellow hair that hung down to his collar, sat in a corner behind the deserted bandstand. There was no one else in the place.

A number of small oil paintings hung on the walls. Their blobs and blocks and whorls and scatterations reminded me of the shapes that dissolve on the retina between sleeping and waking. I felt that I was getting closer to Burke Damis, and I moved from picture to picture looking for his style or his signature.

"*Las pinturas,* they are for sale, señor," a mild voice said behind me.

It belonged to a Mexican youth in a waiter's apron. He had a broken nose and a mouth that had been hurt both physically and morally. Intelligence burned like fever in his black eyes.

"Sorry, I don't buy pictures."

"Nobody buys them. No more. 'Quoth the Raven, "Nevermore." ' "

"You read Poe?"

"In school, señor," he said smiling. " 'My beautiful Annabel Lee, . . . in this kingdom by the sea.' I studied to be a professor but my father lost his nets, I had to give it up. There is very little money, and work is not easy to find. Tourism is slow this summer."

"Why?"

He shrugged. "Who understands the migration of the birds? I only know it is hard to make an honest living. I tried boxing, but it is not for me." He touched his nose.

His story had come fast and slick, and I was expecting a touch. I liked him anyway. His battered face had an incandescence, as if the scattered lights of the dark town had gathered and were burning in him. "Something to drink, señor?"

"I guess a beer."

"Dark or light?"

"Light."

"*Bueno,* we have no dark. We have three bottles of light beer, one *litro* of tequila, and no ice. The beer is cold, however. I borrowed it."

Smiling intensely, he went into a side room and came back with a bottle and a glass. He poured the contents of the one into the other.

"You pour beer well."

"Yessir. Also I can make martinis, margueritas, any kind of drink. I work at parties sometimes, which is how I speak English so good. Please to tell your friends, when they need a first-class *cantinero,* José Perez of the *Cantina* is at your service."

"I'm afraid I have no friends in these parts."

"You are a tourist?"

"Sort of. I'm just passing through."

"An artist, *por ventura?*" he said with an eye on Stacy's sweater. "We used to have many artists here. My boss himself is an artist." He glanced across the room to the solitary drinker in the corner.

"I'd like to talk to him."

"I will tell him, señor."

José darted across the room and said something in Spanish to the long-haired man. He picked up his drink and plodded toward me as if the room was hip-deep in water, or eye-deep in tequila. A woven belt with an amethyst-studded silver buckle divided his globular stomach into two hemispheres.

"Aha," he said. "I spy with my little eye a customer and a fellow American."

"Your eye is sound. My name is Archer, by the way."

He stood over me tall and leaning, a Pisan tower of flesh.

"Why don't you sit down?"

"Thank you." He subsided into a chair. "I am Chauncey Reynolds, no kin to Sir Joshua Reynolds, though I do dabble in paint. I've always considered Sir Joshua a better critic than he was a painter. Or don't you share my opinion?" He hunched forward with a touch of belligerence.

"I wouldn't know, Mr. Reynolds. I'm not too hep artistically."

"I thought you were, since you were looking at the paintings. No matter. It's a pleasure to have a customer."

"What happened to all the other customers?"

"Où sont les neiges d'antan? This place was jumping, honestly, when I took over the lease. I thought I had a gold mine on my hands." He looked down into his pudgy hands as if he was surprised by their emptiness. "Then people stopped coming. If the drought of customers persists, I'll close up and go back to work." He seemed to be delivering an ultimatum to himself.

"You paint for a living?"

"I paint. Fortunately I have a small private income. Nobody paints for a *living*. You have to die before you make a living out of painting. Van Gogh, Modigliani, all the great ones had to die."

"What about Picasso?"

"Picasso is the exception that proves the rule. I drink to Pablo Picasso." He raised his glass and drank from it. "What do you do for a living, Mr. Archer?"

"I'm a detective."

He set down his glass with a rap. His bloodshot eyes watched me distrustfully, like a wounded bull from his *querencia*. "Did Gladys send you to ferret me out? She isn't supposed to know where I am."

"I don't know any Gladys."

"Honestly?"

"And I never heard of you until now. Who's Gladys?"

"My ex-wife. I divorced her in Juarez but the New York courts don't recognize it. Which is why, my friend, I am here. Forever." He made it sound like a long time.

"The one I'm interested in," I said, "is a young man named Burke Damis."

"What's he wanted for?"

"He isn't wanted."

"Kid me not. I read a great deal of mystery fiction in the long night watches, and I recognize that look you have on your face. You have the look of a shamus who is about to put the arm on a grifter."

"How well you express yourself. I take it you know Damis."

"In a casual way. He used to pass the time here, mainly before I took over the leash—the lease." He leaned forward over the table, and his long hair flopped like broken wings. "Why do you suppose

they all stopped coming? Tell me—you're a trained objective observer—do I have an offensive personality?"

"José tells me business is slow all over," I said noncommittally.
"It's like the migrations of the birds."

He looked around for José, who was leaning against the wall, and
called for another drink. José replenished his glass from a bottle of
tequila.

"Did you ever talk to Damis?"

"Not what you'd call intimately. He's an attractive chap but I
never got to know him. He was usually with other people. Do you
know if he's still in Ajijic?"

"No. Can you name some of the other people?"

"The one I saw him with most often was Bill Wilkinson."

"How can I get in touch with Wilkinson?"

"You might find him at The Place. I hear he's taking most of his
business there since we had our little run-in."

"Run-in?"

"Actually, it was Mrs. Wilkinson I had the run-in with. She's one
of those Southern California types who fancies herself as an art col-
lector simply because she has money. I told her what she could do
with her money, and Bill would be better off if he did the same. I'm
not a woman hater—"

"Neither is Damis, I understand. Did you ever see him with
women?"

"Almost invariably. He spent a lot of time with Annie Castle.
That was before he took up with the blonde girl, what was her
name?" He sat locked in combat with his memory.

"It doesn't matter. Who is Annie Castle?"

"She runs an artsy-craftsy shop on the other side of the plaza. As a
matter of fact, Damis has or had his studio on the same premises.
No doubt propinquity did its deadly work. Annie's a cute enough kid
if you like them dark and serious. But he dropped her when the big
little blonde showed up."

"What do you mean, 'big little'?"

"*Quien sabe?* Big girl, little ego, maybe. She hasn't made the
breakthrough, into womanhood, you know." He refreshed his alcoholic insight from his glass. "Whenas she ever does, she could be
quite a thing. Beauty isn't in the features so much as in the spirit, in
the eyes. That's why it's so hard to paint."

"You're quite an observer," I encouraged him.

"I'm a people watcher, my friend. If you're a detective, as you say, you must be something of a people watcher yourself."

"I'm a walking field guide," I said. "You seem to have paid pretty close attention to the blonde girl."

"Oh, I did. What was her name? Miss Blackstone, I believe. Her mother introduced us some time ago. I haven't seen her lately. I tend to take special notice of the tall ones, being rather outsize myself. Gladys is nearly six feet, *mirabile dictu*. She was once a burlesque queen on the Bowery, whence I rescued her and made a model of her, foolish man. With the consequence that I am here on my personal Bowery." His eyes strayed around the empty rooms.

I got up. "Thanks for all the information. Can you tell me how to get to The Place?"

"I can, but look here, man, I'm enjoying this. Drink up your beer, and I'll have José make you a proper drink. Where is José? José!"

"Don't bother. I have to see Bill Wilkinson."

He rose cumbrously. "Whatever you say. Do you feel like telling me what this is all about?"

"I could make up a story for you. But that would be a waste of time." I got out my wallet. "How much do I owe you for the beer?"

"Nothing." He fanned his arm in a lordly gesture which threatened to overbalance him. "You're a stranger within my gates, I couldn't possibly accept your money. Besides, I have a feeling you're going to bring me luck."

"I never have yet, Mr. Reynolds."

He told me how to get to The Place and I set out through the midnight streets. The children had been swallowed up by the doorways. Some men and a very few women were still out. Wrapped in blankets, with faces shadowed by volcano-shaped hats, the men had a conspiratorial look. But when I said *"Buenas noches"* to one small group, a chorus of *"Buenas noches"* followed me.

THE PLACE was closed for the night. Steering a course by dead reckoning and the sound of the town clock chiming the quarter, I made my way back to the central square. It was abandoned except for one lone man locked behind the grille of the unicellular jail.

Followed by his Indian gaze, I took myself for a walk around the perimeter of the square. Seven eighths of the way around, I was stopped by a sign in English hand-lettered on wood: "Anne's Native Crafts." The shutters were up but there was light behind them, and the thump and clack of some rhythmic movement.

The noise stopped when I knocked on the door beside the shutters. Heels clicked on stone, and the heavy door creaked open. A smallish woman peered out at me.

"What do you want? It's very late."

"I realize that, Miss Castle. But I'm hoping to fly out of here in the morning, and I thought since you were up—"

"I know who you are," she said accusingly.

"News travels fast in Ajijic."

"Does it not? I can also tell you that you're here to no purpose. Burke Damis left Ajijic some time ago. It's true I sublet a studio to him for a brief period. But I can tell you nothing whatever about him."

"That's funny. You know all about me, and you never even saw me before."

"There's nothing funny about it. The waiter at the *Cantina* is a friend of mine. I taught his sister to weave."

"That was nice of you."

"It was part of the normal course of my life and work. You are distinctly not. Now if you'll take your big foot out of my doorway, I can get back to my weaving."

I didn't move. "You work very late."

"I work all the time."

"So do I when I'm on a case. That gives us something in common. I think we have something else in common."

"I can't imagine what it would be."

"You're concerned about Burke Damis, and so am I."

"Concerned?" Her voice went tinny on the word. "I don't know what you mean."

"I don't either, Miss Castle. You would have to tell me."

"I'll tell you nothing."

"Are you in love with Burke Damis?"

"I certainly am not!" she said passionately, telling me a great deal. "That's the most absurd statement—question, that anyone ever asked me."

"I'm full of absurd questions. Will you let me come in and ask you some of them?"

"Why should I?"

"Because you're a serious woman, and serious things are happening. I didn't fly down from Los Angeles for fun."

"What *is* happening then?"

"Among other things," I said, "Burke has eloped with a young woman who doesn't know which end is up."

She was silent for a long moment. "I know Harriet Blackwell, and I quite agree with your description of her. She's an emotionally ignorant girl who threw—well, she practically threw herself at his head. There's nothing I can do about it, or want to."

"Even if she's in danger?"

"Danger from Burke? That's impossible."

"It's more than possible, in my opinion, and I've been giving it a good deal of thought."

She moved closer to me. I caught the glint of her eyes, and her odor, light and clean, devoid of perfume. "Did you really come all the way from the States to ask me about Burke?"

"Yes."

"Has he—done something to Harriet Blackwell?"

"I don't know. They've dropped out of sight."

"What makes you suspect he's done something?"

"I'll tell you if you'll tell me. We both seem to have the same idea."

"No. You're putting words into my mouth."

"I wouldn't have to, if you'd talk to me."

"Perhaps I had better," she said to me and her conscience. "Come in, Mr. Archer." She even knew my name.

I followed her into the room behind her shop. A wooden hand loom stood in one corner, with a piece of colored fabric growing intricately on it. The walls and furniture were covered with similar materials in brilliant designs.

Anne Castle was quite brilliant in her own way. She wore a multicolored Mexican skirt, an embroidered blouse, in her ears gold hoops that were big enough to swing on. Black hair cut short emphasized her petiteness and the individuality of her looks. Her eyes were brown and intelligent, and warmer than her voice had let me hope.

She said when we were seated on the divan: "You were going to tell me what Burke has done."

"I'd rather have your account of him first, for psychological reasons."

"You mean," she said carefully, "that I may not want to talk after you've done your talking?"

"Something like that."

"Is it so terrible?"

"It may be quite terrible. I don't know."

"As terrible as murder?" She sounded like a child who names the thing he fears, the dead man walking in the attic, the skeleton just behind the closet door, in order to be assured that it doesn't exist.

"Possibly. I'm interested in your reasons for suggesting it."

"Well," she hedged, "you said Harriet Blackwell was in danger."

"Is that all?"

"Yes. Of course." The skeleton had frightened her away from the verge of candor. She covered her retreat with protestations: "I'm sure you must be mistaken. They seem fond of each other. And you couldn't describe Burke as a violent man."

"How well did you know him, Miss Castle?"

She hesitated. "You asked me, before, if I was in love with him."

"I apologize for my bluntness."

"I don't care. Is it so obvious? Or has Chauncey Reynolds been telling tales out of school?"

"He said that you were seeing a lot of Burke, before Harriet Blackwell entered the picture."

"Yes. I've been trying ever since to work him out of my system.

With not very striking success." She glanced at the loom in the corner. "At least I've gotten through a lot of work."

"Do you want to tell me the story from the beginning?"

"If you insist. I don't see how it can help you."

"How did you meet him?"

"In a perfectly natural way. He came into the shop the day after he got here. His room at the *posada* didn't suit him, because of the light. He was looking for a place to paint. He said he hadn't been able to paint for some time, and he was burning to get at it. I happened to have a studio I'm not using, and I agreed to rent it to him for a month or so."

"Is that how long he wanted it for? A month?"

"A month or two, it wasn't definite."

"And he came here two months ago?"

"Almost to the day. When I think of the changes there have been in just two months—!" Her eyes reflected them. "Anyway, the day he moved in, I had to make a speed trip to Guad. One of my girls has a rheumatic heart and she needed emergency treatment. Burke came along for the ride, and I was impressed by his kindness to the girl— she's one of my best students. After we took her to the hospital we went to the *Copa de Leche* for lunch and really got to know each other.

"He talked to me about his plans as an artist. He's still caught up in abstraction but he's trying to use that method to penetrate more deeply into life. It's his opinion that the American people are living through a tragedy unconsciously, suffering without knowing that we are suffering or what the source of the suffering may be. He thinks it's in our sexual life." She flushed suddenly. "Burke is very verbal for a painter."

"I hadn't noticed," I said. "Who paid for the lunch?"

Her flush deepened. "You know quite a bit about him, don't you? I paid. He was broke. I also took him to an artists' supply house and let him charge four hundred pesos' worth of paints on my account. It was my suggestion, not his, and I don't regret it."

"Did he pay you back?"

"Of course."

"Before or after he attached himself to Harriet Blackwell?"

"Before. It was at least a week before she got here."

"What did he use for money?"

"He sold a picture to Bill Wilkinson, or rather to his wife—she's the one with the money. I tried to persuade him not to sell it or, if he insisted, to sell it to me. But he was determined to sell it to her, and she was determined to have it. She paid him thirty-five hundred pesos, which was more than I could afford. Later on he regretted the sale and tried to buy the picture back from the Wilkinsons. I heard that they had quite a ruction about it."

"When was this?"

"A couple of weeks ago. I only heard about it at second hand. Burke and I were no longer speaking, and I have nothing to do with the Wilkinsons. Bill Wilkinson is a drunk married to a woman older than himself and living on her." She paused over the words, perhaps because they had accidentally touched on her relations with Damis. "They're dangerous people."

"I understand that Wilkinson was Burke's boon companion."

"For a while. Bill Wilkinson is quite perceptive, in the sense that he understands people's weaknesses, and Burke was taken in by him for a while."

"Or vice versa?"

"That was not the case. What would a man like Burke have to gain from a man like Bill Wilkinson?"

"He sold his wife a picture for thirty-five hundred pesos."

"It's a very good picture," she said defensively, "and cheap at the price. Burke isn't ever high on his own work, but even he admitted that it was the kind of tragic painting he was aiming at. It wasn't like his other things, apart from a few sketches. As a matter of fact, it's representational."

"Representational?"

"It's a portrait," she said, "of a lovely young girl. He called it 'Portrait of an Unknown Woman.' I asked him if he'd ever known such a woman. He said perhaps he had, or perhaps he dreamed her."

"What do you think?"

"I think he must have known her, and painted her from memory. I never saw a man work so ferociously hard. He painted twelve and fourteen hours a day. I had to make him stop to eat. I'd walk into the studio with his *comida,* and he'd be working with the tears and sweat running down his face. He'd paint himself blind, then he'd go off on the town and get roaring drunk. I'd put him to bed in the wee hours, and he'd be up in the morning painting again."

"He must have given you quite a month."

"I loved it," she said intensely. "I loved him. I still do."

It was an avowal of passion. If there was some hysteria in it, she had it under control. Everything was under control, except that she worked all the time.

We sat there smiling dimly at each other. She was an attractive woman, with the kind of honesty that chisels the face in pure lines. I recalled what Chauncey Reynolds had said in drunken wisdom about Harriet, that she hadn't made the breakthrough into womanhood. Anne Castle had.

I kept my eyes on her face too long. She rose and moved across the room with hummingbird vitality, and opened a portable bar which stood against the wall:

"May I give you something to drink, Mr. Archer?"

"No, thanks, there's a long night coming up. After you and I have finished, I'm going to try and see the Wilkinsons. I want a look at that portrait they bought, for one thing."

She closed the door of the bar, sharply. "Haven't we finished?"

"I'm afraid not, Miss Castle."

She came back to the divan. "What more do you want from me?"

"I still don't understand Damis and his background. Did he ever talk about his previous life?"

"Some. He came from somewhere in the Middle West. He studied at various art schools."

"Did he name them?"

"If he did, I don't remember. Possibly Chicago was one of them. He knew the Institute collection. But most painters do."

"Where did he live before he came to Mexico?"

"All over the States, I gathered. Most of us have."

"Most of the people here, you mean?"

She nodded. "This is our fifty-first state. We come here when we've run through the other fifty."

"Burke came here from California, we know that. Did he ever mention San Mateo County, or the Bay area in general?"

"He'd spent some time in San Francisco. He was deeply familiar with the El Grecos in the museum there."

"Painting is all he ever talked about, apparently."

"He talked about everything under the sun," she said, "except his past life. He *was* reticent about that. He did tell me he'd been

unhappy for years, that I'd made him happy for the first time since
he was a boy."

"Then why did he turn his back on you so abruptly?"

"That's a very painful question, Mr. Archer."

"I know it, and I'm sorry. I'm trying to understand how the Blackwell girl got into the picture."

"I can't explain it," she said with a little sigh. "Suddenly there she
was, spang in the middle of it."

"Had he ever mentioned her before she arrived?"

"No. They met here, you see."

"And he had no previous knowledge of her?"

"No. Are you implying that he was lying in wait for her or something equally melodramatic?"

"My questions don't imply anything. They're simply questions.
Do you happen to know where they first met?"

"At a party at Helen Wilkinson's. I wasn't there, so I can't tell
you who introduced whom to whom, or who was the aggressor, shall
we say. I do know it was love at first sight." She added dryly: "On
her part."

"What about his part?"

Her clear brow knotted, and she looked almost ugly for a moment.
"It's hard to say. He dropped me like the proverbial hotcake when
she hove into sight. He dropped his painting, too. He spent all his
time with her for weeks, and finally went off with her. Yet the few
times I saw them together—he was still living here, but I arranged to
see as little of him as possible—I got the impression that he wasn't
terribly attracted to her."

"What do you base that on?"

"Base is too definite a word for what I have to go on—the way he
looked at her and the way he didn't look. He struck me as a man
doing a job, doing it with rather cold efficiency. That may be wishful
thinking on my part."

I doubted that it was. I'd seen the lack of interest in his face the
day before, in the Malibu house, when Harriet ran to him across the
room.

"I don't believe you do much wishful thinking, Miss Castle."

"Do I not? But they didn't seem to talk about each other, as people in love are supposed to. As Burke and I did when we were—
together." The ugly darkness caught in her brow again. "They talked

about how much money her father had, and what a beautiful place he maintained at Lake Tahoe. Things like that," she said contemptuously.

"Just what was said about the place at Tahoe?"

"She described it to him in some detail, as if she was trying to sell a piece of real estate. I know I'm being hard on her, but it was hard to listen to. She went on for some time about the great oaken beams, and the stone fireplace where you could roast an ox if you had an ox, and the picture window overlooking the lake. The disheartening thing was, Burke was intensely interested in her very materialistic little recital."

"Did she say anything about taking him there?"

"I believe she did. Yes, I remember she suggested that it would be an ideally secluded place for a honeymoon."

"This may be the most helpful thing you've told me yet," I said. "How did you happen to overhear it, by the way?"

She tugged at one of her earrings in embarrassment. "I didn't mean to let that slip. I might as well confess, though, while I'm confessing all. I eavesdropped on them. I didn't intend to do it, but he brought her to the studio several nights in a row, and my good intentions broke down. I had to know what they were saying to each other." Her voice took on a satiric lilt: "So she was saying that her father had oodles of money and three houses, and Burke was drinking it in. Maybe he had an underprivileged childhood, who knows?"

"It's a funny thing about con men, they often come from respectable well-heeled families."

"He *isn't* a confidence man. He's a good painter."

"I have to reserve my judgment, on both counts. It might be a good idea for you to reserve yours."

"I've been trying, these last weeks. But it's fearfully hard, when you've made a commitment—" She moved her hands helplessly.

"I'd like to have a look at the studio you rented him. Would that be possible?"

"If you think it will help in any way."

On the far side of the courtyard, where a Volkswagen was parked for the night, a detached brick building with a huge window stood against the property wall. She unlocked the door and turned on a lamp inside. The big bare-walled room smelled of insecticide. Several unsittable-looking pigskin-covered chairs were distributed around the tile floor. A cot with its thin mattress uncovered stood in one corner. The only sign of comfort was the hand-woven drapes at the big window.

"He lived frugally enough here," I said.

"Just like a monk in his cell." Her inflection was sardonic. "Of course I've stripped the place since he moved out. That was a week ago Sunday."

"He didn't fly to Los Angeles until the following day."

"I presume he spent the last night with her."

"They were spending nights together, were they?"

"Yes. I don't know what went on in the course of the nights. You mustn't think I spied on them persistently. I only broke down the once." She folded her arms across her breasts and stood like a small monument, determined never to break down again. "You see me in my nakedness, Mr. Archer. I'm the classic case of the landlady who fell in love with her star boarder and got jilted."

"I don't see you in that light at all."

"What other light could you possibly see me in?"

"You'd be surprised. Have you ever been married, Miss Castle?"

"Once. I left Vassar to get married, to a poet, of all things. It didn't work out."

"So you exiled yourself to Mexico?"

"It's not that simple, and neither am I," she said with a complicated smile. "You couldn't possibly understand how I feel about this place. It's as ancient as the hills and as new as the Garden of Eden—the real New World—and I love to be a part of it." She added sadly, her mind revolving around a single pole: "I thought that Burke was beginning to feel the same."

I moved around the room and in and out of the bathroom at the rear. It was all bare and clean and unrevealing. I came back to her.

"Did Damis leave much behind him, in the way of things?"

"He left no personal things, if that's what you're interested in. He had nothing when he came here and not much more when he left, except for his brushes."

"He came here with nothing at all?"

"Just the clothes he had on, and they were quite used up. I persuaded him to have a suit made in Guad. Yes, I paid for it."

"You did a lot for him."

"*Nada.*"

"Did he give you anything in return?"

"I didn't want anything from him."

"No keepsakes or mementos?"

She hesitated. "Burke gave me a little self-portrait. It's only a sketch he tossed off. I asked him for it."

"May I see it?"

"If you like."

She locked up the studio and took me back across the courtyard to her bedroom. Framed in bamboo, the small black and white picture hung on the wall above her smooth bed. The sketch was too stylized to be a perfect likeness, and one eye was for some reason larger than the other, but Burke Damis was easily recognizable in it. He glared out somberly from a nest of crosshatched lines.

Anne Castle stood and answered his look with defensive arms folded across her breasts.

"I have a favor to ask you. A big one."

"You want the sketch," she said.

"I promise you'll get it back."

"But you must know what he looks like. You've seen him, haven't you?"

"I've seen him, but I don't know who I've seen."

"You think he's using a false name?"

"I believe he's using at least two aliases. Burke Damis is one. Quincy Ralph Simpson is another. Did he ever use the Simpson name when he was with you?"

She shook her head. The movement left her face loose and expectant.

"He came to Mexico under the Simpson name. He used it again when he left. There's a strange thing about the name Quincy Ralph Simpson. The man who originally owned it is dead."

Her head moved forward on her neck. "How did he die?"

"Of an icepick in the heart, two months ago, in a town near Los Angeles called Citrus Junction. Did Burke ever mention Citrus Junction to you?"

"Never." Her arms had fallen to her sides. She looked at the bed, and then sat down on it. "Are you trying to tell me that Burke killed him?"

"Burke, or whatever his name is, is the leading suspect in my book, so far the only one. He left the United States shortly after

Simpson disappeared. It's virtually certain he was using Simpson's papers."

"Who was Simpson?"

"A little man of no importance who wanted to be a detective."

"Was he after Burke for—some crime?"

Her voice had overtones and undertones. The dead man was walking in the attic again. The skeleton hung behind her half-shuttered eyes.

"You brought up the subject of murder before," I said. "Is that the crime you have in mind?"

She looked from me to the picture on the wall and back at me. She said miserably: "Did Burke kill a woman?"

"It's not unlikely," I said in a neutral tone.

"Do you know who she was?"

"No. Do you?"

"He didn't tell me her name, or anything else about her. All he said—" She straightened up, trying to discipline her thoughts. "I'll see if I can reconstruct exactly what he did say. It was our first night together. He'd been drinking, and he was in a low mood. Post-coital *tristesse,* I believe they call it."

She was being cruel to herself. Her fingers worked in the coverlet of her bed. One of her hands, still working, went to her breast. She was no longer looking at me.

"You were going to tell me what he said, Miss Castle."

"I can't."

"You already have, in a sense."

"I shouldn't have spoken. Jilted landlady betrays demon lover. I didn't think that was my style. I'm a hopeless creature," she said, and flung herself sideways with her face in the pillow, her legs dragging on the floor.

They were good legs, and I was aware of it, in the center of my body as well as in my head. A wave of feeling went through me; I wanted to comfort her. But I kept my hands off. She had more memories than she could use, and so had I.

The memory I was interested in came out brokenly, half smothered by the pillow. "He said he was bad luck to his women. I should have nothing to do with him if I liked my neck in one piece. He said that that had happened to his last one."

"What happened to her?"

"She was choked to death. It was why he had to leave the States."

"That implies he was responsible for her death. Did he make a confession to you?"

"He didn't say it outright. It was more of a threat to me, or a warning. I suppose he was bullying me. But he never actually hurt me. He's very strong, too. He could have hurt me."

"Did he ever repeat the confession, or the threat?"

"No, but I often thought of it afterward. I never brought it up, though. I was always a little afraid of him after that. It didn't stop my loving him. I'd love him no matter what he'd done."

"Two murders take a lot of doing, and a very special kind of person to do them."

She detached her face from the comfort of the pillow and sat up, smoothing her skirt and then her hair. She was pale and shaken, as if she'd been through a bout of moral nausea.

"I can't believe that Burke is that kind of person."

"Women never can about the men they love."

"Just what evidence is there against him?"

"What I've told you, and what you've told me."

"But it doesn't amount to anything. He might have been simply *talking,* with me."

"You didn't think so at the time, or later. You asked me right off if murder was involved. And I have to tell you that it certainly is. I saw Ralph Simpson's body just twenty-four hours ago."

"But you don't know who the woman was?"

"Not yet. I have no information on Damis's past life. It's why I came here, and why I want to borrow your picture of him."

"What use will you make of it?"

"An acquaintance of mine is art critic on one of the L.A. papers. He knows the work of a lot of young painters, and quite a few of them personally. I want to show the sketch to him and see if he can put a name to your friend."

"Why do you think Burke Damis isn't his name?"

"If he's on the run, as he seems to be, he wouldn't be using his own name. He entered Mexico under the Simpson alias, as I told you. There's one other little piece of evidence. Did you ever notice a shaving kit he had, in a leather case?"

"Yes. It was just about his only possession."

"Do you recall the initials on it?"

"I don't believe I do."

" 'B.C.,' " I said. "They don't go with the name Burke Damis. I'm very eager to know what name they do go with. That picture may do it."

"You can have it," she said, "and you don't have to send it back. I shouldn't have hung it here anyway. It's too much like self-flagellation."

She took it off its hook and gave it to me, talking me out of the room and herself out of her embarrassed pain. "I'm a very self-flagellant type. But I suppose it's better than having other people do it to you. And so very much more economical—it saves paying the middlemen."

"You talk a great deal, Anne."

"Too much, don't I? Much too much too much."

But she was a serviceable woman. She gave me a bag of woven straw to carry the picture in, backed her Volkswagen out over my protests, and drove me out to the Wilkinsons' lake-front house. It was past one but the chances were, she said, that Bill and his wife would still be up. They were late risers and late drinkers.

She turned in at the top of their lane and kept her headlights on the barbed-wire gate while I unfastened it and closed it behind me. Then she gave a little toot on her horn and started back toward the village.

I didn't expect to see her again, and I regretted it.

>>>>>>>>>
>>>>>>>>> *chapter* 12
>>>>>>>>>

MUSIC DRIFTED from the house. It was old romantic music of the twenties, poignant and sweet as the jasmine on the air. The dooryard was thickly planted with shrubbery and trees. Wide terraces descended from it to the lake, which glimmered faintly in the middle distance.

I bumped my head on a low-hanging fruit which was probably a mango. Above the trees the stars hung in the freshly cleared sky like clusters of some smaller, brighter fruit too high to reach.

I knocked on the heavy door. A woman spoke over the music: "Is that you, Bill?"

I didn't answer. After a minute's waiting she opened the door. She was blonde and slim in something diaphanous. She also wore in her right hand a clean-looking .38 revolver pointed at my stomach.

"What do you want?"

"A little talk. My name is Archer and I'm only here overnight and I realize this is a poor time to come bothering you—"

"You haven't told me what you want."

"I'm a private detective investigating a crime."

"We don't have crime here," she said sharply.

"This crime occurred up north."

"What makes you think that I know anything about it?"

"I'm here to ask you, is all."

She moved back, and waved the revolver commandingly. "Come in under the light and let me see you."

I stepped into a room so huge that its far corners were in darkness. Gershwin spilled in a nostalgic cascade from a massive hi-fi layout against one wall. The blonde woman was heavily made up in an old-fashioned way, as if she had been entertaining ghosts. Her triangular face had the taut immobility that plastic surgery often leaves behind.

She looked at my feet and swept her eyes up my body like searchlights, half occulted by eye shadow. I recognized the way she used her eyes. I've seen it a dozen times before through the fallout of old late movies, and earlier still, when I was a juvenile patron of the Long Beach movie houses and she was a western leading lady smirking and ogling her way out of triangular relationships with horses.

I reached deep for her movie name, but I couldn't quite dredge it up.

"You're fairly pretty," she said. "Isn't that Claude Stacy's sweater you're wearing?"

"He lent it to me. My clothes got rained on."

"I gave him that sweater. Are you a friend of Claude's?"

"Not an intimate one."

"That's good. You don't *look* his type. Do you like women?"

"Put the gun away and I'll give you a truthful answer," I said with the necessary smile.

She responded with a smile of her own, a 1929 smile that rested on her mouth like a footnote to history. "Don't let the gun bother you. I learned to handle a gun when I was playing in westerns. My husband insists I keep it handy when I'm alone at night. Which I usually am."

She laid the revolver down on a table near the door and turned back to me. "You haven't told me if you like women or not."

"I like individual women. I've liked you, for example, for a longer time than either of us would care to admit." The name she had used as an actress had come back to me. "You're Helen Holmes, aren't you?"

She lit up coldly and brightly, like a marquee. "You remember me. I thought everyone had forgotten."

"I was a fan," I said, spreading it not too thick.

"How nice!" She clenched her hands at her shoulders and jumped a few inches off the floor, with both feet, her smile immobile. "For that you may sit you down and I'll pour you a drink and tell you anything you want to know. Except about me. Name your poison."

"Gin and tonic, since you're so kind."

"One gin and tonic coming up."

She turned on a gilt chandelier which hung like a barbaric treasure among the ceiling beams. The room was like an auctioneer's warehouse, crowded with furniture of various periods and countries. Against a distant wall stood an ornately carved bar, backed by shelves of bottles, with half a dozen leather-covered stools in front of it.

"Come sit at the bar. It's cozier."

I sat and watched her mix my drink. For herself she compounded something out of tequila and grenadine, with coarse salt sprinkled around the rim of the glass. She stayed behind the bar to drink it, leaning on her forearms and exposing her bosom like a barmaid favoring a customer.

"I won't waste time beating around the bush. I'm interested in Burke Damis. You know him, Mrs. Wilkinson?"

"Slightly. He is, or was, a friend of my husband's."

"Why do you put it in the past tense?"

"They had a quarrel, some time before Mr. Damis left here."

"What about?"

"You ask very direct questions."

"I don't have time for my usual subtlety."

"*That* must be something to experience."

"Oh, it is. What did they quarrel about?"

"Me, if you have to know. Poor little old me." She fluttered her eyelashes. "I was afraid they were going to kill each other, honestly. But Bill contented himself with burning the picture. That way he got back at both of us." She raised one hand like a witness. "Now don't ask me for doing what. There wasn't any *what*. It's just that Bill is very insecure in our relationship."

"He burned the 'Portrait of an Unknown Woman'?"

"Yes, and I haven't forgiven him for it," she said, as though this were proof of character. "He broke up the frame and tore the canvas and put the whole thing in the fireplace and set fire to it. Bill can be quite violent sometimes."

She sipped her drink and licked the salt from her lips with a pale pointed tongue. She reminded me of a cat, not a domestic cat, but one of the larger breeds that could stalk men. Her bright lips seemed to be savoring the memory of violence.

"Did Damis know the picture was destroyed?"

"I told him. It broke him up. He wept actual tears, can you imagine?"

"I wonder why."

"It was his best picture, he said. I liked it, too."

"I heard he'd tried to buy it back."

"He did, but I wouldn't part with it." Between the shadowed lids her eyes were watchful. "Who else have you been talking to?"

"Various people around the village."

"Claude Stacy?"

"No. Not yet."

"Why are you so interested in that particular picture?"

"I'm interested in everything Damis does."

"You mentioned a crime that occurred up north. Do you want to let down your back hair about it? I've been letting down my back hair."

I told her what had happened to Quincy Ralph Simpson. She looked somehow disappointed, as if she'd been expecting something more lurid.

"This is all new to me," she said. "There's nothing I can tell you about Simpson."

"Let's get back to the picture then. Damis called it a portrait. Did he ever say who the subject of it was?"

"He never did," she said shortly.

"Do you have any ideas?"

She shrugged her shoulders and made a stupid face, with her mouth turned down at the corners.

"You must have had a reason for buying the painting and wanting to keep it. Your husband cared enough about it to burn it."

"I don't know who the woman was," she said, too forcefully.

"I think you do."

"Think away. You're getting rather boring. It's late, and I have a headache." She drew her fingers across her forehead. "Why don't you drink up and go?"

I left my drink where it was on the bar between us. "I'm sorry if I pressed too hard. I didn't mean to—"

"Didn't you?" She finished her drink and came around the end of the bar, licking her lips. "Come on, I'll let you out."

It had been a very quick party. Reluctantly I followed her to the door.

"I was hoping to ask you some questions about Harriet Blackwell. I understand Damis met her here at your house."

"So what?" she said, and pulled the door open. "Out."

She slammed it behind me. In the dooryard I bumped my head on the same low-hanging fruit. I picked it—it was a mango—and took it along with me as a souvenir.

It was a long walk back, but I rather enjoyed it. It gave me a chance to think, among other things about Helen Holmes Wilkinson. Our rather tenuous relationship, based on Claude Stacy's sweater and my remembering her movie name, had broken down over the identity of the woman in the burned portrait. I would give odds that she knew who the woman was and what her connection with Damis had been.

I wondered about Helen's own connection with Damis.

Headlights approached me, coming very fast from the direction of the village. They belonged to a beetle-shaped Porsche which swerved in long arcs from one side of the road to the other. I had to slide into the ditch to avoid being run over. As the Porsche went by I caught a glimpse of the driver's face, pale under flying dark hair. I threw my mango at him.

The clock chimed two quarters—half-past two—as I struggled through the village to the *posada*. In the room behind the desk, Claude Stacy was sleeping in his clothes on a mohair couch. It was a couch with one high end, the kind psychiatrists use, and he was curled up on it in foetal position.

I shook him. He grimaced and snorted like a huge old baby being born into a world he never made.

"What is it?"

"I met a friend of yours tonight. Helen Wilkinson. She mentioned you."

"Did she now?" He took a comb out of his pocket and ran it through his thinning hair. "I hope it was complimentary."

"Very," I lied.

He basked in the imaginary compliment. "Oh, Helen and I get along. If Bill Wilkinson hadn't got to her first I might have thought of marrying her myself." He thought about it now. "She used to be in pictures, you know, and she saved her money. I did some acting at one time myself. But I didn't hang on to any money."

"What does Bill Wilkinson do for a living?"

"Nothing. He must be twenty years younger than Helen is," he said by way of explanation. "You'd never know it, she's so beautifully preserved. And Bill has let himself go frightfully. He used to be a Greek god, I mean it."

"Have you known him long?"

"Years and years. It's through him I got to know Helen. He married her a couple of years ago, after his folks stopped sending him money. I wouldn't say he married her for her money, but he married where money is. Tennyson." Stacy giggled. "It drives him out of his mind when Helen even *looks* at another man."

"She looks at other men?"

"I'm afraid she does. She was interested in me at one time." He flushed with vanity. "Of course I wouldn't steal another fellow's wife. Bill knows he can trust me. Bill and I have been buddy-buddy for years."

"Have you seen him tonight?"

"No, I haven't. I think he went to a party in Guadalajara. He has some very good connections. His family are very well-known people in Texas."

"Does he drive a Porsche?"

"If you can call it driving. His driving is one reason he had to leave Texas."

"I can believe it. He almost ran me down on the road just now."

"Poor old Bill. Some night he's going to end up in the ditch with a broken neck. And maybe I'll marry Helen after all, who knows?" The prospect failed to cheer him. "I need a drink, old chap. Will you have one with me?"

"All right. Drinking seems to be the favorite indoor sport around here."

He looked at me to see if I was accusing him of being a drunk. I smiled. He gave me a Mexican-type shrug and got a bottle of Bacardi out from under the high end of the couch. He poured some into paper cups from a dispenser that hung on the wall beside the bottled water. I added water to mine.

"*Salud,*" he said. "If you don't mind my asking, how did you happen to run into Helen Wilkinson?"

"I went to see her."

"Just like that?"

"I happen to be a private investigator."

He sat bolt upright. His drink slopped over the rim of the cup. I wondered what old scandal had the power to galvanize him.

"I thought you were a tourist," he said resentfully.

"I'm a detective, and I came here to investigate a man who calls himself Burke Damis. I think he stayed with you for a night or two."

"One night," Stacy said. "So it's really true about him, after all? I hated to believe it—he's such a fine-looking chap."

"You hated to believe what?"

"That he murdered his wife. Isn't that why you're after him?"

With the aid of a little rum and water I made a quick adjustment. "These rumors get around. Where did you happen to pick that one up?"

"It was going the rounds, as you say. I think it started when Bill Wilkinson told somebody at The Place that he was going to report Damis as an undesirable alien." Stacy sounded like a connoisseur of rumors, who collected them as other men collected notable sayings or pictures of women. "The government has been bearing down on undesirables, rounding them up and sending them back across the border. Like wetbacks in reverse."

"And Wilkinson turned Damis in?"

"I don't believe he actually did, but he threatened to. Which is probably why Damis got out in a hurry. So he really is one jump ahead of the law?"

"A long jump," I said. "This rumor interests me. What exactly was said?"

"Simply that Damis—which wasn't his real name—was wanted for the murder of his wife."

"How do you know it isn't his real name?"

"*I* don't know *any*thing. It was all part of the rumor. I pestered Bill and Helen for more details, but they refused to talk—"

"They know more details, do they?"

"I would say so."

"Where did they get them?"

"I've asked myself that question many times. I know they made their border trip last May and spent a week or so in California. That's when the murder occurred, isn't it? Maybe they read about it in the newspapers. But if they knew all about it, I can't understand why they would get chummy with the man. The three of them were very buddy-buddy for a while, before Bill turned against him. Helen got too interested in Damis."

"But Damis had a girl of his own." Or two. Or three.

He smiled indulgently. "That wouldn't stop Helen."

"Do you know the girl he left here with—Harriet Blackwell?"

"I met her once, at a party."

"Where did Damis meet her?"

"Same party, at Helen Wilkinson's. Helen told me he asked her to invite her."

"Damis asked Helen to invite Harriet to the party?"

"That's what I said."

"So that he could meet Harriet?"

"Apparently. I only know what I hear."

The interview was beginning to depress me. Stacy's eyes had a feeding look, as if he lived on these morsels and scraps of other people's lives. Perhaps I feared a similar fate for myself.

He poured himself more Bacardi and offered me some. I turned it down, politely. If I wanted to get back to California tomorrow—and now I was determined to—I had some further legwork to do tonight.

"Tell me, Mr. Stacy, is there a taxi in the village?"

"There's a man who drives people. You'd have a frightful time routing him out at three in the morning. Why?"

"I have to get out to the Wilkinsons, and I don't feel like walking it again."

"I'll drive you."

"You're very hospitable."

"Think nothing of it. This is *exciting* for me. I'll take you on one condition, that you don't tell Bill or Helen I had any part in this. The connection is important to me, you know."

"Sure."

He brought his battered Ford around to the entrance and drove me out the lake road. Roosters were crowing in the dark countryside. Stacy parked at the head of the Wilkinsons' lane and let me go in by myself.

The Wilkinsons were having an argument which was loud enough to penetrate the walls. I stood outside the front door and listened to it.

She called him an alcoholic. He said she couldn't talk to a Charro like that. She said it took more than a Charro hat to make a Charro, that he was a Charro like she was a member of the DAR.

He called her a sexoholic. She told him if he didn't watch his lip she'd divorce him and turn him loose to beg in the streets. He announced that she'd be doing him a favor, since marriage to her was uphill work at best.

The argument simmered down after a while, so that I could hear the roosters in the distance, yelling with insane glee in the dead dark middle of the night. I balled up the rest of my energy in my fist and knocked on the door.

Wilkinson answered it this time. He was a big man in his thirties who looked older. His Mexican clothes and haircut made him seem to be metamorphosing under my eyes, changing into something that was strange even to himself. He had alcohol in him, red in the eye, sour on the breath, thick on the tongue.

"I don't know you. Go 'way."

"Just give me a minute. I'm a private detective, and I flew down from L.A. to do some checking on Burke Damis. I heard you were a friend of his."

"You heard wrong. He came sucking around for free drinks. Once I caught onto him, I cut him dead. But dead."

Wilkinson had a nasty whining drawl. His red eyes glared with something stronger than drink, perhaps a touch of madness.

"What did you catch on to about Damis?"

"He wormed himself into my good graces so he could get next to my wife. I don't stand for that."

He made a sideways slicing gesture. The edge of his hand struck the doorframe. He put the edge of his hand in his mouth.

"I heard a rumor that he killed his own wife."

"That was no rumor. We were in San Francisco in the spring, and I saw it in the paper with these eyes—the dead woman's picture and all. It said that he shtrangled her. But we didn't know who he was when he came here worming his way. We didn't know till we saw the picture he painted."

"Was it a portrait of his wife?"

"Thass right. Helen reckonized her face, poor little woman. That snake-in-the-grass shtrangled her with his own hands."

Wilkinson made clutching motions, as though he was having a waking dream of strangling or being strangled. His wife called from somewhere out of sight: "Who is it, Bill? Who are you talking to?"

"Man from L.A. He says that he's a detective."

She ran the length of the living room to his side. "Don't talk to him."

"I'll talk to him if I like," he said with the look of a spoiled and sullen child. "I'll put the kibosh on Damis once and for all."

"You stay out of it."

"You were the one that got me into it. If you hadn't tried to blackmail him into—"

"Be quiet. You're a fool."

They faced each other in a rage that created a vacuum around them. He was twice as big as she was, and almost twice as young, but she held her anger better. Her taut and shining face was expressionless.

"Listen to me, Bill. This man was here an hour or so ago. I had to ask him to leave."

"Whaffor?"

"He made a pass at me." Her hooked fingers swept across her bosom.

His attention slopped heavily in my direction. "Izzat true?"

"Don't believe her."

"Now he's calling me a liar. " Her white triangular face was at his shoulder. "Are you going to let him get away with it?"

He threw a wild fist at my head. I let it go by and hit him in the body. He sat down holding his belly with both hands. I shouldn't have hit him. He retched.

"Why you dirty lousy son," the woman said.

She picked her revolver off the table and fired it at me. The bullet tugged at a loose fold of Stacy's sweater, close to my side. I turned and ran.

>>>>>>>>>>
>>>>>>>>>> *chapter* 13
>>>>>>>>>>

IN THE MORNING, the sudden morning, Stacy drove me to the airport. He wouldn't let me pay him for the service, or for the double hole in his sweater. He said it would make a conversation piece.

But he did ask me when I had the time to call a friend of his who managed a small hotel in Laguna Beach. I was to tell the man that Claude was doing all right, and there were no hard feelings.

I tottered on board the plane and slept most of the way to Los Angeles. We landed shortly after one o'clock. It was hot, hotter than it had been in Mexico. Smog lay over the city like the lid of a pressure cooker.

I immured myself in an outside phone booth and made several calls. Colonel Blackwell had had no word from Harriet since she drove off with Damis the day before yesterday. It was possible, he agreed, that they had gone to Tahoe. His lodge there was situated on the lake, on the Nevada side of State Line.

I cut his anxious questions short with a promise to come and see him at his house. Then I called Arnie Walters in Reno. He ran a detective agency which covered that end of Nevada.

Arnie's wife and partner answered the phone. Phyllis Walters had the official-sounding voice of an ex-policewoman, but it didn't quite hide her exuberant femininity.

"How are you, Lew? Where have you been keeping yourself?"

"All over the map. Last night, for instance, I spent a week in Mexico."

"You do get around. Arnie's out. Is it business or just social?"

"Urgent business. You'd better record this."

"All right. Go ahead."

I gave her a description of Harriet and Damis and asked to have them looked for in the Tahoe and Reno area, with special attention to the Blackwell lodge and the wedding chapels. "If Arnie or one of his men runs into Damis, with or without the girl, I want Damis held."

"We can't detain him, you know that."

"You can make a citizen's arrest and turn him over to the nearest cop. He's a fugitive from a murder rap."

"Who did he murder?"

"His wife, apparently. I expect to get the details this afternoon. In the meantime Arnie should be warned that the man is dangerous."

"Will do."

"Good girl. I'll get back to you later, Phyllis."

I called the photographer with whom I'd left my film of Damis's painting. The slides were ready. Finally, I called the art critic Manny Meyer. He said he'd be home for the next hour, and he was willing to look at my exhibits. I picked up the slides in Santa Monica and drove up Wilshire to Westwood.

Manny lived in one of the big new apartment buildings on the hill. The windows of his front room overlooked the UCLA campus. It was the room of a man who loved art and not much besides. Dozens of books had overflowed from the bookshelves onto the furniture, including the closed top of the baby grand piano. The walls were literally paneled with nineteenth-century reproductions and contemporary originals. Entering the room was like stepping into the interior of Manny's head.

He was a small man in a rumpled seersucker suit. His eyes looked deceptively sleepy behind his glasses. They regarded me with quiet waiting patience, as if I was the raw material of art.

"Sit down, Lew."

He waved his hand at the encumbered chairs. I remained standing.

"You would like me to identify a style, is that the problem? It isn't always so easy. You know how many painters there are? I bet you I could find five hundred within a radius of a mile. A thousand, maybe." He smiled slightly. "All of them genuises of the first water."

"This particular genius did a self-portrait, which ought to make it easier for you."

"If I have ever seen him."

I got the bamboo-framed sketch out of my straw bag and showed it to Manny. He held it in his hands, studying it with concentration, like a man peering into a mirror for traces of illness.

"I believe I *have* seen him. Let me look at the transparencies."

I slid them out of their envelope. He held them up to the window one at a time.

"Yes. I know him. He has his own style, though there has been some change in it, perhaps some deterioration. That wouldn't be surprising." When he turned from the window his eyes were sorrowful.

"His name is Bruce Campion. I saw some of his work at a showing of young artists in San Francisco last year. I also met him briefly. I hear since then that he has come to grief, that he is wanted by the police, for murdering his wife. It was in the San Francisco papers. I'm surprised you didn't see it."

"I don't take the San Francisco papers."

"Perhaps you should. You could have saved yourself time and trouble." He gathered together the sketch and the slides and handed them back to me. "I suppose you're hot on his heels?

"On the contrary, the trail is cold."

"I'm glad. Campion is a good painter."

"How good?"

"So good that I don't greatly care what he did to his wife," he said softly. "You live in a world of stark whites and blacks. My world is one of shadings, and the mechanism of punishment is anathema to me. 'An eye for an eye and a tooth for a tooth' is the law of a primitive tribe. If we practiced it to the letter we would all be eyeless and toothless. I hope he eludes you, and goes on painting."

"The danger is that he'll go on killing."

"I doubt it. According to my reading, murderers are the criminals least likely to repeat their offense. Now if you'll excuse me I have a show to cover."

Meyer's parting smile was gentle. He didn't believe in evil. His father had died in Buchenwald, and he didn't believe in evil.

I DROVE ACROSS to Sunset, and up the winding road to Blackwell's house in Bel Air. He opened the front door himself, brushing aside a little maid in uniform. His eyes moved on my face like a blind man's eyes trying to glean a ray of light.

"You've found out something?"

"The news is not good."

His hands came out and clutched both of my arms above the elbows. With the mindless automatism of St. Vitus's dance, he started to shake me. I pushed him away.

"Calm down and I'll tell you about it."

"How can you expect me to be calm? My daughter has been gone for forty-eight hours. I should have used force to stop them. I should have shot him dead at my feet—"

"That's nonsense," I said. "We need to talk. Can we go in and sit down?"

He blinked like a man waking up from troubled sleep. "Yes. Of course."

The drawing room he took me into was furnished with Empire pieces which gave it a museumlike atmosphere. Family portraits looked down their Blackwell noses from the walls. One of them, of an officer in the uniform of the War of 1812, had the weight and finish of a Gilbert Stuart.

Blackwell sat in an armchair under it, as if to call attention to the family resemblance. I parked myself uninvited on a red divan with a curved back, and gave him a brief rundown on my Mexican trip.

"I've put together certain facts I uncovered there with others that cropped up here and come to a definite conclusion about Damis. He's a wanted man traveling under more than one alias. His real name is Bruce Campion, and he's wanted for murder."

Blackwell's jaw moved slackly. I could see the pale insides of his mouth. "What did you say?"

"Damis's real name is Campion. He's wanted in San Mateo County for strangling his wife last spring."

Blackwell's face looked like cracked plaster. Consciousness withdrew from his eyes, leaving them blank as glass. He slipped from the armchair onto his knees, then fell heavily sideways. His white hair spilled like a sheaf on the old rose carpet.

I went to the door and called the maid. She came trotting and skidding on the parquetry, her excited little breasts bobbing under her uniform. She let out a muffled scream when she saw the fallen man.

"Is he dead?"

"He fainted, honey. Bring some water, and a washcloth."

She was back in thirty seconds, half spilling a pan of water on the carpet. I sprinkled some of it on Blackwell's face and swabbed his long forehead. His eyes came open, recognized me, remembered what I had told him. He groaned, and tried to faint again.

I slapped him with the wet cloth. The little maid stood and watched me with wide blue eyes, as if I was committing lese majesty.

"What's your name?" I asked her.

"Letty."

"Where's Mrs. Blackwell, Letty?"

"She does hospital work one day a week. This is the day."

"You'd better try and get in touch with her."

"All right. Should I call the doctor, do you think?"

"He doesn't need a doctor unless he has a heart history."

"Heart history?" she repeated like a lip reader.

"Has he ever had a heart attack, or a stroke?"

Blackwell answered me himself, in a shamed voice: "I've never even fainted before." He sat up laboriously, resting his back against the chair. "I'm not as young as I am—as I was. What you told me came as a fearful shock."

"It doesn't mean that Harriet is dead, you know."

"Doesn't it? I must have jumped to that conclusion." He noticed the young maid standing over him. He smoothed his hair and tried to compose his face. "You may go now, Miss Flavin. Be good enough to take that pot of water with you. It's out of place in here."

"Yessir." She picked it up and marched out.

Blackwell levered himself into the chair. "We have to do something," he said unsteadily.

"I'm glad you feel that way. I've already alerted detectives in the Reno area. I think we should extend the search to the whole Southwest, if not the entire country. That will cost a good deal of money."

He extended his limp fingers. "It doesn't matter. Anything."

"It's time to bring in the police, too, give them all we know and build a fire under them. I suggest you start off by talking to Peter Colton."

"Yes. I'll do that." He rose shakily as if the weight of his years had fallen on him all at once. "Give me a minute. My mind isn't quite clear yet."

"Better get yourself a drink. In the meantime, I have an important call to make. May I use one of your phones?"

"There's one in Isobel's sitting room. You can be private there."

It was a small pleasant room whose French doors opened onto a private terrace. The furniture was well used, shabby rather than antique. It didn't match the nineteenth-century grandeur of the drawing room, and I guessed that Isobel Blackwell had saved it from some less opulent period of her life—a period on which she hadn't turned her back.

I sat at the plain oak desk, called the Hall of Justice in Redwood City, and asked the switchboard operator for Captain Royal. He was San Mateo County's homicide chief, and I had met him on an earlier case.

"What can I do for you?" he said, after a few preliminaries.

"I have some information about Bruce Campion, who is alleged to have strangled his wife last May in your bailiwick. Is that correct?"

"Correct. It happened the night of May fifth. What's your information?"

I heard the small click as Royal switched on his recording machine. There was a second click, that sounded like a receiver being lifed.

"I've been tracing Campion's movements," I said. "He flew from Los Angeles to Guadalajara on May twentieth."

"The airport police were supposed to be watching for him," Royal said impatiently.

"He used false papers and an alias—Quincy Ralph Simpson. Does that name mean anything to you?"

"It does. I found out yesterday that Simpson was icepicked in Citrus Junction two months ago. You telling me Campion did it?"

"The possibility suggests itself," I said. "He must have been carrying Simpson's identification when he crossed the border. Simpson was almost certainly dead by then."

"Is Campion still in Mexico?"

"No. He spent two months there under the name Burke Damis, in Ajijic on Lake Chapala, where he was eventually recognized as a wanted man. In the meantime he'd got a visiting American girl named Harriet Blackwell to fall for him. Nine days ago the two of them flew back to Los Angeles. Campion used the Simpson alias again. Then he switched back to Damis, and spent a week as a guest in the Blackwell's beach house near Malibu. It's possible the Blackwell girl knows something about his past and is protecting him. Campion has her hypnotized, but she could hardly miss the change of names."

"Is she with him now?"

"I hope not. But she probably is. The two of them left her father's house forty-eight hours ago after a serious altercation which involved threats of shooting. They took off in her car, a new green Buick Special." I gave him the license number.

"Who did the threatening?"

"Her father, Mark Blackwell. He's only a retired Colonel but he has money, and I imagine he pulls weight in some circles. I'm calling from his house in Bel Air now."

"Is Blackwell your client?"

"Yes. My immediate job is to find the girl and get her out of danger. She should be easy to spot. She's a big blonde, short-haired, aged twenty-four, about six feet in her shoes, with a tall girl's stoop. Expensively dressed, good figure, but face a little disfigured by a bony protuberance over the eyes. It's a genetic defect—"

"What?"

"The bony eyebrows are a family trait. The old man has 'em, and all the ancestors. Harriet wears dark glasses part of the time. I assume you know what Campion looks like."

"I have him memorized," Royal said.

"Picture?"

"No picture. That's how he got across the border."

"I have one. I'll try to get a copy of it into your hands today. Now there's a possibility that Campion and the girl have doubled back toward Mexico. Nevada is another possibility. They were talking about getting married, and it's an easy state to get married in. They may be married now, or representing themselves as married."

"The girl must be crazy," Royal said, "if she knows what he did to his wife and still wants to marry him."

"I'm not suggesting she knows about the wife. He probably faked a story to explain the aliases, and she would be easily taken in. She's crazy in the sense that she's crazy about him. Also, she's in active revolt against her father. She's twenty-four, as I said, and he treats her as if she was four."

"Isn't twenty-four a little late for the big rebellion?"

"Harriet has been living under military occupation. She's a fugitive from injustice."

"So she takes up with a fugitive from justice. I've seen it happen before." Royal paused. "How much danger do you think she's in?"

"You'd know more about that than I do, Captain. It depends on Campion's motivation. Harriet's due to come into money on her twenty-fifth birthday, so if it's money he's after, she's safe for the next six months. Did Campion kill his wife for money?"

"There wasn't any money, so far as we know. We haven't been able to uncover any motive at all. Which means he could be off his rocker. A lot of these creeps who call themselves artists are nuts. He lived like a bum in a remodeled garage near Luna Bay, everything in one room." Royal's voice was scornful.

"Did he have a record of irrational behavior?"

"I wouldn't know. He has a record, period. A year's hard labor and a dishonorable discharge for assaulting an officer during the Korean War. That's all we've been able to dig up on him, but it shows a history of violence. Also he wasn't getting along with his wife. Put the two together, it's all you need in the way of motive."

"Tell me about the wife."

"That can wait, can't it, Archer? I want to get your info out on the wires."

"You could give me a quick rundown."

Royal said in a clipped, toneless voice: "Her name was Dolly Stone Campion, age about twenty, pretty little blonde, not so pretty when we found her. According to our info, Campion picked her up on the South Shore of Tahoe last summer, and married her in Reno in September. It must have been a marriage of inconvenience—Dolly was three months pregnant at the time. At least their child was born in March, six months after the wedding. Two months after that he knocked her off."

"Tahoe keeps cropping up," I said. "The Blackwells have a lodge there, and Q. R. Simpson spent some time at the lake in May, shortly before he was murdered."

"What was he doing there?"

"I have a hunch he was working on the Dolly Campion case. What happened to her baby, by the way?"

"Her mother took him. Look, Archer, this could go on all day, and I have work to do. A lot more work than I had before," he added wryly. "Will you be coming up this way?"

"As soon as I can make it."

Which wasn't soon. I made a second call to Arnie Walters's office in Reno. I wanted to pass the word on Campion and ask Arnie to add more men to the search. He already had, Phyllis told me, because Campion and Harriet Blackwell had been seen in State Line the previous night. That was all so far.

I dropped the receiver into its cradle. When I picked it up, it felt appeciably heavier. I called the airport and made a reservation on the next flight to Reno. They were going to have to give me flying pay.

As I was getting up from the desk, I noticed a folded newspaper which lay on the back of it. "San Mateo Man," I spelled out upside down. I unfolded the paper.

It was yesterday's issue of the *Citrus Junction News-Beacon*. The full headline ran across the top of the page: "San Mateo Man Killed Here: Police Suspect Gang Murder." The story under it was poorly written and poorly printed, and it told me nothing I didn't already know.

I still had the paper in my hands when Blackwell came into the room. He looked like the ghost of one of his ancestors.

"What are you doing with that newspaper?"

"I was wondering how it got into your house."

"That's no concern of yours, I should think." He snatched it away from me and rolled it up small. "A number of things are no concern of yours. For example, I'm not paying out good money to have myself and my daughter slandered to policemen."

"I thought I heard somebody on another extension. Does everyone in your household eavesdrop on everyone else?"

"That's an insulting remark. I demand that you withdraw it."

Blackwell was shaking with another bout of uncontrollable anger. The rolled newspaper vibrated in his hand. He slapped his thigh with it, as if it was a swagger stick or a riding crop. He looked ready to strike me with it, and challenge me to a duel.

"I can't change facts, Colonel. If you don't like what you heard, you could have stopped listening."

"Are you telling me what to do in my own house?"

"It does sound like it, doesn't it?"

"Then get out of my house. Get out, do you hear?"

"They hear you in Tarzana. Don't you want your daughter found?"

"We'll find her without your help. You're fired."

"You've already had my help," I said. "You owe me three hundred and fifty dollars for time and expenses."

"I'll write you a check, now?"

"You can stop payment on a check. I need cash."

I was playing for time in the faint hope that Blackwell would come to his senses, as he had once before. Though I couldn't knuckle under to him, I was eager to hold on to the case. It was beginning to break, and a breaking case to a man in my trade is like a love affair you can't stay away from, even if it tears your heart out daily.

"I don't have that much in the house," he was saying. "I'd have to cash a check at the hotel."

"Do that. I'll wait here."

"Outside," he said in a monitory tone. "I don't want you prying around in here. You can wait in your car."

I went down the hall and out, with Blackwell making shooing motions at my kidneys. He backed his black Cadillac out of the garage and drove away down the hill. I put in a bad ten minutes deciding where to go from here. It would have to be Tahoe, though I hated to make the trip on my own time.

The mourning dove had returned to the television antenna. He sat there still and perfect as a heraldic bird. I said hoo-hoo to him and got a response, hoo-hoo, and I felt better.

Isobel Blackwell, driving a small foreign car, came into the driveway from the road. I got out of my car to meet her. Her face looked wan in the sunlight, but she made herself smile at me.

"Mr. Archer! What a pleasant surprise."

"Didn't Letty get in touch with you?"

"I left the hospital early. I've been concerned about Mark."

"You have some reason to be. He had a fainting spell a while ago. Then he had a yelling spell."

"Mark fainted?"

"I gave him some information that hit him hard."

She ducked out of her little car and thrust her face up toward mine. "Something has happened to Harriet."

"We don't know that. But something could happen to her any time. She's wandering around Nevada with the man who calls himself Damis. His actual name is Bruce Campion, and he's wanted in Redwood City for murdering his wife."

It took her a minute to absorb this. Then she turned toward the house and noticed the empty garage. "Where is Mark?"

"He went down to the hotel to get some money to pay me off. He fired me."

"What on earth for?"

"The Colonel and I have had it, I'm afraid. We've both had too much Army, in different ways—the worm's-eye view and the god's-eye view."

"But I don't understand. You mean you won't go on with him?"

"I'd have to be asked. Which isn't very likely."

"I know how difficult he can be," she said in a rush of feeling. "Tell me exactly what the trouble was."

"He listened in on a telephone conversation I had with a police officer. I made some critical remarks about his treatment of Harriet. He didn't like them."

"And that's all?"

"All there is on the surface. Of course he was thrown by the information I gave him on Damis-Campion. He couldn't handle it, so he threw it back. He thinks that I'm what hurts him."

She nodded. "That's his standard pattern. It's been getting worse since this began. I'm worried about him, Mr. Archer. I don't know how he's going to survive."

"It's Harriet's survival I'm worried about. She and Campion were seen at State Line last night, and I have some Reno detectives on their trail. We have a chance to take him and rescue her, if we can stay with it."

Her whole body reacted to my words. She clutched her handbag to her breast as if it was a child she could protect. "The man is a murderer, you say?"

"It's a matter of police record."

She moved closer to me. Her hand lit on my wrist, and she said in a voice as low as a mourning dove's: "You said you'd have to be asked. I'm asking you. Will you take me for a client?"

"Nothing would suit me better."

"Then it's a contract." Her hand slid from my wrist to my fingers, and squeezed them. "It would be a good idea to let me tell Mark about this. In my own time, in my own way."

"I agree."

She went into the house and came out and gave me money and went in again. Blackwell's Cadillac rolled into the drive. He climbed out and gave me money. His color was better, and I could smell fresh whisky on him. He must have had a quick one or two at the hotel.

He looked at me as though he wanted to speak, but he didn't say a word.

>>>>>>>>>
>>>>>>>>> *chapter* 15
>>>>>>>>>

ARNIE WALTERS met me at the Reno airport. He was a short broad man in his early fifties who looked like somebody you'd see selling tips at a race track. But he had the qualities of a first-rate detective: honesty, imagination, curiosity, and a love of people. Ten or twelve years in Reno had left him poor and uncorrupted.

On the way to State Line he filled me in on the situation there. A handyman named Sholto, who kept an eye on several lakeside houses for their absentee owners, had talked to Harriet the night before. She had come to Sholto's house to get the key to her father's lodge, and specifically asked him not to tell her father she was there. Campion had been with her, but stayed in the car, her car.

"Apparently," Arnie went on, "they spent the night, or part of the night, in the lodge. There's some dirty dishes on the sinkboard, recently used. Also there's some indication they're coming back, or planned to. He left his suitcase in the entrance hall. I have the place staked out."

"What about her suitcase?"

"Gone. So is her car."

"I don't like that."

Arnie shifted his eyes from the road to my face. "You seriously think he brought her up here to do her in?"

"It's a possibility that can't be ruled out."

"What were the circumstances of the other killing? The wife."

"He strangled her. I don't have the details yet."

"Did he stand to gain by her death?"

"The San Mateo police think not. The only motive they've come up with is incompatibility, or words to that effect. Evidently it was a forced marriage: the girl was about three months pregnant at the time. He married her in Reno last September, by the way, which means that this isn't new territory to Campion."

"You think he's repeating a pattern?"

"Something like that."

"What kind of a character is he?"

"He has me baffled."

"I never heard you say that before, Lew. Not out loud."

"Maybe I'm slipping. I don't pretend to be attuned to the artistic mind. Campion is a good painter, according to a critic who knows what he's talking about."

"You think he could be psycho? A lot of psychos magnetize the broads."

"The psycho broads," I said. "It's hard to tell about Campion. He had himself in control both times I saw him. The second time was under severe provocation. Harriet's father threatened him with a shotgun, and he stood up to it like a little man. But then psychos can be actors."

"Bad actors. Is he as good-looking as the description says?"

"Unfortunately yes. I brought along a picture of him. It's a self-sketch, not a photograph, but it's a good-enough likeness to circularize. I want it back after you have it photographed."

"Sure. Leave it in the car. I'll get it around to our informers and have it posted in the lookout galleries in the clubs. Sooner or later he'll show, if he's hiding out in this area. You realize he could be long gone by now, and so could the girl."

We drove in silence for a while, through country wooded with evergreens. The trees parted at one point, and I caught a first glimpse of the lake. It was the height of the season, and outboards were rioting in the afternoon sun. Skiers drove their plows of spray in eccentric furrows. I couldn't help remembering that Tahoe was deep and cold. Harriet could be long gone, far down, sheathed in black bottom water.

Her father's lodge stood among dense trees at the end of a frost-cracked asphalt lane. It was an imposing timbered building with half-walls of native stone. Concrete steps with iron railings zigzagged down from the terrace to the shore.

A man stepped out of the trees. He had the stubborn thick-bodied presence of an old cop. Arnie introduced him as Jim Hanna, one of his men. The three of us went inside.

Campion's brown suitcase was standing in the hallway under a moose head. I reached for it, but Arnie stopped me.

"It's a waste of time, Lew. Nothing in it but some painting equipment and shaving kit and some old clothes. He was hungry."

The great front room was furnished with handsome rustic pieces, Navajo rugs, animal skins, animal heads staring down at us with sad glass eyes. The picture window that Harriet had described to Campion framed blue sky and blue lake. Her pitch had been too successful, I was thinking.

We went through the other rooms, including the six upstairs bedrooms. Their mattresses lay bare. A closet in the hallway was full of sheets and pillow slips and towels, none of which had been used.

I left Arnie and Hanna in the house and went down the concrete steps to the shore. The lake had been pulling at me since my first sight of it. It was very low this year, and a swath of gravel sloped down from the foot of the steps.

I took a walk along the edge of the gravel. Speedboat waves lapped at the stones and brightened them. I was looking for some trace of Harriet; yet I was shocked when I found it. It was something that looked like a scrap of grey fishnet tangled with some floating sticks about fifty feet offshore.

I stripped to my shorts behind a tree and went in after it. The lake was icy after the summer air. The thing in the nest of sticks did nothing to warm me. It was her hat, with its little veil fluttering in the sun.

I disentangled it and held it out of the water in my left hand as I side-stroked back to shore. There I discovered that the hat had more than the veil attached to it. In the damp silk lining there was a smear of coagulated blood about the size of a thumbnail. Adhering to this was a thin lock of hair about six inches long. It was fair and straight, like Harriet's, and it had been torn out by the roots.

I dressed and went up to the lodge on cold and heavy legs and showed the other men what I had found.

Arnie whistled softly, on a diminuendo. "Looks like we're too late."

"That remains to be proved. How good is the law around here?"

"Spotty. It's been improving, but there's six or seven different jurisdictions around the lake. It spreads the money thin, and also the responsibility."

"Can you bring the Reno P.D. in on this? It needs lab work."

"And a dragging operation. It's not their territory, but I'll see what I can do. You want to come back to town with me?"

"I should talk to Sholto. Does he live in this neighborhood?"

"A couple of miles from here, on the road to State Line. I'll drop you."

Sholto's boxlike little house stood in a clearing far back from the road. Chickens scratched around it. The young woman who answered the door had a baby on her hip and a slightly larger child hanging onto her skirt. She pushed back her hair and gave Arnie a wide slack smile.

"Hank is out back, Mr. Walters. He's building a hutch for the rabbits. Come through the house if you want."

A third child, a girl of eight or nine, was reading a comic book at the kitchen table, simultaneously drinking chocolate milk through a straw. Her bare toes were curled with concentrated pleasure. She regarded us blankly, as though we were less vivid than the characters in her book. I paid particular attention to the child because her towhead was the same color as Harriet's.

A boy of twelve or so was helping his father in the back yard. That is, he sat on a board laid across wooden horses while Sholto used a handsaw on the board. He was a wiry man of indeterminate age, hipless in faded blue levis. His sun wrinkles gave his jay-blue eyes a fiercely questioning look.

"Hi, Mr. Walters. You find her all right?"

"Not yet. This is my associate Lew Archer. He has some more questions to ask you."

Sholto laid down his saw and gave me a wide hard hand. "Shoot away."

"Before you men talk," Arnie said, "I want to show you a picture, Henry."

He produced the self-sketch of Campion which he had brought from the car. "Is this the man you saw with Harriet?"

"Sure looks like him. Something funny about the eyes, though. How come one of 'em is bigger than the other?"

"He drew it that way," I said.

"He drew this himself?"

"That's right."

"Why did he do that to the eyes? It makes him look cockeyed. He's a real nice-lookin' fellow in real life."

Arnie lifted the picture from his hands. "Thanks, Henry. I needed a positive identification."

"Is the guy some kind of a crook?"

"He has a record," I said. "Maybe you'd better send the boy inside."

"I don't wanna go inside."

"Inside," Sholto said.

The boy climbed off his board and went. Arnie followed him into the house, with a curt flick of the hand to us. Sholto said to me: "I hope Miss Blackwell isn't in trouble. She's a nervous young lady, jumpy as a filly. She wouldn't take trouble too well."

"Was she nervous last night when you talked to her?"

He propped one foot up on a sawhorse and rested his arm on his knee. "I'd say she was. Mostly I think she was nervous on account of her father—you know, the young fellow, and them using the lodge. But she had a perfect right—I told Mr. Walters that. And I told her I wouldn't breathe a word to the old man. After all, she's used it before when he wasn't here."

"With men?"

"I dunno about that. This is the first man she ever brought up here, leastways that I saw. What did the two of them have in mind?"

"They talked about getting married."

"Is that a fact?"

"You sound surprised."

"It's just that I never thought of her as the marrying type. I got a sister teaches school in Porterville, she's the same way. She's still living at home."

"Miss Blackwell isn't. How were the two of them getting along when you saw them?"

"I didn't see them together. She came up to the door by herself, wanting the key to the lodge. He stayed in the car." Sholto pushed back his cap and scratched his freckled hairline, as though to promote the growth of an idea. "They did sit out in the car for quite a while after. The wife thought they were having an argument."

"Did you hear any of it?"

"I didn't like to listen," he said delicately. "Besides, I had the radio on."

"Did your wife hear any of it?"

"She must of, or how would she know it was an argument?" He raised his voice: "Molly!"

The woman appeared at the back door with the baby on her hip. From the cover of her other hip, the twelve-year-old peered out resentfully.

"What is it, Hank?"

"Last night, when Miss Blackwell came for the key, and they were sitting out in the car after—did you hear anything they said?"

"Yeah. I told you they were having a battle."

I moved to the foot of the back steps. "Did he hit her?"

"Not that I saw. It was just talk. She didn't want to go to the lodge. He did."

"*She* didn't want to go?"

"That's what she said. She said he was trying to use her or something, said he was taking advantage of her love. He said he wasn't. He said that he was working out his des—destry?"

"Destiny?"

"Yeah, destiny. He said he was working out his destiny or something. I dunno what he meant when he said that. They were talkin' pretty high-falutin'."

"How did his voice sound? Was he excited?"

"Naw, he was real cool and cold. She was more hysterical like."

"Did he threaten her, Mrs. Sholto?"

"I wouldn't say he threatened her. More like he soothed her down. She was okay when they drove off."

"Who was driving?"

"He was. She was at the wheel when they were sitting there, but he changed places with her. He did the driving."

"What time did they leave?"

"I dunno. The clock broke. When are you going to get me a new clock, Hank?"

"Saturday."

"I bet," she said serenely, and retreated into the house.

Sholto turned to me. "It was twilight when they left here, nearly night, I'd say around eight o'clock. I didn't know there was nothin' wrong or I'd of phoned her father. You think the guy did something to her, eh?"

"We have some evidence that points that way. Was Miss Blackwell wearing a hat when you saw her last night?"

"Yeah, a little hat with a veil. I noticed it because the girls don't go in for hats around here much."

"I found her hat in the lake just now," I said. "With blood and hair on it."

His eyes went almost out of sight in their twin nests of wrinkles.

"The man she was with, Campion, is implicated in two other murders. One was his wife. Her maiden name was Dolly Stone, and she's supposed to have spent some time here last summer. Did you ever hear of a Dolly Stone, or Dolly Campion?"

"No, sir. No siree."

"What about Q. R. Simpson?"

"Come again."

"Quincy Ralph Simpson. His wife told me he was up here a couple of months ago."

"Yeah," he said matter-of-factly, "I knew Ralph. He worked for the Blackwells for a little while, in May I think it was. The Colonel opened the lodge early this year, in April. He told me he wanted to give his new little wife a chance to watch the spring come on." He paused, and glanced at the declining sun as though to reorient himself in the present day. "Did something happen to Ralph Simpson?"

"He's the other murder victim. We don't know for certain that Campion was responsible. The chances are he was. What sort of work was Simpson doing for the Blackwells?"

"Chief cook and bottlewasher, while he lasted. He didn't last long."

"Why not?"

Sholto kicked at one of the sawhorses. "I don't like to pass it on about a dead man. There was talk around that Ralph took something. I didn't put much stock in it myself. Ralph may have been a gamblin' fool, but that don't make him no thief."

"He was a gambler?"

"Yeah, he can't stay away from the tables. It was my belief he gambled away his money and got stuck here and had to take any job he could get. He must of had some reason for hiring himself out for a cook—a young fellow with his brains. Now you tell me he's dead," he said with some resentment.

"Did you know him well, Mr. Sholto?"

"We shot the breeze a couple of times when I was doing repair work at the lodge. The kitchen linoleum buckled, and I had to piece it. Ralph Simpson was a likable fellow, full of ideas."

"What kind of ideas?"

"All kinds. Man in space, the atom bomb, he had an opinion on everything. Reincarnation and the hereafter. He had a great understanding. Also, he had a system to beat the tables, for which he was trying to raise the capital."

"How?"

"He didn't say."

"What is he supposed to have stolen from the Blackwells?"

"I dunno. I never got it straight."

"Who did you hear it from?"

"Kito. He's houseboy in one of the other lodges. But you can't always trust these Orientals."

"Still I'd like to talk to Kito."

"He isn't around any more. The family closed the place up last month and went back to Frisco."

"Do you know their address in Frisco?"

"I have it written down in the house."

"Get it for me, will you?"

He went in and came out with a Belvedere address written in

childish longhand on the back of an envelope. I transcribed it in my notebook.

"Is there anything else you can tell me about Simpson?"

"I can't think of anything."

"Or anyone else who can?"

"Well, he did have a girl friend. It wouldn't be fair to pass that on to his wife. Matter of fact, he never mentioned a wife. I thought he was a single man."

"It hardly matters now," I said, with my ball-point poised over the open notebook. "What's the girl friend's name?"

"He called her Fawn. I don't rightly know her last name. I saw her a couple of times in the clubs with Ralph, and once or twice since." He added, with a rueful glance at the house: "I don't go there to gamble. I can't afford to gamble, with my family. But I like to stand around and watch the excitement."

"Can you describe the girl?"

"She's a pretty little thing. She looks something like a real fawn— she has those big brown eyes."

"What color hair?"

"Light blonde, palomino color."

That didn't make it easier. Palomino fillies browsed in herds on the Tahoe shores.

"You say she's little?"

"Yeah, about five foot two or three." He held out a hand at shoulder level. "I call that little in a woman."

"What does she do for a living?"

"I dunno where she works, or if she works. She may not even be here any more. We have a floating population. They drift in and out. I been here for years myself, come here from Porterville when State Line was nothin' more than a wide place in the road."

"When did you last see Fawn?"

"A couple weeks ago, I *think* it was at the Solitaire. She had some older fellow on the string and they were playing the machines, least-ways *she* was. He kept buying silver dollars for her. Yeah, I'm pretty certain it was the Solitaire."

SHOLTO DEPOSITED ME in front of the club and bumped away in his pickup. The main street of State Line was an unstable blend of small-time frontier settlement and big-time carnival. The lake seemed artificial seen from here: a man-made lake dyed a special shade of blue and surrounded by papier-mâché mountains. In this setting it was hard to believe in death, and life itself was denatured.

I went inside the club, where the late afternoon crowd were enjoying themselves, if gamblers can be said to enjoy themselves. They wheedled cards or dice like sinners praying to heaven for one small mercy. They pulled convulsively at the handles of one-armed bandits, as if the machines were computers that would answer all their questions. Am I getting old? Have I failed? Am I immature? Does she love me? Why does he hate me? Hit me, jackpot, flood me with life and liberty and happiness.

A number of men and a few women were hanging around the bar. I waited my turn with one of the overworked bartenders and asked him where the security officer was.

"I saw Mr. Todd on the floor a minute ago." He scanned the big room. "There he is, talking to the character in the hat."

I made my way down one of the aisles of slot machines. Todd was an athletic-looking man in an open-necked shirt. He had iron-grey hair, iron-grey eyes, a face that had been humanized by punishment. The other man, who wore a white Stetson with a rolled brim, was drunk and fat and furious. He had been robbed, the machines were fixed, he'd see the management, invoke his influence with the governor.

With gentle firmness Todd steered him to the front door. I stepped out after Todd, away from the din of the gamblers, and showed him my photostat. He smiled as he handed it back.

"I used to be with the California Highway Patrol. Looking for somebody?"

"Several people." I gave him full descriptions of Campion and Harriet.

"I don't believe I've seen 'em, at least not together. I can't be certain. The turnover in this place is something for the book. Sometimes I think it's the bottleneck where the whole country passes through sooner or later." His eyes were on the drunk, who was weaving across the street through light traffic.

"Try something easier," I said. "A girl named Fawn something. She's a small girl with beautiful brown eyes, I'm told, pale blonde hair. Fawn has been seen in your place."

Todd said with more interest: "What do you want with her?"

"I have some questions to ask her. She knew a man who was murdered in California."

"She involved?"

"I have no reason to think so."

"That's good. She's a nice kid."

"You know her, do you?"

"Sure. She's in and out. Her last name's King, I think, if she hasn't remarried."

"Has she been in today?"

"Not yet. She probably sleeps in the daytime."

"Where?"

"I don't know her that well. She used to work in the beauty parlor down the street. Try there. You'll see it on the left a couple of blocks from here."

He pointed west toward California. I went that way, past gambling houses that resembled supermarkets with nothing to sell. The first effects of night were coming on. Though everything was clearly visible, the fronts of the buildings were stark in their nakedness, as if the light had lost its supportive quality.

Marie's Salon de Paris was closed. I knocked on the glass door. After a while a large woman emerged from a room at the back and minced toward me through the twilit shop.

She turned on a light before she opened the door. Her hair was the color of a spectacular sunset, and she wore it low on her forehead in curled bangs, a dubious advertisement for her trade. Warm air smelling of chemicals and women drifted out past her.

"I'm looking for a woman named Fawn King."

"You're not the first. I hope you'll be the last. Mrs. King doesn't work here any more."

"Where can I put my hands on her?"

It was a bad choice of expression. Her pouched eyes went over me coldly, including my hands. I tried again: "I happen to be a detective—"

"She in trouble?" Marie said hopefully.

"A friend of hers is in the worst kind of trouble. He's dead. Stabbed with an icepick."

She brightened up alarmingly. "Why didn't you say so? Come in. I'll get you King's address."

Fawn lived in an apartment house a mile or so west on the same road. I started to walk, but on the way I noticed a U-drive sign at a gas station. I rented a new-looking Ford that sounded elderly. The attendant said it was the altitude.

The apartment house had a temporary atmosphere, like a motel. It was U-shaped and two-storied. The U enclosed the tenants' parking lot, with its open end facing the street. I drove in and left the Ford in one of the white-marked slots.

Fawn's apartment was number twenty-seven on the second floor. I went up the outside steps and along the railed gallery till I found her door. There was music behind it, the sound of a woman singing a blues. It wasn't quite good enough to be a record, and there was no accompaniment.

The song broke off when I knocked. She appeared at the door, her face still softened by music. Her brown eyes held a puzzled innocence. Perhaps she was puzzled by her body and its uses. It was full and tender under her sweater, like fruit that has ripened too quickly. She held it for me to look at and said in a semiprofessional voice: "Hello. I was just practicing my blues style."

"I heard. You have a nice voice."

"So they all tell me. The trouble is, the competition here is terrif. They bring in recording stars, and it isn't fair to the local talent."

"You're a local girl?"

"This is my third season. My third fabulous season. Which makes me an old-timer."

"And you want to be a singer?"

"Anything," she said. "Anything to get out of the rat race. Do you have any suggestions?"

My usual line was ready, the one I used on aspiring starlets and fledgling nightingales and girls who hoped to model their way into heaven: I was from Hollywood, knew movie people, could help. Her puzzled innocence stopped me.

"Just keep trying."

She regarded me suspiciously, as though I had flubbed my cue. "Did somebody send you?"

"Ralph Simpson."

"What do you know? I haven't heard from Ralph for it must be at least two months." She stepped aside in a quick dancer's movement. "Come in, tell me about him."

It was a hot-plate apartment containing a studio bed that hadn't been made, an open portable record player, a dressing table loaded with cosmetic jars and bottles and a few paperbacked novels with young women like Fawn portrayed on their covers. The calendar on the wall hadn't been changed since April.

I sat on the studio bed. "When did you last hear from Ralph?"

"Couple of months, like I said. He spent the night with me," she went on routinely, "it must of been sometime around the middle of May. That was when he lost his job and didn't have no place—any place to go. I lent him bus fare in the morning, haven't seen him since."

"He must be a good friend of yours."

"Not in the way you think. It's a brother-and-sister act between Ralph and me. We batted around together ever since we were kids in South San Francisco. He was like a big brother to me. Anyway, I wouldn't take a married man away from his wife."

But she posed in front of me as if she was testing out her power to do this.

"I'm not married," I said.

"I was wondering." She sat on the bed beside me, so close I could feel her heat. "You don't talk like a married man and you don't look like a bachelor."

"I had a wife at one time. She looked something like you."

"What was her name?"

"I forget." There was too much pain in the word, and this was no place to deposit it.

"I don't believe you. What happened to your wife?" Her brown eyes were attentive on my face. You'd have thought I was about to tell her fortune.

"Nothing bad happened to her. She left me, but that wasn't bad for her. It was bad for me. Eventually she married somebody else and had some kids and lived happily ever after."

She nodded, as if the story's happy ending might somehow apply to her. "She left you on account of another woman, I bet."

"You'd lose your bet. I treated her badly, but not in that way." The pain stirred like a Santa Ana wind in the desert back reaches of my mind. I'd begun to talk to the girl because she was there. Now I was there, too, more completely than I wanted to be. "Also," I said, "she didn't like my trade. At the moment I'm not too crazy about it myself."

"I wouldn't care what a man did for a living. My ex was just a bookie, but I didn't care. What do you do for a living?"

"I'm a detective."

"How interesting." But her body tensed, and her eyes glazed with distrust.

"Relax," I said. "If I was the kind of detective you're afraid of, I wouldn't be telling you about it, would I?"

"I'm not afraid."

"Good. You have no reason. I'm a private detective from Los Angeles."

"Ralph is interested in that kind of work, too. Is that how you know him?"

"In a way. Let's talk about Ralph. Can you tell me anything about that job he lost?"

"He was a houseboy, more or less. He took jobs like that when he couldn't get anything else. He worked for a mucky-muck up the lake. He showed me the house one night when the family was out. It was quite a layout."

"I've seen the Blackwell place."

"Blackwell. That was the name."

"How long did Ralph work for the Blackwells?"

"A week or so. I didn't keep tabs on him." She smiled in her puzzled way. "I have enough trouble keeping tabs on myself."

"Why did they fire him?"

"He didn't tell *me* he was fired. He said he quit because he had what he wanted. Anyway, the family was going back down south."

"I don't understand."

"They closed the lodge and went back to L.A. or wherever they live. Ralph thought they were going to stay longer, but they changed their minds."

"I mean I don't understand about Ralph getting what he wanted."

"Neither do I. You know Ralph, he likes to act mysterious. Ralph Simpson, boy detective. It's kind of cute."

"Was Ralph doing some sort of detective work at the Blackwell place?"

"So he said. I don't always buy a hundred per cent of what Ralph says. He goes to a lot of movies and sometimes he gets them mixed up with the things he does himself." She added, with an indulgent glance at the paperbacks on the dressing table: "I do the same thing with stories sometimes. It makes life more exciting."

I brought her back to the subject: "Tell me what Ralph said."

"I couldn't—my memory isn't that good. The way he talked, it was all mixed up with the tragedy that happened to Dolly. That hit Ralph hard. He was very fond of Dolly."

"Are you talking about the Dolly who married Bruce Campion?"

The force of the question pushed her off the bed away from me. She went to the far side of the room, which wasn't very far, and stood beside the dressing table in a defensive posture.

"You don't have to shout at a girl. I have neighbors, remember. The management's always breathing down my back."

"I'm sorry, Fawn. The question is important."

"I bet you're working on Dolly's murder, aren't you?"

"Yes. Was Ralph?"

"I guess he thought he was. But Ralph is no great operator. It's time somebody with something on the ball did something. Dolly was a sweet kid. She didn't deserve to die."

She looked up at the low ceiling, as if Dolly's epitaph was also a prayer for herself. Tentatively, almost unconsciously, she drifted back across the room, stood over me with eyes like brimming pools.

"It's a terrible world."

"There are terrible people in it, anyway. Do you know Bruce Campion?"

"I wouldn't say I *know* him. Ralph took me out to their place once, when Dolly was living with him. *She* was crazy about him at that time. She followed him around like a little poodle."

"How did Campion treat her?"

"All right. Actually he didn't pay too much attention to her. I think he kept her around because he needed a model. He wanted me to model for him, too. I told him I hadn't sunk that low yet, to pose for dirty pictures."

"He painted dirty pictures?"

"It sounded like it to me. Dolly said he made her take her clothes off." Her nostrils flared with righteous indignation. "I only know one good reason a girl should uncover herself in front of a man."

"Why did Campion marry her if all he wanted was a model?"

"Oh, he wanted more. They always do. Anyway, he had to marry her. He got her pregnant."

"Did Dolly tell you this?"

"She didn't have to tell me. I could see it already when Ralph and I were out there."

"Do you remember when that was?"

"It was along toward the end of last summer, late August or early September. They weren't married yet, but they were talking about it, at least she was. Ralph brought along a bottle, and we drank a toast to their happiness. It didn't do much good, did it? She's dead, and he's on the run." She touched my shoulder. "Did he really kill her?"

"All the evidence seems to point to him."

"Ralph said that isn't so. He said there was other evidence, but the cops held back on it. He may have been telling the truth, or having one of his movie spells. You never can tell about Ralph, 'specially where one of his friends is concerned." She drew a deep breath.

"When did Ralph say these things to you?"

Using her hand on my shoulder as a pivot, she sat down beside me. "The last night he was here. We sat up talking, after I got in."

"Did he tell you what the other evidence was?"

"No. He kept his lips buttoned. The man of mystery."

"Did he show you anything?"

"No."

"What did he have with him when he left here?"

"Just the clothes that he stood up in. When he came up here he wasn't planning to stay, but then he got this job." She hesitated. "I almost forgot the bundle. He dropped this bundle off with me a day or two before his job folded. I wasn't supposed to open it, he said. I *felt* it, though. It felt like it had clothes in it."

"What kind of clothes?"

"I wouldn't know. It was a great big bundle." She opened her arms. "I tried to ask Ralph about it, but he wasn't talking."

"Was it stolen goods, do you think?"

She shook her head. "Of course not. Ralph's no thief."

"What sort of a man is he?"

"I thought you knew him."

"Not as well as you do."

She answered after a little thought: "I *like* Ralph. I don't want to criticize him. He has a lot of good ideas. The trouble is, he never follows through on them. He keeps changing, because he can't make up his mind what he wants to be. I can remember, when we were kids, Ralph was always talking about how he was going to be a big criminal lawyer. But then he never even made it through high school. It's been like that all his life."

"How long has he known Campion?"

"It goes 'way back," she said. "Ten years or more. I think they were Army buddies in Korea. They did some talking about Korea the day Ralph took me out to the cabin."

"I'm interested in that cabin. Do you think you could find it again?"

"Now?"

"Now."

She looked at the leatherette-covered traveling clock on the dressing table. "I have a date. He's due here any time."

"Stand him up."

"I got rent to pay, mister. Anyway, you won't find Bruce Campion there. He only had the cabin for a while last summer. Somebody lent him the use of it."

"I still want to see it."

"Tomorrow. Buy me brunch tomorrow, and I'll show you where it is. It's real wild on that side of the lake. Buy some sandwiches and we'll have a picnic."

"I like night picnics."

"But I have a date."

"How much do you expect to make out of him?"

She frowned. "I don't think of it that way. They give me money to gamble, that's their business. Nobody says I have to throw it all away."

"I'm asking you how much a couple of hours of your time is worth."

She blinked her innocent eyes. "Twenty?" she said. "And dinner?"

We set out in the rented Ford, along a road which branched north off the highway through thickening timber. Above the broken dark lines of the trees there were almost as many stars as I had seen in Mexico. The night was turning colder, and the girl moved over against me.

"Turn on the heater, will you, mister? I don't even know your name."

"Lew Archer." I switched on the blower.

"That's a nice name. Is it your real one?"

"Naturally not. My real name is Natty Bumppo."

"You're kidding me."

"It's a free country."

"Is there any such person as Natty What'shisname?"

"Bumppo. He's a character in a book. He was a great rifleman and a great tracker."

"Are you?"

"I can shoot a rifle but as for tracking, I do my best work in cities."

"Tracking men?"

"Tracking men."

She huddled closer. "Do you have a gun?"

"Several, but not with me. I wish I had."

"Do you think that Campion is hiding out in the cabin?"

"He may be, and he may be dangerous."

She giggled nervously. "You're trying to scare me. I thought he was kind of a sissy, with that little beret he wears, and all his arty talk."

"He's no sissy. He's something more complicated than that."

"How do you mean?"

"It's time I told you, Fawn. Dolly isn't the only one who was killed. Ralph Simpson was icepicked last May, soon after you saw him last. Campion is the prime suspect."

She had drawn in her breath sharply, and now she was holding it. I could feel her body tighten against my flank. Her breath came out in gusts around her words.

"You must be mistaken. Maybe Bruce Campion did kill Dolly—you never can tell what a man will do to his wife. But he would never do anything like that to Ralph. Ralph idolized him, he thought he was the greatest."

"How did Campion feel about Ralph?"

"He *liked* him. They got along fine. Ralph was proud to have a real artist for a friend. It was one of the things he wanted to be himself."

"I've known a few artists. They can make difficult friends."

"But they don't stick icepicks in people." For the first time, the full meaning of what I had said struck the girl. I could feel it pass through her body, a shuddering aftershock. "Is Ralph really dead?"

"I saw him in the morgue. I'm sorry, Fawn."

"Poor Ralph. Now he'll never make it."

We rode in silence for a time. She began to cry, almost inaudibly. At one point she said to the moving darkness: "All my friends are dying off. I feel like an old woman."

I had starred glimpses of the lake between the trees, like polished steel catching the droppings of infinity.

I said when her grief had subsided: "Tell me more about Dolly."

"What's to tell?" Her voice was hoarse. "She came up here last spring to get a job. She made change at one of the clubs for a while, but her subtraction wasn't too hot, so she got herself a man. It's the same old story."

"This time the ending was different. Did you know her well?"

"There wasn't much to know. She was just a country girl from the sticks. I sort of befriended her when she lost her job. Then Ralph introduced her to Campion, and that was that."

"You said Ralph had a crush on her."

"I wouldn't put it that strong. Dolly was a beautiful kid, but he never made a play for her. He just wanted to look after her. She was pretty helpless. She didn't belong up here."

"Where did she belong?"

"Let's see, she told me once where she came from. It was some place down in the orange belt. She used to talk about the orange blossoms."

"Citrus Junction?"

"Yeah. How did you know?"

"Ralph was murdered in Citrus Junction."

THE CABIN STOOD on a wooded point which projected into the lake below the road. I left the car at the top of the lane and told Fawn to stay in it, out of sight. She crouched down in the front seat, peering like a frightened bush-bunny over the edge of the door.

I made my way down the rutted dirt lane, walking quietly, like Natty Bumppo. Starshine filtering down between the black conifers hung in the air like the ghost of light. A ramp of solider light slanted from the window of the cabin.

I approached it from the side and looked in. A man who wasn't Campion was standing in front of the stone fireplace, in which a low fire burned. He was talking to somebody or something.

"Eat it up, Angelo. Enjoy yourself. We've got to keep your weight up, old boy."

Unless there was someone in the shadowed bunks against the far wall, he seemed to be alone in the room. He was a small man with a dark head and a thin neck like a boy's. He wore a plaid shirt under a sleeveless red vest.

I saw when he moved that he was holding a young hawk, perched on the knuckles of his gauntleted left hand. The brown bird was tearing with its beak at something red held between the man's thumb and forefinger.

"Gorge yourself," he said indulgently. "Daddy wants you to be a big, healthy boy."

I waited until the bird had finished his red meal. Then I knocked on the door. The small man unlatched it and looked out curiously through rimless spectacles. The hawk's flecked golden eyes were impassive. I was just another human being.

"I'm sorry to trouble you," I said to both of them. "I was told a man named Bruce Campion lived here at one time."

His eyes hardened perceptibly behind the glasses. He said in a careful, cultivated voice: "That's true enough. Last summer before I went to Europe I lent Campion the use of my place. He spent August and part of September here, he told me. Then he got married and moved out."

"Do you know what happened to him after that?"

"No. I've been on my sabbatical, and rather completely out of touch with my friends in this country. I spent the entire year in Europe and the Near East."

"Campion is a friend of yours?"

"I admire his talent." He was weighing out his words. "I try to be useful to talent when I can."

"Have you seen Campion recently?"

The question seemed to disturb him. He looked sideways at the hawk perched on his upright fist, as if the bird might provide an answer or an augury. The bird sat unblinking, its great eyes bright and calm.

"I don't wish to be rude," the bird man said. "But I'd certainly feel more comfortable if I knew you had authority to ask me questions."

"I'm a private detective co-operating with several law-enforcement agencies." I gave him my name.

"Co-operating in what?"

"The investigation of a pair of murders, possibly three murders."

He swallowed and grew pale, as though he had swallowed the blood out of his face. "In that case, come in. Don't mind Michelangelo. He's completely indifferent to people."

But the hawk jumped straight up when I entered the room. Held by the leather jesses on its legs, it hung in the air for a moment beating its wings and fanning wind into my face. Then its master thrust his fist up, and the bird returned to its perch.

We sat facing each other with the bird between us.

"I'm Dr. Damis," he said. "Edmund B. Damis. I teach at Berkeley, in the art department." He seemed to be marshaling his professional defenses.

"Is that how you happen to know Campion?"

"I met him some years ago, in Chicago. I was a docent at the Art Institute while he was studying there. I admired his painting, as I said, and I've kept in touch with him. Or rather he has kept in touch with me."

It was a cold account. He was preserving his distance from Campion.

"He's a good painter, I've heard. Is he a good man?"

"I wouldn't care to pass judgment on him. He lives as he can. I took the easy way, myself."

"I'm afraid I don't understand."

"I teach for a living and do my painting, such as it is, on Sundays and on sabbaticals. Campion lives for his work. He cares for nothing else," he said with some feeling.

"You sound almost as though you envied him."

"I almost do."

"It may be a two-way envy, Dr. Damis. Is your middle name Burke, by any chance?"

"It is. My father was an admirer of Edmund Burke."

"Did you know that Campion's been using part of your name as an alias? He's been calling himself Burke Damis."

He flushed with displeasure. "Blast him, I wish he'd leave me and my things alone."

"Has he been at your things?"

"I mean this place. He left it like a pigsty when he moved out last fall. I had to spend most of the last week cleaning it up. Frankly, I've had enough of Bruce and his messy life and his *outré* relationships."

"Are you thinking of his relationships with women?"

"I was, yes. We won't go into them. I've long since given up trying to purge those Augean stables."

"I wish you would go into them."

"I prefer not to. They're excessively boring to me. They invariably follow the same sado-masochistic pattern. Bruce has always regarded women as his legitimate prey."

"Prey is quite a dramatic word. It reminds me of your hawk."

He nodded, as though I'd paid them both a subtle compliment. The hawk sat still as a figurine on his hand. It occurred to me that this Damis might be attached to Campion and the hawk in similar ways, watching through rimless spectacles as the two predators vaulted into space and took their pleasure.

"It brings up the fact," I went on, "that Campion's wife was strangled two months ago. Campion is wanted for the murder. Did you know that, Dr. Damis?"

"I most assuredly did not. I just flew in from Italy last week, and I came directly here." He was pale as bone now, and almost chattering. "I've been utterly out of touch with everyone and everything."

"But you've been in touch with Campion."

"How do you know that?"

"Call it intuition. You'd talk about him differently if you hadn't seen him for a year. Now when and where did you see him?"

"This morning," he said with his eyes on the floor. "Bruce came here this morning. He'd walked halfway around the lake during the night, and he looked perfectly ghastly."

"What did he come to you for?"

"Refuge, I suppose. He admitted that he was in trouble, but he didn't say what kind, and I swear he said nothing about his wife. He wanted to stay here with me. I didn't see that it was possible, or that I owed it to him. He's always been the taker and I've been the giver, as it is. Besides, I've reached a crucial stage in training my hawk." He smoothed the long feathers of its tail.

"When did he leave here?"

"Around noon. I gave him lunch. Naturally I had no idea that I was harboring a fugitive from justice."

"How did he leave?"

"He took my car," Damis said miserably.

"By force?"

"I wouldn't say that. He is bigger than I am, and more—forceful." He had dropped his pride, and he looked very young without it. "Bruce has an ascendancy over me. I suppose you're quite right, I've secretly envied his life, his success with women—"

"You can stop doing that now. Will you please describe your car —make and model?"

"It's a 1959 Chevrolet convertible, red, with a checkered red and black top. California license number TKU 37964." As I was making a note of the number, he added: "Bruce promised I'd have it back within twenty-four hours. He knows I'm stuck out here without transportation."

"I imagine he couldn't care less. I'll see what I can do about getting it back for you. Do you want me to report it as a theft?"

"It wasn't a theft. I was a fool to do it, but I lent it to him voluntarily."

"Did he explain why he wanted the car, or where he was going with it?"

"No." He hesitated. "On second thought, he did give some indication of where he intended to go. He originally proposed that when he was finished with the convertible, he should leave it in Berkeley, in my garage. It certainly suggests that he was headed in that direction."

"And he was alone when he came here and when he left?"

"Oh yes, definitely."

"Did Campion say anything about the girl he'd been with?"

"He didn't mention a girl. As a matter of fact, he did very little talking. Who is she?"

"She is, or was, a tall blonde girl named Harriet Blackwell."

"I never heard of her, I'm afraid. Has something happened to her?"

"The indications are that she's in the lake."

He was shocked, and his feeling communicated itself to the bird on his fist. The hawk spread its wings. Damis calmed it with his hand before he spoke.

"You can't mean that Bruce drowned her?"

"Something like that. When he came here this morning, were there any signs that he'd been in a struggle? Scratch marks on his face, for instance?"

"Yes, his face *was* scratched. His clothes were in bad shape, too."

"Were they wet?"

"They looked as though they had been wet. He looked generally as though he'd had a rough night."

"He's in for rougher ones," I said. "Just in case he does come back this way, we'll want to station a man here. Is it all right with you?"

"I'd welcome it. I'm no more of a physical coward than the next person, but—" His apprehensive look completed the sentence.

"It's unlikely that he will come back," I told him reassuringly. "Assuming he doesn't, I'd like to have your ideas on where to look for him. Also, I want your Berkeley address, in case he follows through on his original plan."

"Couldn't we skip the Berkeley address? My mother lives there with me, and I don't wish her to be alarmed unnecessarily. I'm sure that she's in no danger from him."

"Does she know Campion?"

"Very slightly. Minimally. We had him to dinner, once, a couple of years ago. Mother didn't like him at all—she said he had a dark aura. At that time, though Mother didn't know it, he was living with some black-stockinged tramp in Sausalito. He'd previously lived in Carmel, Santa Barbara, San Diego, Los Angeles, and probably a number of other places. I wouldn't know where to start looking for him. Unless," he added after some thought, "he's gone to his sister."

"Campion has a sister?"

"He has, but it's far from likely that he's with her. She's a very stuffy Peninsula type, he told me. They don't get along."

"Where does she live on the Peninsula, and what's her name?"

"I'd have to look it up. I've never met the woman. I only happen to have her address because Campion used it as a mailing address when he was moving around."

Carrying the hawk with him, Damis went to a table in the corner of the room. He opened a drawer and got out a shabby brown leather address book. I stood beside him as he flipped the pages to the C's.

Bruce Campion was the first name on the page. Scribbled under and around it were addresses in the various cities Damis had mentioned. They were all scratched out except for a Menlo Park address —c/o Mrs. Thor Jurgensen, 401 Schoolhouse Road—which I made a note of.

"I used to think we were good friends," Damis was saying. His eyes were fixed on the hawk, as though it was feeding him his lines by mental telepathy. "But over the years I caught on to the pattern of our relationship. I heard from Bruce only when he wanted something—a loan or a recommendation or the use of something I owned. I'm heartily sick of the man. I hope I never see him again."

I made no comment. He said to the hawk: "Are you hungry, Angelo? How about another sparrow wing?"

I left him communing with the silent bird and drove Fawn into State Line. We had *filets mignons,* carelessly served in one of the gambling clubs. The fat drunk in the white Stetson was balanced precariously on a stool at the bar. He seemed to have shifted gears under his load. His imperfectly focused eyes were watching the girls in the place, especially Fawn.

She had some wine with her meat, and it set her talking about Ralph again. He used to take her fishing at Luna Bay when she was in her early teens and he was in his late ones. Once he rescued her from the San Gregorio surf. Her memories had a dreamlike quality, and I began to wonder if she had dreamed them in the first place. But she ended by saying: "I can't take your twenty dollars. It's the least I can do for Ralph."

"You might as well take it—"

"No. There has to be something I won't do for money. I mean it."

"You're a good girl."

"He said as she lifted his wallet. The hustler with the heart of gold—cold and yellow."

"You're being hard on yourself, Fawn."

"And don't keep calling me Fawn. It isn't my name."

"What do you want me to call you?"

"Don't call me anything."

"Tell me your real name."

"I hate my real name." Her face was as blank as a wall.

"What is it, though?"

"Mabel," she said with disgust. "My parents had to give me the most unglamorous name in the world."

"Where are your parents, by the way?"

"I put them out for adoption."

"Before or after you changed your name to Fawn?"

"If you have to know," she said, "I changed my name the night King went AWOL on me and left me in this hole. The funny thing is, I'm getting sick of calling myself Fawn. I used to think it was glamorous, but now it just sounds like nothing. I'm getting ready to change my name again. Do you have any suggestions?"

"Not on the spur of the moment."

She leaned toward me, smiling intensely and nudging the edge of the table with her papillae. "Let's go to my place and have another drink and talk about it."

"Thanks, but I have work to do."

"It can wait, can't it? I stood up my date for you."

"Also, you're too young for me."

"I don't get it," she said with her puzzled frown. "You're not *old*."

"I'm getting older fast." I rose and laid some money on the table. "Do you want me to drop you anywhere?"

"I'll stay here. It's as good a place as any."

Before I reached the door, the drunk was moving in on her with his white Stetson in his hand and his bald head glowing.

>>>>>>>>>
>>>>>>>>> *chapter* 18
>>>>>>>>>

I FOUND A telephone booth and called Arnie Walters's office in Reno. He answered the telephone himself.

"Walters here."

"This is Lew Archer. I have some information on Campion's movements. He's driving a red Chevvie convertible—"

"We know that." Arnie's voice was low and fast. "Campion's been seen in Saline City, talking to the key boy of one of the local motels. A patrol cop made him but he didn't pick him up right away. He wanted to check with our bulletin, and he had an idea that Campion was checking in. But when he got back to the motel, Campion had cleared out. This happened within the last couple of hours. Do you have later information?"

"You're 'way ahead of me. Did you get the name of the motel?"

"The Travelers, in Saline City. It's a town in the East Bay."

"What about Harriet?"

"Nothing so far. We're starting dragging operations in the morning. The police lab established that the blood in the hat is her type, B, but that doesn't mean much."

"How do you know her blood type?"

"I called her father," Arnie said. "He wanted to come up here, but I think I talked him out of it. If this case doesn't break pretty soon, he's going to blow a gasket."

"So am I."

By midnight I was in Saline City looking for the Travelers Motel. It was on the west side of town at the edge of the salt flats. Red neon outlined its stucco façade and failed to mask its shabbiness.

There was nobody in the cluttered little front office. I rang the handbell on the registration desk. A kind of grey-haired youth came out of a back room with his shirttails flapping.

"Single?"

"I don't need a room. You may be able to give me some information."

"Is it about the murderer?"

"Yes. I understand you talked to him. What was the subject of conversation?"

He groaned, and stopped buttoning up his shirt. "I already told all this to the cops. You expect a man to stay up all night chewing the same cabbage?"

I gave him a five-dollar bill. He peered at it myopically and put it away. "Okay, if it's all that important. What you want to know?"

"Just what Campion said to you."

"Is that his name—Campion? He said his name was Damis. He said he spent the night here a couple months ago, and he wanted me to look up the records to prove it."

"Was he actually here a couple of months ago?"

"Uh-huh. I remembered his face. I got a very good memory for faces." He tapped his low forehead lovingly. "Course I couldn't say for sure what date it was until I looked up the old registration cards."

"You did that, did you?"

"Yeah, but it didn't do him no good. He took off while I was out back checking. The patrol car stopped by, the way it always does around eight o'clock, and it must of scared him off."

"I'd like to see that registration card."

"The cops took it with them. They said it was evidence."

"What was the date on it?"

"May five, I remember that much."

It was evidence. May the fifth was the night of Dolly Campion's death.

"You're sure the man who registered then was the same man you talked to tonight?"

"That's what the cops wanted to know. I couldn't be absotively certain, my eyes aren't that good. But he looked the same to me, and he talked the same. Maybe he was lying about it, though. He said his name was Damis, and it turns out that's a lie."

"He registered under the name Damis on the night of May the fifth, is that correct?"

"They both did."

"Both?"

"I didn't get to see the lady. She came in her own car after he registered for them. He said his wife was gonna do that, so I thought nothing of it. She took off in the morning, early, I guess."

"How do you remember all that, when you're not even certain it was the same man?"

"He sort of reminded me. But I remembered all right when he reminded me."

He was a stupid man. His eyes were glazed and solemn with stupidity. I said: "Do you have any independent recollections of the night of May the fifth?"

"The date was on the registration card."

"But he could have registered another night, and said that it was May the fifth? And the man who signed in on May fifth could have been another man?"

I realized that I was talking like a prosecutor trying to confuse a witness. My witness was thoroughly confused.

"I guess so," he said dejectedly.

"Did Campion tell you why he was so interested in pinning down the date?"

"He didn't say. He just said it was important."

"Did he give you money?"

"He didn't have to. I said I'd help him out. After all, he was a customer."

"But you'd only seen him once before?"

"That's right. On the night of May five." His voice was stubborn.

"What time did he check in that night?"

"I couldn't say. It wasn't too late."

"And he stayed all night?"

"I couldn't say. We don't keep watch on the guests." He yawned, so wide I could count his cavities.

"What's your name?" I said.

"Nelson Karp."

"My name is Archer, Nelson. Lew Archer. I'm a private detective, and I have to ask you to return the five dollars I gave you. I'm sorry.

You're probably going to be a witness in a murder trial, and you'll want to be able to tell the court that nobody paid you money."

He took the bill out of his pocket and dropped it on the counter. "I might of known there was a catch to it."

"I said I was sorry."

"You and who else is sorry?"

"Anyway, the State pays witnesses."

I didn't say how little, and Nelson Karp cheered up.

"When Campion left here tonight, which way did he go?"

" 'Crost San Mateo Bridge. I heard them say that."

"By 'them' you mean the cops?"

"Yeah. They did a lot of telephoning from here." He gestured toward the pay phone on the wall.

I stepped outside and looked across the flats, where piles of salt rose like ephemeral pyramids. The lights of the Peninsula winked blearily in the haze across the Bay. As the crow flies, or the hawk, I wasn't more than ten miles from Menlo Park.

I went back into the office and got some change from Karp and placed a toll call under the name John Smith to Campion's sister Mrs. Jurgensen. Her phone rang thirteen times, and then a man's voice answered.

"Hello."

"I have a person-to-person call for Mrs. Thor Jurgensen," the operator intoned.

"Mrs. Jurgensen isn't here. Can I take a message?"

"Do you wish to leave a message, sir?" the operator said to me.

I didn't. Campion knew my voice, as I knew his.

Shortly after one o'clock I parked in the three-hundred block of Schoolhouse Road in Menlo Park. I crossed into the next block on foot, examining the mailboxes for the Jurgensens' number. It was a broad and quiet street of large ranch-type houses shadowed by oaks that far predated them. Bayshore was a murmur in the distance.

At this hour most of the houses were dark, but there was light in a back window of 401. I circled the house. My footsteps were muffled in the dew-wet grass. Crouching behind a plumbago bush, I peered through a matchstick bamboo blind into the lighted room.

It was a big country-style kitchen divided by a breakfast bar into cooking and living areas. A used-brick fireplace took up most of one wall. Campion was sleeping peacefully on a couch in front of the fireplace. A road map unfolded on his chest rose and fell with his breathing.

He had on the remains of his grey suit. There were dark stains on it, oil or mud or blood. His face was scratched, and charred with beard. His right arm dragged on the floor and he had a gun there at his fingertips, a medium-caliber nickel-plated revolver.

No doubt I should have called the police. But I wanted to take him myself.

A detached garage big enough for three cars stood at the rear of the property. I approached it through a flower garden and let myself in through the unlocked side door. One of the two cars inside had the outlines of a Chevrolet convertible.

It was Dr. Damis's car. I read his name on the steering post in the light of my pencil flash. The keys were in the ignition. I took them out and pocketed them.

I looked around for a weapon. There was a work bench at the rear of the garage, and attached to the wall above it was a pegboard hung with tools. I had a choice of several hammers. I took down a light ball-peen hammer and hefted it. It would do.

I went back to the Chevrolet and stuck a matchbook between the horn and the steering wheel. It began to blow like Gabriel's horn. I moved to the open side door and flattened myself against the wall beside it, watching the back of the house. My ears were hurting. The enclosed space was filled with yelling decibels which threatened to crowd me out.

Campion came out of the house. He ran through the garden, floundering among camellias. The nickel-plated revolver gleamed in his hand. Before he reached the garage he stopped and looked all around him, as though he suspected a trick. But the pull of the horn was too strong for him. He had to silence it.

I ducked out of sight and saw his shadowy figure enter the doorway. I struck him on the back of the head with the hammer, not too hard and not too easily. He fell on his gun. I got it out from under him and dropped it in my jacket pocket. Then I unjammed the horn.

A man was swearing loudly in the next yard. I stepped outside and said: "Good evening."

He turned a flashlight on me. "What goes on? You're not Thor Jurgensen."

"No. Where are the Jurgensens?"

"They're spending the night in the City. I was wondering who was using their house."

He came up to the fence, a heavy-bodied man in silk pajamas, and looked me over closely. I smiled into the glare. I was feeling pretty good.

"A wanted man was using it. I'm a detective, and I just knocked him out."

"Evelyn's brother?"

"I guess so."

"Does Evelyn know he was here?"

"I doubt it."

"Poor Evelyn." His voice held that special blend of grief and glee which we reserve for other people's disasters. "Poor old Thor. I suppose this will be in the papers—"

I cut him short: "Call the Sheriff's office in Redwood City, will you? Tell them to send a car out."

He moved away, walking springily in his bare feet.

>>>>>>>>>
>>>>>>>>> *chapter* 19
>>>>>>>>>

ROYAL AND I waited outside the hospital room while Campion returned to consciousness. It took him the better part of an hour. I had time to fill the Captain in on my activities, and Campion's.

Royal was unimpressed by my findings in Saline City. "He's trying to fake an alibi for his wife's murder."

"Or establish one. I think you should talk to the key boy Nelson Karp, and see if that registration card is genuine. It's in the hands of the Saline City police."

Royal said without much interest: "Alibis like that one come a dime a dozen and you know it. He could have checked in at this motel and even spent part of the night, then driven back to Luna Bay and done her in. It's only about thirty miles between the two places."

"Which makes it all the easier to check."

"Look," he said, "I've got other things on my mind. Take it up with Deputy Mungan if you like. He's in charge of the substation at Luna Bay, and he's been handling the evidential details."

I didn't pursue the argument. Royal was a good cop but like other good cops he had an inflexible mind, once it was made up. We sat in uneasy silence for a few minutes. Then a young resident wearing a white coat and a high-minded expression came out of Campion's room and announced that, in view of the importance of the case, his patient could be questioned.

Royal and I went in past the uniformed guard. It was an ordinary small hospital room, with the addition of heavy steel screening on the window. Campion's bed was slightly raised at the head. He lay still and watched us. His heavy eyes recognized each of us in turn, but he didn't speak. His head was bandaged, and the flesh around his eyes was turning purple. Scratches stood out on his pale cheeks.

I said: "Hello, Campion."

Royal said: "Long time no see, Bruce."

Campion said nothing. The turbanlike bandage on his head, the grimace of pain on his mouth, made him look a little like an Indian fakir lying on a bed of spikes.

Royal's shadow fell across him. "What did you do with Harriet Blackwell, Bruce?"

"I didn't do anything with her."

"She was last seen in your company."

"I can't help it."

"You can't help killing people, you mean?"

"I've never killed anyone."

"What about your little wife Dolly?"

"I didn't kill Dolly."

"Come on now, Bruce. We know different. You've had your little burst of freedom. This is the end of the trail. The end of the trail and the beginning of the trial." Royal grinned at his own bad joke. "Anything you say can be used against you, true, but I'm advising you to speak out now, tell us the whole thing freely. It'll be easier on you in the long run."

"Sure," Campion said. "They'll put a cushion on the chair in the gas chamber and perfume the cyanide."

Royal leaned over the bed, his wide shoulders blotting out Campion's face. "You know you're headed for the gas chamber, eh? So why not give me the full story, Bruce? I been waiting a long time to hear it. Just come clean about Dolly, and I'm your friend. I'll do what I can to save you from the green room."

"Don't do me any favors, cop. And get away from me. You have bad breath."

Royal's open hand jerked up. "Why, you dirty little bas—" He bit the word in two and backed away, with a sideways glance at me.

Campion said: "Go ahead and hit me. Hitting people is what you people are for. I've hated you people all my life. You sell out justice to the highest bidder and let the poor people take the gaff."

"Shut up, you." Royal was shouting. "You lie there crying about justice with women's blood on your hands."

Campion flapped his hands in front of his face. "I don't see any blood."

"That's right, you didn't shed any blood when you killed Dolly. You used a stocking around her neck. Her own stocking." Royal made a spitting noise. "What goes on in a mind like yours, Bruce? I'd like to know."

"You never will. You're too ignorant."

"I'm not too ignorant to know a psycho when I see one, fooling around with paintboxes and living on women. Why don't you do a man's work?"

"Like vagging prostitutes and shaking them down?"

"Don't talk to me about prostitutes. I read a book about that whoring psycho French painter—the one that cut off his ear and committed suicide. How psycho can you get?"

Campion sat up in bed. "If you weren't so ignorant you'd speak of Van Gogh with respect. Incidentally, he wasn't a Frenchman. He was a Dutchman, and a great religious genius."

"And you're another? Is that what you're trying to say? You're a great religious genius who goes in for human sacrifice?"

"You're the one who puts people in the gas chamber."

"I'm the one, and that's where you're going."

I stepped between them, facing Royal. His face was congested with blood, and his eyes had an oily sheen. I'd never seen him out of control before. Campion had lain back and closed his eyes.

I opened them with a question: "How did the blood get on Harriet's hat?"

"What hat?"

"The hat I fished out of the lake today. What was it doing in the lake, and how did her blood and hair get on the lining?"

"You better ask *her*. It's her hat."

"You knew it was in the lake?"

"You just told me, and I know you wouldn't lie. Cops never lie."

"Change the record, boy. How did that hat get into the lake?"

"I said, why don't you ask her?"

"She isn't available. Where is she, Campion?"

"I wouldn't know. I have a suggestion, however."

"What is it?"

"Disappear. I'm a sick man. I need rest."

"The doctor says you're questionable."

"Not me. I'm incommunicado. It's my reputation that's questionable."

"Stop playing word games."

"Why? A man needs some amusement in the long night watches. Storm troopers make dull companions."

Hot blood rose in my face. I felt a growing solidarity with Royal.

"You don't show much concern for your fiancée."

"My what?"

"You were going to marry her, weren't you?"

"Was I?"

"Answer me."

"You already know all the answers. Cops always do."

"If you weren't going to marry her, why did you take her to Tahoe? Because the lake is deep?"

Campion looked up at me with a deathly boredom. Royal spoke behind me in a new quiet voice: "Mr. Archer deserves an answer, Bruce. He's gone to a lot of trouble to ask you that question."

"Mr. Archer can take a running jump in the lake."

"Is that what Harriet did," I said, "with a little help from you?"

"I don't know what she did. I never touched her."

"How did you get those marks on your face?"

One of his hands crawled up to his face. His fingers explored it like a blind man's fingers palpating a strange object.

"I was wandering around in the woods last night. I must have scratched myself on the bushes."

"This was after your trouble with Harriet?"

He nodded almost imperceptibly.

"What was the trouble about?"

He lay and looked at me. "What trouble?"

"You mentioned trouble with Harriet."

"You were the one who mentioned trouble," he said.

"But you agreed that trouble had occurred."

"You must have been hearing things."

"I saw you nod your head."

"I have a slight tremor. Please excuse it. It comes from being beaten half to death by storm troopers. Now why don't you go away?"

"We're not going away," Royal said at my shoulder. "You admitted you had trouble with the girl. You've taken the first step toward the truth. You might as well give us the rest of it and get it over with. How about it, Bruce?"

"Don't call me Bruce."

"Bruce is your name, isn't it?"

"Not to you. To my friends."

"What friends?" Royal said in bitter contempt.

"I have friends."

"Where are they? Under the ground?"

Campion turned his face away.

"Did Ralph Simpson call you Bruce?" I said.

"What?" he said to the wall.

"Did Ralph Simpson call you Bruce?"

"Yes, he did."

"You were friends?"

"Yes."

"Then why did you knock him off and steal his papers?"

His eyes rolled in my direction. "I didn't steal his papers."

"We found his birth certificate in your pocket," Royal said.

"Ralph lent it to me."

"The same night you stuck the icepick in him?"

Campion's mouth became rectangular. I could see the red tongue curled behind his teeth. He raised his voice and cried out. His eyes turned up, and their veined whites glared at us as he went on yelling inarticulately.

Royal and I exchanged shameful looks. For some reason we were feeling guilty, at least I was. When Campion stopped his noise and fell back onto the pillow, other noises could be heard in the corridor. A woman seemed to be arguing with more than one man.

Royal started for the door. It was flung open before he reached it. The woman who burst in resembled Campion, though she was older and softer and better cared for.

"What are you doing to my brother?"

"Nothing, ma'am," Royal said. "That is, we had some questions—"

"Have you been torturing him?"

"It's been more like the other way around."

She moved past him to the bed. "They've hurt you, Bruce."

Campion looked at her bleakly. "If I can stand it, you can. Go away."

"He's right, Mrs. Jurgensen," Royal said. "You shouldn't be in here, you know."

The guard spoke up from the doorway. "That's what I was trying to tell her, Captain. I didn't know if I should use physical force."

Royal shook his head curtly. A tall man came in past the guard. He had greying blond crewcut hair and a long face. His mouth was pinched as though he'd been sucking a lemon. He took the woman by the arm and tried to drag her away from the bed.

She resisted his efforts without looking at him. She was staring hungrily at her brother's face.

"Don't you want me to help you?"

"You were among the missing when I needed it. You know what you can do with it now. Get lost."

"You heard him, Evelyn," the tall man said. He had a faint Scandinavian accent, more a lack of timbre than an accent. "He wants no part of us. We want no part of him."

"But he's my brother."

"I *know* that, Evelyn. Do you want everyone in the Bay area to know it? Do you want young Thor to lose his fraternity connection? Do you want people pointing me out on Montgomery Street?"

"You hear your husband," Campion said. "Why don't you am-scray, sister? Fold your tensions like the Arabs and silently steal away."

The resident doctor appeared with a nurse in tow. He cast a withering glance around the room.

"May I remind you this is a hospital, Captain. This man is your prisoner but also my patient. I gave you permission to question him on the understanding that it would be quiet and brief."

Royal started to say: "I'm not responsible—"

"I am. I want this room cleared immediately. That includes you, Captain."

"I'm not finished with my interrogation."

"It can wait till morning."

Royal dropped the issue. He had the trial to think of, and the use that Campion's defense could make of the doctor's testimony. He walked out. The rest of us went along.

Not entirely by accident, I met the Jurgensen couple in the parking lot. They pretended not to see me, but I planted myself between them and their Mercedes sedan and made a fast pitch to her.

"I'm a private detective working on this case and it's come to my attention that there are some holes in the case against your brother. I'd like very much to talk to you about it."

"Don't say a word, Evelyn," her husband said.

"If we could sit down and have an exchange of views, Mrs. Jurgensen—"

"Pay no attention, Evelyn. He's simply trying to pump you."

"Why don't you stay out of this?" I said. "He isn't your brother."

She turned to him. "I'm worried about him, Thor, and I'm ashamed. All these months we've pretended he didn't exist, that we had no connection—"

"We *have* no connection. We decided that between us and that's the way it's going to be."

"Why don't you let the lady to her own talking?" I said.

"There isn't going to be any talking. You get out of the way."

He took me by the shoulder and pushed me to one side. There was no point in hitting him. The Mercedes whisked them away to their half-acre earthly paradise.

I checked in at a Camino Real motel and went to sleep trying to think of some one thing I could do that would be absolutely right and final. I dreamed that Campion was innocent and I had to prove it by re-enacting the crimes with paper dolls that stuck to my fingers.

Then I found Harriet's body in the lake. She had talon marks on her head.

I awoke in a cold sweat. The late night traffic whirred with a sound like wings along the highway.

>>>>>>>>>
>>>>>>>>> *chapter* 20
>>>>>>>>>

I GOT UP into the sharp-edged uncertainties of morning and drove across the county to Luna Bay. Patrick Mungan, the deputy in charge there, was a man I knew and trusted. I hoped the trust was reciprocal.

When I entered the bare stucco substation, his broad face generated a smile which resembled sunlight on a cliff.

"I hear you've been doing our work for us, Lew."

"Somebody has to."

"Uh-huh. You look kind of bedraggled. I keep an electric razor here, in case you want to borrow it."

I rubbed my chin. It rasped. "Thanks, it can wait. Captain Royal tells me you handled the evidence in the Dolly Campion murder."

"What evidence there was. We didn't pick up too much. It wasn't there to be picked up."

Mungan had risen from his desk. He was a huge man who towered over me. It gave me the not unpleasant illusion of being small and fast, like a trained-down welterweight. He opened the swinging door at the end of the counter that divided the front office.

"Come on in and sit down. I'll send out for coffee."

"That can wait, too."

"Sure, but we might as well be comfortable while we talk." He summoned a young deputy from the back room and dispatched him for coffee. "What got you so involved in the Campion business?"

"Some Los Angeles people named Blackwell hired me to look into Campion's background. He'd picked up their daughter Harriet in Mexico and was romancing her, under an alias. Three days ago they ran away together to Nevada, where she disappeared. The indications are that she's his second victim, or his third."

I told Mungan about the hat in the water, and about the dusty fate of Quincy Ralph Simpson. He listened earnestly, with the corners of his mouth drawn down like a bulldog's, and said when I'd done: "The Blackwell girl I don't know about. But I don't see any reason why Campion would stab Ralph Simpson. It may be true what he said about Simpson lending him his papers to use. They were friends. When the Campions moved here last fall, it was Simpson who found them a house. Call it a house, but I guess it was all they could afford. They had a tough winter."

"In what way?"

"Every way. They ran out of money. The wife was pregnant and he wasn't working, unless you call painting pictures work. They had to draw welfare money for a while. The county cut 'em off when they found out Campion was using some of it to buy paints. Ralph Simpson helped them out as much as he could. I heard when the baby was born in March, he was the one paid the doctor."

"That's interesting."

"Yeah. It crossed my mind at the time that maybe Simpson was the baby's father. I asked him if he was, after Dolly got killed. He denied it."

"It's still a possibility. Simpson was a friend of Dolly's before she knew Campion. I found out last night that Simpson was responsible for bringing them together in the first place. If Simpson got her pregnant and let Campion hold the bag, it would give Campion a motive for both killings. I realize that's very iffy reasoning."

"It is that."

"Have you had any clear indication that Campion wasn't the father?"

Mungan shook his ponderous head. "All the indications point the other way. Remember she was well along when he married her in September. A man doesn't do that for a woman unless he's the one."

"I admit it isn't usual. But Campion isn't a usual man."

"Thank the good Lord for that. If everybody was like him, the whole country would be headed for Hades in a handbasket. A hand-painted handbasket." He laid his palm on the desk as if he was covering a hole card. "Personally I have my doubts that those two killings, Dolly and Simpson, are connected. I'm not saying they aren't connected. I'm only saying I have my doubts."

"They have to be connected, Pat. Simpson was killed within a couple of weeks of Dolly—a couple of weeks which he apparently spent investigating her death. Add to that the fact that he was found buried in her home town."

"Citrus Junction?"

I nodded.

"Maybe he went to see the baby," Mungan said thoughtfully. "The baby's in Citrus Junction, you know. Dolly's mother came and got him."

"You seem to like my idea after all."

"It's worth bearing in mind, I guess. If you're going down that way, you might drop in on Mrs. Stone and take a look at the little tyke. He's only about four months old, though, so I wouldn't count on his resembling anybody."

The young deputy came back with a hot carton in a paper bag. Mungan poured black coffee for the three of us. In response to unspoken signals, the young deputy carried his into the back room and closed the door. Mungan said over his paper cup: "What I meant a minute ago, I meant the two killings weren't connected the way you thought, by way of Campion. This isn't official thinking, so I'm asking you to keep it confidential, but there's some doubt in certain quarters that Campion killed Dolly."

"What quarters are you talking about?"

"These quarters," he said with a glance at the closed door. "Me personally. So did Ralph Simpson have his doubts. We talked about it. He knew that he was a suspect himself, but he insisted that Campion didn't do it. Simpson was the kind of fellow who sometimes talked without knowing what he was talking about. But now that he's dead, I give his opinion more weight."

I sipped my coffee and kept still while Mungan went on in his deliberate way: "Understand me, Lew, I'm not saying Bruce Campion didn't kill his wife. When a woman gets herself murdered, nine times out of ten it's the man in her life, her boy friend or her husband or her ex. We all know that. All I'm saying, and I probably shouldn't be saying it, we don't have firm evidence that Campion did it."

"Then why was he indicted?"

"He has his own stupidity to thank for that. He panicked and ran, and naturally it looked like consciousness of guilt to the powers that be. But we didn't have the evidence to convict him, or maybe even arraign him. After we held him twenty-four hours, I recommended his release without charges. The crazy son-of-a-gun took off that same night. The Grand Jury was sitting, and the D.A. rushed the case in to them and got an indictment. They never would have indicted if Campion hadn't run." Mungan added with careful honesty: "This is just my opinion, my unofficial opinion."

"What's Royal's unofficial opinion?"

"The Captain keeps his opinion to himself. He's bucking for Sheriff, and you don't get to be Sheriff by fighting the powers that be."

"And I suppose the D.A. is bucking for Governor or something."

"Something. Watch him make a circus out of this."

"You don't like circuses?"

"I like the kind with elephants."

He finished his coffee, crumpled the cup in his fist, and tossed it into the wastebasket. I did the same. It was a trivial action, but it seemed to me to mark a turning point in the case.

"Exactly what evidence do you have against Campion?"

Mungan made a face, as if he had swallowed and regurgitated a bitter pill. "It boils down to suspicion, and his lack of an alibi, and his runout. In addition to which, there's the purely negative evidence: there was no sign that the place had been broken into, or that Dolly had tried to get away from the killer. She was lying there on the floor in her nightgown, real peaceful like, with one of her own silk stockings knotted around her neck."

"In her bedroom?"

"The place has no bedroom. I'll show you a picture of the layout."

He went to his files in the back room and returned with several photographs in his hands. One was a close-up of a full-breasted young blonde woman whose face had been savagely caricatured by the internal pressure of her own blood. The stocking around her neck was almost hidden in her flesh.

In the other pictures, her place on the floor had been taken by a chalk outline of her figure. They showed from various angles a roughly finished interior containing an unmade bed, a battered-looking child's crib, a kitchen table and some chairs, a gas plate and a heater, a palette and some paints on a bench by the single large window. This window, actually the glazed door opening of the converted garage, had a triangular hole in a lower corner. Unframed canvases hung on the plasterboard walls, like other broken windows revealing a weirdly devastated outside world.

"How did the window get broken, Pat?"

"Ralph Simpson said that it had been broken for weeks. Campion just never got around to fixing it. He was too high and mighty, too busy throwing paint at the wall to see that the wife and child got proper care."

"You don't like him much."

"I think he's a bum. I also think he's got a fair shake coming to him."

Mungan tossed the pictures onto his desk. He took a button out of the pocket of his blouse and rolled it meditatively between his thumb and forefinger. It was a large brown button covered with woven leather, and it had a few brown threads attached to it. I'd seen a button like it in the last few days, I couldn't remember where.

"Apparently the baby slept in the same room."

"There's only the one room. They lived like shanty Irish," he said in the disapproving tone of a lace-curtain Irishman.

"What happened to the child on the night of the murder?"

"I was going to bring that up. It's one of the queer things about the case, and one reason we suspected Campion from the start. Somebody, presumably the killer, took the baby out of his crib and stashed him in a car that was parked by the next house down the road. The woman who lives there, a Negro woman name of Johnson, woke up before dawn and heard the baby crying in her car. She knew whose baby it was—her and Dolly were good neighbors—so naturally she took it over to the Campions'. That's how Dolly's body was discovered."

"Where was Campion that night, do you know?"

"He said he was gone all night, drinking until the bars closed, and then driving, all over hell and gone. It's the kind of story you can't prove or disprove. He couldn't or wouldn't name the bars, or the places he drove afterward. He said along toward dawn he went to sleep in his car in a cul-de-sac off Skyline. That wouldn't be inconsistent with him doing the murder. Anyway, we picked him up around nine o'clock in the morning, when he drove back to his place. There's no doubt he had been drinking. I could smell it on him."

"What time was his wife killed?"

"Between three and four A.M. The Deputy Coroner was out there by eight, and he said she couldn't have been dead longer than four or five hours. He went by body temp. and stomach contents, and the two factors checked each other out."

"How did he know when she'd eaten last?"

"Campion said they ate together at six the previous night. He brought in a couple of hamburgers—some diet for a nursing mother —and the carhop at the drive-in confirmed the time. Apparently he and Dolly had an argument over the food, so he took what money there was in the house and went and got himself plastered."

"What was the argument about?"

"Things in general, he said. They hadn't been getting along too well for months."

"He told you this?"

"Yeah. You'd think he was trying to make himself look bad."

"Did he say anything about another woman?"

"No. What's on your mind, Lew?"

"I think we can prove he was lying about what he did on the night of May the fifth. Have you talked to Royal this morning?"

"He phoned to tell me he had Campion. He wants me to go over to Redwood City and take a hand in the questioning."

"Has Campion admitted anything yet?"

"He's not talking at all. Royal's getting kind of frustrated."

"Did he say anything to you about the Travelers Motel in Saline City?"

"Not a word." Mungan gave me a questioning look.

"According to their night clerk, Nelson Karp, Campion spent the night of May fifth there with a woman. Or part of the night. They registered as Mr. and Mrs. Burke Damis, which is one of the aliases Campion has been using. The Saline City police lifted the registration card last night after Campion was seen there. He seems to have been trying to set up an alibi."

"A good one or a phony?"

"You can find that out quicker than I can."

Mungan stood up and looked down the rocky slopes of his face at me. "Whyn't you give me the word on it in the first place?"

"I gave the word to Royal last night. He wasn't interested. I thought I'd wait and see if you were."

"Well, I am. But if this is no phony, why did Campion hold it out until now?"

"Ask him."

"I think I will."

He dropped the leather button he had been playing with on his desk. It rolled onto the floor, and I picked it up.

"Is this part of the evidence, Pat?"

"I honestly don't know. The baby had it in his fist when Mrs. Johnson found him in her car. She didn't know where it came from. Neither did anybody else."

I was still trying to remember where I had seen a button or buttons like it. I dredged deep in my memory, but all that came up was the smell of the sea and the sound of it.

"May I have this button?"

"Nope. I read a story once about a button solving a murder, and I have a special feeling about this button."

"So have I."

"But I'm holding onto it." His smiling eyes narrowed on my face. "You sure you don't want to borrow the use of my razor before you go?"

"I guess I'd better."

He got the electric razor out of the bottom drawer of his desk. I took it into the washroom and shaved myself. All I uncovered was the same old trouble-prone face.

>>>>>>>>>
>>>>>>>>> *chapter* 21
>>>>>>>>>

MUNGAN WAS GONE when I came out. I used his telephone to call Vicky Simpson's house. No answer. The young deputy in the back room told me that so far as he knew Vicky was still in Citrus Junction waiting for the authorities to release her husband's body. I turned in the U-drive car at the San Francisco airport, caught a jet to Los Angeles, picked up my own car at the airport there, and drove out through the wedding-smelling orange groves to Citrus Junction.

I went first to see the baby. His grandmother lived on the west side of town in the waste that the highway builders had created. It was mid-afternoon when I got there. Earth movers were working in the dust like tanks in a no man's land.

An overgrown pittasporum hedge shielded the house from the road. The universal dust had made its leaves as grey as aspen. The house was a two-story frame building which needed paint. Holes in the screen door had been repaired with string. I rattled it with my fist.

The woman who appeared behind the screen looked young to be a grandmother. The flouncy dress she wore, and her spike heels, were meant to emphasize her slender figure. She had a blue-eyed baby face to which the marks of time clung like an intricate spider web. She was blonder than the picture I'd seen of her daughter.

"Mrs. Stone?"

"I'm Mrs. Stone."

I told her my name and occupation. "May I come in and talk to you for a bit?"

"What about?"

"Your daughter Dolly and what happened to her. I know it must be a painful subject—"

"Painful subject is right. I don't see any sense in going over and over the same old ground. You people know who killed her as well as me. Instead of coming around torturing me, why don't you go and catch that man? He has to be some place."

"I took Campion last night, Mrs. Stone. He's being held in Redwood City."

A hungry eagerness deepened the lines in her face and aged her suddenly. "Has he confessed?"

"Not yet. We need more information. I'm comparatively new on the case, and I'd appreciate any help you can give me."

"Sure. Come in."

She unhooked the screen door and led me across a hallway into her living room. It was closely blinded, almost dark. Instead of raising a blind, she turned on a standing lamp.

"Excuse the dust on everything. It's hard to keep a decent house with that road work going on. Stone thought we should sell, but we found out we couldn't get our money out of it. The lucky ones were the people across the way that got condemned by the State. But they're not widening on this side."

An undersong of protest ran through everything she said, and she had reason. Grey dust rimed the furniture; even without it the furniture would have been shabby. I sat on a prolapsed chair and watched her arrange herself on the chesterfield. She had the faintly anachronistic airs of a woman who had been good-looking but had found no place to use her looks except the mirror.

At the moment I was the mirror, and she smiled into me intensively. "What do you want me to tell you?"

"We'll start with your son-in-law. Did you ever meet him?"

"Once. Once was enough. Jack and me invited the two of them down for Christmas. We had a hen turkey and all the trimmings. But that Bruce Campion acted like he was on a slumming expedition. He hauled poor Dolly out of here so fast you'd think there was a quarantine sign on the house. Little did he know that some of the best people in town are our good friends."

"Did you quarrel with him?"

"You bet I did. What did he have to act so snooty about? Dolly told me they were living in a garage, and we've owned our own house here for twenty-odd years. So I asked him what he planned to do for her. When was he going to get a job and so on? He said he married her, didn't he, and that was all he planned to do for her, said he already had a job doing his own work. So I asked him how much money he made and he said not very much, but they were getting along with the help of friends. I told him my daughter wasn't a charity case, and he said that's what *I* thought. Imagine him talking like that to her own mother, and her six months pregnant at the time. I tried to talk her into cutting her losses and staying here with us, but Dolly wouldn't. She was too loyal."

Mrs. Stone had the total recall of a woman with a grievance. I interrupted her flow of words: "Were they getting along with each other?"

"*She* was getting along with him. It took a saint to do it and that's what she was, a saint." She rummaged in a sewing basket beside her. "I want to show you a letter she wrote me after Christmas. If you ever saw a devoted young wife it was her."

She produced a crumpled letter addressed to her and postmarked "Luna Bay, Dec. 27." It was written in pencil on a sheet of sketching paper by an immature hand:

Dear Elizabeth,

I'm sorry you and Bruce had to fight. He is moody but he is really A-okay if you only know him. We appresiate the twenty—it will come in handy to buy a coat—I only hope Bruce does not get to it first—he spends so much on his painting—I realy need a coat. Its colder up here than it was in Citrus J. I realy appresiate you asking me to stay (I'm a poet and don't know it!) but a girl has to stick with her "hubby" thru thick and thin—after all Bruce stuck with me. Maybe he is hard to get along with but he is a lot better than "no hubby at all." Dont you honestly think hes cute? Besides some of the people we know think his pictures are real great and he will make a "killing"—then you will be glad I stuck with Bruce.

Love to Jack
Dolly
(*Mrs. Bruce Campion*)

"Doesn't it tear your heart out?" Mrs. Stone said, plucking at the neighborhood of hers. "I mean the way she idolized him and all?"

I assumed a suitably grim expression. It came naturally enough. I was thinking of the cultural gap between Dolly and Harriet, and the flexibility of the man who had straddled it.

"How did she happen to marry him, Mrs. Stone?"

"It's the old old story. You probably know what happened. She was an innocent girl. She'd never even been away from home before. He corrupted her, and he had to take the consequences." She was a little alarmed by what she had said. She dropped her eyes, and added: "It was partly my own fault, I admit it. I never should have let her go off to Nevada by herself, a young girl like her."

"How old?"

"Dolly was just twenty when she left home. That was a year ago last May. She was working in the laundry and she wasn't happy there, under her father's thumb. She wanted to have more of a life of her own. I couldn't blame her for that. A girl with her looks could go far."

She paused, and her eyes went into long focus. Perhaps she was remembering that a girl with her own looks hadn't. Perhaps she was remembering how far Dolly had gone, all the way out of life.

"Anyway," she said, "I let her go up to Tahoe and get herself a job. It was just to be for the summer. She was supposed to save her money, so she could prepare herself for something permanent. I wanted her to go to beauty school. She was very good at grooming herself—it was the one real talent she had. She took after me in that. But then she ran into *him,* and that was the end of beauty school and everything else."

"Did she make any other friends up at the lake?"

"Yeah, there was one little girl who helped her out, name of Fawn. She was a beauty operator, and Dolly thought very highly of her. She even wrote me about her. I was glad she had a girl friend like that. I thought it would give her some ambition. Beauty operators command good money, and you can get a job practically anywhere. I always regretted I didn't take it up myself. Jack makes a fair salary at the laundry, but it's been hard these last years, with inflation and all. Now we have the baby to contend with."

She raised her eyes to the ceiling.

"I'd like to see the baby."

"He's upstairs sleeping. What do you want to see him for?"

"I like babies."

"You don't look the type. I'm not the type myself, not any more. You get out of the habit of attending to their needs. Still," she added in a softer voice, "the little man's a comfort to me. He's all I have left of Dolores. You can come and take a look—long as you don't wake him."

I followed her up the rubber-treaded staircase. The baby's room was dim and hot. She turned on a shaded wall light. He was lying uncovered in the battered crib which I had seen in Mungan's glaring photographs. As Mungan had predicted, he didn't resemble anyone in particular. Small and vulnerable and profoundly sleeping, he was simply a baby. His breath was sweet.

His grandmother pulled a sheet up over the round Buddha eye of his umbilicus. I stood above him, trying to guess what he would look like when he grew up. It was hard to imagine him as a man, with a man's passions.

"This was Dolly's own crib," Mrs. Stone was saying. "We sent it up with them at Christmas. Now we have it back here." I heard her breath being drawn in. "Thank God his crazy father spared him, anyway."

"What's his name?"

"Dolly called him Jack, after her father. Dolly and her father were always close. What do you think of him?"

"He's a fine healthy baby."

"Oh, I do for him the best I can. It isn't easy to go back to it, though, after twenty years. My only hope is that I can bring him up properly. I guess I didn't do such a good job of bringing Dolly up."

I murmured something encouraging as we started downstairs. Like other women I had known, she had the strength to accept the worst that could happen and go on from there. Moving like a dreamer into the living room, she went to the mantel and took down a framed photograph.

"Did you ever see a picture of my daughter?"

"Not a good one."

The picture she showed me was an improvement on Mungan's, but it wasn't a good one, either. It looked like what it was, a small-town high-school graduation picture, crudely retouched in color. Dolly smiled and smiled like a painted angel.

"She's—she was pretty, wasn't she?"

"Very," I said.

"You wouldn't think she'd have to settle for a Bruce Campion. As a matter of fact, she didn't have to. There were any number of boys around town interested. There used to be a regular caravan out here. Only Dolly wasn't interested in the boys. She wanted to get out of Citrus for life. Besides, she always went for the older ones. I think sometimes," she said quite innocently, "that came from being so fond of her father and all. She never felt at home with boys her own age. The truth is, in a town this size, the *decent* older ones are already married off."

"Was Dolly friends with some of the other kind?"

"She most certainly was not. Dolly was always a good girl, and leery of bad company. Until that Campion got ahold of her."

"What about her friends at Tahoe? Were there other men besides Campion in her life?"

"I don't know what you mean by in her *life*." Almost roughly, she took the picture of Dolly out of my hands and replaced it on the mantel. With her back still turned, she said across the width of the room: "What are you getting at, mister?"

"I'm trying to find out how Dolly lived before she married Campion. I understand she lost her job and got some help from friends, including Fawn King. You said she wrote you about Fawn. Do you have the letter?"

"No. I didn't keep it."

"Did she mention any other friends besides Fawn?"

She came back toward me shaking her head. Her heels made dents in the carpet. "I think I know what you're getting at. It's just another one of his dirty lies."

"Whose lies?"

"Bruce Campion's lies. He's full of them. When they were here Christmas, he tried to let on to Jack that he wasn't the father, that he married her out of the goodness of his heart."

"Did he say who the father was?"

"Of course he didn't, because there wasn't anybody else. I asked Dolly myself, and she said *he* was the father. Then he turned around and admitted it then and there."

"What did he say?"

"He said he wouldn't argue, said he made his bargain and he would stick to it. He had his gall, talking about her like she was a piece of merchandise. I told him so, and that was when he marched her out of the house. He didn't want her talking any more. He had too much to hide."

"What are you referring to?"

"His lies, and all his other shenanigans. He was a drinker, and heaven knows what else. Dolly didn't say much—she never complained—but I could read between the lines. He went through money like it was water—"

I interrupted her. "Did Dolly ever mention a man named Quincy Ralph Simpson?"

"Simpson? No, she never did. What was that name again?"

"Quincy Ralph Simpson."

"Isn't that the man they found across the street—the one that was buried in Jim Rowland's yard?"

"Yes. He was a friend of your daughter's."

"I don't believe it."

"He was, though. Simpson was the one who introduced her to

Campion. After they got married, Simpson gave them a good deal of help, including financial help."

"That doesn't prove anything."

"I'm not trying to make it prove anything. But I'm surprised that Dolly never mentioned Simpson to you."

"We didn't keep in close touch. She wasn't much of a letter writer."

"When did you see Dolly and Campion last?"

"Christmas. I told you about that."

"You didn't see Campion in May?"

"I did not. Jack drove me up there the day they found her, but I shunned *him* like a rattlesnake."

"And he wasn't here in Citrus Junction, after the police released him?"

"How would I know? He wouldn't come to us."

"He may have, in a sense. He may have been across the road burying Ralph Simpson. Whoever buried Simpson must have had a reason for picking the house across from yours."

She squinted at me, as if the light had brightened painfully. "I see what you mean."

"Are you sure Ralph Simpson never came here to your house?"

"There's no reason he should. We didn't even know him." Mrs. Stone was getting restless, twining her hands in her lap.

"But he knew Dolly," I reminded her. "After she was killed, and you brought the baby here, he may have been watching your house."

"Why would he do that?"

"It's been suggested that he was the baby's father."

"I don't believe it." But after a pause, she said: "What kind of a man *was* Ralph Simpson? All I know about him is what I read in the papers, that he was stabbed and buried in the Rowlands' yard."

"I never knew him in life, but I gather he wasn't a bad man. He was loyal, and generous, and I think he had some courage. He spent his own last days trying to track down Dolly's murderer."

"Bruce Campion, you mean?"

"He wasn't convinced that it was Campion."

"And you aren't, either," she said with her mouth tight.

"No. I'm not."

Her posture became angular and hostile. I was trying to rob her of her dearest enemy.

"All I can say is, you're mistaken. I *know* he did it. I can feel it, here." She laid her hand over her heart.

"We all make mistakes," I said.

"Yes, and you made more than one. I *know* that Bruce Campion was the baby's father. Dolly wouldn't lie to me."

"Daughters have been known to lie to their mothers."

"Maybe so. But if this Simpson was the father, why didn't he marry her? Answer me that."

"He was already married."

"Now I *know* you're wrong. Dolly would never mess with a married man. The one time she did—" Her eyes widened as though she had frightened herself again. She clamped her mouth shut.

"Tell me about the one time Dolly messed with a married man."

"There was no such time."

"You said there was."

"I'm saying there wasn't. I was thinking about something entirely different. I wouldn't sully her memory with it, so there."

I tried to persuade her to tell me more, with no success. Finally I changed the subject.

"This house across the way where Simpson was found buried—I understand it wasn't occupied at the time."

"You understand right. The Rowlands moved out the first of the year, and the house was standing empty there for months. It was a crying shame what happened to it and the other condemned houses. Some of the wild kids around were using them to carry on in. Jack used to find the bottles and the beer cans all around. They smashed the windows and everything. I hated to see it, even if it didn't matter in the long run. The State just tore the houses down anyway." She seemed to be mourning obscurely over the changes and losses in her own life. "I hated to see them do it to the Jaimet house."

"The Jaimet house?"

She made a gesture in the direction of the road. "I'm talking about that same house. Jim Rowland bought it from Mrs. Jaimet after her husband died. It was the original Jaimet ranch house. This whole west side of town used to be the Jaimet ranch. But that's all past history."

"Tell me about Jim Rowland."

"There's nothing much to tell. He's a good steady man, runs the Union station up the road, and he's opening another station in town.

Jack always swears by Rowland. He says he's an honest mechanic, and that's high praise from Jack."

"Did Dolly know him?"

"Naturally she knew him. The Rowlands lived across the street for the last three-four years. If you think it went further than that, you're really off. Jim's a good family man. Anyway, he sold to the State and moved out the first of the year. He wouldn't come back and bury a body in his own yard, if that's what you're thinking."

I was thinking that you never could tell what murderers would do. Most of them were acting out a fantasy which they couldn't explain themselves: destroying an unlamented past which seemed to bar them from the brave new world, erasing the fear of death by inflicting death, or burying an old malignant grief where it would sprout and multiply and end by destroying the destroyer.

I thanked Mrs. Stone for her trouble and walked across the road. The earth movers had stopped for the day, but their dust still hung in the air. Through it I could see uprooted trees, houses smashed to rubble and piled in disorderly heaps. I couldn't tell where Rowland's house had stood.

>>>>>>>>>
>>>>>>>>> *chapter* 22
>>>>>>>>>

THE DEPUTY on duty at the Citrus Junction courthouse was a tired-looking man with his blouse open at the neck and a toothpick in his mouth. A deep nirvanic calm lay over his office. Even the motes at the window moved languidly. The ultimate slowdown of the universe would probably begin in Citrus Junction. Perhaps it already had.

I asked the tired man where Sergeant Leonard was. He regarded me morosely, as if I'd interrupted an important meditation.

"Gone to town on business."

"Which town?"

"L.A."

"What business?"

He looked me over some more. Perhaps he was estimating my Bertillon measurements. He belonged to the Bertillon era.

"Anything to do with the Simpson case?" I said.

He removed his toothpick from between his teeth and examined it for clues, such as toothmarks. "We don't discuss official business with the public. You a newspaper fellow?"

"I'm a private detective working with Leonard on the Simpson case."

He was unimpressed. "I'll tell the Sergeant when he comes in. What's your name?"

"S. Holmes."

He reinserted his toothpick in his mouth and wrote haltingly on a scratch pad. I said: "The 'S.' stands for Sherlock."

He looked up from his laborious pencil work. The old crystal set he was using for a brain received a faint and far-off signal: he was being ribbed.

"What did you say the first name was?"

"Sherlock."

"That supposed to be funny? Ha ha," he said.

I started over: "My name is Archer, and Leonard will want to see me. When are you expecting him back?"

"When he gets here."

"Oh, thanks."

"You're welcome." He tore up the paper he had been writing on and let the pieces flutter down onto the counter between us.

"Can you give me Leonard's home address?"

"Sure I can. But you're the great detective. Find it for yourself."

Archer the wit. Archer the public relations wizard. I took my keen sense of humor and social expertise for a walk down the corridor. There was nobody at the information desk inside the front door, but a thin telephone directory was chained to the side of the desk. Wesley Leonard lived on Walnut Street. An old man watering the courthouse chrysanthemums told me where Walnut Street was, a few blocks from here. Archer the bloodhound.

It was a middle-middle-class street of stucco cottages dating from the twenties. The lawn in front of Leonard's cottage was as well kept as a putting green. A stout woman who was not so well kept answered the door.

Pink plastic curlers on her head gave her a grim and defiant expression. She said before I asked: "Wesley's not here. And I'm busy cooking supper."

"Do you know when he'll be back?"

"He's generally home for supper. Wesley likes a good hot supper."

"What time would that be?"

"Six. We eat an early supper." Supper was a key word in her vocabulary. "Who shall I tell him?"

"Lew Archer. I'm the detective who brought Vicky Simpson here last Monday night. Is Mrs. Simpson still with you?"

"No. She only stayed the one night." The woman said in a sudden gush of confidence: "Wesley's such a good Samaritan, he doesn't realize. Are you a real good friend of Mrs. Simpson's?"

"No."

"Well, I wouldn't want to insult her. She has her troubles. But it's hard on an older woman having a younger woman in the house. A younger woman with all those troubles, it puts a strain on the marriage." She ran her fingers over her curlers, as if they were holding the marriage precariously together. "You know how men are."

"Not Wesley."

"Yes, Wesley. He's not immune. No man is." She looked ready to be disappointed in me at any moment. "Wesley was up half the night letting her cry on his shoulder. Heating milk. Making a grilled cheese sandwich at four A.M. He hasn't made me a sandwich in ten years. So after she woke up at noon and I gave her her lunch I tactfully suggested that she should try the hotel. Wesley says I acted hardhearted. I say I was only heading off trouble in the marriage."

"What's she using for money?"

"Her boss wired her an advance on her wages, and I guess the boys in the courthouse chipped in some. Mrs. Vicky Simpson is comfortably ensconced."

"Where?"

"The Valencia Hotel, on Main Street."

It had stood there for forty or fifty years, a three-story cube of bricks that had once been white. Old men in old hats were watching the street through the front window. Their heads turned in unison to follow my progress across the dim lobby. It was so quiet I could hear their necks, or their chairs, creak.

There was nobody on duty at the desk. I punched the handbell. It didn't work. One of the old men rose from his chair near the window and shuffled past me through a door at the back. He reappeared behind the desk, adjusting a glossy brown toupee which he had substituted for his hat. It settled low on his forehead.

"Yessir?"

"Is Mrs. Simpson in?"

He turned to inspect the bank of pigeonholes behind him. The back of his neck was naked as a plucked chicken's.

"Yessir. She's in."

"Tell her there's someone who wants to speak to her."

"No telephone in her room. I guess I could go up and tell her," he said doubtfully.

"I'll go. What's her number?"

"Three-oh-eight on the third floor. But we don't like gentlemen visitors in a lady's room." Somehow his toupee made this remark sound lowbrow and obscene.

"I'm no gentleman. I'm a detective."

"I see."

He and his friends by the window watched me go up the stairs. I was the event of the day. A red bulb lit the third-floor corridor. I tapped on the door of 308.

"Who is it?" Vicky said in a dull voice.

"Lew Archer. Remember me?"

Bedsprings made a protesting noise. She opened the door and peered out. Her face had thinned.

"What do you want?"

"Some talk."

"I'm all run out of talk."

Her eyes were enormous and vulnerable. I could see myself mirrored in their pupils, a tiny red-lit man caught in amber, twice.

"Let me in, Vicky. I need your help."

She shrugged and walked away from the open door, sprawling on the bed in a posture that seemed deliberately ugly. Her breasts and hips stood out under her black dress like protuberances carved from something hard and durable, wood or bone. A Gideon Bible lay open on the bed. I saw when I sat down in the chair beside it that Vicky had been reading the Book of Job.

"I didn't know you were a Bible reader."

"There's lots of things you don't know about me."

"That's true. Why didn't you tell me Ralph was a friend of the Campions?"

"That should be easy to figure out. I didn't want you to know."

"But why?"

"It's none of your business."

"We have business in common, Vicky. We both want to get this mess straightened out."

"It'll never get straightened out. Ralph's dead. You can't change that."

"Was he involved in Dolly's murder? Is that why you covered for him?"

"I didn't cover for him."

"Of course you did. You must have recognized Campion from the description I gave you. You must have known that Dolly had been murdered. You knew that Ralph was close to her."

"He wasn't—not in the way you mean."

"In what way was he close to her?"

"He was more like her financial adviser," she said in a halting voice.

"Dolly had no use for a financial adviser. She was stony broke."

"That's what you think. I happen to know she was loaded at the time she was killed. Ralph told me she had at least a thousand dollars in cash. She didn't know what to do with it, so she asked Ralph."

"You must be mistaken, Vicky. The Campions had no money. I was told that Ralph had to pay the doctor when their child was born."

"He didn't *have* to. He had a good day at the race track and gave them the money. When Ralph won a little money he thought he was Santa Claus. Don't think I didn't put up a squawk. But she paid him back after all."

"When?"

"Just before she was killed. Out of the money she had. That's how he financed his trip to Tahoe."

It was a peculiar story, peculiar enough to be true.

"Did Ralph actually see all the money Dolly claimed she had?"

"He saw it. He didn't count it or anything, but he saw it. She asked him to take it and hold it for her, so she could make a down payment on a tract house. Ralph didn't want the responsibility. He advised her to put it in the bank, but she was afraid Bruce would find out, and it would be gone with the wind. Like the other money —the money she had when he married her."

"I didn't know she had any."

"What do you think he married her for? She had plenty, according to Ralph, another thousand anyway. Bruce took it and blew it. She was afraid he'd do the same with the new money."

"Where did all the money come from?"

"Ralph said she got it out of a man. She wasn't saying who."

"Was the man the father of her child?"

She lowered her eyes demurely. "I always thought Bruce was the father."

"Bruce denied it."

"I never heard that."

"I did, Vicky. Do you have any idea who the father was if it wasn't Bruce?"

"No."

"Could it have been Ralph?"

"No. There was nothing between him and Dolly. For one thing, he had too much respect for Bruce."

"But the child was conceived long before she married Campion. Also you tell me she confided in Ralph about her money problems. Didn't you say she wanted him to look after her thousand dollars?"

"Yes, and maybe he should have." She glanced around the little room as if someone might be spying at the keyhole or the window. She lowered her voice to a whisper: "I think she was killed for that money."

"By Bruce, you mean?"

"By him, or somebody else."

"Did Ralph tell the police about it?"

"No."

"And you didn't either?"

"Why should I ask for trouble? You get enough trouble in this life without coming out and asking for it."

I rose and stood over her. Late afternoon sunlight slanted in through the window. She sat rigid with her legs under her, as if the shafts of light had transfixed her neck and shoulders.

"You were afraid Ralph killed her."

Her eyes shifted away from mine and stayed far over in the corners of her head. "Deputy Mungan made Ralph come down to the station and answer a lot of questions. Then Ralph went off to Nevada right after. Naturally I was scared."

"Where was Ralph the night Dolly was killed?"

"I don't know. He was out late, and I didn't wake up when he came in."

"You still think Ralph murdered her?"

"I didn't say I *thought* it. I was scared."

"Did you ask him?"

"Of course I didn't ask him. But he kept talking about the murder. He was so upset and shaky he couldn't handle a cup of coffee. This was the night after it happened. They had Bruce Campion in the clink, and Ralph kept saying that Bruce didn't do it, he knew Bruce didn't do it."

"Did Ralph see Bruce before he left for Tahoe?"

"Yeah, Bruce came to the house in the morning when they let him out. I wouldn't of let him *in* if I'd been there."

"What happened between Bruce and Ralph that morning?"

"I wouldn't know. I was at work. Ralph phoned me around noon and said he was going up to Tahoe. Maybe Bruce went with him. He dropped out of sight that same day, and I never saw him again. A couple of days after that, the papers were full of him running away, and the Grand Jury brought in a murder conviction."

"The Grand Jury indicted him," I said. "There's a big difference between an indictment and a conviction."

"That's what Ralph said, the day he came back from the lake. I thought a week or so away from it all would get it off his mind. But he was worse than ever when he came back. He was obsessed with Bruce Campion."

"Just how close were they?"

"They were like brothers," she said, "ever since they were in Korea together. Bruce had more on the ball than Ralph had, I guess, but somehow it was Ralph who did the looking after. He thought it was wonderful to have Bruce for a friend. He'd give him the shirt off his back, and he practically did more than once."

"Would Ralph give Bruce his birth certificate to get out of the country?"

She glanced up sharply. "Did he?"

"Bruce says he did. Either Ralph gave it to him voluntarily, or Bruce took it by force."

"And killed him?"

"I have my doubts that Bruce killed either one of them. He had no apparent motive to kill Ralph, and the money Dolly had puts a new complexion on her case. It provides a motive for anyone who knew she had it."

"But why would anybody want to kill Ralph?"

"There's one obvious possibility. He may have known who murdered Dolly."

"Why didn't he say so, then?"

"Perhaps he wasn't sure. I believe he was trying to investigate Dolly's murder, up at the lake and probably here in Citrus Junction. When he came back from Tahoe, did he say anything to you about the Blackwells?"

"The Blackwells?" There was no recognition in her voice.

"Colonel Mark Blackwell and his wife. They brought me into this case, because their daughter Harriet had taken up with Campion. The Blackwells have a lodge at Tahoe, and Harriet was there with Campion the night before last. Then she disappeared. We found her hat in the lake with blood on it. Campion has no explanation."

Vicky rose on her knees. Moving awkwardly, she backed away to the far side of the bed. "I don't know nothing about it."

"That's why I'm telling you. The interesting thing is that Ralph spent some time in the Blackwells' lodge last May. He worked as their houseboy for a week or so. They fired him, allegedly for stealing."

"Ralph might of had his faults," she said from her corner, "but I never knew him to steal anything in his life. Anyway, there's no sense trying to pin something on a dead man."

"I'm not, Vicky. I'm trying to pin murder on whoever killed him. You loved him, didn't you?"

She looked as though she would have liked to deny it and the pain that went with it. "I couldn't help it. I tried to help it, but I couldn't stop myself. He was such a crazy guy," she murmured, so softly that it sounded like an endearment. "Sometimes when he was asleep, when he was asleep and out of trouble, I used to think he was beautiful."

"He's asleep and out of trouble now," I said. "What about the bundle of clothes he brought back from Tahoe?"

"There was no bundle of clothes, there was just the coat. He had this brown topcoat with him. But I know he didn't steal it. He never stole in his life."

"I don't care whether he stole it or not. The question is where did he get it?"

"He *said* somebody gave it to him. But people don't give away that kind of a coat for free. It was real good tweed, imported like. Harris tweed, I think they call it. It must of cost a hundred dollars new, and it was still in new condition. The only thing the matter with it, one of the buttons was missing."

"Can you describe the buttons?"

"They were brown leather. I wanted to try and match the missing one so he could wear it. But he said leave it as it was, he wasn't going to wear it." Tears glistened in her eyes. "He said he wasn't going to wear it and he was right."

"Did he bring it with him when he came down south?"

"Yeah. He was carrying it over his arm when he got on the bus. I don't know why he bothered dragging it along with him. It was warm weather, and anyway it had that button missing."

"Which button on the coat was missing, Vicky?"

"The top one." She pointed with her thumb between her breasts.

I wished I had Mungan's button with me. I remembered now where I had seen other buttons like it, attached to a coat that answered Vicky's description. One of the girls in the zebra-striped hearse had been wearing it.

>>>>>>>>
>>>>>>>> *chapter* 23
>>>>>>>>

I DROVE BACK to the coast and hit the surfing beaches southward from the fork of 101 and 101 Alternate. Some of the surfers recalled the black-and-white hearse, but they didn't know the names of any of the occupants. Anyway they claimed they didn't—they're a closemouthed tribe.

I had better luck with the Highway Patrol in Malibu. The owner of the hearse had been cited the previous weekend for driving with only one headlight. His name was Ray Buzzell, and he lived in one of the canyons above the town.

"Mrs. Sloan Buzzell" was stenciled on the side of the rustic mailbox. An asphalt driveway zigzagged down the canyon side to her house. It was a redwood and glass structure with a white gravel roof, cantilevered over a steep drop. A small Fiat stood in the double carport, but there was no hearse beside it.

A violently redheaded woman opened the front door before I got to it, and stepped outside. Her hard, handsome face was carefully made up, as though she'd been expecting a visitor. I wondered what kind of visitor. Her black Capri pants adhered like oil to her thighs and hips. The plunging neckline of her shirt exhibited large areas of chest and stomach. She was carrying a half-full martini glass in her hand and, to judge by her speech, a number of previous martinis inside of her.

"Hello-hello," she said. "Don't I know you from somewhere?"

"I'm just a type. How are you, Mrs. Buzzell?"

"Fine. Feen. Fane." She flexed her free arm to prove it, and inflated her chest, which almost broke from its moorings. "*You* look sort of beat. Come in and I'll pour you a drink. I hope you drink."

"Quantities, but not at the moment, thanks. I'm looking for Ray."

She frowned muzzily. "People are always looking for Ray. Has he done something?"

"I hope not. Where can I find him?"

She flung out her arm in a gesture which included the whole coast. From the height we stood on, we could see a good many miles of it. The sun was low in the west, and it glared like a searchlight through barred clouds.

"I can't keep track of my son any more," she said in a soberer voice. "I haven't seen him since breakfast. He's off with his crowd somewhere. All they care about is surfing. Some weeks I don't set eyes on him for days at a time." She consoled herself with the rest of her martini. "Sure you won't come in for a drink? I just made a fresh shaker, and if I have to drink it all by myself I'll be smasherooed."

"Pour it out."

"The man is mad." She studied my face with exaggerated interest. "You must be a wandering evangelist or something."

"I'm a wandering detective investigating a murder. Your son may be able to help me."

She moved closer to me and whispered through her teeth: "Is Ray involved in a murder?"

"That I doubt. He may have some information that will help me. Are you expecting him home for dinner?"

"I never know. Sometimes he's out all night with his crowd. They have bedrolls in the hearse." She burst out angrily: "I could *kill* myself for letting him buy that thing. He practically *lives* in it." Her mind veered back to the point. "Who do you mean, he has information?"

"I said he may have."

"Who was murdered?"

"A man named Simpson, Quincy Ralph Simpson."

"I never heard of any such man. Neither did Ray, I'm sure."

I said: "When Simpson was last seen alive by his wife, he was carrying a brown Harris tweed topcoat with brown leather buttons; the top button was missing. That was two months ago. The other day I saw one of the girls in Ray's crowd wearing that topcoat, or one exactly like it."

"Mona?"

"She was a big chesty blonde."

"That's Ray's girl, Mona Sutherland. And the coat is his, too. I know it well. His father gave it to him the last time Ray visited him, so you see you've made a mistake. It's a different coat entirely."

"Now tell me where Ray really got it, Mrs. Buzzell."

The manifestations of mother love are unpredictable. She threw her empty glass at my head. It missed me and smashed on the flagstones. Then she retreated into the house, slamming the door behind her.

I got into my car and sat. The sun was almost down, a narrowing red lozenge on the cloud-streaked horizon. It slipped out of sight. The whole western sky became smoky red, as if the sun had touched off fires on the far side of the world.

After a while the front door opened. The lady appeared with a fresh glass in her hand.

"I've just been talking to my ex on the long-distance telephone. He'll back me up about the coat."

"Bully for him."

She looked at the glass in her hand as if she was considering throwing it, too. But it had liquor in it.

"What right have you got sitting on my property? Get off my property!"

I turned the car and drove up past her mailbox and parked at the roadside and watched the horizontal fires die out and the dark come on. The sky was crowded with stars when the woman came out again. She plodded up the slope and balanced her teetering weight against the mailbox.

"I'm smasherooed."

I got out and approached her. "I told you to pour it out."

"I couldn't do that to good gin. It's been my dearest friend and beloved companion for lo these many yea-hears." She reached for me like a blind woman. "I'm frightened."

"I didn't mean to frighten you, and I don't believe your son is involved in this murder. But I have to know where he got the tweed topcoat. His father had nothing to do with it, did he?"

"No. Ray told me he found it."

"Where?"

"On the beach, he said."

"How long ago was this?"

"About two months. He brought it home and brushed the sand out of it. That's why I got so frightened, on account of the timing. You said two months. That's why I lied to you."

She was leaning on me heavily, one hand on my shoulder, the other clutching my upper arm. I let her lean.

"Ray couldn't murder anyone," she said. "He's a little hard to regiment but he's not a bad boy really. And he's so *young.*"

"He's not a murder suspect, Mrs. Buzzell. He's a witness, and the coat is evidence. How he got it may be significant. But I can't establish that without talking to him. You must have some idea where I can find him."

"He did say something this morning—something about spending the night at Zuma. I know he took along some things to cook. But what he says and what he actually does are often two different things. I can't keep track of him any more. He needs a father."

She was talking into the front of my coat, and her grip had tightened on me. I held her for a bit, because she needed holding, until a car came up the road and flashed its headlights on her wet startled face.

The striped hearse was standing empty among other cars off the highway above Zuma. I parked behind it and went down to the beach to search for its owner. Bonfires were scattered along the shore, like the bivouacs of nomad tribes or nuclear war survivors. The tide was high and the breakers loomed up marbled black and fell white out of oceanic darkness.

Six young people were huddled under blankets around one of the fires. I recognized them: one of the girls was wearing the brown tweed coat. They paid no attention when I approached. I was an apparition from the adult world. If they pretended I wasn't there, I would probably go away like all the other adults.

"I'm looking for Ray Buzzell."

One of the boys cupped his hand behind his ear and said: "Hey?"

He was an overgrown seventeen- or eighteen-year-old with heavy masculine features unfocused by any meaning in his eyes. In spite of his peroxided hair, he looked like an Indian in the red firelight.

"Ray Buzzell," I repeated.

"Never heard of him." He glanced around at the others. "Anybody ever hear of a Ray Buzzell?"

"*I* never heard of a Ray Buzzell," the girl in the coat said. "I knew a man named Heliogabalus Rexford Buzzell. He had a long grey beard and he died some years ago of bubonic plague."

Everybody laughed except me and the girl. I said to the boy: "You're Ray, aren't you?"

"Depends who you are." He rose in a sudden single movement, shedding his blanket. The three other boys rose, too. "You fuzz?"

"You're getting warm, kid."

"Don't call me kid."

"What do you want me to call you?"

"Anything but kid."

"All right, Mr. Buzzell. I have some questions to ask you, about the coat Miss Sutherland is wearing."

"Who you been talking to? How come you know our names?"

He took a step toward me, his bare feet noiseless in the sand. His little comitatus grouped themselves behind him. They crossed their arms on their chests to emphasize their muscles, and the red firelight flickered on their biceps.

With a little judo I thought I could handle all eight of their biceps, but I didn't want to hurt them. I was an emissary from the adult camp. I flashed the special-deputy's badge which I carried as a souvenir of an old trouble on the San Pedro docks.

"I've been talking to your mother, among other people. She said you found the coat on the beach."

"Never believe her," he said with one eye on the girls. "Never believe a mother."

"Where did you get it then?"

"I wove it underwater out of sea lettuce. I'm very clever with my hands." He wiggled his fingers at me.

"I wouldn't go on playing this for laughs, Buzzell. It's a serious matter. Have you ever been in Citrus Junction?"

"I guess I passed through."

"Did you stop over long enough to kill and bury a man?"

"Bury a man?" He was appalled.

"His name was Quincy Ralph Simpson. He was found buried in Citrus Junction last week, with an icepick wound in his heart. Did you know him?"

"I never heard of him, honest. Besides, we've had the coat for a couple of months." His voice had regressed five years, and sounded as though it was changing all over again. He turned to the girl. "Isn't that right, Mona?"

She nodded. Her sea-lion eyes were wide and scared. With scrabbling fingers she unbuttoned the coat and flung it off. I held out my hands for it. Ray Buzzell picked it up and gave it to me. His movements had lost their certainty.

The coat was heavy, with matted fibers that smelled of the sea. I folded it over my arm.

"Where did you get it, Ray?"

"On the beach, like Moth—like the old lady said. It was salvage, like. I'm always living off the beach, picking up salvage and jetsam. Isn't that right, Mona?"

She nodded, still without breaking silence.

His voice rushed on in an adolescent spate: "It was soaked through, and there were stones in the pockets, like somebody chunked it in the drink to get rid of it. But there was a strong tide running, and the waves washed it up on the beach. It was still in pretty good condition, this Harris tweed is indestructible, so I decided to dry it out and keep it. It was like salvage. Mona wears it mostly—she's the one that gets cold."

She was shivering in her bathing suit now, close by the fire. The other girl draped a plaid shirt over her shoulders. The boys were standing around desultorily, like figures relaxing out of a battle frieze.

"Can you name the beach?"

"I don't remember. We go to a lot of beaches."

"I know which one it was," Mona said. "It was the day we had the six-point-five and I was scared to go out in them and you all said I was chicken. *You* know," she said to the others, "that little private beach above Malibu where they have the shrimp joint across the highway."

"Yeah," Ray said. "We ate there the other day. Crummy joint."

"I saw you there the other day," I said. "Now let's see if we can pin down the date you found the coat."

"I don't see how. That was a long time ago, a couple months."

The girl rose and touched his arm. "What about the tide tables, Raybuzz?"

"What about them?"

"We had a six-point-five tide that day. We haven't had many this year. You've got the tide tables in the car, haven't you?"

"I guess so."

The three of us went up the beach to the zebra-striped hearse. Ray found the dog-eared booklet, and Mona scanned it under the dashboard lights.

"It was May the nineteenth," she said positively. "It couldn't have been any other day."

I thanked her. I thanked them both, but she was the one with the brains. As I drove back toward Los Angeles, I wondered what Mona was doing on the beach. Perhaps if I met her father or her mother I could stop wondering.

THE BLACKWELL HOUSE was dark. I pressed the bell push, and the chimes inside gave out a lonely tinkling. I waited and rang again and waited and rang and waited.

Eventually I heard footsteps inside. The veranda light went on over my head, and the little maid looked out at me sleepily. She was out of uniform and out of sorts.

"What do *you* want?"

"Are the Blackwells in?"

"She is. He isn't."

"Tell her Mr. Archer would like to speak to her."

"I can't do that. She's in bed asleep. I was asleep myself." She yawned in my face, and hugged her rayon bathrobe more closely around her.

"You go to bed early, Letty."

"I had to get *up* early this morning, so I thought I might as well catch up on my rest. Mrs. Blackwell took some sleeping pills and left strict orders not to be disturbed. She went to bed right after dinner."

"Is Mrs. Blackwell all right?"

"She said she had a blinding headache but she gets those from time to time."

"How many sleeping pills did she take?"

"A couple."

"What kind?"

"The red kind. Why?"

"Nothing. Where's the lord and master?"

"He left early this morning. He had a phone call, about Miss Harriet, and he made me get up and make breakfast for him. It isn't a regular part of my duties but the cook sleeps out—"

I cut in on her explanations: "Do you know where he is now?"

"He went up to Tahoe to help them search for her body. That's where the phone call was from."

"They haven't found her, then?"

"No. What do you think happened to her?"

"I think she's in the lake."

"That's what he said." She stepped outside, partly closing the door behind her. "He was in bad shape at breakfast. He couldn't eat he was so broken up. I didn't think he should go off there by himself. But he wouldn't let me wake up Mrs. Blackwell, and what could I do?"

She crossed the veranda and looked up at the stars. She sighed, and laid a hand on her round pink rayon bosom.

"How long have you been working for the Blackwells?"

"Two months. It seems like longer. I mean with all the trouble in the house."

"Trouble between Mr. and Mrs. Blackwell?"

"They've had their share. But it don't behoove me to talk about it."

"Don't they get along?"

"They get along as well as most, I guess. A-course they've only been married eight or nine months. It's the long pull that counts, my daddy says, and the Colonel must be twenty years older than her."

"Is that an issue between the Blackwells?"

"No, I don't mean that. Only it makes you wonder why she married him. Mrs. Blackwell may have her faults, but she's not the gold-digging type."

"I'm interested in what you think of her and her faults."

"I don't talk behind people's backs," she said with some spirit. "Mrs. Blackwell treats me good, and I try to treat her good back. She's a nice lady to work for. He isn't so bad either."

"Did they take you up to Tahoe in May?"

"That was before I started with them. Just my luck. They were talking about going up again in September, but it's probably all off now. They wouldn't want to stay in the lodge so soon after what happened there. I wouldn't want to myself."

"Were you fond of Harriet?"

"I wouldn't say that. I never saw much of her. But I felt kind of sorry for her, even before this happened. She was a real sad cookie, even with all that money. It's too bad she had to die before she had any happiness in life. She put on a pretty good front, but you ought to seen the crying tantrums she threw in the privacy of her own room. My mother is a practical nurse, and I tried to calm her down a couple of times."

"What was she crying about?"

"Nobody loved her, she said. She said she was ugly. I told her she had a real nice figure and other attractive features, but she couldn't see it. This was in June, before she went to Mexico. It's easy to understand why she was such a pushover for that artist guy—the one with all the names that murdered her." She looked at the stars again, and coughed at their chilliness. "I think I'm catching cold. I better get back to bed. You never can tell when they'll get you up around here."

She went back into the dark house. I went down the hill and turned left on Sunset toward my office. I drove automatically in the light evening traffic. My mind was sifting the facts I'd scraped together, the facts and the semi-facts and the semi-demi-semi-facts. One of the semi-facts had become a certainty since I'd learned that the tweed coat had been found near the Blackwells' beach house: the Blackwell case and the Dolly Campion case and the Ralph Simpson case were parts of one another. Dolly and Ralph and probably Harriet had died by the same hand, and the coat could be used to identify the hand.

I spread it out on the desk in my office and looked at it under the light. The leather buttons were identical with the one Mungan had shown me. Where the top one had been pulled off there were some strands of broken thread corresponding with the threads attached to Mungan's button. I had no doubt that an identification man with a microscope could tie that button and this coat together.

I turned the coat over, scattering sand across the desk and the floor. It had a Harris label on the right inside breast pocket, and under it the label of the retailers: Cruttworth, Ltd., Toronto. My impulse was to phone the Cruttworth firm right away. But it was the middle of the night in Toronto, and the best I could hope for was a chat with the night watchman.

I searched in vain for cleaners' marks. Perhaps the coat had never been cleaned. In spite of its rough usage on the beach, the cuffs and the collar showed no sign of wear.

I tried the thing on. It was small for me, tight across the chest. I wondered how it would fit Campion. It was a heavy coat, and a heavy thought, and I began to sweat. I struggled out of the coat. It hugged me like guilt.

I knew a man named Sam Garlick who specialized in identifying clothes and connecting them with their rightful owners in court. He was a Detective Sergeant in the L.A.P.D. His father and his grandfather had been tailors.

I called Sam's house in West Los Angeles. His mother-in-law informed me that the Garlicks were out celebrating their twenty-second wedding anniversary. She was looking after the three smaller children, and they were a handful, but she'd finally got them off to bed. Yes, Sam would be on duty in the morning.

While the receiver was in my hand, I dialed my answering service. Both Arnie Walters and Isobel Blackwell had called me earlier in the day. The most recent calls were from Sergeant Wesley Leonard and a woman named Mrs. Hatchen, who was staying at the Santa Monica Inn. Mrs. Hatchen. Harriet's mother. The long loops were intersecting, and I was at the point of intersection.

I put in a call to the Santa Monica Inn. The switchboard operator told me after repeated attempts that Mrs. Hatchen's room didn't answer. The desk clerk thought she'd gone out for a late drive. She had checked into a single late that afternoon.

I returned Leonard's call. He answered on the first ring.

"Sergeant Leonard here."

"Archer. You wanted to talk to me?"

"I thought you wanted to talk to me. The wife mentioned you were here this afternoon."

"I had some evidence that should interest you. I have more now than I had then."

"What is it?"

"The coat Ralph Simpson had with him when he left home. I'm hoping it will lead us to the killer."

"How?" he said, rather competitively.

"It's a little complicated for the phone. We should get together, Sergeant."

"I concur. I've got something hotter than the coat." He was a simple man, and simple pride swelled in his voice. "So hot I can't even tell you over the phone."

"Do you come here or do I go there?"

"You come to me. I have my reasons. You know where I live."

He was waiting for me on the lighted porch, looking younger and taller than I remembered him. There was a flush on his cheeks and a glitter in his eyes, as if the hotness of his evidence had raised his temperature.

I suspected that he was letting me in on it because he secretly doubted his competence to handle it. He had anxiety in him, too. He pumped my hand, and seemed to have a hard time letting go.

Mrs. Leonard had made lemonade and egg-salad sandwiches, and laid them out on a coffee table in the small overfurnished living room. She poured two glasses of lemonade from a pitcher clinking with ice. Then she retreated into the kitchen, shutting the door with crisp tact. I had forgotten to eat, and I wolfed several sandwiches while Leonard talked.

"I've found the murder weapon," he announced. "I didn't find it personally, but it was my own personal idea that led to its disclosure. Ever since we uncovered Simpson's body, I've had a crew of county prisoners out there mornings picking over the scene of the crime. This morning one of them came across the icepick and turned it in."

"Let me see it."

"It's down at the courthouse, locked up. I'll show it to you later."

"What makes you certain it's the weapon?"

"I took it into the L.A. crime lab today. They gave it a test for blood traces, and got a positive reaction. Also, it fits the puncture in Simpson's body."

"Any icepick would."

"But this is it. This is the one." He leaned toward me urgently across the plate of sandwiches. "I had to be sure, and I made sure."

"Fingerprints?"

"No. The only prints were the ones from the prisoner that found it. It was probably wiped clean before the murderer stuck it in the dirt. I've got something better than fingerprints. And worse, in a way."

"You're talking in riddles, Sergeant."

"It's a riddle for sure." He glanced at the closed door to the kitchen, and lowered his voice. "The icepick was part of a little silver bar set which was sold right here in town last October. I had no trouble tracking down the store because there's only the one good hardware store here in town. That's Drake Hardware, and Mr. Drake identified the icepick personally tonight. He just had the one set like it in stock, and he remembered who he sold it to. She's a local citizen—a woman my wife has known for years."

"Who is she?"

Leonard raised his hand as if he was back on traffic point duty. "Not so fast. I don't know that I'm justified telling you her name. It wouldn't mean anything to you, anyway. She's a Citrus Junction woman, lived here all her life. Always had a clean record, till now. But it looks dark for her, or maybe her husband. There's more than the icepick tying them into the murder. They live directly across the road from the site where we found the icepick *and* the body."

"Are we talking about Mr. and Mrs. Stone?"

He looked at me in surprise. "You know Jack and Liz Stone?"

"I interviewed her this afternoon. He wasn't there."

"What were you doing—questioning her about the Simpson killing?"

"We discussed it, but I didn't consider her a suspect. We talked mostly about her daughter Dolly—and what happened to her."

Leonard made a lugubrious face. "That was a bad blow to the Stone couple. The way I figure it, psychologically speaking, the murder of their girl could of drove them over the edge. Maybe Simpson had something to do with that murder, and they killed him in revenge."

"It's a possible motive, all right. Simpson was definitely involved with Dolly and her husband. Have you questioned the Stones?"

"Not yet. I just got Mr. Drake's identification of the icepick tonight. I talked it over with the Sheriff and he says I should wait until the D.A. gets back from Sacramento. He's due back tomorrow. We wouldn't want to make a serious mistake, the Sheriff says." Clear sweat, like distilled anxiety, burst out on his forehead. "The Stones aren't moneyed folks but they've always had a good reputation and plenty of friends in town. Liz Stone is active in the Eastern Star." He took a long gulp of lemonade.

"Somebody ought to ask her about the icepick."

"That's my opinion, too. Unfortunately my hands are tied until the D.A. gets back."

"Mine aren't."

He regarded me appraisingly. Clearly he was asking himself how far he could trust me. He tossed down the rest of his lemonade and got up.

"Okay. You want to take a look at it first?"

We rode in my car to the courthouse. The icepick was in Leonard's second-floor office, where a map of Citrus County took up one whole wall. He got the thing out of a locker and set it on the table under a magnifying glass on a flexible arm.

A tag bearing Leonard's initials was wired to the handle, and the wire sealed with lead. The square-cut silver handle felt cold to my fingers. The point of the icepick was sharp and dirty, like a bad death.

"There's a corkscrew that goes with it, part of the set," he said. "If Liz and Jack Stone have the corkscrew, it ties it up."

"Maybe. Are they the sort of people that would use a silver bar set, or any kind of a bar set?"

"I never heard that they drank, but you never can tell. One of them could be a secret drinker."

"Secret drinkers don't fool around with fancy accessories. Do I have your permission to show them this thing, and ask for an explanation?"

"I guess so." He wiped his forehead. "Long as you don't go to them in my name, I guess it's all right. But don't make any accusations. We don't want them to panic and go on the run."

I let him out on the sidewalk in front of his house and drove to the west side. The Stones had an upstairs light on. The man who came to the front door was in his pajamas. He was a thin man with bushy sandy hair and defeated eyes.

"Mr. Stone?"

"Yessir."

"I had some conversation with your wife today."

"You're the detective, are you?" he said in a flat voice.

"Yes. I'd appreciate a few minutes more with your wife, and with you, too."

"I dunno, it's getting pretty late. Mrs. Stone is on her way to bed." He glanced up the stairs which rose from the hallway. "Is it about Dolly?"

"It's connected with Dolly."

"Maybe I can handle it, eh?" He squared his narrow shoulders. "It was a terrible sorrow to my wife what happened to Dolly. I hate to see her dragged back to it all the time."

"I'm afraid it's necessary, Mr. Stone."

He took my word for it and went upstairs to fetch her, climbing like a man on a treadmill. They came down together wearing bathrobes. He was holding her arm. Her face and neck were shiny with some kind of cream or oil.

"Come in," she said. "You shouldn't keep a man waiting on the doorstep, Jack. It isn't polite."

We went into the living room, where the three of us stood and looked at each other. The awkwardness developed into tension. The woman pulled at the oily skin of her throat.

"What brings you here so late? Have you found something out?"

"I keep trying, Mrs. Stone." I got the icepick out of my pocket and held it out by the tip. "Have you seen this before?"

"Let me look at it."

She reached out and took it from me by the handle. Her husband leaned at her shoulder, one arm around her waist. He seemed to depend on physical contact with her.

"It looks like the one you bought for Mrs. Jaimet," he said.

"I believe it is. What's this little wire tag doing on it?"

"It's just to identify it. Where did you buy it, Mrs. Stone?"

"At Drake Hardware. It's part of a set I got for Mrs. Jaimet as a wedding gift. Jack thought I spent too much money on it, but I wanted to get her something nice for once. She was always good to us and Dolly. Twelve dollars wasn't too much for all she's done." Her eye was on her husband, and she was speaking more to him than to me.

"It cost sixteen," he corrected her. "I work all day for sixteen dollars take-home. But I'm not kicking. She *was* a good friend to Dolly."

His wife took up the sentiment and breathed more life into it. "She was *wonderful* to Dolly, a second mother. Remember when Dolly used to call her Aunt Izzie? Not every woman in Izzie Jaimet's position would permit that, but she's no snob. She gave our Dolly some of her happiest hours."

They clung to each other and to this warm fragment of the past. The icepick in her hand brought her back to the sharp present.

"How did you get ahold of this? I sent it to Mrs. Jaimet for a wedding gift. She doesn't even live in town any more."

"She used to live in town?"

"Right across the road," Stone said. "We were neighbors with the Jaimets for close to twenty years. She sold out to the Rowlands after

Jaimet died, and moved to Santa Barbara. But Liz and her kept in touch. She even invited Liz to attend her wedding. Liz didn't go though. I convinced her she'd be out of place—"

His wife interrupted him: "Mr. Archer didn't come here to listen to a lot of ancient history." She said to me: "You haven't answered my question. Where did you get ahold of this?"

She shook the icepick at me. I held out my hand, and she relinquished it. I put it away in my pocket.

"I can't answer that question, Mrs. Stone."

"I've been answering *your* questions, all day and half the night."

"It hasn't been quite that bad. Still I'm sorry that I can't make things even with you. You'll find out soon enough what this is about."

"Is it the man they found across the road?"

I didn't affirm it or deny it. "This may be important to you personally. It may lead to a solution of Dolly's murder."

"I don't understand how."

"Neither do I. If I did, I wouldn't be here asking you questions. How well and how long did Mrs. Jaimet know Dolly?"

"All her life." She sat down suddenly on the chesterfield. The net of time had drawn tight on her face, cutting deep marks. "That is, until about three and a half years ago, when she moved to Santa Barbara. But it didn't stop then. She invited Dolly to come and visit her in Santa Barbara. I tried to talk Dolly into it—Mrs. Jaimet could do a lot for her—but Dolly never made the trip."

"How could Mrs. Jaimet do a lot for her?"

"The way she did do a lot for her. Mrs. Jaimet is an educated woman; her husband was the principal of the high school. She used to give Dolly books to read, and take her on picnics and all. I was working in those days, and she was a real good neighbor. She just loved Dolly. So if you're thinking she had anything to do with Dolly's death, you're 'way off the beam."

" 'Way off the beam," her husband echoed. "She was like a second mother to Dolly, being she had no children of her own."

"Which was her secret sorrow. She never will have children now—she's too old."

Elizabeth Stone looked down at her own body. Jack Stone put his arm around her shoulders. She crossed her legs.

"Where can I get in touch with Mrs. Jaimet?"

"She's living in L.A. with her new husband. I ought to have her address some place. She remembered me with a card at Christmastime. I think I still have that card in the bureau." She started to get up, and froze in a leaning posture. "If I give you the address, you have to promise you won't tell her who gave it to you."

"I could promise, but it's bound to come out. Nearly everything does in the long run."

"Yeah, you have something there." She turned to her husband. "Jack, will you get it for me? It's in the top drawer of the bureau with the other special cards I saved—the one with the silver bells."

He rose quickly and left the room, and she subsided onto the chesterfield. Her baby-blue eyes were strained and speculative.

"The man across the road was stabbed with an icepick. It said so in the paper. The icepick you have there, the one I bought for Mrs. Jaimet's wedding—it couldn't be the one, could it?"

"Yes. It could be."

"I don't get it. How would a lady like her get mixed up in a killing?"

"Some of the darnedest people do."

"But she's a real lady."

"What makes you so sure?"

"I may not be a lady myself, but I know one when I see one. Isobel Jaimet has class, the kind that doesn't have to flaunt itself. I happen to know she has very good connections. Matter of fact, she married one of them the second time around. Her second husband was her first husband's second cousin, if you can follow that. I met him years ago when he was staying with the Jaimets. He was very important in the military. The Jaimet family itself used to own the whole west side, before they lost it."

"What is her second husband's name?"

"Let's see, it's on the tip of my tongue. Anyway, it's on the card she sent me."

"Would it be Blackwell?"

"That's it! Blackwell. You know him?"

I didn't have to answer her. Her husband's slippered feet were clop-clopping down the stairs. He came into the room carrying a square envelope, which he handed to his wife. She opened it.

"Merry Christmas and Happy New Year," the bright card said. "Colonel and Mrs. Mark Blackwell."

SERGEANT LEONARD was waiting for me at the front of his house. He was wearing an eager expression, which sharpened when our eyes met under the light.

"Did they break down and confess?"

"They had nothing to confess. Elizabeth Stone bought the bar set as a wedding present for an old neighbor."

"It sounds like malarkey to me. They don't have the money to buy that kind of presents for the neighbors."

"They did, though."

"Who was the neighbor?"

"Mrs. Jaimet."

"Mrs. Ronald Jaimet? That's malarkey. She couldn't have had anything to do with this."

I would have liked to be able to agree with him. Since I couldn't, I said nothing.

"Why, her and her husband were two of our leading citizens," he said. "They had a front-page editorial in the paper when he died. He was a member of a pioneer county family and the best principal we ever had at the union high school."

"What did he die of?"

"He was a diabetic. He broke his leg in the Sierra and ran out of insulin before they could get him back to civilization. It was a great loss to the town, and just about as big a loss when Mrs. Jaimet moved away. She was the head of the Volunteer Family Service and half a dozen other organizations." He paused reflectively. "Did the Stones say where she is now?"

I lit a cigarette and considered my answer. Between my duty to the law and a man who trusted me, and my duty to a client I no longer trusted, my ethics were stretched thin. Leonard repeated his question.

"I think they said she was married in Santa Barbara last year. You'd better talk to them yourself."

"Yeah. I better. In the morning." He scratched at his hairline. "It just came to my mind, the Jaimets lived right across the road from the Stones. We found Simpson buried right spang in their back yard, their use-to-was back yard. What do you make of that?"

"I don't like it," I said honestly, and changed the subject before he could ask me further questions. "I have that coat in the car if you want to look it over."

"Yeah. Bring it in."

I spread it out on the carpet in his living room. While I told him what I knew of its history, he was down on his knees, examining it inside and out.

"Too bad there's no cleaners' marks," he said. "But we may be able to trace the ownership through these Cruttworth people in Toronto. Another long trip for somebody."

"I'm getting used to long trips."

Leonard rose with his hands in the small of his back, then got down on his knees beside the coat again.

"Sometimes," he said, "the older-established cleaners put their marks inside the sleeves."

He turned back the right cuff. Several code letters and figures were written in indelible ink in the lining: BX1207. He stood up smiling.

"It's a lucky thing I looked."

"Do you recognize the mark, Sergeant?"

"No, it isn't local. But we can trace it. I know an officer in L.A. who has a pretty complete collection of these marks."

"Sam Garlick."

"You know Sam too, do you? We'll get to work on it first thing in the morning. You may not have to go to Toronto after all."

I left the coat with Leonard and went back to Bel Air. The Blackwell house had lights in it, and there was a taxi standing in the drive. The sound of my feet in the gravel woke the driver. He looked at me as if I might be about to hold him up.

"It's a nice night," I said.

"Uh-huh."

"Who are you waiting for?"

"A fare. Any objections?" His broken sleep had made him a little surly. He had a seamed dark face, and the eyes of a loner.

"I have no objections."

He said with aggressive politeness: "If I'm in your way I can move. Just say the word."

"You're not in my way. What happened, brother—did a bear bite you?"

"I don't like these long waits. These dames have no consideration. She must of been in there nearly an hour." He looked at his watch. "Over an hour."

"Who is she?"

"I dunno. Some big blonde dame in a leopard coat. I picked her up in Santa Monica."

"Is she old or young?"

"She isn't young. You ask a lot of questions."

"I'll bet you two dollars you didn't pick her up at the Santa Monica Inn."

"You lose. Are you her husband?"

"A friend." I gave him two dollars and went back to my car. We sat and had a waiting competition which lasted another fifteen or twenty minutes. Then the front door opened.

Pauline Hatchen backed out saying good night to Isobel Blackwell. I had a good look at Isobel before she closed the door. She was fully and formally dressed in a dark suit. Her heavy make-up didn't entirely hide her pallor or the patches of funeral crepe under her eyes. She didn't notice me.

I was waiting beside the cab when Pauline Hatchen reached it. "How are you, Mrs. Hatchen? I'm not as surprised to see you here as you might think. I got your call, and tried to return it."

"It's Mr. Archer. How nice." But she didn't sound too happy. "I've been wanting to talk to you again. It was one of my main reasons for coming back. The other night, in Ajijic, I didn't truly *real*ize the situation. I suppose I'm what they call slow on the up-take."

"Did you fly in?"

"Yes. Today." She looked around at the large and quiet night. The lights in the Blackwell house were going out progressively. "Is there somewhere we can go and talk?"

"Will my car do? I prefer not to leave here right now. I want to see Isobel before she goes back to bed."

"I suppose it will have to do." She turned to the driver. "Do you mind waiting a few more minutes?"

"It's your time, ma'am. You're paying for it."

We walked back to my car. She seemed very tired, so tired that she had forgotten her self-consciousness. She leaned on my arm, and let me help her into the lighted front seat. Her leopard coat was genuine but shabby. She pulled it around her not inelegant legs, and I shut the door.

I sat behind the wheel. "You want to talk about Harriet."

"Yes. Is there any word from her? Anything at all?"

"Nothing that will give you any comfort."

"So Isobel said. I thought perhaps she was holding back on me. She's always been a great one for deciding what other people ought to know. And I had the very devil of a time getting in touch with her. She'd gone to bed and refused to answer the phone. How any woman can *sleep* through a thing like this! But of course she's not Harriet's mother. That makes the difference. Blood is thicker than water."

She sounded like an algebra student quoting a formula which she was just learning how to apply.

"Do you know Isobel well?"

"I've known her for a long time. That isn't quite the same thing, is it? Her first husband, Ronald Jaimet, was Mark's cousin, and incidentally one of his best friends. Mark is a very family-minded man, and naturally we saw a good deal of the Jaimets. But Isobel and I were never close. I always felt she envied me my position as Mark's wife. Ronald was a decent-enough fellow, but he was nothing but a high-school teacher. He was one of those dedicated souls. Perhaps his diabetes had something to do with it."

"Do you know anything about his death?"

"Not much. He had an accident in the mountains. Mark was with him at the time. Why don't you ask Mark?"

"Mark isn't available. Or is he?"

"No, he's not here. According to Isobel, he's gone up to Tahoe." She leaned toward me, and her clothes emitted a gust of perfume. "Just what is the situation up there, Mr. Archer?"

"I haven't been in touch with it today. They're searching for Harriet, of course. She was last seen there, and a bloodstained hat belonging to her was found in the water. I found it myself."

"Does that mean she's been killed?"

"I keep hoping it doesn't. All we can do is hope."

"You think Harriet's dead." Her voice was low and dull. "Did Burke Damis kill her?"

"He says he didn't."

"But what would he have to gain?"

"Not all murders are for profit."

We sat in close silence, listening to each other breathe. I was keenly aware of her, not so much as a woman, but as a fellow creature who had begun to feel pain. She had lost her way to the happy ending and begun to realize the consequences of the sealed-off past.

"You came a long way to ask me a few questions, Mrs. Hatchen. I'm sorry I can't give you better answers."

"It isn't your fault. And it wasn't just to ask questions that I came back. I heard from Harriet, you see. It brought home to me—"

"You heard from Harriet? When?"

"Yesterday, but please don't get your hopes up. She wrote the letter last Sunday, before this thing erupted. It was a very touching little letter. It made me see myself, and Harriet, in quite a new light."

"What did she have to say?"

"I can't repeat it verbatim, though I must have read it a dozen times on the plane. You can read it yourself if you like."

I turned on the overhead light. She rummaged in her leopard bag and produced a crumpled airmail envelope. It was addressed to Mrs. Keith Hatchen, Apartado Postal 89, Ajijic, Jalisco, Mexico, and had been postmarked in Pacific Palisades the previous Monday morning at 9:42. The envelope contained a single sheet crowded with writing. The first few lines slanted up to the right; the rest slanted down increasingly, so that the concluding lines were at a thirty-degree angle from the bottom of the page.

Dear Mother,

This is a difficult letter to write because we've never talked to one another as woman to woman (all my fault) and it was stupid and childish of me to leave without saying good-by. I was afraid (it seems I'm always afraid of something, doesn't it?) you would disapprove of me and Burke, and that I couldn't bear. He's my moon and stars, my great brilliant moon and my cruel

bright stars. You didn't know I had such feelings, did you? Well,
I do. I love him and I'm going to marry him, I don't care what
Mark says. When I'm with Him I feel quite different from my
ordinary sad shy self (alliteration's artful aid!)—he's a Prince, a
dark Prince, who fits crystal slippers on my Cinderella feet and
teaches me to dance to music I never heard before—the music
of the spheres. When he touches me the dead cold world comes
alive, dead cold Harriet comes alive.

That sounds like gibberish, doesn't it, but believe me I mean
every word of it, but I will try to write more calmly. I need your
help, Mother. I know I can count on you, in spite of all the
wasted years between us. You have known passion and suffered
for it—but here I am going on again like a nineteenth-century
romance. The point is, we need money and we need it right
away if we are to get married. Burke is in some sort of trouble
(nothing serious) and I should never have brought him back to
this country. We plan to fly to South America—keep this under
your hat!—if we can get the money, and you are the only one we
can turn to. Mark is no help at all. He hates Burke, I even think
he hates me, too. He says he'll hire detectives to stop the wedding! Since he is one of the controllers of Aunt Ada's trust, I
can't do anything in that direction until I'm twenty-five. So I
am asking you to lend me five thousand dollars till January. If
you will do this please have it ready for me and I will get in
touch with you when we reach Mexico. We have enough money
to reach Mexico.

Dear Mother, please do this. It's the only thing I've ever
asked of you. It's the only thing I ask of life, that Burke and I
have a chance to be happy together. If I can't have him, I'll die.

> Your loving daughter,
> *Harriet.*

I folded the letter along its creases and tucked it into the envelope.
Mrs. Hatchen watched me as if it was a live thing which I might injure.

"It's a strangely beautiful letter, isn't it?"

"It didn't strike me in quite that way. I'm not too crazy about some of the implications. Harriet wasn't thinking too well when she wrote it."

"What do you expect?" she said defensively. "The poor girl was under great strain. She'd just had a fearful battle with her father—Isobel told me something about it. Harriet was fighting for everything she holds dear."

"So was Campion. Everything that he holds dear seems to be five thousand dollars."

"Campion?"

"Campion is Burke Damis's real name. He's in jail in Redwood City at the moment. What about the five thousand dollars, Mrs. Hatchen? Would you have been willing to lend it to her?"

"Yes. I still am, if she is alive to use it. I brought it with me. Keith and I went into Guadalajara yesterday afternoon and took it out of the bank. It's part of my settlement from Mark, and Keith had no real objection."

"I hope you're not carrying it around."

"It's in the safe at the hotel."

"Leave it there. Harriet certainly won't be needing it. I don't believe it was her idea, anyway." I turned to look at her under the light. "You're a generous woman, Mrs. Hatchen. I took you for something different."

"I am something different." She narrowed her eyes and drew down the corners of her mouth. "Please turn off the light and don't look at me. I'm an ugly old woman, trying to buy back the past. But I came back here about fifteen years too late. I had no right to leave Harriet. Her life would have turned out better if I'd stayed."

"You can't be sure of that." I switched off the light, and noticed that all the lights in the Blackwell house had gone out. "Do you mind telling me just why you left Mark Blackwell? Did it have anything to do with Isobel?"

"No, he wasn't interested in her. He wasn't interested in any woman, and that includes me." Her voice had become harsher and deeper. "Mark was a mother's boy. I know that sounds like a peculiar statement to make about a professional military man. Unfortunately it's true. His mother was the widow of the late Colonel, who was killed in the First War, and Mark was her only son, and she really lavished herself on him, if 'lavish' is the word. 'Ravish' may be closer.

"She spent the first years of our marriage with us, and I had to sit in the background and watch him dance to her tune, playing skip-rope with the silver cord. It's a common story—I've heard it from other women, in and out of the service. You marry them because they're idealistic and make no passes. The trouble is, they stay that way. Mark was like a little boy in bed. You'll never know the contortions I had to go through to get a child. But we won't go into that.

"When his mother died, I thought he'd turn to me. I was a dreamer. He transferred his fixation—yes, I've talked to the doctors—he transferred his fixation to poor little Harriet. It's a terrible thing to see a person converting another person into a puppet, a kind of zombie. He supervised her reading, her games, her friends, even her thoughts. He made her keep a diary, which he read, and when he was away on duty she had to send it to him. He got her so confused that she didn't know whether she was a girl or a boy, or if he was her father or her lover.

"He was worse than ever after the war, when he got back from Germany. The war was a disappointment to Mark; it didn't do what he'd hoped for his career. Actually he only chose that career because it was a family tradition and his mother insisted on it. I think he would have been happier doing almost anything else. But by the time they retired him, he thought it was too late to start something new. And he had money, so he didn't have to. There's always been scads of money in the family, and he could afford to spend all his time on Harriet. He conceived the grand idea of turning her into a sort of boy-girl who would make everything come right in the end for him. He taught her to shoot and climb mountains and play polo. He even took to calling her Harry.

"It sickened me. I'm not the aggressive type, and I'd always been afraid of him—you get that way living with a man you don't love. But I finally forced a showdown. I told him I would divorce him if he didn't get some help, psychiatric help. Naturally he thought I was the one who was crazy—he couldn't afford to think otherwise. Maybe I was, to stay with him for twelve years. He told me to go ahead and divorce him, that he and Harriet were enough for each other. She was only eleven years old at the time. I wanted to take her with me, but Mark said he would fight me to the limit. I couldn't afford a court battle. Don't ask why. Everything catches up with you in the end. So I lost my daughter, and now she's really lost."

We sat and let the darkness soak into our bones. I tried to relieve it.

"There's a small chance that Harriet's all right," I said. "She and Campion may have decided to travel separately. It would account for his refusal to say what happened to her. She may turn up in Mexico after all."

"But you don't really think she will?"

"No. It's just one of several possibilities. The others aren't so pleasant to contemplate."

There was a stir of life in the cab ahead. The driver got out and slouched toward us.

"You said a few minutes, ma'am. I don't mind waiting if I know how long I got to wait. It's this uncertainty that makes me nervous."

"Things are rough all over," I said.

"I was speaking to the lady." But he went back to his cab.

Mrs. Hatchen opened the door on her side. "I've kept you longer than I meant to. You said you wanted to talk to Isobel."

"Yes."

"Do you think she knows something she hasn't told?"

"People nearly always do," I said. "It's why I have a hard life, and an interesting one."

She reached for the letter, which was still in my hand. "I'd like that back if you don't mind. It's very important to me."

"I'm sorry. The police will have to see it. I'll try to get it back to you eventually. Will you be staying at the Santa Monica Inn?"

"I don't know. Isobel asked me to stay with her, but that's impossible."

"Why?"

"We don't get along. We never have. She thinks I'm a silly flibbertigibbet. Maybe I am. *I* think *she* is a hypocrite."

"I'd be interested in your reasons."

"They're simple enough. Isobel has always pretended to despise money and the things it can buy. Plain living and high thinking was her motto. But I notice she grabbed Mark and his money the first good chance she got. Please don't quote me to Isobel. In fact, you better not tell her that you saw me."

I said I wouldn't. "One more question, Mrs. Hatchen. What happens to Ada's trust fund if Harriet doesn't live to enjoy it?"

"I suppose it reverts to Mark. Nearly everything does."

THE MAID reluctantly let me in. I waited in the hallway, counting the pieces in the parquetry and wishing that I had never seen Isobel Blackwell, or taken her money, or liked her. She finally appeared, wearing the same dark suit and the same dark patches under her eyes. Her movements were carefully controlled, as if she was walking a line.

She said with unsmiling formality: "I hope the importance of your news justifies this late-night visit."

"It does. Can we sit down?"

She took me into the drawing room, under the eyes of the ancestors. I said to them as well as to her: "I'm doing you a favor coming here. If you weren't my client, there'd be policemen instead, and reporters trampling the roses."

"Am I supposed to understand that?" Her speech was slurred, and her eyes had a drugged look. "If I am, you'll have to explain it to me. And please bear in mind that I may not be thinking too clearly—I'm full of chloral hydrate. Now what were you saying about policemen and newspapermen?"

"They'll be here tomorrow. They'll be wanting to know, among other things, if you have an icepick with a square-cut silver handle."

"We do have, yes. I haven't seen it lately, but I assume it's somewhere in the kitchen, or one of the portable bars."

"I can tell you now it isn't. It's in the hands of Sergeant Wesley Leonard of the Citrus County Sheriff's Department."

I was watching her closely, and she seemed genuinely perplexed. "Are you trying to threaten me in some way? You sound as though you were."

"The word is warn, Mrs. Blackwell."

Her voice sharpened. "Has something happened to Mark?"

"Something has happened to Ralph Simpson and Dolly Stone. I think both those people were known to you."

"Dolly Stone? I haven't even seen the girl in years."

"I hope you can prove that, because Dolly was murdered last May."

She lowered her head and moved it from side to side, as if she was trying to dodge the fact. "You must be joking." She stole a look at my face and saw that I was not. "How? How was she murdered?"

"She was strangled, by unknown hands."

Isobel Blackwell looked at her hands. They were slender and well kept, but the knuckles suggested a history of work. She massaged the knuckles, as if she might be trying to erase the history.

"You surely can't imagine that I had anything to do with it. I had no idea that Dolly was dead. I *was* quite close to her at one time—she was virtually my foster daughter—but that was years ago."

"She was your foster daughter?"

"That may be putting it too strongly. Dolly was one of my projects. The Stones lived across the road from us, and I couldn't help noticing the beginnings of antisocial tendencies in the child. I did my best to provide her with an example and steer her clear of delinquency." Her voice was cool and careful. "Did I fail?"

"Somebody failed. You sound a little like a social worker, Mrs. Blackwell."

"I was one before I married my first husband."

"Ronald Jaimet."

She raised her brows. Under them, her eyes appeared strangely naked. "Suddenly you know a great deal about my affairs."

"Suddenly your affairs are at the center of this case. When I found out tonight that you knew Dolly Stone and her parents, it knocked most of my ideas sideways. I'm trying to work up a new set of ideas, and I can't do it without your co-operation."

"I'm still very much in the dark. I'm not even sure what case we're talking about."

"It's all one case," I said, "Harriet's disappearance and Dolly's death and the murder of Ralph Simpson, who was stabbed with an icepick—"

"*My* icepick?"

"That's the police hypothesis. I share it. I'm not accusing you of doing the actual stabbing."

"How good of you."

"The fact remains that you knew Ralph Simpson, you were almost certainly aware of his death, and you said nothing about it."

"Is this the same Ralph Simpson who worked for us at Tahoe in the spring?"

"The same. A day or two after he left you he was stabbed to death and buried in the back yard of the house you used to own in Citrus Junction."

"But that's insane, utterly insane."

"You knew about it, didn't you?"

"I did not. You're quite mistaken."

"There's an account of the Simpson killing on the front page of the Citrus Junction paper in your sitting room."

"I haven't read it. I take the paper, to keep track of old friends, but I'm afraid I seldom look at it. I haven't even glanced at it this week."

I couldn't tell if she was lying. Her face had become a stiff mask which refused to tell what went on in the mind behind it. Her eyes had veiled themselves. Guilt can effect those changes. So can innocent fear.

"You have sharp eyes, don't you, Mr. Archer? Unfriendly eyes."

"Objective eyes, I hope."

"I'm not fond of your objectivity. I thought there was a—degree of confidence between us."

"There was."

"You put that emphatically in the past tense. Since you've been operating with my money, operating on *me* in fact, I would have expected a little more tolerance, and sympathy. You realize my connection with Dolly proves nothing whatever against me."

"I'd be glad to see that proved."

"How can I prove it?"

"Tell me more about Dolly. For instance, what were the antisocial tendencies you noticed in her?"

"Must I? I've only just learned of her death. It's distressing to rake over the past under the circumstances."

"The past is the key to the present."

"You're quite a philosopher," she said with some irony.

"I'm simply a detective with quite a few murder cases under my belt. People start out young on the road to becoming murderers.

They start out equally young on the road to becoming victims. When the two roads intersect, you have a violent crime."

"Are you suggesting that Dolly was a predestined victim?"

"Not predestined, but prepared. What prepared her, Mrs. Blackwell?"

"*I* didn't, if that's what you're thinking." She paused, and took a deep breath. "Very well, I'll try to give you a serious answer. I *was* concerned about Dolly, from the time she was four or five. She wasn't relating too well to other children. Her relationship with adults wasn't right, either, and it got worse. It showed up particularly in her contacts with my husband. Dolly was a pretty little thing, and her father had treated her seductively and then rejected her. It's a common pattern. The Stones aren't bad people, but they're ignorant people, lacking in insight. They were our good neighbors, however, and Ronald and I believed in helping our neighbors as best we could. We tried to provide Dolly with a more normal family constellation—"

"And yourselves with a daughter?"

"That's an unkind remark." Her anger showed through her mask. She forced it back. "It's true, we couldn't have children; Ronald had a diabetic condition. I'm also aware of the ease with which good white magic turns into bad black magic. But we made no attempt to take Dolly from her parents, emotionally or otherwise. We merely tried to give her some things they couldn't—books and music and recreation and the company of understanding people."

"Then your husband died, and you moved away."

"I'd already lost her by that time," she said defensively. "It wasn't I who failed Dolly. She'd begun to steal money from my purse and lie about it, and she did other things I prefer not to go into. She's dead: *nil nisi bonum.*"

"I wish you would go into the other things."

"I'll put it this way. I wasn't able to protect her against degrading influences—I only had a part of her life after all. She ran with the wrong crowd in high school and picked up gutter ideas of sex. Dolly was already mature at the age of fifteen."

She didn't go on. Her mouth was grave, her eyes watchful. It was possible, I thought, that Dolly had made a play for Ronald Jaimet before he died. It was possible that Jaimet had fallen for it. A daughterless man in middle age can take a sudden fall, all the way down to the bottom of the hole. It would be a suicidal hole, but suicide came easily to a diabetic. He simply had to forget his dose and his diet.

Being a murder victim came easily to a diabetic, too.

"You have that look again," Isobel Blackwell said. "That objective look, as you call it. I hope I'm not the object of your thoughts."

"In a way you are. I was thinking about Ronald Jaimet's death."

"Apparently you've come here tonight determined to spare me nothing. If you must know, Ronald died by accident. And incidentally, since I think I know what's on your mind, Ronald's relations with Dolly were pure—wonderfully pure. I knew Ronald."

"I didn't. What were the circumstances of his death? I understand Mark was with him."

"They were on a pack trip in the Sierra. Ronald fell and broke his ankle. What was worse, he broke his insulin needle. By the time Mark got him down the hill to Bishop, he was in a coma. He died in the Bishop hospital, before I could get to him."

"So you have the story from Mark."

"It's the truth. Ronald and Mark were good friends as well as cousins. Ronald was the younger of the two, and he'd always admired Mark. I could never have married Mark if that hadn't been the case."

Under the increase in pressure of my questions, she seemed to feel the need to justify the main actions of her life. I brought her back to Ronald Jaimet's death.

"Diabetics don't usually go on pack trips in the mountains. Aren't they supposed to lead a fairly sheltered life?"

"Some of them do. Ronald couldn't. I realize, I realized then, that it was risky for him to expose himself to accidents. But I couldn't bring myself to try and stop him. His annual hike was important to him, as a man. And Mark was there to look after him."

I sat for a minute and listened to the echoes of her last sentence. Perhaps she was hearing them, too.

"How did Ronald happen to take a spill?"

"He slipped and fell on a steep trail." She jerked her head sideways as if to deflect the image of his fall. "Please don't try to tell me that it was accident-proneness or unconscious suicide. I've been over all that in my mind many times. Ronald had a great sense of life, in spite of his illness. He was happy in his life. I made him happy."

"I'm sure you did."

She went on stubbornly, justifying her life and its meanings: "And please don't try to tell me that Mark had anything to do with Ronald's death. The two men were deeply fond of each other. Mark was like an older brother to Ronald. He carried him on his back for miles over rugged trails, back to the jeep. It took him most of a day and a night to bring him down the hill. When Harriet and I finally reached the hospital—she drove me up to Bishop that day—Mark was completely broken up. He blamed himself for not taking better care of Ronald. So you see, you're wandering far afield when you suggest that Mark—"

"The suggestion came from you, Mrs. Blackwell."

"No, it was you."

"I'm sorry, but you brought it up."

"I did?" She dragged her fingers diagonally across her face, pressing her eyes closed, drawing down one corner of her mouth. Her lipstick was smeared like blood there. "You're probably right. I'm very tired, and confused. I only have about half a lobe working."

"It's the chloral hydrate," I said, thinking that the drug had some of the properties of a truth serum.

"It's partly that and partly other things. Before you arrived, I had a very wearing hour with Harriet's mother. Pauline flew all the way from Guadalajara to find out what had happened. I didn't know she had so much maternal feeling."

"What went on in that hour?"

"Nothing, really. She seems to blame me for the family trouble, and I suppose I blame her. Someday, in the brave new world, we'll all stop blaming each other."

She tried to smile, and the faltering movement of her mouth charmed me. I would have preferred not to be charmed by her.

"Someday," I said, "I can stop asking questions. As it stands, I have to go on asking them. What kind of a houseboy was Ralph Simpson?"

"Adequate, I suppose. He worked for us such a short time, it's hard to say. I don't like using servants, anyway, which is why we have only the one living in. I'm accustomed to doing things for myself."

"Is that why Simpson was fired?"

"Mark thought he was too familiar. Mark likes to be treated as a superior being; Ralph Simpson was very democratic. I rather liked it.

I'm not really used to the stuffy life." She glanced up at the ancestors.

"I heard a rumor at Tahoe that Ralph was fired for stealing."

"Stealing what, for heaven's sake?"

"It may have been a topcoat," I said carefully. "When Ralph got home from the lake, he had a man's topcoat which he told his wife was given him. It was brown Harris tweed with woven brown leather buttons. One of the buttons was missing. Do you know anything about the coat?"

"No. Obviously you do."

"Did your husband ever buy clothes in Toronto?"

"Not to my knowledge."

"Has he ever been in Toronto?"

"Of course, many times. We passed through there on our honeymoon last fall."

"This coat was bought from a Toronto firm named Cruttworth. Did your husband have dealings there?"

"I couldn't say. Why is this topcoat so important to you?"

"I'll tell you if you'll let me look at your husband's clothes."

She shook her head. "I couldn't possibly, without his permission."

"When do you expect him back?"

"I don't believe he'll leave Tahoe until Harriet is found."

"Then he may be there for a long time. The chances are better than even that she's dead and buried like Ralph Simpson, or sunk in the lake."

Her face was ugly with dismay. "You think Burke Damis did this to her?"

"He's the leading suspect."

"But it isn't possible. He couldn't have."

"That's his contention, too."

"You've talked to him?"

"I ran him down last night. He's in custody in Redwood City. I thought that was going to close the case, but it didn't. The case keeps opening up, and taking in more people and more territory. The connections between the people keep multiplying. Damis's real name is Campion, as you may know, and he married Dolly Stone last September. She had a child in March, and two months later she was strangled. Campion was the main suspect in her death."

"That's incredible."

"What I find hard to believe, Mrs. Blackwell, is that you were to-tally unaware of all this."

"But I was. I hadn't been in touch with Dolly."

"There has to be a further connection, though. You see that. Bruce Campion alias Burke Damis married your one-time foster daughter last year. This year he planned to marry your stepdaughter, with your support, and got as far as eloping with her. Coincidences come large sometimes, but I'm not buying that one."

She said in a small voice: "You're really suspicious of me."

"I have to be. You tried to keep me off Campion's back. You promoted his marriage to Harriet."

"Only because she had no one else. I was afraid of what would happen to her, to her emotions, if she went on being so bitterly lonely."

"Perhaps you were playing God with her, the way you did with Dolly? Perhaps you met Campion through Dolly, and put him up to marrying Harriet?"

"I swear I never saw him before he came to this house last Satur-day night. I admit I rather liked him. People make mistakes. I seem to have made a mistake about you as well."

Her look was complexly female, asking me for renewed assurances of loyalty and fealty. Under the threat of the situation she was using all her brains now, and the full range of her temperament. I guessed that she was defending herself, or something just as dear to her as herself.

"Anyway," she said, "what possible advantage could I derive from serving as a marriage broker to Mr. Damis-Campion?"

The question was rhetorical, but I had answers for it. "If your hus-band disinherited Harriet, or if she was killed, you could inherit ev-erything he has. If Harriet and your husband were killed, in that order, you could inherit everything they both have."

"My husband is very much alive."

"At last report he is."

"I love my husband. I won't say I loved Harriet, but I cared for her."

"You loved your first husband, too, and you survived him."

Tears started in her eyes. She made an effort of will which con-torted her face, and cut the tears off at the source. "You can't believe these things about me. You're just saying them."

"I'm not saying them for fun. We've had two murders, or three, or four. Ralph Simpson and Dolly, Harriet, Ronald Jaimet. All of the victims were known to you; three were close."

"But we don't know that Harriet has been murdered. Ronald definitely was not. I told you the circumstances of Ronald's death."

"I heard what you told me."

"My husband will confirm my account, in detail. Don't you believe it?"

"At this point I'd be silly to commit myself."

"What kind of a woman do you think I am?" Her eyes were intent on mine, with a kind of scornful ardor.

"I'm trying to develop an answer to that question."

"I don't admire your methods. They're a combination of bullying and blackmail and insulting speculation. You're trying to make me out a liar and a cheat, perhaps even a murderer. I'm none of those things."

"I hope you're not. The facts are what they are. I don't know all of them yet. I don't know you."

"I thought you liked me, that we liked each other."

"I do. But that's my problem."

"Yet you treat me without sympathy, without feeling."

"It's cleaner that way. I have a job to do."

"But you're supposed to be working for me."

"True. I've been expecting you to fire me any minute."

"Is that what you want?"

"It would free my hand. You can't pull me off the case—I guess you know that. It's my case and I'll finish it on my own time if I have to."

"You seem to be using a great deal of my time, too. And as for freeing your hand, I have the impression that your hand is already excessively free. I can feel the lacerations, Mr. Archer."

Her voice was brittle, but she had recovered her style. That bothered me, too. Chloral hydrate or no, an innocent woman holding nothing back wouldn't have sat still for some of the things I had said. She'd have slapped my face or screamed or burst into tears or fainted or left the room or ordered me out. I almost wished that one or several of these things had happened.

"At least you're feeling pain," I said. "It's better than being anaesthetized and not knowing where the knife is cutting you."

"You conceive of yourself as a surgeon? Perhaps I should call you doctor."

"I'm not the one holding a knife. I'm not the one, either, who took your silver icepick and stabbed Ralph Simpson with it."

"I trust you've relinquished the idea that it was I."

"You're the most likely suspect. It's time you got that through your head. You knew Simpson, it was your icepick, it was your old stamping ground where he was buried."

"You don't have to get rough," she said in a rough voice. Her voice was as mutable as any I'd ever heard.

"This is a picnic compared with what you're going to have for breakfast. I kept the police out of your hair tonight by suppressing your present name and whereabouts—"

"You did that for me?"

"You are my client, after all. I wanted to give you a chance to clear yourself. You haven't used the chance."

"I see." A grim look settled like age on her mouth. "What was my motive for stabbing Ralph Simpson and burying him in the yard of our old house?"

"Self-protection of one kind or another. Most murderers think they're protecting themselves against some kind of threat."

"But why did I bury him in the yard of our house? That doesn't make any sense, does it?"

"You could have arranged to meet him there, knowing the house was empty, and killed him on the spot."

"That's a pretty picture. Why would I rendezvous with a man like Ralph Simpson?"

"Because he knew something about you."

"And what would that delightful something be?"

"It could have to do with the death of Dolly Stone Campion."

"Are you accusing me of murdering her?"

"I'm asking you."

"What was my motive?"

"I'm asking you."

"Ask away. You'll get no further answers from me."

Her eyes were bright and hard, but the grinding interchange had hurt her will. Her mouth was tremulous.

"I think I will, Mrs. Blackwell. A queer thing occurred the night Dolly was murdered—queer when you look at it in relation to murder. When the strangler had done his strangling, he, or she, noticed that Dolly's baby was in the room. Perhaps the child woke up crying. The average criminal would take to his heels when that happened. This one didn't. He, or she, went to some trouble and ran considerable risk to put the child where he'd be found and looked after. He, or she, picked up the baby and carried him down the road to a neighbor's house and left him in a car."

"This is all new to me. I don't even know where the murder took place."

"Near Luna Bay in San Mateo County."

"I've never even been there."

I threw a question at her from left field: "The Travelers Motel in Saline City—have you been there?"

"Never." Her eyes didn't change.

"Getting back to the night of Dolly's murder, a woman might think of the child's safety at such a time. So might the child's father. I'm reasonably sure it wasn't Campion. Are you willing to discuss the possible identity of the child's father?"

"I have nothing to contribute."

"I have, Mrs. Blackwell. We have evidence suggesting that the strangler was wearing the Harris tweed topcoat I mentioned. Apparently one of the buttons was loose, about to fall off. The baby got hold of it when the murderer was carrying him down the road. The neighbor woman found the brown leather button in the baby's fist." I paused, and went on: "You see why the identification of that topcoat is crucial."

"Where is the topcoat now?"

"The police have it, as I said. They'll be showing it to you tomorrow. Are you certain you've never seen one like it? Are you certain that your husband didn't buy a coat from Cruttworth's in Toronto?"

Her eyes had changed now. They were large and unfocused, looking a long way past me. Under her smudged make-up the skin around her mouth had a bluish tinge, as if my hammering questions had literally bruised her. She got to her feet, swaying slightly, and ran out of the room on awkward high heels.

I followed her. The threat of violence, of homicide or suicide, had been gathering in the house for days. She flung herself along the hallway and through the master bedroom into a bathroom. I heard her being sick there in the dark.

A light was on in the great bedroom. I opened one of the wardrobe closets and found Mark Blackwell's clothes. He had a couple of dozen suits, hanging in a row like thin and docile felons.

I turned back the right cuff of one of the jackets. Written in the lining in indelible ink was the same cleaner's code that Leonard had found in the sleeve of the topcoat: BX1207.

>>>>>>>>>
>>>>>>>>> *chapter* 27
>>>>>>>>>

THE MAID APPEARED in the doorway. She was back in uniform but still using her unzipped personality.

"Now what?"

"Mrs. Blackwell is ill. You'd better see to her."

She crossed the bedroom to the dark bathroom, dragging her feet a little. I waited until I heard the two women's voices. Then I made my way back through the house to the telephone I had used before. The Citrus Junction paper with the Simpson story on the front page lay untouched on Isobel Blackwell's desk. If she had guilty knowledge of it, I thought wishfully, she would have hidden or destroyed the newspaper.

Arnie Walters answered his phone with a grudging "Hello."

"This is Archer. Have you seen Blackwell?"

He ignored the question. "It's about time you checked in, Lew. I heard you took Campion last night—"

"I want to know if you've seen Mark Blackwell, Harriet's father."

"No. Was I supposed to?"

"He set out early Thursday morning for Tahoe, at least that was his story. Check with the people there, will you, and call me back. I'm at Blackwell's house in L.A. You know the number."

"Is he on the missing list, too?"

"Voluntary missing, maybe."

"Too bad you can't keep track of your clients. Have they all flipped?"

"Everybody's doing it. It's the new freedom."

"Stop trying to be funny. You wake me up in the middle of the night, and you don't even tell me what Campion had to say."

"He denies everything. I'm inclined to believe him."

"He can't deny the blood on the hat. It's Harriet's blood type, and she was last seen with him. He can't deny the murder of his wife."

"That was a bum beef, Arnie."

"You know that for a fact?"

"A semi-fact, anyway. Campion's no Eagle Scout, but it looks as though somebody made a patsy out of him."

"Who?"

"I'm working on it."

"Then what's your theory about Harriet? She's vanished without a trace."

"She may have met with foul play after Campion left her. She was carrying money and driving a new car. We ought to bear down on finding that car. One place to look would be the airport parking lots at Reno and San Francisco."

"You think she flew some place?"

"It's a possibility. Look into it, will you, but call me back right away on Blackwell. I have to know if the Tahoe authorities have seen him."

Isobel Blackwell spoke behind me as I hung up: "Do you doubt everything and everyone?"

She had washed her face and left it naked of make-up. Her hair was wet at the temples.

"Practically everything," I said. "Almost everyone. It's a little habit I picked up from my clients by osmosis."

"Not from me. I've never learned the habit of distrust."

"Then it's time you did. You've been deliberately cutting yourself off from the facts of life, and death, while all hell has been breaking loose around you."

"At least you believe I'm innocent."

She came all the way into the room and sat in the chair I'd vacated, turning it sideways and resting her head on her hand. She had drenched herself with cologne. I stood over her with the distinct feeling that she had come to place herself in my power or under my protection.

"Innocence is a positive thing, Mrs. Blackwell. It doesn't consist in holding back information out of a misplaced sense of loyalty. Or shutting your eyes while people die—"

"Don't lecture me." She moved her head sideways as though I'd pushed her. "What kind of woman do you think I am? I've asked you that before."

"I think we're both in the process of finding out."

"I already know, and I'll tell you. I'm an unlucky woman. I've known it for many years, since the man I loved told me he was diabetic and couldn't or shouldn't have children. When he died it confirmed my unluck. I made up my mind never to marry anyone or love anyone again. I refused to expose myself to suffering. I'd had it.

"I moved to Santa Barbara and went on schedule. My schedule was chock full of all the activities a widowed woman is supposed to fill up her time with—garden tours and bridge and adult education classes in mosaic work. I got myself to the point where I was reasonably content and hideously bored. I forgot about my basic unluck, and that was my mistake.

"Mark came to me late last summer and told me that he needed me. He was in trouble. My heart, or whatever, went out to him. I allowed myself to feel needed once again. I'd always been fond of Mark and his blundering boyish ways. That may sound like a queer description of him, but it's the Mark I know, the only one I've known. At any rate I married him and here I am."

She turned her head up to meet my eyes. The tendons in her neck were like wires in a taut cable. An obscure feeling for her moved me. If it was pity, it changed to something better. I wanted to touch her face. But there were still too many things unsaid.

"If you've been unlucky," she said, "you become unwilling to move for fear the whole house will come tumbling down."

"It's lying in pieces around you now, Mrs. Blackwell."

"I hardly need you to tell me that."

"Was Mark in trouble with a girl last summer?"

"Yes. He picked her up at Tahoe and got her pregnant. She was plaguing him for money, naturally. He didn't care about the money, but he was afraid she'd press for something more drastic. Marriage, perhaps, or a lawsuit that would ruin him in the public eye. What people think is very important to Mark. I suppose he thought that marriage to me would protect him and tend to silence the girl." Stubbornly, she refrained from naming her.

"Did he have the gall to spell this out to you?"

"Not in so many words. His motives are usually quite transparent. He gives himself away, especially when he's afraid. He was terribly afraid when he came to my house in Santa Barbara. The girl, or one of her friends, had threatened him with criminal charges. Apparently he'd driven her across the state line."

"Did you know the girl was Dolly Stone?"

"No." The word came out with retching force. "I'd never have married Mark—"

"Why did you marry him?"

"I was willing to feel needed, as I said. He certainly needed me, and so did Harriet. I thought a marriage that started badly couldn't fail to improve. And Mark was so desperately afraid, and guilty. He believed he was on the moral skids, that he might end by molesting little children on the streets. He said I was the only one who could save him, and I believed him."

"You didn't save him from murdering Dolly. I think you know that by now."

"I've been afraid of it."

"How long have you suspected?"

"Just tonight, when we were talking about his topcoat, and I got sick. I'm not feeling very well now."

A greenish pallor had invaded her face, as though the light had changed. Without thinking about it, I touched her temple where the hair was wet. She leaned her head against my hand.

"I'm sorry you're not feeling well," I said. "You realize we have to go on to the end."

"I suppose we do. I lied to you about the topcoat, of course. He bought it when we were on our honeymoon—we ran into some cold weather in Toronto. Mark said it would come in handy when we went up to Tahoe in the spring. I suppose Ralph Simpson found it there, and brought it to Mark for an accounting. Mark took the icepick the Stones had given us—" Her voice broke. "These things are all mixed up with our marriage," she said. "You'd think he was trying to make a Black Mass of our wedding ceremony."

She shuddered. I found myself crouching with my arms around her, her tears wetting my collar. After a while the tears stopped coming. Later still she drew away from me.

"I'm sorry. I didn't mean to let my emotions go at your expense."

I touched the tragic hollow in her cheek. She turned away from my hand.

"Please. Thank you, but also please. I have to think of just one thing, and that's my duty to Mark."

"Isn't that pretty well washed out?"

She raised her eyes. "You've never been married, have you?"

"I have been."

"Well, you've never been a woman. I have to follow through on this marriage, no matter what Mark has done to it. For my sake as well as his." She hesitated. "Surely I won't have to stand up in court and testify about these things—the icepick, and the coat, and Dolly?"

"A wife can't be forced to testify against her husband. You probably know that from your social-working days."

"Yes. I'm not thinking too well. I'm still in shock, I guess. I feel as though I'd been stripped naked and was about to be driven through the streets."

"There will be bad publicity. It's one reason I had to get the facts from you tonight. I'd like to protect you as much as possible."

"You're a thoughtful man, Mr. Archer. But what can you do?"

"I can do your talking to the police for you, up to a point."

Her mind caught on the word police. "Did I understand from your telephone conversation just now that you're asking the Tahoe police to arrest Mark?"

"I asked a friend in Reno, a detective I've been using, to find out if your husband is up there. He's going to call me back."

"Then what?"

"Your husband will be arrested, if he's there. He may not be within five thousand miles of Tahoe."

"I'm sure he is. He was so concerned about Harriet."

"Or about his own skin."

She looked at me with sharp dislike.

"You might as well face this, too," I said. "There's a very good chance that your husband left here this morning with no intention of ever coming back. What time did he leave, by the way?"

"Early, very early. I wasn't up. He left me a note."

"Do you still have the note?"

She opened the top drawer of her desk and handed me a folded piece of stationery. The writing was a hasty scratching which I could hardly decipher:

Isobel,

I'm off to Tahoe. It is too grinding to sit and wait for news of Harriet. I must do something, anything. It's best you stay here at home. I'll see you when this is over. Please think of me with affection, as I do you.

Mark

"It could be a farewell note," I said.

"No. I'm sure he's gone to Tahoe. You'll see."

I dropped the subject, pending Arnie's call. Some time went by. I sat in a straight-backed chair by the French doors. The dark sky was turning pale. House lights pierced the emerging hills, like random substitutes for the fading stars.

Isobel Blackwell sat with her head on her arms. She was as quiet as a sleeper, but I knew by the rhythm of her breathing that she was awake.

"There's one thing I'd like to have clear," I said to her back. "Is it possible that Mark killed Ronald Jaimet?"

She pretended not to hear me. I repeated the question in the same words and the same tone. She said without raising her head: "It isn't possible. They were dear friends. Mark went to enormous trouble to bring Ronald down from the high country. He was almost dead from exhaustion when he got to Bishop. He needed medical attention himself."

"That doesn't prove anything about the accident. Was there any indication that it was a planned accident?"

She turned on me fiercely. "There was not. What are you trying to do to me?"

I wasn't sure myself. There were obscure areas in the case, like blank spaces on a map. I wanted to fill them in. I also wanted to wean Isobel Blackwell away from her marriage before she went down the drain with it. I'd seen that happen to sensitive women who would rather die in a vaguely hopeful dream than live in the agonizing light of wakefulness.

I tried to tell her some of these things, but she cut me short.

"It's quite impossible. I know how Ronald died, and I know how Mark felt about it. He was completely broken up, as I told you."

"A murder can do that to a man. A first murder. Was Mark in love with you four years ago when Ronald died?"

"He most assuredly was not."

"Can you be certain?"

"I can be very certain. He was infatuated with—a girl."

"Dolly Stone?"

She nodded, slowly and dismally. "It wasn't what you think, not at that time. It was more of a father-daughter thing, the kind of relationship he had with Harriet when she was younger. He brought Dolly gifts when he came to visit us, he took her for little outings. She called him uncle."

"What happened on the little outings?"

"Nothing. Mark wouldn't sink that low—not with a young girl."

"You used the word 'infatuated.'"

"I shouldn't have. It was Ronald's word really. He took a much stronger view of it than I did."

"Ronald knew all about it then?"

"Oh yes. He was the one who put a stop to it."

"How?"

"He talked to Mark. I wasn't in on the proceedings, but I know they weren't pleasant. However, their friendship survived."

"But Ronald didn't."

She got to her feet blazing with anger. "You have a vile imagination and a vicious tongue."

"That may be. We're not talking about imaginary things. Did the Dolly issue come up shortly before Ronald's death?"

"I refuse to discuss this any further."

The telephone punctuated her refusal. It buzzed like a rattlesnake beside her; she started as though it was one. I walked around her and answered it.

"Arnie here, Lew. Blackwell didn't turn up at the dragging operations. Sholto was there all day, and he says that Blackwell hasn't been at the lodge since the middle of May. Got that?"

"Yes."

"Get this. Harriet's car has been spotted. It was found abandoned off the highway north of Malibu. We just got word from the CHP. What does that mean to you?"

"More driving. I'll go out there and take a look at the car."

"About Blackwell, what do we do if he shows up?"

"He won't. But if he does, stay close to him."

Arnie said with a strain of grievance in his voice: "It would help if I knew what the problem was."

"Blackwell is a suspect in two known murders, two other possibles. The ones I know about for sure are Dolly Stone and Ralph Simpson. He's probably armed and dangerous."

Isobel Blackwell struck me on the shoulder with her fist and said: "No!"

"Are you all right, Lew?" Arnie's voice had altered, become soothing, almost caressing. "You haven't been sitting up all night with a bottle?"

"I'm sober as a judge, soberer than some. You ought to be getting official confirmation in the course of the day."

I hung up before he could ask me questions I wasn't ready to answer. Isobel Blackwell was looking at me strangely, as if I had created the situation and somehow made it real by telling Arnie about it. The light from the windows was cruel on her face.

"Has my husband's car been found?"

"Harriet's. I'm going out to Malibu to look at it."

"Does it mean she's alive?"

"I don't know what it means."

"You suspect Mark of killing Harriet, too."

"We'd better not discuss what I suspect. I'll be back. If your husband should come home, don't tell him what's been said here tonight."

"He has a right to know—"

"Not from you, Mrs. Blackwell. We can't predict how he'd react."

"Mark would never injure me."

But there was a questioning note in her voice, and her hand went to her throat. Her head moved from side to side in the collar of her fingers.

I DROVE OUT to Malibu through the chilly dawn. The zebra-striped hearse was still parked by the roadside at Zuma. The sight of it did nothing for me at all.

The HP dispatcher working the graveyard shift had an open paperback on the desk in front of him, and seemed to begrudge his answers to my questions. Harriet's Buick Special was impounded in a local garage; it wouldn't be available for inspection until the garage opened at eight.

"When was it picked up?"

"Last night, before I came on duty."

"You came on at midnight?"

"That's correct."

His eyes kept straying downward to his book. He was a fat man with a frowzy unwed aura.

"Can you tell me where it was found?"

He consulted his records. "Side road off the highway about six miles north of here. According to the officer, the woman in the lunchroom said it was there all day. She got around to reporting it when she closed up for the night."

"What lunchroom is that?"

"It's one of those jumbo shrimp traps. You'll see the sign on the right as you go north."

He picked up his book. It had a picture on the cover of a man riding a horse into a kind of nuclear sunset.

I drove out of the straggling beachfront town and north on the highway to the jumbo shrimp place. It was the same establishment in which I had sat and drunk coffee long ago at the beginning of the case. Harriet's car had been abandoned within a few hundred yards of her father's beach house.

I turned left down the hill, nosed my car into the parking area, and parked at the railing beside a black Cadillac. The tide was high, and the sea brimmed up like blue mercury. Some pelicans were sailing far out over it, tiny within the amplitude of the sky.

The Cadillac had Blackwell's name on the steering post. I walked along the gangway to his beach house. I was keenly aware of every sound and movement, my own, the thumping and shushing of the waves, the distant cry of a scavenger gull following the pelicans. Then my knocking on Blackwell's door was the only sound.

Finally I let myself in with his key. Nothing had been changed in the high raftered room, except for what had been done to Campion's painting. Someone had slashed it so that the morning sun came jaggedly through it like lightning in a cloud.

I went to the head of the stairs and called down: "Blackwell! Are you there?"

No answer.

I called Harriet. My voice rang through the house. I felt like a self-deluded medium trying to summon up the spirits of the dead. I moved reluctantly down the steps and more reluctantly through the big front bedroom into the bathroom. I think I smelled the spillage before I saw it.

I turned on the bathroom light. A towel in the sink was soaked and heavy with coagulating blood. I lifted it by one corner, dropped it back into the sink. Splatters of blood were congealed on the linoleum floor. I stepped across them and opened the door into the back bedroom. It had a broken lock.

Blackwell was there, sitting in his shirtsleeves on the edge of a bare mattress. His face was white, except where it was shadowed by black beard. He looked at me like a thief.

"Good morning," he said. "It would have to be you."

"Bad morning. Who have you been killing this morning?"

He screwed up his face, as if a glare had fallen across it. "No one."

"The bathroom is a shambles. Whose blood is it?"

"Mine. I cut myself shaving."

"You haven't shaved for at least twenty-four hours."

He touched his chin absently. I sensed that he was out of contact, trying to fill the gap between himself and reality with any words he could think of from moment to moment.

"I cut myself shaving yesterday. That's old blood. Nobody died today."

"Who died yesterday?"

"I did." He grimaced in the invisible glare.

"You're not that lucky. Stand up."

He rose obediently. I shook him down, though I hated to touch his body. He had no weapon on him. I told him to sit again, and he sat.

The angry will had gone out of him. A sort of fretfulness had taken its place. I had seen that fretfulness before, in far-gone men. It was like a rat gnawing their hearts and it made them dangerous, to others and themselves.

A slow leakage of water glazed his eyes. "I've had a lonely night."

"What have you been doing?"

"Nothing in particular. Waiting. I hoped that daylight would give me the strength to get up and move. But the daylight is worse than the darkness." He sniffed a little. "I don't know why I'm talking to you. You don't like me."

I didn't try to pretend anything. "It's good you're able and willing to talk. We have the business of the confession to get over."

"Confession? I have nothing to confess. The blood in the bathroom is old blood. I didn't spill it."

"Who did?"

"Vandals, possibly. Vandals must have broken in. We've had a lot of vandalism over the years."

"We've had a lot of murders over the years. Let's start with the first one. Why did you kill Ronald Jaimet?"

He looked up like a white-haired child horribly ravaged by age. "I didn't kill him. His death was the result of an accident. He fell and broke his ankle, and his needle. It took me a day and a night to get him out of the mountains. Without his insulin he became very sick. He died of his illness. It was all completely accidental."

"Just how did the accident happen?"

"Ronald and I had a scuffle, a friendly scuffle. His foot slipped on a stone and went over the edge of the trail. His weight came down on his ankle. I actually heard it snap."

"What was the friendly scuffle about?"

"Nothing, really. He was joshing me a bit, about my affection for a young protégée of his. It's true I was fond of the girl, but that was as far as it went. I never—I never did her any physical harm. My feelings were pure, and I told Ronald this. I think I pushed him, in a playful way, to emphasize what I was saying. I had no idea of making him fall."

"And no intention of killing him?"

He puzzled over the question. "I don't see how I could have wanted to kill him. Wouldn't I have left him there if I had?" He added, as if this would clinch it: "Ronald was my favorite cousin. He greatly resembled my mother."

He gave me a peculiar wet look. I was afraid he was going to talk about his mother. They often did.

I said: "When did you start having sexual relations with Dolly Stone?"

His eyes shifted away. They were almost lost in the puffiness around them, as if he had been beaten by intangible fists. "Oh. That."

"That."

He lay back on the bed, curling his body sideways so that his head rested on the uncovered striped pillow. He said in a hushed voice: "I swear to heaven I didn't touch her when she was a child. I merely adored her from a distance. She was like a fairy princess. And I didn't go near her after Ronald died. I didn't see her again till we met last spring at Tahoe. She was grown up, but I felt as though I'd found my fairy princess once again.

"I invited her to the lodge, simply with the idea of showing it to her. But I was too happy. And she was willing. She came back more than once on her own initiative. I lived in pure delight and pure misery—delight when I was with her, and misery the rest of my waking hours. Then she turned against me, and I was in utter misery all the time." He sighed like an adolescent lover.

"What turned her against you?"

"We ran into difficulties."

I was weary of his euphemisms. "You mean you got her pregnant."

"That, and other things, other difficulties. She turned against me finally and completely." He drew up his legs. "I went through hell last summer. She put me through hell."

"How did she do that?"

"I was fearful of losing her, and just as fearful of what would happen if I tried to hold her. I was utterly at her mercy. It was a very tense period. I couldn't stomach some of the things she said. She called me a dirty old man. Then my daughter Harriet joined me at the lodge, and the whole thing became impossible. Dolly wouldn't come to me any more, but she kept threatening to tell Harriet about us."

He squirmed and tossed like a restless sleeper. The bed creaked under him in harsh mimicry of the noises of passion.

"Was Dolly blackmailing you?"

"I wouldn't put it that way. I gave her money, altogether a good deal of money. Then I stopped hearing from her entirely. But I was still on tenterhooks. The thing could erupt publicly at any time. I didn't know she'd married until this spring."

"In the meantime you married Isobel Jaimet as a buffer."

"It was more than that," he insisted. "Isobel was an old and trusted friend. I was—I am genuinely fond of Isobel."

"Lucky Isobel."

He looked up at me with hatred in his eyes. But he was too broken to sustain it. He turned his face into the pillow. I had the queer impression that under the tangled white hair at the back of his head was another face made of blind bone.

"Tell me the rest of it," I said.

He lay so still that he didn't appear to be breathing. It occurred to me that he was holding his breath as angry children did when the world turned unpermissive.

"Tell me the rest of it, Blackwell."

He began to breathe visibly. His shoulders rose and fell. His body jerked in occasional little spasms. It was the only response I could get from him.

"Then I'll tell you, and I'll make it short, because the police will be eager to talk to you. Dolly renewed her demands for money this spring—she'd had a hard winter. You decided to put a final stop to the demands and the uncertainty. You went to her house in the middle of the night of May the fifth. Her husband wasn't there—he was out with another woman. I suppose Dolly let you in because she thought you were bringing her money. You strangled her with one of her stockings."

Blackwell groaned as though he felt the nylon around his withering neck.

"Then you noticed the baby, your own bastard son. For some reason you couldn't bear to leave him in the room with the dead woman. Perhaps you had the child's safety and welfare in mind. I'd like to think so. At any rate you picked him up and carried him down the road to a neighbor's car. The child got hold of a button on your coat which may have been loosened during your struggle with Dolly. It was still in his fist when the neighbor woman found him. The button has brought this whole thing home to you.

"When Dolly's husband was indicted for her murder, his friend Ralph Simpson set out to track down its source. He probably knew of your affair with Dolly, and had a pretty good idea where the button came from. He went up to Tahoe and got you to employ him and eventually found the coat where you had hidden it. Perhaps he confronted you with it. You fired him and came back here. Instead of taking the coat to the police, as he ought to have, he followed you south with it. He may have had a dream of solving the crime by himself—Simpson was a failure who needed a success—or maybe the dream went sour in him and turned into money-hunger. Did he attempt to blackmail you?"

He spoke inarticulately into the pillow.

"It doesn't greatly matter now," I said. "It will come out at the trial. It will come out that you took a silver icepick from your house when you went to meet Simpson. I think it was no accident that the icepick was a wedding present from Dolly's parents. It was certainly no accident that you buried his body in what had been Ronald Jaimet's back yard. I don't know what was going on in your head. I don't believe you could tell me if you tried. A psychiatrist would be interested in what went on in that back yard when Dolly was a child."

Blackwell cried out. His voice was thin and muffled. It sounded like a ghost trapped in the haunted house of his mind. I remembered his saying that he was dead and I pitied him as you pity the dead, from a long way off.

He turned his head sideways. His visible eye was open, but featureless as a mollusk in the harsh shell of his brow.

"Is that how it was?" he said. There seemed to be no irony in his question.

"I don't claim to know all the details. If you're willing to talk now, correct me."

"Why should I correct your errors for you?"

"You're talking for the record, not for me. Is that Harriet's blood in the bathroom?"

"Yes."

"Did you kill her?"

"Yes. I cut her throat." His voice was flat and unemotional.

"Why? Because she caught on to you and had to be silenced?"

"Yes."

"What did you do with her body?"

"You'll never find it." A kind of giggle rattled out of his throat and made his lips flutter. "I'm a dirty old man, as Dolly said. Why don't you put me out of my misery? You have a gun, don't you?"

"No. I wouldn't use it on you if I had. You're not that important to me. Where is your daughter's body?"

The giggle erupted again, and amplified itself into a laugh. Whoops of laughter surged up into his throat and choked him. He sat up coughing.

"Get me some water, for pity's sake."

For pity's sake I started into the bathroom. Then I heard the furtive rustle of his movement. One of his hands was groping under the pillow. It came out holding a revolver which wavered in my direction and then held steady.

"Get out of here or I'll shoot you. You don't want to be the fifth one."

I backed through the doorway.

"Close the door. Stay in there."

I obeyed his orders. The bathroom seemed hideously familiar. The towel lay like a maimed thing in the sink.

Blackwell's gun went off on the other side of the door. It was still in his mouth when I reached him, like a pipe of queer design which he had fallen asleep smoking.

>>>>>>>>>
>>>>>>>>> *chapter* 29
>>>>>>>>>

I GOT BACK to Isobel Blackwell around noon. All morning county cars had bumped down the old blacktop road, and county men had tramped back and forth along the gangway to the beach house. I told my story, and Blackwell's, till it grated on my tongue. If I had any doubts of Blackwell's credibility, I suppressed them. I was bone-tired, and eager to see the case ended.

They trundled his body away. We searched for Harriet's body in the house and under it, and up and down the beach. We went back to Malibu and examined her car. It told us nothing.

"The consensus is that Harriet's in the sea," I told Isobel Blackwell, "that he disposed of her body in the same way he disposed of the topcoat. And like the topcoat it will probably come in with the next big tide."

We were in her sitting room. The drapes were closed, and she had left the lights off. Perhaps she didn't want me to see her face; perhaps she didn't want to see mine. She sat in a long chair and peered at me through the artificial gloom as if I was as monstrous as the things I had had to tell her. The side-to-side movement of her head, the gesture of incomprehension and denial, was threatening to become habitual.

"I'm sorry, Mrs. Blackwell. I thought you'd rather hear it from me than get it from the police or read it in the newspapers."

"Does it have to be in the newspapers?"

"It will be. You don't have to read them. After you've gathered yourself together, you ought to take a long trip, put all this behind you." My suggestion sounded feeble in my own ears.

"I couldn't face a journey now." After a pause, she said in a softer voice: "I thought horrors like this only occurred in Greek plays."

"The horrors will pass. Tragedy is like a sickness, and it passes. Even the horrors in the Greek plays are long since past."

"That's not much comfort to me here and now."

"It's something to think about."

"I don't want to think." But she sat locked in thought, as still as ancient marble, her mind transfixed by the Medusa fact: "How could he bring himself to kill Harriet? He loved her."

"In a sick way. Where girls were concerned, even his own, he was a mother's boy playing with dolls in the attic. Love like that can change to hatred if it's threatened. You cut off the doll's head—"

"He cut off her head?"

"I was speaking figuratively. Apparently he cut her throat with an old razor blade. He used the same blade to slash Campion's painting."

Her head had begun its sidewise movement again. "I can understand why Mark had to kill Dolly, or thought he had to. Once he'd used her, she threatened him by her very existence. Ralph Simpson was a threat, and even Ronald must have seemed to be. But Harriet was his own daughter."

"I suspect she was another threat to him, the most intimate one of all. Did Harriet know about his affair with Dolly?"

"I'm afraid so. Mark had a horrible habit of confession. I don't suppose he poured it all out, but he did say something to Harriet last spring. He may have felt it was bound to come out, and it was his duty to prepare her. It didn't have the desired effect."

"How do you know?"

"Because Harriet came to me with it. She said she had to talk to someone. She was greatly upset, much more deeply upset than I'd ever seen her. She regressed to a very low age level; she was literally bawling with her head in my lap. I didn't think she should be encouraged to throw childish fits at her age. I told her she ought to be able to take it if I could."

"How did she handle that?"

"She got up and left the room. We didn't discuss the subject again. I felt that Mark had made a mistake in telling her. It didn't improve the situation among the three of us."

"When did this happen?"

"Some time in March or April. I imagine Mark was concerned about the birth of the child, and that's why he spoke to Harriet, though he never said a word about it to me. Looking back, it does throw some light on what Harriet was feeling. Dolly had displaced her in Mark's affections, as she thought. A couple of months later she attached herself to Dolly's widower. Do you suppose she was aware of what she was doing?"

"Yes," I said, "and Campion knew what he was doing, but neither of them told the other. I believe that Campion took up with her in Mexico precisely because she was Mark's daughter. He suspected Mark of killing his wife, and cooked up an affair with Harriet in order to get close to him. He surely wouldn't have come back from Mexico, with an indictment hanging over him, unless he hoped to clear himself."

"Why didn't he ever say anything?"

"He did, last Monday afternoon, when your husband turned a

shotgun on him. I failed to get the message. He hasn't talked since then because he knew he wouldn't be believed. Campion's a maverick, an authority-hater, with a certain pride of his own. But he'll be talking now, and I want to be there when he spills over. You can pay my time and expenses if you like."

"I'll be glad to."

"You're a generous woman. After some of the things I said to you last night—"

She cut me short with a movement of her head. "They helped me, Mr. Archer. You were cruel at the time, but actually you were preparing me—for this."

"I was doing more than that. I considered you a possible murder suspect."

"I know. The point is that you don't any more. It's over."

"Almost over. Campion's testimony should wind up the case."

"What do you suppose he will have to say?"

"He probably made the mistake of speaking out to Harriet at the lodge, accusing Mark of Dolly's murder. She couldn't take it; it completely destroyed her image of her father. It must have been a shock, too, to learn that Campion had been using her, that his interest in her was mainly on his dead wife's account. They quarreled, violently. Campion got his face scratched, she was hit on the head, somehow her hat got knocked into the water. She couldn't have been badly hurt—she was well enough to drive to Malibu—but Campion didn't know that. Judging by his attitude the other night, he may have thought he killed her, or injured her seriously."

"But she drove herself from Tahoe to Malibu?"

"Apparently. It took her more than twenty-four hours. She may have had her head wound attended to on the way. She reached the beach house early yesterday morning and telephoned her father. Perhaps she accused him of murder over the phone, or asked him to deny it. He left you a note to put you off the track, went to the beach house, and killed her. He carried her body down to the beach and let it go out with the tide.

"But he had killed once too often. This doll bled. It was his daughter's blood, and it was real. He was so paralyzed he couldn't clean up after his final murder. He sat in the back bedroom all day and all night trying to gather the strength to kill himself. Perhaps he had to talk to someone before he did. I happened to be the one."

"I'm glad it was you, Mr. Archer. And I'm glad he didn't kill you. Truly glad."

She rose up in the ruins of her life and gave me her hand. I said I would be seeing her again. She didn't deny it, even with a movement of her head.

>>>>>>>>
>>>>>>>> *chapter* 30
>>>>>>>>

CAMPION HAD BEEN MOVED to the San Mateo County jail. He still wasn't talking. After some palaver with Captain Royal and his chief, and telephone calls to their opposite numbers in Los Angeles, I got permission to interview him alone. Royal brought him into the interrogation room and left us together, locking the steel-sheathed door behind him.

Campion stood with his back to the door. He didn't say hello or nod his head. Bad nights had left their nightmare tracks on his face, but he still had a kind of frayed intensity. He looked at me as though I might lunge at him with a rubber hose.

"How are you, Bruce? Sit down."

"Is that an order?"

"It's an invitation," I said in a mollifying tone. "Mark Blackwell has confessed your wife's murder. Did Royal tell you?"

"He told me. It came a little late. I'm going to sue you all for false arrest."

"That doesn't sound like such a wise idea. You're pretty vulnerable."

"Then when are they going to let me out? I've got work to go on with."

"You've got some talking to do first. If you'd leveled with the cops, you wouldn't be here—"

"Don't snow me. I know cops. They make patsies out of the little ones and let the big ones go."

"You made a patsy out of yourself. Think about it."

I left him standing and moved around the bright barred room.

Campion's eyes followed me warily. After a while he sat down at a metal table, resting his bandaged head on one hand.

I approached him and touched his shoulder. "Listen, Bruce—"

He raised both arms to protect his head.

"Relax. I'm not your enemy."

He twisted under my hand. "Then don't stand over me. I've always hated people standing over me."

I sat down across the table from him. "I assume you're a serious man in spite of the cop-hater nonsense. You've been through some rough experiences, and I respect that. You could have spared yourself some of the roughness by trusting other people."

"Who was there to trust?"

"Me, for one. Royal can be trusted, too. He's not a bad cop. Why didn't you tell us the truth the night before last? You let us believe that Harriet was dead and you had drowned her."

"You would have gone on believing it no matter what I said."

"But you didn't give us a chance. You didn't give her a chance, either. You might have saved her life."

His right fist clenched on the table. "I tried. I tried to stop her. But I can't swim too well. She got away from me in the dark."

"We seem to be talking past each other. When did she get away from you?"

"That night at the lake, Tuesday night I think it was. She went berserk when I told her I suspected her father of killing Dolly. She came at me clawing—I had to hit her to get her off me. It was a bad scene, and it got worse. Before I knew what she was doing, she ran out of the lodge and down to the lake. I plunged in after her, but she was already gone. I'm afraid I panicked then."

"Is this the truth?"

His eyes came up to mine. "I swear it is. I didn't tell you and Royal because you would have taken any such admission as a confession of guilt." He looked at his fist; slowly it came unclenched. "I still can't prove I didn't knock her out and drown her."

"You don't have to. She didn't drown in Tahoe. If suicide was in her mind that night, she changed her mind. Evidently she came out of the water after you'd gone."

"Then she's still alive!"

"She's dead, but you didn't kill her. Her father did. He confessed it along with his other murders before he shot himself."

"Why in the name of God did he do that?"

"God only knows. She probably accused him to his face of murdering Dolly."

Emotions warred across Campion's face: incredulity and relief and self-reproach. He tried to wipe them away with his hand.

"I should never have told Harriet about her father," he said. "I see now why I should have been honest with you. But I thought you were working for Blackwell, covering up for him."

"We were both mistaken about each other. Do you want to straighten me out about a few other matters?"

"I suppose so. I seem to be on the truth kick."

"You were in serious trouble during the Korean War," I said by way of testing him. "What was it?"

"It was after the war. We were sitting around in Japan waiting for transport." He made an impatient outward gesture with his arm. "To make a long story short, I hit the officer in charge of the staging point. I broke his nose. He was a Colonel."

"Did you have a reason, apart from the fact that you don't like Colonels?"

"My reason may sound foolish to you. He caught me sketching one day and thought it would be dandy if I painted his portrait. I told him I didn't take orders about my work. We got into a battle of wills. He threatened to keep me over there till I painted him. I hit him. If he'd had a little less rank, or a little more, or if he'd belonged to our unit, it wouldn't have been so bad. But face had to be saved and I got a year in a detention camp and a D.D. I didn't paint him, though," he added with bitter satisfaction.

"You're a pretty good hater. What do you like?"

"The life of the imagination," he said. "It's all I'm good for. Every time I try to do something in the actual world I make a mess of it. I never should have married Dolly, for instance."

"Why did you?"

"It's a hard question. I've been thinking about the answers to it ever since I got into this jam. The main thing was the money, of course—I'd be a hypocrite if I denied that. She had a little money, call it a dowry. I was trying to prepare a series of pictures for a show, and I needed money to do it. You always need money, at least I do, and so we struck a bargain."

"You knew about her pregnancy?"

"It was one of the attractions, in a way."

"Most men would feel the opposite way."

"I'm not most men. I liked the idea of having a child but I didn't want to be anybody's father. I didn't care who the father was, so long as it wasn't me. Does that sound foolish? It may have something to do with the fact that my old man did the disappearing-father act when I was four years old." There was a growl of resentment in his voice.

"Did your father have trouble with the law?"

He said with a sour mocking grin: "My father was the law. He was a lousy Chicago cop, with both front feet in the trough. A bad act. I remember the last time I saw him. I was eighteen at the time, hacking my way through art school. He was helping a blonde into a Cadillac in front of an apartment hotel on the Gold Coast." He cleared his throat. "Next question."

"Getting back to Dolly—I'm not quite clear how you felt about her."

"Neither am I. I started out feeling sorry for her. I thought it might develop into something real—that's an old boyish dream of mine." His mouth curled in self-irony. "It didn't. You know the pity that chills the heart? Oddly enough I never went to bed with her. I loved to paint her, though. That's my way of loving people. I'm not much good at the other ways."

"I thought you were a devil with the ladies."

He flushed. "I've done my share of rutting. A lot of them think it's artistic to bed with an artist. But there was only one in my life I cared about—and that one didn't last. I was too fouled up."

"What was her name?"

"Does it matter? Her first name was Anne."

"Anne Castle."

He gave me a bright astonished look. "Who told you about her?"

"She did. I was in Ajijic two or three nights ago. She spoke of you with great affection."

"Well," he said. "That's a fresh note for a change. Is Anne all right?"

"She probably would be if she didn't have you to worry about. It broke her heart when you decamped with Harriet. The least you can do is write her a letter."

He sat quiet for a time. I think he was composing the letter in his head. To judge by his frowning concentration, he was having a hard time with it.

"If Anne was important to you," I said, "why did you take up with Harriet?"

"I'd already made a commitment." His eyes were still turned inward on himself.

"I don't follow you, Campion."

"I didn't meet Harriet in Mexico, as you seem to think. I met her in my own house in Luna Bay several weeks before I went to Mexico. She came to see Dolly and the baby. She and Dolly were old friends. But Dolly wasn't there that afternoon—she'd taken the baby in for his monthly checkup. Harriet stood around watching me paint. She was an amateur painter herself, and she got very excited over what I was doing. She was quite an excitable girl."

"So?"

Campion looked at me uneasily. "I couldn't help thinking what she could do for me, with a little encouragement. I was broke, as usual, and she obviously wasn't. I thought it would be pleasant to have a patroness. I could stop worrying about the light bill and simply do my work. I made a date with her before Dolly got back with the baby. I saw her that night, and before long we were spending nights together.

"I didn't know what I was letting myself in for. Harriet acted as though she'd never been with a man. She fell so hard it scared me. She drove over from Tahoe a couple of times a week, and we were in and out of the motels. I should have had the sense to pull out of the situation. I had a feeling that it would lead to trouble." He drew in a deep breath.

"What kind of trouble?"

"I didn't know. But she was a serious girl, too serious, and terribly passionate. I shouldn't have led her on."

"Did you suspect that Blackwell was the baby's father?"

He hesitated. "I may have, more or less subconsciously. Harriet said something once, when she was holding the baby in her arms. She called him little brother. It stuck in my mind, though I didn't realize she was speaking literally."

"And Dolly never told you?"

"No. I didn't press the point, while she was alive. I didn't really want to know who the father was. I thought I could love the baby better if he was anonymous. But it turned out I couldn't love him too well. Him or anybody. Then I messed the whole thing up when I tried to go into orbit with Harriet. I should have stayed home and looked after Dolly and the baby."

His voice was low, and I thought I heard the growl of manhood in it. He rose and struck his open left palm with his closed right fist. Shaking hands with himself in an embarrassed way, he went to the window.

"I was with Harriet the night Dolly was killed," he said with his back turned.

"Harriet was the woman you slept with in the Travelers Motel?"

"That's right. Slept isn't quite accurate. We had an argument, and she started back to Tahoe in the middle of the night. I stayed in the room and got drunk. She'd brought me a bottle of her father's Scotch." He seemed to take a painful pride in spelling out the details of his humiliation.

"What was the argument about?"

"Marriage. She wanted to buy me a Reno divorce. I won't deny I was tempted, but when it came to a showdown I found I couldn't do it. I didn't love Harriet. I didn't love Dolly, either, but I had made a bargain with her to give the boy my name. I kept hoping if I stuck with it I'd learn to love the boy. But it was already too late. When I sobered up enough to drive myself home, Dolly was dead and the boy was gone and the cops were there."

"Why didn't you tell them where you'd spent the night? You had an alibi of sorts."

"It didn't look as if I'd have to use it. They questioned me and let me go. As soon as I was free, I got in touch with Harriet at Tahoe. She said I mustn't on any account drag her or her family into it. She was protecting her father, obviously, though she didn't say so. She sold me the idea of hiding out after they indicted me, and I spent a bad couple of weeks shut up in their beach house. I wanted to go on to Mexico—Ralph lent me his birth certificate with that in mind—but I had no money.

"Harriet finally gave me the money for the flight. She said that she would join me in Mexico later, and we could pretend to be strangers, and pick up where we'd left off. We could stay in Mexico or go further down into South America." He turned from the window—his face had been opened by the light. "I suppose she saw her chance to sew me up for life. And I was tempted, again. I'm a very ambivalent guy."

"I'm wondering about Harriet's motive. You suggested she was protecting her father. Did she know, at that time, that he had murdered Dolly?"

"I don't see how she could have." He fingered the scratches on his face. "Look how she reacted when I told her about my suspicions the other night."

"Just when did you develop those suspicions?"

"It happened over a period of time. Ralph Simpson brought up the name before I left Luna Bay. He'd seen Dolly with Blackwell last summer. Ralph fancied himself as a detective, and he was very interested in a leather button that was found at the scene of the crime. The police mentioned it, too. Do you know anything about that button?"

"Too much." I summarized the history of the wandering topcoat. "So Blackwell killed Ralph."

"He confessed the murder this morning, along with the others."

"Poor old Ralph." Campion lowered himself into a chair and sat for a while in blank-eyed silence. "Ralph should never have got mixed up with me. I'm a moral typhoid carrier."

"It's a thought," I said. "But you were telling me about your suspicions of Blackwell and how they grew."

After another silence he went on: "Ralph started me thinking about Blackwell. Bits and pieces, associations, began to gather, and eventually I had a sort of Gestalt. Some of the things that went into it were Harriet's interest in the baby, and the slip she made, if it was a slip, about her little brother. Then Dolly started getting money from somewhere, about the time that Harriet turned up at our house. I didn't understand the relationship between Dolly and Harriet. It was pleasant enough on the surface, but there was a good deal of hostility under it."

"That would be natural enough, if Dolly knew you were making love to Harriet."

"She didn't. Anyway, the relationship didn't change from the first afternoon Harriet came to the house. They greeted each other like two sisters who hated each other but refused to admit it. I can see now why that would be: Harriet knew about Dolly's fling with her father, and Dolly knew she knew."

"You still haven't told me when you found out."

"I got my Gestalt one night in Mexico, after Harriet came. We were talking in my studio, and the subject of her father's lodge at Tahoe came up, I don't know how." He turned his head to one side, as though he had overheard a distant voice. "Yes, I do know. She was hot on the marriage trail again, in spite of the fact that I was wanted for murder. She was fantasying about going back to the States where we could settle down in the lodge and live happily ever after. She got quite lyrical in her descriptions of the place. Oddly enough, I'd heard it all before."

"From Harriet?"

"From Dolly. Dolly used to tell me stories about the sweet old lady who befriended her when she was on her uppers in State Line last summer. She gave me detailed descriptions of the sweet old lady's house—the beamed ceilings, the lake view, the layout of the rooms. It suddenly hit me that it was Blackwell's house and that Blackwell was the sweet old lady and probably the father of my"—he swallowed the word—"the father of Dolly's child. I didn't say a word to Harriet at the time, but I decided to go back to the States with her. I wanted to find out more about the sweet old lady. Well, I have."

A complex grief controlled the lines of his face like a magnetic field.

>>>>>>>>>
>>>>>>>>> *chapter* 31
>>>>>>>>>

GETTING OUT OF my cab at the San Francisco airport, I saw a woman I vaguely recognized standing with a suitcase in front of the main terminal building. She was wearing a tailored suit whose skirt was a little too long for the current fashion. It was Anne Castle, minus her earrings and with the addition of a rakish hat.

I took the suitcase out of her hand. "May I carry this, Miss Castle?"

She looked up at my face. Her own was so deeply shadowed by trouble that her vision seemed clouded. Slowly her brow cleared.

"Mr. Archer! I intended to look you up, and here you are. Surely you didn't follow me from Los Angeles?"

"You seem to have followed me. I imagine we both came here for the same reason. Bruce Campion, alias Burke Damis."

She nodded gravely. "I heard a report yesterday on the Guadalajara radio. I decided to drop everything and come here. I want to help him even if he did kill his wife. There must be mitigating circumstances."

Her upward look was steady and pure. I caught myself on the point of envying Campion, wondering how the careless ones got women like her to care for them so deeply. I said: "Your friend is innocent. His wife was murdered by another man."

"No!"

"Yes."

Tears started in her eyes. She stood blind and smiling.

"We need to talk, Anne. Let's go some place we can sit down."

"But I'm on my way to see him."

"It can wait. He'll be busy with the police for some time. They have a lot of questions to ask him, and this is the first day he's been willing to answer."

"Why do they have to question him if he's innocent?"

"He's a material witness. He also has a good deal of explaining to do."

"Because he used a false name to cross the border?"

"That doesn't concern the local police. It's the business of the Justice Department. I'm hoping they won't press charges. A man who's been wrongly indicted for murder has certain arguments on his side —what you called mitigating circumstances."

"Yes," she said. "We'll fight it. Has he done anything else?"

"I can't think of anything that's actionable. But there are some things you should know before you see him. Let me buy you a drink."

"I don't think I'd better. I haven't been sleeping too well, and I have to keep my wits about me. Could we have coffee?"

We went upstairs to the restaurant, and over several cups of coffee I told her the whole story of the case. It made more sense in the telling than it had in the acting out. Reflected in her deep eyes, her subtle face, it seemed to be transformed from a raffish melodrama into a tragedy of errors in which Campion and the others had been caught. But I didn't whitewash him. I thought she deserved to know the worst about him, including his sporadic designs on Harriet's money and his partial responsibility for her death.

She reached across the table and stopped me with her hand on my sleeve. "I saw Harriet last night."

I looked at her closely. Her eyes were definite, alive with candor. "Harriet isn't dead. Her father must have been lying, or hallucinating. I know I wasn't."

"Where did you see her?"

"In the Guadalajara airport, when I went in to make my reservation. It was about nine-thirty last night. She was waiting for her bag at the end of the ticket counter. I heard her call out that it was *azul* —blue—and I knew her voice. She'd evidently just come in on the Los Angeles plane."

"Did you speak to her?"

"I tried to. She didn't recognize me, or pretended not to. She turned away very brusquely and ran out to the taxi stands. I didn't follow her."

"Why not?"

She answered carefully: "I felt I had no right to interfere with her. I was a little frightened of her, too. She had that terribly bright-faced look. I don't know if I'm making myself clear, but I've seen that look on other people who were far out."

>>>>>>>>>
>>>>>>>>> *chapter* 32
>>>>>>>>>

I FOUND HER late Monday afternoon in a village in Michoacán. The village had an Aztec name which I forget, and a church with Aztec figures carved in some of its ancient stones. A roughly cobbled road like the bed of a dry creek ran past the church.

A beggar woman in widow's black met me at the door and followed me into the nave reciting griefs I couldn't understand, though

I could see the scars they had left on her. Her face broke up in wrinkled smiles and blessings when I gave her money. She went out and left me alone in the church with Harriet.

She was kneeling on the stone floor close to the chancel. She had a black *rebozo* over her head, and she was as still as the images of the saints along the walls.

She scrambled to her feet when I said her name. Her mouth worked stiffly, but no words came out. The shawl covering her hair accentuated the stubborn boniness of her face.

"Do you remember me?"

"Yes." Her small voice was made smaller by the cavernous space around us. "How did you know—?"

"The *posadero* told me you've been here all day."

She moved her arm in an abrupt downward gesture. "I don't mean that. How did you know I was in Mexico?"

"You were seen—by other Americans."

"I don't believe you. Father sent you to bring me back, didn't he? He promised that he wouldn't. But he never kept his promises to me, not once in my life."

"He kept this one."

"Then why have you followed me here?"

"I didn't make any promises, to you or anyone."

"But you're supposed to be working for Father. He said when he put me on the plane that he would call off the dogs once and for all."

"He tried to. There isn't anything more he can do for you now. Your father is dead, Harriet. He shot himself Friday morning."

"You're lying! He can't be dead!"

The force of the words shook her body. She raised her hands to cover her face. I could see in her sleeves the flesh-colored tape securing the bandages at her wrists. I had seen such bandages before on would-be suicides.

"I was there when he shot himself. Before he did, he confessed the murders of Ralph Simpson and Dolly. He also said that he had murdered you. Why would your father do that?"

Her eyes glittered like wet stone between her fingers. "I have no idea."

"I have. He knew that you had committed those two murders. He tried to take the blame for them and arrange it so we wouldn't press the search for you. Then he silenced himself. I don't think he wanted to live in any case; he had too much guilt of his own. Ronald Jaimet's death may have been something less than a murder, but it was something more than an accident. And he must have known that his affair with Dolly led indirectly to your murdering her and Ralph Simpson. He had nothing to look forward to but your trial and the end of the Blackwell name—the same prospect you're facing now."

She removed her hands from her face. It had a queer glazed look, as if it had been fired like pottery. "I hate the Blackwell name. I wish my name was Smith or Jones or Gomez."

"It wouldn't change you or the facts. You can't lose what you've done."

"No." She shook her head despondently. "There's no hope for me. No deposit, no return, no nothing. I've been in here since early morning, trying to make contact. There is no contact."

"Are you a member of this Church?"

"I'm not a member of anything. But I thought I could find peace here. The people seemed so happy yesterday coming out of Mass—so happy and peaceful."

"They're not running away from another life."

"You call it life, what I had?" She screwed up her face as though she was trying to cry, but no tears came. "I did my best to end my so-called life. The first time the water was too cold. The second time Father wouldn't let me. He broke in the bathroom door and stopped me. He bandaged my wrists and sent me here; he said that Mother would look after me. But when I went to her house in Ajijic she wouldn't even come out and talk to me. She sent Keith out to the gate to fob me off with a lie. He tried to tell me that she had gone away and taken the money with her."

"Keith Hatchen told you the truth. I've talked to him, and your mother as well. She went to California to try and help you. She's waiting in Los Angeles."

"You're a liar." Her sense of grievance rose like a storm in her throat. "You're all liars, liars and betrayers. Keith betrayed me to you, didn't he?"

"He said that you had been to his house."

"See!" She pointed a finger at my eyes. "Everybody betrayed me, including Father."

"I told you he didn't. He did his best to cover up for you. Your father loved you, Harriet."

"Then why did he betray me with Dolly Stone?" She stabbed the air with her finger like a prosecutor.

"Men get carried away sometimes. It wasn't done against you."

"Wasn't it? I know better. She turned him against me when we were just little kids. I wasn't so little, but she was. She was so pretty, like a little doll. Once he bought her a doll that was almost as big as she was. He bought me a doll just like it to make it up to me. I didn't want it. I was too old for dolls. I wanted my daddy."

Her voice had thinned to a childish treble. It sounded through the spaces of the old building like an archaic voice piping out of the crypts of the past.

"Tell me about the murders, Harriet."

"I don't have to."

"You want to, though. You wouldn't be here if you didn't."

"I tried to tell the priest. My Spanish wasn't good enough. But you're no priest."

"No, I'm just a man. You can tell me, anyway. Why did you have to kill Dolly?"

"At least you understand that I did *have* to. First she stole my father and then she stole my husband."

"I thought Bruce was her husband."

She shook her head. "It wasn't a marriage. I could sense that it wasn't a marriage as soon as I saw them with each other. They were just two people living together, facing in opposite directions. Bruce wanted out of it. He told me so himself, the very first day."

"Why did you go there that first day?"

"Father asked me to. He was afraid to go near her himself, but he said that no one could criticize me if I paid her a visit and gave her a gift of money. I had to see the baby, anyway. My little brother. I believed that seeing him would make me feel—differently. I was so terribly torn asunder when Father told me about him." She raised both fists beside her head and shook them, not at me. She said between her fists: "And there Bruce was. I fell in love with him as soon as I saw him. He loved me, too. He didn't change till afterward."

"What changed him?"

"*She* did, with her wiles and stratagems. He turned against me suddenly one night. We were in a motel on the other side of the

Bay, and he sat there drinking my father's whisky and said he wouldn't leave her. He said he'd made a bargain he couldn't break. So I broke it for him. I took it into my hands and broke it."

She brought her fists together and broke an invisible thing. Then her arms fell limp at her sides. Her eyes went sleepy. I thought for a minute she was going to fall, but she caught herself and faced me in a kind of shaky somnambulistic defiance.

"After I killed her, I took the money back. I'd seen where she hid it, in the baby's mattress. I had to move him to get at it, and he started crying. I took him in my arms to quiet him. Then I had an overmastering urge to take him out of that place and run away with him. I started down the road with him, but suddenly I was overcome by fear. The darkness was so dense I could hardly move. Yet I could see myself, a dreadful woman walking in darkness with a little baby. I was afraid he'd be hurt."

"That you would hurt him?"

Her chin pressed down onto her chest. "Yes. I put him in some-body else's car for safekeeping. I gave him up, and I'm glad I did. At least my little brother is all right." It was a question.

"He's all right. His grandmother is looking after him. I saw him in Citrus Junction the other day."

"I almost did," she said, "the night I killed Ralph Simpson. It's funny how these things keep following you. I thought I was past the sound barrier but I heard him crying that night, in Elizabeth Stone's house. I wanted to knock on the door and visit him. I had my hand lifted to knock when I saw myself again, a dreadful woman in outer darkness, in outer space, driving a man's dead body around in my car."

"You mean Ralph Simpson."

"Yes. He came to the house that night to talk to Father. I recognized the coat he was carrying and intercepted him. He agreed to go for a drive and discuss the situation. I told him Bruce was hiding in the beach house—he said any friend of Bruce was a friend of his, poor little man—and I drove him out to the place above the beach. I stabbed him with the icepick that Mrs. Stone gave my father." Her clenched fist struck weakly at her breast. "I intended to throw his body in the sea, but I changed my mind. I was afraid that Bruce would find it before I got him out of there. I threw the coat in the sea instead and drove to Citrus Junction."

"Why did you pick Isobel's yard to bury him in?"

"It was a safe place. I knew there was nobody there." Her eyes, her entire face, seemed to be groping blindly for a meaning. "It kept it in the family."

"Were you trying to throw the blame on Isobel?"

"Maybe I was. I don't always know why I do things, especially at night. I get the urge to do them and I do them."

"Is that why you wore your father's coat the night you killed Dolly?"

"It happened to be in the car. I was cold." She shivered with the memory. "It isn't true that I wanted him to be blamed. I loved my father. But he didn't love me."

"He loved you to the point of death, Harriet."

She shook her head, and began to shiver more violently. I put my arm around her shoulders and walked her toward the door. It opened, filling with the red sunset. The beggar woman appeared in it, black as a cinder in the blaze.

"What will happen now?" Harriet said with her head down.

"It depends on whether you're willing to waive extradition. We can go back together, if you are."

"I might as well."

The beggar held out her hands to us as we passed. I gave her money again. I had nothing to give Harriet. We went out into the changing light and started to walk up the dry riverbed of the road.

THE
INSTANT
ENEMY

chapter 1

THERE WAS LIGHT early morning traffic on Sepul-
veda. As I drove over the low pass, the sun came up glaring behind
the blue crags on the far side of the valley. For a minute or two, before regular day set in, everything looked fresh and new and awesome
as creation.

I left the freeway at Canoga Park and stopped at a drive-in for a
ninety-nine-cent breakfast. Then I went on up to the Sebastians'
place in Woodland Hills.

Keith Sebastian had given me detailed instructions on how to find
his house. It was an angular contemporary house cantilevered out
over a slope. The slope ran steeply down to the edge of a golf course,
green from the first of the winter rains.

Keith Sebastian came out of the house in shirt sleeves. He was a
handsome man of forty or so, with thick curly brown hair frosted at
the sides. He hadn't shaved yet, and his growth of beard looked like
fibrous dirt that his lower face had been rubbed in.

"It's good of you to come right out," he said when I had introduced myself. "I realize it's an ungodly hour—"

"You didn't pick it, and I don't mind. I gather she hasn't come
home yet."

"No, she hasn't. Since I called you I've found out something else
is missing. My shotgun, and a box of shells."

"You think your daughter took them?"

"I'm afraid she must have. The gun cabinet wasn't broken, and
nobody else knew where the key to it was. Except my wife, of
course."

Mrs. Sebastian had appeared as if on cue at the open front door.
She was thin and dark and rather beautiful in a haggard sort of way,
and she was wearing fresh lipstick and a fresh yellow linen dress.

"Come in," she said to both of us. "It's *cold* out."

She made a shivery self-hugging gesture which didn't end when it should have. She went on shivering.

"This is Mr. Lew Archer," Sebastian was saying. "The private detective I called." He spoke as if he was presenting me to her as a kind of peace offering.

She answered him impatiently: "I guessed that. Come in, I've made some coffee."

I sat between them at the kitchen counter and drank the bitter brew from a thin cup. The place seemed very clean and very empty. The light pouring in through the window had a cruel clarity.

"Can Alexandria fire a shotgun?" I asked them.

"Anybody can," Sebastian said glumly. "All you have to do is pull the trigger."

His wife cut in. "Actually Sandy's a fair shot. The Hacketts took her quail hunting earlier this year. Much against my wishes, I might add."

"You might and did," Sebastian said. "I'm sure the experience was good for her."

"She hated it. She said so in her diary. She hates to kill things."

"She'll get over it. And I know it gave pleasure to Mr. and Mrs. Hackett."

"Here we go again."

But before they did, I said: "Who in hell are Mr. and Mrs. Hackett?"

Sebastian gave me a self-revealing look, partly offended, partly patronizing.

"Mr. Stephen Hackett is my boss. That is, he controls the holding company that controls the savings and loan company I work for. He owns quite a few other things, too."

"Including you," his wife said. "But not my daughter."

"That's unfair, Bernice. I never said—"

"It's what you do that counts."

I got up and walked around to the other side of the counter and stood facing them. They both looked a little startled and ashamed.

"All this is very interesting," I said. "But I didn't get out of bed at five o'clock in the morning to referee a family argument. Let's concentrate on your daughter Sandy. How old is she, Mrs. Sebastian?"

"Seventeen. She's in her senior year."

"Doing well?"

"She was until the last few months. Then her grades started slipping, quite badly."

"Why?"

She looked down into her coffee cup. "I don't really know why." She sounded evasive, unwilling even to give herself an answer.

"Of course you know why," her husband said. "All this has happened since she took up with that wild man. Davy what's-his-name."

"He isn't a man. He's a nineteen-year-old boy and we handled the whole thing abominably."

"What whole thing, Mrs. Sebastian?"

She held out her arms as if she was trying to encompass the situation, then dropped them in despair. "The business of the boy. We mishandled it."

"She means *I* did, as usual," Sebastian said. "But I only did what I had to do. Sandy was starting to run wild. Skipping school to have afternoon dates with this fellow. Spending her nights on the Strip and God knows where else. Last night I went out and hunted them down—"

His wife interrupted him. "It wasn't last night. It was the night before last."

"Whenever it was." His voice seemed to be weakening under the steady cold force of her disapproval. It shifted gears, to a kind of chanting shout. "I hunted them down in a weird joint in West Hollywood. They were sitting there in public with their arms around each other. I told him if he didn't stay away from my daughter I'd take my shotgun and blow his bloody head off."

"My husband watches a good deal of television," Mrs. Sebastian said dryly.

"Make fun of me if you want to, Bernice. Somebody had to do what I did. My daughter was running wild with a criminal. I brought her home and locked her in her room. What else could a man do?"

His wife was silent for once. She moved her fine dark head slowly from side to side.

I said: "Do you know the young man is a criminal?"

"He served time in the county jail for auto theft."

"Joy riding," she said.

"Call it what you like. It wasn't a first offense, either."

"How do you know?"

"Bernice read it in her diary."

"I'd like to see this famous diary."

"No," Mrs. Sebastian said. "It was bad enough for me to have read it. I shouldn't have." She took a deep breath. "We haven't been very good parents, I'm afraid. I'm just as much to blame as my husband is, in subtler ways. But you don't want to go into that."

"Not now." I was weary of the war of the generations, the charges and countercharges, the escalations and negotiations, the endless talk across the bargaining table. "How long has your daughter been gone?"

Sebastian looked at his wrist watch. "Nearly twenty-three hours. I let her out of her room yesterday morning. She seemed to have calmed down—"

"She was furious," her mother said. "But I never thought when she started out for school that she had no intention of going there. We didn't really catch on until about six o'clock last night when she didn't come home for dinner. Then I got in touch with her home-room teacher and found out she'd been playing hooky all day. By that time it was dark already."

She looked at the window as if it was still dark, now and forever. I followed her glance. Two people were striding along the fairway, a man and a woman, both white-haired, as if they'd grown old in the quest for their small white ball.

"One thing I don't understand," I said. "If you thought she was going to school yesterday morning, what about the gun?"

"She must have put it in the trunk of her car," Sebastian said.

"I see. She's driving a car."

"That's one of the reasons we're so concerned." Sebastian pushed his face forward across the counter. I felt like a bartender being consulted by a drunk. But it was fear he was drunk on. "You've had some experience in these matters. Why would she take my shotgun, for heaven's sake?"

"I can think of one possible reason, Mr. Sebastian. You told her you'd blow her friend's head off with it."

"But she couldn't have taken me seriously."

"*I* do."

"So do I," his wife said.

Sebastian hung his head like a prisoner in the dock. But he said under his breath: "By God, I will kill him if he doesn't bring her back."

"Good thinking, Keith," his wife said.

>>>>>>>>>
>>>>>>>>> *chapter* 2
>>>>>>>>>

THE FRICTION BETWEEN the two was starting to rasp on my nerves. I asked Sebastian to show me his gun cabinet. He took me into a small study which was partly library and partly gun room.

There were light and heavy rifles standing upright behind glass in the mahogany gun cabinet, and an empty slot where a double-barreled shotgun had fitted. The bookshelves held a collection of best sellers and book-club editions, and one drab row of textbooks in economics and advertising psychology.

"Are you in advertising?"

"Public relations. I'm chief PR officer for Centennial Savings and Loan. Actually I should be there this morning. We're deciding on our program for next year."

"It can wait one day, can't it?"

"I don't know."

He turned to the gun cabinet, opening it and the drawer under it where he kept his shells. They unlocked with the same brass key.

"Where was the key?"

"In the top drawer of my desk." He opened the drawer and showed me. "Sandy knew where I kept it, of course."

"But anybody else could easily have found it."

"That's true. But I'm sure she took it."

"Why?"

"I just have a feeling."

"Is she gun-happy?"

"Certainly not. When you're properly trained in the use of guns, you don't become gun-happy, as you call it."

"Who trained her?"

"I did, naturally. I'm her father."

He went to the gun cabinet and touched the barrel of the heavy rifle. Carefully he closed the glass door and locked it. He must have caught his reflection in the glass. He backed away from it, scouring his bearded chin with his cupped palm.

"I look terrible. No wonder Bernice has been picking at me. My face is coming apart."

He excused himself and went away to put his face together. I took a peek at my own face in the glass. I didn't look too happy. Early morning was not my best thinking time, but I formulated a vague unhappy thought: Sandy was middle girl in a tense marriage, and at the moment I was middle man.

Mrs. Sebastian came softly into the room and stood beside me in front of the gun cabinet.

"I married a boy scout," she said.

"There are sorrier fates."

"Name one. My mother warned me not to take up with a good-looking man. Marry brains, she told me. But I wouldn't listen. I should have stuck with my modeling career. At least I can depend on my own bones." She patted the hip nearest me.

"You have good bones. Also, you're very candid."

"I got that way in the course of the night."

"Show me your daughter's diary."

"I will not."

"Are you ashamed of her?"

"Of myself," she said. "What could the diary tell you that I can't tell you?"

"If she was sleeping with this boy, for instance."

"Of course she wasn't," she said with a little flash of anger.

"Or anybody else."

"That's absurd." But her face went sallow.

"Was she?"

"Of course not. Sandy's remarkably innocent for her age."

"Or was. Let's hope she still is."

Bernice Sebastian retreated to higher ground. "I—we didn't hire you to pry into my daughter's morals."

"You didn't hire me, period. In a chancy case like this, I need a retainer, Mrs. Sebastian."

"What do you mean, chancy?"

"Your daughter could come home at any time. Or you and your husband could change your minds—"

She stopped me with an impatient flick of her hand. "All right, how much do you want?"

"Two days' pay and expenses, say two hundred and fifty."

She sat at the desk, got a checkbook out of the second drawer, and wrote me a check. "What else?"

"Some recent pictures of her."

"Sit down, I'll get you some."

When she was gone, I examined the checkbook stubs. After paying me my retainer, the Sebastians had less than two hundred dollars left in their bank account. Their smart new house cantilevered over a steep drop was an almost perfect image of their lives.

Mrs. Sebastian came back with a handful of pictures. Sandy was a serious-looking girl who resembled her mother in her dark coloring. Most of the pictures showed her doing things: riding a horse, riding a bicycle, standing on a diving board ready to dive, pointing a gun. The gun looked like the same .22 rifle as the one in the gun cabinet. She held it as if she knew how to use it.

"What about this gun bit, Mrs. Sebastian? Was it Sandy's idea?"

"It was Keith's. His father brought him up to hunt. Keith passed on the great tradition to his daughter." Her voice was sardonic.

"Is she your only child?"

"That's right. We have no son."

"May I go through her room?"

The woman hesitated. "What do you expect to find? Evidence of transvestitism? Narcotics?"

She was still trying to be sardonic, but the questions came through literally to me. I'd found stranger things than those in young people's rooms.

Sandy's room was full of sunlight and fresh sweet odors. I found pretty much what you'd expect to find in the bedroom of an innocent, serious high-school senior. A lot of sweaters and skirts and books, both high-school books and a few good novels like *A High Wind in Jamaica*. A menagerie of cloth animals. College pennants, mostly Ivy League. A pink-frilled vanity with cosmetics laid out on the top of it in geometrical patterns. The photograph of another young girl smiling from a silver frame on the wall.

"Who's that?"

"Sandy's best friend, Heidi Gensler."

"I'd like to talk to her."

Mrs. Sebastian hesitated. These hesitations of hers were brief but tense and somber, as if she was planning her moves far ahead in a high-stakes game.

"The Genslers don't know about this," she said.

"You can't look for your daughter and keep it a secret both at the same time. Are the Genslers friends of yours?"

"They're neighbors. The two girls are the real friends." She made her decision suddenly. "I'll ask Heidi to drop over before she goes to school."

"Why not right away?"

She left the room. I made a quick search of possible hiding places, under the pink oval lamb's-wool rug, between the mattress and springs, on the high dark shelf in the closet, behind and under the clothes in the chest of drawers. I shook out some of the books. From the center of *Sonnets from the Portuguese* a scrap of paper fluttered.

I picked it up from the rug. It was part of a lined notebook page on which someone had written in precise black script:

> *Listen, bird, you give me a pain*
> *In my blood swinging about.*
> *I think I better open a vein*
> *And let you bloody well out.*

Mrs. Sebastian was watching me from the doorway. "You're very thorough, Mr. Archer. What *is* that?"

"A little verse. I wonder if Davy wrote it."

She snatched it from between my fingers and read it. "It sounds quite meaningless to me."

"It doesn't to me." I snatched it back and put it in my wallet. "Is Heidi coming?"

"She'll be here in a little while. She's just finishing breakfast."

"Good. Do you have any letters from Davy?"

"Of course not."

"I thought he might have written to Sandy. I'd like to know if this verse is in his handwriting."

"I have no idea."

"I'm willing to bet it is. Do you have a picture of Davy?"

"Where would I get a picture of him?"

"The same place you got your daughter's diary."

"You needn't keep flinging that in my face."

"I'm not. I'd simply like to read it. It could give me a lot of help."

She went into another of her somber hesitations, straining her eyes ahead over the curve of time.

"Where is the diary, Mrs. Sebastian?"

"It doesn't exist any longer," she said carefully. "I destroyed it."

I thought she was lying, and I didn't try to conceal my thought. "How?"

"I chewed it up and swallowed it, if you must know. Now you've got to excuse me. I have a dreadful headache."

She waited at the doorway for me to come out of the room, then closed and locked the door. The lock was new.

"Whose idea was the lock?"

"Actually it was Sandy's. She wanted more privacy these last few months. More than she could use."

She went into another bedroom and shut the door. I found Sebastian back at the kitchen counter drinking coffee. He had washed and shaved and brushed his curly brown hair, put on a tie and a jacket and a more hopeful look.

"More coffee?"

"No thanks." I got out a small black notebook and sat beside him. "Can you give me a description of Davy?"

"He looked like a young thug to me."

"Thugs come in all shapes and sizes. What's his height, approximately?"

"About the same as mine. I'm six feet in my shoes."

"Weight?"

"He looks heavy, maybe two hundred."

"Athletic build?"

"I guess you'd say that." He had a sour competitive note in his voice. "But I could have taken him."

"No doubt you could. Describe his face."

"He isn't too bad-looking. But he has that typical sullen look they have."

"Before or after you offered to shoot him?"

Sebastian moved to get up. "Look here, if you're taking sides against me, what do you think we're paying you for?"

"For this," I said, "and for a lot of other dull interrogations. You think this is my idea of a social good time?"

"It's not mine, either."

"No, but it belongs to you. What color is his hair?"

"Blondish."

"Does he wear it long?"

"Short. They probably cut it off in prison."

"Blue eyes?"

"I guess so."

"Any facial hair?"

"No."

"What was he wearing?"

"The standard uniform. Tight pants worn low on the hips, a faded blue shirt, boots."

"How did he talk?"

"With his mouth." Sebastian's thin feelings were wearing thinner again.

"Educated or uneducated? Hip or square?"

"I didn't hear him say enough to know. He was mad. We both were."

"How would you sum him up?"

"A slob. A dangerous slob." He turned in a queer quick movement and looked at me wide-eyed, as if I'd just applied those words to him. "Listen, I have to get down to the office. We're having an important conference about next year's program. And then I'm going to have lunch with Mr. Hackett."

Before he left, I got him to give me a description of his daughter's car. It was a last year's Dart two-door, light green in color, which was registered in his name. He wouldn't let me put it on the official hot-car list. I wasn't to tell the police anything about the case.

"You don't know how it is in my profession," he said. "I have to keep up a stainless-steel front. If it slips, I slip. Confidence is our product in the savings and loan industry."

He drove away in a new Oldsmobile which, according to his check stubs, was costing him a hundred and twenty dollars a month.

A FEW MINUTES LATER I opened the front door for Heidi Gensler. She was a clean-looking adolescent whose yellow hair hung straight onto her thin shoulders. She wore no makeup that I could see. She carried a satchel of books.

Her pale-blue gaze was uncertain. "Are you the man I'm supposed to talk to?"

I said I was. "My name is Archer. Come in, Miss Gensler."

She looked past me into the house. "Is it all right?"

Mrs. Sebastian emerged from her room wearing a fluffy pink robe. "Come in, Heidi dear, don't be afraid. It's nice of you to come." Her voice was not maternal.

Heidi stepped inside and lingered in the hallway, ill at ease. "Did something happen to Sandy?"

"We don't know, dear. If I tell you the bare facts, I want you to promise one thing: you mustn't talk about it at school, or at home, either."

"I wouldn't. I never have."

"What do you mean by that, dear: 'You never have'?"

Heidi bit her lip. "I mean—I don't mean anything."

Mrs. Sebastian moved toward her like a pink bird with a keen dark outthrust head. "Did you know what was going on between her and that boy?"

"I couldn't help it."

"And yet you never told us? That wasn't very friendly of you, dear."

The girl was close to tears. "*Sandy* is my friend."

"Good. Fine. Then you'll help us get her safely home, won't you?"

The girl nodded. "Did she run away with Davy Spanner?"

"Before I answer that, remember you have to promise not to talk."

I said: "That's hardly necessary, Mrs. Sebastian. And I really prefer to do my own questioning."

She turned on me. "How can I know you'll be discreet?"

"You can't. You can't control the situation. It's out of control. So why don't you go away and let me handle this?"

Mrs. Sebastian refused to go. She looked ready to fire me. I didn't care. The case was shaping up as one on which I'd make no friends and very little money.

Heidi touched my arm. "You could drive me to school, Mr. Archer. I don't have a ride when Sandy isn't here."

"I'll do that. When do you want to go?"

"Any time. If I get there too early for my first class I can always do some homework."

"Did Sandy drive you to school yesterday?"

"No. I took the bus. She phoned me yesterday morning about this time. She said she wasn't going to school."

Mrs. Sebastian leaned forward. "Did she tell you where she *was* going?"

"No." The girl had put on a closed, stubborn look. If she did know anything more, she wasn't going to tell it to Sandy's mother.

Mrs. Sebastian said: "I think you're lying, Heidi."

The girl flushed, and water rose in her eyes. "You have no right to say that. You're not my mother."

I intervened again. Nothing worth saying was going to get said in the Sebastian house. "Come on," I told the girl, "I'll drive you to school."

We went outside and got into my car and started downhill toward the freeway. Heidi sat very sedately with her satchel of books between us on the seat. She'd probably remembered that she wasn't supposed to get into an automobile with a strange man. But after a minute she said: "Mrs. Sebastian blames *me*. It isn't fair."

"Blames you for what?"

"For everything Sandy does. Just because Sandy tells me things doesn't mean I'm responsible."

"Things?"

"Like about Davy. I can't run to Mrs. Sebastian with everything Sandy says. That would make me a stool pigeon."

"I can think of worse things."

"Like for instance?" I was questioning her code, and she spoke with some defiance.

"Like letting your best friend get into trouble and not lifting a finger to prevent it."

"I didn't *let* her. How could I stop her? Anyway, she isn't in trouble, not in the way you mean."

"I'm not talking about having a baby. That's a minor problem compared with the other things that can happen to a girl."

"What other things?"

"Not living to have a baby. Or growing old all of a sudden."

Heidi made a thin sound like a small frightened animal. She said in a hushed voice: "That's what happened to Sandy, in a way. How did you know that?"

"I've seen it happen to other girls who couldn't wait. Do you know Davy?"

She hesitated before answering. "I've met him."

"What do you think of him?"

"He's quite an exciting personality," she said carefully. "But I don't think he's good for Sandy. He's rough and wild. I think he's crazy. Sandy isn't any of those things." She paused in solemn thought. "A bad thing happened to her, is all. It just *happened.*"

"You mean her falling for Davy?"

"I mean the other one. Davy Spanner isn't so bad compared with the other one."

"Who's he?"

"She wouldn't tell me his name, or anything else about him."

"So how do you know that Davy's an improvement?"

"It's easy to tell. Sandy's happier than she was before. She used to talk about suicide all the time."

"When was this?"

"In the summer, before school started. She was going to walk into the ocean at Zuma Beach and swim on out. I talked her out of it."

"What was bothering her—a love affair?"

"I guess you could call it that."

Heidi wouldn't tell me anything further. She'd given Sandy her solemn oath never to breathe a word, and she had already broken it by what she'd said to me.

"Did you ever see her diary?"

"No. I know she kept one. But she never showed it to anybody, ever." She turned toward me in the seat, pulling her skirt down over her knees. "May I ask you a question, Mr. Archer?"

"Go ahead."

"Just what happened to Sandy? This time, I mean?"

"I don't know. She drove away from home twenty-four hours ago. The night before, her father broke up a date she was having with Davy in West Hollywood. He dragged her home and locked her up overnight."

"No wonder Sandy left home," the girl said.

"Incidentally, she took along her father's shotgun."

"What for?"

"I don't know. But I understand Davy has a criminal record."

The girl didn't respond to the implied question. She sat looking down at her fists, which were clenched in her lap. We reached the foot of the slope and drove toward Ventura Boulevard.

"Do you think she's with Davy now, Mr. Archer?"

"That's the assumption I'm going on. Which way?"

"Wait a minute. Pull over to the side."

I parked in the sharp morning shadow of a live oak which had somehow survived the building of the freeway and the boulevard.

"I know where Davy lives," Heidi said. "Sandy took me to his pad once." She used the shabby word with a certain pride, as if it proved that she was growing up. "It's in the Laurel Apartments in Pacific Palisades. Sandy told me he gets his apartment free, for looking after the swimming pool and stuff."

"What happened when you visited his place?"

"Nothing happened. We sat around and talked. It was very interesting."

"What did you talk about?"

"The way people live. The bad morals people have today."

I offered to drive Heidi the rest of the way to school, but she said she could catch a bus. I left her standing on the corner, a gentle creature who seemed a little lost in a world of high velocities and low morals.

I LEFT SEPULVEDA at Sunset Boulevard, drove south to the business section of Pacific Palisades, and made a left turn on Chautauqua. The Laurel Apartments were on Elder Street, a slanting street on the long gradual slope down to the sea.

It was one of the newer and smaller apartment buildings in the area. I left my car at the curb and made my way into the interior court.

The swimming pool was sparkling. The shrubs in the garden were green and carefully clipped. Red hibiscus and purple princess flowers glowed among the leaves.

A woman who sort of went with the red hibiscus came out of one of the ground-floor apartments. Under her brilliant housecoat, orange on black, her body moved as though it was used to being watched. Her handsome face was a little coarsened by the dyed red hair that framed it. She had elegant brown legs and bare feet.

In a pleasant, experienced voice that hadn't been to college she asked me what I wanted.

"Are you the manager?"

"I'm Mrs. Smith, yes. I own this place. I don't have any vacancies at the moment."

I told her my name. "I'd like to ask you some questions if I may."

"What about?"

"You have an employee named Davy Spanner."

"Do I?"

"I understood you did."

She said with a kind of weary defensiveness: "Why don't you people leave him alone for a change?"

"I've never laid eyes on him."

"But you're a policeman, aren't you? Keep after him long enough and you'll push him over the edge again. Is that what you want?" Her voice was low but full of force, like the mutter of a furnace.

"No, and I'm not a policeman."

"Probation officer then. You're all the same to me. Davy Spanner's a good boy."

"And he's got at least one good friend," I said, hoping to change the tone of the interview.

"If you mean me, you're not wrong. What do you want with Davy?"

"Just to ask him a few questions."

"Ask me instead."

"All right. Do you know Sandy Sebastian?"

"I've met her. She's a pretty little thing."

"Is she here?"

"She doesn't live here. She lives with her parents, someplace in the Valley."

"She's been missing from home since yesterday morning. Has she been here?"

"I doubt it."

"What about Davy?"

"I haven't seen him this morning. I just got up myself." She peered up at the sky like a woman who loved the light but hadn't always lived in it. "So you are a cop."

"A private detective. Sandy's father hired me. I think you'd be wise to let me talk to Davy."

"I'll do the talking. You don't want to set him off."

She led me to a small apartment at the rear beside the entrance to the garages. The name "David Spanner" had been inscribed on a white card on the door, in the same precise hand as the verse that had fallen out of Sandy's book.

Mrs. Smith knocked lightly and when she got no answer called out: "Davy."

There were voices somewhere behind the door, a young man's voice and then a girl's which set my heart pounding for no good reason. I heard the soft pad of footsteps. The door opened.

Davy was no taller than I was, but he seemed to fill the doorway from side to side. Muscles crawled under his black sweatshirt. His blond head and face had a slightly unfinished look. He peered out at the sunlight as if it had rejected him.

"You want me?"

"Is your girl friend with you?" Mrs. Smith had a note in her voice which I couldn't quite place. I wondered if she was jealous of the girl.

Apparently Davy caught the note. "Is there something the matter?"

"This man seems to think so. He says your girl friend is missing."

"How can she be missing? She's right here." His voice was flat, as though he was guarding his feelings. "Her father sent you, no doubt," he said to me.

"That's right."

"Go back and tell him this is the twentieth century, second half. Maybe there was a time when a chick's old man could get away with locking her up in her room. The day's long past. Tell old man Sebastian that."

"He isn't an old man. But he's aged in the last twenty-four hours."

"Good. I hope he dies. And so does Sandy."

"May I talk to her?"

"I'll give you exactly one minute." To Mrs. Smith he said: "Please go away for a minute."

He spoke to both of us with a certain authority, but it was a slightly manic authority. The woman seemed to feel this. She moved away across the court without an argument or a backward glance, as if she was deliberately humoring him. As she sat down by the pool I wondered again in exactly what capacity she employed him.

Blocking the doorway with his body, he turned and called to the girl: "Sandy? Come here a minute."

She came to the doorway wearing dark glasses which robbed her face of meaning. Like Davy, she had on a black sweatshirt. Her body thrust itself forward and leaned on Davy's with the kind of heart-broken lewdness that only very young girls are capable of. Her face was set and pale, and her mouth hardly moved when she spoke.

"I don't know you, do I?"

"Your mother sent me."

"To drag me back home again?"

"Your parents are naturally interested in your plans. If any."

"Tell them they'll find out soon enough." She didn't sound angry in the usual sense. Her voice was dull and even. Behind the dark glasses she seemed to be looking at Davy instead of me.

There was some kind of passion between them. It gave off a faint wrong smoky odor, like something burning where it shouldn't be, arson committed by children playing with matches.

I didn't know how to talk to them. "Your mother's pretty sick about this, Miss Sebastian."

"She'll be sicker."

"That sounds like a threat."

"It is. I guarantee that she'll be sicker."

Davy shook his head at her. "Don't say anything more. Anyway his minute is up." He made an elaborate show of checking his wrist watch, and I caught a glimpse of what went on in his head: large plans and intricate hostilities and a complicated schedule which didn't always jibe with reality. "You've had your minute. Good-bye."

"Hello again. I need another minute, or maybe two." I wasn't deliberately crossing the boy, but I wasn't avoiding it, either. It was important to know how wild he really was. "Do me a favor, Miss Sebastian. Take off your glasses so I can see you."

She reached for her glasses with both hands, and lifted them from her face. Her eyes were hot and lost.

"Put them back on," Davy said.

She obeyed him.

"You take orders from me, bird. From nobody else." He turned on me. "As for you, I want you to be out of sight in one minute. That's an order."

"You're not old enough to be giving orders to anybody. When I leave, Miss Sebastian goes along."

"You think so?" He pushed her inside and shut the door. "She's never going back to that dungeon."

"It's better than shacking up with a psycho."

"I'm not a psycho!"

To prove it he swung his right fist at my head. I leaned back and let it go by. But his left followed very quickly, catching me on the side of the neck. I staggered backward into the garden, balancing the wobbling sky on my chin. My heel caught on the edge of the concrete deck around the pool. The back of my head rapped the concrete.

Davy came between me and the sky. I rolled sideways. He kicked me twice in the back. I got up somehow and closed with him. It was like trying to wrestle with a bear. He lifted me clear off my feet.

Mrs. Smith said: "Stop it!" She spoke as if he really was some half-tamed animal. "Do you want to go back to jail?"

He paused, still holding me in a bear hug that inhibited my breathing. The redheaded woman went to a tap and started a hose running. She turned it full on Davy. Some of the water splashed on me.

"Drop him."

Davy dropped me. The woman kept the hose on him, aiming at the middle of his body. He didn't try to take it away from her. He was watching me. I was watching a Jerusalem cricket which was crawling across the deck through the spilled water, like a tiny clumsy travesty of a man.

The woman spoke to me over her shoulder: "You better get the hell out of here, troublemaker."

She was adding insult to injury, but I went. Not very far: around the corner where my car was parked. I drove around the block and parked it again on the slanting street above the Laurel Apartments. I couldn't see the inner court or the doors that opened onto it. But the entrance to the garage was clearly visible.

I sat and watched it for half an hour. My hot and wounded feelings gradually simmered down. The kick-bruise in my back went right on hurting.

I hadn't expected to be taken. The fact that I had been meant I was getting old, or else that Davy was pretty tough. It didn't take me half an hour to decide that both of these things were probably true.

The name of the street I was parked on was Los Baños Street. It was a fairly good street, with new ranch houses sitting on pads cut one above another in the hillside. Each house was carefully different. The one across the street from me, for example, the one with the closed drapes, had a ten-foot slab of volcanic rock set into the front. The car in the driveway was a new Cougar.

A man in a soft leather jacket came out of the house, opened the trunk of the car, and got out a small flat disk which interested me. It looked like a roll of recording tape. The man noticed my interest in it and slipped it into the pocket of his jacket.

Then he decided to make something more of it. He crossed the street to my side, walking with swaggering authority. He was a large heavy man with a freckled bald head. In his big slack smiling face the sharp hard eyes came as a bit of a shock, like gravel in custard.

"You live around here, my friend?" he said to me.

"I'm just reconnoitering. You call it living around here?"

"We don't like strangers snooping. So how would you like to move along?"

I didn't want to attract attention. I moved along. With me I took the license number of the Cougar and the number of the house, 702 Los Baños Street.

I have a good sense of timing, or timing has a good sense of me. My car had just begun to move when a light-green compact backed out of the garage of the Laurel Apartments. As it turned downhill toward the coastal highway, I could see that Sandy was driving and Davy was with her in the front seat. I followed them. They turned right on the highway, went through a yellow light at the foot of Sunset, and left me gritting my teeth behind a red light.

I drove all the way to Malibu trying to pick them up again, but I had no luck. I went back to the Laurel Apartments on Elder Street.

>>>>>>>>
>>>>>>>> *chapter* 5
>>>>>>>>

THE CARD ON THE DOOR of Apartment One said: "Mrs. Laurel Smith." She opened the door on a chain and growled at me:

"You drove him away. I hope you're satisfied."

"You mean they're gone for good?"

"I'm not talking to you."

"I think you'd better. I'm not a troublemaker by choice, but trouble can be made. If Davy Spanner's on probation, he broke it when he swung on me."

"You were asking for it."

"That depends on which side you're on. You're obviously on Davy's side. In which case you better cooperate with me."

She thought about this. "Cooperate how?"

"I want the girl. If I get her back in reasonable shape, in a reasonable period of time—like today—I won't bear down hard on Davy. Otherwise I will."

She unhooked the chain. "Okay, Mr. God. Come in. The place is a mess but then so are you."

She smiled with one side of her mouth and one eye. I think she wanted to be angry with me, but so many things had happened in her life that she couldn't stay angry. One of the things that had happened to her, I could tell by her breath, was alcohol.

The clock on her mantel said it was half past ten. The clock was under a bell jar, as if to shield Laurel Smith from the passage of time. The other things in the living room, the overstuffed furniture and the gewgaws and the litter of magazines, had an unlived-with feeling. It was like a waiting room where you couldn't relax, for fear that the dentist would call you in any minute. Or the psychiatrist.

The small television set in one corner of the room was on, with the sound turned off. Laurel Smith said apologetically:

"I never used to watch TV. But I won this thing in a contest a couple of weeks ago."

"What kind of a contest?"

"One of those telephone contests. They called me up and asked me what was the capital of California. I said Sacramento, and they told me I'd won a portable TV set, just like that. I thought it was a gag, but within the hour they turned up here with the set."

She switched it off. We sat facing each other at opposite ends of the chesterfield.

There was a cloudy glass on the coffee table between us. The picture window behind us was full of blue sky and blue sea.

"Tell me about Davy."

"There isn't much to tell. I took him on a couple of months ago."

"In what sense took him on?"

"To do the clean-up work around the place. He needed a part-time job, he's planning to start at junior college the first of the year. You wouldn't know it the way he acted this morning, but he's an ambitious young man."

"Did you know he'd been in jail when you hired him?"

"Naturally I did. That's what got me interested in his case. I've had my own share of troubles—"

"Troubles with the law?"

"I didn't say that. And let's not talk about me, eh? I've had a little luck in real estate, and I like to spread the luck around a little. So I gave Davy a job."

"Have you talked to him at any length?"

She let out a short laugh. "I'll say I have. That boy will talk your arm off."

"What about?"

"Any subject. His main subject is how the country is going to the dogs. He may be right at that. He says his time in jail gave him a worm's-eye view of the whole business."

"He sounds like a poolroom lawyer to me."

"Davy's more than that," she said defensively. "He's more than just a talker. And he isn't the poolroom type. He's a serious boy."

"What's he serious about?"

"He wants to grow up and be a real man and do something useful."

"I think he's conning you, Mrs. Smith."

"No." She shook her artificial head. "He isn't conning me. He may be conning himself a little. God knows he's got his problems. I've talked to his probation officer—" She hesitated.

"Who is his probation officer?"

"I forget his name." She went to the telephone directory in the hall and consulted the front of it. "Mr. Belsize. Do you know him?"

"We've met. He's a good man."

Laurel Smith sat down nearer me. She seemed to be warming up slightly, but her eyes were still watchful. "Mr. Belsize admitted to me that he was taking a chance on Davy. Recommending him for probation, I mean. He said Davy might make it and then again he might not. I said I was willing to take my chances, too."

"Why?"

"You can't just live for yourself. I found that out." A sudden smile lit her face. "I sure picked a hot potato, didn't I?"

"You sure did. Did Belsize say what was the matter with him?"

"He has emotional trouble. When he gets mad he thinks we're all his enemies. Even me. He never lifted his hand against me, though. Or anybody else until this morning."

"That you know of."

"I know he's been in trouble in the past," she said. "But I'm willing to give him the benefit. You don't know what that boy's been through—orphanages and foster homes and getting kicked around. He never had a home of his own, he never had a father or a mother."

"He still has to learn to handle himself."

"*I* know that. I thought you were beginning to sympathize."

"I do sympathize, but that won't help Davy. He's playing house and other games with a young girl. He's got to bring her back. Her parents could hang a rap on him that would put him away until he's middle-aged."

She pressed her hand against her breast. "We can't let that happen."

"Where would he have taken her, Mrs. Smith?"

"I don't know."

She raked her dyed head with her finger, then rose and went to the picture window. With her back to me, her body was simply an object, an odalisque shape against the light. Framed in dark-red curtains, the sea looked old as the Mediterranean, old as sin.

"Has he brought her here before?" I said to her black-and-orange back.

"He brought her to introduce her to me last week—week before last."

"Were they planning to get married?"

"I don't think so. They're too young. I'm sure Davy has other plans."

"What are his plans?"

"I told you, about going to school and all. He wants to be a doctor or a lawyer."

"He'll be lucky if he just stays out of jail."

She turned to me, clutching and pulling at her hands. Their friction made a dry anxious sound. "What can *I* do?"

"Let me search his apartment."

She was silent for a minute, looking at me as if she found it hard to trust a man.

"I guess that is a good idea."

She got her keys, a heavy clinking loop like an overgrown charm bracelet. The card with "David Spanner" written on it was missing from his door. That seemed to imply that he wasn't coming back.

The apartment was a single room with two convertible beds at right angles in a corner. Both beds had been slept in and left unmade. Mrs. Smith pulled back the covers and examined the sheets.

"I can't tell if they were sleeping together," she said.

"I assume they were."

She gave me a worried look. "The girl isn't Quentin quail, is she?"

"No. But if he takes her someplace against her will—or if she wants out and he uses force—"

"I know, that's kidnapping. But Davy wouldn't do that to her. He likes her."

I opened the closet. It was empty.

"He didn't have much in the way of clothes," she said. "He didn't care about clothes and things like that."

"What did he care about?"

"Cars. But on probation he isn't allowed to drive. I think that's one reason he took up with the girl. She has a car."

"And her father had a shotgun. Davy has it now."

She turned so quickly that the skirt of her housecoat flared out. "You didn't tell me that before."

"What makes it so important?"

"He might shoot somebody."

"Anyone in particular?"

"He doesn't *know* anybody," she said foolishly.

"That's good."

I went through the rest of the place. There were sliced ham and cheese and milk in the little refrigerator in the kitchenette. I found a few books on the desk by the window: *The Prophet,* and a book about Clarence Darrow, and one about an American doctor who had built a hospital in Burma. Meager wings to fly on.

Tacked up over the desk was a list of ten "Don'ts." They were written out in the precise hand I recognized as Davy's:

1. *Don't drive cars.*
2. *Don't drink alcoholic beverages.*
3. *Don't stay up too late—the night is the bad time.*
4. *Don't frequent crummy joints.*
5. *Don't make friends without careful investigation.*
6. *Don't use dirty language.*
7. *Don't use 'ain't' and other vulgarisms.*
8. *Don't sit around and brood about the past.*
9. *Don't hit people.*
10. *Don't get mad and be an instant enemy.*

"You see what kind of a boy he is?" Laurel said at my shoulder. "A real trier."

"You're fond of him, aren't you?"

She didn't answer directly. "You'd like him, too, if you only got to know him."

"Maybe." Davy's list of self-regulations was kind of touching, but I read it with a different eye from Laurel's. The boy was beginning to know himself, and didn't like what he saw.

I went through the desk. It was empty except for a sheet of paper jammed into the back of the bottom drawer. I spread it out on the desk top. It was covered with a map, crudely drawn in ink, of a ranch or large estate. Its various features were labeled in a girlish unformed hand: "main house," "garage with L.'s apt.," "artificial lake and dam," "road from highway" passing through a "locked gate."

I showed the map to Laurel Smith. "Does this mean anything to you?"

"Not a thing." But her eyes had grown small and intent. "Should it?"

"It looks as if they've been casing some joint."

"More likely they were just doodling."

"Some doodle." I folded the map and put it in my inside pocket.

"What are you going to do with that?" she said.

"Find the place. If you know where it is you could save me a lot of trouble."

"I don't," she said abruptly. "Now if you're finished in here, I've got other things to do."

She stood by the door till I went out. I thanked her. She shook her head gloomily; "You're not welcome. Listen, how much would you take to lay off Davy? Lay off the whole damn business?"

"I can't."

"Sure you can. I'll give you five hundred."

"No."

"A thousand? A thousand cash, no taxes to pay."

"Forget it."

"A thousand cash and me. I look better without my clothes on." She nudged my arm with her breast. All it did was make my kidneys hurt.

"It's a handsome offer but I can't take it. You're forgetting about the girl. I can't afford to."

"To hell with her and to hell with you." She walked away to her apartment, swinging her keys.

I went into the garage. Against the dim rear wall was a workbench littered with tools: hammer, screwdrivers, pliers, wrenches, a hacksaw. A small vise was attached to the bench. Under it and around it, bright new iron filings mixed with saw dust were scattered on the concrete floor.

The filings suggested a queer idea to my mind. I made a further search, which ended up in the rafters of the garage. Wrapped in a dirty beach towel and a rolled-up carpet remnant I found the two barrels and the stock which Davy had sawed off the shotgun. They gave me an ugly moment: they were like the leavings of a major amputation.

>>>>>>>>>
>>>>>>>>> *chapter* 6
>>>>>>>>>

I PUT THE SEVERED BARRELS and stock in the trunk of my car and drove to my office on Sunset. From there I phoned Keith Sebastian at Centennial Savings and Loan. His secretary told me he had just gone out for lunch.

I made an appointment with Sebastian for early afternoon. In order not to waste the noon hour I put in a call to Jacob Belsize before I left my office.

Belsize remembered me. When I mentioned Davy Spanner's name, he agreed to meet me for lunch at a restaurant near his building on South Broadway.

I found him waiting for me in a booth. I hadn't seen Jake Belsize in several years, and he had aged in the interval. His hair was almost white now. The lines around his mouth and eyes reminded me of the fissured clay surrounding desert water holes.

The Special Businessman's Dollar Lunch was a hot beef sandwich with French fries and coffee. Belsize ordered it, and so did I. When the waitress had taken our order, he spoke under the clatter and buzz of eating, talking men:

"You weren't too clear on the phone. What's Davy been up to?"

"Aggravated assault. He stomped me in the kidneys."

Jake's dark eyes jumped. He was one of the good ones who never could stop caring. "You going to press charges?"

"I may. But he's got heavier charges to worry about. I can't mention names because my client won't let me. His daughter is a high-school girl. She's been gone for a day and a night—a night which she spent with Davy in his apartment."

"Where are they now?"

"Driving around in her car. When I lost them, they were on the coast highway headed for Malibu."

"How old is the girl?"

"Seventeen."

He took a deep breath. "That isn't good. But it could be worse."

"It is worse, if you knew all the details. It's much worse."

"Tell me the details. What kind of a girl is she?"

"I saw her for two minutes. I'd say she's a nice girl in serious trouble. This seems to be her second go-round with sex. The first go-round made her suicidal, according to a friend of hers. This time could be worse. I'm guessing, but I'd say that the girl and Davy are spurring each other on to do something really wild."

Belsize leaned across the table toward me. "What do you think they might do?"

"I think they're building up to some kind of crime."

"What kind of crime?"

"You tell me. He's your boy."

Belsize shook his head. The lines in his face deepened, like cracks in his conception of himself. "He's mine in a very limited sense. I can't follow him down the street or out on the highway. I have a hundred and fifty clients, a hundred and fifty Davy Spanners. They walk through my dreams."

"I know you can't make it for them," I said, "and nobody's blaming you. I came here to get your professional judgment on Davy. Does he go in for crimes against the person?"

"He never has, but he's capable of it."

"Homicide?"

Belsize nodded. "Davy's pretty paranoid. When he feels threatened or rejected he loses his balance. One day in my office he almost jumped *me*."

"Why?"

"It was just before his sentencing. I told him I was recommending that he be sent to jail for six months as a condition of probation. It triggered something in him, something from the past, I don't know what. We don't have a complete history on Davy. He lost his parents and spent his early years in an orphanage, until foster parents took him on. Anyway, when I told him what I was going to do, he must have felt abandoned all over again. Only now he was big and strong and ready to kill me. Fortunately I was able to talk him back to his senses. And I didn't revoke my recommendation for probation."

"That took faith."

Belsize shrugged. "I'm a faith healer. I learned a good many years ago that I have to take my chances. If I won't take a chance on them, I can't expect them to take a chance on themselves."

The waitress brought our sandwiches, and for a few minutes we were busy with them. At least I was busy with mine. Belsize picked at his as if Davy and I had spoiled his appetite. Finally he pushed it away.

"I have to learn not to hope too much," he said. "I have to school myself to remember that they have two strikes on them before I ever see them. One more and they're whiffed." He raised his head. "I wish you'd give me all the facts about Davy."

"They wouldn't make you any happier. And I don't want you putting out an alarm for him and the girl. Not until I talk to my client, anyway."

"What do you want me to do?"

"Answer a few more questions. If you were high on Davy, why did you recommend six months in jail?"

"He needed it. He'd been stealing cars on impulse, probably for years."

"For sale?"

"For joy riding. Or grief riding, as he calls it. He admitted when we'd established rapport that he had driven all over the state. He told me he was looking for his people, his own people. I believed him. I hated to send him to jail. But I thought six months in a controlled situation would give him a chance to cool off, time to mature."

"Did it?"

"In some ways. He finished his high-school education and did a lot of extra reading. But of course he still has problems to work out—if he'll only give himself the time."

"Psychiatric problems?"

"I prefer to call them life problems," Belsize said. "He's a boy who never really had anybody or anything of his own. That is a lot of not-having. I thought, myself, a psychiatrist could help him. But the psychologist who tested him for us didn't think he'd be a good investment."

"Because he's semi-psychotic?"

"I don't pin labels on young people. I see their adolescent storms. I've seen them take every form that you could find in a textbook of abnormal psychology. But often when the storms pass, they're different and better people." His hands turned over, palms upward, on the table.

"Or different and worse."

"You're a cynic, Mr. Archer."

"Not me. I was one of the ones who turned out different and better. Slightly better, anyway. I joined the cops instead of the hoods."

Belsize said with a smile that crumpled his whole face: "I still haven't made my decision. My clients think I'm a cop. The cops think I'm a hood-lover. But we're not the problem, are we?"

"Do you have any idea where Davy would go?"

"He might go anywhere at all. Have you talked to his employer? I don't recall her name at the moment but she's a redheaded woman—"

"Laurel Smith. I talked to her. How did she get into the picture?"

"She offered him a part-time job through our office. This was when he got out of jail about two months ago."

"Had she known him before?"

"I don't believe so. I think she's a woman who wanted someone to help."

"And what did she expect in return?"

"You are a cynic," he said. "People often do good simply because it's their nature. I think Mrs. Smith may have had troubles of her own."

"What makes you think so?"

"I had an inquiry on her from the sheriff's office in Santa Teresa. This was about the time that Davy got out of jail."

"An official inquiry?"

"Semi-official. A sheriff's man named Fleischer came to my office. He wanted to know all about Laurel Smith and all about Davy. I didn't tell him much. Frankly, I didn't like him, and he wouldn't explain why he needed the information."

"Have you checked Laurel Smith's record?"

"No. It didn't seem necessary."

"I would if I were you. Where did Davy live before he went to jail?"

"He'd been on his own for a year or more after he dropped out of high school. Living on the beaches in the summer, taking odd jobs in the winter."

"Before that?"

"He lived with foster parents, Mr. and Mrs. Edward Spanner. He took their name."

"Can you tell me where to find the Spanners?"

"They live in West Los Angeles. You can find them in the phone book."

"Is Davy still in touch with them?"

"I don't know. Ask them yourself." The waitress brought our checks, and Belsize stood up to go.

>>>>>>>>>>
>>>>>>>>>> *chapter* 7
>>>>>>>>>>

THE CENTENNIAL SAVINGS building on Wilshire was a new twelve-story tower sheathed with aluminum and glass. An automatic elevator took me up to Sebastian's office on the second floor.

The violet-eyed secretary in the outer room told me that Sebastian was expecting me. "But," she added in an important tone, "Mr. Stephen Hackett is with him now."

"The big boss himself?"

She frowned and shushed me. "Mr. Hackett came back from lunch with Mr. Sebastian. But he likes to stay incognito. This is just the second time I ever saw him myself." She sounded as if they were having a visit from royalty.

I sat on a settee against the wall. The girl got up from her type-writer desk and, to my surprise, came and sat down beside me.

"Are you a policeman or a doctor or something?"

"I'm a something."

She was offended. "You don't have to tell me if you don't want to."

"That's true."

She was silent for a time. "I'm concerned about Mr. Sebastian."

"So am I. What makes you think I'm a doctor or a cop?"

"The way he talked about you. He's very anxious to see you."

"Did he say why?"

"No, but I heard him crying in there this morning." She indicated the door of the inner office. "Mr. Sebastian is a very cool person in general. But he was actually crying. I went in and asked him if I could help. He said nothing could help, that his daughter was very ill." She turned and looked deep into my eyes with her ultraviolet ones. "Is that true?"

"It could be. Do you know Sandy?"

"I know her to see. What's the matter with her?"

I didn't have to offer a diagnosis. There was a soft scuffling of feet in the inner office. By the time Sebastian had opened the door the girl was back at her desk, looking as permanent as a statue in a niche.

Stephen Hackett was a well-kept man of forty or so, younger than I expected. His thick body borrowed some grace from his well-tailored tweeds, which looked like Bond Street. His scornful eyes flicked over me as if I was a misplaced piece of furniture. He gave the impression of wearing his money the way other men wear eleva-tor shoes.

Sebastian clearly hated to see him go, and tried to follow him out to the elevator. Hackett turned at the door and gave him a quick handshake and a definite, "Good-bye. Keep up the good work."

Sebastian came back to me with bright dreaming eyes. "That was Mr. Hackett. He likes my program very very much." He was bragging to the girl as well as me.

"I knew he would," she said. "It's a brilliant program."

"Yeah, but you never can tell."

He took me into his office and closed the door. It wasn't large, but it was a corner room overlooking the boulevard and the parking lot. I looked down and saw Stephen Hackett step over the door of a red sports car and drive away.

"He's a terrific sportsman," Sebastian said.

His hero worship annoyed me. "Is that all he does?"

"He keeps an eye on his interests, of course. But he doesn't bother with active management."

"Where does his money come from?"

"He inherited a fortune from his father. Mark Hackett was one of those fabulous Texas oilmen. But Stephen Hackett is a moneymaker in his own right. Just in the last few years, for example, he bought out Centennial Savings and put up this building."

"Good for him. Jolly good for him."

Sebastian gave me a startled look and sat down behind his desk. On it were stand-up photographs of Sandy and his wife, and a pile of advertising layouts. The top one said in archaic lettering: "We respect other people's money just as profoundly as we respect our own."

I waited for Sebastian to shift gears. It took a while. He had to shift from the world of money, where being bought out by a millionaire was the finest thing you could hope for, back to his difficult private world. I liked Sebastian better since I learned that he had tears inside his curly head.

"I've seen your daughter within the last few hours."

"Really? Is she okay?"

"She seemed to be all right physically. Mentally, I don't know."

"Where did you see her?"

"She was with her friend in his apartment. I'm afraid she was in no mood to come home. Sandy seems to have quite a grudge against you and your wife."

I meant this to be a question. Sebastian picked up his daughter's photograph and studied it as if he could find the answer there.

"She always used to be crazy about me," he said. "We were real pals. Until last summer."

"What happened last summer?"

"She turned against me, against both of us. She practically stopped talking entirely, except when she flared up and called us bad things."

"I've heard she had a love affair last summer."

"A love affair? That's impossible at her age."

"It wasn't a happy love affair," I said.

"Who was the man?"

"I was hoping you could tell me."

His face underwent another change. His mouth and jaw went slack. His eyes were intent on something behind them, in his head.

"Where did you hear this?" he said.

"From a friend of hers."

"Are you talking about actual sexual relations?"

"There isn't much doubt that she's been having them, beginning last summer. Don't let it throw you."

But something had. Sebastian had a hang-dog look, and real fear in his eyes. He turned Sandy's picture face down on the desk as if to prevent it from seeing him.

I got out the amateurish map I'd found in Davy's desk and spread it out on top of Sebastian's desk. "Take a good look at this, will you? First of all, do you recognize the handwriting?"

"It looks like Sandy's writing." He picked up the map and studied it more closely. "Yes, I'm sure it's Sandy's. What does it mean?"

"I don't know. Do you recognize the place with the artificial lake?"

Sebastian scratched his head, with the result that one large curly lock fell down over one eye. It made him look furtive and a little shabby. He pushed the hair back carefully, but the shabbiness stayed on him.

"It looks like Mr. Hackett's place," he said.

"Where is it?"

"In the hills above Malibu. It's quite a showplace. But I don't know why Sandy would be drawing a map of it. Do you have any idea?"

"I have one. Before we talk about it I want you to see something. I got your shotgun back, or parts of it."

"What do you mean, parts of it?"

"Come down to the parking lot and I'll show you. I didn't want to bring it into the building."

We went down in the elevator and out to my car. I opened the trunk and unwrapped the sad amputated stock and barrels.

Sebastian picked them up. "Who did this?" He sounded shocked and furious. "Did Sandy do this?"

"More likely it was Davy."

"What kind of a vandal *is* he? That shotgun cost me a hundred and fifty dollars."

"I don't think this was vandalism. But it may lead to something worse. It almost certainly means that Davy's carrying a sawed-off shotgun. Put that together with Sandy's map of the Hackett place—"

"Good Lord, do you think they're planning to hold him up?"

"I think he should be warned of the possibility."

Sebastian made an abortive movement toward the building, then turned back toward me. He was full of anxiety, and some of it spilled. "We can't do that. You can't expect me to tell him my own daughter—"

"She drew the map. Does she know the place well?"

"Very well. The Hacketts have been very good to Sandy."

"Don't you think you owe them a warning?"

"Certainly not at this stage." He tossed the pieces of shotgun into the trunk, where they made a clanking noise. "We don't know for sure that they're planning anything. In fact, the more I think about it, the less likely it sounds. You can't expect me to go out there and ruin myself with the Hacketts—not to mention Sandy—"

"She'll really be ruined if her friend pulls a heist on the Hacketts. And so will you."

He went into deep thought, looking down at the asphalt between his feet. I watched the traffic go by on Wilshire. It usually made me feel better to watch traffic and not be in it. Not today.

"Does Hackett keep money and jewels in the house?"

"He wouldn't keep much money there. But his wife has diamonds. And they have a valuable art collection. Mr. Hackett has spent a lot of time in Europe buying pictures." Sebastian paused. "What would you say to Hackett if you told him about this? I mean, could you keep Sandy out of it?"

"That's the whole point of what I'm trying to do."

"Why didn't you bring her home when you saw her?"

"She didn't want to come. I couldn't force her. I can't force you to go to Hackett with this information, either. But I think you should. Or else take it to the police."

"And get her thrown in jail?"

"They won't put her in jail if she hasn't done anything. Anyway, there are worse places than jail."

He looked at me with dislike. "You don't seem to realize, you're talking about my daughter."

"She's the only thing on my mind. You seem to have quite a few other things on yours. So here we stand while the whole thing slips away."

Sebastian bit his lip. He looked up at the metal and glass building as if for inspiration. But it was just a monument to money. He came closer to me and palpated my upper arm. He squeezed the muscle as if to compliment me and at the same time estimate my strength, in case we might come to blows.

"Look here, Archer, I don't see why you can't go out and talk to Mr. Hackett. Without telling him who's involved. You wouldn't have to mention my name *or* Sandy's."

"Is that what you want me to do?"

"It's the only sensible course. I can't believe that they're really planning anything drastic. Sandy's not a criminal."

"A young girl is whatever she runs with, usually."

"Not my daughter. She's never been in any kind of trouble."

I was tired of arguing with Sebastian. He was a man who believed whatever made him feel better at the moment.

"Have it your way. Was Hackett on his way home when he left you?"

"Yes, I think he was. You will go and see him then?"

"If you insist."

"And keep us out of it?"

"I may not be able to. Remember, Hackett saw me in your office."

"Give him a story. You stumbled across this information and brought it to me because I work for his company. You and I are old friends, nothing more."

A good deal less. I made no promises. He told me how to find Hackett's place, and gave me his unlisted telephone number.

I CALLED THE NUMBER from Malibu. A woman answered, and told me in a foreign accent that her husband wasn't home but she expected him at any moment. When I mentioned Sebastian's name she said she'd have someone meet me at the gate.

It was only a couple of miles from downtown Malibu. The gate was ten feet high, topped with barbed wire. On either side of it, a heavy wire fence plastered with "NO TRESPASSING" signs stretched off into the hills as far as I could see.

The man who was waiting for me at the gate was a lean Spanish type. His tight pants and loose haircut gave a youthful impression which his dark and ageless eyes repudiated. He made no attempt to conceal the heavy revolver in the belt holster under his jacket.

Before he opened the gate he made me show him the photostat of my license. "Okay, man. I guess it's okay."

He unlocked the gate and let me drive in, relocked it as I waited behind his jeep.

"Is Mr. Hackett here yet?"

He shook his head, got into his jeep, and led me up the private blacktop road. Once we had rounded the first curve, the place seemed almost as remote and untouched as back-country. Quail were calling in the brush, and smaller birds were eating the red berries off the toyon. A couple of soaring vultures balanced high on a thermal were keeping an eye on things.

The road mounted a low pass and ran along the crest of the wide earth dam which held back the water of the artificial lake. There were ducks on the water, pintails and cinnamon teal, and mud hens in the grass around its shore.

My escort drew his revolver and, without stopping his jeep, shot the nearest mud hen. I think he was showing off to me. All the ducks flew up, and all the mud hens but one ran like hell into the water, like little animated cartoons of terrified people.

The house was on a rise at the far end of the lake. It was wide and low and handsome, and it fitted the landscape so well that it looked like a piece of it.

Mrs. Hackett was waiting on the terrace in front of the house. She had on a brown wool suit, and her long yellow hair was done up in a loose bun at the nape of her neck. She was in her early thirties, pretty and plump and very fair. She called out angrily to the man in the jeep: "Was it you who fired that gun?"

"I shot a mud hen."

"I've asked you not to do that. It drives away the ducks."

"There's too many mud hens."

She went pale. "Don't talk back to me, Lupe."

They glared at each other. His face was like carved saddle leather. Hers was like Dresden porcelain. Apparently the porcelain won. Lupe drove away in the jeep and disappeared into one of the outbuildings.

I introduced myself. The woman turned to me, but Lupe was still on her mind. "He's insubordinate. I don't know how to handle him. I've been in this country for over ten years and I still don't understand Americans." Her accent was Middle European, probably Austrian or German.

"I've been here for over forty," I said, "and I don't understand Americans, either. Spanish-Americans are particularly hard to understand."

"I'm afraid you're not much help." She smiled, and made a small helpless gesture with her fairly wide shoulders.

"What's Lupe's job?"

"He looks after the place."

"Singlehanded?"

"It isn't as much work as you might think. We have a bonded maintenance service for the house and grounds. My husband dislikes to have servants underfoot. I miss having servants myself, we always had servants at home."

"Where's home?"

"Bayerne," she said with heavy nostalgia. "Near München. My family has lived in the same house since the time of Napoleon."

"How long have you lived here?"

"Ten years. Stephen brought me to this country ten years ago. I'm still not used to it. In Germany the servant classes treat us with respect."

"Lupe doesn't act like a typical servant."

"No, and he isn't typical. My mother-in-law insisted that we hire him. He knows that." She sounded like a woman who needed someone to talk to. She must have heard herself. "I'm afraid I'm talking too much. But why are you asking me these questions?"

"It's a habit of mine. I'm a private detective."

Her eyes blurred with apprehension. "Has Stephen had an accident? Is that why he hasn't come home?"

"I hope not."

She looked at me accusingly. I was the messenger who brought bad news.

"You said on the telephone you were a friend of Keith Sebastian's."

"I know him."

"Has something happened to my husband? Is that what you're trying to say?"

"No. I suppose I'd better tell you why I'm here. May I sit down?"

"Of course. But come inside. It's getting cold out here in the wind."

She led me through a glass door, up a short flight of steps, and along a well-lit gallery hung with pictures. I recognized a Klee and a Kokoschka and a Picasso, and thought it was no wonder the place had a fence around it.

The living room commanded a broad view of the sea, which seemed from this height to slant up to the horizon. A few white sails clung to it like moths on a blue window.

Mrs. Hackett made me sit in an austere-looking steel-and-leather chair which turned out to be comfortable.

"Bauhaus," she said instructively. "Would you like a drink? Benedictine?"

She got a stone bottle and glasses out of a portable bar and poured small drinks for us. Then sat down confidentially with her round silk knees almost touching mine. "Now what is all this business?"

I told her that in the course of an investigation which I didn't specify, I'd stumbled on a couple of facts. Taken together they suggested that she and her husband might be in danger of robbery or extortion.

"Danger from whom?"

"I can't name names. But I think you'd be well advised to have the place guarded."

My advice was punctuated by a distant sound that resembled machine-gun fire. Hackett's red sports car came into view and scooted around the lake toward the house.

"*Ach!*" Mrs. Hackett said. "He's brought his mother with him."

"Doesn't she live here?"

"Ruth lives in Bel-Air. We are not enemies but neither are we friends. She is too close to Stephen. Her husband is younger than Stephen."

I seemed to have won Mrs. Hackett's confidence, and wondered if I really wanted it. She was handsome but a little fat and dull, and full of unpredictable emotions.

Her husband had stopped below the terrace and was helping his mother out of the car. She looked about his age, and dressed it. But if Hackett was forty, his mother had to be at least fifty-six or seven. As she came across the terrace on his arm, I could see the years accumulate behind her youthful façade.

Mrs. Hackett went to the window and waved at them rather lifelessly. The sight of her husband's mother seemed to drain her of energy.

The mother was introduced to me as Mrs. Marburg. She looked at me with the arithmetical eye of an aging professional beauty: would I be viable in bed?

Her son's eye was equally cold and calculating, but he was interested in other questions: "Didn't I see you in Keith Sebastian's office?"

"Yes."

"And you followed me out here? Why? I see you've made yourself cozy."

He meant the glasses on the coffee table. His wife flushed guiltily. His mother said in chiding coquetry: "I know you have a passion for privacy, Stephen. But don't be nasty, now. I'm sure the nice man has a very good explanation."

She reached for his hand. Hackett winced away from her touch, but it seemed to ground some of his static. He said in a more reasonable tone: "What *is* your explanation?"

"It was Sebastian's idea." I sat down and repeated the story I'd told his wife.

It seemed to upset all three of them. Hackett got a bottle of bourbon out of the portable bar and, without offering any of it around, poured himself a solid slug which he knocked back.

His German wife began to weep, without any sound, and then her hair came loose and flooded her shoulders. Hackett's mother sat down beside his wife and patted her broad back with one hand. The other hand plucked at her own throat where crepe had gathered in memory of her youth.

"It would help," Mrs. Marburg said to me, "if you'd lay out all the facts for us. By the way, I didn't catch your name."

"Lew Archer. I'm sorry I can't tell you much more than I have."

"But who are these people? How do we know they exist?"

"Because I say so."

Hackett said: "You could be angling for a bodyguard job."

"Guarding bodies isn't my idea of a decent job. I can give you the name of a good firm if you like." None of them seemed interested. "Of course you can do as you choose. People generally do."

Hackett saw that I was getting ready to leave.

"Now don't rush away, Mr. Archer. I really do appreciate your coming here." The whisky had humanized him, softening his voice and his perspective. "And I certainly don't mean to be inhospitable. Have a drink."

"One was enough, thanks." But I felt more friendly toward him. "You haven't had any threatening phone calls? Or letters asking for money?"

Hackett looked at his wife, and they both shook their heads. He said: "May I ask a question? How do you know this-ah-criminal plot is directed against me?—against us?"

"I don't. But the people involved had a map of your place."

"*This* place, or the beach cottage?"

"This place. I thought that was good enough reason to come out here and talk to you."

"You're very thoughtful," Ruth Marburg said. Her voice was pleasant and a little coarse, a blend of Western drawls ranging from the Pacific Coast to the Gulf Coast. Under the sound of money, her voice remembered times when there hadn't been any. "I think we should pay Mr. Archer for his time."

Hackett got his wallet out and from the assortment of bills it contained selected a twenty. "This will take care of your time."

"Thanks, it's already taken care of."

"Go ahead, take it," Mrs. Marburg said. "It's good clean oil money."

"No thanks."

Hackett looked at me in surprise. I wondered how long it had been since anyone had refused a small piece of his money. When I made a move to leave he followed me into the gallery and started to name the artists represented.

"Do you like pictures?"

"Very much."

But Hackett's recital bored me. He told me how much each picture cost and how much it was worth now. He said he had made a profit on every picture he'd bought in the past ten years.

"Bully for you."

He cocked a pale eye at me. "Is that supposed to be funny?"

"No."

"That's good." But he was peeved. I'd failed to show proper respect for him and his money. "After all, you said that you were interested in paintings. These are some of the most valuable modern paintings in California."

"You told me."

"Very well, if you're not interested." He turned away, and then came back to me. "One thing I don't understand. Where does Keith Sebastian come in on all this?"

I told the lie I'd hoped to avoid telling: "I knew Keith worked for one of your companies. I went to him, and he sent me out here."

"I see."

Before Hackett saw too much, I got into my car and started for the gate. Lupe followed me in his jeep.

The ducks had not returned to the lake. The frightened mud hens had crossed to the far shore. In the distance they looked like a congregation of mourners.

ON MY WAY BACK into the city I stopped at the Laurel Apartments to see if Davy and Sandy had come back there. The door of Laurel Smith's apartment was standing partly open. She didn't answer when I knocked. I listened, and heard the sound of snoring deep inside the place. I guessed that Laurel had drunk herself unconscious.

But when I went in and found her in the bathtub, I saw that she'd been hit by something heavier than alcohol. Her nose was bleeding and swollen; her eyes were puffed shut, her lips cut. The bathtub was dry, except for splashes of blood. Laurel still had on her orange and black housecoat.

I went to the phone and called the police, and asked at the same time for an ambulance. In the minutes before they arrived I gave the place a quick shakedown. The first thing I looked at was the portable television set. Laurel's account of winning it in a contest had sounded to me like a plant.

I took the back off. Glued to the inside of the cabinet was a plastic-encased bug, a miniature radio transmitter no larger than a pack of cigarettes. I left the bug where it was, and replaced the back of the set.

The other unusual thing I found was a negative fact. Nothing I came across in my hurried search suggested that Laurel Smith had a personal history: no letters or old photographs or documents. I did find, in a purse in a bedroom drawer, a savings bank book with deposits totaling over six thousand dollars, and a dog-eared Social Security card in the name of Laurel Blevins.

The same drawer contained a sparsely populated address-book in which I found two names I recognized: Jacob Belsize, and Mr. and Mrs. Edward Spanner. I made a note of the Spanners' address, which wasn't too far from my own apartment in West Los Angeles. Then I put everything back in the drawer and pushed it shut.

I could hear the sound of the police siren rising from Pacific Coast Highway. It was a sound I hated: the howl of disaster in the urban barrens. It climbed Chautauqua and died like a wolf in Elder Street. The ambulance was whining in the distance.

I knew the two policemen who came in. Janowski and Prince were detective-sergeants from the Purdue Street station, men in their late thirties who were proud of their work and good at it. I had to tell them what I was doing there, but I suppressed Sandy's name. I gave them Davy Spanner's.

Prince said: "Did Spanner do that?" He jerked his thumb toward the bathroom, where by now two ambulance men were getting Laurel Smith onto a stretcher.

"I doubt it. They were good friends."

"How good?" Janowski said. He was a homely broad-faced Baltic type with a fair delicate skin.

"She gave him a job when he got out of jail."

"That's pretty good friends," Prince said. "What was he in for?"

"Car theft."

"So now he's doing postgraduate work in mayhem." Prince took crime personally. He was a former Golden Gloves welterweight who could have gone either way in his own life. Like me.

I didn't argue with them. If they picked up Davy, they'd probably be doing him a favor. And the afternoon was slipping away. I wanted to see the Spanners before it got too late.

We went outside and watched Laurel Smith being lifted into the ambulance. Three or four of the apartment dwellers, all women, had drifted out onto the sidewalk. Laurel was their landlady, and they undoubtedly knew her, but they didn't come too near. The snoring woman gave off the germs of disaster.

Janowski said to one of the attendants: "How bad is she hurt?"

"It's hard to say, with head injuries. She has a broken nose, and jaw, maybe a fractured skull. I don't think it was done with fists."

"With what?"

"A sap, or a truncheon."

Prince was questioning the women from the apartment building: none of them had heard or seen a thing. They were quiet and sub-dued, like birds when a hawk is in the neighborhood.

The ambulance rolled away. The women went into the building.

Prince got into the police car and made a report in a low-pitched monotone.

Janowski went back into Laurel's apartment. I walked up to Los Baños Street for a second look at the house with volcanic rock built into the front. The drapes were still drawn. The Cougar was no longer in the driveway.

I wandered around to the back and found an unblinded sliding glass door. The room inside contained no furniture. I looked around the small back yard. It was overgrown with dry crabgrass, which the rains had failed to revive, and surrounded by a five-foot grapestake fence.

A woman looked over the fence from the next yard. She was an attempted blonde whose eyes were magnified by purple eye shadow.

"What do *you* want?"

"I'm looking for the man of the house."

"Big fellow with a bald head?"

"That's him."

"He left about an hour ago. It looked to me like he was moving out. Which would suit me just fine."

"How so?"

She threw me a sorrowful purple look over the grapestake fence. "You a friend of his?"

"I wouldn't say that."

"What do you want with him?"

"He was the one who wanted me. He called me out here to do some repairs."

"On that electronic equipment he had?"

"Right."

"You're too late. He took it with him. Piled it in the trunk of his car and took off. Good riddance, I say."

"Did he cause you any trouble?"

"Nothing you could put your finger on. But it was creepy having him next door, sitting all alone in an empty house. I think he's cracked myself."

"How do you know the house was empty?"

"I have my two good eyes," she said. "All he took in when he moved in was a camp cot and a folding chair and a card table and that radio equipment. And that was all he took out when he left."

"How long was he here?"

"A couple of weeks, off and on. I was getting ready to complain to Mr. Santee. It runs down the neighborhood when you don't put furniture in a house."

"Who's Mr. Santee?"

"Alex Santee. The agent I rent from. He's agent for that house, too."

"Where can I find Mr. Santee?"

"He has an office on Sunset." She pointed toward the Palisades downtown. "You've got to excuse me now, I've got something on the stove."

I went to the other side of the yard and looked downhill across several other back yards. I could see Laurel Smith's apartment. Her open door was in my direct line of vision. Detective-Sergeant Janowski came out and closed the door.

>>>>>>>>>
>>>>>>>>> *chapter* 10
>>>>>>>>>

ALEX SANTEE was a small middle-aged man with a bold stare masked by glasses. He was just closing his real-estate office when I arrived, but he was glad to stay open for a prospect.

"I only have a few minutes, though. I've an appointment to show a house."

"I'm interested in a house on Los Baños Street. 702, the one with the lava front."

"It is distinctive, isn't it? Unfortunately it's rented."

"Since when? It's standing empty."

"Since November 15 of this year. Do you mean the party hasn't moved in yet?"

"He's been and gone, according to the neighbors. Moved out today."

"That's peculiar." Santee shrugged. "Well, that's his privilege. If Fleischer has moved out, the house will be available for rental on the fifteenth of this month. Three hundred and fifty a month on a one-year lease, first and last months payable in advance."

"Maybe I better talk to him first. Did you say his name was Fleischer?"

"Jack Fleischer." Santee looked it up in his file and spelled it out. "The address he gave me was the Dorinda Hotel in Santa Monica."

"Did he say what business he was in?"

"He's a retired sheriff from someplace up north." He consulted the file again. "Santa Teresa. Maybe he decided to go back there."

The desk clerk at the Dorinda Hotel, a sad man with an exuberant pompadour hairpiece, didn't remember Jack Fleischer at first. After some research in the register he established that about a month ago, early in November, Fleischer had stayed there two nights.

In a passageway at the rear of the lobby, I found a phone booth and called the Spanners' number. A man's deep voice answered: "This is the Edward Spanner residence."

"Mr. Spanner?"

"Yes."

"This is Lew Archer. Mr. Jacob Belsize gave me your name. I'm conducting an investigation and I'd like very much to talk to you—"

"About Davy?" His voice had thinned.

"About Davy and a number of other things."

"Has he done something wrong again?"

"His employer has been beaten up. They just took her to the hospital."

"You mean Mrs. Smith? He never hurt a woman before."

"I'm not saying he did this. You know him better than anybody does, Mr. Spanner. Please give me a few minutes."

"But we were just sitting down to supper. I don't know why you people can't leave us alone. Davy hasn't lived with us for years. We never did adopt him, we're not legally responsible."

I cut him short: "I'll be there in half an hour."

The sun was setting as I left the hotel. It looked like a wildfire threatening the western edge of the city. Night comes quickly in Los Angeles. The fire was burnt out when I reached the Spanner house, and evening hung like thin smoke in the air.

It was a prewar stucco bungalow squeezed into a row of other houses like it. I knocked on the front door, and Edward Spanner opened it reluctantly. He was a tall thin man with a long face and emotional eyes. He had a lot of black hair, not only on his head but on his arms and on the backs of his hands. He was wearing a striped shirt with the sleeves rolled up, and gave off an old-fashioned impression, almost an odor, of soured good will.

"Come in, Mr. Archer. Welcome to our abode." He sounded like a man who had taught himself to speak correctly by reading books.

He took me through the living room, with its threadbare furnishings and its mottoes on the walls, into the kitchen where his wife was sitting at the table. She wore a plain housedress which emphasized the angularity of her body. There were marks of suffering on her face, relieved by a soft mouth and responsive eyes.

The Spanners resembled each other, and seemed very much aware of each other, unusually so for middle-aged people. Mrs. Spanner seemed rather afraid of her husband, or afraid for him.

"This is Mr. Archer, Martha. He wants to talk about Davy."

She hung her head. Her husband said by way of explanation: "Since you called me, my wife has made a little confession. Davy was here this afternoon while I was working. Apparently she wasn't going to tell me." He was speaking more to her than to me. "For all I know he comes here every day behind my back."

He'd gone too far, and she caught him off balance. "That isn't so, and you know it. And I was *so* going to tell you. I simply didn't want it to spoil your dinner." She turned to me, evading the direct confrontation with Spanner. "My husband has an ulcer. This business has been hard on both of us."

As if to illustrate her words, Spanner sat down at the head of the table and let his arms hang loose. A half-eaten plate of brown stew lay in front of him, glazing. I sat facing his wife across the table.

"When was Davy here?"

"A couple of hours ago," she said.

"Was anybody with him?"

"He had his girl friend with him. His fiancée. She's a *pretty* girl." The woman seemed surprised.

"What kind of a mood were they in?"

"They both seemed quite excited. They're planning to get married, you know."

Edward Spanner uttered a dry snortlike laugh.

"Did Davy tell you that?" I asked his wife.

"They both did." She smiled a little dreamily. "I realize they're young. But I was glad to see he picked a nice girl. I gave them a ten-dollar bill for a wedding present."

Spanner cried out in pain: "You gave him ten dollars? I cut ten heads of hair to clear ten dollars."

"I saved up the money. It wasn't your money."

Spanner shook his doleful head. "No wonder he went bad. From the first day he came into our household you spoiled him rotten."

"I didn't. I gave him affection. He needed some, after those years in the orphanage."

She leaned over and touched her husband's shoulder, almost as if he and Davy were the same to her.

He rebounded into deeper despair: "We should have left him in the orphanage."

"You don't mean that, Edward. The three of us had ten good years."

"Did we? Hardly a day went by that I didn't have to use the razor strap on him. If I never heard of Davy again, I'd—"

She touched his mouth. "Don't say it. You care about him just as much as I do."

"After what he *did* to us?"

She looked across him at me. "My husband can't help feeling bitter. He put a lot of stock in Davy. He was a real good father to him, too. But Davy needed more than we could give him. And when he got into trouble the first time the Holy Brethren of the Immaculate Conception asked Edward to step aside as a lay preacher. That was a terrible blow to him, and with one thing and another we left town and moved here. Then Edward came down with his ulcer, and after that he was out of work for a long time—most of the last three years. Under the circumstances we couldn't do much for Davy. He was running loose by that time, anyway, running loose and living on his own most of the time."

Spanner was embarrassed by his wife's candor: "This is all ancient history."

"It's what I came to hear. You say you moved here from another town?"

"We lived most of our lives in Santa Teresa," she said.

"Do you know a man named Jack Fleischer?"

She looked at her husband. "Isn't that the name of the man who was here last month?"

I prompted them: "Big man with a bald head? Claims to be a retired policeman."

"That's him," she said. "He asked us a lot of questions about Davy, mainly his background. We told him what little we knew. We got him out of the Santa Teresa Shelter when he was six years old. He didn't have a last name, and so we gave him ours. I wanted to adopt him, but Edward felt we weren't up to the responsibility."

"She means," Spanner put in, "that if we adopted him the county wouldn't pay us for his board."

"But we treated him just like he was our own. We never had any children of our own. And I'll never forget the first time we saw him in the supervisor's office at the Shelter. He came right over to us and stood beside Edward and wouldn't go away. 'I want to stand beside the man,' was what he said. You remember, Edward."

He remembered. There was sorrowful pride in his eyes.

"Now he stands as tall as you do. I wish you'd seen him today."

She was quite a woman, I thought: trying to create a family out of a runaway boy and a reluctant husband, a wholeness out of disappointed lives.

"Do you know who his real parents were, Mrs. Spanner?"

"No, he was just an orphan. Some fieldworker died and left him in the tules. I found that out from the other man—Fleischer."

"Did Fleischer say why he was interested in Davy?"

"I didn't ask him. I was afraid to ask, with Davy on probation and all." She hesitated, peering into my face. "Do you mind if I ask you the same question?"

Spanner answered for me: "Mrs. Laurel Smith got beat up. I told you that."

Her eyes widened. "Davy wouldn't do that to Mrs. Smith. She was the best friend he had."

"I don't know what he'd do," Spanner said morosely. "Remember he hit a high-school teacher and that was the beginning of all our trouble."

"Was it a woman teacher?" I said.

"No, it was a man. Mr. Langston at the high school. There's one thing you can't get away with, and that's hitting a teacher. They wouldn't let him back in school after that. We didn't know what to do with him. He couldn't get a job. It's one reason we moved down here. Nothing went right for us after that." He spoke of the move as if it had been a banishment.

"There was more to it than hitting a teacher," his wife said.

"Henry Langston wasn't a teacher really. He was what they call a counselor. He was trying to counsel Davy when it happened."

"Counsel him on what?"

"I never did get that clear."

Spanner turned to her: "Davy has mental trouble. You never faced up to that. But it's time you did. He had mental trouble from the time we took him out of the Shelter. He never warmed up to me. He was never a normal boy."

Slowly she wagged her head from side to side in stubborn negation. "I don't believe it."

Their argument had evidently been going on for years. Probably it would last as long as they did. I interrupted it: "You saw him today, Mrs. Spanner. Did he seem to have trouble on his mind?"

"Well, he's never cheerful. And he seemed to be pretty tense. Any young man is, these days, when he's getting ready to marry."

"Were they serious about getting married?"

"I'd say very serious. They could hardly wait." She turned to her husband: "I didn't mean to tell you this, but I guess it should all come out. Davy thought that maybe you would marry them. I explained you had no legal right, being just a lay preacher."

"I wouldn't marry him to anybody, anyway. I've got too much respect for the race of females."

"Did they say anything more about their plans, Mrs. Spanner? Where did they plan to get married?"

"They didn't say."

"And you don't know where they went after they left here?"

"No, I don't." But her eyes seemed to focus inward, as if she was remembering something.

"Didn't they give you some inkling?"

She hesitated. "You never answered *my* question. Why are you so interested? You don't really think he beat up Mrs. Smith?"

"No. But people are always surprising me."

She studied my face, leaning her elbows on the table. "You don't talk like a policeman. Are you one?"

"I used to be. I'm a private detective now—I'm not trying to pin anything on Davy."

"What *are* you trying to do?"

"Make sure the girl is safe. Her father hired me for that. She's only seventeen. She should have been in school today, not bucketing around the countryside."

No matter how unrewarding their own married lives may be, women seem to love the idea of weddings. Mrs. Spanner's wedding dream died hard. I watched it die.

"When I was out here in the kitchen making tea for them," she said, "I heard them talking in the living room. They were reading the wall mottoes out loud and making fun of them. That wasn't very nice, but maybe I shouldn't have been listening to them. Anyway, they made a joke about the Unseen Guest. Davy said that Daddy Warbucks was going to have an unseen guest tonight."

Spanner exploded: "That's blasphemy!"

"Was anything else said on the subject?"

"He asked the girl was she sure she could get him in. She said it would be easy, Louis knew her."

"Louis?" I said. "Or Lupe?"

"It could have been Lupe. Yes, I'm pretty sure it was. Do you know who they were talking about?"

"I'm afraid I do. May I use your telephone?"

"Long as it isn't long distance," Spanner said prudently.

I gave him a dollar and called the Hacketts' number in Malibu. A woman's voice which I didn't recognize at first answered the phone. I said:

"Is Stephen Hackett there?"

"Who is calling, please?"

"Lew Archer. Is that Mrs. Marburg?"

"It is." Her voice was thin and dry. "You were a good prophet, Mr. Archer."

"Has something happened to your son?"

"You're such a good prophet I wonder if it's prophecy. Where are you?"

"In West Los Angeles."

"Come out here right away, will you? I'll tell my husband to open the gate."

I left without telling the Spanners where I was going or why. On my way to Malibu I stopped at my apartment to pick up a revolver.

THE HACKETTS' GATE was standing open. I expected to find police cars in front of the house, but the only car standing under the floodlights was a new blue Mercedes convertible. The young man who went with it came out of the house to meet me.

"Mr. Archer? I'm Sidney Marburg."

He gave me a hard competitive handshake. On second look he wasn't so very young. His smile was probably porcelain, and the smile-lines radiating from it could just as well have been worry-lines. His narrow black eyes were opaque in the light.

"What happened, Mr. Marburg?"

"I'm not too clear about it myself, I wasn't here when it happened. Apparently Stephen's been kidnapped. A young chick and a boy with a shotgun took him away in their car."

"Where was Lupe?"

"Lupe was here. He still is—lying down with a bloody head. The boy got out of the trunk of their car and held a sawed-off shotgun on him. The girl hit him over the head with a hammer or a tire iron."

"The girl did that?"

He nodded. "What makes it even queerer, it seems to be someone the family knows. My wife wants to talk to you."

Marburg took me into the library where his wife was sitting under a lamp, with a phone and a revolver at her elbow. She seemed calm, but her face had a look of chilled surprise. She forced a smile.

"Thank you for coming. Sidney's a charming boy, but he's not much practical use." She turned to him. "Now run along and play with your paints or something."

He stood resentfully between her and the door. His mouth opened and closed.

"Go on now like a good boy. Mr. Archer and I have things to discuss."

Marburg walked out. I sat on the leather hassock that matched her chair. "Where's Mrs. Hackett?"

"Gerda went to pieces—par for the course. Fortunately I always carry chloral hydrate. I gave her a couple of capsules and she cried herself to sleep."

"So everything's under control."

"Everything's busted wide open, and you know it. Are you going to help me put it back together?"

"I have a client."

She disregarded this. "I can pay you a good deal of money."

"How much?"

"A hundred thousand."

"That's too much."

She gave me a narrow, probing look. "I saw you turn down twenty dollars today. But nobody ever turned down a hundred grand."

"It isn't real money. You're offering it to me because you think I may be in on an extortion deal. No such luck."

"Then how did you know about it before it happened?"

"I came across the evidence. They left the map of this place lying around, almost as if they wanted to be stopped. Which doesn't make them any less dangerous."

"I know they're dangerous. I saw them. The two of them came right into the living room and marched Stephen out to their car. In their dark glasses they looked like creatures from another planet."

"Did you recognize either of them?"

"Gerda recognized the girl right away. She's been a guest here more than once. Her name is Alexandria Sebastian."

She turned and looked at me in surmise. I was glad the secret was coming out.

"Keith Sebastian is my client."

"And he knew about this?"

"He knew his daughter had run away. Then he knew what I told him, which wasn't much. Let's not get involved in recriminations. The important thing is to get your son back."

"I agree. My offer stands. A hundred thousand if Stephen comes home safe."

"The police do this work for free."

She pushed the idea away with her hand. "I don't want them. So often they solve the case and lose the victim. I want my son back alive."

"I can't guarantee it."

"I *know* that," she said impatiently. "Will you try?" She pressed both hands to her breast, then offered them to me, empty. Her emotion was both theatrical and real.

"I'll try," I said. "I think you're making a mistake, though. You should use the police."

"I've already said I wouldn't. I don't trust them."

"But you trust me?"

"Shouldn't I? Yes, I do, up to a point."

"So does Keith Sebastian. I'm going to have to check with him on this."

"I don't see why. He's one of our employees."

"Not when he's on his own time. His daughter is missing, remember. He feels about her just as strongly as you do about your son." Not quite, perhaps, but I gave Sebastian the benefit of the doubt.

"We'll get him out here." Abruptly she reached for the phone. "What's his number?"

"We're wasting time."

"I asked you for his number."

I looked it up in my black book. She dialed, and got Sebastian on the first ring. He must have been sitting beside the telephone.

"Mr. Sebastian? This is Ruth Marburg. Stephen Hackett's mother. I'm at his Malibu place now, and I'd very much like to see you . . . Yes, tonight. Immediately, in fact. How soon can you get here? . . . Very well, I'll look for you in half an hour. You won't disappoint me, will you?"

She hung up and looked at me quietly, almost sweetly. Her hand was still on the phone, as if she was taking Sebastian's pulse by remote control.

"He wouldn't be in on this with his daughter, would he? I know that Stephen isn't always popular with the hired help."

"Is that what we are, Mrs. Marburg?"

"Don't change the subject. I asked you a straight question."

"The answer is no. Sebastian doesn't have that kind of guts. Anyway he practically worships your son."

"Why?" she asked me bluntly.

"Money. He has a passion for the stuff."

"Are you *sure* he didn't put the girl up to this?"

"I'm sure."

"Then what in hell does she think she's doing?"

"She seems to be in revolt, against everyone over thirty. Your son was the biggest target within reach. I doubt that she picked the target, though. Davy Spanner's probably the main instigator."

"What does he want? Money?"

"I haven't figured out what he wants. Do you know of any connection between him and your son? This could be a personal thing."

She shook her head. "Maybe if you tell me what you know about him."

I gave her a quick rundown on Davy Spanner, son of a migrant laborer, orphaned at three or four and institutionalized, then taken by foster parents; a violent dropout from high school, a wandering teenager, car thief, jail graduate, candidate for more advanced felonies, possibly somewhat crazy in the head.

Ruth Marburg listened to me with a suspicious ear. "You sound almost sympathetic."

"I almost am," I said, though my kidneys were still sore. "Davy Spanner didn't make himself."

She answered me with deliberate roughness: "Don't give me that crap. I know these psychopaths. They're like dogs biting the hands that feed them."

"Has Spanner had previous contact with your family?"

"No. Not that I know of."

"But the girl has."

"Not with me. With Gerda, Stephen's wife. The girl was interested in languages, or pretended to be. Gerda took her under her wing last summer. She'll know better next time, if the family survives this."

I was getting impatient with the conversation. We seemed to have been sitting in the room for a long time. Book-lined, with the windows heavily draped, it was like an underground bunker cut off from the world of life.

Ruth Marburg must have sensed or shared my feeling. She went to one of the windows and pulled back the drapes. We looked out at the broken necklace of lights along the shore.

"I still can't believe it happened," she said. "Stephen has always been so careful. It's one reason they don't have servants."

"What's Lupe?"

"We hardly think of him as a servant. He's really the manager of the estate."

"A friend of yours?"

"I wouldn't say that, exactly. We get along." Her half-smile, and the way she held her body, gave the words a sexual connotation.

"May I talk to Lupe?"

"Not now. He's a pretty sick man."

"Should he have a doctor?"

"I'm going to get him one." She turned and faced me, visibly shaken by her own angry force. "You needn't take responsibility for things you're not responsible for. I'm hiring you to get my son back alive."

"You haven't hired me yet."

"And I may not." She turned back to the window. "What's keeping him?" She clenched her hands and rapped the knuckles together, making a noise which reminded me that she contained a skeleton.

As if he'd heard it, or felt her impatient will, Sebastian turned up almost immediately. His big car threw its lights up over the pass, came around the dark lake, and stopped under the floodlights.

"You took your time," Mrs. Marburg said at the door.

"I'm sorry. I had a phone call as I was leaving. I had to take it."

Sebastian seemed tremendously excited. He was pale and brilliant-eyed. He looked from the woman to me.

"What's up?"

Ruth Marburg answered grimly: "Come in, I'll tell you what's up." She led us into the library and closed the door emphatically, like a warder. "Your precious daughter has stolen my son."

"What do you mean?"

"She drove in here with her bully-boy hidden in the trunk of her car. Knocked out our manager with a tire iron. Walked into the house with bully-boy and marched Stephen out to their car and took him away."

"But that's insane."

"It happened."

"When?"

"Just before sundown. That was about five thirty. It's after eight now. The question is, what are you going to do about it?"

"Anything. I'll do anything."

A delayed rush of tears almost blinded him. He wiped them with his fingers, stood swaying in the light with his hands covering his eyes.

"You're *sure* it was Sandy?"

"Yes. My daughter-in-law knows her well. Mr. Archer here virtually predicted it was going to happen. Which brings me to the reason why you're here. I want Mr. Archer to get my son back for me."

"This means," I told him, "that you and I may be on opposite sides. Your daughter has helped to commit a major crime. I'm afraid I can't protect her from the consequences."

"But I'll expect you to cooperate with Archer," Mrs. Marburg told him. "If you hear from your daughter, for example, you've got to let him know."

"Yes." He nodded several times. "I promise I'll cooperate. Thank you for—thank you for telling me."

She waved him away, out of her sight.

"Well," she said to me when he had left the room, "do you think he put her up to it?"

"You know he didn't."

"Don't tell me what I know. People are capable of anything. Even the nicest people, and he's not one of them." She added: "Neither am I, in case you were in doubt."

"We're wasting time."

She had the last word: "You're on my time. On your way out, will you tell my husband to bring me a double Scotch. I'm as tired as death."

She slumped into her chair and let her face and body droop like Plasticine. Her husband was in the lighted gallery looking at the pictures. I delivered her message to him.

"Thanks, old fellow. Don't work too hard on this assignment, will you? If Stephen doesn't come back, all this comes to Ruth and me. I love good paintings."

Marburg was half-serious, which was all he'd ever be. I went outside where Sebastian was waiting in my car. He was gnawing at a thumbnail. It was bleeding.

I got in behind the wheel. "Do you have something to tell me?"

"Yes. I was afraid to say it in front of her. That telephone call just before I left my house—it was from Sandy. She wanted me to come and get her."

"Where?"

"Santa Teresa. She was cut off before she could give me directions."

"Did she say where she was calling from?"

"No, but it was a collect call and the operator was able to trace it for me. Sandy used the office phone in the Power Plus station on this side of Santa Teresa. We've often driven up weekends, and stopped at that very station."

"I'd better get up there now."

"Take me along," he said. "Please."

I turned and looked into his face. I didn't like him much, or trust him very far. But I was liking him better as time passed.

"How well do you drive?"

"I don't have accidents, and I haven't been drinking."

"Okay, we'll take my car."

Sebastian left his in a Malibu parking lot next door to a drive-in. I had a quick sandwich, which tasted of highway fumes, while he phoned his wife. Then he phoned the Power Plus station in Santa Teresa.

"They're open till midnight," he told me. "And the man remembered Sandy."

My watch said nine fifteen. It had been a long day, and I expected to be up most of the night. I climbed into the back seat and went to sleep.

>>>>>>>>>
>>>>>>>>> *chapter* 12
>>>>>>>>>

THE TURNING OFF of the engine woke me from dreams of supersonic flight. My car was standing beside the pumps in the hard white glare of the Power Plus station. A young man in coveralls came out of the office. He had one thin leg and wore a special boot. He moved with great rapidity, though it was late and his face was drawn.

"What can I do for you?" he asked Sebastian.

"I called you earlier. About my daughter." His voice was low and uncertain, like a beggar's.

"I see." The pain and fatigue in the attendant's face turned into sympathy, and altered the quality of the transaction. "Is she a runaway, something like that?"

"Something like that." I got out of the car to talk to him. "Was she driving a green compact?"

"Yeah. She stopped it right where your car is standing, asked me to fill the tank. It was nearly empty, it took over nineteen gallons."

"Did you see the others?"

"There was only the one other, the big fellow with the crew cut. He stayed in the car until he saw her phoning. She *said* she wanted to go to the ladies' room. I left the pump running and went to the office to get the key for her. Then she asked me if she could use the phone for a distance call. I said, if she made it collect, which she did. I stayed there to monitor her, like. Then the other one came charging in and made her quit."

"Did he use force?"

"He didn't hit her. He put his arms around her, more like a hug. Then she broke down and cried, and he took her back to the car. She paid for the gas and drove away herself, in the direction of town." He gestured toward Santa Teresa.

"You didn't see a gun?"

"No. She acted afraid of him, though."

"Did he say anything?"

"Just when he came charging into the office. He said she was crazy to call her folks, that they were her worst enemies."

Sebastian muttered something inarticulate.

"Hers, or his?" I said.

"Both of them. I think he said '*their* worst enemies.'"

"You're a good witness. What's your name?"

"Fred Cram."

I offered him a dollar.

"You don't have to pay me." He spoke with gentle force. "I'm sorry I couldn't do more. Maybe I should have tried to stop them, or called the police or something. Only I didn't think I had the right."

An old Chevrolet painted with brown undercoat rolled in from the street and stopped beside the pumps. A couple of teen-age boys occupied the front seat. The bare feet of two others projected from the rear window. The driver honked for service.

I asked Fred Cram again: "Are you sure there wasn't a third person in the car?"

He pondered the question. "Not unless you count the dog."

"What kind of a dog?"

"I don't know. It sounded like a big one."

"You didn't see it?"

"It was in the trunk. I could hear it breathing and kind of whining."

"How do you know it was a dog?"

"She said so."

Sebastian groaned.

"You mean it was a human being in there?" the young man said.

"I don't know."

Fred Cram gave me a long questioning look. His face saddened as he realized the depth of the trouble he had dipped into. Then the teen-ager honked again, imperiously, and he swung away on his mismatched legs.

"Jesus," Sebastian said in the car. "It really happened. We've got to get her back, Archer."

"We will." I didn't let him hear my doubts, the doubt that we could find her, the graver doubt that the law would let him keep her if we did. "The best contribution you can make is to get in touch with your wife and stay by a telephone. Sandy phoned home once, she may again."

"If he lets her."

But he accepted my suggestion. We checked into adjoining rooms in a beach motel near the center of Santa Teresa. It was the depth of the winter season, and the place was almost deserted. The yacht harbor under my window hung in the starlight like a dim white fantasy of summer.

The keyboy opened the door between our two rooms. I listened to Sebastian talking to his wife on the telephone. He told her with brisk cheerfulness that the case was progressing rapidly and she had nothing to worry about at all. The fine front he was putting on reminded me somehow of the young man with the thin leg, limping faster than other men could walk.

"I love you, too," Sebastian said, and hung up.

I went to the doorway. "How is your wife taking this?"

"Terrific. She's terrific."

But his gaze wandered around the room, taking in the details of his catastrophe: the lonely bed, the homeless walls, and my face watching him.

I tried to smile. "I'm going out for a bit. I'll check back with you later."

"What are you planning to do?"

"Pay a couple of visits to people in town."

"It's late for visiting."

"All the better. They're more likely to be home."

I went back into my room, got the directory out of the drawer in the telephone table, and looked up Henry Langston, the counselor who had had a run-in with Davy Spanner. A young girl answered Langston's phone, and for a moment I thought by some remarkable coincidence it was Sandy.

"Who is that?" I asked her.

"Elaine. I'm just the baby-sitter. Mr. and Mrs. Langston are out for the evening."

"When do you expect them back?"

"They *promised* by midnight. You want to leave a message?"

"No thanks."

Coincidences seldom happen in my work. If you dig deep enough, you can nearly always find their single bifurcating roots. It was probably no coincidence that Jack Fleischer had taken off, presumably for his home in Santa Teresa, immediately after Laurel Smith was beaten. I looked him up in the directory and found his address: 33 Pine Street.

It was a street of older middle-class houses, appropriately pine-shaded, within walking distance of the courthouse. Most of the houses in the block were dark. I parked at the corner in front of an old church, and walked along the street looking for Fleischer's number with my flashlight.

I found two rusty metal three's attached to the porch of a two-story white frame house. There was light in the house, dim yellow behind drawn blinds. I knocked on the front door.

Uncertain footsteps approached the door and a woman's voice spoke through it: "What do you want?"

"Is Mr. Fleischer home?"

"No."

But she opened the door in order to peer out at me. She was a middle-aged blond woman whose face had been carefully made up at some point earlier in the day. Erosion had set in. In the midst of it her eyes regarded me with that steady look of hurt suspicion which takes years to develop.

There was gin on her breath, and it triggered an association in my mind. She looked enough like Laurel Smith to be her older sister.

"Mrs. Fleischer?"

She nodded grimly. "I don't know you, do I?"

"I'm better acquainted with your husband. Do you know where I can find him?"

She spread her hands. Under her quilted pink housecoat her body was sullen. "Search me."

"It's pretty important. I've come all the way from Los Angeles."

Her hand came out and clenched on my arm. I felt like a stand-in for Fleischer. "What's Jack been doing down there?"

"I'm afraid that's confidential."

"You can tell me. I'm his wife." She jerked at my arm. "Come in, I'll give you a drink. Any friend of Jack's—"

I let her take me into the large drab living room. It had an air of not being lived in, just being endured. The main ornaments of the room were Fleischer's shooting trophies on the mantel.

"What will you have? I'm drinking gin on the rocks."

"That will suit me."

She padded out of the room and came back with lowball glasses full of ice and gin.

I sipped at mine. "Cheers."

"Here, have a seat." She indicated a slip-covered davenport and sat down crowding me. "You were going to tell me what Jack is up to."

"I don't know all the ramifications. He seems to be doing an investigative job—"

She shut me off impatiently. "Don't let him fool you. And don't you cover up for him, either. There's a woman in it, isn't there? He's got another place in L.A. and that woman is living with him again. Isn't that right?"

"You know him better than I do."

"You bet I do. We've been married for thirty years, and for half of those thirty years he's been chasing the same skirt." She leaned toward me with an avid mouth. "Have you see the woman?"

"I've seen her."

"Say I show you a picture of her," she said, "are you willing to tell me if it's the same woman?"

"If you'll help me locate Jack."

She gave my question serious thought. "He's headed for the Bay area, God knows why. I thought at least he'd be staying overnight. But he took a shower and changed his clothes and ate the dinner I cooked for him, and then he was off again."

"Where in the Bay area?"

"The Peninsula. I heard him call Palo Alto before he left. He made a reservation at the Sandman Motor Hotel. That's all I know. He doesn't tell me anything any more, and I know why. He's after that piece of skirt again. He had that light in his eye." Her voice buzzed with resentment, like a hornet caught in a web. She drowned it with gin. "I'll show you her picture."

She set down her empty glass on a table inset with polished bits of stone, left the room and came back. She thrust a small photograph at me, and turned up the three-way lamp.

"That's her, isn't it?"

It was a full-face picture of Laurel Smith, taken when she was a dark-haired girl in her twenties. Even in this small and carelessly printed photograph, her beauty showed through. I remembered her beaten face as they lifted her into the ambulance, and I had a delayed shock, a sense of something valuable being destroyed by time and violence.

Mrs. Fleischer repeated her question. I answered her carefully: "I *think* it is. Where did you get this picture?"

"I got it out of Jack's wallet while he was taking his shower. He started carrying it again. It's an old picture he's had for a long time."

"How long?"

"Let's see." She counted on her fingers. "Fifteen years. It was fifteen years ago he picked her up. He kept her in Rodeo City, claimed she was a witness, that everything he did was strictly business. But the only crime *she* ever witnessed was Deputy Jack Fleischer taking off his pants."

There was sly satisfaction in her eyes. She was betraying her husband to me just as completely as he had betrayed her. And as an old cop's wife, she was betraying herself.

She took the picture and laid it on the table and picked up her glass. "Drink up. We'll have another."

I didn't argue. Cases break in different ways. This case was opening, not like a door or even a grave, certainly not like a rose or any flower, but opening like an old sad blonde with darkness at her core.

I emptied my glass, and she took it out to the kitchen for a refill. I think while she was out of the room she sneaked an extra drink for herself. Coming back she bumped the doorframe of the living room and spilled gin on her hands.

I took both glasses from her and set them down on the stony table. She swayed in front of me, her eyes unfocused. She forced them back into focus, the cobweb of fine lines surrounding them cutting deep into her flesh.

"It's the same woman, isn't it?" she said.

"I'm pretty sure it is. Do you know her name?"

"She called herself Laurel Smith in Rodeo City."

"She still does."

"Jack's living with her in L.A., isn't he?"

"Nobody's living with her that I know of."

"Don't try to kid me. You men are always covering up for each other. But I know when a man's spending money on a woman. He took more than a thousand dollars out of our savings account in less than a month. And I have to beg him for twelve dollars to get my hair done." She pushed her fingers through her fine dry wavy hair. "Is she still pretty?"

"Pretty enough." I gathered my élan together, and paid her a compliment. "As a matter of fact, she looks quite a bit like you."

"They always do. The women he goes for always look like me. But that's no comfort, they're always younger." Her voice was like a flagellant's whip, turned against herself. She turned it against Fleischer: "The dirty creep! He has the almighty guts to spend our hard-earned money on that bag. Then he comes home and tells me he's investing it, going to make us rich for the rest of our lives."

"Did he say how?"

"You ought to know. You're one of his cronies, aren't you?"

She picked up her glass and drained it. She looked ready to throw the empty glass at my head. I wasn't her husband, but I wore pants.

"Drink up your drink," she said. "I drank up mine."

"We've had enough."

"That's what *you* think."

She carried her glass out of the room. Her mules slid along the floor and her body leaned as if she was on an irreversible slope, sliding away forever into the limbo of deserted women. I heard her smashing something in the kitchen. I looked in through the open door and saw her breaking dishes in the sink.

I didn't interfere. They were her dishes. I went back through the living room, took Laurel's picture from the table, and left the house.

On the porch next door, a white-haired man wearing a bathrobe stood in a listening attitude. When he saw me, he turned away and went into the house. I heard him say before he closed the door:

"Jack Fleischer's home again."

>>>>>>>>>
>>>>>>>>> *chapter* 13
>>>>>>>>>

HENRY LANGSTON's one-story house was in a newer tract on the northern outskirts of the city. The lights were on, both inside and out. The doors of the attached garage were open but there was no car in it, only a child's tricycle standing against one wall.

A young woman wearing a fur-collared coat came out of the house. She had bright dark eyes and a piquant oval face. She stopped short before she reached me, ready to be alarmed.

"I'm looking for Mr. Langston," I told her.

"Why? Has something happened?"

"I've no reason to think so."

"But it's so *late*."

"I'm sorry. I tried to get him earlier. Is he home now?"

She glanced over her shoulder at the open front door. She was disturbed by me, as if I carried trouble like a communicable disease from the last house I had visited.

I smiled a midnight smile. "Don't get upset. This has nothing to do with you. I have some questions to ask him about one of his former students."

"I'm sure he won't want to talk to you tonight."

"I'm sure he will. Tell him it has to do with Davy Spanner."

"Him again." She tossed her head like a rival, then bit her lip. "Is Davy in trouble again, or is it still?"

"I prefer to discuss that with your husband. You *are* Mrs. Langston?"

"Yes, and I'm cold and tired and ready to go to bed, and we had a lovely evening with some friends, and now it's spoiled." Perhaps she had had a drink or two, but she was deliberately indulging her feelings. She was pretty enough to do that.

"I'm sorry."

"If you're so sorry, go away."

She went inside and slammed the door with a carefully calculated degree of force, between six and seven on the Richter scale. I stood where I was on the flagstone walk. Mrs. Langston reopened the door, carefully, like somebody reopening a law case.

"I apologize. I know it must be important or you wouldn't be here. Are you a policeman?"

"A private detective. My name is Archer."

"Henry should be back any minute. He's just driving the baby-sitter home. Come in, it's a chilly night."

She backed into the living room. I followed her. The room was jammed with furniture and books. A closed baby grand piano was its central feature.

Mrs. Langston stood beside it like a nervous soloist. "Let me make you some coffee."

"Please don't bother. And please don't be afraid."

"It's not *your* fault. I'm scared of Davy Spanner."

"You were scared before his name came up."

"Was I? I guess you're right. You looked at me in such a strange way, as if I was going to die."

I didn't bother reminding her that she was going to. She took off her coat. She looked about six months pregnant.

"If you'll excuse me, I'm just plain going to bed. Please don't keep Henry up all night."

"I'll try not to. Good night."

She fluttered her fingers at me, leaving a kind of tremulous feeling in the room. When I heard the car in the driveway I went outside.

Langston got out, leaving his station wagon outside the garage with the headlights on and the engine running. A sense of alarm seemed to be in the air, and I could see it reflected in his face. He was a large, homely, sandy-haired young man with sensitive eyes.

"Is Kate all right?"

"Your wife is fine. She let me in and went to bed." I told him who I was. "Davy Spanner was in town tonight."

Langston's eyes seemed to withdraw, as if I'd touched invisible antennae. He went back to his wagon and turned off the engine and the headlights.

"We'll talk in the car, okay? I don't want to disturb her."

We got into the front seat, closing the doors without slamming them.

"You didn't see Davy tonight by any chance?"

He hesitated before answering. "Yes, I did. Briefly."

"Where?"

"He came here to my house."

"About what time?"

"Eight o'clock. Kate had gone to pick up Elaine—that's the high-school girl who sits with Junior—and I was just as glad she was out of the house. Fortunately he left before she got back. Davy upsets Kate basically, you know?"

"She isn't the only one."

Langston gave me a sideways look. "Has he been beating his head on the wall again?"

"If that's what you call it."

"Davy's a self-destroyer."

"It's the other people I'm worried about. Was the girl Sandy with him?"

"Very much so. She's one of the reasons he came to me tonight. He wanted me to look after her for him. Me and Kate, that is. He said that they were going to get married but first he had a job to do. It would take a day or two."

"Did he say what the job was?"

"No. I gathered it was going to be rough. He thought it would be nice if Sandy stayed with us until he got through with it."

"Why you?"

"It's what I often ask myself," he said with a quick wry smile. "Why me? The answer is, I asked for it. I got very deeply involved with Davy's problems, years ago, and once that happens it's very hard to, you know, wean your affections. It almost broke up my marriage at one point. Never again. I told him what he suggested was impossible. He took it hard, as if I was letting him down. But it was a question of who—of whom—I was going to let down, Davy or my own family."

"How did the girl react?"

"I never did get a chance to talk to her. I could see her sitting in their car, looking rather pale and tense." He pointed with his thumb toward the street where my car was standing. "But I couldn't take the responsibility for her. The truth is I wanted them out of here before Kate returned. She's going to have another child, and she had a very hard time with the first—with Junior. I have to protect her from too much excitement—alarms and excursions."

"Of course."

"There have to be priorities," he went on. "Otherwise you spread yourself thin and the whole structure collapses." He sounded like an overconscientious man repeating a hard lesson he was trying to learn. But he couldn't help caring about the girl. "She really is his fiancée, isn't she?"

"They think so. She's a runaway, though, and only seventeen. Her parents originally hired me to get her back."

"And that's why you're here?"

"Partly. What other reasons did Davy have for coming to you?"

"Other reasons?"

"You said the girl was one reason. What were the others?"

"It had to do with history," he said rather obscurely. "He wanted some information, essentially information about himself. As I was saying, I delved pretty deeply into his case several years ago, when he was one of our students at the high school. I realize now I went too deep. I'd had some therapy when I was in college, and I thought I could use it to help him. But something happened, I don't know how to explain it."

His look was puzzled and inward, as if he was trying to explain the past to himself: "Something seemed to tear like a membrane in between us. There were times when our identities seemed to get mixed up. I could actually feel his feelings and think his thoughts, and I felt this terrible empathy—" He broke off. "Has that ever happened to you?"

"No. Unless you count women, in very special circumstances."

"Women?" he said in his puzzled way. "Kate is as strange to me as the mountains of the moon. That doesn't mean I don't love her. I worship her."

"Fine. You were going to tell me about Davy's history."

"He didn't have any history, that was the trouble. I thought I could help him by providing some. But it turned out he couldn't handle it. Neither could I, really. I was the one who mishandled the situation, since I was the counselor and he was just a troubled sixteen-year-old."

Langston was troubled, too. His mind seemed to be struggling through magnetic fields of memory which put a twist on everything he said. I prompted him again: "Is it true his father was killed?"

He gave me a quick stabbing look. "You know about his father's death?"

"Just that. How did it happen?"

"I never did find out for sure. Apparently he fell under a train near Rodeo City. The train wheels passed over him and cut his head off." Langston drew his fingers across his own throat. "He was a young man, younger than I am now."

"What was his name?"

"Nobody seems to know. He wasn't carrying any identification. According to the theory of the deputy sheriff who handled the case—"

"Jack Fleischer?"

"Yes. Do you know him?"

"I'm looking forward to knowing him. What was his theory?"

"That the man was a migrant worker who was riding the rods and accidentally fell off. But there's one big trouble with that theory. He had a three-year-old boy with him and if *he* fell off the moving train, Davy must have fallen off, too. But he was unhurt, at least in the physical sense.

"In the psychic sense," he added, "Davy was badly hurt. I'm sure it's the root of his trouble. He sat beside the railroad tracks all night with that headless corpse." His voice had dropped so low I could barely hear him.

"How do you know that?"

"Deputy Fleischer found him beside the body. Davy confirmed this himself. I helped him to dredge up the memory. I thought it would be good for him. But I'm afraid it wasn't. I realize now I was playing God, practicing psychiatry without a license." His voice was contrite.

"He went completely wild and attacked me. We were in my office at the high school, and there wasn't any way I could keep it quiet. As a matter of fact he gave me quite a beating. The school expelled him, over my protests. It was all I could do to keep him out of reform school."

"Why did you want to?"

"I felt guilty, of course. I'd been playing with black magic—these repressed memories are as powerful as any magic—and the thing blew up in both our faces. He suffered permanent damage."

"That happened long before. You're still playing God," I said.

"I know the extent of my responsibility. I helped to bring that terrible memory back to his conscious mind. He's been fixed on it ever since."

"You don't know that."

"I do, though. That's the hell of it. He came here tonight and insisted I tell him exactly where his father's corpse was found. It's still the dominant thing in his mind."

"Did you tell him?"

"Yes. It was the only way to get rid of him."

"Can you take me to the place? Tonight?"

"I could. But it's at least an hour's drive up the coast." He looked at his watch. "It's past twelve thirty. If I take you, I won't get home before three. And I have to be at school at a quarter to eight."

"Forget about school. You said yourself there are priorities. This one has to do with a man's life or death."

"What man?"

I told Langston about the breathing in the trunk. "I thought at first it was a snatch for money. The people who pull them are getting younger all the time. But the motives for kidnapping are changing with the times, too. More and more of them are naked power plays, for the sheer sake of dominating another person. God knows what goes on in Davy's mind. Or the girl's, for that matter. They may be planning to re-enact his father's death."

I had Langston's full attention. He couldn't resist the psychological bait. "You may be right. He was terribly urgent about finding the right place. Are the police in on this?"

"No. The victim's family asked me to handle it myself."

"Who is he?"

"A Los Angeles financier. The girl's father works for one of his companies."

"It does sound more complex than a crime for money."

"Will you help me?" I said.

"I don't have much choice. We'll take your car, okay?"

"Whatever you say, Mr. Langston."

"Please call me Hank, everybody else does." He got out of the car. "Come into the house for a moment, won't you? I have to leave a note for my wife."

He wrote it on top of the baby grand while I looked over his books. They covered a surprising range including law and history. His psychology and sociology books emphasized the freer spirits in those fields: Erik Erikson and Erich Fromm, Paul Goodman, Edgar Z. Friedenberg.

He left the note to his wife on the music rack of the piano, with a small light shining on it. I read it on the way out:

Dearest:

Just in case you wake up and wonder where I am, I've gone for a little spin with Mr. Archer. If anybody comes to the door, don't answer. Please don't worry. I love you with all my heart, in case you were wondering. Back soon.

Love,
H.
(12:30 a.m.)

I DROVE THE CAR, and told Langston he could sleep. He claimed that he wasn't sleepy, but soon after we got onto the highway he butted his cigarette and dozed off.

The highway left the sea for a while, looping inland through a mountain pass, and then returned to the sea. The railroad ran between the sea and the mountains, and I caught the gleam of the tracks from time to time.

There was very little traffic. This northern part of the county was mostly open country. On the ocean side a few oil stations and gas flares broke up the darkness. Inland, the fields sloped up to the rocky flanks of the headless mountains. There were cattle in the fields, as still as stones.

"No!" Langston said in his sleep.

"Wake up, Hank."

He seemed dazed. "Terrible dream. The three of us were in bed to—" He stopped in mid-sentence, and watched the night rush by.

"Which three of you?"

"My wife and I, and Davy. It was a rotten dream."

I said after some hesitation: "Are you afraid that Davy might go to your house?"

"The thought did occur to me," he admitted. "But he wouldn't do anything to anyone I love."

He was talking against the darkness. Perhaps I should have left him at home, I thought, but it was too late now. Since leaving his house I'd added over fifty miles to the odometer.

"How much further, Hank?"

"I can't say exactly. I'll know the place when I see it. You have to make a left turn onto a gravel road. It crosses the tracks." He peered ahead through the windshield.

"How long is it since you've visited the place?"

"About three years. Deputy Fleischer drove me up."

"Why did you go to all the trouble?"

"I wanted to know exactly what had happened. The people at the Shelter told me Davy was practically autistic when he was admitted —mute and almost unreachable. I wanted to know why. Fleischer hadn't told them much, if anything."

"Did he talk freely to you?"

"Policemen never do, do they? And I can understand an officer getting quite possessive about a case. At the time he brought me up here, he'd been working on this one for twelve years."

"Did he say so?"

"Yes."

"Then he couldn't have thought it was an accident."

"I don't know what he thought, really." Langston thrust his head forward. "Slow down. We're coming to the place."

Several hundred yards ahead in the lights of an approaching truck I could make out a gravel road sloping away to the left. A lonely hitchhiker was at the corner. It was a girl, standing with her back to us and frantically signaling to the truck driver. The truck passed her, and then us, without slackening speed.

I made a left turn onto the side road and got out. The girl was wearing sunglasses, as if the natural darkness wasn't deep enough for her. Her body made a jerky movement. I thought she was going to run. But her feet seemed to be stuck fast in the gravel.

"Sandy?"

She didn't answer me, except with a little moan of recognition. I had a vision of myself seen from above, a kind of owl's-eye view of a man moving in on a frightened girl at a deserted crossroads. Somehow my motives didn't enter the picture.

"What happened to the others, Sandy?"

"I don't know. I ran away and hid in the trees." She pointed toward a grove of Monterey pines on the far side of the railroad tracks. I could smell their odor on her. "He laid Mr. Hackett across the railroad tracks, and I got really scared. I thought he was pretending, until then. I didn't think he really meant to kill him."

"Is Hackett unconscious?"

"No, but he's all taped up—his hands and feet and mouth. He looked so helpless lying across the rail. He knew where he was, too, I could tell by the noises he made. I couldn't stand it, so I ran away. When I came back they were gone."

Langston moved up beside me. His feet crackled in the gravel. The girl shied away.

"Don't be afraid," he said.

"Who are you? Do I know you?"

"I'm Henry Langston. Davy wanted me to take care of you. It seems to be working out that way after all."

"I don't want to be taken care of. I'm all right. I can get a ride." She spoke with a kind of mechanical assurance which seemed to be unconnected with her real feelings.

"Come on," he said. "Don't be so stand-offish."

"Have you got a cigarette?"

"I have a whole pack."

"I'll come with you if you give me a cigarette."

He brought out his cigarettes and solemnly handed them over. She got a cigarette out of the pack. Her hands were shaking.

"Give me a light?"

Langston handed her a book of matches. She lit one and dragged deep. The end of her cigarette was reflected double like little hot red eyes in the lenses of her dark glasses.

"All right, I'll get into your car."

She sat in the front seat, with Langston and me on either side of her. She gulped her cigarette until it burned her fingers, then dropped it in the ashtray.

"You didn't have very good plans," I said. "Who made your plans?"

"Davy did, mostly."

"What did he have in mind?"

"He was going to kill Mr. Hackett, like I said. Leave him across the track and let the train cut him up."

"And you went along with this?"

"I didn't really believe he was going to do it. He didn't do it, either."

"We'd better check on that."

I released the emergency brake. The car rolled down the grade toward the crossing, which was marked by an old wooden sign with drooping crosspieces.

"Where did he put Mr. Hackett?"

"Right here beside the road." Sandy indicated the north side of the crossing.

I got out with my flashlight and looked over the railbed. There were fresh marks in the gravel which could have been gouged by heels. Still it was hard to imagine the scene that the girl had described.

I went back to the car. "Did Davy tell you why he picked this place?"

"He thought it would be a good place to kill him, I guess. Then he probably changed his mind when I ran away."

"Why did he choose Mr. Hackett as a victim?"

"I don't know."

I leaned in at the open door. "You must have some idea, Sandy. Mr. Hackett is or was a friend of your family."

"He's not my friend," she said guardedly.

"You've made that fairly clear. What did Hackett do, if anything?"

She turned to Langston. "I don't have to answer that, do I? I'm only a juvenile but I've got a right to a lawyer."

"You've not only got a right," I said. "You've got a need for one. But you're not going to help yourself by keeping quiet. If we don't head your boyfriend off, you'll end up going to trial with him for everything he pulls."

She appealed again to Langston, the cigarette king. "That isn't true, is it?"

"It could happen," he said.

"But I'm just a juvenile."

I said: "That's no protection against a capital charge. You already own a piece of a kidnapping. If Hackett gets killed, you'll be an accomplice in murder."

"But I ran away."

"That won't be much help, Sandy."

She was shocked. I think she was realizing that the place and the time were real, that this was her life and she was living it, badly.

I felt a certain empathy with her. The scene was becoming a part of my life, too: the grove of trees standing dark against the darkness, the rails reaching like iron strands of necessity from north to south. A late moon like an afterthought hung in the lower quarter of the sky.

Away off to the north the beam of a train's headlight was flung around a curve. It came toward us swinging, cutting the darkness into illegible patterns, pulling a freight train behind it. My own headlights were shining on the rails, and I could see them dip under the weight of the diesels. The overwhelming noise of the train completed the drastic reality of the scene.

Sandy let out a strangled cry and tried to fight her way past me. I forced her back into the car. She scratched at my face. I slapped her. We were both acting as if the noise had shut us off from the human race.

Langston said when the train had gone south: "Take it easy, now. There's no need for violence."

"Tell that to Davy Spanner."

"I have, many times. Let's hope it took." He said to the girl: "Mr. Archer is perfectly right, Sandy. If you can help us, you'll be helping yourself. You must have some idea where Davy went from here."

"He didn't know himself." She was breathing hard. "He did a lot of talking, about this place in the hills where he used to live. He didn't know where it was, though."

"Are you sure it existed?"

"*He* thought so. I don't know."

I got in behind the wheel. Our brief struggle had warmed her, and I could feel her body glowing beside me. It was too bad, I thought, that her parents hadn't been able to keep her on the back burner for another year or two. Too bad for her, and too bad for them.

I asked Sandy some further questions as we drove south. She was reticent about herself, and about her relations with Davy. But her answers established one thing to my own satisfaction: if Davy Spanner was the one who had beaten Laurel Smith, Sandy didn't know about it. And she had been with Davy right through the day, she said.

>>>>>>>>
>>>>>>>> *chapter* 15
>>>>>>>>

IT WAS PAST THREE when we got back to Santa Teresa. I asked Langston to come along to the motel. He seemed to have a calming effect on the girl.

Sebastian heard us coming, and opened the door of his room before I could knock. Light spilled out over his daughter. She stood in it boldly with one round hip out.

He reached for her with open arms. She moved back abruptly. In a long-drawn-out gesture of contempt she lit a cigarette and blew smoke in his direction.

"I didn't know you smoked," he said lamely.

"I smoke pot when I can get it."

We all went into Sebastian's room, with me bringing up the rear. He turned to me.

"Where did you find her?" he asked.

"Up the highway a piece. This is Mr. Langston. He helped to locate her."

The two men shook hands. Sebastian said he was very grateful. But he looked at his daughter as if he wondered what he was grateful for. She sat on the edge of the bed with her knees crossed, watching him.

"We're still in trouble," I said. "And I'm going to make a few suggestions. First, take your daughter home and keep her there. If you and your wife can't control her, hire some help."

"What kind of help?"

"A psychiatric nurse, maybe. Ask your doctor."

"He thinks I'm crazy," Sandy said to the room. *"He* must be crazy."

I didn't look at her. "Do you have a good lawyer, Mr. Sebastian?"

"I don't have any lawyer. I've never really needed one."

"You need one now. Get someone to recommend a criminal lawyer, and give him a chance to talk to Sandy today. She's in serious trouble, and she's going to have to cooperate with the law."

"But I don't want her involved with the law."

"You don't have any choice."

"Don't tell me that. Mrs. Marburg told *you* to keep this whole thing private."

"I'm going to talk to Mrs. Marburg, too. The case is too big for me to handle alone."

Sandy made a break for the door. Langston caught her before she reached it, with one arm around her waist. She burned his wrist with her cigarette butt. He swung her around, pushed her down on the bed and stood over her panting. I could smell singed hair.

Somebody rapped on the other side of the wall. "Knock it off, swingers!"

Sebastian looked at his daughter with pained interest. She had suddenly grown up into a source of trouble. He must have been wondering how large the trouble was going to become.

"I think we better get out of here," I said. "Do you want to phone your wife?"

"I really should, shouldn't I?"

He went to the phone and after a good deal of receiver-banging managed to rouse the switchboard. His wife answered right away.

"I have wonderful news," he said in a shaky voice. "Sandy is with me. I'm bringing her home." The words brought mist to his eyes. "Yes, she's fine. We'll see you in a couple of hours. Get some sleep now."

He hung up and turned to Sandy. "Your mother asked me to give you her love."

"Who needs it?"

"Don't you care for us at all?"

She rolled over, face down on the bed, and lay stiff and silent. I went into the adjoining room to make a phone call of my own.

It was to Willie Mackey, who ran a San Francisco detective agency. His answering service took the call, but shifted it to Willie's California Street apartment. He answered in a sleep-fogged voice: "Mackey here."

"Lew Archer. Are you going to be free today?"

"I can make myself free."

"Good. I have a job on the Peninsula. It's just a tail job but it could turn out to be important. Got a pencil?"

"Hold it just a minute." Willie went away and came back. "Go ahead."

"You know the Sandman Motor Hotel in Palo Alto?"

"Yeah, it's on Camino Real. I've stayed there."

"A man named Jack Fleischer, a retired sheriff's deputy from Santa Teresa, is supposed to be checking in there some time tonight. I want to know why if possible. I want to know where he goes and who he talks to and what about. And I don't want you to lose him even if you have to spend some money."

"How much is some?"

"Use your own discretion."

"Do you want to tell me what it's all about?"

"Jack Fleischer may know. I don't, except that a man's life is at issue."

"Who's the man?"

"His name is Hackett. He's been kidnapped by a nineteen-year-old named Davy Spanner." I described the two of them, in case they turned up in Willie's territory. "Hackett is very well-heeled, but this doesn't seem to be a ransom kidnapping. Spanner's a sociopath with schizoid tendencies."

"They're always fun. I'll get right down to Palo Alto, Lew."

I went back into Sebastian's room. The girl was still lying face down on the bed with Langston standing over her.

"I'll drop you off at your house," I said to him. "I'm sorry I ruined the night for you."

"You didn't. I was glad to help, and that still goes. One thing. I feel I should talk to the local police."

"Let me handle that part. Okay?"

"Okay."

The girl got up when I told her to, and the four of us drove across town. The lights were on in Langston's house. His wife came running out to greet him, wearing a red Chinese robe.

"You shouldn't run," he told her. "Haven't you been to bed?"

"I couldn't sleep. I was scared something would happen to you." She turned on me. "You promised you wouldn't keep him up all night."

"No I didn't. Anyway it's only four."

"*Only* four!"

"You shouldn't be standing out here in the cold." Langston took her into the house, lifting his hand to me before he closed the door.

It was a dreary ride south to Malibu. The girl sat silent between me and her father. He made a few attempts to talk to her, but she pretended to be deaf.

One thing was clear. By changing the rules of the game to include outrage, she had gained an advantage over him. He had more to lose than she had. He was losing it, but he hadn't lost hope of holding on to something. She acted as if she had.

I dropped them off in the parking lot where Sebastian had left his car. I waited until they were in it, and blue smoke puffed from its exhaust. Sandy made no attempt to run. Perhaps she realized there was no place to run to.

Below the narrow town a high tide was roaring on the beach. I caught glimpses of the breakers between the buildings, faintly phosphorescent in the beginning light.

It was too soon for another day to start. I checked into the first motel I came to.

>>>>>>>>>>
>>>>>>>>>> *chapter* 16
>>>>>>>>>>

I WOKE UP PROMPTLY at eight. It was still too early, but my stomach was groaning. I went out and had a slice of grilled ham, two eggs fried over easy, a pile of toast, a side order of dollar-size pancakes with raspberry syrup, and several cups of black coffee.

By this time I felt as ready as I would ever feel to talk to Mrs. Marburg. Without phoning her in advance, I drove out to the Hackett place. The gate was standing open. I had a heavy *déjà-vu* feeling as I drove up past the artificial lake. The ducks had not returned, and the mud hens were still on the far side of the water.

A Cadillac coupe displaying a doctor's caduceus was standing in front of the house. A youthful-looking man with clever eyes and iron-gray hair met me at the door.

"I'm Dr. Converse. Are you from the police?"

"No, I'm a private detective working for Mrs. Marburg." I told him my name.

"She didn't mention you." He stepped outside and pulled the door shut behind him. "Exactly what has been going on around here? Has something happened to Stephen Hackett?"

"Didn't Mrs. Marburg tell you?"

"She gave me some intimations of disaster. But she seems to think she can undo the mischief by not talking about it. She made a fearful row when I insisted on calling the police."

"What's her big objection to the police?"

"She has a fixed idea that they're corrupt and incompetent. I suppose she's entitled to it, after what happened to her previous husband."

"What happened to him?"

"I assumed you knew. He was shot to death on the beach about fifteen years ago. I'm not too clear about the details—it was before my time—but I don't believe the killer was ever found. Anyway, getting back to the present, I explained to Mrs. Marburg that the law requires physicians and hospitals to report all serious injuries."

"Are we talking about Lupe?"

"Yes. I called an ambulance and sent him to the hospital."

"Is he seriously hurt?"

"I wouldn't attempt to say. I'm an internist, not a brain surgeon, and these head injuries can be tricky. I'm putting him in the hands of a competent man, Dr. Sunderland at St. John's Hospital."

"Is Lupe conscious?"

"Yes, but he refuses to talk about what happened." The doctor's fingers tweezered my upper arm. He was wearing some piny scent which made me want to sneeze. "Do you know who hit him over the head?"

"It was a seventeen-year-old girl. Lupe's probably ashamed of it."

"Do you know her name?"

"Sandy Sebastian."

He frowned in a puzzled way. "Are you sure?"

"Yes."

"But Sandy isn't a rough girl at all."

"How well do you know her, doctor?"

"I've seen her once or twice, professionally. That was some months ago." His fingers tightened on me. "What happened with her and Lupe, anyway? Did he attempt to attack her?"

"You've got it turned around. Sandy and her boyfriend were on the attack. Lupe was defending himself and I assume Mr. Hackett."

"What's happened to Mr. Hackett? Surely you can tell me, I'm his physician." But Converse lacked authority. He looked and sounded like a society doctor who made his living by talking to money in the proper tone of voice. "Has he been injured, too?"

"He's been kidnapped."

"For ransom?"

"For kicks, apparently."

"And Miss Sebastian and her friend are responsible?"

"Yes. I caught Sandy last night and brought her home. She's with her parents in Woodland Hills. She's not in very good shape emotionally, and I think a doctor should see her. If you're her doctor—"

"I'm not." Dr. Converse let go of me and moved away as if I'd suddenly become contaminated. "I saw her just once, last summer, and I haven't seen her since. I can't call up her home and force my professional attentions on her."

"I suppose not. What did you treat her for last summer?"

"It would hardly be professional to tell you."

Communications had suddenly broken down. I went inside to talk to Mrs. Marburg. She was in the living room, half lying on a long chair with her back to the window. There were bluish bulges under her eyes. She hadn't changed her clothes since the night before.

"No luck, eh?" she said hoarsely.

"No. Did you sleep at all?"

"Not a wink. I had a bad night. I couldn't get a doctor to come out here. When I finally got Dr. Converse, he insisted on informing the police."

"I think it's a good idea. We should lay the whole thing out for them. They can do things I couldn't do if I hired a thousand men. They have a new statewide computer system for spotting cars, for example. The best chance we have is to pick up Sebastian's car."

She drew air hissingly between her teeth. "I wish I'd never heard of that creep or his wretched little daughter."

"I caught the girl, if that's any comfort to you."

Mrs. Marburg sat up straight. "Where is she?"

"At home with her mother and father."

"I wish you'd brought her to me. I'd give a good deal to know what goes on in her head. Did you question her?"

"Some. She won't talk freely."

"What was her motivation?"

"Sheer malice, as far as I can see. She wanted to hurt her father."

"Then why in God's name didn't they kidnap *him?*"

"I don't know. Did the girl have any trouble with your son?"

"Certainly not. Stephen treated her very well. It was Gerda who was her special friend, of course."

"Where is Mrs. Hackett?"

"Gerda's still in her room. She might as well sleep, she's no particular help to anybody. She's no better than Sidney."

She spoke with the fretful impatience of near-despair. Mrs. Marburg was evidently one of those stubborn souls who reacted to trouble by trying to take charge of a situation and make all the decisions. But the thing was slipping out of her hands, and she knew it.

"You can't stay up forever and do everything yourself. This could turn into a long siege. And it could end badly."

She leaned sideways toward me. "Is Stephen dead?"

"We have to face that possibility. Spanner isn't playing games. He's homicidal, apparently."

"How do you know that?" She was angry. "You're trying to frighten me, aren't you? So I'll cooperate with the police."

"I'm giving you the facts, so you can make a good decision. In the course of the night Spanner laid your son out across a railroad track. He intended to let a freight train run over him."

She looked at me in astonishment. "A freight train?"

"I know it sounds wild, but it happened. The girl saw it happen. She got scared and ran out on Spanner at that point, which makes it fairly certain she isn't lying."

"What happened to Stephen?"

"Spanner changed his mind when the girl got away. But he could try it again. There's a lot of railroad track in California, and freight trains are running all the time."

"What is he trying to do to us?"

"I doubt that he could tell you if you asked him. He seems to be acting out a childhood memory."

"That sounds like phony psychology to me."

"It isn't, though. I've talked to Davy Spanner's high-school counselor in Santa Teresa. His father was killed by a train at that same spot, when he was three. Davy saw it happen."

"Where is the place?"

"In the northern part of Santa Teresa County, near Rodeo City."

"I'm not familiar with that territory."

"Neither am I. Of course they may be hundreds of miles away from there by now. In northern California or out of the state in Nevada or Arizona."

She pushed my words away as if they were flies buzzing around her head. "You *are* trying to frighten me."

"I wish I could, Mrs. Marburg. You have nothing to gain by keep-ing this business private. I can't find your son by myself, I don't have the leads. The leads I do have should go to the police."

"I haven't had good luck with the local police."

"You mean in the death of your husband?"

"Yes." She gave me a level look. "Who's been talking?"

"Not you. I think you should. The murder of your husband and the taking of your son may be connected."

"I don't see how they could be. The Spanner boy couldn't have been more than four or five when Mark Hackett was killed."

"How was he killed?"

"He was shot on the beach." She rubbed her temple as if her hus-band's death had left a permanent sore spot in her mind.

"Malibu Beach?"

"Yes. We have a beach cottage, and Mark often went for an eve-ning stroll down there. Someone came up behind him and shot him in the head with a handgun. The police arrested a dozen or more suspects—mostly transients and beach bums—but they never got enough evidence to lay charges."

"Was he robbed?"

"His wallet was taken. They never recovered it either. You can see why I'm not a great admirer of the local police."

"Still they have their uses, and they're coming out here anyway. I need your permission to talk to them, freely."

She sat still and solemn. I could hear her breathing, measuring out the slow seconds.

"I have to take your advice, don't I? If Stephen was killed because I decided wrong, I couldn't live with it. Go ahead, Mr. Archer, do what you want to do." She dismissed me with a wave of her hand, then called me back from the door. "I want you to stay with it, of course."

"I was hoping you would."

"If you do find Stephen yourself, and bring him home safely, I'm still prepared to pay you a hundred thousand. Do you need money for expenses, now?"

"It would help. I'm co-opting another man, a San Francisco detec-tive named Willie Mackey. Do you want to advance me a thou-sand?"

"I'll write you a check. Where's my bag?" She raised her voice and called: "Sidney! Where's my bag?"

Her husband came from the adjoining room. He was wearing a paint-daubed smock and had a spot of red paint on his nose. His eyes looked through us as if we were transparent.

"What is it?" he said impatiently.

"I want you to find my bag."

"Find it yourself. I'm working."

"Don't use that tone on me."

"I wasn't aware of any particular tone."

"We won't argue. Go and find my bag. It will do you no harm to do something useful for a change."

"Painting is useful."

She half-rose from the long chair. "I said we wouldn't argue. Get my bag. I think I left it in the library."

"All right, if you want to make a major issue out of it."

He went and got her bag, and she wrote me a check for a thousand dollars. Marburg went back to his painting.

Then two deputies arrived from the sheriff's office, and Mrs. Marburg and I talked to them in the main living room. Dr. Converse stood listening just inside the door, his clever glance moving from face to face.

Later I talked to an officer of the highway patrol, and after that to a sheriff's captain named Aubrey. He was a big middle-aged man with a big man's easy confidence. I liked him. Dr. Converse was gone by this time, and with a single exception I held nothing back from Aubrey.

The single exception was the Fleischer angle. Jack Fleischer was a recently retired officer of the law, and officers of the law tend to hang together protectively in a pinch. I felt that Fleischer's role in the case should be investigated by freelances like me and Willie Mackey.

To keep everything even, I stopped by the Purdue Street station on my way into town. Detective-Sergeant Prince was in a rage so black that his partner Janowski was worried about him. Laurel Smith had died during the night.

I CLIMBED THE STAIRS to my second-floor office on knees that shook under me. It was a few minutes past ten by the wall clock. I called my answering service. A few minutes before ten, Willie Mackey had called me from San Francisco. I returned the call now, and got Willie in his Geary Street office.

"Nice timing, Lew. I was just trying to phone you. Your man Fleischer checked in at the Sandman about 3 a.m. I put a man on him and made a deal with the night keyboy. The keyboy handles the switchboard after midnight. Fleischer left a call for seven thirty and as soon as he got up he phoned a certain Albert Blevins at the Bowman Hotel. That's in the Mission District. Fleischer came up to the city and he and Blevins had breakfast together in a cafeteria on Fifth Street. Then they went back to Blevins's hotel and apparently they're still there, in his room. Does all this mean anything to you?"

"The name Blevins does." It was the name on Laurel's Social Security card. "Find out what you can about him, will you, and meet me at San Francisco Airport?"

"What time?"

I got a plane schedule out of my desk. "One o'clock, in the bar."

I made an airline reservation and drove out to Los Angeles International. It was a clear bright day at both ends of the flight. When my jet came down over San Francisco Bay I could see the city standing up like a perpendicular dream and past it to the curved dark blue horizon. The endless roofs of the bedroom towns stretched southward along the Peninsula farther than I could see.

I found Willie in the airport bar drinking a Gibson. He was a smart experienced man who copied his style of life from the flamboyant San Francisco lawyers who often employed him. Willie spent his money on women and clothes, and always looked a little overdressed, as he did now. His gray hair had once been black. His very sharp black eyes hadn't changed in the twenty years I'd known him.

"Albert Blevins," he said, "has lived in the Bowman Hotel for about a year. It's a pensioners' hotel, one of the better ones in the Mission District."

"Just how old is he?"

"Maybe sixty. I don't know for sure. You didn't give me much time, Lew."

"There isn't much time."

I told him why. Willie was a money player, and his eyes shone like anthracite coal when he heard about Hackett's wealth. A chunk of it would buy him a new young blonde to break his heart with again.

Willie wanted another Gibson and some lunch, but I steered him to an elevator and out to the parking lot. He backed his Jaguar out of its slot and headed up Bayshore to the city. The aching blue water and the endless mud flats gave me the pang of remembered younger days.

Willie broke into my thoughts. "What's Albert Blevins got to do with the Hackett snatch?"

"I don't know, but there has to be some connection. A woman named Laurel Smith who died last night—homicide victim—used to call herself Laurel Blevins. Fleischer knew her in Rodeo City fifteen years ago. Around the same time, and the same locality, an unidentified man was decapitated by a train. Apparently he was Davy Spanner's father. Deputy Fleischer handled the case, and put it in the books as accidental death."

"And you say it wasn't?"

"I'm suspending judgment. There's still another connection. Spanner was Laurel Smith's tenant and employee, and I suspect they were closer than that, maybe very close."

"Did he kill her?"

"I don't think so. The point is that the people and the places are starting to repeat." I told Willie about the midnight scene at the railroad crossing. "If we can get Fleischer and Blevins to talk, we may be able to shut the case down in a hurry. Particularly Fleischer. For the past month he's been bugging Laurel's apartment in Pacific Palisades."

"You think he killed her?"

"He may have. Or he may know who did."

Willie concentrated on the traffic as we entered the city. He left his car in an underground garage on Geary Street. I walked up to his office with him to see if the tail on Fleischer had called in. He had. Fleischer had left Blevins at the Bowman Hotel, and at the time of the call was inside the shop of the Acme Photocopy Service. This was Fleischer's second visit to the Acme Photocopy Service. He had stopped there on his way to the Bowman Hotel.

I did the same. The Acme Service was a one-man business conducted in a narrow store on Market Street. A thin man with a cough labored over a copying machine. For five quick dollars he told me what Fleischer had had copied. On his first visit it was the front page of an old newspaper, on his second an even older birth certificate.

"Whose birth certificate?"

"I don't know. Just a minute. Somebody called Jasper, that was the first name, I think."

I waited, but nothing else came. "What was in the newspaper?"

"I didn't read it. If I read everything I copy, I'd go blind."

"You say it was old. How old?"

"I didn't look at the date, but the paper had turned pretty yellow. I had to handle it carefully." He coughed, and lit a cigarette in reflex. "That's all I can tell you, mister. What's it all about?"

I took that question to the Bowman Hotel. It was a grimy white brick building whose four rows of evenly spaced front windows had a view of the railroad yards. Some of the windows had wooden boxes nailed to their outside sills in lieu of refrigerators.

The lobby was full of old men. I wondered where all the old women were.

One of the old men told me that Albert Blevins's room was on the second floor at the end of the hall. I went up and knocked on the door.

A husky voice said: "Who is it?"

"My name is Archer. I'd like to talk to you, Mr. Blevins."

"What about?"

"Same thing as the other fellow."

A key turned in the lock. Albert Blevins opened the door a few inches. He wasn't terribly old, but his body was warped by use and his seamed face was set in the cast of permanent stubborn failure. His clear blue eyes had the oddly innocent look of a man who had never been completely broken in to human society. You used to see such men in the small towns, in the desert, on the road. Now they collected in the hollow cores of the cities.

"Will you pay me same as the other fellow?" he said.

"How much?"

"The other fellow gave me fifty dollars. Ask him yourself if you don't believe me." A horrible suspicion ravaged his face. "Say, you're not from Welfare?"

"No."

"Thank Jehosophat for that. You get a lucky windfall, they take it off your Welfare and that wipes out your luck."

"They shouldn't do that."

My agreement pleased Blevins. He opened the door wider and beckoned me into the room. It was a ten-foot cube containing a chair, a table, and a bed. The iron fire escape slanted across the single window like a cancellation mark.

There was a faint sour odor of time in the room. So far as I could tell, it came from the leatherette suitcase which lay open across the bed. Some of its contents were on the table, as if Blevins had been sorting through his memories and laying them out for sale.

I could recognize some of the things on sight: a broad-bladed fisherman's knife to which a few old fish scales were clinging like dry tears, a marriage certificate with deep foldmarks cutting across it, a bundle of letters tied together with a brown shoestring, some rifle bullets and a silver dollar in a net sack, a small miner's pick, a couple of ancient pipes, an ineffectual-looking rabbit's foot, some clean folded underwear and socks, a glass ball that filled itself with a miniature snowstorm when you shook it, a peacock feather watching us with its eye, and an eagle's claw.

I sat at the table and picked up the marriage certificate. It was signed by a civil registrar, and stated that Albert D. Blevins had married Henrietta R. Krug in San Francisco on March 3, 1927. Henrietta was seventeen at the time; Albert was twenty; which made him just over sixty now.

"You want to buy my marriage paper?"

"I might."

"The other fellow gave me fifty for the birth certificate. I'll let this one go for twenty-five." He sat on the edge of the bed. "It's of no great value to me. Marrying her was the big mistake of my life. I never should of married any woman. She told me that herself a hundred times, *after* we got hitched. But what's a man to do when a girl comes to him and tells him he got her pregnant?" He spread his hands out incompletely on his faded denim knees. His painfully uncurling fingers reminded me of starfish torn from their moorings.

"I shouldn't complain," he said. "Her parents treated us right. They gave us their farm and moved into town. It wasn't Mr. Krug's fault that we had three straight years of drought and I couldn't afford to bring in water and feed and the cattle died. I don't even blame Etta for leaving me, not any more. It was a miserable life on that dry farm. All we had between us was going to bed together, and that dried up before the baby was born. I delivered him myself, and I guess it hurt her pretty bad. Etta never let me come near her again."

He was talking like a man who hadn't had a chance to reveal himself for years, if ever. He rose and paced the room, four steps each way.

"It made me mean," he said, "living with a pretty girl and not being able to touch her. I treated her mean, and I treated the boy even worse. I used to beat the living bejesus out of him. I blamed him, see, for cutting off my nooky by being born. Sometimes I beat him until the blood would flow. Etta would try to stop me, and then I'd beat her, too."

His calm blue eyes looked down into mine. I could feel the coldness of his innocence.

"One night I beat her once too often. She picked up the kitchen lamp and threw it at my head. I ducked, but the kerosene splashed on the hot stove and set fire to the kitchen. Before I got the fire out, most of the house was gone, and so was Etta."

"You mean she burned to death?"

"No, I don't mean that." He was impatient with me for failing to divine his thoughts. "She ran away. I never saw hide nor hair of her again."

"What happened to your son?"

"Jasper? He stayed with me for a while. This was right at the beginning of the depression. I got a government job working on the roads, and I found some boards and bought some tarpaper and roofed over what was left of the house. We lived there for a couple more years, little Jasper and me. I was treating him better, but he didn't like me much. He was always scared of me, I can't say I blame him. When he was four he started to run away. I tried tying him up, but he got pretty good at untying knots. What could I do? I took him to his grandparents in L.A. Mr. Krug had a watchman job with one of the oil companies and they agreed to take him off my hands.

"I went down to see Jasper a few times after that, but he always got upset. He used to run at me and hit me with his fists. So I just stopped going. I left the state. I mined silver in Colorado. I fished for salmon out of Anchorage. One day my boat turned over and I made it to shore all right but then I came down with double pneumonia. After that I lost my poop and I came back to California. That's my sad story. I been here going on ten years."

He sat down again. He was neither sad nor smiling. Breathing slowly and deeply, he regarded me with a certain satisfaction. He had lifted the weight of his life and set it down again in the same place.

I asked him: "Do you know what happened to Jasper?" The question made me conscious of its overtones. I was fairly sure by now that Jasper Blevins had died under a train fifteen years ago.

"He grew up and got married. Etta's parents sent me a wedding announcement, and then about seven months after that they sent me a letter that I had a grandson. That was close to twenty years ago, when I was in Colorado, but that seven months stuck in my mind. It meant that Jasper had to get married, just the same as I did in my time.

"History repeating itself," he said. "But there was one way I didn't let it repeat. I kept away from my grandson. I wasn't going to make him a-scared of me. And I didn't want to get to know him and then get cut off from seeing him either. I'd rather stay alone right on through."

"You wouldn't have that letter, would you?"

"I might. I think I have."

He untied the brown shoelace that held his bundle of letters together. His awkward fingers sorted them and picked out a blue envelope. He took the letter out of the envelope, read it slowly with moving lips, and handed it to me.

The letter was written in faded blue ink on blue notepaper with a deckled edge:

> *Mrs. Joseph L. Krug*
> *209 West Capo Street*
> *Santa Monica, California*
> *December 14, 1948*

Mr. Albert D. Blevins
Box 49, Silver Creek, Colorado

Dear Albert:

> *It's a long time since we heard from you. Here's hoping this finds you at the same address. You never did let us know if you got the wedding announcement. In case you did not, Jasper married a lovely girl who has been staying with us, nee Laurel Dudney. She's only seventeen but very mature, these Texas girls grow up fast. Anyway they got married and now they have a darling baby boy, born the day before yesterday, they called him David which is a biblical name as you know.*

> *So now you have a grandson, anyway. Come and see him if you can, you really should, we'll all let bygones be bygones. Jasper and Laurel and the babe will be staying at our house for a while, then Jasper wants to have a try at ranching. We hope you are taking care of yourself, Albert, in those mines. Your loving mother-in-law,*

> *Alma R. Krug,*

P.S. We never hear from Etta.

> *A.R.K.*

"Do you have the wedding announcement?" I asked Blevins.

"I had, but I gave it to the other fellow. I threw it in along with the birth certificate."

"Whose birth certificate?"

"Jasper's. Jasper is the one he's interested in."

"Did he say why?"

"No. This Fleischer fellow plays his cards very close to his vest. Is he really a policeman?"

"An ex-policeman."

"What's in it for him?"

"I don't know."

"You know what's in it for *you*," Blevins said. "You didn't come here to listen to the story of my life."

"I sort of have, though, haven't I?"

"I guess you have." He smiled, so widely I could count his six upper teeth. "This business of Jasper churned up a lot of memories. Why is everybody so interested in Jasper? Why are you fellows willing to pay me money? Or are you?"

Instead of answering his questions, I took three twenties from my wallet and spread them out on a bare part of the table. Blevins opened the front of his shirt and pulled out an oilskin pouch which hung around his neck on a piece of soiled rawhide. He folded the twenties small and put them in the pouch, replacing it against the sparse gray fur of his chest.

"That's twenty-five for the marriage certificate," I said, "twenty-five for the letter, and ten for the autobiography."

"Come again?"

"The life story," I said.

"Oh. Thank you very much. I been needing some warm clothes. Sixty dollars goes a long way at the rummage stores."

I felt a little cheap when he handed me the letter and marriage certificate. I put them in my inside breast pocket. My hand came in contact with the picture Mrs. Fleischer had given me. I showed it to Albert Blevins, remembering with a pang that Laurel was newly dead.

"Do you recognize her, Mr. Blevins?"

"No."

"It's the girl Jasper married."

"I never met her."

Our hands touched as he gave the picture back to me. I felt a kind of short-circuit, a buzzing and burning, as if I had grounded the present in the actual flesh of the past.

Time blurred like tears for an instant. Davy's father had died a violent death. His mother had died in violence. Davy the child of violence was roaring down the trail which led back to Albert Blevins. In the buzzing and the burning and the blur I got my first real feeling of what it was like to be Davy, and it jolted me.

"No," Blevins said, "I never saw Jasper's wife. She's a handsome filly."

"She was."

I took the picture and left before either of us could ask the other more questions.

>>>>>>>>>
>>>>>>>>> *chapter* 18
>>>>>>>>>

I TOOK A CAB back to Willie Mackey's office, buying a paper on the way. Stephen Hackett's disappearance had made the headlines. The story underneath was weak in detail. I did learn from it, though, that Hackett was alleged to be one of the richest men in California.

From Willie Mackey I learned that Jack Fleischer had checked out of the Sandman Motor Hotel and headed south. Willie's operative had lost Fleischer on the highway above San José.

I talked to the operative when he came in. He was an earnest crew-cut young man named Bob Levine, and he was deeply frustrated. Not only had Fleischer eluded him; Fleischer's car was faster than his. He looked ready to kick Willie's ornate red-upholstered office furniture.

"Don't take it so hard," I told Levine. "I know where Fleischer lives, I can pick him up down south. It would have been a wasted trip for you."

"Really?"

"Really. During the time you tailed him, did Fleischer visit anyone besides Albert Blevins?"

"Not unless you count the Acme copying shop. I haven't had a chance to check back on them."

"I have. You might try the man again. He may have been holding back on me. He may have copies of the newspaper page and the birth certificate that Fleischer took in to him."

"If he had I'll get them," Levine said. "Now is there anything else I can do for you?"

"Drive me to the airport." I looked at my watch. "We've got time to stop at the Sandman Motor Hotel on the way."

It was worth making the detour to Camino Real. The maid was cleaning out Fleischer's room at the Sandman. The only thing he had left behind in the wastebasket was a copy of the same paper I had bought. The Hackett story had been torn out of it.

Whatever Fleischer's interests were, they were steadily converging with mine. At the moment he was a step ahead of me, and I calculated how much time I would have in Los Angeles before Fleischer could possibly get there by car. Three hours, anyway.

I used up nearly all of the first hour driving in slow traffic from Los Angeles International Airport to the Sebastian house in Woodland Hills. I hadn't phoned ahead because I didn't want to be told by Sebastian that I couldn't talk to his daughter. It was daylight when I left the airport, and full night when my overheated engine toiled up Sebastian's hill.

A Los Angeles County sheriff's car was parked in front of Sebastian's house. Its radio was talking brokenly, as if the car itself had developed a voice and begun to complain about the state of the world. When I rang Sebastian's doorbell, it was a grim-looking sheriff's deputy who answered the door.

"Yes sir?"

"I'd like to talk to Mr. Sebastian."

"Mr. Sebastian is busy right now. You the lawyer?"

"No." I told him who I was. "Mr. Sebastian will want to see me."

"I'll ask him."

The deputy closed the door until it clicked. I waited for a couple of minutes, listening to the mutterings of the patrol car. Sebastian opened the door. He kept changing, like a fighter undergoing a fifteen-round beating. The clump of hair on his forehead needed combing. His face was pale. His eyes were hopeless. The deputy stood behind him formally, like a keeper.

"They're taking her away," Sebastian said. "They're going to put her in prison."

"It isn't a prison," the deputy said. "It's a home."

I asked Sebastian: "Can't you get bail?"

"Yes, but I can't raise twenty thousand dollars."

"That's high."

"Assault with intent is a very serious charge," the deputy said. "And then there's the kidnapping charge—"

"It's still high."

"The judge didn't think so," the deputy said.

I said: "Would you go away, please? I want to talk to Mr. Sebastian in private."

"You said you weren't a lawyer. You got no right to give him legal advice."

"Neither have you. Give us a little leeway, officer."

He retreated out of sight if not out of hearing. I asked Sebastian: "Who is your lawyer?"

"I called a man in Van Nuys. Arnold Bendix. He said he'd come out tonight."

"This is tonight. What have you been doing all day?"

"I hardly know." He looked back into the house as if the day was still there waiting for him like a maze or a puzzle. "The D.A. sent two men out. Then we did a lot of talking to Sandy, of course, trying to make sense of this whole terrible mess."

"You won't do that by sitting around talking. Get your lawyer out here. And a doctor. You should be able to persuade the law to let you keep your daughter overnight. That will give your lawyer time to get back to the court and see if he can get the bail reduced. You can swing ten thousand bail. A bondsman will let you have it for one thousand."

He was appalled by the amount. "How can I possibly raise a thousand dollars? I'm sure to be fired from my job."

"Go to a loan shark. This is what they're for."

"And how much will that cost me?" he said wretchedly.

"A hundred or two more, perhaps. But we're not talking about money. We're talking about keeping your daughter out of jail."

He got the message, dimly at first, as if it had reached him by way of a communications satellite: he was at the crux of his life. The realization entered his eyes and took the place of hopelessness. There were still things he could do.

He went to the telephone and called his family doctor, a Dr. Jeffrey in Canoga Park. Dr. Jeffrey didn't want to come out to the house. Sebastian told him he had to. Then he called the lawyer and told him the same thing.

We went into the living room, accompanied by the deputy sheriff, who seemed to suspect that all of us might be planning a mass getaway. Bernice Sebastian was there, looking strained and gaunt and exceedingly well-groomed in a black sheath. With her was a pert blonde about my age who wore a blue suit that resembled a uniform.

She introduced herself as Mrs. Sherrill from the probation office. I told her I knew Jake Belsize.

"I was talking to him this afternoon," she said. "He's very upset about this whole affair. He blames himself for not keeping closer tabs on Spanner."

"He *should* blame himself," Mrs. Sebastian said.

"That's water under the bridge," I said to both of them; and to Mrs. Sherrill: "Does Belsize have any suggestions?"

"My being here was his suggestion. The girl won't talk to me, unfortunately. I tried to explain to her parents that if Sandy would give some sign of cooperation, it would be a lot easier for her."

Sebastian spoke up: "Sandy's in no condition to be questioned. She's in bed under sedation. Dr. Jeffrey's on his way over. So is my lawyer, Arnold Bendix."

"We can't wait around all night," the deputy said. "We've got a warrant, and it's our duty to take her in."

"No, we better wait, Tom," Mrs. Sherrill said. "See what the doctor has to say."

The deputy sat down in a corner by himself. A heavy silence settled over the room. It was like a funeral, or a deathbed scene. By getting into trouble Sandy had converted herself into an unforgettable presence, a kind of presiding deity of the household. I wondered if that had been her real intention.

Dr. Jeffrey arrived, a young man in a hurry. He went into Sandy's bedroom with her mother. The lawyer came close on the doctor's heels. Between the two of them, they persuaded the deputy and Mrs. Sherrill to let the whole thing lie over until morning.

The doctor was the first to leave: his time was the most expensive. I followed him out to his Rover, and he gave me a reluctant couple of minutes.

"What's Sandy's mental condition?"

"She's frightened and confused, naturally. A bit hysterical, and very tired."

"Is it all right for me to question her, doctor?"

"Is it necessary?"

"A man's life may depend on it. You may not know what's going on—"

"It's in tonight's paper. But it sounds pretty farfetched to me. How could a girl like that be involved in a kidnapping?"

"There's no doubt she is. Can I talk to her?"

"For five minutes, no longer. She needs rest."

"What about psychiatric care?"

"We'll see about that tomorrow. These adolescents have great recuperative powers."

Jeffrey turned to get into his car. But I had more questions for him.

"How long have you been treating her, doctor?"

"Three or four years, since she left her pediatrician."

"Last summer she was treated by a doctor named Converse in Beverly Hills. Did you know that?"

"No." I had succeeded in interesting Jeffrey. "I never heard of any Dr. Converse. What was he treating her for?"

"He wouldn't tell me. But he'd probably tell you. It could have a bearing on this mess."

"Really? Perhaps I'll give him a call."

The deputy and Mrs. Sherrill came out to the patrol car, and Jeffrey's Rover led them down the hill. Bernice Sebastian stood in the open doorway and watched them go.

"Thank God we've got them out of here for tonight. Thank you, too, Mr. Archer, for taking charge."

The expression of feeling came hard to her. Her eyes had a dull overexposed look.

"Your husband took charge. I gave him some advice. I've sat in on quite a few of these family evenings."

"Do you have children of your own?"

"No. I used to feel deprived."

She let me in and closed the door and leaned on it, as if she was countering the pressure of the night outside. "Will they let us keep her?"

"It depends on several things. You have trouble in the family, and Sandy isn't the only source of it. The trouble is between her and you."

"It's Keith she's angry with, mainly."

"That makes it three-way trouble. You've got to resolve it some way."

"Who says so?"

"Probation will say so, if she's lucky enough to be taken on as a risk. What's Sandy got against her father?"

"I don't know." But she veiled her eyes and looked down.

"I don't believe you, Mrs. Sebastian. Do you want to show me Sandy's diary?"

"I destroyed it, as I told you this morning—yesterday morning." She closed her eyes and covered them with her fine narrow hand. She had lost a day, for a moment, and it worried her.

"Tell me what was in it that made you destroy it."

"I can't. I won't. I won't put up with this humiliation."

She tried to rush blindly past me. I stepped sideways, and she ran into me. We stood in close contact, her body taut and elegant against mine. A spreading heat climbed from my groin to my heart and into my head.

We stepped back away from each other by sudden mutual consent. But there was a difference in our relation now, the difference of a possibility.

"I'm sorry," she said without explaining what she was sorry for.

"It was my fault. We haven't finished." Possibility put a curve on the meanings of the words.

"Haven't we?"

"No. The most important thing in determining what happens to Sandy is what happens to Stephen Hackett. If we can get him back alive—" I let the sentence finish itself in her mind. "Sandy may be able to tell me something. I have the doctor's permission to question her."

"What about?"

"She said last night that Davy Spanner was looking for a place where he used to live. I'm hoping she can pin it down a bit."

"Is that all?"

"It's all for now."

"Very well. You can talk to her."

We passed the door of the living room, where Sebastian and the lawyer were talking about bail. The door of Sandy's room was locked and the key was in the door. Her mother turned the key and gently pushed the door open.

"Sandy? Are you still awake?"

"What do you think?"

"That's not a nice way to answer me." The mother's tone was strangely mixed, as if she was talking to an immensely powerful idiot. "Mr. Archer wants to talk to you. *You* remember Mr. Archer."

"How could I forget him?"

"Sandy, *please* talk like yourself."

"This is the new me. Send in the fuzz."

The girl's toughness was clearly an act, generated by guilt and terror and self-disgust, and a rather bullying contempt for her mother. But for the time, at least, the tough act had taken over her personality. I went in hoping to reach the original girl, the one who collected Ivy League pennants and cloth animals.

She was sitting up in bed with one of the cloth animals hugged to her chest: a brown velvet spaniel with drooping ears, button eyes, a red felt tongue. Sandy was flushed and heavy-eyed. I sat on my heels by the bed, so that our eyes were almost on a level.

"Hello, Sandy."

"Hello. They're going to put me in jail." Her voice was matter-of-fact, wooden. "That should make you happy."

"Why do you say that?"

"It's what you wanted, isn't it?"

Her mother spoke from the doorway: "You mustn't talk like that to Mr. Archer."

"Go away," the girl said. "You give me a headache."

"*I'm* the one with the headache."

"I think I'm getting one, too," I said. "Please let me talk to Sandy alone for a minute."

The woman withdrew. The girl said: "What are we supposed to talk about?"

"You may be able to help me and help yourself at the same time. Everyone will be a lot better off if we can find Davy before he kills Mr. Hackett. Do you have any idea where they are?"

"No."

"You said last night, early this morning, that Davy was looking for a certain place, a place where he used to live. Do you know where it is, Sandy?"

"How should I know? He didn't know himself."

"Did he remember anything about it?"

"It was in the mountains someplace, up north of Santa Teresa. Some kind of a ranch where he used to live before they put him in the orphanage."

"Did he describe the place?"

"Yes, but it didn't sound like much of a place to me. The house burned down a long time ago. Somebody put a roof over part of it."

"The house burned down?"

"That's what he said."

I stood up. The girl recoiled, clutching the velvet dog as if it was her only friend and guardian.

"Why did he want to go back there, Sandy?"

"I don't know. He used to live there with his father. And his mother. I guess he thought it was heaven or something, you know?"

"Was Laurel Smith his mother?"

"I guess she was. She said she was his mother. But she ran out on him when he was a little boy." Sandy took a quick audible breath. "I told him he was lucky to have that happen."

"What have you got against your parents, Sandy?"

"We won't talk about it."

"Why did you throw in with Davy on this? You're not that kind of a girl."

"You don't know me. I'm bad clear through."

The tough act, which she'd forgotten for a minute, was coming on strong again. It was more than an act, of course. Her mind was caught between darkness and light, spinning like a coin she had tossed herself.

Outside in the hallway, where Bernice Sebastian was waiting, I remembered that something was missing from Sandy's room. The silver-framed picture of Heidi Gensler had been taken down.

chapter 19

WITH BERNICE SEBASTIAN'S permission, I shut my-
self up in the study and put in a call for Albert Blevins at the Bowman
Hotel. The long silence on the line was broken by a succession of
voices. Albert would be right down. Albert wasn't in his room but he
was being searched for. Albert has apparently gone out, and nobody
knew when he was expected back. He'd gone to a triple feature on
Market Street, it was thought.

I left a message for Albert, asking him to call my answering service
collect, but I doubted that I'd be hearing from him tonight.

There was another possible source of information. I got out the
papers I'd acquired from Albert Blevins and laid them on Sebastian's
desk. I reread the letter which Alma R. Krug, Albert's mother-in-law,
had sent him in 1948 from her house at 209 West Capo Street in
Santa Monica.

"Jasper and Laurel and the babe will be staying at our house for a
while," Mrs. Krug had written; "then Jasper wants to have a try at
ranching."

I looked for Alma Krug's name in the telephone directory, and
tried Information, in vain. Mrs. Krug's letter had been written nearly
twenty years ago. The lady must be very old, or dead.

I could think of only one way to find out which. I said good night
to the Sebastians and headed back toward Santa Monica. The traffic
on the freeway was still heavy but it was flowing freely now. The
headlights poured down Sepulveda in a brilliant cataract.

I felt surprisingly good. If Mrs. Krug was alive and able to tell me
where the ranch was, I could break the case before morning. I even
let a part of my mind play with the question of what I might do
with a hundred thousand dollars.

Hell, I could even retire. The possibility jarred me. I had to admit
to myself that I lived for nights like these, moving across the city's
great broken body, making connections among its millions of cells. I

had a crazy wish or fantasy that some day before I died, if I made all the right neural connections, the city would come all the way alive. Like the Bride of Frankenstein.

I left Sepulveda at Wilshire and drove down San Vicente to Capo Street. 209 West Capo was a two-story apartment building. Transplanted palm trees lit by green floodlights leaned across the new-looking stucco front.

I found the manager in Apartment One, a middle-aged man in shirt sleeves with his finger in a book. I told him my name. He said his was Ralph Cuddy.

Cuddy had a Southern accent, probably Texan. There were crossed pistols over the mantelpiece, and several moral sayings on the walls. I said: "A Mrs. Alma Krug used to live at this location."

"That's right."

"Do you know where she lives now?"

"In a home."

"What kind of a home?"

"A convalescent home. She broke her hip a few years back."

"That's too bad. I'd like to talk to her."

"What about?"

"Family matters."

"Mrs. Krug has no family left." He added with a self-conscious smirk: "Unless you count me."

"She has a son-in-law in San Francisco." And a great-grandson named Davy, God knows where. "Did she ever mention a ranch she owns in Santa Teresa County?"

"I've heard of the ranch."

"Can you tell me how to find it?"

"I've never been there. They let it go for taxes years ago."

"Are you related to Mrs. Krug?"

"Not exactly. I was close to the family. Still am."

"Can you give me the address of her convalescent home?"

"Maybe. Just what do you want to see her about?"

"I ran into her son-in-law Albert Blevins today."

Cuddy gave me a wise look. "That would be Etta's first husband."

"Right."

"And where does the ranch come in?"

"Albert was talking about it. He lived there once."

"I see."

Ralph Cuddy laid down his open book—its title was *The Role of the Security Officer in Business*—and went to a desk on the far side of the room. He came back to me with the address of the Oakwood Convalescent Home neatly written on a slip of paper.

The Home turned out to be a large California Spanish house dating from the twenties. It occupied its own walled grounds in Santa Monica. The driveway was overarched by Italian stone pines. There were ten or a dozen cars in the lighted parking lot, a drift of music from the main building. You could almost imagine that time had been reversed and there was a party going on.

The illusion faded in the big reception hall. Old people sat around in groups of two or three, chatting, keeping life warm. They made me think of refugees who had been given shelter in some baronial manor.

A very contemporary-looking nurse in white nylon led me down a corridor to Mrs. Krug's room. It was a spacious and well furnished bed-sitting room. A white-haired old lady wearing a wool robe was sitting in a wheel chair with an afghan over her knees, watching the Merv Griffin Show on television. She held an open Bible in her arthritic hands.

The nurse turned down the sound. "A gentleman to see you, Mrs. Krug."

She looked up with keen inquiring eyes magnified by her glasses. "Who are you?"

"My name is Lew Archer. Remember Albert Blevins, who married your daughter Etta?"

"Naturally I remember him. There's nothing the matter with my memory, thank you. What about Albert Blevins?"

"I was talking to him in San Francisco today."

"Is that a fact? I haven't heard from Albert in nearly twenty years. I asked him to come and see us when Jasper's boy was born, but Albert never answered."

She was silent, listening to silence. The nurse left the room. I sat down and Mrs. Krug leaned toward me, into the present.

"How is Albert, anyway? Is he still the same old Albert?"

"Probably. I didn't know him when he was younger."

"You weren't missing much." She smiled. "My husband always said that Albert was born too late. He should have been an old-time cowpoke. Albert was always a loner."

"He still is. He lives in a hotel room by himself."

"I'm not surprised. He should never have married anybody, let alone Etta. At first I blamed Albert for all the trouble between them, when he threw the lamp and set fire to the house. But when I saw the things that my daughter did later—" She closed her mouth with a click, as if to bite back memory. "Did Albert send you here to me?"

"Not exactly. In the course of our conversation, he mentioned the ranch you gave him, or let him use."

She nodded briskly. "That was in 1927, the year Albert married Etta. I was sick of the ranch myself, if you want the truth. I was a city girl, and a trained teacher. Twenty years of feeding chickens was all I could take. I made Krug move down here. He got a good job, a security job, which he held until he retired. Albert and Etta took over the ranch. They lasted about two years, and then they split. It was a bad-luck ranch. Did Albert tell you?"

"Tell me what?"

"The things that happened at that ranch. No." She shook her head. "Albert couldn't tell you because he didn't know, at least not all of them. First he burned down the house, and Etta ran out on him. She left him to look after little Jasper. When that broke down my husband and I took over Jasper and raised him, which wasn't easy, I can tell you. He was a handful.

"Then when Jasper settled down and married Laurel Dudney, he took it into his head to go back to the ranch. He didn't plan to work it, you understand. He thought it would be a cheap place to live while he painted pretty pictures of the countryside. I guess it was cheap enough, for him, with my husband and me sending him money after he used up Laurel's." Her veined hands closed on the arms of the wheel chair. "Do you know how that spoiled grandson of ours showed his gratitude?"

"Albert didn't tell me."

"Jasper took Laurel and the little boy and shook the dust from his heels. I haven't heard from any one of them since. Jasper is like his mother—and I say it even if she is my daughter—an ingrate through and through."

I didn't try to tell Alma Krug about Jasper's death, or Laurel's. The old woman's eyes were getting too bright. They knew too much already. A bitter frozen expression had settled on her mouth like a foretaste of her own death.

After another silence, she turned to me. "You didn't come here to listen to me complaining. Why *did* you come?"

"I want to see that ranch."

"What for? It's wornout land. It never was any better than semi-desert. We raised more buzzards than we did cattle. And after Jasper and Laurel took off into the blue we let it go for taxes."

"I think your great-grandson David may be there."

"Really? Do you know David?"

"I've met him."

She calculated rapidly. "He must be a young man now."

"A very young man. Davy is nineteen."

"What's he doing with himself?" she asked with the kind of hopeful interest that wasn't betting too heavily on the answer.

"Nothing much."

"I suppose he takes after his father. Jasper always had big dreams and nothing much to show for them afterwards." She rotated one wheel of her chair and turned to face me. "If you know where David is, do you know where Jasper is?"

"No. And I don't know where David is. I was hoping you could tell me how to find the ranch."

"Sure, if it hasn't blown away, the way that wind comes roaring down the wash. You know Rodeo City?"

"I've been there."

"Go into the middle of town to the main corner, that's the Rodeo Hotel with the sheriff's office right across from it. Take a right turn there and drive out past the rodeo grounds and over the pass and inland about twenty miles, to a little settlement called Centerville. I taught school there once. From Centerville you drive north another twelve miles on a county road. It's not too easy to find, especially after dark. Are you thinking of going there tonight?"

I said I was.

"Then you better ask in Centerville. Everybody in Centerville knows where the Krug ranch is." She paused. "It's strange how the generations of the family keep homing to that place. It's a bad-luck place, I guess we're a bad-luck family."

I didn't try to deny this. The little I knew of the family—Albert Blevins' solitary life, the ugly fates of Jasper and Laurel fifteen years apart, Davy's penchant for violence—only confirmed what Mrs. Krug had said.

She was sitting with her fists pressed against her body, as if she could feel the memory of labor. She shook her white head.

"I was thinking, if you see David, you could tell him where his great-grandma is. But I don't know. I just have enough for myself. I pay six hundred a month here. Don't tell him about me unless he asks. I wouldn't want Jasper back on my hands again. Or Laurel. She was a sweet girl, but she turned out to be an ingrate, too. I took her into my home and did my best for her, and then she turned her back on me."

"Was Laurel related to you, too?"

"No. She came from Texas. A very wealthy man was interested in Laurel. He sent her to us."

"I don't understand."

"You're not supposed to. I won't tell on Laurel. She wasn't my daughter or granddaughter, but I liked her better than any of them."

She was whispering. The past was filling the room like a tide of whispers. I got up to leave.

Alma Krug gave me her knobbed, delicate hand. "Turn up the sound on your way out, please. I'd rather listen to *other* people talk."

I turned up the sound and closed her door after me. Behind another door, halfway down the corridor, a quavering old man's voice rose: "Please don't cut me."

The old man pulled the door open and came out into the corridor. His naked body was the shape of an elongated egg. He flung his arms around me, and pressed his almost hairless head into my solar plexus.

"Don't let them cut me to pieces. Tell them not to, Momma."

Though there was nobody else there, I told them not to. The little old man let go of me and went back into his room and closed the door.

IN THE RECEPTION HALL, the refugees from the war of the generations had dwindled to half a dozen. A middle-aged male orderly was quietly herding them back to their rooms.

"It's bedtime, folks," he said.

Jack Fleischer came in the front door. His eyes, his entire face, were glazed with weariness and alcohol.

"I'd like to see Mrs. Krug," he said to the orderly.

"I'm sorry, sir. Visiting hours are over."

"This is important."

"I can't help that, sir. I don't make the decisions around here. The manager's in Chicago at a convention."

"Don't tell me that. I'm a law-enforcement officer."

Fleischer's voice was rising. His face was swelling with blood. He fumbled in his pockets and found a badge which he showed to the orderly.

"That makes no difference, sir. I have my orders."

Without warning, Fleischer hit the orderly with his open hand. The man fell down and got up. Half of his face was red, the other half white. The old people watched in silence. Like actual refugees, they were more afraid of physical force than anything.

I moved up behind Fleischer and put an armlock on him. He was heavy and powerful. It was all I could do to hold him.

"Is he a friend of yours?" the orderly asked me.

"No."

But in a sense Fleischer belonged to me. I walked him outside and released him. He pulled out an automatic pistol.

"You're under arrest," he told me.

"What for? Preventing a riot?"

"Resisting an officer in the performance of his duty."

He was glaring and sputtering. The gun in his hand looked like a .38, big enough to knock me down for good.

"Come off it, Jack, and put the gun away. You're out of your county, and there are witnesses."

The orderly and his charges were watching from the front steps. Jack Fleischer turned his head to look at them. I knocked the gun from his hand and picked it up as he dove for it. On his hands and knees, like a man changing into a dog, he barked at me: "I can put you away for this. I'm an officer."

"Act like one."

The orderly came toward us. He was just a whitish movement in the corner of my vision. I was watching Fleischer as he got up.

The orderly said to me: "We don't want trouble. I better call the police, eh?"

"That shouldn't be necessary. How about it, Fleischer?"

"Hell, I am the police."

"Not in this bailiwick you're not. Anyway, I heard that you were retired."

"Who the hell are you?" Fleischer squinted at me. His eyes gleamed like yellowish quartz in the half light.

"I'm a licensed private detective. My name is Archer."

"If you want to stay licensed, give me back my gun." He held out his thick red hand for it.

"We better have a talk first, Jack. And you better apologize to the man you hit."

Fleischer lifted one corner of his mouth in a snarl of pain. For a spoiled old cop, having to apologize was cruel and unusual punishment.

"Sorry," he said without looking at the man.

"All right," the orderly said.

He turned and walked away with formal dignity. The old people on the steps followed him into the building. The door sucked shut behind them.

Fleischer and I moved toward our cars. We faced each other in the space between them, each with his back to his own car.

"My gun," he reminded me. It was in my pocket.

"First we talk. What are you after, Jack?"

"I'm working on an old case, a fatal accident which happened years ago."

"If you know it was an accident, why did you open it up again?"

"I never closed it. I don't like unfinished business."

He was fencing, talking in generalities. I tried to jolt him. "Did you know Jasper Blevins?"

"No. I never met him," he said levelly.

"But you knew his wife Laurel."

"Maybe I did. Not as well as some people think."

"Why didn't you get her to identify her husband's body?"

He didn't answer for quite a while. Finally he said: "Are you recording this?"

"No."

"Come away from your car, eh, pal?"

We walked down the driveway. The overarching stone pines were like a darker sky narrowing down on us. Fleischer was more voluble in the almost total darkness.

"I admit I made a mistake fifteen years ago. That's the only thing I'm going to admit. I'm not going to dig up the garbage and spread it all over my own front porch."

"What was the mistake, Jack?"

"I trusted that broad."

"Did Laurel say it wasn't her husband who died under the train?"

"She said a lot of things. Most of them were lies. She conned me good."

"You can't blame her for everything. It was your job to get the body identified."

"Don't tell me what my job was. In the thirty years I worked for the sheriff's department, close to a hundred hoboes died under trains in our county. Some had identification on them, and some didn't. This one didn't. How was I to know it was different from the others?"

"What makes it so different, Jack?"

"You know damn well what makes it different."

"Tell me."

"I've told you all I'm going to. I thought we could have a meeting of the minds. But you're all take and no give."

"You haven't given me anything I can use."

"You haven't given me anything, period," he said. "What's your angle?"

"No angle. I'm working on the Stephen Hackett snatch."

"The what?" He was stalling.

"Don't kid me, you know about Hackett. You read about it in the San Francisco paper."

He made a quarter-turn and faced me in the darkness. "So you're the one that had me tailed in Frisco. What in hell are you trying to do to me?"

"Nothing personal. Your case and mine are connected. Jasper Blevins's little boy Davy, the one who got lost in the shuffle, has grown up into a big boy. He took Hackett yesterday."

I could hear Fleischer draw in his breath quickly, then let it out slowly. "The paper said this Hackett is really loaded." It was a question.

"He's loaded all right."

"And Jasper Blevins's boy is holding him for ransom?"

"There hasn't been any talk of ransom, that I know of. I think he's planning to kill Hackett, if he hasn't already."

"Christ! He can't do that!" Fleischer sounded as if his own life had been threatened.

I said: "Do you know Hackett?"

"I never saw him in my life. But there's money in it, pal. We should throw in together, you and me."

I didn't want Fleischer as a partner. I didn't trust him. On the other hand, he knew things about the case that were unknown to anyone else alive. And he knew Santa Teresa County.

"Do you remember the Krug ranch, near Centerville?"

"Yeah, I know where it is."

"Davy Blevins may be holding Stephen Hackett on the ranch."

"Then let's get up there," Fleischer said. "What are we waiting for?"

We went back to our cars. I handed Fleischer his gun. Facing him in the semi-darkness, I had the feeling that I was looking at myself in a bleared distorting mirror.

Neither of us had mentioned the death of Laurel Smith.

WE AGREED TO DOUBLE UP in Fleischer's car, which was new and fast. I left mine at an all-night station in Canoga Park, not too far from Keith Sebastian's house. Whatever happened, I'd be coming back there.

I drove while Fleischer dozed in the front seat beside me. Up the San Fernando Valley, over the main pass, back by way of Camarillo to the dark sea. When we crossed the Santa Teresa County line, Fleischer woke up as if he could smell home territory.

A few miles south of Santa Teresa, as we were traversing a lonely stretch of highway, Fleischer told me to stop by a eucalyptus grove. I assumed it was a call of nature. He didn't get out of the car, though, when I pulled off on the shoulder.

He twisted toward me in the seat and chopped at my head with the loaded butt of his gun. I went out, all the way. After a while the darkness where I lay was invaded by dreams. Huge turning wheels, like the interlocking wheels of eternity and necessity, resolved themselves into a diesel locomotive. I was lying limp across the tracks and the train was coming, swinging its Cyclops eye.

It honked its horn at me. It wasn't a train sound, though, and I wasn't lying on a track, and it was no dream. I sat up in the middle of the northbound lane of the highway. A truck lit up like a Christmas tree was bearing down on me, honking repeatedly.

Its brakes were shrieking, too, but it wasn't going to be able to stop before it got to me. I lay down and watched it blot out the stars. Then I could see the stars again, and feel the blood pounding all through my body.

More traffic was coming up from the south. I crawled off the road, feeling small and awkward as a Jerusalem cricket. The eucalyptus trees muttered and sighed in the wind like witnesses. I felt for my gun. It was missing.

Fleischer's treachery had touched a paranoid nerve which twanged and jangled in my injured head. I reminded it and myself that I had been ready to turn on Fleischer when it suited me to. His timing had been a little faster than mine.

By now the driver of the truck had pulled his rig off the road and set out a flare. He ran toward me with a flashlight.

"Hey, are you all right?"

"I think so." I stood up, balancing the angry weight of my head.

He shone the flashlight in my face. I closed my eyes and almost fell under the slap of light.

"Hey, there's blood on your face. Did I hit you?"

"You missed me. A friend of mine knocked me out and left me on the highway."

"I better call the police, eh? You need an ambulance?"

"I don't need anything if you'll give me a lift to Santa Teresa."

He hesitated, his face torn between sympathy and suspicion. The blood on my face cut two ways. Nice people didn't get hurt and left on the highway.

"Okay," he said without enthusiasm. "I can do that much for you."

He drove me to the outskirts of Santa Teresa. The Power Plus station was still lit up, and I asked the driver to let me off there.

Fred Cram, the attendant with the special boot, was on duty. He didn't seem to recognize me. I went into the men's room and washed my face. There was a swollen cut above my temple, but it had stopped bleeding.

Someone had printed on the wall: MAKE SENSE NOT WAR. I laughed. It hurt my head.

I went outside and asked Fred Cram for permission to use the phone. He recognized me now.

"Did you find the girl?"

"I found her. Thanks very much."

"You're welcome. Is there anything I can do for you?"

"Just let me use the phone, for a local call."

The electric clock in the office had its hands straight up on midnight. Midnight was my time for calling the Langstons. I looked up their number in the directory, and dialed it. Henry Langston answered, in a muffled voice:

"Langston residence."

"Archer. You're going to hate me."

His voice brightened. "I've been wondering about you. Davy is all over the local paper."

"I think I know where he is, Hank. So does Fleischer—he's on his way there now. Do you feel like another midnight drive?"

"Where to?"

"A ranch near Centerville in the northern part of the county."

"And Davy's there with Hackett?"

"I'd say there's a fifty per cent chance of it. Bring a gun."

"All I have is a .32 target pistol."

"Bring it. And bring a flashlight."

I told him where I was. While I was waiting outside the office, Fred Cram locked the pumps and turned out the overhead lights.

"I'm sorry," he said to me. "It's time to close."

"Go right ahead. I expect to be picked up in a few minutes."

But the young man lingered, eying my head wound. "Did Davy Spanner do that to you?"

"No. I'm still looking for him."

"That was him with the girl last night. I didn't know him at first, he's changed so much. But when I read about him in the paper—he really did have somebody in the trunk."

"He really did. Do you know Davy?"

"I knew him in high school one year. He was a freshman and I was a senior. He wasn't a delinquent back in those days. He was real little and small, before he got his growth, which is why I didn't recognize him last night."

"If you see him again let me know, Fred." I gave him my card. "You can call my answering service any time, collect."

He took the card, but the look on his face rejected it. "That isn't really what I had in mind."

"What did you have in mind?"

"The way things turn out in life. I mean, here I am pumping gas for a living and Davy's turned into a criminal."

Having put himself on record, he turned out the office lights and locked the door. He stayed around, politely, until Langston's station wagon came in off the highway and pulled up beside his jalopy.

I said good night to Fred and climbed into the wagon. Langston's sensitive eyes took in my face and head.

"You've been hurt. Do you need a doctor?"

"Not now. I'm at least half an hour behind Fleischer already."

"How did he get into this?"

"He's been in it from the beginning. You know that. I made the mistake of trying to work with him. That lasted about an hour. He knocked me out and left me on the highway."

Hank whistled. "Shouldn't you tell the police?"

"Then we'd never get away. Did you bring your flashlight and pistol?"

"In the dash compartment. I feel like a crimebuster's apprentice."

His humor sounded a little forced, but I went along with it. "Let's go, apprentice."

Langston turned onto the highway and headed north. He'd caught a few hours' sleep before I called, and was full of energy and curiosity. He wanted to talk at length about Davy and his psychological problems. I was weary of such palaver. My answers got shorter and shorter. After a while I crawled into the back seat and tried to sleep. But every time a truck went by I woke up with a start.

Where the highway looped inland, we ran into a spatter of rain. Above the mountains to the north, the sky was very black, lit by occasional stabs of lightning. The highway brought us back to the coast. Here the night sky was still clear, and the moon's white eye peered over the rim of the sea. I recognized the crossroads where we had picked up Sandy the night before.

The thought of the girl was heavy on my mind. She was swinging through all the changes of the moon. The moon was white and shining, the very symbol of purity, but it had its dark side, too, pocked and cold and desolate and hidden. The girl could turn either way, depending on the outcome of our journey.

If we could bring Hackett out alive, she'd have a chance for probation. If Hackett died, her future died with him.

IT WAS AFTER ONE when we got to Rodeo City. It was a seaside motel town strung out between the highway and the shore. We went down a ramp to the main street, which ran parallel to the highway and just below it. Three motorcyclists in bowler hats roared past us down the middle of the street. Girls with blowing hair clung to their backs like succubi.

We found the turning and the sign: CENTERVILLE 20 MIS., and we turned inland. The blacktop road passed rodeo stands which loomed like an ancient amphitheater in the darkness. Gradually it looped up through the foothills, then more abruptly into a mountain pass. Before we reached the summit of the pass we were in a dense cloud. It gathered like rain on the windshield, and slowed us to a crawl.

On the far side of the summit actual rain began to pound on the roof. The windshield and the windows fogged up. I climbed into the front seat and wiped them every few minutes, but it was slow going.

It rained all the way to Centerville. Every now and then a flash of lightning would show the timbered walls of the valley slanting up above us.

Centerville was one of those Western hamlets that hadn't changed much in two generations. It was a street of poor frame houses, a general store with a gas pump, closed for the night, a schoolhouse with a bell housing on the roof-peak, and a small white steepled church shining wetly in our headlights.

The only lighted building was a lunch counter with a beer sign, beside the general store. The place had its CLOSED sign out, but I could see a white-aproned man swinging a mop inside. I ran through the downpour and knocked on the door.

The aproned man shook his head, and pointed at the CLOSED sign. I knocked some more. After a while he leaned his mop against the bar and came and opened up.

"What is this, anyway?" He was a man past middle age with a foxy weathered face and a talker's mouth.

I stepped inside. "I'm sorry to bother you. Can you tell me how to get to the Krug ranch?"

"I can tell you, but it doesn't mean you'll get there. Buzzard Creek will be running by now."

"So?"

"The wash crosses the road to the ranch. You can try it if you want to. The other fellow made it, leastwise he hasn't come back."

"You mean Jack Fleischer?"

"You know Jack, do you? What's going on up at the ranch?" He nudged me confidentially. "Has Jack got a woman up there? It wouldn't be the first time."

"Could be."

"It's a hell of a night for a party, and a hell of a place."

I called Hank Langston in from the car. The man in the apron introduced himself. His name was Al Simmons, and he made it very clear that he owned the place, as well as the store next door.

Simmons spread out a paper napkin on the bar and drew a crude map for us. The entrance to the ranch was twelve miles north of Centerville. Buzzard Creek ran, when it ran, just this side of the ranch. It rose very quickly in a heavy rain. But we might make it across, since it hadn't been raining long.

Simmons said as we were leaving: "If you get stuck, I have a tractor that can pull you out. Of course that will cost you money."

"How much money?" Hank wanted to know.

"Depends on how long it takes. I generally get ten an hour with the tractor. That's portal to portal. But if your car gets carried away downriver, there's nothing anybody can do. So don't let that happen, eh?"

We drove forever up a gravel road that badly needed resurfacing. The rain came hissing down from the sky. The lightning made frightening meaningless signs.

We crossed several small streams which ran through dips in the road. Exactly twelve miles from Centerville by the odometer, we came to the creek. It flowed across the road, sliding brown and steady under the headlights, dappled by falling rain. It looked at least a hundred feet wide.

"Do you think you can make it, Hank?"

"I don't know how deep it is. I'd hate to lose the car."

"We might do better wading. I'll try first."

I got out my gun and flashlight and put them in the inside breast pockets of my jacket. Then I removed my shoes and socks and trousers and left them in the wagon. When I stepped out in front of the headlights, jacketed but trouserless, Hank laughed out loud at me.

The water was cold, and the gravel hurt my feet. Still I felt a certain pleasure which went back a long way, to my first infantile wades in Long Beach, holding my father's hand.

I could have used a hand to hold on to now. Though the water never rose higher than my thighs, it pulled at my legs and made it hard to walk. At the deepest part, in the middle of the stream, I had to brace my legs apart and lean into it. It was like a second force of gravity pulling me at right angles to the first.

When I got beyond the middle I paused for a moment to rest and get my bearings. Peering ahead to the far shore, I could see a grayish bundle lying beside the road. I moved closer. It was a man, or the body of a man, wearing gray clothes. I splashed toward him and got the flashlight out.

It was Hackett, lying face up to the rain. His face was so badly battered that he was hardly recognizable. His clothes were sodden. There was mud in his hair.

He responded to the light, though, by trying to sit up. I got down and helped him, with an arm around his shoulders.

"I'm Archer. Remember me?"

He nodded. His head lolled against me.

"Can you talk?"

"Yes, I can talk." His voice was thick, as though he had blood in his mouth, and pitched so low I had to lean close to hear it.

"Where's Davy Spanner?"

"He ran away. Shot the other one and ran away."

"He shot Jack Fleischer?"

"I don't know his name. An older man. Spanner blew his head off. It was terrible."

"Who beat you, Mr. Hackett?"

"Spanner did. He beat me unconscious and left me for dead, I guess. The rain brought me to. I got this far, but then I pooped out."

Hank shouted at me from the other bank. The headlights of the station wagon blinked. I yelled at him to cool it, and told Hackett to wait where he was.

He said in utter dismay: "You're not going to leave me here?"

"Just for a few minutes. We'll try and bring the station wagon across. If Spanner's gone, there's nothing to be afraid of."

"He's gone. Thank God for that."

Hackett's bad experience seemed to have humbled him. I felt a sympathy for him which had been lacking before, and I lent him my jacket.

I started back across the river with the flashlight in one hand and the gun in the other. Then I remembered Fleischer's car. If he was dead, I might as well use it.

I came back to Hackett. "Where's the dead man's car?"

"I think I saw a car beside the barn."

Waveringly, he pointed off to the right.

I walked up the road a hundred yards or so and came to a lane branching off to the right. Rains past and present had worn it down to bare rocks. I went up the lane, dreading what I would find at the end of it.

The barn was the first building I came to. It was sagging and old, with great holes in its walls. I shone my flashlight around. A barn owl flew out of one of the holes: a blank flat oddly human face flying on silent wings through the beam of light. It startled me, as if it had been Jack Fleischer's ghost.

His car was parked below the barn, unlocked, with no key in the ignition. This probably meant the key was in Fleischer's pocket. I almost gave up my plan to use his car. But I forced myself to go on up to the house.

Apart from one small flat-roofed section, there was nothing left of the building but its old stone foundations. Even the part still standing had taken a beating from the weather. Torn roofing paper flapped in the wind, and the warped door hung ajar.

When I found Jack Fleischer inside, prone on the wet concrete floor, he had become a part of the general ruin. In the weak flashlight beam, his face and head seemed to have been partly rusted away. Water dripped down on him from the leaking roof.

I found when I went through Fleischer's pockets that his body was still warm. His car keys were in his trousers, and in the breast pocket of his jacket were the documents he had had copied at the Acme shop in San Francisco. I kept a copy of each of them.

Before leaving the shack, I took a final look around with the flashlight. Built into one corner was a two-level board bed like those you see in old Western bunkhouses. There was a sleeping bag in the lower bunk. The only other furniture was a chair made from a cut-down wooden barrel. Looped and coiled beside this chair was a lot of used adhesive tape. Some cigarette butts lay on the floor by the bunk.

I left Fleischer where he was, for the police, and made my way down the muddy slope to his car. The engine started on the first try. I drove in low gear down the gullied lane to the road, and back to the spot where Hackett was waiting. He sat with his head leaning forward on his knees.

I helped him to his feet and into the front seat. Hank shouted from the other bank:

"Don't try it, Lew. It's too deep."

I had to try it. I couldn't leave Hackett where he was. I didn't trust myself to carry him across. One slip and he'd be gone downriver, and all our efforts lost.

I eased the car forward slowly into the water, aiming straight for Hank Langston's headlights and trusting there were no curves in the road. For one frightening instant in the middle, the car seemed to be floating. It shifted sideways, then jarred to rest on a higher part of the invisible road.

We got across without further incident. Supporting Hackett between us, Langston and I transferred him to the back seat of the wagon. After putting on my trousers I took back my jacket and wrapped Hackett in a car rug. Fortunately the wagon had a good heater.

I locked the doors of Fleischer's car and left it in the road. Then I went back to it and searched the trunk. No tapes. I slammed the trunk lid down. We made the slow twelve-mile journey back to Centerville.

We must have been gone about two hours, but the lights were still on in Al Simmons' place. He came to the door yawning. He looked as if he'd been sleeping in his clothes.

"I see you made it back."

"We did. Jack Fleischer didn't. He's been shot."

"Dead?"

"Half his head was blasted away with a sawed-off shotgun."

"At the Krug place?"

"That's correct."

"What do you know? I always reckoned that place would get him in the end."

I didn't take time to ask Simmons what he meant. He showed me his telephone at the back of the counter, and gave me the number of the nearest sheriff's office, in Rodeo City. The officer on duty was a Deputy Pennell. I told him that Jack Fleischer had been killed by a shotgun blast.

"Jack?" he said in a shocked voice. "But I was just talking to Jack tonight. He dropped by earlier in the evening."

"What did he say?"

"Said he was on his way to the old Krug ranch. He wouldn't tell me what was on his mind. But he said if he didn't come back by morning, I was to come up after him, with a couple of extra men."

"You better do just that. Don't wait for morning."

"I can't. I got no patrol car available. My car broke down, and the county won't budget another till January." Pennell sounded upset and confused. "I'll have to have a car sent up from Santa Teresa."

"What about an ambulance?"

"That has to come up from Santa Teresa, too. But if Jack's dead he don't need an ambulance."

"Not everybody's dead. I have an injured man with me." I didn't mention Hackett's name, since I was hoping somehow to get him home before the news broke. "I'll bring him into Rodeo City. We'll meet the ambulance and the patrol car at your office."

Al Simmons sat at the counter listening openly to my end of the conversation. When I hung up he spoke in a meditative tone:

"It's funny how things turn out in a man's life. Jack held that same post in Rodeo for over fifteen years. Rory Pennell was his sidekick."

"What was Jack's connection with the Krug ranch?"

"I don't hardly like to say." But his eyes were bright with desire to deliver his story. "Jack's dead and all, and he's—he was a married man. I wouldn't want it to get back to Mrs. Fleischer."

"Another woman?"

"Yeah. Jack had his good qualities, I guess, but he was always a

skirt-chaser. Back in the early fifties, he was chasing the woman who
lived on the Krug place. I think he caught her, too," Simmons said
with a sideways grin. "He used to stop off here for a case of beer, and
then he'd go up and spend the night with her. I can't hardly blame
him. Laurel Blevins was a pretty piece."

"Didn't her husband object?"

"I don't think he knew. Blevins was gone a lot of the time. He
killed all his own meat. When he wasn't hunting, he was tramping
around the hills with a painter's whatever-you-call-it."

"Easel?"

"Yeah. He pretended to be some kind of an artist. But him and
his wife, and the little boy, they lived like Digger Indians in that
burned-out old ranch house. You can't hardly blame the woman for
going for Jack. He was a good-looking fellow fifteen years ago, and he
always had money from the Rodeo houses. After Blevins left her, he
kept the woman in Mamie Hagedorn's house. I got that from
Mamie Hagedorn herself."

"What happened to Blevins?"

"He traveled on. He was a born loser."

"And the little boy?"

"I don't know. He got lost in the shuffle."

He should have stayed lost, I was thinking, instead of coming back
to revenge himself on a past he couldn't change even with a shotgun.

I questioned Al Simmons about Davy, and Simmons remembered
him. At least he'd seen a man or boy, driving a green compact, take
the turn to the ranch early the previous morning. No, he hadn't seen
or heard him come out tonight.

"Is there another way out?"

"There's the northwest pass. But it takes a four-wheel drive, 'specially in weather like this."

Langston was honking outside. I had one more thing to do. I
phoned Hackett's house in Malibu and got Ruth Marburg on the
line and told her I was bringing her son home.

She burst into tears. Then she started to ask me questions, which I
cut short. I told her we were coming down by ambulance. While
Hackett didn't seem to be seriously hurt, he was exhausted and
suffering from exposure. She'd better have a doctor on hand when we
got there.

I gave her six a.m. as our E.T.A.

chapter 23

DEPUTY RORY PENNELL was a rawboned man of
forty or so with a heavy chestnut mustache and a bad stammer. The
stammer had probably been intensified by Jack Fleischer's death.
Pennell seemed genuinely upset. As we talked, his big right hand
kept going back to the butt of the gun he wore on his hip.

I would have liked to spend more time in Rodeo City, talking to
Pennell and Mamie Hagedorn and anyone else who might help me
to reconstruct the past. It was beginning to look as though Jack
Fleischer had been deeply implicated in the death of Jasper Blevins.
But the question was fairly academic now, and it would have to wait.
The important thing was to get Stephen Hackett home.

The two sheriff's men from Santa Teresa would have been glad to
escort him. It was a relatively safe and easy job, high in publicity
value. I reminded them that Jack Fleischer's body was lying alone on
the Krug place. Somewhere in the hills north of there the boy who
killed him was probably stuck in the mud.

I said good-bye to Hank and rode the ambulance south, sitting on
the floor beside Hackett's pallet. He was feeling better. He had had
some first aid on his face, and sucked a cup of broth through a straw.
I asked him a few of the questions that had to be asked.

"Did Sandy Sebastian hit Lupe?"

"Yes. She knocked him out with a tire iron."

"Did she use violence on you?"

"Not directly. She did tape me while the boy held the shotgun on
me. She taped my wrists and ankles and mouth, even my eyes." He
raised his hand from the blanket and touched his eyes. "Then they
put me in the trunk of her car. It was hellish being shut up like
that." He lifted his head. "How long ago did it start?"

"About thirty-six hours. Did she have any special grudge against
you?"

He answered slowly. "She must have. But I can't understand what."

"What about the boy?"

"I never saw him before. He acted crazy."

"In what way?"

"He didn't seem to know what he was doing. At one point he laid me out across a railroad track. I know it sounds like Victorian melodrama. But he clearly intended to kill me, by letting a train crush me. The girl ran away, and he changed his mind. He took me up to the—the other place and kept me prisoner there.

"For most of the day—yesterday?—he treated me pretty well. He took the tape off and let me move around some. Gave me water to drink, and some bread and cheese. Of course the shotgun was always in evidence. He lay on the bunk and held the gun on me. I sat in the chair. I'm not a coward, ordinarily, but it got pretty nerve-wracking after a while. I couldn't understand what he had in mind."

"Did he mention money, Mr. Hackett?"

"I did. I offered him a good deal of money. He said he didn't want it."

"What did he want?"

Hackett took a long time to answer. "He didn't seem to know. He seemed to be living out some kind of a dream. In the evening he smoked marijuana, and he got dreamier. He seemed to be hoping for some kind of mystic experience. And I was the burnt offering."

"Did he say so?"

"Not directly. He said it as a joke, that he and I should form a musical group. He suggested several names for it, such as The Human Sacrifice." His voice faded. "It was no joke. I believe he meant to kill me. But he wanted to see me suffer as long as possible first."

"Why?"

"I'm not a psychologist, but he seemed to regard me as a substitute father. Toward the end, when he got high on marijuana, he started calling me Dad. I don't know who his real dad is or was, but he must have hated him."

"His dad died under a train when he was three. He saw it happen."

"Good Lord!" Hackett sat up partly. "That explains a lot of things, doesn't it?"

"Did he talk about his father?"

"No. I didn't encourage him to talk. Eventually he dozed off. I was planning to jump him when the other chap—Fleischer?—came in. He must have thought there was nobody there. The boy let him have both barrels. He had no chance at all. I ran outside. The boy caught me and beat me unconscious."

He fell back onto the pallet and raised both elbows defensively, as if Davy's fists were in his face again. We rode the rest of the way in silence. Hackett's hoarse breathing quieted down, lengthening out gradually into the rhythms of sleep.

I spread a blanket on the vibrating floor and slept, too, while the world turned toward morning. I woke up feeling good. Stephen Hackett and I had come back together and alive. But he was still full of fear. He moaned in his sleep and covered his head with his arms.

The red sun was coming up behind the Malibu hills. The ambulance stopped in West Malibu near a sign which said "PRIVATE COLONY: NO TRESPASSING." The driver didn't know where to make his turn, and he gestured through the window.

I went up front with him. The other attendant got into the back with Hackett. We found our left turn and climbed through the hills to Hackett's gate.

It was just a few minutes past six. Coming over the pass we were met by the full blaze of the morning sun, like an avalanche of light.

Ruth Marburg and Gerda Hackett came out of the house together. Ruth's face was lined and bleary-eyed and joyful. She ran heavily toward me and pressed my hands and thanked me. Then she turned to her son, who was being lifted out of the ambulance by the attendants. She bent over him and hugged him, crying and exclaiming over his wounds.

Gerda Hackett stood behind her. She looked a little piqued, as if she felt upstaged by Ruth's display of emotion. But she got her hug in, too, while Sidney Marburg and Dr. Converse stood and watched.

There was a third man, fortyish and heavy-shouldered, with a square unsmiling face. He acted as if he was in charge. When Hackett stood up shakily and insisted on walking into the house, instead of being carried, the heavy-shouldered man assisted him. Dr. Converse followed them in, looking rather ineffectual.

Ruth Marburg surprised me. I'd temporarily forgotten about the money she'd promised. She hadn't. Without having to be reminded, she took me into the library and wrote a check.

"I've postdated this a week." She stood up, waving the check to dry the ink. "I don't keep this much in the bank. I'm going to have to transfer some funds and sell some securities."

"There's no hurry."

"Good." She handed me the little yellow slip. It was for the amount she had promised.

"You're an unusual rich woman," I said. "Most of them scream bloody murder over a nickel."

"I haven't always been rich. Now I have more money than I can spend."

"So have I, now."

"Don't let it fool you. A hundred grand is chicken feed these days. Uncle Sam will cut it in half for you. If you take my advice you'll put the rest in real estate and watch it grow."

Somehow, I didn't think I would. I put the check away in my wallet. It excited me in a way I didn't quite like. Underlying the excitement was a vague depression, as if I belonged to the check in a way, instead of having it belong to me.

Ruth Marburg reached up and touched my cheek. It wasn't a pass, but it was a gesture of possession. "Aren't you happy, Lew? May I call you Lew?"

"Yes and yes."

"You don't look happy. You should be. You've done a wonderful thing, for all of us. I'm eternally grateful to you."

"Good." But it wasn't so good. Even her repeated thanks were a subtle form of possession, taking and not giving.

"How on earth did you pull it off?" she said.

I told her, very briefly, about the series of leads, from Fleischer to Albert Blevins and Alma Krug, which took me to the shack where her son was held; and what I found there.

"You've had a terrible night. You must be exhausted." She touched my cheek again.

"Don't do that please."

She withdrew her hand as if I'd tried to bite it. "What's the matter?"

"You bought your son with this check. Not me."

"I didn't mean anything by it. It was a friendly gesture. Heavens, I'm old enough to be your mother."

"The hell you are."

She chose to take this as a compliment, and it soothed her injured feelings. "You really are tired, aren't you, Lew? Did you get any sleep at all?"

"Not much."

"I'll tell you what. Why don't you go to bed and get some sleep now? Stephen and Gerda have plenty of room."

The invitation sounded so good that I started yawning, like an addict for a fix. But I told her I preferred my own bed.

"You're very independent, aren't you, Lew?"

"I guess I am."

"I feel the same way myself. I only wish Sidney had some of the same spirit."

She sounded like a mother talking about her backward little boy.

"Speaking of Sidney, I wonder if I can get him to drive me. My car's over in the Valley."

"Of course. I'll tell him. There's just one thing before you leave," she said. "Mr. Thorndike will want to talk to you."

She went and got the heavy-shouldered man. Thorndike introduced himself as a special agent of the FBI. Ruth left us together in the library and Thorndike debriefed me, recording what I said on a portable tape recorder.

"I don't mean to be critical," he said, "since it all worked out. But that was kind of a wild idea, going up against a kidnapper with nobody but a high-school counselor to back you up. You could have got what Fleischer got."

"I know that. But this is a peculiar kind of kidnapper. I don't believe he'd shoot Langston."

"Anyway, he didn't get a chance to."

Thorndike's manner was a little superior, like a teacher giving an oral quiz to a not very apt pupil. I didn't mind. I had brought Hackett in. He hadn't.

CAPTAIN AUBREY of the sheriff's department arrived, and Thorndike went to talk to him. I closed the door of the library behind Thorndike and pushed the button in the knob which locked the door. It was the first time I'd been alone in a lighted place since I took the photocopies from Jack Fleischer's body.

I spread them out on a table by the windows and pulled back the drapes. The copy of the birth certificate stated that Henrietta R. Krug had been born in Santa Teresa County on October 17, 1910, the daughter of Joseph and Alma Krug. It was signed by Richard Harlock, M.D., of Rodeo City.

The other photocopy was more interesting. It showed a part of the front page of the *Santa Teresa Star* for May 28, 1952. Under the heading "Oil Tycoon Slaying Still Unsolved" and the subheading "Youth Gang Sought," was the following short account, datelined Malibu:

"The May 24 beach shooting of Mark Hackett, well-known Malibu citizen and Texas oil millionaire, is still under investigation by the police. According to Deputy Robert Aubrey of the sheriff's Malibu substation, more than a dozen suspects have been arrested and released. A gang of motorcyclists which was reported in the Malibu area on the night of May 24 is being sought for questioning.

"Hackett was shot to death while walking on the beach on the evening of May 24. His wallet was taken. Police have recovered a revolver which has been identified as the murder weapon. The dead man is survived by his widow and his son, Stephen."

On the same page there was a story, with the dateline "Rodeo City (by Special Correspondent)," under the heading "Death on the Rails Strikes Again":

"Riding the rails, which is reputed to be the cheapest way to travel, is costing some travelers their lives. Over the past several years, the lonely stretch of tracks south of Rodeo City has been the scene of a number of fatal accidents. Beheadings, dismemberments, and other mutilations have occurred.

"The most recent victim of the railroad jinx, and the second to die this year, was found early this morning by Sheriff's Deputy Jack Fleischer of the Rodeo City substation. The body, which bore no identification, was that of a man in his middle twenties. His head had been severed from his body.

"According to Deputy Fleischer, the man's clothes marked him as a transient laborer. He had more than twenty dollars in his pockets, ruling out suspicion of foul play.

"A touching aspect of the accident was revealed by Deputy Fleischer to this reporter. The victim was accompanied by a small boy, approximately three years old, who apparently spent the night by his father's body. The child has been placed in Children's Shelter pending further investigation."

Besides confirming what I already knew, this second story suggested that Fleischer had deliberately closed off the investigation. He must have known who the victim was; possibly he removed identification. The money in the dead man's pockets didn't rule out the possibility of murder, or the possibility that Fleischer himself had committed it.

I was struck by the sequence of the two deaths, three or four days apart. It could have been a coincidence, but it was clear enough that Fleischer hadn't thought so. Also it seemed very likely that Captain Aubrey was that same Deputy Aubrey who had dealt with Mark Hackett's murder fifteen years ago.

I found Captain Aubrey in the living room with Thorndike and Dr. Converse. Hackett wasn't seriously injured, the doctor was telling them, but he was suffering from a certain degree of shock. He didn't feel that his patient should be questioned any further until he'd had some rest. The policemen didn't argue.

When Converse had finished, I drew him into the next room, out of earshot.

"What is it now?" he said impatiently.

"The same old question, about Sandy Sebastian. What did you treat her for last summer?"

"I can't possibly tell you. It wouldn't be ethical without the patient's permission." Converse paused, and his eyebrows went up. "Did you put Dr. Jeffrey up to calling me last night?"

"Not exactly. I asked him the same question I'm asking you."

"Well, I'm not answering either of you," Converse said flatly. "The girl's in enough trouble as it is."

"I'm trying to get her out of trouble."

"You're going about it rather strangely, aren't you?"

I threw him a question from left field. "Was she taking drugs last summer, something like that?"

"I refuse to answer." But his clever eyes flickered in a way that said yes.

"Psychedelic drugs?"

His curiosity overcame his ethics, or whatever they were. "What makes you suggest that?"

"I heard she was suicidal. A bad trip on LSD sometimes has that effect. I'm sure you know that, doctor."

"Of course."

"Will you sit down and talk about it with me?"

"No, sir, I will not. I have no right to discuss my patient's private affairs."

"Sandy's affairs are pretty public now. And I'm on her side, remember."

Converse shook his head. "You really must excuse me. I have hospital rounds to make."

"How's Lupe?"

"He's doing fine now."

"Is Lupe on drugs by any chance?"

"How on earth should I know?"

Converse turned abruptly and went away.

Captain Aubrey was waiting for me in the living room. Thorndike had filled him in on my report, but he had some further questions.

"You've been close to this case from the beginning," he said. "How do you think it all started?"

"It started the day that Davy Spanner and Sandy Sebastian got together. They're both badly alienated, young people with a grudge."

"I know something about Spanner. He's a psycho with a record. He shouldn't have been out on the streets." His eyes were a cold gray. "Fortunately he won't be out much longer. I've been in touch with Rodeo City. They found the Sebastian girl's car north of the ranch, hub-deep in the mud. Spanner won't get far without it. The Santa Teresa County authorities expect to take him today."

"Then what?"

"Spanner's their baby." Aubrey's phrase hit me queerly, and broke into multiple meanings. "They want him for first-degree murder, and that takes care of him. The problem of the girl is more complicated. For one thing, she's a juvenile, with a clean record. Also she ran out on Spanner before the Fleischer murder was committed. Lucky for her."

"Sandy's no criminal. She wanted to quit as soon as she saw crime was for real."

"You've talked to her, haven't you? What gets into a girl like that?" Aubrey was genuinely disturbed. "I've got a daughter sixteen. She's a good girl. So was this one apparently. How do I know my own daughter won't walk up to somebody some fine day and crack his skull with a tire iron?"

"I think Sandy had a grudge against Lupe. The case may have started right there."

"What did she have against him?"

"I better not say until I can prove it, Captain."

He leaned toward me, red in the face, remembering his own daughter. "Did he have sexual congress with her?"

"Not that I know of. Whatever happened between them will all come out in the wash. The probation people will be going over her with a fine-tooth comb."

Aubrey gave me an impatient look, and turned to leave.

I detained him. "There's another thing I wanted to talk to you about. Let's go out to your car. It's more private."

He shrugged. We went outside. Aubrey got in behind the wheel of his unmarked car, and I slid in beside him.

"Are you the same Aubrey who used to work out of the Malibu station?"

"I am. It's why I was assigned to this one."

"This is the second major crime in the Hackett family, I've been told."

"That's right. The senior Mr. Hackett—his name was Mark—was shot on the beach."

"Did you ever get a line on the killer?"

"No. These hit-and-run crimes are hard to solve." Aubrey sounded apologetic. "The trouble is there's generally no provable connection between the robber and his victim."

"Was robbery the motive?"

"Apparently. Hackett's wallet was taken, and he carried a lot of money. Which wasn't the wisest thing to do under the circumstances. He had a hideaway cottage on the beach, and he made a habit of walking down there at night, all by himself. Some thief with a gun caught onto the habit, and took him for his roll."

"Did you arrest anyone?"

"We picked up dozens of suspects. But we couldn't pin the crime on any one of them."

"Do you remember any of their names?"

"Not at this late date."

"I'll try one on you, anyway. Jasper Blevins."

He shook his head. "I'm afraid it rings no bell. Who is Jasper Blevins?"

"Davy Spanner's father. According to an old Santa Teresa newspaper, he died under a train near Rodeo City, about three days after Mark Hackett was murdered."

"So?"

"It's an interesting coincidence."

"Maybe. I run into these coincidences all the time. Sometimes they mean something, other times they don't."

"This one does."

"Do you mean there's a causal connection between these two crimes—Mark Hackett's murder and his son's kidnapping?"

"Some kind of a connection, anyway. According to a newspaper account, you recovered the revolver Mark Hackett was shot with."

Aubrey turned and looked at me appraisingly. "You do your homework, don't you?"

"Did you ever trace the revolver to its owner?"

Aubrey was slow in answering. "The queer thing is," he said finally, "the gun belonged to Hackett himself, in a sense—"

"That suggests a family affair."

Aubrey lifted the flat of his hand above the wheel. "Let me finish. The gun belonged to Hackett in the sense that one of his oil companies had purchased it. They stored it in an unlocked drawer in their Long Beach office. It wasn't kept proper track of, and it simply disappeared, apparently some time before the murder."

"Disgruntled employee?"

"We went into that pretty thoroughly. But we didn't come up

with anything tangible. The trouble was, Hackett had quite a number of disgruntled employees. He'd recently moved here from Texas, and he was riding herd on them Texas style. He was very unpopular with his people. But we couldn't prove that any one of them killed him. He had nearly five hundred employees in Long Beach alone, and a good half of them hated his guts."

"What was the name of his company?"

"Corpus Christi Oil and Gas. Mark Hackett originally came from Corpus Christi. He should have stayed there."

Aubrey punched my arm in a friendly way, and turned his ignition key. I wandered into the house.

>>>>>>>>>
>>>>>>>>> *chapter* 25
>>>>>>>>>

GERDA HACKETT was in the picture gallery, standing absorbed in front of a painting. It showed a man in a geometrical maze, and seemed to show that the man and the maze were continuous with each other.

"Are you interested in painting, Mrs. Hackett?"

"Yes. Particularly in Klee. I sold this picture to Mr. Hack—to Stephen."

"Really?"

"Yes. I worked in a gallery in München, a very good gallery." Her voice was thick with nostalgia. "It was how I met my husband. But if I had a second chance I would stay in Germany."

"Why?"

"I don't like it here. Such dreadful things happen to people."

"At least you got your husband back."

"Yes." But this failed to cheer her. She turned to me with a vague ambiguous light in her blue eyes. "I'm very grateful, really. You saved his life and I want to thank you. *Vielen Dank.*"

She pulled my face down and kissed me. This gesture was unexpected, perhaps even by her. It may have started out as a thank-you kiss, but it turned into something more involved. Her body leaned

into me. Her tongue pushed into my mouth like a blind worm looking for a home.

I didn't like the woman that well. I took her by the arms and
released myself. It was like handling a soft statue.

"Am I no good?" she said. "Am I not attractive?"

"You're very attractive," I said, stretching the truth a little. "The
trouble is, I work for your husband and this is his house."

"He wouldn't care!" The ambiguous light in her eyes crystallized
in a kind of helpless anger. "Do you know what they're doing? She's
on the bed beside him feeding him soft-boiled eggs with a spoon."

"That sounds like an innocent pastime."

"It's no joke! She is his mother. He has an Oedipus fixation on her,
and she encourages it."

"Who told you that?"

"I can see it with my own eyes. She is the seductive mother. The
soft-boiled eggs are symbolic. Everything is symbolic!"

Gerda was disheveled and close to tears. She was one of those
women who dishevel easily, as if the fronts they turned to the world
were precarious to begin with. She would never be the equal of her
mother-in-law.

But that was not my problem. I changed the subject: "I understand you're a friend of Sandy Sebastian's."

"No more. I helped her with her languages. But she is a little
ingrate."

"Did she spend any time with Lupe?"

"Lupe? Why do you ask?"

"Because it may be important. Did she see much of him?"

"Certainly not, not in the way you mean. He used to go and get
her sometimes, and drive her home."

"How often?"

"Many times. But Lupe isn't interested in girls."

"How do you know?"

"I can tell." She flushed. "Why do you ask?"

"I'd like to have a look at Lupe's room."

"For what reason?"

"Nothing to do with you. Does he have a room in the house?"

"His apartment is over the main garage. I don't know if it's open.
Wait, I'll get our key."

She was gone for a few minutes. I stood and looked at the Klee, and found that it grew on me. The man was in the maze; the maze was in the man.

Gerda Hackett came back carrying a key with a tab attached: "Garage apt." I went out to the garage and used the key to open Lupe's door.

It was what is called a studio apartment, consisting of one large room with a pullman kitchen. It was furnished in bold colors with Mexican fabrics and artifacts. Some pre-Columbian masks hung over the serape-covered bed. If Lupe was a primitive, he was a sophisticated one.

I went through the chest of drawers and found nothing unusual except some pornographic pictures of the handcuff school. The bathroom medicine cabinet yielded only a jar of something labeled Psychedelic Love Balm. But some of the sugar cubes in the bottom of the bowl in the pullman kitchen were amateurishly wrapped in aluminum foil.

There were six wrapped cubes. I took three, tied them in my handkerchief, and put them away in an inside pocket.

I hadn't heard anyone coming up the stairs, and was mildly surprised by the door opening behind me. It was Sidney Marburg, wearing tennis shoes.

"Gerda said you were out here. What's with Lupe?"

"Just checking."

"Checking what?"

"His morals and his manners. He's no ordinary houseman, is he?"

"You can say that again. Personally I think he's a creep." Marburg walked toward me silently. "If you get something on him, I'd like to know about it."

"Are you serious?"

"You're bloody right I'm serious. He puts on a show of being interested in art, because my wife is, but she's the only one that's taken in."

"Is there something between the two of them?"

"I think there is. He comes to our house in Bel-Air sometimes when I'm away. Our houseboy keeps me posted."

"Are they lovers?"

"I don't know," Marburg said in pain. "I do know she gives him money, because I've seen some of the canceled checks. According to the houseboy, Lupe tells her everything that goes on here in her son's house. It isn't a healthy situation, and that's putting it mildly."

"How long have they known each other?"

"Practically forever. He's worked here, if you can call it work, as long as I can remember."

"How long is that?"

"Fifteen—sixteen years."

"Did you know the Hacketts when Mark was still alive?"

For some reason, the question irritated him. "I did. That's hardly relevant to what we were talking about. We were talking about Lupe."

"So we were. What do you suspect him of, besides spying for your wife? Does he mess around with drugs?"

"I wouldn't be surprised," Marburg said, a little too readily. "I've seen him high more than once. He was either manic or on drugs."

"Did you ever see him with the Sebastian girl?"

"I never did."

"I understand he chauffeured her quite a bit."

"No doubt he did. She spent a lot of time here in the summer." He paused, and gave me a questioning look. "You think he tampered with her?"

"I haven't come to any conclusion about it."

"Boy, if you can get that on him—!"

I didn't like his eagerness. "Slow down. I'm not going to shove the facts around to suit you."

"Nobody asked you to." But he sounded angry. I suspected he was angry with himself for talking to me too freely. "If you're finished here, I'll drive you bloody well home."

"Since you put it so charmingly."

"I don't have to be charming. I'm a serious painter, and that's all I have to be."

In spite of his lousy manners, I felt a certain liking for Sidney Marburg, or a tolerance bordering on liking. Perhaps he had sold out for money in marrying Ruth, who was nearly twenty years older. But like a shrewd agent he'd held back a percentage of himself.

"That sounds like a declaration of independence," I said.

His angry grimace changed to a smile, but there was self-deprecation in it. "Come on, let's go. I didn't mean to take it out on you." We went out to his Mercedes. "Where do you live?"

"In West Los Angeles, but I'm not going home. My car's in Woodland Hills."

"That's where the Sebastian girl lives, isn't it?"

"Yes."

"What's the matter with her? Schitzy?"

"I'm trying to find out."

"More power to you. Excuse my little flareup a minute ago. I'm glad to drive you. But this place has bad associations for me."

As if he hoped to leave them behind forever, he started the Mercedes' engine with a roar. We rocketed along the shore of the lake, across the dam, and down the long winding grade to the gate, where Marburg braked the car to a jarring halt.

"Okay," I said, "you win the Distinguished Flying Cross."

"Sorry if I alarmed you."

"I've had a rough two days. I was hoping this one would be some improvement."

"I said I was sorry."

Marburg drove more carefully down to the coastal highway and turned north. At Malibu Canyon he turned inland again. In a few minutes we were surrounded by the hills.

I said that they would make a pretty picture.

Marburg corrected me. "No. Anything that would make a pretty picture makes a bad picture. The picturesque things have all been done. You have to do something new. Beauty is difficult, as somebody said."

"That Klee in the gallery, for instance?"

"Yes. I advised Stephen to buy Klee ten years ago." He added: "Stephen needs advice. His taste is terrible, in everything."

"Women?"

Marburg groaned. "Poor Gerda. When she came back from Germany with him, she thought she was going to live *la vie en rose*. She had a rude awakening. They live like recluses, never go anywhere, never see anyone."

"Why?"

"I think he's frightened—frightened of life. Money does that to some people. And then of course there's what happened to his father. It's strange, for fifteen years Stephen's been acting as if the same thing was going to happen to him. And it almost did."

"Almost."

"You've had considerable experience, Mr. Archer. Is it possible for people to bring disaster down on their own heads? You know, by assuming a disaster-prone posture?"

"It's an interesting idea."

"You haven't answered my question."

"Ask me again when I've finished with this case."

He gave me a swift startled look, during which the car almost left the road. He concentrated on driving for a minute, slowing down.

"I thought you *had* finished."

"Not with Spanner still at large, and several unsolved murders."

"Several?"

I let the question hang. We passed the Probation Camp, off the road to the left. Marburg looked at the buildings in a worried way, as if I might be tricking him into custody.

"Did you say several murders?"

"There are at least two others besides Mark Hackett."

Marburg drove until we were out of sight of the camp. He found a turnout point, pulled off the road, and stopped the car.

"What about these other murders?"

"One was a woman named Laurel Smith. She owned a small apartment building in the Palisades. She was beaten to death there the day before yesterday."

"I read about her in this morning's *Times*. The police think she was beaten by a kook—some sadist who didn't even know her."

"I don't think so. Laurel Smith was once married to a man named Jasper Blevins. He died under a train fifteen years ago—just a few days after Mark Hackett was killed. As far as I can make out, Laurel Smith and Jasper Blevins were Davy Spanner's parents. I think all these crimes, including the one against Stephen, are tied together."

Without moving, except for his fingers drumming on the wheel, Marburg gave the impression of squirming. His eyes came up to mine and gave me a quick unguarded look, like a spurt of darkness. "Am I being paranoid, or are you accusing me of something?"

"Maybe I am. What am I accusing you of?"

"It isn't so funny," he said in an aggrieved tone. "This isn't the first time I've been accused of something I didn't do. The cops gave me a really bad time after Mark was killed. They took me down to the station and questioned me most of the night. I had a perfectly good alibi, but to them it looked like one of those open-and-shut

cases—you know, the standard triangle. I don't deny, and I didn't deny then, that Ruth and I were very close and I adore her passionately," he said in a rather perfunctory way. "But the fact is she was planning to divorce Mark."

"And marry you?"

"And marry me. So I had nothing to gain by Mark's death."

"Ruth had."

"Not really. He left her as little as he legally could. Mark changed his will, on account of me, shortly before he died, and left the bulk of his estate to Stephen. Anyway, Ruth had a perfectly good alibi, just as I had, and I resent your imputation for both of us."

But there was no real force in Marburg's anger. Like his passion, it belonged to the part of himself he had sold. He was watching me and talking carefully, like a hired advocate for himself.

"Tell me about the alibis, just for fun."

"I don't have to, but I will. Gladly. At the time that Mark was killed, Ruth and I were having dinner with some friends in Montecito. It was a large dinner party, with over twenty guests."

"Why didn't the police accept your alibi?"

"They did when they got around to checking it out. But that wasn't until the next day. They wanted me to be guilty, I know how their minds work. They were afraid to tackle Ruth directly, but they thought they could get at her through me."

"Whose side was Stephen on?"

"He was out of the country, had been for several years. At the time of his father's death he was studying economics at the London School. I'd never even met him at that time. But he was close to his father, and Mark's death hit him hard. He actually broke down and wept on the transatlantic phone. That was about the last time I ever knew him to show any real emotion."

"When was this?"

"Ruth called him immediately after Lupe phoned her, before we left her friends' house in Montecito. As a matter of fact I put in the call to London for her, and then she took it on another extension. The news came as a terrible blow to Stephen. Frankly, I felt sorry for him."

"How did he feel about you?"

"I don't think Stephen even knew I existed, at that time. And I kept out of sight for nearly a year afterwards. That was Ruth's idea, and it was a good one."

"Why? Because she's financially dependent on Stephen?"

"That may have played a part in it. But the fact is she's very fond of him. She wanted to arrange her life so she could have us both, and that's what she's done." Marburg spoke of his wife as if she was some kind of natural force, a demiurge or deity. "She gave me a—well, a kind of personal scholarship, at San Miguel de Allende. A few minutes after Stephen flew in from London, I flew out for Mexico City. Ruth kept us separate at the airport, but I caught a glimpse of Stephen when he got off the plane. He was a lot less conventional in those days. He wore a beard and a mustache and had let his hair grow long. By the time I finally met him he'd stiffened up a good deal—money ages a man."

"How long were you gone?"

"Nearly a year, as I said. Actually that year was the making of me. I'd never had any decent instruction before, or painted from a model, or had a chance to talk to genuine painters. I loved the light in Mexico, and the colors. And I learned to paint them." The part of Marburg that belonged to himself was talking to me now. "I changed from a Sunday painter into an artist. And Ruth made it possible for me."

"What did you do before you became an artist?"

"I was a geological draftsman. I worked for a—an oil company. It was dull work."

"Corpus Christi Oil and Gas?"

"That's right, I worked for Mark Hackett. It's how I met Ruth." He paused, and hung his head in depression. "So you have been researching me?"

I answered him with another question; "How do you and Stephen get along?"

"Fine. We follow our separate courses."

"Night before last, you suggested it would be nice if he never came back. You'd own his art collection then, you said."

"I was joking. Don't you recognize black humor?" When I failed to reply, he peered into my face. "You don't think I had anything to do with what happened to Stephen?"

I still didn't answer him. He sulked the rest of the way to Woodland Hills.

I WENT INTO a chain restaurant on Ventura Boulevard and ordered a rare steak for breakfast. Then I reclaimed my car from the station where I had left it and drove up the long hill to Sebastian's street.

It was Saturday, and even at this time in the morning the fairways beyond the street were sprinkled with golfers. A mailbox bearing the name Gensler stopped me before I reached Sebastian's house. I knocked on the door of the Gensler house instead.

A fair-haired man of about forty came to the door. He had an anxious vulnerable look which was accentuated by prominent blue eyes and almost invisible eyebrows.

I explained who I was, and asked if I could see Heidi.

"My daughter isn't here."

"When will she be back?"

"I don't really know. I've sent her out of town to stay with relatives."

"You shouldn't have done that, Mr. Gensler. The probation people will want to talk to her."

"I don't see why."

"She's a witness."

His face and neck reddened. "She certainly is not. Heidi's a nice clean-living girl. Her only connection with the Sebastian girl is that we happen to live on the same street."

"It's no disgrace to be a witness," I said. "Or even to know someone in trouble."

Gensler closed the door abruptly in my face. I drove my car up the street to Sebastian's house, thinking that Heidi must have told her father something that frightened him.

Dr. Jeffrey's Rover was parked in front of the house. When Bernice Sebastian let me in, I could see that her face reflected some further disaster. Its flesh was being eaten away from inside so that the bones had become more prominent: her eyes were like lights in a cage.

"What happened?"

"Sandy attempted suicide. She hid one of her father's razor blades in her dog."

"Her dog?"

"Her little cloth spaniel. She must have got the blade when she went to the bathroom. She tried to cut her wrist with it. Fortunately I was listening at the door. I heard her cry out and I stopped her before she hurt herself too terribly."

"Did she say why she did it?"

"She said she didn't deserve to live, that she was a terrible person."

"Is she?"

"No."

"Did you tell her that?"

"No. I didn't know what to say."

"When did all this happen?"

"Just now. The doctor's still with her. Please excuse me."

It was her daughter, but my case. I followed her to the door of Sandy's room and looked in. Sandy was sitting on the edge of her bed. She had a gauze bandage on her left wrist, a sprinkling of blood on the front of her pajamas. She had changed in other ways in the course of the night. Her eyes were darker in color. Her mouth was set hard. She wasn't very pretty now.

Her father was sitting beside her, holding her hand in an unreal sort of way. Dr. Jeffrey was standing over them, telling them both that Sandy would have to be hospitalized:

"I recommend the Psychiatric Center in Westwood."

"Isn't that terribly expensive?" Sebastian said.

"No more so than other hospitals. Good psychiatric treatment is always expensive."

Sebastian shook his head: his face swung loosely. "I don't know how I'm going to pay for it. It was all I could do to raise bail money."

Sandy lifted her heavy eyes. Barely moving her lips, she said: "Let them take me to jail. That doesn't cost anything."

"No," her mother said. "We'll sell the house."

"Not on this market," Sebastian said. "We wouldn't even get our equity out."

His daughter pulled her hand away from his. "Why didn't you let me die? That would solve all the problems."

"The hard way," Jeffrey said. "I'll order an ambulance."

Sebastian got to his feet. "Let me drive her. Ambulances cost money."

"I'm sorry, this is an ambulance case."

I followed Jeffrey to the telephone in the study. He made his call and hung up.

"Yes?" His look was hard and questioning.

"How sick is she?"

"I don't know. There's been some slippage, obviously. But I'm not a psychiatrist. That's why I want to get her to one right away. She needs security precautions."

"You think she'll try again?"

"We have to go on that assumption. I'd say she's very likely to repeat. She told me she's been planning this for months. She took some LSD last summer and had a bad reaction. She's still not over it."

"She told you this?"

"Yes. It may account for the change in her personality over the last few months. One dose can do it if it hits you wrong. She claims that's all she had—one dose in a sugar cube."

"Did she tell you where she got it?"

"No. Obviously she's covering up for somebody."

I got out the sugar cubes I'd taken from Lupe's kitchen and handed one of them to the doctor. "This almost certainly came from the same source. Can you have it analyzed?"

"I'll be happy to. Where did you find it?"

"In Lupe Rivera's apartment. He's the man she clobbered the other night. If I can prove that he fed her LSD—"

Jeffrey rose impatiently. "I get the point. Why don't I ask her?"

We went back to Sandy's bedroom where the little family sat frozen in each other's company. The girl, who was in the middle, looked up at us.

"Did you send for the wagon to the booby hatch?"

"As a matter of fact I did," Jeffrey said unexpectedly. "Now it's my turn to ask you a question."

She waited in silence.

"That sugar cube you took last August—did Lupe Rivera give it to you?"

"What if he did?"

The doctor put his hand under her chin, very gently, and tipped it up. "Did he? I want a yes or no answer, Sandy."

"Yes. I freaked out. I blew my mind."

"Did he do anything else to you, Sandy?"

She withdrew her chin from the doctor's hand and hung her head. Her face was impassive, her eyes very dark and fixed. "He said he would kill me if I told anyone."

"Nobody's going to kill you."

She looked at the doctor in disbelief.

"Did Lupe take you to Dr. Converse?" I said.

"No, Gerda—Mrs. Hackett—took me. I tried to jump out of the car on the freeway. Dr. Converse put me in a straitjacket. He kept me in his clinic all night."

Bernice Sebastian groaned. When the ambulance came for her daughter, she rode along.

>>>>>>>>>
>>>>>>>>> *chapter* 27
>>>>>>>>>

I WENT BACK to the freeway, where I seemed to live. I was running out of initiative, and sorely tempted to go home. Instead I drove to Long Beach on the bleakest stretch of pavement in the world.

The Corpus Christi Oil building was a massive four-story structure overlooking the waterfront and its slums. I was born and raised in Long Beach, within walking distance of the waterfront, and I could remember when the building had been put up, the year after the earthquake.

I parked in a visitor's slot and went into the lobby. Just inside the front door, a uniformed security officer sat behind a counter. When I gave him a second look I found that I knew him. He was Ralph

Cuddy, who managed Alma Krug's apartment building in Santa Monica.

He knew me too. "Couldn't you find Mrs. Krug?"

"I found her, thanks."

"How is she? I haven't had a chance to visit her this week. My two jobs keep me humping."

"She seems to be doing pretty well for her age."

"Good for her. She's been like a mother to me all my life. Did you know that?"

"No."

"She has been." His emotional gaze narrowed on my face. "What sort of family matters did you discuss with her?"

"Various relatives of hers. Jasper Blevins, for instance."

"Hey, do you know Jasper? Whatever happened to him?"

"He died under a train."

"I'm not surprised," Cuddy said moralistically. "Jasper was always in trouble. He was a trouble to himself and a trouble to other people. But Alma was good to him anyway. Jasper was always her favorite." His eyes grew small and grudging, in a kind of rivalry.

"What kind of trouble?"

Cuddy started to say something and then decided not to. He was silent for a moment, his face groping for an alternative reply.

"Sex trouble, for example. Laurel was pregnant when he married her. I almost married her myself, till I found out she was in trouble." He added in mild surprise, as if he hadn't thought of the fact for some years: "I never did marry. Frankly, I never found a woman worthy of my standards. I've often said to Alma Krug, if only I wasn't born too late—"

I interrupted him: "How long have you worked here, Mr. Cuddy?"

"Twenty years."

"In security?"

"After the first three, four years, yep."

"Do you remember the summer when Mr. Hackett was killed?"

"I sure do." He gave me a rather worried look. "I had nothing to do with it. I mean, I didn't even know Mr. Hackett personally. I was just an underling in those days."

"Nobody's accusing you of anything, Mr. Cuddy. I'm trying to find out what I can about a certain revolver. Apparently it was stolen from this office and used to shoot Mr. Hackett."

"I wouldn't know anything about that."

His face closed up into a stiff mask of righteousness. I suspected he was lying.

"You have to remember the search for the gun if you were in security at the time."

"Don't tell me what I have to remember." He manufactured a quick rage and stood up full of it. Cuddy was wearing a sidearm, which added weight to his rage. "What are you trying to do, force thoughts into my head?"

"That would be a hopeless task," I said unfortunately.

He put his hand on his gun butt. "You get out of here. You got no right to come in here and brainwash and insult me."

"I'm sorry if I said the wrong thing. I take it back. Okay?"

"No, it's not okay."

"You seem to think I'm after your scalp or something. The man I'm interested in is Sidney Marburg. He worked here as a draftsman."

"I never heard of him. And I'm not answering any more questions."

"Then I'll try personnel." I started toward the elevator. "What floor is the personnel manager on?"

"He's out to lunch."

"It's only the middle of the morning."

"I mean he hasn't come in yet. He isn't coming in today."

I turned and faced Cuddy. "This is ridiculous. What do you know that you don't want me to know?"

He lifted a hinged section of the counter and came out, pulling his gun. His mouth was mean.

"Go away," he said in a yammering voice. "You're not going to smear my friends, see."

"Is Marburg a friend of yours?"

"There you go again, twisting the thoughts in my mind. I never even heard of any Marburg. Is he a Jew?"

"I don't know."

"I'm a Christian. You can thank the Lord I am. If I wasn't a religious man, I'd shoot you down like a dog."

She drank most of hers down. "I'm glad he's dead," she said without gladness. "I mean it. Jack only got what was coming to him."

"How so?"

"You know as well as I do. Come on, drink up your drink."

She finished hers. I drank a little of the oily mixture in my glass. I like to drink but that particular drink, in Jack Fleischer's house and his widow's company, reminded me of taking castor oil.

"You say you were working with Jack," she said. "Did you help him make the tapes?"

"Tapes?"

"Don't try to kid me. A policeman called me from L.A. this morning. He had a funny name, a Polish name, Junkowski, something like that. Know him?"

"I know a Sergeant Janowski."

"That's the name. He wanted to know if Jack left any tapes around the house. He said they could be important in a homicide. Laurel got it, too." She thrust her face toward me, as though to affirm her own continued existence. "Did you know that?"

"I found it out."

"Jack beat her to death, didn't he?"

"I don't know."

"Of course you do. I can see it in your face. You don't have to be so tight-mouthed with me. I was married to Jack, remember. I lived with him and his wildness for thirty years. Why do you think I started drinking? I was a teetotaler when we got married. I started drinking because I couldn't bear the thought of the things he did."

She leaned so close her eyes crossed. She had a cool way of saying outrageous things, but her version of events was too subjective to be entirely true. Still I wanted to hear more from her, and when she told me to finish my drink I did.

She went out to the kitchen and returned with another dose of the stuff for me, and another for her.

"What about those tapes?" she said. "Are they worth money?"

I made a quick decision. "They are to me."

"How much?"

"A thousand dollars."

"That isn't very much."

"The police won't pay you anything for the tapes. I might raise

my offer, depending on what's on them. Have you played them back?"

"No."

"Where are they?"

"I'm not telling. I need much more than a thousand. Now that Jack is dead and gone, I'm planning to do some traveling. He never took me anywhere, not once in the last fifteen years. And you know why? Whenever he went someplace, *she* was there waiting for him. Well, now she isn't waiting any more." After a moment, she added in mild surprise: "Jack isn't waiting, either. They're both dead, aren't they? I wished it on them so often I can't believe it happened."

"It happened."

"Good."

She went through the motions of drinking a toast and stood swaying, tangle-footed. I took the glass from her hand and put it down on the table inset with stones.

"Sanctuary muchly."

She did a little dance step to inaudible music. She seemed to be trying hard to find something to do that would make her feel human again.

"I never thought I'd feel sorry for *her*," she said. "But I kind of do feel sorry for her. She resembled me, did you know that? I was much more beautiful when I was young, but Laurel had fifteen years on me. I used to pretend to myself that I was her in bed with Jack. But it wasn't all fun and frolic even for her. He put her through the ropes and over the jumps just like he did with any of his women. And in the end he caved in her pretty face for her."

"Do you really believe your husband did that?"

"You don't know the half of it." She plopped down on the settee beside me. "I could tell you things that would make your flesh crawl. It's a terrible thing to say, but I hardly blame that boy for blowing his head off for him. You know who the boy is?"

"His father was Jasper Blevins. His mother was Laurel."

"You're smarter than I thought." She gave me a crinkled look. "Or did I tell you all this the other night?"

"No."

"I bet I did, though, didn't I? Or did they tell you in the north county? It's common knowledge in Rodeo City."

"What is, Mrs. Fleischer?"

"Jack and his tricks. He was the law, there was no way they could stop him. He killed that Blevins man, shoved him under a train so he could have his wife. He got Laurel to say it wasn't her husband's body. He put their little boy in the orphanage, because he got in the way of the big romance."

I didn't believe her. I didn't disbelieve her. Her words hung in the unreal room, perfectly at home there, but unconnected with the daylight world.

"How do you know all this?"

"Some of it I figured out for myself." One of her eyes gave me a wise look: the other was half closed and idiotic. "I have friends in law enforcement, or used to have. Other deputies' wives—they did some whispering."

"Why didn't their husbands bring your husband to book?"

The idiotic eye closed entirely in a frozen wink; she peered at my face with the wise one. "Jack knew where too many bodies were buried. The north county's rough territory, mister, and he was the king of it. Anyway, what could they prove? The woman Laurel said the body didn't belong to her husband. Said she never saw him before in her life. The head was all smashed up, unrecog—" She stumbled over the word—"unrecnizable. They put it down as just another accidental death."

"Do you know for a fact it wasn't?"

"I know what I know." But her one closed eye seemed to mock her seriousness.

"Are you willing to pass this on to the police?"

"What would be the use? Jack's dead. Everybody's dead."

"You're not."

"I wish I was." The statement surprised or alarmed her. She opened both eyes and glared at me, as if I'd threatened her with loss of life.

"And Davy Spanner isn't dead."

"He soon will be. There's a fifty-man posse out after him. I talked to Rory Pennell on the phone this morning. He promised they'd shoot to kill."

"You want them to?"

"He killed Jack, didn't he?"

"But you said you hardly blamed him."

"Did I?" The question was directed to herself as well as me. "I couldn't have. Jack was my husband."

This was where I came in. Her single life and mind were as deeply split as her marriage had been. I got up to leave.

She followed me to the door. "What about the tapes?"

"What about them? Do you have them?"

"I think I can put my hands on them."

"For a thousand?"

"It isn't enough," she said. "I'm a widow now, I have to look out for myself."

"Let me play the tapes. Then I'll make you another offer."

"They're not here."

"Where are they?"

"That's for me to know and you to find out."

"Okay, sit on them. I'll be back, or I'll phone you. Do you remember my name?"

"Archer," she said. "Jack Archer."

I left it at that. She went back into the artificial twilight of her living room.

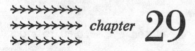 *chapter* 29

BEFORE I LEFT Santa Teresa I called Henry Langston's house from a gas-station telephone booth. His wife answered, formally: "This is the Langston residence."

"Is your husband at home?"

"Who is calling, please?" But she probably knew my voice. Her voice was hostile.

"Lew Archer."

"No, he isn't here, and you're responsible. He's still up in the north county, trying to save that precious murderer of his. He'll end up getting shot himself."

She was semi-hysterical, and I tried to soothe her. "That isn't very likely, Mrs. Langston."

"You don't know," she said. "I have this terrible feeling of fatality, that nothing will ever go right for us again. And it's your fault, you got him into this."

"Not really. He's been involved with Davy Spanner for years. He made a commitment to him, and he's trying to follow through."

"What about *me?*" she cried.

"Is there something specific bothering you?"

"There's no use telling you," she said in a kind of angry intimacy. "You're not a doctor."

"Are you ill, Mrs. Langston?"

She answered by hanging up on me. I was tempted to go to her house, but that would only lead to further involvement and loss of time. I sympathized with her but I couldn't help her. Only her husband could do that.

I got onto the freeway headed north. My body was beginning to rebel against continuous action without enough rest. It felt as if my right foot on the accelerator pushed the car uphill all the way to Rodeo City.

Deputy Pennell was in the back room of his office, listening to his dispatcher's radio. I gathered he had been sitting there ever since I talked to him in the middle of the night. His mustache and his eyes gave the impression that they were taking over his face, which was paler and thinner and needed a shave.

"What's the word, Deputy?"

"They lost him." His voice was edged with disgust.

"Where?"

"There's no telling. The rain washed out his tracks. It's still raining in the north pass."

"Where does that lead to?"

"He'd have to come back to the coast. Inland there's nothing but more mountain ranges. It's snowing in the back country above five thousand feet."

"So?"

"We head him off when he hits the highway. I'm requesting the highway patrol to set up roadblocks."

"Is there any chance that he's still in the valley?"

"Could be. The p-professor seems to think so, anyway."

"Do you mean Henry Langston?"

"Yeah. He's still hanging around the old Krug ranch. He's got a

theory that Spanner is kind of cracked on the subject of that place, and that he'll head back there."

"But you don't buy that theory?"

"Naw. I never saw a p-professor yet that knew what he was talking about. They get soft in the head from reading too many books."

I didn't argue, and this encouraged Pennell to go on. Langston had upset him, it appeared, and he needed reassurance.

"You know what the professor tried to tell me? That Spanner had j-j-justification for doing what he did to poor old Jack. On account of Jack putting him in the orphanage."

"Didn't that happen?"

"Sure, but what else could Jack do with the kid? His father got killed by a train. Jack wasn't responsible for him."

I could hear a little slippage, a trace of double-talk. "Jack wasn't responsible for what, Deputy?"

"For either of them, father *or* son. I know there were dirty rumors at the time, and now this Langston is trying to start them up again, before old Jack is even in his grave."

"What kind of rumors?"

He raised his hot sorrowful eyes. "I wouldn't even pass them on, they're so crazy."

"Rumors that Jack killed the man himself?"

"Yeah. That's all a lot of malarkey."

"Would you swear to it, Deputy?"

"Sure I would," he said with some bravado, "I'd swear to it on a stack of Bibles. I told the p-professor that, but he wasn't satisfied."

Neither was I. "Would you take a lie-detector test?"

Pennell was disappointed in me. "So you think I'm a liar. And that poor old Jack was a murderer."

"Who killed Jasper Blevins if he didn't?"

"Plenty of people could have."

"Who were the suspects?"

"There was a wild-looking character with a beard hanging around the ranch. He looked like a Russian, I heard."

"Come on now, Deputy. I'm not buying any bearded anarchists. I know Jack hung around the ranch. Later, I've been told, he stashed the woman at Mamie Hagedorn's place."

"What if he did? Blevins didn't want his wife; he made that clear."

"Did you know Blevins?"

"I saw him once or twice."

"Did you see him after he was dead?"

"Yeah."

"Was it Blevins?"

"I couldn't swear to it, one way or the other." He added with a shifty look in his eye: "Mrs. Blevins said it wasn't. She ought to know."

"What did the little boy say?"

"Never said a word. He couldn't talk; he was just a dummy."

"That was convenient, wasn't it?"

Pennell stood up with his hand on his gun butt. "I've heard enough of that kind of t-talk. Jack Fleischer was like an older b-brother to me. He t-taught me to shoot and drink. He g-got me my first woman. He m-made a m-man of me."

"I was wondering who to blame."

Pennell cursed me and got his gun out. I retreated. He didn't follow me out of the office, but I was a little shaken. This was the second gun that had been pulled on me today. Sooner or later one was bound to go off.

I walked across the street to the Rodeo Hotel and asked the desk clerk where Mamie Hagedorn lived.

He looked up brightly. "Mamie retired from business."

"Good. My intentions are social."

"I see. She lives up the road a piece, on the way to Centerville. It's a big red-brick house, the only red-brick house on that side of town."

I drove out of town past the rodeo grounds and up into the hills. The red-brick house stood high on one of them, commanding the whole scene. It was a gray overcast day, and the sea was like a worn-out mirror reflecting the sullen sky.

I went up the gravel drive and knocked on the door of the big house. It was answered by a Spanish American woman wearing a black uniform and white cap with a black velvet bow. She was the first maid in uniform I'd seen in quite a while.

She started to give me an oral quiz on who and what I was, and why I was here. It was interrupted by a woman's voice which came from the front parlor: "Send him in! I'll talk to him."

The maid took me into a room filled with ornate Victorian furniture, complete with antimacassars. It underlined the feeling I had

when I came to the north county, though the gantries of Vandenberg were just over the county line, that I was stepping back into prewar time.

Mamie Hagedorn sustained the illusion. She was sitting on a couch, a small woman whose gold-slippered feet dangled clear of the parquet floor. She was wearing a rather formal high-necked dress. She had a pouter pigeon bosom, a rouged and raddled face, hair or a wig which was a peculiarly horrible shade of iridescent red. But I liked the way her smile broke up her face.

"What's on your mind?" she said. "Sit down and tell Mamie."

She raised her hand, on which a diamond winked. I sat beside her.

"I was talking to Al Simmons last night in Centerville. He mentioned that you once knew Laurel Blevins."

"Al talks too much for his own good," she said cheerfully. "As a matter of fact I knew Laurel very well. She lived with me after her husband died."

"Then it was her husband who died under the train?"

She thought about this. "I'm not *sure* it was. It never came out officially."

"Why not?"

She moved uneasily. Her dress rustled and gave off a whiff of lavender. To my stretched nerves she seemed like the past itself stirring in its shroud.

"I wouldn't want to queer things for Laurel. I always liked Laurel."

"Then you'll be sorry to hear that she's dead."

"Laurel? She's just a young woman."

"She didn't die of old age. She was beaten to death."

"Holy cripes!" the woman said. "Who did that?"

"Jack Fleischer's a prime suspect."

"But he's dead, too."

"That's right. You can't hurt either of them by talking, Mrs. Hagedorn."

"*Miss.* I never married." She put on horn-rimmed glasses which made her look severe, and studied my face. "Just who are you, anyway?"

I told her. Then she asked me about the case. I laid it out for her, with the names and the places.

"I knew most all of those people," she said in a rusty voice, "going

all the way back to Joe Krug and his wife Alma. I liked Joe. He was a fine figure of a man. But Alma was a Bible-thumping sobersides. Joe used to come and visit me sometimes—I ran a house in Rodeo City in case you didn't know—and Alma never forgave me for leading him astray. I think I was one of the main reasons she made him move to Los Angeles. Cripes, that was forty years ago. What happened to Joe?"

"He's dead now. Alma's alive."

"She must be old. Alma's older than I am."

"How old is that?"

She answered with her broken smile: "I never tell my age. I'm older than I look."

"I bet you are."

"Don't flatter me." She took off her glasses and wiped her eyes with a lace handkerchief. "Joe Krug was a good man, but he never had any luck in this neck of the woods. I heard he had a little before he died, after he moved to Los Angeles."

"What kind of luck?"

"Money luck. Is there any other? He got himself a job with some big company and married his daughter Etta to the boss."

"Etta?"

"Henrietta. They called her Etta for short. She was married before to a man named Albert Blevins. And he was the father of Jasper Blevins who married Laurel, poor dear." The old woman seemed to take pride in her genealogical knowledge.

"Who killed Jasper, Miss Hagedorn?"

"I don't know for sure." She gave me a long shrewd look. "If I tell you what I do know, what do you plan to do with it?"

"Open up the case and let the daylight in."

She smiled a little sadly. "That reminds me of a hymn, an old revival hymn. I was converted once, would you believe it? It lasted until the boy evangelist ran away with the week's offerings and my best friend. What are you after, Mr. Evangelist? Money?"

"I'm being paid."

"Who by?"

"Some people down south."

"Why are they paying you?"

"It would take all day to explain."

"Then why not drop it, leave it lay? Let the dead people rest in peace."

"There are getting to be too many of them. It's been going on for a long time now. Fifteen years." I leaned toward her and said in a quiet voice, "Did Laurel kill her husband? Or was it Jack Fleischer?"

She countered with another question, which seemed to contain an answer hidden in it: "You said Laurel is dead. How do I know you're telling me the truth?"

"Call the L.A.P.D., Purdue Street Station. Ask for Sergeant Prince or Sergeant Janowski."

I recited the number. She slid off the couch, with the help of a needlepoint footstool, and left the room. I heard a door close down the hall. A few minutes later I heard the same door open.

She came back much more slowly. The rouge stood out on her slack cheeks. She climbed back onto the couch, reminding me for an instant of a child dressed up in attic finery, wearing an ancestor's wig.

"So Laurel really is dead," she said heavily. "I talked to Sergeant Prince. He's going to send somebody up here to interview me."

"I'm here now."

"I know that. With Laurel dead, and Jack, I'm willing to answer your question. The answer is yes. She killed Jasper Blevins, smashed in his head with the blunt end of an ax. Jack Fleischer got rid of the body under a train. He put it down on the books as an accident, victim unknown."

"How do you know all this?"

"Laurel told me herself. Before she left here Laurel and I were as close as mother and daughter. She told me how she killed Jasper, and she told me why. I didn't ever blame her for a minute." Mamie Hagedorn took a deep shuddering breath. "The only thing I blamed her for was leaving the little boy the way she did. That was a terrible thing to do. But she was bound to travel light and make her way in the world. The little boy was evidence against her."

"She came back to him finally," I said. "By that time it was too late for either of them."

"You think her own boy killed her?"

"I didn't until now. He had no motive. But if he found out that she killed his father—" I left the sentence unfinished.

"She didn't, though."

"You just said she did."

"No, I said she killed her husband, Jasper Blevins. He wasn't the little boy's father."

"Who was?"

"Some rich fellow in Texas. Laurel got herself pregnant by him before she ever left there. His family gave her some money and shipped her off to California. Jasper married her for that money, but he never had normal relations with her. I never could respect a man who didn't like normal meat-and-potatoes—"

I interrupted her. "How do you know all this?"

"Laurel told me after she killed him. He did things to her that no woman has to put up with. That was why she killed him, and I don't blame her."

>>>>>>>>>
>>>>>>>>> *chapter* 30
>>>>>>>>>

I THANKED MAMIE HAGEDORN and went out to my car. I'd let some daylight into the case, all right. But the main effect had been to change the color of the daylight.

I headed over the pass toward the Krug ranch. It was the place where all the trouble had started, where Albert Blevins had thrown a lamp at his wife (or vice versa) and ruined his house and his marriage and his son Jasper, where Jasper's marriage had ended in murder, where Davy Spanner was born and Jack Fleischer died. I wanted to see the place in the different-colored daylight.

It wasn't raining in the valley. The cloud cover was breaking up, letting the sky show through in places.

I went through Centerville and made my turn without pausing. I didn't stop till I got to Buzzard Creek.

Henry Langston's station wagon was parked on the side of the road. The creek had shrunk to a shallow stream meandering across the road through several channels cut in the mud it had deposited.

I waded through the mud, following footprints which were probably Langston's, and climbed the rocky lane to the old ranch. The fields around it looked fresh and new. Each blade of grass, each oak leaf, was brilliantly distinct. The sky was luminous, and even the scattering clouds were like floes of light.

Only the human structures were dilapidated. They were dwarfed by the sky, which seemed to arch like a great span of time across the valley.

Henry Langston's footsteps led past the barn to the ruined house. Before I reached the house, he came out carrying his .32 target pistol in his left hand and a sawed-off shotgun on his right arm. For a moment I entertained the wild idea that he intended to shoot me.

Instead, he waved the shotgun at me in a friendly way and spoke my name with pleasure. "I found the murder weapon."

"In the house?"

"No. He threw it in the river. I saw it sticking out of the mud when I came across."

I took the shotgun out of his hands and broke it. There were two expended cartridges in the breech. The short ugly double muzzle was choked with mud.

"Any other sign of him?"

Hank shook his head. "I had a hunch that he might come back to the ranch here. It seemed to be the place he was looking for. But I was wrong."

"Where's the posse?"

Hank pointed toward the mountains in the northeast. Over them I could see black clouds whose trailing edges were ragged with rain.

"They may be bogged down," he said with some satisfaction.

"You don't want him caught, do you, Hank?"

"I'm of two minds about Davy. Of course I want him caught. He's dangerous. But I don't want him shot and killed without a trial. There are mitigating circumstances, remember."

I knew that. It was one of my reasons for going on with the case. There wasn't much chance of saving Davy from a first-degree conviction, but I hoped the girl was still reclaimable.

"Let's get out of here," I said. "I stopped in Santa Teresa, by the way, talked to your wife on the phone."

Hank gave me a quick guilty look. "Is Kate all right?"

"No, she isn't. She's worried about you and worried about herself."

"What's the matter with her?"

"It may be only nerves. She said she wouldn't tell me because I wasn't a doctor."

"She's concerned about losing the baby," he said gravely. "She was bleeding a little before I left last night."

He started walking with long strides past the barn toward the road. The barn owl flew out, his eyes wide in his flabbergasted face. Hank took a shot at the owl with his target pistol. He missed the bird, but I didn't like the action. It reminded me of Lupe's shot at the mud hen.

We drove to Centerville in separate cars. Hank parked his wagon in front of Al Simmons's beer and sandwich place. When I followed him in, he was already talking into the bar telephone: "Make it collect, please. My name is Henry Langston."

There was a long silence, stitched by the telephone ringing at the far end of the line, and the mutter of a turned-down radio at this end. Al Simmons leaned across the bar:

"More trouble?"

"I hope not."

The operator's voice came over the line like a second answer to Al's question: "Your party does not answer, sir. Do you wish me to try again?"

"I'll try again myself, thanks." Hank hung up and turned to me: "She must be at the nursery school picking up Henry, Jr. It's early for that, though."

Moving abruptly, as if he was pulled or driven, he started for the door. Al Simmons detained me.

"What's on your friend's mind?"

"He's worried about his wife."

"On account of the shotgun killer?"

"Yes."

"I guess a lot of people will be worried. He made it out over the north pass, did you know that? The radio said he hitched a ride on a truck."

"Headed which way?"

"South. The truck driver says he dropped him in Santa Teresa."

I went outside to tell Hank. He was already roaring up the county blacktop. By the time I reached the summit of the pass, his car was far down the twisting road, crawling like a flea on the mountain's scarred flank.

Perhaps I should have stopped in Rodeo City. The trouble was that I didn't trust Pennell's judgment. Assuming that Davy had holed up in Langston's house, the last thing needed was the kind of shoot-out in which innocent people could get hurt.

Once on the highway and past the roadblock which Pennell had ordered too late, I pushed the speedometer up to ninety and held it till I reached the outskirts of Santa Teresa. I took the first off-ramp and drove to the Langstons' neighborhood.

Hank's wagon was standing in the road with steam blowing out from under the hood. Hank was halfway between the wagon and his front door, running with his pistol in his hand.

He shouted: "Kate! Are you all right?"

Kate Langston came out screaming. She lunged toward her husband, fell on the flagstone walk before she reached him, got up bloody-kneed and crying piteously: "I'm going to lose the baby. He's making me lose the baby."

Hank gathered her against him with his left arm. Davy appeared in the doorway. He was muddy and unshaven, and awkward, like an actor dying of stage fright.

Hank raised his right arm, pointing the pistol like a dark elongated finger. Davy looked at him shyly, and opened his mouth to speak. Hank shot him several times. The third shot broke his left eye. He sat down on the threshold and died there very quickly.

An hour or so later, I was inside the house with Hank. The local police had come and, after getting a statement from Hank and congratulating him, had taken the body away. Kate was in the emergency ward of the hospital under sedation for shock.

With the same general idea in mind, I was pouring whisky for Hank but not drinking much myself. On top of everything else, the whisky hit him hard. He wandered around the living room, looking for something that probably wasn't there. He paused at the grand piano, with closed fists began to hammer the keys.

I yelled at him: "Is that necessary?"

He turned with his fists raised. His eyes were dark and wild, as wild as Davy's had been.

"I shouldn't have killed him, should I?"

"I'm not your conscience. There is a kind of economy in life. You don't spend more than you have, or say more than you know, or throw your weight around more than necessary."

"He was wrecking my marriage, driving my wife crazy. I had to make a decision, do something decisive."

"You certainly did that."

"The police didn't blame me."

"They're not your conscience either."

He sat swaying on the piano bench. I was disappointed in Hank, and worried about him. The second self that most of us have inside of us had stepped into the open and acted out its violence. Now he had to live with it, like an insane Siamese twin, for the rest of his life.

The telephone rang. I answered it: "Langston residence."

"Is that you, Mr. Langston?" a woman said.

"I'm a friend of the family. There's illness in the family."

"I was wondering why Mrs. Langston didn't pick up Junior."

"Is that the nursery school?"

The woman said it was, and that she was Mrs. Hawkins.

"Just keep the boy for now. Keep him overnight."

"We can't do that. We don't have the facilities."

"Give it a try, will you? Mrs. Langston's in the hospital."

"What about Mr. Langston?"

"He's not well, either."

I hung up and went back to him. His eyes had a dark used look, like burned ends. He was beginning to feel the change in himself and in his life.

I said good-bye and left the house, stepping wide over the threshold where some of Davy's blood was turning brown in the sun that had rejected him now forever.

>>>>>>>>>
>>>>>>>>> *chapter* 31
>>>>>>>>>

BEFORE HEADING BACK to Los Angeles, I paid a final visit to Mrs. Fleischer. She came to the door wearing a black hat and coat. Her face was freshly made up but under the makeup it looked pasty and inert.

She seemed almost completely sober, but very nervous. "What do you want?"

"The tapes."

She spread her gloved hands. "No havey, no savvy."

"Don't give me that, Mrs. Fleischer. You said they're where you could put your hands on them."

"Well, they're not any more."

"Did you turn them over to the police?"

"Maybe I did and maybe I didn't. You've got to let me go now. I'm expecting a taxi."

She started to close the door on me. I leaned against it casually but firmly. Her eyes moved sluggishly up to my face.

"What is this, anyway?"

"I've decided to raise my offer. I'll give you two thousand."

She laughed joylessly. "That's peanuts. Chicken feed. If I wasn't a lady I'd tell you what you can do with your lousy two thousand."

"Who have you been talking to?"

"A very nice young man. He treated me like a gentleman, which is more than some people do." She gave the door a fretful shove, which my shoulder blocked. "And he told me how much those cans of tape were really worth."

"How much?"

"Ten grand," she said with the pride of a daily-double winner putting down a loser.

"Did he buy them from you?"

"Maybe he did."

"I know. And maybe he didn't. Can you describe him to me?"

"He's very good-looking, with nice brown curly hair. Much better looking than you are. And quite a few years younger," she added, as if she could score off her husband through his old buddy Jack Archer.

Her description failed to evoke anyone, unless it was Keith Sebastian, which seemed unlikely. "What name did he use?"

"He didn't mention his name."

That probably meant she had been paid in cash, if she had been paid. "Ten grand is a lot of cash," I said. "I hope you're not planning to carry it around loose."

"No, I'm gonna—" She bit her lower lip and got lipstick on her

front teeth. "It's none of your business what I'm gonna do. And if you don't lay off me, I'll call the police."

That was the last thing she was likely to do. But I was weary of her, and of myself talking to her. I drove around the block and parked at the corner. After a while a yellow cab came from the other direction. It stopped in front of her house and honked gently.

Mrs. Fleischer came out carrying a light-blue traveling bag. She got into the taxi. I followed it across town to the freeway and north along the freeway to the local airport.

I didn't try to find out where Mrs. Fleischer was flying to. I didn't care. She wouldn't be leaving town if she hadn't sold the tapes.

I drove south to Woodland Hills, feeling empty and light and futile. I think I'd been harboring a secret wish that I could somehow pull it out for Davy, save his life at least, give him a long-term chance for rehabilitation.

Such wishes for other people were always going sour. Langston's wish for Davy had turned into a secret triangle which meant the opposite of what it seemed to mean. I was beginning to worry about my wish for the girl.

Bernice Sebastian let me into her house. She was sallow and desolate, with black glittering eyes. Her grooming was coming apart for the first time that I'd seen. She had cigarette ashes down the front of her dress, and her hair needed combing.

She took me into the living room and seated me in a golden drench of late afternoon sunlight which came in through the high glass.

"Would you like some coffee?"

"No thanks. A glass of water would taste good."

She brought it to me formally, on a tray. She gave the impression of trying to hold together, by such formalities, all the centrifugal pieces of her life. I drank the water and thanked her.

"Where's your husband?"

"Off on one of his missions," she said dryly.

"He didn't go to Santa Teresa, by any chance?"

"I don't know where he went. We had a quarrel."

"Do you want to talk about it?"

"No. It isn't the sort of talk I'd care to repeat, to anyone. Essentially we were blaming each other, for this disaster."

She sat down on a hassock facing me, folding her knees and hold-

ing them with locked fingers. Nothing she did was graceless, as she knew. She turned her pretty, disheveled head self-consciously under my eyes.

"I'll tell you what our quarrel was about, if you promise not to do anything."

"What do you want me not to do?"

"I don't want you to do anything to stop Keith. That would be treachery."

"Stop him doing what?"

"Promise first."

"I can't, Mrs. Sebastian. I will promise this: I won't do anything that would harm your daughter."

"But not Keith?"

"If their interests turn out to be separate, I'll do my best for Sandy."

"Then I'll tell you. He's planning to take her out of the country."

"Jump bail?"

"I'm afraid so. He's talking in terms of South America."

"It isn't a good idea. She'd have a hard time ever coming back, and so would he."

"I know that. I told him that."

"How is he planning to finance the trip?"

"I'm afraid he's thinking about embezzling money. Keith seems to be breaking up. He simply can't bear the idea of Sandy standing trial and possibly going to jail."

"She's still in the Psychiatric Center, isn't she?"

"I don't know."

"Call them and find out."

Bernice went into the study and closed the door behind her. I heard her talking, too dimly to know what she said. She came out with a frightened grimace pulling at her mouth.

"He took her out of the Center."

"When?"

"About an hour ago."

"Did he say where he was taking her?"

"No."

"Or give you any clue?"

"This morning he talked about flying to Mexico City, and then

perhaps on to Brazil. But he wouldn't go without telling me first. He expects me to go along."

"Do you want to?"

She shook her head. "I don't think any of us should go. We should stay here and fight it out."

"You're a good girl."

Her eyes filled up with feeling but what she said was: "No. If I were a good person, my family wouldn't have got into this mess. I made all the mistakes in the book."

"Do you feel like naming them?"

"If you can bear to listen." She sat quiet for a minute, ordering her thoughts. "I don't really want to talk it out at any length. This isn't the time, and I doubt that you're the person."

"Who is?"

"Keith should be. He's still my husband. The trouble is we stopped talking years ago. We started a game of let's pretend, without ever admitting it to each other. Keith was to be the rising young executive and I was to be his model homemaker, making him feel like a man, which is hard for Keith. And Sandy was to make us both feel good by doing well in school and never doing or saying anything wrong. What that boils down to is exploitation. Keith and I were exploiting each other and Sandy, and that's the opposite of loving each other."

"I still say you're a good girl."

"Don't try to make me feel better. I have no right to."

But she closed her eyes and leaned her face toward me. I held it between my hands. I could feel her mouth and her breathing warm on my fingers.

After a while she straightened up. Her face was more composed. It had recovered some of the pride that made it beautiful.

She said: "Are you hungry? Let me fix you something to eat."

"It wouldn't be a good idea."

"Why not?"

"You said it yourself just now. People shouldn't play let's pretend."

"Is that what I'd be doing?"

"That's what I'd be doing, Bernice. There's something else we should be doing."

She misunderstood me, and gave me a quick-frozen quizzical look. "Really?"

"That wasn't a pass. But I have to ask you a question that may embarrass you. It has to do with Sandy's sex experience."

She was startled. She stood up and walked away from me, to the far side of the room.

"How much did your daughter know about sex?"

Slowly, she turned to face me. "I haven't the faintest idea. We never discussed the matter."

"Why not?"

"I assumed she learned all about it in school. She took a course on the subject. Anyway, I didn't feel qualified."

"Why?"

She looked at me angrily. "I don't know why you're insisting on this catechism. It has nothing to do with anything."

"People are always telling me that about their central concerns."

"Sex is *not* one of my central concerns. I can take it or leave it. Keith and I—" She heard herself, and paused.

"What about you and Keith?"

"Nothing. You have no right to ask me these questions."

I moved toward her. "Tell me one thing. What happened to Sandy last summer—the incident you've been suppressing in her diary?"

"It hardly matters any more."

"Everything matters."

She looked at me with a kind of incredulity. "You really believe that, don't you? I never met a man like you before."

"Let's not get off on the personal. Did she write about her LSD experience?"

"That was part of it. Incidentally, I forgot to tell you, the doctor left a message for you. The substance you gave him for analysis was LSD of a poor quality. He said that helped to account for Sandy's reaction."

"I'm not surprised. What else helped to account for it?"

"He didn't say."

"I'm asking you, Bernice. What was the rest of it?"

Her face darkened. "I can't tell you. Honestly I can't."

"If Sandy could do it or have it done to her, you should be able to say it. Are we talking about her sexual relations with Lupe?"

She bowed her head. "There were more than one of them: They took turns at her, doing—different things."

"And she spelled this out in her diary?"

"Yes."

"May I see it?"

"I destroyed it. Honestly. I was so terribly ashamed."

"Why do you suppose she wrote it out?"

"To shame me. She knew I read her diary."

"Don't you think she may have been asking you for help?"

"I don't know. It came as such a shock, I couldn't think clearly about it. I still can't." Her voice was hurried and monotonous, with a shrill note of panic running through it.

"Why, Bernice?" I wondered if the same sort of thing had ever happened to her.

She raised her head and looked at me with black dislike. "I don't want to talk to you any more. Go away."

"Promise me one thing first. Let me know when you hear from Keith. All I want is a chance to talk to him and Sandy."

"I'll call you. I promise that much."

I told her I would wait for her call in my office, and went outside. Late afternoon sunlight spilled over the mountains to the west. The light had a tarnished elegiac quality, as if the sinking sun might never rise again. On the fairway behind the house the golfers seemed to be hurrying, pursued by their lengthening shadows.

chapter **32**

I BOUGHT A plastic basket of fried chicken and took it to my office. Before eating it, I checked in with my answering service. The girl on the switchboard told me I'd had a call from Ralph Cuddy.

I called the Santa Monica number that Cuddy had left for me. He answered the phone himself:

"Good evening. This is Ralph Cuddy."

"Archer here. I wasn't expecting to hear from you again."

"Mrs. Krug asked me to call you." His voice was stiff with embarrassment. "I told her Jasper was dead. She wants to talk to you about it."

"Tell her I'll get in touch with her tomorrow."

"Tonight would be better. Mrs. Krug is very anxious to see you. You know that missing gun you were asking me about? She has some information on that, too."

"How could she have?"

"Mr. Krug was security chief at Corpus Christi Oil at the time the gun was stolen."

"Who stole it? Jasper Blevins?"

"I'm not authorized to tell you anything. You better get it direct from Mrs. Krug."

I drove through heavy early-evening traffic to the Oakwood Convalescent Home. As the nurse conducted me down the corridor, I got a whiff of some patient's dinner. It reminded me of the chicken I had left untouched on my desk.

Alma Krug looked up from her Bible when I entered the room. Her eyes were grave. She dismissed the nurse with a movement of her hand.

"Please shut the door," she said to me. "It's good of you to visit me, Mr. Archer." She indicated a straight chair, which I took, and turned her wheel chair to face me. "Ralph Cuddy says my grandson Jasper was killed in a train wreck. Is that true?"

"His body was found under a train. I've been told he was murdered somewhere else, and that Laurel did the killing. That's hearsay evidence, but I'm inclined to believe it."

"Has Laurel been punished?"

"Not directly and not immediately. The local sheriff's man covered up for her, or so I'm told. But Laurel was killed herself the other day."

"Who killed her?"

"I don't know."

"This is terrible news." Her voice had a rustling sibilance. "You say that Laurel was killed the other day. You didn't tell me that when you came to see me before."

"No."

"And you didn't tell me Jasper was dead."

"I wasn't sure, and I didn't want to hurt you unnecessarily."

"You should have told me. How long ago did he die?"

"About fifteen years. Actually his body was found on the tracks near Rodeo City in late May of 1952."

"A bad end," she said.

"Other bad things have happened." I went on slowly and carefully, watching her face. "Three or four days before Jasper was killed, Mark Hackett was shot on Malibu Beach. Perhaps we've both been holding back, Mrs. Krug. You didn't tell me your husband was security officer for Mark Hackett's oil company. I admit I should have been able to work it out for myself, but for some reason I didn't. I think you're the reason."

Her eyes flinched. "I have a lot on my conscience. It's why I asked you to come here, Mr. Archer. The still small voice wouldn't let me rest, and now that my grandson Jasper's dead—" She let the sentence trail off into silence.

"Did Jasper steal the gun from Hackett's company?"

"Joe always thought so. Jasper had stolen before—I had to lock up my purse when he was with us. And he visited Joe at the office that same day."

"The day Mark Hackett was killed?"

She nodded very slowly. "The day before that he had a terrible quarrel with Mr. Hackett."

"How do you know?"

"He told Joe. He wanted Joe to intercede for him with Mr. Hackett."

"What was the problem?"

"Money. Jasper thought he had a legitimate claim on Mr. Hackett, for raising the boy. Actually Mr. Hackett gave Jasper a good deal of money at the time he married Laurel. That was all part of the bargain."

"Are you telling me that Davy was Mark Hackett's illegitimate son?"

"His grandson," she corrected me soberly. "Davy was Stephen Hackett's natural son. Laurel Dudney was one of the Hacketts' servants back in Texas. She was a pretty little thing, and Stephen got her with child. His father sent him off to study in Europe. He sent Laurel out to us, to find a husband before she got too big.

"Jasper decided to marry her himself. He was barbering at the
time, and he hardly made enough to keep body and soul together.
Mr. Hackett gave them five thousand dollars for a wedding present.
Later, Jasper thought he should get more. He was badgering Mr.
Hackett the day before—" Her precise mouth closed without com-
pleting the sentence.

"The day before he killed him?"

"That's what Joe always thought. It shortened my husband's life.
Joe was an honest man, but he couldn't bring himself to accuse his
own daughter's son. He asked me if he should, and I told him not to.
That's on my conscience, too."

"You did what most grandparents would do."

"That isn't good enough. But we were in the habit of making excuses for Jasper. From the time that he was a little boy and first
came to us, he was a Tartar. He stole and fought and tortured cats
and got in trouble at school. I took him to a head doctor once and
the doctor said he should be sent away. But I couldn't bear to do
that to him, the poor boy wasn't all bad." She added after some
thought: "He had some artistic talent. He got that from his
mother."

"Tell me about his mother."

Mrs. Krug was confused for a moment. She looked at me with displeasure. "I prefer not to talk about my daughter. I have some right
to the privacy of my feelings."

"I already have some facts, Mrs. Krug. Your daughter was born in
1910 in Rodeo City. Oddly enough, I have a copy of her birth
certificate. She was christened Henrietta R. Krug. You called her
Etta, but at some point in her life she dropped that name."

"She always hated it. She started using her middle name after she
left Albert Blevins."

"Her middle name is Ruth, isn't it?"

The old woman bowed her head in assent. Her eyes refused to
meet mine.

"And her second husband was Mark Hackett."

"There was another one in between," she said with an old
woman's passion for accuracy. "She took up with a Mexican boy from
San Diego. That was over twenty-five years ago."

"What was his name?"

"Lupe Rivera. They only stayed together a few months. The po-

Righteous anger and a loaded gun: the combination scared me: it always had. I went.

My office on Sunset was beginning to look abandoned. A spider was working in the corner of the waiting room. Flies drowsed in the window, making a noise like time running down. A thin patina of dust had gathered on all the horizontal surfaces.

I wiped the top of my desk with a piece of Kleenex and sat and looked at the check Ruth Marburg had given me. Since I couldn't deposit a postdated check in the bank, I put it in my safe. It didn't make me feel rich.

I called Corpus Christi Oil in Long Beach and got in touch with the head of the drafting department, a man named Patterson. He remembered Sidney Marburg but was careful in what he said about him. Sid was a good worker, talented draftsman, always wanted to be a painter, glad he made it.

"I understand he married the former Mrs. Hackett."

"So I heard," Patterson said noncommittally.

"Did he work for you at the time of Mark Hackett's death?"

"Yeah, he quit about that time."

"Why did he quit?"

"Told me he had a chance to go to Mexico, on an art scholarship."

"Do you remember a gun that was missing? A gun that was used in the killing of Mark Hackett?"

"I heard something about it." His voice was getting fainter, like a receding spirit. "It wasn't the responsibility of the drafting department. And if you're pointing a finger at Sid, you couldn't be wronger, mister. Sid wouldn't kill anybody."

"I'm glad to hear it. Whose responsibility was that gun?"

"It belonged to security. It was their responsibility to look after it. But don't go running to them and quoting me. I don't want any trouble with the head security man."

"You mean Ralph Cuddy?"

"Listen, you've made me say more than I should already. Who is this calling, anyway? Did you say you were with the L.A. police?"

"I said I was working with them. I'm a private detective."

Patterson hung up.

I sat and tried to do some thinking. My mind went around in a circle, and I had the frustrating feeling that there was a missing connection just beyond the circle. Or deep inside the circle, at its center, buried as deep as the dead.

I dug and groped for the missing connection, sure that it was in my memory if I could only recognize it. But you can't force your unconscious mind to rap out information like a computer. It only retreats growling further into its lair.

I was stoned with weariness and frustration. I stretched out on the settee in the waiting room. I tried to stretch out, that is. The settee was a foot too short, and I lay with my legs hanging over the wooden arm, as usual.

I watched the spider in the corner of the ceiling, and wished my case was as neat and controlled as his web. I dropped off to sleep and dreamed that I was caught in a larger web, whose radii were hung with the husks of dead men. The web spun like a roulette wheel, and the spider at the center of the web had a croupier's rake in each of his eight hands. He raked me in toward him.

I woke up wet under my shirt. The spider was still working in the corner of the ceiling. I got up, intending to kill him, but both my feet were asleep. By the time they came awake, my mind was awake, too. I let the spider be. Perhaps he'd catch the flies buzzing in the window.

My brief, nightmare-ridden sleep had somehow refreshed me. I discarded my damp shirt, shaved with an electric razor, and put on a fresh shirt that I kept in the closet. Then I went to the window to see what the weather was like.

It was fair and clear, only faintly tinged with smog. Early noon traffic was roaring along the boulevard.

Detective-Sergeant Prince and his partner Janowski got out of a police car on the far side of the street. I hoped they weren't coming to see me; I was aware that I hadn't been cooperating with them. But of course they were coming to see me.

They crossed the boulevard as if they were invulnerable or oblivious to traffic. Prince walked a step ahead, like a keen dog pulling Janowski along on a kind of moral leash.

I put on a jacket, and met them at the outside door of my office. They came in without being asked. Prince was wan with barely controlled anger. Even Janowski's fair skin was blotched with feeling. He said:

"You haven't been taking us into your confidence, Archer. We decided to come and ask you why."

"I had other things to think about."

"Such as?" Prince said unpleasantly.

"Such as trying to save a man's life. His life got saved, incidentally."

"Lucky for you it did," Prince said. "Your neck was out a mile. It still is."

I was getting tired of being sounded off at. The blood was pounding in my stomach and my sore kidneys.

"Moderate your tone, Sergeant."

Prince looked ready to slug me. I almost wished he would. Like most Americans, I was a counter-puncher.

Janowski stepped between us. "Let me do the talking," he said to his partner. He turned to me: "We won't cry over spilt milk, but we'd like to have your cooperation now. There are places you can go, things you can do, that we can't."

"What do you want done?"

"This retired deputy sheriff, the one who was knocked off in the snatch—"

"Jack Fleischer."

"Right. You probably know all this, but I'll tell you anyway. Fleischer has had Laurel Smith's apartment under electronic surveillance for several weeks. Apparently he recorded it all on tapes. Anyway, we know he bought the tapes and the other equipment. Those tapes could be very helpful to us, I think."

"I think so, too."

Prince spoke across Janowski: "Do you have them?"

"No."

"Where are they?"

"I don't know. They may be in Fleischer's house in Santa Teresa."

"That's our opinion, too," Janowski said. "His widow denies it, but that doesn't prove anything. I talked to her on the phone, and she was pretty evasive. I tried to get some action from the Santa Teresa police, but they won't touch it. Fleischer had political connections, or so I gather, and now that he's dead he's a hero. They won't even admit the possibility that he was bugging the dead woman's apartment. Of course we could kick it up to the higher echelons—"

"Or kick it down to the lower," I said with a smile. "You want me to go to Santa Teresa and talk to Mrs. Fleischer?"

"That would be very cooperative of you," Janowski said.

"It's no chore. I was planning to see her anyway."

Janowski shook my hand, and even Prince smiled a little. They had forgiven me, to the extent that policemen ever forgive anything.

>>>>>>>>>>
>>>>>>>>>> *chapter* 28
>>>>>>>>>>

I GOT TO SANTA TERESA shortly after one o'clock. I had a cold sandwich in a restaurant near the courthouse, and walked from there to Fleischer's house, slowly. I wasn't looking forward to another interview with Fleischer's widow.

The drapes pulled over the front windows gave the house a shut and deserted look. But there was life inside of it. Mrs. Fleischer answered the door.

She was drinking again, or still, had passed through various stages of drunkenness into a kind of false sobriety. She was decently clothed in a black dress. Her hair was brushed and in place. The tremor in her hands wasn't too obvious.

But she didn't seem to remember me at all. Her eyes looked right through me, as if there was someone behind me and I was a ghost.

I started over. "You may not remember me. I was working with your husband on the Davy Spanner case."

"He killed Jack," she said. "Did you know that? He killed my husband."

"Yes. I'm sorry."

She glanced at the neighbor's house, and leaned toward me, conspiratorially, twitching at my sleeve. "Didn't you and I have a talk the other night? Come in, I'll pour you a drink."

I followed her into the house reluctantly. The lights were on in the living room, as if she preferred to live in permanent evening. The drinks she brought were gin faintly tinctured with tonic. We seemed to be picking up where we had left off.

lice arrested him for smuggling, and Etta got a divorce from him. Then came Mark Hackett. Then came Sidney Marburg." Her voice rang harshly, as if she was reciting an indictment.

"Why didn't you tell me Ruth Marburg was your daughter?"

"You didn't ask me. It makes no difference, anyway. I haven't had much to do with Etta since she threw herself at Mr. Hackett and rose in the world and became a great lady. She never comes to see me, and I know why. She's ashamed of the life she leads, with young men half her age. I might as well not have a family. I never even see my grandson Stephen."

I said I was sorry, and left her warming her hands at her Bible.

>>>>>>>>>
>>>>>>>>> *chapter* 33
>>>>>>>>>

I DROVE TO MALIBU, forgetting that I was hungry and tired. Just before I reached the Hacketts' gate, I passed a car going in the other direction. The man at the wheel looked like Keith Sebastian. I turned in the entrance to the Hacketts' driveway and chased him down the hill.

I caught him at the highway STOP sign. He turned right on the highway and then left on a secondary road that looped down along the beach. He parked behind a lighted beach house and knocked on the back door. For an instant, as she opened the door for him, his daughter was silhouetted against the light.

I got out of my car and approached the house. The blinds and drapes were closed. A good deal of light leaked out but I couldn't hear anything because of the waves marking time on the beach.

The name on the mailbox was Hackett. I knocked on the back door, trying the knob at the same time. It was locked.

Keith Sebastian said through the door: "Who is it?"

"Archer."

There was another wait. Inside the house a door closed. Sebastian unlocked the outer door and opened it.

I stepped in past him without waiting to be asked. "What are you doing, Keith?"

He had no decent cover story. "I decided I better get away from it all for a day or two. Mr. Hackett loaned me the use of his private cottage."

I moved from the kitchen into the next room. There were dirty dishes, set for two, on a round poker table. One of the coffee mugs had a half-moon of lipstick at the rim.

"Do you have a girl with you?"

"As a matter of fact I have." He looked at me with hopeful foolish guile. "You won't tell Bernice now, will you?"

"She knows, and so do I. It's Sandy, isn't it?"

He picked up Sandy's coffee mug. For a moment his face was open. I think he was planning to brain me, and I stepped back out of close range. He set the mug down on the table.

"She's my daughter," he asserted. "I know what's best for her."

"Is that why her life is working out so beautifully? This is a lousy substitute for treatment."

"It's better than jail. She'd get no treatment at all."

"Who's been telling you horror stories?"

He wouldn't answer me. He stood there shaking his stupid handsome head. I sat down at the table uninvited. After a minute he sat down opposite me. We faced each other like bluffing poker players.

"You don't understand. Sandy and I aren't planning to stay *here*. Everything's all worked out."

"To leave the country?"

He frowned. "Bernice told you then."

"It's a good thing someone did. If you skip you'll virtually lose your citizenship. Sandy will, anyway. And how will you support yourself in a foreign country?"

"That's all taken care of. If I look after what I've got, and live in the right place, I'll never have to work again."

"I thought you were flat broke."

"Not any more. The whole thing's working out." He spoke with the deaf and blind assurance of terrible anxiety. "So please don't try to stop me, Mr. Archer. I know exactly what I'm doing."

"Is your wife going with you?"

"I hope so. She hasn't decided. We're flying out tomorrow, and she's going to have to make up her mind in a hurry."

"I don't think either of you should decide in a hurry."

"Nobody asked for your advice."

"You did, though, in a way, when you brought me into this case. I'm afraid you're stuck with me."

We sat and looked at each other, two poker players with lousy hands who were too far behind to quit. For a moment I could hear the sea more clearly, and a cold draft touched my ankles. Something jarred in another part of the house, and the draft was cut off.

"Where is your daughter?"

He crossed the room and opened a door. "Sandy!"

I followed him into a lighted bedroom. It was a strange room, as strange as Lupe's. Wild color exploded on the walls and ceiling. A round bed stood like an altar in the middle. Sandy's clothes were scattered across the bed.

Sebastian opened the sliding glass door. We ran down to the water. The girl was out past the surf line, swimming for her life, or for her death.

Sebastian waded in in his clothes, then turned to me helplessly. "I can't swim very well."

A wave knocked him down. I had to drag him out of the sucking water.

"Go and call the sheriff."

"No!"

I slapped him. "Call the sheriff, Keith. You have to."

He floundered up the beach. I tore off my shoes and most of my clothes, and went in after the girl. She was young, and hard to catch. By the time I reached her, we were a long way out and I was tiring.

She didn't know I was there until I touched her. Her eyes were wide and dark as a seal's. "Go away. I want to die."

"I'm not going to let you."

"You would if you knew all about me."

"I almost do, Sandy. Come on in with me. I'm too tired to drag you."

The eye of a searchlight winked open on the beach. It roved the sea and found us. Sandy swam away from me. Her body was white and faintly phosphorescent, shimmering like moonlight in the water.

I stayed close to her. She was the only one left. A man in a black rubber wet-suit came out on a paddleboard and took her in unresisting through the surf.

Sebastian and Captain Aubrey were waiting for us with blankets. I rescued my clothes from under the feet of the onlookers and followed Sebastian and his daughter toward the beach cottage. Captain Aubrey walked with me.

"Suicide attempt?" he said.

"She's been talking about it for months. I hope this gets it out of her system."

"Don't count on it. Her family better take security precautions."

"I've been telling them that."

"You say it's been on her mind for months. That means it antedates the current mess."

"Correct."

We had reached the cottage. I was shivering in my blanket, but Aubrey detained me outside. "What made her suicidal in the first place?"

"I want to talk to you about that, Captain. First I need a hot shower and a chance to get Sebastian squared away. Where will you be in the next hour?"

"I'll wait for you in the substation."

I opened the glass door and stepped up into the colored bedroom. Sebastian was on the far side of the room. He stood like a sentry beside an open door through which I could hear a shower running. His clothes were dripping. He had wet sand in his hair, and in his eyes a look of maniacal dutifulness.

"What do you plan to do for the next five or ten years, Keith? Stand suicide watch?"

He gave me a puzzled look. "I don't quite follow."

"We almost lost her just now. You can't go on taking chances with her life. And you can't stand around and watch her twenty-four hours a day."

"I don't know what to do."

"Take her back to the Psychiatric Center tonight. Forget about South America. You wouldn't like it."

"But I made a promise."

"To Sandy? She'd rather die than go on this way. Literally."

"She isn't the only one involved," he said miserably. "I don't have any choice about South America. It's part of the whole ball of wax."

"You'd better explain that."

"I can't. I promised not to talk about it."

"Who did you make these promises to? Stephen Hackett?"

"No. It wasn't Mr. Hackett."

I moved around the bed toward him. "I can't do anything more for you, if you won't open up. I think you're being taken for a ride, you and your daughter both."

He answered me doggedly: "I know what I'm doing. I don't want or need your help."

"You may not want it, but you certainly need it. Are you going to take Sandy back to the Center?"

"No."

"Then I'll have to make you."

"You can't. I'm a free citizen."

"You won't be for long. Captain Aubrey is waiting to talk to me now. When he finds out that you've been buying and selling evidence in a murder case—"

"What do you mean?"

"I mean the tapes you bought from Mrs. Fleischer."

It was a guess, but an educated one, that the tapes were part of the ball of wax he'd referred to. His face confirmed my guess.

"Who did you buy them for, Keith?"

He didn't answer.

"Who's paying you to take your daughter out of the country?"

He still refused to answer. Sandy appeared in the doorway behind him. She had on a clean yellow terrycloth robe and was rosy from her shower. Clearly the night swim had been good for her. I found this hard to forgive.

She said to her father: "Is somebody paying you to leave? You didn't tell me that. You said your company was giving you some separation money."

"That's what it is, dear, separation money." He stood between us, looking from one to the other.

"How much money?"

"That's none of your business, dear. I mean, let me handle the business. You don't have to trouble your mind—"

"Gee thanks. Is Mr. Hackett giving you this money?"

"You might say so. It's his company."

"And you get the money if you take me to South America? Is that right? Otherwise you don't?"

"I don't like this cross-questioning," Sebastian said. "After all I am your father."

"Sure you are, Dad." Her voice was sardonic, darkened by the authority of experienced pain. "But I don't want to go to South America."

"You said you did."

"I don't any more." Brusquely she turned her attention to me. "Get me out of here, will you? I've had it with this scene. This is where I freaked out last summer, right here in this very room. This is the bed where Lupe and Steve took turns at me. In the vulva and the anus." She touched those parts of herself like a child showing where she'd been hurt.

The words and gestures were addressed to me but meant for her father. Sebastian was appalled. He sat on the bed, then stood up quickly and brushed away the sand he had deposited.

"You can't mean Mr. Hackett."

"Yes I can. I blew my mind and I hardly knew what was happening. But I know old Steve Hackett when I see him."

Like lenses in a sophisticated camera, Sebastian's eyes were changing. He wanted not to believe her, to find a credibility gap in her story. But the truth was there, and we both knew it.

"Why didn't you tell me, Sandy?"

"I'm telling you now."

"I mean last summer, when it happened."

She regarded him with scorn. "How do you know it happened last summer? I haven't mentioned that tonight."

He looked around rather wildly, and rushed into speech: "Your mother said something, I don't mean she spelled it out. But there was something in your diary, wasn't there?"

"*I* spelled it out," she said. "I knew Bernice read my diary. But neither of you ever said a word to me. Never ever a word."

"I took your mother's lead in that, Sandy. After all I'm only a man and you're a girl."

"I know I'm a girl. I found it out the hard way."

She was angry and troubled, but she sounded more like a woman than a girl. She wasn't afraid. It occurred to me that she had suffered a sea-change into a woman, and that her storm would pass.

I went into the bathroom for a hot shower. The stall was warm and fragrant from Sandy's use of it.

Then, while Sebastian took a shower, I talked to his daughter across the poker table.

We both had our clothes on now, and they seemed to impose a certain formality on the conversation. Sandy started out by thanking me, though, which wasn't a bad sign.

I told her not to mention it, I'd been dying for a swim. "Have you decided to give life a try?"

"I'm not making any promises," she said. "It's a stinking world."

"You don't improve it by committing suicide."

"I do for me." She was still and silent for a while. "I thought I could break away from it all with Davy."

"Whose idea was that?"

"It was his. He picked me up on the Strip because somebody told him that I knew the Hacketts. He needed a way to get to Steve, and I was glad to help."

"Why?"

"You know why. I wanted to get back at him and Lupe. But it didn't really make me feel any better. It only made me feel worse."

"What did Davy want?"

"It's hard to tell. He always has three or four reasons for everything, three or four different versions. It isn't his fault. Nobody ever told him the truth, about who he was, until Laurel did. And even then he didn't *know* it was true. Laurel was drunk when she told him."

"Told him that Stephen Hackett was his father?"

"I don't know what she told him. Honestly." It was her mother's word, and she said it with her mother's intonation. "Davy and I weren't talking much at the end. I was afraid to go with him, and afraid to quit. I didn't know how far he would go. Neither did he."

"He's gone further now." I thought it was time to tell her, before the changes of the night had crystallized. "Davy was shot dead this afternoon."

She looked at me dully, as if her capacity to react was used up for the time being. "Who shot him?"

"Henry Langston."

"I thought he was a friend of Davy's."

"He was, but he had troubles of his own. Most people do."

I left her with the thought and went into the bedroom where her father was trying on clothes. He settled for a turtleneck sweater and a pair of slacks. The sweater made him look young and bold, like an actor.

"What's on the agenda, Keith?"

"I'm going up to Hackett's place and give him back his check."

His statement astonished me. He looked slightly astonished himself.

"I'm glad you feel that way. But you better let me have the check. It's evidence."

"Against me?"

"Against Hackett. How much money is involved?"

"The check is for a hundred thousand."

"Plus how much cash for the tapes?"

He barely hesitated. "Ten thousand cash. I paid it over to Mrs. Fleischer."

"What story did Hackett give you about the tapes?"

"He said Fleischer was trying to blackmail him."

"For doing what?"

"He didn't say. I gather he was having an affair, though."

"When did you deliver the tapes to him?"

"Just now. Just before you came."

"Who was there, Keith?"

"Mr. Hackett and his mother were the only ones I saw."

"Do they have a tape recorder?"

"Yes. I saw them try the tapes on it for size."

"How many tapes are there altogether?"

"Six."

"Where did you put them?"

"I left them with Mrs. Marburg in the library. I don't know what they did with them after that."

"And they gave you a check? Right?"

"Yes. Hackett did."

He took the yellow slip out of his wallet and handed it over. It was very like the one in my office safe, except that it was signed by Stephen Hackett instead of his mother, and not postdated.

The moral force required to part with the money generated more of the same in Sebastian. He followed me into the living room, moving eagerly. "I'll go along with you. I want to tell that Hackett creep what I think of him."

"No. You've got better things to do."

"What do you have in mind?"

"Taking your daughter back to the Center," I said.

"Can't I just simply take her home?"

"It's too soon for that."

"It always will be," Sandy said. But she was looking at her father with changing eyes.

>>>>>>>>>
>>>>>>>>> *chapter* 34
>>>>>>>>>

CAPTAIN AUBREY was waiting for me at the wicket which opened onto the porch of the Sheriff's substation. We talked in the dingy hallway of the old building, out of hearing of the officer on duty. Aubrey, when I sketched out what I knew and some of what I guessed, wanted to go along to the Hackett place.

I reminded him that he'd have to get a search warrant, and that might take some doing. Meanwhile Hackett could be destroying the tapes or erasing the sound from them.

"What makes the tapes so important?" Aubrey wanted to know.

"The death of Laurel Smith. I found out tonight that Stephen Hackett had an affair with her about twenty years ago. Davy Spanner was their illegitimate son."

"And you think Hackett killed her?"

"It's too early to say. I know he paid ten grand for the tapes."

"Even so, you can't just go in and seize them."

"I don't have to, Captain. I've been working for Mrs. Marburg. I can get into the house."

"Can you get out again?" he said with a grim half-smile.

"I think I can. I may need some backstopping though. Give me some time alone with them first."

"Then what?"

"We'll play it by ear. If I need help I'll holler."

Aubrey followed me out to my car and leaned in at the window: "Watch out for Mrs. Marburg. At the time of her second husband's death I—" he cleared his throat and edited the slander out of his warning—"there was some suspicion that she was involved."

"She may have been. Mark Hackett was killed by her son by her first husband—a man named Jasper Blevins."

"You know this for a fact?"

"Just about. I got it from Jasper Blevins's grandmother, and it cost her some pain to tell me. She held back until she knew Jasper was dead."

"Too many people have been dying," Aubrey said. "Don't you be one of them."

His unmarked car followed me to the Hacketts' gate. I drove on up the private road to the pass and across the dam. The house beyond the lake had lights in it, faint behind drawn curtains. As I knocked on the door I felt I was coming there for the last time.

Gerda Hackett answered the door. She looked anxious and lonely, like an overweight ghost haunting the wrong house. She brightened up unnervingly when she saw me:

"Mr. Archer! *Kommen Sie nur 'rein.*"

I stepped inside. "How's your husband?"

"Much better, thank you." She added in a disappointed tone: "It's Stephen you wish to see?"

"And Mrs. Marburg."

"They're in the library. I'll tell them you're here."

"Don't bother. I know where it is."

I left her standing like a stranger at the doorway of her house. Moving through the massive building with its institutional feeling, I could guess why Hackett had married a girl from another country. He didn't want to be known.

The library door was closed. I could hear a voice behind it, a woman's voice, and when I pressed my ear against the oak door I recognized the voice of Laurel Smith. It made the hair on the back of my neck bristle. Then my heart began to pound with the crazy hope that Laurel had survived.

I was close to breaking down, like a man coming near to the end of a long climb: an inverted downward climb into the past. I could hardly breathe the air there, and I leaned against the library door.

"Thank you, Mrs. Lippert," Laurel was saying. "You want me to give you a receipt?"

"It isn't necessary," another woman's voice said. "I'll be getting the check back from the bank."

"How about a little drink?"

"No thanks. My husband doesn't like it when he comes home and I have liquor on my breath."

"You can't smell vodka," Laurel said.

"*He* can. He's got a nose like a beagle. Good night now."

"Take care."

A door closed. Laurel began to hum an old song about whistling in the dark. She must have been moving around her apartment, because her voice faded and returned.

I started to turn the knob of the library door. Ruth Marburg said: "Who is that out there?"

I had to go in, smiling. Mrs. Marburg was sitting beside the telephone. There was no revolver in sight.

Hackett was sitting at the table where the tape recorder stood. His battered smile looked as ghastly from the outside as mine felt from the inside. He switched off Laurel's singing.

"Mrs. Hackett told me where to find you. I hope I'm not interrupting anything."

Hackett started to tell me that I wasn't, but Mrs. Marburg's voice overbore his: "As a matter of fact you are interrupting something. My son and I are playing some old family tapes."

"Go right ahead."

"You wouldn't be interested. They're very nostalgic, but just to members of the family." Her voice sharpened: "Do you want something?"

"I came to give you my final report."

"This is a bad time. Come back tomorrow, eh?"

"I'd like to hear what he has to say." Hackett looked uneasily at his mother. "As long as we're paying him so much we might as well get the benefit of it."

"I'd rather hear what Laurel has to say."

Mrs. Marburg flapped her false eyelashes at me. "Laurel? Who on earth is Laurel?"

"Jasper's wife. You've just been listening to her. Let's all listen."

Mrs. Marburg leaned toward me urgently. "Close the door behind you. I want to talk to you."

I closed the door and leaned on it, watching them. Mrs. Marburg rose heavily, using her arms as well as her legs. Hackett reached for the tape recorder.

"Leave it alone."

His hand hovered over the controls, and then withdrew. Mrs. Marburg walked toward me.

"So you've dug up a little dirt and you think you can raise the ante. You couldn't be more wrong. If you don't watch yourself you'll be in jail before morning."

"Somebody will."

She thrust her face close to mine. "My son and I buy up people like you two for a nickel. That check I gave you is postdated. Are you too stupid to know what that means?"

"It means you didn't trust me to stay bought. Nobody's staying bought these days." I got out Keith Sebastian's check and showed it to her. "Sebastian gave me this."

She snatched at the check. I held it out of her reach and put it away. "Don't be grabby, Etta."

Her whole face scowled under its mask of paint. "You mustn't call me that name. My name is Ruth."

She went to her chair. Instead of sitting down she opened the drawer of the telephone table. I reached her before she got the revolver out and ready to fire, and tore it out of her hands.

I backed away from her and turned to Hackett. He was on his feet, moving on me. I didn't have to fire the gun. He started to walk backwards, rather tentatively, toward the table where he'd been sitting.

"Get away from the table, Hackett. I want you on the other side of the room, near your mother."

He crossed in front of her and leaned against all of Dickens, then sat on a three-stepped stool in the corner, like a dunce. Mrs. Marburg stood resistant, but eventually sank back into her chair.

I took her son's place on the chair by the tape recorder, and switched it on. Fleischer's recording apparatus must have been noise-activated: there were no long breaks or lacunae in the sound. Laurel's singing was followed by the small noise of Laurel making herself a drink, then by the larger noise of her making another drink.

She sang a song of her own invention, with the refrain of "Davy, Davy, Davy."

The door of her apartment opened and closed, and Davy himself was in the room. "Hi, Laurel."

"Call me Mother."

"It doesn't sound right. Hey, you don't have to kiss me."

"I have a right to. Haven't I treated you like a mother?"

"Lately, you have. Sometimes I wonder why."

"Because I *am* your mother. I'd cut off my right hand to prove it."

"Or your head?"

She cried out, "Ah!" as if he had hurt her physically. "It isn't very nice of you to talk like that. I didn't have anything to do with killing your father."

"But you know who did kill him."

"I told you the other night, it was the young man—the beatnik with the beard."

"They didn't have beatniks in those days." Davy's voice was flat and incredulous.

"Whatever you want to call him—he was the one."

"Who was he?"

After some hesitation she said: "I don't know."

"Then why did you cover up for him?"

"I didn't."

"Yes, you did. You told Fleischer and the law that the dead man wasn't my father. But you told me he was. Either you lied to them or you're lying to me. Which is it?"

Laurel said in a small voice: "You mustn't be so hard on me. I didn't lie either time. The man the train ran over—"

Mrs. Marburg groaned, so loudly that I missed the end of Laurel's sentence. I switched the recorder off as Mrs. Marburg started to speak:

"Do I have to sit here all night and listen to this soap opera?"

"It's a family tape," I said. "Very nostalgic. Your grandson and his mother are talking about what happened to your son. Don't you want to know what happened to him?"

"That's nonsense! I only have the one son."

She turned to Hackett in his corner and showed her teeth in what was probably meant to be a maternal smile. He moved uneasily under it. Finally he spoke, for the second time, very carefully:

"There's not much use pretending, Mother. He can find out about

Jasper quite easily. I think he already has. I also think it's time I made a clean breast of it."

"Don't be a fool!"

"A clean breast of what?" I said.

"The fact that I killed my half-brother, Jasper Blevins. If you'll give me a chance to explain what happened, I think you'll take a different view of the matter. Certainly no jury would convict me."

"Don't be too sure of that," his mother said. "I say you're making a big mistake if you trust this s.o.b."

"I have to trust someone," he said. "And this man saved my life. I don't agree with you, by the way, that we should stop payment on his check. He earned the money."

I cut in: "You were going to tell me how you killed Jasper."

He took a deep breath. "Let me start with why I killed him. Jasper murdered my father. My father and I had been very close, though I hadn't seen him for a long time. I was living in London, studying economics in preparation for taking over the business eventually. But Dad was a man in his prime, and I didn't expect him to die for many years. When I got the word that he'd been murdered, it just about pushed me over the edge. I was still very young, in my early twenties. When I flew home I was determined to track down my father's murderer."

Hackett was talking like a book, which made it hard to believe him. "How did you track him down?"

"It turned out to be quite easy. I found out Jasper had quarreled with Dad."

"Who told you?"

He looked at his mother. She pushed air away with the flat of her hand. "Leave me out of this. If you take my advice, you'll shut up here and now."

"What are you afraid of, Mrs. Marburg?"

"You," she said.

Hackett went on with a faint whine in his voice: "I want to finish what I had to say. I learned that Jasper was at the ranch with his wife, and I drove up there. This was the second or third day after he murdered Dad. I accused him of the crime. He came at me with an ax. Fortunately I was stronger than he was, or luckier. I got the ax away from him and crushed his skull with it."

"So you were the man with the beard?"

"Yes. I'd grown a beard when I was a student in London."

"Was Laurel there when you killed Jasper?"

"Yes. She saw it happen."

"And the boy Davy?"

"He was there, too. I can hardly blame him for what he did to me." Hackett touched his swollen mouth and discolored eyes.

"What happened between you and Davy?"

"He gave me a very bad time, as you know. At first he meant to put me under a train. Then he changed his mind and forced me to show him the way to the ranch. He seemed to be trying to reconstruct what happened, and he made me confess what I've just told you. He gave me a terrible beating. He talked as if he meant to kill me but he changed his mind again."

"Did you tell him you were his father, his natural father?"

A one-sided grin of surprise pulled up the corner of Hackett's mouth and narrowed one eye. It resembled the effects of a mild paralytic stroke. "Yes, I did. I am."

"What happened after you told him that?"

"He untaped my wrists and ankles. We had a talk. He did most of the talking. I promised him money, and even recognition, if that was what he wanted. But he was mainly interested in getting at the truth."

"The fact that you killed Jasper?"

"Yes. He didn't remember me consciously at all. He'd blacked out on the whole thing."

"It isn't entirely clear to me," I said. "The way you tell it, you killed Jasper in self-defense. Even without that, I agree that no jury would have convicted you, of anything worse than manslaughter. Why did you cover up, and go to such lengths to dispose of the body?"

"That wasn't my doing. It was Laurel's. I suppose she felt guilty about our affair in Texas. And I admit I felt guilty, about that and everything else. Don't forget that Jasper was my brother. I felt like Cain himself."

He may have felt like Cain, once long ago, but at the moment he sounded phony to me. His mother stirred and erupted again:

"Talk is expensive. Haven't you learned that yet? You want this s.o.b. to own you outright?"

Hackett watched my face as he answered her: "I don't believe Mr. Archer is a blackmailer."

"Hell, he doesn't call it that. None of them do. They call it investigation, or personal research, or scratch-my-back-and-I'll-scratch yours. So we buy him an apartment house to live in, and an office building to keep his files in, and he pays us five cents on the dollar." She stood up. "What's the ante, this time, you s.o.b.?"

"Don't keep saying that, Etta. It spoils the maternal image. I've been wondering where Laurel got her apartment building and where your mother got hers."

"Leave my mother out of this, my mother has nothing to do with this." I seemed to have touched Mrs. Marburg on a nerve. "Have you been talking to Alma?"

"A little. She knows a lot more than you think she does."

For the first time in our acquaintance, Mrs. Marburg's eyes reflected real fear. "What does she know?"

"That Jasper killed Mark Hackett. And I think she thinks that you put Jasper up to it."

"The hell I did! It was Jasper's own idea."

Mrs. Marburg had blundered, and she knew it. The fear in her eyes began to spill across the rest of her face.

"Did Jasper tell you he killed Mark?" I said.

She considered the long-term consequences of her answer and finally said: "I don't remember. It was a long time ago, and I was very upset."

"So you're taking the Fifth. Maybe the tape will remember." I reached for the recorder, intending to switch it on.

"Wait," Mrs. Marburg said. "What will you take to stop right here? Just walk out and forget about us? How much?"

"I haven't given the matter any thought."

"Think about it now. I'm offering you a million dollars." She held her breath, and added: "Tax-free. You could live like a king."

I looked around the room. "Is this the way kings live?"

Hackett spoke from his dunce's stool: "It's no use, Mother. It's going to be our word against his. So we better stop talking to him, just as you said."

"You hear that?" Mrs. Marburg said to me. "A million, tax-free. That's our final offer. You don't have to do a thing for it. Just walk away."

Hackett was watching my face. "You're wasting your time," he said. "He doesn't want our money. He wants our blood."

"Be quiet, both of you."

I switched on the recorder, turned the tape back a little, and heard Davy's voice say again: "—or you're lying to me. Which is it?"

Then Laurel's voice: "You mustn't be so hard on me. I didn't lie either time. The man the train ran over really was your father."

"That's not what you said the other night. You said that Stephen Hackett was my father."

"He was."

I looked at Hackett. He was listening intently, his eyes still focused on my face. His own face seemed queerly starved. The scorn in his eyes had changed to a chilly loneliness.

Davy said: "I don't understand."

"I don't want you to, Davy. I don't want to dig up the past."

"But I have to know who I am," he said in a chanting rhythm. "I have to, it's important to me."

"Why? You're my son and I love you."

"Then why won't you tell me who my father was?"

"I have. Can't we leave it at that? We'll only stir up trouble."

The door opened.

"Where are you going?" Laurel said.

"My bird is waiting. Sorry."

The door closed. Laurel cried a little, then made a drink. She yawned. There were night movements, an inner door closing. Night sounds, cars in the street.

I speeded up the tape and jumped it ahead and heard a voice which had to be my own, saying: "—sounds like a poolroom lawyer to me."

Laurel's voice answered mine: "Davy's more than that. He's more than just a talker. And he isn't the poolroom type. He's a serious boy."

"What's he serious about?"

"He wants to grow up and be a man and do something useful."

"I think he's conning you, Mrs. Smith," I heard my strange voice say, a long time ago.

I moved the tape ahead again and heard the familiar noise of the apartment door being opened. Laurel said: "What do you want?"

No answer, except the sound of the door being closed. Then Hackett's voice:

"I want to know who you've been talking to. I had a phone call last night—"

"From Davy?"

"From Jack Fleischer. Who the hell is Davy?"

"Don't you remember, Jasper?" Laurel said.

The sound of a blow on flesh was followed by Laurel's sigh, then other blows until the sighing changed to snoring. I was watching the man who called himself Stephen Hackett. He sat tense on his stool. He seemed to be excited by the noises, emotionally transported to Laurel's apartment.

I broke the spell: "What did you hit her with, Jasper?"

He let his breath out in a kind of soughing whine. Even his mother had turned her eyes away from him.

I said to her: "What did he hit her with?"

"How in God's name should I know?"

"He went to you immediately afterward. He probably disposed of the weapon at your house. But mainly I think he wanted moral support. When he came back here that afternoon he brought you along with him."

"That doesn't make me responsible."

"You are, though. You can't profit from murder without taking part of the blame."

"I didn't *know* he killed Laurel," she said with some force.

"You knew he killed Mark Hackett. Didn't you?"

"I found out about it."

"But you didn't turn him in."

"He was my son," she said.

"Stephen was your son, too. But your maternal instincts didn't work for him. You conspired with Jasper to kill Stephen and put Jasper in his place."

She gave me a shocked look, as if the truth of what they had done was just occurring to her, fifteen years too late. "How could I possibly do a thing like that?"

The sentence was meant to be a denial, but it was also a question; which I answered. "You were headed for the rocks. Mark Hackett knew about your affair with Sidney Marburg. He was going to divorce you and cut you off financially. Simply killing Mark wouldn't help you very much. The bulk of his estate was going to Stephen. So Stephen had to go.

"Nobody in California knew Stephen. He'd been out of the country for several years, and at the time he left for Europe you were all living in Texas. But your lover Sid had sharp eyes, and you didn't want to have to knock him off, so you sent him to Mexico for the transition period. Sid caught one glimpse of Stephen wearing a beard when Stephen flew in from England.

"You shunted Stephen off to the ranch where Jasper was waiting for him. Jasper had more than money to gain from Stephen's death. His brother's identity was a perfect mask for the murderer of Mark Hackett. He killed Stephen and shaved his beard off." I looked past Mrs. Marburg to her son. "You were a barber at one time, weren't you, Jasper?"

He looked back at me with eyes as empty as a skull's. I said to him: "You left Laurel behind to con the local law and came down here and took your brother's place. It couldn't have been too hard, with your mother vouching for you. I imagine the hardest part was learning to forge your brother's signature. But then you were a bit of an artist, too. You were a bit of just about everything. But you found your real *métier* as a killer and conman."

The man in the corner spat at me and missed. His role as a rich and lucky man had ended. The room with its books and pictures no longer belonged to him. He was Albert Blevins's son, alone in blank space.

"For fourteen or fifteen years," I said, "nothing much happened to threaten your success. You lived quietly in seclusion, developed a taste for good pictures, visited Europe. You even got up nerve enough to make a bigamous marriage.

"No doubt you were paying off Laurel all those years. You owed her a lot, really, for keeping Jack Fleischer off your trail. Unfortunately she got lonely with nothing but a little money to keep her company. And she had some pangs of conscience about the boy she'd abandoned.

"In the end she made a move toward the boy. It was enough to tip Jack Fleischer off. I'm sure he'd been suspicious of both of you from the start. His retirement freed him to act. He put Laurel's apartment under surveillance, and started to dig into the whole background.

"We know from the tape what happened after that. Fleischer called you. You silenced Laurel. Later you got your chance to silence Fleischer. Do you want to talk about that?"

Hackett made no response of any kind. He was leaning forward with his hands on his knees. I went on:

"It isn't hard to imagine what happened. Davy believed he had found his father, that his life was just beginning. He laid the shotgun down and untied you. You made a grab for the gun and got hold of it. But Davy got away.

"Jack Fleischer was older and not so quick. Or maybe he was paralyzed by the sudden confrontation. Did he recognize you, Jasper, and know in the moment before he died who shot him? We know, anyway. You killed Fleischer and threw the gun in the creek. Then you collapsed on the creek bank and waited to be rescued."

"You can't prove any of this," Mrs. Marburg said.

Her son was doubtful. He slid off the stool and tried to rush me, clumsy and almost reluctant, trotting in slow motion toward his own revolver in my hand.

I had time to decide where to shoot him. If I had liked the man I might have shot to kill. I shot him in the right leg.

He fell at his mother's feet, clutching his knee and moaning. She didn't reach out to touch him or comfort him. She sat looking down at him in the way I imagine the damned look down, with pity and terror only for themselves, into lower circles than their own.

The sound of the shot brought Aubrey into the house. He arrested both of them and took them in on suspicion of conspiracy to commit murder.

Later I made my way through the crowds of night-blooming young people on the Strip and climbed the stairs to my office. The basket of cold chicken, washed down with a slug of whisky, tasted better than I expected it to.

I had a second slug to fortify my nerves. Then I got Mrs. Marburg's check out of the safe. I tore it into small pieces and tossed the yellow confetti out the window. It drifted down on the short hairs and the long hairs, the potheads and the acid heads, draft dodgers and dollar chasers, swingers and walking wounded, idiot saints, hard cases, foolish virgins.

A NOTE ABOUT THE AUTHOR

Ross Macdonald was born near San Francisco in 1915. He was educated in Canadian schools, traveled widely in Europe, and acquired advanced degrees and a Phi Beta Kappa key at the University of Michigan. In 1938 he married a Canadian who is now well known as the novelist Margaret Millar. Mr. Macdonald (Kenneth Millar in private life) taught school and later college, and served as communications officer aboard an escort carrier in the Pacific. For nearly thirty years he has lived in Santa Barbara and written mystery novels about the fascinating and changing society of his native state. Among his leading interests are conservation and poli-tics. He is a past president of the Mystery Writers of America. In 1964 his novel The Chill *was given a Silver Dagger award by the Crime Writers' Association of Great Britain. Mr. Macdonald's* The Far Side of the Dollar *was named the best crime novel of 1965 by the same organization.* The Moving Target *was made into the highly successful movie* Harper *(1966). And* The Goodbye Look *(1969),* The Underground Man *(1971), and* Sleeping Beauty *(1973) were all national best sellers.*